Praise for *Hælend's Ballad*

"A powerful inspection of moral, ethical, and spiritual paths, readers receive a fine story that embraces and contrasts dark appetites, terrible memories, and beauty alike . . . *Hælend's Ballad* [is] a compelling force to contend with." —**D. Donovan, Senior Reviewer,** *Midwest Book Review*

"A spiraling story of bloody histories . . . fantasy fans will not be disappointed with this masterfully imagined realm . . . Meticulously written, with unexpected turns of phrase and instantly authentic dialogue, this hefty tome from Conrey is an impressive, immersive, and impeccably penned tale." —*Self-Publishing Review*

"A triumphant debut . . . Conrey's fantasy world is morbidly gripping and enriched by darkness, intrigue, and poignant emotions and enlivened by bloody action . . . Gritty and well-constructed, this makes a rich treat for lovers of dark fantasy." —*The Prairies Book Review*

"Complex and highly-developed dark fantasy . . . full of heroism, tragedy, love, loss, intrigue and fantastic battle scenes." —**Tenkara Smart, author of** *She Named Me Wolf*

"High fantasy told at a dark level . . . Conrey's prose is atmospheric and gorgeous . . . full of adventure and twists . . . but most of all, great depth of character is exposed." —**Amanda Adam, author of** *Merewif*

HÆLEND'S BALLAD

Ian V. Conrey

To Triston

Table of Contents

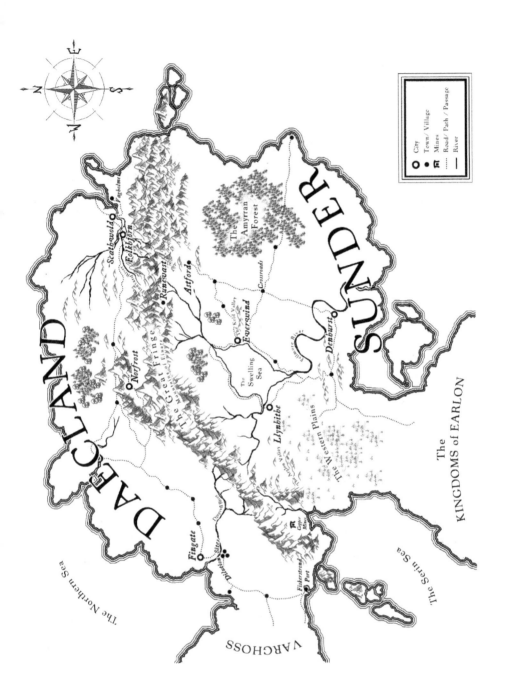

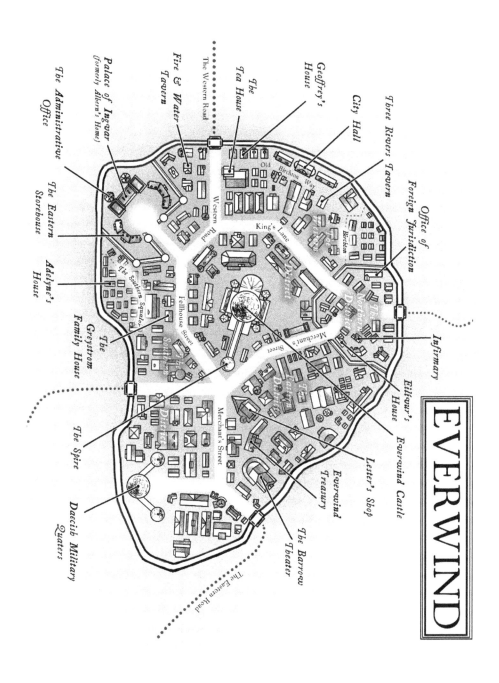

EVERWIND

Office of
Foreign Jurisdiction

Three Rivers Tavern

City Hall

Geoffrey's
House

The
Tea House

Fire & Water
Tavern

The Western Road

Palace of Ingvar
(formerly Allen's Home)

The Administrative
Office

The Eastern
Storehouse

Adelyne's
House

The
Greystrom
Family House

The Spire

Daccib Military
Quaters

Old
Birchton
Way

Western
Road

King's Lane

Birchton

The Northern District

Infirmary

Eillour's
House

Everwind Castle

Lester's Shop

Everwind
Treasury

The Barrow
Theater

The Southern Square

Fellhouse Street

Southern
District

Merchant's Street

Merchant's Street

Merchant's Street

The Eastern District

The Eastern Road

He turned rivers into a desert,
flowing springs into thirsty ground,
and fruitful land into a salt waste,
because of the wickedness of those who lived there.
He turned the desert into pools of water
and the parched ground into flowing springs;
there he brought the hungry to live,
and they founded a city where they could settle.
They sowed fields and planted vineyards
that yielded a fruitful harvest;
he blessed them, and their numbers greatly increased,
and he did not let their herds diminish.

—Psalm 107:33-38

Dark Horses

As the breeze blew the tails of Eilívur's coat behind him, he peered across the Llynhithe port docks to the rising tides of the Swelling Sea. He pulled the letter from his pocket and fiddled with the corner as his gaze wandered to a group of sailors, gesturing and shouting while they raised the sails upon the foremast of a great ship. A boatswain pointed toward the outhaul, and several men gripped the rope, tightening the sail which billowed out in the wind.

"Blasted air's gone chilly again," came a voice from behind.

Eilívur turned as Commander Jótham approached in his black uniform, which only seemed to accentuate his pale skin, even by Daecish standards. "Llynhithe isn't so bad," he replied. "At least you can see the sun."

Jótham grinned, revealing his ghastly brownish-gray teeth—unfit for an officer. "With all due respect, Commander Tyr, you haven't been here but two days. You'll grow to hate it, too." He pointed to the letter in Eilívur's hand. "Are those my orders?"

Eilívur faintly nodded and scratched his cleanshaven face. His eyes wandered to a row of crooked wooden buildings. Gray thatched roofs sagged around the seemingly rotting beams beneath them. "Anywhere we can get a drink?"

Jótham let out a hack, which Eilívur assumed was meant to be a chuckle. "A drink? Commander, this isn't Everwind."

Eilívur didn't bother replying.

Jótham rolled his eyes and pointed down the road. "There's a tavern not far from here."

Stepping through the open entryway, the smell of sour milk and lantern oil filled Eilívur's nose. Several Sunderian men, clothed in brown leather tunics and jerkins, sat at the bar. As with just about everyone else in Sunder, they looked like poor farmers. One man, with a leathery face, smiled, revealing his toothless gums. Another man chewed on something, probably tobacco. Eilívur never smoked, but even he knew tobacco was for smoking in pipes, not chewing raw.

Jótham motioned for the barman to bring them a drink as they sat at the table situated beside a hand-blown window wrapped in a rotting frame. Gazing back at the port docks, Eilívur could almost make out the reflection of his graying blonde hair in the glass.

"I've about had it with this country," Jótham whispered as he glanced over his shoulder at the men at the bar.

The barman brought two mugs of ale and set them on the table. "You want to go back to Daecland?" Eilívur asked before taking a sip of ale. He frowned as he forced the liquid down his throat. Jótham was right. This tasted little better than bilge water. A hot cup of tea would have been nicer.

"I don't know," he replied with a sigh. "At least out of Llynhithe. But anyway," he pointed to the letter again, "what have you got for me?"

"Greystrom's arrest papers."

Jótham raised an eye. "Lombard Greystrom? Has he been found?"

"A scout found him and his family nearly forty leagues due west of here in the Western Plains, just north of the Arglen Valley."

"The Western Plains? We should have known."

"We've always been pretty certain. But finding a homestead in the vastness of the plains isn't easy."

"Well, it's about time," Jótham replied. "This Black Horse will wish—"

Eilívur lifted a finger. "Dark Horse, you mean?"

Jótham waved his finger away. "Whatever you want to call the leaders of the Slithering," he rolled his hand for the word. "The Slithering—"

"The Silent Hither?"

"Yes, that's what I said."

"Anyway," Eilívur interrupted, "I had planned on arresting Greystrom myself, but as soon as I arrived in Llynhithe, I was asked to take on a series of training courses for the Nautical Armada, effective immediately."

"You're a man of many talents, aren't you?"

Eilívur sighed. "Unfortunately. So, I must find a replacement for arresting Greystrom."

"And that would be me?"

"I thought you would be a good fit. And you did mention that you'd like to spend some time outside of Llynhithe."

Jótham laughed. "I'm not so sure the Western Plains were what I had in mind." He interlocked his fingers, cracking his knuckles. "But I guess it's better than nothing. When do I depart?"

Eilívur pushed the letter toward Jótham. "Next week."

Jótham slid his mug out of the way and unfolded the letter, reading through its contents. "Certainly gives me enough time to prepare. Do you already have a team lined up?"

"Three men, fully armored and equipped, as well as yourself. You shouldn't have any problems."

"Sounds reasonable for the arrest of one man. And the family?"

Eilívur threw Jótham a stern look. "The family is to be untouched, obviously, unless you're using self-defense."

Jótham nodded but said nothing as he continued reading.

"That's very important, Jótham. We don't need the blood of women and children on our hands."

"Of course not," he replied, waving his hand in the air.

Eilívur sat back. "One other thing," he said. "One of your men will be Ulnleif."

Jótham glanced up, a cocked grin on his face.

"It's his first mission outside of Llynhithe."

"Look," Jótham said, "it isn't a secret that you're protective of your brother. You want me to give him a special role or something?"

"No, no," Eilívur replied. "Treat him like the others. I just want to be sure everything is done right. He's still young."

Jótham took a last draught of ale, tipping it up as he finished. "Don't worry, Commander. Your brother will do fine, and we'll have Lombard in the gallows before you get back to Everwind."

* * *

Although the sun lay hidden behind the hills, it still managed to cast a thin light against the fleeting darkness. Lombard gazed across the rolling landscape, dotted with sparse withered plants. A sad memory lay in those hills as if they could remember when the land once stood green and lush before it faded into a barren death. But maybe it was his own conscience that made it seem that way—a reflection of his own life. It was a constant internal battle, having to fight off the temptation to wonder whether his hiding in the Western Plains was a punishment from Theos.

It had been five years since the Fellhouse Cellar was sacked by the Daecish, breaking the backbone of the Dark Horses. Landon was murdered, Galvin fled to Denhurst, and Porter and himself were hiding out in this wasteland. The Silent Hither in Everwind was now at its weakest. And as much as he didn't want to admit it, he regretted leaving Wesley in charge. It was a foolish act of sympathy, and he should've put a stronger man in his place—someone who knew how to keep the Dark Horses going in Everwind—to keep the cause of the

Silent Hither alive. Hopefully, Drake and Morgan would keep the poor fool straight.

Lombard couldn't help but let out a low groan. He needed to get back to Everwind as soon as possible.

Approaching a wide depression, he knelt down. Arnon squatted beside him as he notched a cedar arrow on his bowstring. His dark brown hair, as straight as the arrow in his hand, reached down to his lower jaw. Like himself, Arnon was a Sunderian in the fullest sense. It was said that Sarig blood even ran through their clan's veins, and he was proud of it. He pat Arnon on the back. During these early morning hunts, he had more in mind than just teaching his only son how to kill a deer. He was teaching him how to survive. How to be a Dark Horse when he was gone.

Arnon lifted his bow and drew back the bowstring, his back muscles tightening. Gazing through the tall grass, Lombard caught sight of a doe rising from her bedding, seemingly unaware of the hunters in her midst. With both eyes open, Arnon looked down the shaft of the arrow and let it go with a deep twang as it hissed through the grass and pierced the deer just behind the ribcage. Stumbling, it bolted out of the grass and over the ridgeline above. Lombard pulled the long grass he'd been chewing on from his mouth and gave Arnon a solid clap with the palm of his hand. "Barely nineteen and already surpassing your old man!"

Arnon laughed, rubbing his shoulder. "You said that last year. You sure I haven't always been the better shot?"

Although Lombard smiled, he never could get over the softening accents of the younger generation. "Maybe, but you'll never be stronger than me," he replied.

Arnon began to disassemble his bow. "I wouldn't be so sure. You've gotta get old at some point."

Lombard laughed. "Not even then, boy."

They began the steep climb up the ridge, following the blood trail. The dried grass crunched beneath their boots as dust whipped in the wind behind them.

"You ever wonder what this place might have looked like when Burgess first arrived?" Arnon asked.

"Well, being thirteen-hundred years ago, I reckon it would've been greener. Likely more trees, too."

Reaching the top of the ridge, they paused as the view opened before them. The wind rushed from the west, blowing Lombard's bearskin behind him. The Serin Sea could barely be made out as it stretched across the horizon like a thin gray thread. To the north towered the vast, impenetrable mountain range—the Great Fringe, his own people called it. Its icy jagged peaks marched from east to west, as far as he could see. There was a rumor that several new Daecish copper mines were operating nearby where the mountains plunged into the sea, and he made a point never to travel too far in that direction.

Dozens of tales about trekking parties looking for a pass through those mountains had been laid down over the ages. But as far as he knew, they never returned with success, nor without several deaths to show for it. Winds were too strong, and the natural paths went too high. The few returning survivors almost always came back with blackened toes and fingers, which would either be amputated or rot off on their own. His grandfather once told him of a man who returned sickened, mumbling and gripping his head as he coughed up blood before falling into an agonizing death.

Despite the casualties, in the early centuries, his people never gave up their search. They craved to know what secrets were hidden on the other side of those mountains. But it soon brought out the worst in them. Of course, all of that ended when the Daecish arrived from over the mountains, and the mystery turned into resentment.

Lombard shook the thoughts from his mind and looked across the ridge, following the blood trail into another holler thirty yards ahead. Next to a rotting tree lay the dying deer, caught up in briar and blackbrush.

"Why didn't the Earlonians ever speak of why they left the Southern Kingdoms?" Arnon asked, looking south.

Lombard almost laughed. Could Arnon read his thoughts?

"Do you really think they were running away from something?"

"Aye. When Burgess and our ancestors arrived in this land, they brought with them many tales. But the one thing they swore to never talk about was why they left. I, and other like-minded folk, believe it was something they were ashamed of. Something wrong they did which they hoped to forget. Perhaps it's why they named this land Sunder?" He tapped the side of his head. "It's all in the name."

They continued the trek down into the holler. As they approached the trunk, Arnon pulled the shaft of the arrow from below the ribs of the doe.

"That was a good shot," Lombard said. "But remember you want to aim behind the shoulder." He pointed to his chest. "Right in the heart."

"I know how to shoot a deer," replied Arnon shortly.

Lombard raised his eyebrows and set his boot on the trunk of the tree, crossing his thick arms.

"Look here, boy."

Arnon swallowed as if he immediately regretted his comment.

"Don't get put out. You're a fine shot, but your pride gets in the way. You need to work that out of yourself." He peered into Arnon's eyes. "Pride ain't strength; it's weakness. And from it can spring forth all kinds of evil thoughts. All a prideful man shows me is that he cares too much about himself, you understand?"

"Yes, sire."

"Your grandfather told me the same thing. See, he was a learned man and spoke wise counsel. It's something we all have to battle."

"Yes, sire."

"Good, now grab your knife, and let's clean that deer."

By mid-day, they were welcomed by the view of their cottage, situated at the bottom of a low bluff, yet perched on its own little hill. Built of wattle and daub and topped with a thatched roof of grass and willow branches, the cottage didn't look like much, but he built it himself, and it held strong against the changing seasons. On the west side sat a stable built of a thick layer of sod; it housed two cows, several chickens, and his own bay horse, whom he named Ansel. Out front stood a maple tree with few leaves of a dark and shriveled olive green. Lombard walked up to the front door as Arnon followed.

"Where you heading to?" Lombard asked.

Arnon groaned. "Firewood?"

"Can't cook without it." Lombard took the meat from Arnon and walked inside.

* * *

Setting up a hickory log, Arnon swung his ax with a great heave, splitting the log in two. The high sun helped warm the autumn air, but the occasional northern gust from the Fringe pierced through his jerkin. Just as he set up another log to split, he turned, hearing his youngest sister, Hazel, skipping through the tall grass. Her light brown hair whipped in the wind above her woolen gown.

"What's taking you so long?" She smirked.

"Well, here." Arnon handed her the ax. "Think you can go quicker?"

"It's your job." She stuck out her tongue.

"Then don't interrupt."

She placed her hands behind her back and dug her toe into the earth.

Arnon lifted his ax but glanced at her. "I know what you want," he said, "but I've got to finish chopping this wood first."

"Oh, but please!" she replied with wide blue eyes. Although only six, she had mastered the art of getting her way with him.

"Hazel, I really need—"

"But we ain't played Burrow Hunt for a whole week. Pretty please?"

Arnon sighed and dropped his ax. "One quick game."

Hazel jumped as she threw her arms in the air. "Thank you!"

Arnon turned over several logs until he found one with a clean flat top and began drawing out the lines with a piece of charcoal. "Do you have the pieces?"

Hazel searched in her pockets and pulled out a handful of dyed figurines carved from oak. She set them on the log. "I lost a couple more yesterday."

"It'll be all right. We'll just have to improvise."

As fun as this game was for him when he was younger, it was really pretty dull—just mindlessly moving pieces until one player had the opponent's fox cornered with no way to escape. It didn't help that Hazel still couldn't get the rules right, so it always took longer than normal. And when she did win, which she always did because he let her, she never let him live it down.

Hazel knocked his red fox over. "Ha!" she shouted as she jumped up and jabbed a finger at him. "You lost."

"Very good, Hazel. Now help me put the pieces away."

Of course, she didn't help and just ran back to the house, hollering something Arnon couldn't understand.

With chopped logs in his hand, Arnon stepped inside the cottage and breathed in the savory smell of roasting venison and smoke. Their family home may have been small, but it had two rooms, one of which was the bedroom on the left side, with a single thick door built from oak planks. Four years ago, his father had felled that oak about a league east of there, and it took him and Arnon a dozen trips to haul it all back to the homestead. In the family room sat a little hearth in the center, with a large trestle table behind it. Arnon tossed several split logs over the hot coals and made his way to his father, who stood salting the venison.

"Give that back, Hazel!" Fleta hollered as she chased Hazel around the hearth. "That one's mine! You've got your own!"

Hazel stopped and faced Fleta. Her face shone almost purple. "You tore her arm off last time!"

"Mama sewed it back on!" Fleta snapped back, snatching her doll from Hazel's grasp. Hazel broke out in a cry.

"Girls!" called out his mother. "Outside!"

Arnon chuckled and stood beside his father. "Is the pit ready?" he asked.

"Cleaned it out this morning before we set out." He handed Arnon a thick loin. "But we'll need to salt and wrap the deer first."

Arnon stepped around him, grabbing the raw meat. He brushed aside a pile of grass and broken pine needles from the counter, which he assumed was Hazel's. Reaching between several clay jars of honey and cream, he grabbed the half-empty jar of salt. Above his head hung several bundles of rosemary and basil, which filled the corner of the room with a rich, earthy scent. "This deer will give us enough meat for a while," Arnon said, massaging the salt into the meat.

"Enough for a few weeks, certainly," his father replied, laying another strip of meat next to the salt jar. "On the 'morrow at dawn, we'll take Ansel to Rock Hill and work on our archery."

"While riding?" he asked.

"Why else would I take Ansel? One day you'll be the head of your kin and help lead the Silent Hither among the Dark Horses. You need to be ready."

Arnon grinned. Nearly every day, for as long as he could remember, his father took him to Rock Hill; whether it was hunting, stalking, building, or survival, he taught him everything he knew, and his knowledge and talents seemed limitless. He happened to also be the strongest man Arnon had ever known.

Flipping over the loin, Arnon began to salt the other side until he felt a bump against his side.

"Excuse me," came Hazel's voice from below. She reached up over the meat, grabbing at her pile of grass and needles. "You're getting blood on the seasoning!"

"The seasoning?" Arnon asked.

Hazel frowned and raised her grass-filled hand toward Arnon's face. "For our pottage." She marched toward the hearth.

Arnon glanced at his father, who only shrugged with a smile.

"Hazel!" shouted Fleta from the dining table. "Now look at what you done! You spoiled it!"

"I did not! Mama said I could season it."

"Not with grass!"

Both Lombard and Arnon burst into laughter.

Myla hurried over to the hearth. "Hazel, dear," she said, peering into the cooking pot as she held back her long, wavy brown hair. "Thank you very much. I'm sure it'll taste just fine. Now do me a favor and bring in the milk from the stable. Can you do that for me?"

Hazel stuck her tongue out at Fleta before stepping outside.

"Hurry," said Myla to Fleta. "I think we can get most of it out."

With the sun set over the Serin Sea, Lombard lit a lantern as the family gathered around the table.

"Which story will you tell us tonight, papa?" Fleta asked, looking up from her bowl. The lantern light flickered against her green eyes. Even with her black hair tucked behind her ears, he could barely see the faint freckles dotting across her nose. When she was five, Arnon once chased her across their home in Everwind. She slipped and hit her face on the edge of a door frame. A large bump formed on the upper bridge of her nose, and it'd never gone away since. She'd always been self-conscious about it, and one time, when she and Arnon had gotten into an argument, he said she looked like a horse. It upset her so badly she didn't speak to him for a week. Despite the passing years, he knew it had an effect on her confidence, and he'd never forgiven himself.

"How 'bout a ballad?" Lombard asked.

Hazel grunted. "I don't like the singing ones. They're boring."

"Hazel," Myla said, "as you get older, you'll learn to. Just listen."

"I like ballads," Fleta added.

Hazel shot a glare at her.

Lombard crossed his arms and leaned toward Hazel. "It's the ballads that capture not only the past but the hearts and desires of those who shaped it. But don't worry," he laughed, "I'll only sing part of one." He then closed his eyes, and in a low, resonant voice, began to hum. His family soon joined in, and together, they sang:

I shall tell ye now a tragic tale
From Ashfirth village on the dale
In the distant kingdoms, south
By the Cymford river's mouth
When young Brigham of Colgate
Left poor Orla to her dreadful fate

In early spring, at the break of dawn
Before the birds broke out in song
Stood young Orla with curling hair
Eyes of brown and smooth skin fair
Her dress of sage and tasseled ends
Blew against the gentle winds

On the Isen road, her people left
For the north, their hearts were set
To forget a dark and troubled past
And settle a country fair and vast
Yet by the southern river flowing
There poor Orla stood sorrowing

With cunning words and a handsome grin
Brigham had stolen her love for him
But when her womb stirred with life
He would not take her as his wife
To the north, he'd join his people
And leave her behind weak and feeble

She had no means for food or care
So she wept with a pleading prayer
No such journey could she endure
Her coming death was set and sure
Yet still, he left with a heart of ice
And spoke no more of his shame and vice

By early winter, starved and cold
She ventured north, in vain yet bold
To find that man before she died
And plead once more to be his bride
But of his fate, she could not tell
For she knew not where he dwelled

She soon grew weary with aching pain
And searched for shelter from the rain
By the road, she lay down and wept
With tears, all spent, she finally slept

Under a dying weeping willow
Her beating heart began to slow

Early one morn', a man walked by
And saw poor Orla beneath the sky
He laid aside his hunting bow
And knelt beneath that weeping willow
In his arms, he took ahold
Her body stiffened with lifeless cold

Along the hills and through the dew
He hurried north, for her face he knew
By evening he found her family clan
And laid her body beneath that man
Who left poor Orla and child to die
As his new dame stood by his side

When Lombard finished, Arnon opened his eyes as he let his mind drift back to the room. In Everwind, at their old family home, fast-paced tunes, plucked and whistled with homemade fiddles and fifes, could keep everyone dancing for hours. But old ballads were always sung in the late night after the crowd had quieted down. His father still had an old gourd cut out and fitted with gut strings. He even had a bow made of mule's hair to go with it. But since they left for the plains, he hardly ever played it anymore. No one even danced much either, except for maybe Fleta, when she thought no one else was looking. But even so, ballads and tales were either told or sung every night, and Lombard always insisted the whole family should sing together so that they would never forget their past.

Fleta sighed as her chin rested on her hands.

Hazel rolled her eyes. "It don't even make sense. Why'd she go and get herself pregnant in the first place?"

Arnon burst out in an unexpected laugh.

Lombard lifted Hazel's chin. "She made a terrible mistake and fell too easily for a worthless man who sought only to satisfy himself."

"If you say so," Hazel replied.

"It's all right," said Myla as she stood up, picking up her bowl. "We don't all have to—" she began to say but froze at the sound of Ansel whinnying in the stable. Arnon shot a glance at his father. The whole family held their breath.

"Surely, it's just a wolf or a—" Arnon began to say before Lombard raised his hand.

In the distance grew the thudding sound of galloping hooves.

"Someone's coming," Lombard said in a low voice. He slid back his chair and hurried to the door, blowing out the hanging lantern. "Arnon, go out back and stay outta sight."

"Father, I am not going to leave—"

"Now!" he snapped.

"Listen to your father and go," Myla whispered as she threw Arnon's bowl in a basket.

Arnon knew why he needed to hide, but he hated the idea. He climbed through a back window and ran north against the howling wind. After ascending a steep path to the top of the bluff, he positioned himself out of sight but still had a decent view of the homestead below. Four horses galloped along the road, coming to a trot as they paused just in front of the cottage. Their uniforms looked black. Daecish.

Gunborg Orphanage

Mathios brought the back of his hand across the boy's cheek. Quietness filled the sleeping quarters, and Søren stood still as he looked down at his bare feet, his blanket still in his hands. He couldn't remember the new boy's name, but he obviously hadn't learned that the younger orphans don't talk back to Mathios.

"Learn your place!" Mathios hollered before looking at the others. "If we aren't downstairs in two minutes, there will be no breakfast for none of us!" Walking between the line of boys and iron-framed cots, each step came with a heavy limp as he forced his knocked knees to carry him through the room. He paused and looked at Søren with his freckled face and cheeks as red as his hair. "And don't even think about dodging work today," he mumbled before heading out of the room.

As soon as Mathios disappeared, Søren walked over and grabbed his sweat-stained feather pillow. Slipping two fingers into a rip, he poked around the chicken feathers until he found a brass ring. Pulling it out, he examined the empty socket that once held a small gem. Every time he looked at it, he felt as empty and lonely as the socket, but he treasured it more than anything else. It was his last thread of hope.

Jokith hammered his shoulder into him. "Don't lose your mother's ring!" He laughed.

"That isn't his mother's ring!" another boy said as Søren clambered back to his feet. "He just found it in the street!"

"It is t—too my mother's!" Søren defended. "And she's coming back for me!" He didn't care what the boys thought. They may have had parents who didn't care about them, but he was different.

Jokith sneered. The hairy birthmark over his right eyebrow somehow looked uglier today. "You're just a cocker! Why don't you run off to Eirún like you always do?" He punched Søren in the shoulder and walked off.

Rotating his shoulder, Søren swore that if he was any bigger, he'd smack that stupid birthmark right off Jokith's face. In the least, he could exaggerate the pain, and maybe Jokith would get a few lashings from the headmaster.

As the boys left the room and approached the dark wooden steps, Søren stuffed the ring in his pants pocket and followed behind, trying to force a tear out of his eye as he rubbed his arm. Maybe one of the maids would notice. As he continued down the stairway, the railing opened into the dining hall to his left. He let out an exaggerated sigh and dropped his hand from his shoulder. No grown-up in sight. But that's the way it always seemed to work out.

Three doors opened into the dining hall, but he only cared about two. One led to the kitchen; the other, called the southern door, led to Eirún's and the other maids sleeping quarters. The boys made their way to the low benches on either side of the table, and Søren sat, facing away from the fireplace. Trying to ignore the heat on his back, he glanced toward the swinging door to the kitchen, hoping Eirún would walk through soon.

Long, leaky pipes clanked and hammered along the ceiling, keeping the orphanage humid with the constant lingering scent of mold. But this morning, the smell of something pungent from the kitchen overpowered the room. With grim faces, they all peered through the open kitchen door at a large steaming copper pot.

Jokith pulled something from his nose and flicked it to the floor. "What do you think is in the stew today?"

Stígr sighed. "Let's just hope it isn't leather laces."

Several of the younger boys went wide-eyed. Jokith's birthmark looked like a patch of leather, and the thought of it cooking in stew made Søren almost gag.

"I've seen it once," Stígr continued in a low whisper, "chopped up laces, straight off the boots." He glanced at Mathios. "You remember Olle? The one that got stuck in the chimney and died last winter?"

"Yea," Mathios replied. "Which is why I'm glad I'm too big to be a chimney sweep."

"They were his laces. I saw Headmaster Baulfr take them off his boots."

Mathios shook his head. "Stígr. . ."

"What?"

At that moment, a couple of maids set steaming wooden bowls of stew in front of the boys.

"Eat up, Søren," Mathios said. "You're nearly ten, and you haven't grown since you were, like what, six?"

Several of the boys laughed with their faces in their bowls, but Søren only stared at the few strips of thin meat swirling around in the brown broth. Maybe it was leather laces. But it did look a bit like Jokith's birthmark, didn't it? Perhaps if he drank quickly, he wouldn't taste it.

He slowly dipped his spoon up and down. Did Eirún make this stew? Certainly not. It must have been Adis. He never could figure out how that maid got so chubby. It definitely wasn't from eating her own cooking. Eirún, on the other hand, was the best cook in the world, even if the other boys said otherwise. But then again, she was perfect at everything. She was the only reason he didn't mind living in that terrible place. But he wished she'd spend more time with him. She always seemed busy and—

"Søren?" asked Stígr. The grandfather clock gave a low chime, and Søren looked up with a jerk. The boys burst into laughter. Everyone had finished eating, and they were now stacking their bowls. Søren dipped his finger into the now cool stew.

Mathios walked by and smacked his hand on Søren's back. "Always somewhere else than here."

Still chuckling, the boys carried their bowls to the kitchen, and Søren drank down as much stew as he could. He coughed, wiping his mouth on his sleeve. With the other boys getting in line in front of the stairwell, he hurried his bowl to the kitchen and joined them. Reluctantly, he had to stand next to Stígr, who scratched at an infected rash scabbing around the back of his neck. Søren sighed. Where was Eirún?

Headmaster Baulfr finally walked in through the southern door. His feet thudded with each step, and the nauseating aroma of some spicy fragrance over the sour stench of dried sweat filled Søren's nose. Baulfr's greasy brown hair, a unique look among the mostly fair-haired Daecish, matched the dark buttons along his gray vest, which struggled to hold the threading together as his gut protruded forward. As always, Mathios straightened himself and raised his chin. It was as if he thought Baulfr would actually be proud of him.

The maids began to clean the dining table, obviously trying to appear busy. Baulfr stood before the boys with his thick muscled arms crossed over his chest. Being a quiet man, this was often the only instance Søren heard him speak throughout the day; if he heard him talk at any other time, it was probably because he did something wrong.

"First six on the left," Baulfr rumbled in a deep voice, "you're working on the fence. I want it running up to the smokehouse by dinner . . ." He kept giving orders, but his voice seemed to go distant and muffled. Søren gazed into the embers in the fireplace—reds and oranges waving in and out of each coal. He hated the feeling of hard labor. Most of the time, he managed to get out of breaking rocks or stacking the fence. Maybe he should rub his shoulder. It didn't even hurt, but if Baulfr saw him, he might feel sorry for him. Or maybe he should—

"Søren!"

"Y—Yes, Sir!" he stuttered, turning from his gaze.

"You're scrubbing my floor."

"Floor?"

"In my sleeping quarters."

As Baulfr marched to the kitchen, the boys hurried to their various tasks. Søren headed to the broom closet behind the stairwell and grabbed a bucket, and filled it with cold water. It was supposed to be hot, but that took too much time.

With bucket and brush in hand, Søren stepped inside the sleeping quarters. To his dismay, Baulfr sat at his small black desk situated by a tall shelf, which housed numerous plates and several imported trinkets from Norfrost. Becoming overly aware of what his hands and feet were doing, Søren slowly kneeled and began scrubbing between the cracks of the oak floor. Too much grime came out. This would take all day. He glanced up occasionally at Baulfr, who seemed occupied with writing and scribbling. Excess ink dribbled over the jar as he dipped his pen.

Søren had barely begun working, and he was already certain his arms might fall off. And the dirt only smeared around, making the wood look nastier. At this rate, it would take him a week to finish this job. Wiping his dry eyes, he moaned, just loud enough so that Baulfr might hear. But Baulfr never said a word, and what should have taken a couple of hours took Søren the better part of the day.

He worked straight through lunch, and by close to evening time, he managed to work his way around the bed to the far-end corner, now scrubbing the last few boards which bordered the tall shelf. Although Baulfr had left for a couple of hours, he soon returned to sit once again at his desk, grumbling as he read over some letter.

Søren heard a soft ting as something fell beneath him. He looked around but couldn't see what it was. Then a dreaded weight sank into his stomach. He slipped his hand into his pocket, but his ring was gone. Frantically, he swept his eyes across the floor, hoping it didn't slip through one of the cracks. He broke into a sweat, and his eyes watered as he sunk low and peered beneath the shelf, hoping it rolled beneath it.

Abruptly, Baulfr stood up, shifting his chair back. Startled, Søren banged his head on the low-lying shelf, bringing several plates crashing down to the floor. His heart pounded, and he slowly looked up. Through his blurred watery eyes, Baulfr grimly stared at him.

"Get up!" he bellowed in a cold, deep voice. He crumpled the letter and threw it on the floor. Søren stood, his eyes fixed on the ground and his chin quivering.

"You muck up every task I give you, you scamp," Baulfr spat out. "You never listen. Always crying, always dodging work!"

"I'm sorry, sir," he cried. "I t—try to listen! I t—t—" His words stumbled into a mess.

"You need to grow up!" Baulfr kicked the bucket at Søren, splashing soiled water across the floor. With trembling knees, Søren thought he should pick up the bucket, but he couldn't move. Baulfr leaned toward him. His breath smelled as sour as the floor. "If it weren't for the few aracs I get every month for housing you, I would have buried you in that ditch in the back when your father dropped you on my doorstep! Just wait 'til I—"

Adis and Eirún pushed opened the door.

"Supper's ready, Mr. Baulfr!" said Adis in a nervous tone.

Eirún glanced at Søren with worry in her eyes.

Baulfr shot a stern glare at the maids, and Adis shrank back.

"Come, Søren," Eirún told him. "It's time to wash up,"

He lowered his head and ran toward her.

Adis hurried over and picked up the bucket, and began to gather the broken ceramic fragments. "Don't you worry, sir," she said. "I'll get this whole place cleaned up for you. Why don't you go eat before your supper gets cold?"

Standing beside Eirún in the kitchen, Søren washed his face and hands. Grabbing the towel from the shelf, he tried to dry out the tears as they formed in his eyes. But as he looked at Eirún, he couldn't hide his trembling chin.

"Don't worry," she said with a steady voice. She tidied her long blonde hair, held up with sapphire blue pins. In her late twenties, she looked younger than the other maids, with her delicate face and high cheekbones, but her deep green eyes seemed tired. Whenever he was around her, the troubles of the world seemed to melt away. She was his haven, and he often pretended that she was his mother. "The plates will get cleaned up, and the headmaster will forget about it. You'll see. Everything will turn out all right."

Søren faked a smile, but it wasn't the plates that upset him. Would he really never see his ring again? Then, almost instinctively, he felt that familiar bitter tendency come out of him. "Where were you this morning?"

"You know I have work to do, and I can't always be there for breakfast. Sometimes Baulfr needs me in the kitchen or outside cleaning the coop."

"But I thought you would be there." Even before he said it, he felt guilty. He knew she didn't do anything wrong, but it was as if he believed that making her feel bad would somehow make him feel like a better person. But it didn't, and yet it never seemed to stop him.

Eirún's eyes went sorrowful, almost hurt. "I'm sorry," she said. She glanced behind for a second, then she turned back with a bright smile. "But I think this will make you feel better." She pulled a folded note from her apron and slipped it into his olive coat pocket. "I want you to read it, just as I taught you. But not until after you finish your meal.

When you're alone. And don't share it with anyone else. Do you understand?"

Søren nodded.

"I mean it," she insisted in a more serious tone. "Remember what we talked about last week."

"T—to be thoughtful of the other boys' feelings?"

"That's right," she replied. "We must always be kind to others."

Søren nodded again, but the boys were never kind to him, so why should he be?

"Why don't you go back to the dining hall?" she continued. "I must get supper ready."

Søren held his hand over his pocket, feeling the note. He was just about to open his mouth to ask her to stay with him a while longer, but she gave him a quick wink, kissed him on the head, and walked him through the door.

Taking his seat at the far end of the table, he peered at the other boys as they tore into their bread, shoving massive chunks into their mouths. The dining hall filled with the hazy sound of munching and moaning, but he only took small bites. What did the note say? As he stirred his spoon in the stew, he kept looking down at his pocket, until by chance, he glanced across the table and saw Stígr peering at him.

Søren didn't say anything, but he liked the idea of Stígr being jealous. That's right. He was loved. He was special. He slid his fingers into his pocket and slightly pulled up the note for a second, pretending to observe it. But when he noticed Mathios glance at it, he slipped it back down and swallowed, keeping his eyes fixed on his bowl.

He subconsciously rubbed the outside of his pant pocket and lost his appetite as he imagined the ring laying in a dark pile of dust beneath the floorboards.

Soon, the boys stood up and carried their dishes to the kitchen, but Mathios stayed in his seat. Eirún walked into the dining hall, and Søren looked up. She laid her hand on his shoulder. "Go, read it now," she whispered. She took his bowl and disappeared through the kitchen door.

Søren raced up the stairs.

Entering the empty sleeping quarters, he slipped off his shoes and hurried past the rows of cots and whitewashed walls. His feet felt raw against the rough grain of the wooden boards. In the back corner, he sat behind the cast-iron furnace and pulled out the note.

He tried to read the words. Thump, thump, thump came the sound of water hammering through the steam pipes. The rising heat of the furnace burned against his face. Was someone walking up the stairs? He glanced at the door. Seeing nothing, he took a calming breath and looked back at the note again. With a finger, he slowly pointed to each word and read aloud:

Søren,

After supper, pack your clothes and meet me in the front entryway. I have a surprise for you.

"Pack my clothes?" he asked out loud.

"What do you have there?" came the voice of Mathios from the far side of the room.

Startled, Søren gripped the note in his hand but didn't speak.

"Come on now, you can share it."

Søren said nothing.

"Look here," Mathios said as he bent down and grabbed Søren by the collar. "You think that since you've got some letter from Eirún, that she loves you more, but she doesn't! Can't you see that?"

Søren remained quiet but couldn't keep his shoulders from trembling.

Mathios's face turned that familiar red, and he lunged forward as Søren turned his back, balling up against the wall. "Give it here!" Mathios shouted as he pulled Søren back toward him by the face. His fingers felt like talons, but he suddenly screamed as Søren sunk his teeth into the flesh of his palm. Mathios slammed him against the hot iron, searing the skin on his right hand and lower forearm. Søren cried out and crumpled onto the floor as the note fell behind the furnace.

The other boys suddenly entered the room with Baulfr behind them.

"What's going on?" he bellowed, pushing himself past the boys.

Mathios sat on the floor, gripping his bleeding hand, while Søren lay prostrate, weeping onto the dust-laden floor. The room stood silent while Baulfr marched forward. His voice cracked as he shouted louder, "What's going on?"

Mathios raised his hand, showing the gash of teeth marks. "Søren bit me!"

Baulfr grabbed Mathios by the hand and dragged him across the floor toward Søren.

"S—Sir!" Mathios whimpered.

"Keep your mouth shut!" Baulfr snapped, grabbing Søren's hand and dragging him alongside Mathios. Attempting to stand, Søren's feet only tripped behind him along the ground. Baulfr took them both out of the room, down the stairs, and into the dining hall.

"Sit there, and don't move," he said, shoving them against the table and tying their hands to the back of the chair. He walked into the kitchen and a moment later returned with that old switch in his right hand. Up and down its shaft poked out several thick barbs and sharp slivers from where he failed to fully smooth it.

Time seemed to slow as Baulfr stood in front of them, bowing the switch in his hands as if to stretch the snap back into it. The grandfather clock began to chime. It was at least past seven, but Søren was too afraid to worry about counting.

With the last chime, the room fell quiet and heavy as the rest of the boys peered down from behind the safety of the stairway banister. With his chin on the back of the chair and his arms tied around it, Søren tried to focus on the crumbs scattered along the oaken tabletop in front of him. All he could hear was his own quickening breath.

The switch swung down onto the table with a loud crack causing Søren to jolt in his seat. Baulfr walked behind the boys, and Søren closed his eyes and held his breath. The sudden sound of the switch whipping through the air was quickly followed by a snap and a cutting pain that ripped into Søren's lower back like a burning knife. He wailed as he pressed his face against the tabletop.

Rotating every three or four blows, Baulfr whipped the switch across the lower and upper backs of both boys. With snot and tears flooding down his face, Søren clenched his teeth so hard he thought they'd crack. Soon his head went dizzy, and his skin broke as warm blood dripped down into the back of his pants. Upstairs, the boys covered their ears to muffle the cries.

After a while, Baulfr untied Mathios' hands as he crumpled onto the floor. The maids stood behind the kitchen door, weeping with handkerchiefs over their mouths. Baulfr walked beneath the stairway for a moment, only to come back with a large stone attached to a short rope with a loop on one end.

"You want to be a big man, Mathios," said Baulfr in a low voice, adjusting the loop in the rope. "Let's see how big you feel after tonight."

Mathios didn't say anything. His body struggled to hold himself straight as his knocked knees quivered beneath him. Baulfr pushed him toward the stairs and hung the rope around his neck. The stone, nearly the size of his head, hung down to his knees.

"Begin!" Baulfr hollered.

Adis opened the kitchen door with Yrsa and Eirún standing behind her. Søren's eyes met Eirún's as she covered her mouth and wept. She attempted to push past Adis, but she held her back.

"Mr. Baulfr, please!" Eirún cried, clenching a handkerchief against her chest.

"Get out!" he shouted.

The women trembled but stood their ground.

"I will not leave the boys!" Eirún exclaimed. "I'll stay until you're finished!"

With his chin still on the chair, Søren closed his eyes, feeling the burning heat from his swelling back. He couldn't see Mathios, but he listened to each heavy step as Mathios slowly dragged his warped legs up and down the stairs. He knew Mathios had to be careful not to knock the stone against his knees—it's how he got the warp in the first place. The best way was to bend your neck down and bow yourself over.

After what felt like an hour, he heard Mathios collapse and his body tumble down the stairs with a sickening thud.

A Lion in the Dark

M yla," Lombard whispered. "Take the girls to the bedroom. If anything happens to me, go out the window and flee to Porter's house."

"What's going on?" cried Hazel.

"Shush now," said Myla, taking the girls' hands and walking them into the bedroom. "Don't worry. It'll be all right."

Now standing alone in the family room, Lombard glanced toward the bedroom. His wife's face looked pale in the moonlight glowing through the window. He never saw such an expression of fear in her eyes. The sound of several men dismounting their horses came from outside the door.

"Lombard Greystrom!" bellowed a voice.

From the table, he grabbed Arnon's hunting knife and slipped it into his boot. With a deep breath, he walked out the front door. Outside, the air bit with cold. He narrowed his eyes, peering at the four armored men—two swordsmen with hands on their hilts and two archers who held torches that blew violently as the wind rushed from the mountains. The light flickered against their black leather brigandines, fastened over with many small plates crafted from Daecish steel. At their knees and elbows, he could just make out the underlying hauberks. Etched in white, the Daecish emblem of the three stripes almost glared against the leather of their upper right shoulders.

As Lombard's breath condensed into a fog before him, one of the swordsmen, who appeared to be a commander, stepped forward, motioning for the other swordsman to stand between Lombard and the house. The two archers each notched an arrow in their bow. Peering through the commander's barbute, he could not make out what he looked like, except that his face was deathly pale and his stature tall, as with most of the Daecish.

"We've been hunting you a long time, Lombard," said the commander with a hollow and gristly voice. He pulled out a scroll and cleared his throat as he unrolled the paper. "By command of the king, as written in Article Forty-Three, all citizens of Sunder, participating, exchanging, or assisting in the Silent Hither are hereby declared traitors of Sunder and Daecland, and have forfeited their rights as citizens, unto payment of death for high-treason."

From behind, the swordsman bound Lombard's hands behind his back and patted his legs and sides. Closing his eyes, Lombard silently prayed for Theos to protect his family.

"He's clear," the soldier said to the commander.

"And what of my own?" asked Lombard, keeping calm. "You have me, but let them go."

The commander walked toward Lombard, lifted his barbute above his mouth, and twisted his colorless face into a nasty grin. His stained teeth, jutting out from his receding gums, glistened in the torchlight. "Don't worry about your family," he said. "I assure you they will be taken care of."

Lombard knew by the commander's tone that his family was in danger. "Don't your own law ensure the safekeeping of women and children?"

The commander laughed and wiped his arm across his mouth. "Daecish law doesn't apply to Sunderian peasants."

Lombard's mind raced to find words to reason with the commander. "But am I not wanted alive in Llynhithe? If I give my full cooperation, will you not let my family be?"

"You have been a thorn in our side for a long time," the commander replied as he took a step forward. "And an especial annoyance to me. It's because of men like you that I've been stuck in this forsaken wilderness for as long as I have. The less of you there are, the better. Do you really think they will care if I bring you back dead?"

"Fine," Lombard's heartbeat quickened. "Kill me. But swear you will not bring harm to my family."

"And let them grow up to follow in your footsteps? I'm afraid that's not how this is going to work." The commander nodded to the swordsman behind Lombard.

As Lombard listened to the blade slide from its sheath, he took in a deep breath. With the thought of the soldiers slaughtering his family, blood surged through his body as he slammed the back of his head into the nose of the swordsman, knocking him to the ground. Clenching his arms, Lombard ripped the leather straps.

The commander stumbled back, pulling his own sword from its sheath. "Shoot him!" the commander spat out. "Now!"

Reaching for the hunting knife, Lombard bolted toward the commander just as the archers released their arrows. One pierced his shoulder as the other bore into his heart. Lombard tripped and collapsed at the commander's feet.

* * *

Peering down with hard eyes, Arnon watched his father collapse, and every muscle in his body trembled. He needed to do something, but like a fool, he left his bow in the house. Trying desperately to figure out what to do, he clenched his fists white as fury swelled within him. He suddenly remembered leaving the ax at the bottom of the hill. Rising to a crouch, he hurried down the bluff in the darkness of the shadow. He picked up his ax and glanced up in the direction of the soldiers. Then he peered to the back of the house and made his way to the open bedroom window. His mother and sisters huddled in the back corner, and he tapped the wooden frame. Myla jumped, grabbing her heart. He put his finger on his lips and motioned for them to climb through the window.

Hurrying forward, Myla shook her head with a quivering chin. "I heard it," she whispered, breaking into a quiet sob. "They shot him!"

Hazel cried out, but Fleta covered her mouth.

"Take the backtrail to Porter's house." His voice trembled. "He'll know what to do."

His mother shook her head.

"For the girls, mother, you must go!"

Fleta grabbed her and Hazel's hand and looked up at Arnon. "I've got 'em," she said with a confidence that surprised Arnon.

He kissed her on the head. "Be careful."

As they hurried up the path and over the ridgeline, Arnon climbed through the window and into the bedroom. Behind the door, he peered through the crack, just beneath the wooden hinge, and waited. He tightened his grip on the ax and prayed the soldiers would take their horses and leave.

A commander and swordsman stepped up to the front door. "Archers," the commander ordered, "go check the stable. Kill anyone you see." He stepped into the house, followed by the swordsman who gazed toward the dying hearth. They took slow steps as the wood creaked beneath their feet.

Walking around the right side of the hearth, the commander peered into the dark corners while the swordsman walked over to the dining table, just in front of the bedroom door. Arnon held his breath as the commander looked in his direction and pointed a finger. He stepped forward. Arnon's heart almost beat straight out of his chest. His palms turned wet, and his head felt light. The commander slowly pushed the door open. With his back now against the wall and his ax held high, Arnon let the door open against him. When it paused, the first thing Arnon saw was the tip of a sword enter the bedroom.

When the side of the commander came into view, Arnon summoned all of his strength and rammed his shoulder into the door, knocking the commander off balance. The commander shouted as Arnon swung his ax and the iron head lodged into the man's chest, reducing his shout to a desperate shriek.

Just as he wrenched his ax from the body, the swordsman rushed in with his blade swinging down. Arnon blocked the swing with his ax, but the force of the blow shattered the neck of the handle. Dropping it, Arnon tackled the swordsman as the back of his head slammed against the ground.

In a burning rage, Arnon wildly beat his fists against the swordsman's nose and eyes. The soldier reached up to defend himself, but Arnon gripped him by the wrists. Raising his head high, he brought it back down against the swordsman's face with a heavy thud. Several times he did this until the swordsman's body went limp.

Leaning back, his head went dizzy. He took in long breaths, not bothering to wipe away the warm blood which flowed down his face, dripping off his nose. Slowly opening his eyes, he watched the two archers stumble into the front door. The moonlight spilled in from outside and shed a silver glow on their armor. They both paused as they faced the darkness.

The first archer gripped the hilt of a short sword and darted his gaze to either side of the room; he took a single step forward. The other took a step back and pulled an arrow from his quiver.

"Commander!" shouted the archer in the front.

"Eyes sharp, Lieutenant!" said the archer in the back. "Eyes sharp!"

Keeping his eyes on the archers, Arnon picked up the swordsman's blade, gripping it in his right hand. With quaking muscles, he narrowed his eyes and lunged forward.

The first archer was turned away when Arnon slammed into him with a great thud, goring him through the stomach. Both Arnon and the archer crashed through the front wall, propelling wattle and dried mud in all directions as they collapsed on the cold ground outside.

Arnon flung himself up, but his body tingled with numbness. Collapsing back onto the archer, his head swirled. As he crawled off of the body, the searing pain of an arrow lodged into the side of his left shoulder.

The second archer, now standing outside, dropped his bow and reached for his sword. Arnon shook the dizziness from his head and felt around the dry ground. His right hand gripped a stone about twice the size of his fist. The archer ran forward, rearing his blade. As the blade swung down, Arnon swung the stone in his right hand toward the archer's temple.

The sword went limp in the archer's hand as the stone collided with his soft flesh. There was a muffled crack, and the archer's body fell over in a heap, sending dust particles swirling in the moonlight. Arnon's body wavered as his heavy breaths condensed before him. Their blood ran over his arms and hands. He could see the arrows shoot into his father.

Overwhelmed, he pulled himself to his feet and let out an aching howl as he stumbled backward. The venison pottage finally rushed up from his gut as he threw up onto the ground. His throat burned, and his knees gave out beneath him. He collapsed with a thud.

The Journey East

When Arnon opened his eyes, the air was still and quiet. His head pounded, and his body was sore. For the better part of an hour, he laid there gazing across the lawn at his father, whose eyes were half-open and still. Blood seeped from his nose, mingling with his black mustache and beard. That couldn't be his father. It was just a lifeless body with no soul. No light in the gray eyes, like the deer they slaughtered the day before.

He knew he needed to get up, but he just laid there, numb. It was strange to think that he would never hear his father's voice again.

At last, he tried to sit up, but his shoulder gave way, and he cringed as the fresh scab surrounding the arrow cracked, spilling blood down his arm. With shallow breaths, he checked the sagging shaft. The head of the arrow sunk deep but not into the bone. Picking up a small stick from the ground, he placed it in his mouth and rolled over onto his back. Grabbing hold of the wooden shaft, he closed his eyes in hesitation. Screaming through his teeth, he pulled the arrow out.

Gasping for air, he dropped it to the ground. His head swam, but there was no time to waste. He tore off what remained of his left sleeve, dressing the wound tightly. Pulling himself to his feet, he took a moment to compose himself as he stared down at the lifeless body of the archer before him. Beneath the tangle of bloody hair, the left side of his head was dark and sunken in. He was young, possibly younger than Arnon. Tearing his face away from the scene, Arnon gazed at the other soldier he had gored through the stomach near the broken wall—dark, hollow eyes gazing in the distance. The blood which seeped from the body had already turned a ghastly brown.

A mountain of guilt fell over Arnon, and he forced himself to take in what had happened. He'd kept his family safe. He'd avenged his father. It was necessary, and he knew it. But he couldn't shake the growing conviction that when he killed those men, something dark crept out of his heart. It wasn't what he did. It was why. There was a hatred in him he had never felt before.

Struggling to hold down his stomach, he hobbled back over to his father, and as best he could, lifted him from beneath the shoulders. From inside his father's cloak, his hunting knife fell to the ground. Arnon looked at it for a moment, examining the antler handle his father had carved. He picked it up, slid it through his belt, and carried his father into the house. After he undressed his father's shirt, he pulled out the arrows and cleaned his wounds. Afterward, he grabbed his hunting knife and pressed the tip against his father's chest, just breaking the skin, but he hesitated. He closed his eyes and swallowed, then he pushed the blade in and cut out his heart.

The air had warmed by the time Arnon crossed the bluff. He walked alongside Ansel with the reins in his left hand, and his father's sword sheathed through his belt. The wool blanket which concealed his father's body flapped in the wind—his heart wrapped in a cloth in a leather satchel.

The path to Porter's stretched nearly two leagues, but it seemed to pass too quickly. Watching his feet stride across the brown grass, he thought about the look on his mother's face when she knew her husband had been killed. She used to always joke that Arnon would never cry, even at her own funeral. He hated the fact that she was right. As much as he wanted to, he could never get it out of him. Whenever he did feel sorrowful, it usually came out as anger.

Just as the sun reached its full height, he rounded a low hill, and a small log cabin came into view, situated at the bottom of a shallow holler. Smoke seeped from the open windows beneath the straw and twig roof.

He made his way down the gentle slope. His mother stood with her back to him on the front porch by the left side of the house. When she turned and looked at him, his knees suddenly buckled, and his chest sank. A desire for the innocence he had as a child overwhelmed him, and even though he had washed himself before he left, he wiped his hands as if he feared that the blood of those men would stain him forever.

"Arnon!" Myla shouted as she ran toward him. Just as she embraced him in her arms, Hazel and Fleta ran through the front door as they followed after with tears streaming from their eyes.

"I'm sorry," was all Arnon could say. "I'm so sorry."

The next morning, Arnon awoke to the smell of pottage boiling over the open fire. His mother and sisters set up the table as Porter kept busy by the fire. Based on her dazed look and the rings around her eyes, he knew his mother hadn't slept that night. After they had buried Father, just before sunset, she had asked him what happened to the soldiers. He couldn't bring himself to tell them anything other than that they didn't have to worry about them anymore.

"The morn's leaving us," said Porter, looking down at Arnon with dark eyes and a white beard. "I don't mean to be blunt, but we got to eat in haste."

Before Arnon had a chance to stand up, Myla walked over and gave him a hug, kissing him on the forehead. "I don't care what happened, I still love you." She looked at him in the eyes. "And I'll always love you."

"I know." Arnon barely got the words out. His sisters smiled as if to try to make him feel better. He couldn't smile back, but he wanted to.

Myla poured the thin pottage into Arnon's wooden bowl with a thick chunk of rye bread, then ushered the girls outside.

Porter peered toward him, then to Myla. "We need to act now," he said, forking in a mouthful with his spoon. "How they found your location, I can't figure, but the authorities in Llynhithe will soon realize those who were sent out to bring in Lombard haven't returned. I'll give it three days before this place is swarming with them pale-faces."

Arnon swallowed. It was on him now to take care of the family—and to become a Dark Horse. He knew it was coming, but not so soon.

"I didn't plan on leaving 'til winter," Porter went on, "but given our current situation, I think we ought'a leave today. And I think going to Galvin and Kent will be the wisest course. Everwind's crucial, no doubt, but there be strength in Denhurst. Galvin sent word, more than once, asking for my help among 'em."

No one responded. Arnon tried to hide his discontent because he knew that his father wanted to go to Everwind.

"The oppression from the Daecish has grown since you all have left Everwind," Porter continued as if he could read Arnon's mind. "Galvin sent word that a draft will be enacted soon. For sure in Everwind. Perhaps other towns as well. But we've no details. The only possible rumor is that Daecland's at war with another country, and they'll be sending natives of Sunder to fight."

Arnon clenched his jaw. "They're sending our own people? Why don't they just order their soldiers back from Sunder and fight their own war?"

"You know very well, just as your father did, that Daecland isn't going to use up its own men before ours." Porter wiped the broth from his beard.

"But it's not our war!" Arnon snapped.

Myla laid her hand on his arm.

"You're right, but that don't matter," Porter continued. "The Daecish own us now. They're the elite class in our cities, not us. Save the few dastards in Everwind willing to sell their souls for a Daecish suit." He sniffed hard as if to take out a bad taste. "You can't hardly recognize her. Every building and street corner in Everwind's starting to look Daecish. And that was six years ago. Theos knows what she looks like now."

"But that's what many wanted," spoke up Myla with a sound of regret. "The Daecish brought new materials, ores, metals. In one way, many saw a better life after the invasion."

"But what about the families they're forcing into the mines and slums?" Arnon asked. "Or banning our festivals?" His face grew hot. "Or the fact that they are now sending our men to some war which we have nothing to do with?"

"I'm not saying they're right, son," Myla replied. "I'm simply saying that not all Sunderians have been treated the same, which makes the cause more difficult, especially in Everwind. If they see their own families prospering, why would they stand against the Daecish?"

Porter gave a sour laugh. "Some folks are masters at justifying their own actions."

Myla wiped off her mouth with her hands. "We must face the fact that many aren't going to stand up. Not unless something stirs 'em."

Porter set his elbows on the table. "People are too quick to act on immediate benefits, and they'll pay for it dearly. The mines are just the beginning. It's as if they forgot about the day they invaded." There was a long silence as Porter peered across the table. He took a long drink of mead. "I remember when it happened," he continued. "I's just outside Everwind. Shadows slithered on the ground, and I looked up. Everyone looked up. I remember the horror as we set our eyes upon thousands of what looked like beasts, soaring toward us betwixt the peaks of the Great Fringe. Wisps, they called them. Monsters birthed out of machine. Canons were mounted on their sides. I'd never seen or heard anything so destructive in my whole life." He groaned. "Within a few weeks, our kingdom was theirs. King Albern didn't do a thing; the last heir of the House of Burgess just let 'em come in and take over." He paused. "Still can't believe that was sixteen years ago."

Arnon frowned. He was only three when the War of the Wisps took place. He had never known a Sunder without Daecland. And since then, wisps were hardly ever flown. He only saw one once when he was about eight or so. It looked like a ship sailing through the air. Losing his appetite, he looked over at Porter. "Have you heard anything from Everwind lately?"

Porter stood up, setting his bowl on a small table. "Wesley reported to me not long ago. Though he didn't have any details regarding the draft, he did say that Dark Horse leadership's been weak since the Daecish sacked the Fellhouse Cellar. The Silent Hither's still active, but it don't seem to be growing. It'll need some more strength, likely from Denhurst, if it's gonna stand against the Daecish." He leaned over his chair and spit something on the ground. "However, Wesley did bring some interesting news. It seems they may have the support of a man, Geoffrey, who's actually an investigator for King Albern."

"For the king?" asked Arnon. "Then he must have some power."

"Well, power ain't quite right. Our king's a puppet for that pale-face Ónarr, at best. But Geoffrey's position may help the Silent Hither. We'll just have to see."

"Come on," Myla said. "The rest of this can wait until we get going to Denhurst."

"I'm not going to Denhurst," said Arnon. "Take the girls, but I'm going to Everwind to meet up with the Wesley and the court. That's where Father would have gone."

Myla's eyes grew wide. "No, you're not!" she exclaimed, planting her hands on the table.

"Mother—"

"I've lost my husband, and I'll not lose you! You can't possibly go on your own right now."

Arnon looked at her as gently as he could.

Porter cleared his throat. "If I may," he started as Myla glanced scornfully at him. "Ah, well." He cleared his throat again. "I think I understand Arnon's meaning. Lombard was one of the most influential Dark Horses in Everwind. They'll expect Arnon's arrival. And Lombard, I think, meant for him to go there."

Myla looked down at the table. Her chest shook. After a moment, she stood up and walked toward the front door. "Why don't you go to Everwind?" she asked as she stared into the open landscape. "And Arnon will go with us to Denhurst?"

"That's a good plan," he replied as he sat back down. "But unfortunately, I got no choice. I wouldn't make it within ten leagues of Everwind before I'd be spotted and killed. Arnon, however, he's not that well-known among the Daecish. He's grown up these past few years and'll have a better chance of getting through without being noticed."

"And if neither of us go, who will bring news of father's death to them?" Arnon added.

Porter chuckled. "And as far as I've heard, neither Drake nor Morgan has been impressed with Wesley's leadership, and it makes us all a bit nervous. They could use Arnon."

Myla wiped a tear from her face, and a heavy silence filled the room. She walked back in and sat back down in her chair. "My husband always believed in Wesley, and he wouldn't have put him on the court with Drake and Morgan if he doubted his ability."

Arnon had known Wesley all his life, and Lombard had always treated him like a younger brother. But as close as they were, Wesley had issues. Even as a child, Arnon knew something wasn't quite right with him. When they left for the Western Plains, Lombard finally told him how Wesley had been beaten as a child by his own father. Lots of kids were beaten. Even Lombard had given Arnon the occasional pounding when he deserved it, but apparently, Wesley's was bad enough to leave more than just physical scars. Some of the other men, Galvin and Porter included, had always been rough and stern with him—probably to try and toughen him up. But his own mother always thought it made it worse. Like his father, she pitied Wesley.

"Father knew I would be among the Dark Horses in Everwind," Arnon said in a softer tone. "I don't think he expected it to happen this way, but it did. What better plan do we have?"

Myla slightly nodded as she let another tear slip down her face.

Porter took a deep breath. "Right then. We'll leave immediately for Denhurst. There, we'll meet with Galvin and be an aid wherever he needs us. I don't have enough information to make any more of a plan than that. A few months ago, Galvin did send me encouraging numbers, though. Their movement's growing, and their leadership's strong. Denhurst's the light this dark land needs." He looked at Arnon. "As soon as I find out more, we'll send word to Drake. Let you in on what's going on." He leaned forward and spoke in a quieter tone. "You must remember that you're young. You've never seen battle, and you've never dealt with leading men, especially of the sort who have the strength and stubbornness to stand up to the Daecish."

Pride swelled in Arnon as he swallowed. "Of course," he replied, but he thought of all the training his father had given him and that now would be a good time to share that with Porter. He opened his mouth just as Porter stood up, but his eyes caught Myla's glare.

"Hold your tongue," she whispered.

Arnon closed his mouth.

That afternoon, Arnon helped the girls load their few belongings into a wagon pulled by two mules.

Porter walked up beside him. "If I need to ride by your homestead to get supplies," he said, keeping his eyes on the girls, "is it safe? You sure they're all dead?"

Arnon scarcely nodded. "Just don't let the girls see the bodies."

"Your father would be proud of you." He patted Arnon on the back and walked back to the wagon. Arnon could only look down. His father may have been, but he wasn't. His actions only made him feel wrong. Or something worse.

As he watched them ride south, he threw on his father's bearskin cloak over his shoulders. He would miss all of his family, but Hazel was the hardest to say goodbye to. She was still too young to understand it all.

When his family had rolled out of sight, he turned Ansel around and headed up the hill and back down the other side. He stopped at a small well, which Porter had dug several years ago. Even in the driest months, it ran cold and clear. With filled skins, he gave Ansel a kick and galloped east against the sun.

For three days, he rode, stopping only at night and to let Ansel rest. By the fourth morning, patches of low-lying pines and shrubs occasionally sprouted up along the now green landscape, marking the end of the Western Plains. Thin, steep tributaries cascaded down from the Great Fringe, eventually finding their end in the Swelling Sea to the south. Always, he remained close to the base of the mountains, with its black rocky crags rising above into the clouds. Although there were quicker paths to Everwind, he knew he needed to stay as far away from Daecish patrols as he could.

The fifth day brought clear skies and a chill from the mountains. Entering into a hemlock wood, Arnon dismounted Ansel at the mossy bank of a shallow stream that crept through thickets of overhanging rhododendron. On the far bank, several stone foundations of Sarig-make, dating to an age almost entirely forgotten, sat scattered in an overgrown glade.

Arnon closed his eyes; only the wind and rush of water flowing over bare rock into bubbling eddies surrounded him. Limbs high above creaked and sighed. Something small scurried through the dead leaves. He took in a long breath as a gust blew from the north, bringing with it the rich scent of evergreens. It'd been five years since he last stood in a forest.

With only a few hours of sunlight left, he gathered dried branches and twigs and scraped a piece of flint across a fire-iron, creating a spark in a pile of tinder. Cupping it in his hands, he blew gently until it birthed into flame. With the fire now going on its own, he pulled out a few apples from a satchel and roasted them over the crackling wood. Although the apples warmed his stomach, after eating them for four days, they began to grow tasteless. He was hungry for something else.

Walking over to Ansel, he pulled out a fine, meshed net that his father had given him when they still lived in Everwind. He was thankful he had taught him how to set a fish trap with it.

It took him a few hours, but he soon found himself roasting two brook trout stuffed with mint and wild ginger. As the wood crackled and hissed, Arnon heard the sudden loud snap of a branch about ten yards downstream. He stood up and notched an arrow in his bow.

At first, all he could make out was the silhouette of a man, hunched over. As he stepped forward, the firelight revealed an old man with a clean-shaven face. Thin white hair ran down the sides of his face beneath a worn blue cloak. Leaning on a small hiking stick, his free hand gripped a large brown sack thrown over his back. Arnon lowered his bow.

"Pardon my intrusion," said the old man in a hollow and dry voice. "I saw your fire and figured you a nice feller who might have some food to share."

Arnon knew to trust no one in the wild, but the last thing he wanted to do was show his own fear. "Sire, you're welcome to join me," Arnon replied but kept his bow close at hand.

The old man set his bag down on the opposite side of the fire. With a low groan, he lowered himself to the ground, still holding on to his stick. There was something unusual about the man's appearance. His large eyes seemed to observe everything he looked at in wonder. Almost childlike.

"Where you from?" Arnon asked. "If you don't mind."

"Before the Daecish came, I lived in Everwind. I had a nice wife and children then." He nodded slightly, but it didn't stop, as if he couldn't help it. "But they're now dead. After the invasion, they caught the plague, so I took to traveling. That's where I've been since."

Arnon had heard about the Daecish bringing over certain illnesses when they came over. It spread quickly. Killed thousands. Then one day, it just left. He handed the old man a trout, wrapped in a green fern. "Where do you like to travel to?"

"Nowhere, particularly. In my heart, I long for a place, but it's not to be found in Sunder."

"Earlon?"

"Afraid not."

"Daecland?"

The old man looked up at him with a crooked grin. "I should hope not."

"Which place is it?"

He took a bite of the trout. "A place where my family is alive."

Arnon slouched as he thought of his own father. He knew the old man meant a restored Sunder—a paradise, where many people would be raised from the dead. But the only hint of such a thing was found in Hælend's Ballad or some of the later chronicles written about the ballad. And even those were vague.

The old man pointed to the other trout in Arnon's hand. "You going to eat that?"

He looked at the trout. Not wanting to eat apples again, he almost hesitated but held in his sigh. "Eat as much as you want." He handed the trout over.

"Thank you, young lad," he replied as he took a bite.

Soon after, the old man threw the remaining bones into the fire and pulled a frayed gray blanket from his sack, littered with damp leaves, and laid down. "I hope you don't mind me sleeping here tonight," he said. "The fire's warm."

"Not at all," Arnon replied. "I'm Arnon Greystrom, by the way."

The old man sat up on his elbow and reached a hand out to Arnon. "I'm Benedict," he replied.

Arnon had never heard that name before. "What does your name mean?"

"It means 'the one who is blessed.'" He snickered. "A bit ironic, given my situation, ain't it?"

Arnon peered at the dark limbs beneath the starry sky. His own family name meant 'dark stream,' but that was common enough; clans were often named for the area they lived around. "I know what you mean," he said in response to the meaning of Benedict's name. "But maybe blessings don't always look the way we expect them to."

Benedict only chuckled.

"Is there anything else you do on your travels?" Arnon asked.

"Not really, but I enjoy sharing stories and learning new ones from those I meet."

"You're a storyteller?" His eyes piqued in interest.

"Some may call me that."

"How many of the old stories do you know?"

"Oh, quite a few." Benedict pointed upstream. "There're some old ruins just a stone's throw away from here."

"One of the old Sarig ruins," Arnon interrupted.

Benedict laughed. "I'm impressed. There are few who know that. Tell me, do you know any of their stories?"

Arnon thought for a moment. "I know part of Haiden and Aart."

Benedict laid once again on his back. "I'm old and tired, so how about I rest, and you tell me a story."

"Well," Arnon began, recollecting the way his father always told him the story. "Before our ancestors arrived from Earlon, the Sarig people lived here in this land. They were simple and peaceful, and they built these structures; halls cut into the rock of the mountains, houses of wood and earth built in the trees." Arnon longed to see such a site.

"My father said that the first Earlonians who set their eyes on these wonders described it in such a way that it was difficult to see where nature ended and where the structures began. It was as if the Sarig people raised their homes from the world itself. But soon after the Earlonians arrived, they quickly began to grow in number. It didn't take long before they overthrew a Sarig village by the Serin Sea, where they built a city."

"Everwind," added Benedict.

Arnon respectfully nodded. "Soon, our people desired to find a way through the Great Fringe, and there was a rumor that an isolated village, possibly in this very spot, knew of a path. The Earlonians sent out expeditions to search for the village but couldn't find it. Then one day, an expedition, led by a young captain named Aart, came upon a young maiden. Haiden, she was called, the daughter of a village chieftain. She was said to have auburn hair and green eyes. One of the most beautiful of all the Sarig people."

Arnon hesitated. He almost didn't want to tell the rest of the story. "It was late spring, and she was betrothed to be married. As was the custom of her people, as far as we know, the day before her wedding, she went from her village to praise and give thanks to Theos in the wild. That was when the expedition found her, singing near Sefa's Rill. Fearing their intentions, she refused to reveal where her village was. Because of this, the men believed her village knew a path through the Fringe. It was said that Aart tried to dissuade his men, but tired of their search, they mutinied and took her captive. They continued to search the foothills for her village, and they eventually found it. Holding Haiden as a ransom, they demanded to know the path through the mountains, but the villagers insisted that there was no such path. In a fury, the men slaughtered the villagers, including Haiden's betrothed, and burned their homes to the ground."

Arnon paused again, looking across the stream. He pictured the old ruins. "Whether by an act of mercy or malice," he continued, "they let Haiden go. Although some of the traditions differ, it's most commonly said that with a broken spirit, she wandered alone in the forest for many days until she came upon the brink of a steep cliff. There she wept and threw herself to the bottom."

There followed a long silence until Benedict spoke up. "And what happened to Aart?"

"After the men returned to Everwind, they weren't punished. Angered, Aart renounced his rank as captain. He left his own people and went to look for Haiden. When he couldn't find her, he found a Sarig village and remained with them for the rest of his life."

"And also," added Benedict, "Aart was the first to give them the name Sarig."

"The People of Sorrow," Arnon replied. He picked up a stick and stirred the coals in the dying fire. "My father once told me that the people of Earlon left their kingdom because they were running away from something they had done. Something they were ashamed of."

"It's possible," Benedict said.

"Sometimes I hear our history and I wonder if we're any different than the Daecish. They've invaded our land, but we did the same thing to the Sarig. Maybe committing even worse crimes."

"You're a good storyteller," was all Benedict said. He rolled over and closed his eyes.

The next morning, Arnon awoke with a shiver. Cold invaded the air and penetrated through his damp clothes. He wanted to rotate the soreness out of his left shoulder, but he knew if he did, the wound may open again. The fire had long gone out. Benedict was nowhere to be found—only shallow footprints headed north before disappearing behind a thicket of rhododendron.

After a short breakfast of apples, Arnon mounted Ansel and continued east. He figured it would be another three days before he'd reach the eastern edge of the Swelling Sea. By then, he would finally turn south toward Everwind.

The Finnvard River

Eirún sat in the shadowed corner of the kitchen, keeping her eyes on both boys. That morning, Adis had given them each a long swig of liquor, keeping them sound asleep on their low cots situated side-by-side. The cruelty of Baulfr brought an ache in her chest she couldn't shake. But she was angry about more than that. She had just learned that Søren foolishly showed off his note at the dining table. Why didn't he listen to her? Was it just to make the other boys jealous? Did he want a beating from Baulfr?

And as angry as she was at Mathios for even attacking him, one look at his swollen neck, discolored into blotches of purple and brown, forced her to feel pity. Born to a mother who had a thing for sailors, Mathios met a lot of men, and he probably never knew which one his real father was. When he showed up at the orphanage, barely five years old, one of those men had beaten him so badly she didn't think he'd make it through the night. But he healed, and although the orphanage should have been a haven, the poor boy shattered his own soul when he attached himself to Baulfr. It was as if he'd take any man at that point to fill the role of the father he needed. Someone to imitate. Even if that man despised him.

Her own father died when she was still young. And just four years ago, her mother joined him. She had no siblings. Other than Adis and Yrsa, no friends. Really, she was no different than the orphans she took care of.

The kitchen door swung open, and Adis walked in with the doctor. She glanced in Eirún's direction with a sympathetic smile. Although Eirún didn't speak, she listened intently.

Peering through his thin wire spectacles, the doctor examined Mathios's neck. "There's deep bruising beneath the rash. This is the worst I have seen from Gunborg in a while." He sighed. "There is certainly injury, a neck strain at the very least. Keep it supported, watch for any signs of concussion, and most importantly, let him rest." He peered at Adis. "You would think with all of the progression our country has made in the last century, the General Assembly would have passed a law to protect the children in our orphanages." He added in a lower voice, "If I had the say so, I would have had Baulfr locked up in a prison years ago."

Adis glanced to the closed kitchen door. "Mr. Baulfr's already told me that both boys are to be working in the ditches by the end of the week. If he sees them in this kitchen for longer than that, he'll—"

"With their backs in this condition, they will be lucky if they're even able to walk in two weeks." He clasped the leather strap to his medical satchel. "Especially Mathios. I'll talk to Baulfr myself. Do your best to keep them clean and bandaged to prevent infection." He approached Søren and skillfully removed the burn dressing on his right arm, coating the wound in a dark-colored, pungent oil before taking his leave through the back of the kitchen door. He paused, looking down at Eirún. "Keep an eye on those boys. They'll need plenty of broth. Mix it with liquor if the pain gets too bad."

"I will." She barely got the words out.

Over the course of the next few days, Eirún did as she said but spent most of her time waving air over their backs when they complained that their skin felt too hot. Even though there was a constant whistling of steam and the foul smell of old food wasting in a large tin bucket, the boys slept for long lengths. When they woke, they seemed to never speak to one other. To her relief, and undoubtedly to theirs as well, Baulfr never showed his face in the kitchen.

On the evening of the sixth day, she was sitting by Søren's cot, and the sound of the other boys in the dining hall crept through the open door. Apparently, Jokith was saying that Baulfr had thrown both Mathios and Søren in the hole for a week. Another suggested that they had been chopped up and fed to the dogs.

Eirún turned her attention to Søren, who seemed to not be listening to the boys as he traced his finger through the grout of the clay bricks. All of her plans seemed to be on the verge of ruin. Having accepted a new job at the textile mill, she had planned to move away with him to Vagholme. She had everything in place, but now her position may be given to someone else. Why did Søren have to act so foolishly? Why did any of this have to happen?

Letting the thoughts go, she pulled out a small leather-bound book, laced in gold threading. From a middle page stuck out her feather bookmark.

A glint appeared in Søren's hazel eyes. "Is that?" he asked.

"Just because you're both stuck in this bed doesn't mean we can't go over a few lessons."

Mathios strained to roll onto his side and kept his eyes on her.

"What are w—we going to learn?" Søren asked.

"Let's see." She thought as she opened the book, pulling out the feather. "Last week, we did arithmetic. How about we do some reading this time? Just some basic words?"

Both boys nodded.

After half an hour or so, Eirún looked up as Mathios's eyes went heavy, and he rolled onto his back. She set the book down and adjusted his blanket.

"Please don't stop reading," whispered Søren.

Eirún leaned forward, running her fingers through Søren's dark-blonde hair. "It's getting late."

Søren sighed. "Eirún?"

"Yes?"

"Why did you want me t—to pack my clothes? Do you remember? You said so in the note you gave me."

Eirún looked over at Mathios, who now seemed fast asleep. "We'll talk about that when you get better." Søren frowned, but she was too upset to talk about it. "Don't worry," she continued. "You'll heal soon enough." She placed her hand over Søren's, feeling his trembling fingers beneath her palm. "What's wrong?"

His chin slightly quivered. "I lost . . ." he hesitated. "I lost a ring that meant a lot to me."

"Do you know where you lost it?"

He nibbled on his fingernail. "The headmaster's quarters."

Eirún knew about his ring. Despite finding it out in the street, he told the boys it was his mother's, and he probably half-believed it himself. But Søren never met his mother and likely never would. Eirún saw it often, but it was always terrible to witness such young minds be filled with so much hopelessness that they made up false hopes just to survive.

She reached her hands behind her neck and unclasped a thin leather necklace hidden beneath her blouse. At its end hung a lens, which she handed to Søren. Numerous holes had been drilled through the outer plate, one of which the leather cord had been strung through. "Here," she said. "I don't know if we'll be able to find your ring again, but I want you to have this."

"What is it?" Søren asked.

Though it was barely larger than a gold coin, his palm recoiled under its weight. "My father gave it to me when I was a young girl. It's a lens to a camera. One of the earliest models. The glass has long been cracked, though." She pointed to a thin crack along the outer edge. "He bought it from a merchant when he traveled to Norfrost."

"What's it for?"

"Well, it makes pictures."

"Like the one by your bed?" he asked as he ran a finger along the ribbed edges of the brass.

"Yes," she smiled. "Just like that one."

He raised the lens to his eye and looked at her but brought it back down with a look of surprise. "You were upside-down."

Eirún laughed and hung the leather cord around his neck. Fresh blood from his tiny back had already stained his clean shirt. "There," she said, forcing to keep her smile. "Now get some sleep." She lifted the lantern off the shelf and bent down to kiss Søren on the head once again. "I love you."

"I love you, too."

Stepping into the darkness of the empty dining hall, Eirún paused as she stood in front of the fireplace, where a few glowing embers still smoldered beneath the ashes. She placed her hand on the mantle and closed her eyes, sniffing in the sobs that yearned to burst out.

For a second, the darkness threatened to creep back over her. In the past, she occasionally fell into depressions she couldn't seem to come out of. There was no reason for it; her life seemed to go well enough, relatively speaking. All she could remember was that it was like a madness of contradictions. She was lonely and yet refused to see anyone. She wanted to feel happy but clung to her sorrows like a lover. And through it all, her emotions felt more like mocking ghosts, for deep down, she felt nothing. Just tired and weary.

After a moment, she took in a deep breath and wiped her cheeks. Everything will work out. There's no reason the job position won't be open in a couple of weeks. She'll take Søren, and everything will be fine.

Turning up the lantern wick, she continued through the hall and opened the southern door, already able to hear Baulfr snoring from inside his room. The narrow rug felt soft beneath her bare feet as she continued to the maid's quarters. She turned the knob, pushing the heavy door against its iron hinges as it creaked. Inside, two large lanterns were lit, bouncing a golden glow against the deep green walls. In their nightgowns, Adis and Yrsa both sipped their tea.

"How's the little one?" Adis asked as she pulled back her long gray hair.

Eirún sat down and rubbed her toes. She wanted to reply but already felt herself fighting back tears again.

Setting her teacup on a short stack of old books, Yrsa sat beside her and rubbed the back of her shoulders. "He'll be just fine."

"If he doesn't get infected."

"Adis!" Yrsa snapped, widening her brown eyes.

Adis waved her chubby hand. "I wasn't thinking, I'm sorry." She grunted as she lowered herself onto her bed, and the rusted springs screeched beneath her weight. "He'll get well before you know it. You remember when he came down with that fever? How old was he?"

"He was four," Eirún replied as she gazed between her feet at the dark wooden floor. It had just been swept yesterday, and clumps of dust were already collecting.

"I didn't think he'd make it," Yrsa added.

"He broke that fever in no time." Adis laughed. "And remember? As soon as it broke, Baulfr had to go off to Scathwold, and you took that boy right out into town!"

"We thought you'd lost your mind!" Yrsa exclaimed. "If Baulfr had of found out . . ." She shook her head.

Eirún laughed as she wiped away a tear.

"Where'd you take him to again?"

Eirún thought back, remembering his round face beneath that wild blonde hair. His tiny feet couldn't carry him fast enough down the streets. "We just walked around. I showed him some of the shops." Suddenly her lips trembled. "He never let go of my hand. All day he held it. And he was always singing to himself." She sniffed with another short laugh. "Most of it made no sense. But he had this wonder in his eyes. This excitement of what life had to offer." She finally let go and wept into her hands until she could taste the salt in her tears.

"There, there," Yrsa said, squeezing her shoulder. "You're the closest thing to a mother that boy's ever had. Have you mentioned your plans to him yet?"

She wiped her nose on a handkerchief. "I gave him a note. I wanted to surprise him, but since his injuries, I don't know what's going to happen."

"I'm sure everything's going to be fine," Yrsa encouraged. "Have you written to your employer? About the delay?"

"I have," Eirún replied. "But I haven't heard anything back yet."

"I'm sure it'll be fine," Adis added. "And we all know that textile mill will be good for him. Help him get rid of the stutter and teach him to toughen up a little bit. You think Baulfr's harsh?" She laughed. "The moment Søren tries to make up some excuse in a place like that, he'll wish he were back here!"

"And it'll teach him a little humility and respect," Yrsa exclaimed. She fiddled with the laced sleeves of her nightgown. "I know you love that boy, but the way he talks to you sometimes—you can't let him keep doing that."

Adis shook her head. "He can be a little manipulator, that's for sure. Always trying to make you feel bad for him."

Eirún didn't respond. Normally, when Adis or Yrsa said such things, she let the words roll off with no thought. She had always known that Søren pitied himself too much. She also knew he had a problem trying to make others feel guilty as if he was always the victim. But she had often done the same thing, especially when she went through her bouts of depression. Maybe that's why she babied him too much. But this time, his carelessness had gone too far, and Yrsa and Adis' words sank into her heart. This incident may have very well lost them their opportunity to move to Vagholme. "I only wish we could have left a week ago."

"You won't forget to write to us, now, will you?" asked Yrsa.

"Of course, I won't forget."

* * *

It had been nearly three weeks since the flogging incident, and Søren was beginning to feel stronger. Even Mathios had occasionally walked around the kitchen. But on this evening, his weariness seemed to get the better of him, and he fell asleep just after dinner.

Eirún soon stepped into the kitchen and sat down on Søren's cot. "Do you remember asking about the note the other day?" she asked in a whisper.

"Yes," Søren replied.

"Do you know why I wanted you to pack your clothes?"

Søren shook his head.

"Because I have a new job in Vagholme, on the bay."

Søren stared at Eirún, widening his eyes. "You're not going to leave me, are you?"

"Not at all." She rubbed his cheek. "I've made arrangements for you to come with me."

"As an, um . . ." He thought for a moment. "An apprentice?"

"Yes, there's a textile mill there, and you will be under Mr. Solveig. He's agreed to take us both on. The original plan was to leave the evening I gave you the note. I wanted it to be a surprise. But due to this little incident, we were delayed and almost lost our opportunity." She grinned. "But yesterday morning, I received a telegram that we are still welcome, and Mr. Solveig will expect our arrival next week."

Søren's heart began to race, but he also felt overwhelmed. "Was that why Mr. Baulfr said he was glad to get rid of me?"

Eirún sighed. "Don't worry about what Mr. Baulfr said. All will be made right, and you'll forget this place." She tucked him in. "Now, get some sleep."

"Eirún?"

"Yes?"

"When, um," he fiddled with his fingers, "when we get to Vagholme, can I call you mother?"

Her expression softened. "Of course."

Feeling warmth in his chest, Søren could hardly contain his joy. "And . . ." he hesitated. "Can I tell the other boys?"

Eirún's face suddenly hardened, and Søren bit his lip. It was a look he had never seen on her. "Have you not learned your lesson?" she said in a hoarse whisper, but her eyes watered as if she was sad. "No, you can't tell the other boys. How would that make them feel? Can you not see that all of this has happened because you're always trying to make other boys jealous? If you hadn't of been acting foolish and shown off your note, none of this would have happened in the first place."

Søren tried to hold back his tears as his stomach churned. The only person who had ever been kind to him suddenly looked at him like everyone else. His heart broke, and he felt like crawling under the bed and bawling. With a quivering mouth, he tried to say something, but only tears came out.

"Stop it!" she suddenly snapped.

Her tone made him lose his breath.

"You won't make me feel bad this time! You will not make me feel guilty."

"But . . ." he tried to get out, still sobbing. He didn't want her to feel guilty, and he wished, more than anything, that he could take back his question.

She stood up and walked to the door. Tears flowed down her own face as she looked back at him. "If the only reason you want to call me mother is to make the other boys envious of you, then you can't. Do you understand?" She walked out the door, shutting it behind her.

Mathios moaned as he shifted his legs beneath the blanket. Did he hear their conversation? Ignoring the thought, Søren buried his face into his pillow and wept.

At the end of the week, he knew his time to depart with Eirún was drawing close. But she had barely spoken to him. It didn't help that he didn't say anything to her. He couldn't even say he was sorry. He wasn't sure why, though. Maybe he was scared, or maybe he wanted her to apologize instead. That was the meanest she had ever been with him.

Mathios was picking at his breakfast, but Søren couldn't even touch his. For the past two days, they had both been allowed to walk around the kitchen, and Søren felt his strength returning.

The maids pushed through the kitchen door carrying piles of bowls and plates. Søren looked toward Mathios, who stared blankly in his direction, but his eyes seemed to be fixed on nothing as the maids walked back and forth through the kitchen. He had barely touched his food. It was then that Søren noticed that Mathios was staring at his chest. Søren glanced down and wrapped his fingers around the lens, then tucked it behind his shirt.

After the maids had finished the dishes, they walked into the dining hall. Mathios blinked out of his daze and stretched his arms. Though he still looked tired, he got out of his cot and stood up, looking out the back-kitchen door.

"We should go outside," he said. "Just for a moment, to get some fresh air."

Søren thought Mathios sounded weak and shaky. "Do you think that's a good idea? You don't look very well."

"I feel fine," he insisted.

Søren looked at the door leading to the dining hall. "Do you think they'll let us?"

"I don't mean go out for the whole day." His eyes dropped to Søren's chest again, but he quickly looked away. "I just mean stretch our limbs and feel the air again. We've been trapped in this hot kitchen for weeks. Come on, it'll be fun."

The tone of Mathios's voice made Søren feel uneasy, but the thought of fresh air beckoned him. They both headed out the door without even slipping on their boots.

Outside, the sun flashed in Søren's eyes, and he lifted a hand above his brow. Despite the sound of steam-powered carriages puttering along the streets on the other side of the orphanage, green meadows stretched out before him, with the Finnvard River winding swift and deep like a silver ribbon. Birds sang in thin chirps as they darted around the yellowing leaves of a thick elm tree. A small fire burned beside several large pots, and the scent of the smoke filled his nostrils. Feeling the soft, thick grass below his feet, he sighed in relief as he took in the breeze once again.

"Sure is a nice day for autumn," remarked Mathios. "Would be nice to cool off in the river."

Søren thought that wetting his feet wasn't such a bad idea, but he didn't want to stay out too long. He turned to Mathios to suggest another time, but he wasn't there. "Mathios?" he asked aloud. There was no reply. He wasn't by the kitchen door. A rustling noise came from around the side of the orphanage.

As Søren walked around the corner, he startled. Mathios stood with a raised hammer while tears filled his eyes.

"Mathios?" Søren felt a dread fall over him as he took a step back.

"What makes you think you're so special?" Mathios hollered as he swung the hammer against Søren's jaw. Bones in his face cracked, and he collapsed to the ground. Mathios gripped him by the legs. "Eirún doesn't love you! No one does!"

Disorientation swept over Søren as blood spewed from his mouth and his tender back scraped across rocks and dirt. He flailed his arms, trying to grasp at Mathios in a pitiful attempt to break free.

Approaching the river, he tried to call out for Eirún, but no words came out.

For a second, he thought he heard her voice scream from the kitchen door. Then, with a great plunge, the coldness of rushing water surged over his body, seizing his breath. Mathios gripped Søren's hair at the back of his head and shoved his face underwater as he cried out inaudible curses with a cracking voice. Søren could not think, save the desperate will to breathe. He soon kicked his last, and his lungs filled with water.

Ghosts of Birchton

Geoffrey stood before the broken remains of what used to be a small cottage on the southern end of Birchton. The Capital Guard had already removed the bodies of the family that had lived there, or at least the ones they could find. The same pungent fumes, like a grotesque mixture of sulfur and rotting earth, filled the air and burned his nose—just like the other two houses before it. In some accounts, apparently, the earth trembled as far as Three Rivers. He scratched his short beard and pulled out a leather-bound book, issued by the Daecish, as he scribbled down descriptions of the incident.

"Who taught ye that?" came a sudden voice from behind.

Geoffrey turned to see an old man wrapped in a grimy wool cloak. All but two teeth seemed to be missing. "I'm sorry?" he asked.

The old man pointed to the book. "Did the Daecish teach ye how to write?"

He closed the book and slid it back into the outer pocket of his dark blue coat. "I was fortunate to have an education when I was younger," he replied. In truth, it was the reason he was made an officer of the Capital Guard.

The old man didn't say anything as he walked past Geoffrey along the mud streets and into a ruined shelter across from the rubble. Beside it ran a narrow alley, from where a woman stepped forward, revealing a thin body beneath her sunken cheeks and dark hair. Several bruises marred her neck, and her gown looked little better than worn rags. She motioned an inviting finger for Geoffrey to walk over, but he went on his way.

The loneliness and sorrow of Birchton lay so thick he could feel it on his skin. As if it was yesterday, he remembered when the Daecish, along with the few remaining elite Sunderians, ruled by their blindness and greed, cleaned the lower class out of Everwind. In their attempt to create a new Everwind, they forced whole families out of their homes, deporting them to designated slums like Birchton and the Southern Squalor. Or worse, they were sent to the coal and iron mines outside the city.

As Geoffrey headed west, the streets remained mostly empty, save a half-starved dog ill with mange lying on the doorstep of an abandoned home. The thatched roof sagged within the broken half-timber walls. On the other side of the street, a few families peered out of their bare windows in the direction of the rubble. A young girl, no more than five, stared at Geoffrey with eyes far beyond her years, clumsily holding a doll against her chest. Her sparse clothing fluttered against the cool breeze, which crept into their homes like fingers of death. Before long, she'd be in the streets with the other women, doing whatever it took to survive.

Geoffrey felt ashamed of his cotton-lined coat and brick home, which he had just moved his family into. It was hypocritical. As a full-blooded Sunderian, he couldn't stand the Daecish, and yet he not only depended on them for his income, he was living well compared to most others.

Now passing the southern edge of Birchton, the city took a drastic change within a single block as the mud streets turned to smooth cobblestone laid down seven years ago. The decorative lampposts and white trimmed buildings, all of Daecish fashion, lined the streets of the remaining Western District. Almost every building was adorned with ornate windows, and many of the oiled parchment panes were now refitted with blown glass. Stepping in and out of warm, lit taverns and shops, crowds of people seemed to walk along the streets so casually, as if Birchton was just a ghost—a figment they could neither see nor wished to believe in.

With the sun now beginning to set, Geoffrey picked up his pace to Three Rivers. He had been waiting too long to get a confession from Hal, and he knew that the tavern would be the place to do it. Picturing the scene in his mind, he thought of a perfect line to say to Hal as he was being arrested.

"It's a lot harder to keep a lie when you're drunk," he said to himself with a wink. That sounded good.

Stepping up to the tavern door, he hid his grin and cleared his throat, nodding to two sentries of the Capital Guard standing on either side. He walked inside, and they followed him in as the door closed behind him. Smoke and sour ale filled the air. Despite the crowd of loud and arrogant men, Three Rivers was a reminder that the Everwind of old was still alive in the hearts of many Sunderians. The thatched roof leaked, and the floorboards were badly built, but it was once one of the nicer buildings in Everwind. A glimpse of home. Geoffrey relished the warm burning fire, the clucking chickens weaving themselves around the trestle tables, and the fact that the Daecish rarely walked within its walls. The owner, Old Bale, was even kind, which was hard to find in the realm of tavern owners. On this particular evening, the tavern was crowded with men discussing the incident Geoffrey had just returned from.

"I'm telling you," said an old man sitting by a table situated by the hearth. "It's Hælend's Ballad. Alphyns are coming soon." He cocked an eye. "With their long mouths and jagged teeth. Few appeared in the old days, but Hælend said that they'll be coming in droves, and then," he lifted a mug, "it'll be the Day of Reckoning. They're the ones causing these cave-ins. They're already moving."

Another man laughed. "Old man, what do you know of Hælend's Ballad? It ain't alphyns but wyrms that'll come, and that's not for another thousand years at least!"

The old man looked down at the bottom of his mug. "Alphyns first, then the wyrms. All led by the Bane of Sunder. You jus' wait and see."

"You can both quit your blabbing," said another man on the far side of the room. "I ain't seen enough signs for it to be the end yet. These are jus' natural quakes, that's all. Happen all the time."

"Neither quakes nor creatures," murmured another man at a table just beside Geoffrey. He leaned in and whispered to his friend. "It's them pale-faces. They're the real alphyns the chronicles spoke of. They be Sunder's Bane." He waved his hands toward the door. "They're the ones causing all these the cave-ins."

The old man's face furrowed into a frown. "Don't ye be a fool. Sunder's Bane'll be a man riding an alphyn, and you know it!"

At that moment, several other men joined the debate, and the conversation quickly turned to an unintelligible rumble as everyone spoke over the other. Like any other Sunderian, Geoffrey had a deep love for Hælend's Ballad, as well as for the chronicles, but he was hesitant to add his opinion on what happened in Birchton. His guess was as good as theirs, but it could have been anything.

Passing through the crowd, he walked over to the bar. There was the man he was looking for. "How's the mare doing, Hal?" he asked, sitting beside him.

Hal turned toward him with lazy eyes and a sluggish sneer. His black hair was so greasy it looked wet. "With them clothes and proper speaking, I thought you was a pale-face for a second."

Geoffrey glared at his own uniform with a frown. He may have worked for the Daecish, but he resented that comment.

"But she's much better now," Hal continued. "I'll have her riding again in no time. Did you find out who did it?"

Geoffrey shook his head. "We've been questioning those on your list, but nothing's come up, which is actually why I'm here. I'd like you to answer a few questions for me."

Hal stiffened and seemed to try to give him a stern glare, but his head wavered. His sweat reeked of alcohol. "You got questions for me?"

Geoffrey pulled his book out and flipped through a few pages of scribbled notes, scratching his beard. "You said you were here in Three Rivers the night your brother was killed, right?"

"That's right." Hal took a drink from his mug.

"What time did you get here?"

He rolled his eyes up in thought. "I told you already. Four in the evening, and here I stayed until nine."

"And then you left and found your brother in his home, dead?"

"Yes," replied Hal shortly as he set his mug on the table with a thud, splattering ale on the bar top.

"Why did you go to your brother's house?"

"Why you asking me these questions, again?" Hal replied with a raised voice, at which point several ears in the tavern turned toward him, and the patrons brought their conversations to a low murmur. "I already told you! He owed me and said he'd pay that night. I went to collect my due, and I found him dead."

"Well, Hal, I have to be honest with you. I first grew suspicious when everyone you put on the list of possible suspects was someone you owed money to. What was it? A total of," he glanced at his notes, "two-hundred aracs between four different lenders?" Geoffrey almost chuckled at the thought of Hal's plan. He motioned for the barman to bring him a drink. "But when you say you went to your brother's house at nine at night to collect his debt, that doesn't add up."

Hal laid his palms on his thighs. Geoffrey grabbed the tankard and took a long draught of a dark lager, wiping the foam from his mustache. "Through my investigations," he continued, "I've learned that you'd already visited your brother that morning and asked for your debt, which you did not share with the officials. And I was told by several witnesses that your brother said he couldn't pay you until next week. So, why did you go back that same night?"

The red in Hal's cheeks sallowed. He remained silent.

"It must be difficult to owe so many debts and to have your own brother evade you week after week." Geoffrey glanced to a table beside him. The men stared into their mugs, frozen in obvious interest.

"You don't know what it's like!" Hal hollered out in sudden rage, knocking his mug over. He stood up and stabbed his finger toward Geoffrey. "Those men were gonna kill me if I didn't pay. My good-fer-nothing kin owed me!"

There was an abrupt commotion among the crowd while the two sentries rushed toward Hal, slamming him against the bar. They bound his hands and carried him out as he hollered out curses.

Geoffrey threw his hands up. He forgot to say his line. An old man sitting several seats over stared at him, and Geoffrey raised his tankard to him. "It's a lot harder to keep a lie when you're drunk."

The old man frowned. "What makes you think I'm drunk?"

"No." Geoffrey chuckled. "Not you as in *you*." He pointed to the door. "I meant . . ."

The old man waved a dismissing hand and turned his attention away.

". . . Hal," Geoffrey barely mumbled. He took another draught. It sounded funnier when it was in his head.

Geoffrey continued to finish his drink while the crowd's excitement dwindled. Old Bale hauled a wooden keg on his shoulder and disappeared into a back room. Beneath Geoffrey's stool clucked a chicken, pecking at stale bread crumbs. A conversation picked up from the table just to his left, where three men were talking. Geoffrey recognized two of them—Lester, a wealthy businessman and head of the Merchant's Guild. He had a large reputation among the few Sunderians who still held some form of power, and his secretary, Miles, sat beside him.

"I'll tell ya, business is as good as ever these days," Lester said, running his hand through his slicked back, white hair. He looked seventy but dressed as if he was some twenty-year-old Daecish lord. "Every year for the past four, I've had a profit increase. In fact, we just opened up a new shop in the Eastern District, isn't that right, Miles?"

"Indeed, it is, sire," Miles replied as he glanced over to the third man, who sat across from him. "Wouldn't you say so, Mr. Claude?"

Geoffrey laughed to himself. It was as if they were trying to sound Daecish.

"Well, Mr. Lester," said Claude, dabbing the corner of his mouth with a handkerchief. Due to his overly large gut, he had to sit further back from the table than the others. "I got to give it to you. You've built yourself a fine empire."

Lester gave only a slight shrug but compensated with an overly wide grin.

"With fine businessmen like you," Claude continued, "it'll be no time before this city is trimmed to a proper state."

"Indeed, Mr. Claude. Indeed," said Miles as he ran his fingers through his thinning hair. "Mr. Lester here's taken a point to volunteering his time for the government in cleaning up the streets. With these designated slums, proper gentlemen don't have to worry about casting their eyes on them unruly folk any longer."

Claude nodded. "Filthy, they are."

"Pile 'em up nicely and keep 'em out of sight," exclaimed Lester. "One of the best things the new government's done for us, those slums. This city was ripe with scum. A gentleman couldn't hardly walk out his doors without being bombarded with beggars."

"Agreed," said Miles. "It's no wonder the government don't send them all to the mines. It would be good for 'em, you know. Give 'em some work to do for a change. Then maybe they might put food on their table instead of begging us proper working men."

Both Claude and Lester nodded in agreement.

"Most of the folk in the Slums are part of that Silent Hither anyway," said Lester, sitting back and patting his stomach. "We don't need their violence and crimes in these areas. You remember that Dark Horse uprising several years ago?"

"Like it was yesterday," Claude replied.

Geoffrey's face grew hard. Wishing to listen no longer, he finished his drink. "How much?" he asked Old Bale.

"Just an arac."

Geoffrey pulled out a three-arac note and slapped it on the bar.

"I'd be glad to go back to bartering," Old Bale said, grabbing the note. "More efficient than this Daecish garbage.

"That would be a good day," Geoffrey replied.

Old Bale brought back his change. "I hear Denhurst's still on the barter system."

"Not for long," Geoffrey replied. He stood up to walk out the door but paused by Lester's table. "You were there?" he asked. "You saw the Dark Horses' riot, and the Daecish soldiers take them down?"

"Of course, I did," Lester replied, clearing his throat. "And who might you be?"

"Where was it? Where were the Dark Horses attacking?"

Lester shot a sour look Geoffrey's way. "You best remember who you're talkin' to." He waved a hand. "But none the matter. It was four blocks down from the Western gate. I saw them attacking the merchants of the produce shops."

"Funny," Geoffrey replied, "because I was there on the street corner, and I remember watching the soldiers drag the already dead men out onto the streets from Fellhouse Cellar. There were no attacks except what spread through the rumors you obviously drew your account from."

Lester's face went red as he glanced at his two companions. Geoffrey walked out the door, not bothering to wait for a reply. He cursed himself, suddenly feeling foolish. Just because he supported the Silent Hither didn't mean he had to announce it.

Stepping into the night air, a cold shiver ran down his limbs. He headed south. Up above, the stars shone brightly, and the full moon cast a pale light on the shops as their owners closed their doors and blew out their entry lanterns. Daecish soldiers were posted on nearly every corner. Why did they even bother keeping the Capital Guard?

"We're just puppets," he said to himself.

Reaching City Hall, he hurried up the steps. For as long as he could remember, the Capital Guard operated out of the castle. But when the Daecish arrived, despite their numerous renovations, they found it too impractical. So, they had this building erected about ten years ago over an old foundation. The new City Hall was tall, built of stone and brick, and covered with a steep shingled roof. Two spire towers stood on either side with black Daecish banners hanging down their face.

Stepping inside, Geoffrey's footsteps echoed along the marble floor. Just ahead were two winding staircases rising on either side until they joined on the upper floor. Daecish architecture at its finest. To his right sat the main office for the Capital Guard.

"Where've you been all day?" came the voice of Barnaby, a short, plump, elderly man who wore a new pair of spectacles seated on his round nose. Thick, white hair wrapped around the back and sides of his head, but the top was as clean as his face. He had been on the Capital Guard longer than any other man on staff, and he made sure they all knew it.

"When did you get those?" Geoffrey pointed to the spectacles.

"You like them?" He took them off with a smile. "Commander Veurðr gave them to me as a gift. Made in Scathwold, he said."

"Where?"

Barnaby slid the spectacles back on as they walked into the main office. "Not sure. Somewhere in Daecland." His expression quickly changed as he pointed a finger at Geoffrey. "But don't change the subject. Where've you been?"

"I closed the case with Hal," replied Geoffrey, sitting down in front of Barnaby's desk. "He admitted to the murder."

"I knew you'd break him," Barnaby said with a laugh, but he glanced sharply toward the Daecish guards by the front entry and motioned for Geoffrey to follow him to a back storeroom. Geoffrey rolled his eyes as he stood up and followed Barnaby through the open door. Descending to the bottom of a set of old stone stairs, Barnaby lit a lantern. "Geoffrey, you've been gone the entire day. Now, I know you weren't investigating Hal's case for eight hours. Please tell me you weren't over at the incident in Birchton."

Geoffrey looked at Barnaby but didn't respond.

"Geoffrey," he hissed. "You got to stop meddling in affairs which you are not assigned to. Especially in the slums!"

"Why especially the slums?"

"What do you mean, 'especially the slums?'" Barnaby shook in frustration, his glasses almost shaking off his nose. "Because that's where the Silent Hither folks assemble! Do you want King Ónarr to think you a spy? Because that's what you look like." He paused, taking a deep breath. "We have to be careful, Geoffrey. The Daecish watch our every move, and I know you'd never do anything to bring ruin on yourself or your own people, but when you disappear all day in Birchton, you begin to look suspicious."

Geoffrey sighed. "So, when did you start calling that Daecish tyrant your king instead of Albern?"

Barnaby almost looked shocked. "Because Albern's not our king anymore. He lost his mind years ago, and we've been conquered, Geoffrey. You seem to have forgotten that."

Geoffrey knew that. He also knew Albern's father had lost his mind as well. They did a good job hiding it from the public, but the kingdom suffered because of it. For the last twenty-eight years leading up to Daecish occupation, Sunder was ruled by mentally deranged men, bent on spending the last ounces of their wealth on every vile lust imaginable. Geoffrey never liked to admit it, but the kingdom was falling apart when the Daecish invaded. "I haven't forgotten anything," he replied coolly.

"What you need to realize," Barnaby interrupted, "is that Albern is a puppet at best. At least what's left of him. He can do nothing without Ónarr—I mean *King* Ónarr. And if you're caught snooping around places like Birchton, you'll find yourself arrested along with anyone else who has talked to you—namely me!"

"So, we just ignore the fact that holes have opened up in the city, sinking the homes above them?"

"If it happens in a slum, then yes!"

Geoffrey clenched his fists. "We've had three of these incidents in the past week. At least seven people have died, Barnaby, seven. How can we ignore that?"

Barnaby slid his glasses back up his nose as he peered at Geoffrey. "I don't like it any more than you do. But we must watch our every step. The slums are off-limits." He rubbed his forehead. "Geoffrey, I've known you since you were still wetting your trousers. Your father, before he passed, Theos bless him, was like a brother to me. Please trust me. Keep your nose out of trouble. You're a good man, a good man. Things'll look up. You'll see."

Geoffrey gazed at the mostly empty shelves in the old room. They once held scrolls and books containing hundreds of years of Sunder's culture and history, some of which were penned when his people were still in Earlon. Books were rare in Sunder, and although a few still remained in the Spire, the Daecish threw most of them out like trash, including the last copy of the Acwellen Chronicles. All his people had left now were what the older generations had put to memory. Just the thought of it cut Geoffrey to the heart. There was a long silence until he finally spoke up. "Of all people," he said, opening the door. "I thought you would see it as I do."

He walked out of the room.

Three blocks down from City Hall, Geoffrey found himself on the doorstep to his townhome nestled near the Western Gate. The outside was built of brick and half-timber with a tiled roof. He opened the thick oak door, and a warm light flooded out upon his feet. The crackling wood burned in the fireplace room to his left, and his wife, Sarah, was cooking dinner in the indoor kitchen in a room on the right—a rare addition to most Sunderian homes. Lilly, their only child, was crying for something, but she could not yet form her words.

"Hi, dear," said Sarah, "I hope you're hungry."

"Very!" Geoffrey replied. He sat down at the wooden table across from the brick oven.

Sarah straightened her blue woolen linsey as Lilly tugged at her, pointing to the cobbler she just pulled from the oven. She stood in an awkward posture as the weight of being seven months pregnant began to take a strain on her back. "How was your day?" she asked, patting Lilly's hand away.

Geoffrey smiled while he watched Lilly stretch to the tip of her toes, reaching up in vain. "It was all right," he said as he stood up and took a spoonful of cobbler and handed it to Lilly. He placed a hand on Sarah's belly, feeling a little kick. "That's my boy."

"You mean girl?"

"Nope, I meant boy. Acton."

"Acton?"

"You don't like it?"

"Well . . ." Sarah smirked.

"I can't believe you don't like it." He slumped his shoulders in disbelief. "Acton was a hero." He chuckled. "You must not like the name because you're pregnant."

She dropped her jaw and laughed. "You can't blame everything on me being pregnant."

"But you know it's true," Geoffrey said in the kindest tone he could muster. "You get more emotional; your tastes change. Things you like when you're pregnant aren't the same things you like when you're not."

"Fair enough," she conceded, "but I clearly remember not liking the name Acton even before I was pregnant."

Geoffrey knew he wouldn't win. Besides, if he kept this going, she might actually get emotional. Pregnant women were unpredictable. "Fine, I give in." He bent down and kissed his daughter on the head. "I'm sure we'll think of a name we all agree on. Isn't that right, Lilly?"

She jabbed her spoon at him for more cobbler.

"Did you even eat any?" he asked. "You're wearing it all. Come on now. No more 'til dinner!" Geoffrey picked her up and wiped off her face while Sarah set the table.

As they ate, Geoffrey stared at his wife. Her faint smile lines didn't even begin to sap the youthfulness in those slender green eyes. And he loved how she always held her long brown hair up in a wooden pin. It gave her a look of elegance.

Sarah kept glancing up and blushed. "Are you going to keep looking at me like that?"

"I can't help it." He broke a piece of bread. A short silence followed as Geoffrey's mind wandered. "I went to Birchton today," he said. "I saw this child, a young girl."

Sarah glanced up, wiping cream from her fingers.

"Her eyes looked so hopeless," he continued. "I couldn't help but think of Lilly." He shook his head and changed the subject. "Do you need help packing bread for in the morning? The meats are all salted, aren't they?"

"It's already taken care of," she replied. "Paige has the bread at her house."

"Where you going?"

"Southern Squalor."

"Nowhere else?"

"Don't worry, Chloe's handing the food out at Birchton. We won't forget about them, I promise."

Geoffrey furrowed his brow. "Just be careful."

"You know I will." She wiped off Lilly's face. "So, this girl you saw—what about her?"

It's like she could read his thoughts. "I don't know, I just—" He glanced out the window. "I can't keep doing what I'm doing. Something has to change. Children are starving to death while everyone pretends like it's not happening. I saw that girl, and I felt guilty. I wanted to take her and everyone else there and bring them home."

"I know," she replied, "but what more can we do? We're going to them as often as we can with food."

Lilly smacked her cobbler with her wooden spoon as the strawberry filling splattered through the air.

"It's keeping some of them alive." He wiped cobbler off his sleeve. "But it won't fix the problem. Most will still starve or be sent to the mines, which only Theos knows what goes on there. No, I need to do something." He paused in thought. "I want to meet with Wesley again and see what help I can offer."

Sarah took his hand. He felt a slight tremble in her fingers. "Whatever you decide to do," she said, "I love you, and I'll support you."

Although her words encouraged him, a weight sank in his gut. All he needed was her affirmation. Now he knew he had to do it.

Sarah stood up to clean the dishes but paused, looking out the window. "Did you hear that?"

Outside, a small crowd gathered in the street, peering north. Several Daecish officers, followed by large, iron-barred carriages, with soldiers lined on either side, marched north toward Birchton.

Geoffrey walked out the front door as Sarah grabbed hold of Lilly, keeping watch from the window. The soldiers continued marching north, out of sight. Geoffrey ran back in and grabbed his coat.

"I'll be right back," he said.

"Be careful!" Sarah shouted after him.

Geoffrey followed the crowds along the road. Some of the women were still in their nightgowns. Others wrapped thick cloaks around themselves in the chill of the autumn night. Rounding a corner, one block past the City Hall, the carriages and soldiers made their way north until the last carriage stopped between two quiet homes. Further down, another stopped, and then another, until all the carriages stretched across the southern end of Birchton.

Geoffrey ran up behind a barrel situated next to a lamppost and squatted, watching the commanders bark out orders in the moonlight while their breath condensed in the air. Lanterns lit up here and there from within the dark homes. The soldiers lined up before a dozen houses and drew their swords.

They pounded their fists against the doors and window frames. Geoffrey's stomach sloshed like water when one soldier kicked a front door down. A shrill scream cut the air—a woman or maybe even a young child. More screams eventually broke out as the soldiers entered each home.

When they marched back out, they gripped the bound wrists of men. Some were only in their shirts; others had nothing on, having likely been pulled from their beds. Every one of them was loaded into the empty carriages until their bodies pressed against the iron bars on all sides.

The shock of the scene caused Geoffrey's arms to tremble, and he ran south. A heaviness weighed on his chest while images of being torn from his family raced through his mind. He ran past City Hall, but as he neared his house, he stopped. Another set of screams and cries erupted from the south. Down where Old Birchton Way ran into Western Road, women helplessly pointed to another set of iron carriages, filled with men, rolling toward the gate and out of sight.

* * *

With a flat wooden shovel slung across his back and a hammer through his belt, Drake punched Darragh in the right eye once again, then he glanced up and down the dark alleyway. Although night had fallen, the full moon threw enough light to make him nervous. There were distant shouts, but he ignored them. They were too far to bother him right now. He grabbed Darragh by the wrists and dragged him west toward the outer city wall. Darragh feebly waved his legs, but he was too drunk to actually do anything.

"Where . . ." he slurred. "Where you takin' me?"

"Far away from here," Drake replied in his deep rough voice.

Reaching the city wall, he removed several loose stones at the base. There soon appeared a hole, barely enough for a man to crawl through. Eyeing his surroundings again, he shoved Darragh through the hole before following after him. He had known about the hole since he was a boy. It was well hidden and easy enough to remove the stones to prove a useful escape out of the city if one needed to.

As soon as he stood on the green grass, the wind blew from the north across a deep silvery blue landscape. The scattered dark shapes of boulders dotted the rolling hills, which slowly descended to the shores of the Swelling Sea. Drake peered north and watched as Daecish carriages rolled out of the Western Gate. He sneered at Darragh, then grabbed him by the throat and drug him down a hill, between two boulders. There, he squatted and looked back to the dark shadow of the encircling stone wall of the city, ensuring no one followed him through the hole. Then he glanced across the other side of the boulder at the carriages until they disappeared out of sight. The wail of women echoed from inside the city. Darragh helplessly tried to lift himself off the ground.

"What are ye doing?" he grunted with a scowl on his face. Drake kicked him in the stomach as he rolled onto his back with a deep groan. "Yer gonna kill me, aren't you?" He coughed up thick mucus from his lungs.

Drake couldn't help but hate what he was about to do. Wiping his damp cheek, he pulled the hammer from his belt and raised it up high.

A sudden look of fear came upon Darragh's face. "I ain't gonna do it again!" He raised his hand. "I swear. I love her!"

"Sorry, Darragh, but I can't trust you. I gotta make sure you keep your promise."

He swung the hammer down hard and swift.

Afterward, he took the shovel and dug a hole, burying Darragh's body between the two boulders.

Brine and Blood

Søren's mind clouded with memories, dark and mournful, as the tide shifted his motionless body. He thought back as long as he could remember—his mother he never knew, his father turned away as he reached out for him. He couldn't even remember what his face looked like. Suddenly, the imprisonment of the orphanage walls clamped around him. At first, the colors were vibrant and the voices loud. Everyone moved around busily. Never looking at him. Never taking notice. He passed through the hall and through many other rooms until the faces of the boys blurred with distant laughter, and the colors began to fade. Then he heard her voice; clear and beautiful. The voice he had been searching for. But as he reached to grab hold of that memory, it faded with the rest until all was lost.

A surge of coldness rushed upon Søren when he awoke. He opened his mouth to gulp for air, but only saltwater clogged and burned his throat. He threw out his arms, but the water strained his efforts. He opened his eyes and frantically swam toward the light. When he broke the surface, he let out a hoarse cough as saltwater spewed out of his lungs. He took in a sharp, gasping breath.

"Eirún!" he tried to cry out, but his jaw cracked behind his teeth. He screamed out in pain as he choked on the brackish mix of brine and blood. His broken jaw throbbed as the copper taste warmed his tongue. Losing strength, he looked ahead and could just make out the shore not far in the distance. When he glanced over his shoulder, the water stretched endlessly to the horizon, mirroring the vast emptiness which began to fester inside of him. His panic slowly transformed into hopelessness, and he peered back to the shore through his blurred vision. Lifting his heavy arms, he attempted to paddle toward the land, struggling to draw breath against each rising swell. But he knew he couldn't make it. He never learned how to swim.

Continuous swells rose behind and crashed over him as the water drove into his stinging eyes. With sputtering coughs and quick desperate breaths, he finally collapsed beneath the power of the sea and tumbled along the sandy bottom. He fought his way back up, but wave after wave continued to push him down and stir him beneath the murky water. Before long, he found himself struggling less as the power of the sea overwhelmed him. He could no longer sense which way was up or down, and with no strength left in him, he gave up and closed his eyes.

Then, as if he had made it up in his own mind, a sudden tug yanked at him, enveloping his entire body. Pulling him up. Breaking the surface once again, a cool breeze brushed against his face with rushing water flowing across his fingertips. It had to be a dream. Maybe he was dead. But soon, a bed of warm sand coddled him. He closed his eyes and slept for an unnatural length of time. As the sun rose above the rim of the world, Søren opened his eyes, though his vision was blurred. How many days had passed since he fell asleep, he did not know. The sand gently brushed against his body as the wind blew from the south. He went to lift a finger, but his numb body lay motionless.

Seeing something in the distance through the corner of his eyes, he startled and blinked several times. At first, he only noticed a dark shadow, like a hovering black mist over the beach. Then, from within it, walked forward a large beast, almost wolf-like, but bigger. Søren's breathing quickened as he turned his eyes toward it. The creature still walked towards him, but the black shadow behind it vanished. He was sure it was going to eat him, but he had no strength to move. There he waited and watched as it drew ever closer. Now only a step away, Søren held his breath as he waited for it to swallow him whole. But it wasn't just fear that seized his breath, but a sour, foul smell that burned his nostrils.

With a gag, he attempted to breathe as little as possible. And although his vision still blurred the edges of things, and his head swirled as if it was spinning in water; he thought he could see the beast lowering its back beside him. And there it waited.

Was any of this real? He hoped the beast would get up and leave, but it stayed. Maybe Eirún would come for him. Maybe she was close by.

By the time the sun was high, Søren lifted a finger before resting it once again on the sand. Then he lifted two fingers. Soon he summoned the strength to lift his hand. At which point, he carefully reached out toward the beast, patting the air. Thick, bristly fur poked against his fingertips. Other than soft panting, the beast made no sound as its hide raised and lifted with each breath. Søren tried to make out its features, but his eyes still couldn't focus. Whether the smell faded, or he was just getting used to it, he soon found it easier to breathe.

After a time, the beast shifted closer to him, keeping its back low. Surprised by his own actions, almost as if he was possessed by some greater will, Søren found himself climbing onto the beast. His heart fearfully pounded through his chest, but he somehow knew he was supposed to do this.

As he shifted his weight over its back, he laid his head down, exhausted. Cracking his eyes open, all he could make out was thick matted fur against his cheek. The beast's muscles rippled beneath the bristly hide as it stood up on all fours and carried Søren beyond the beach and into the land ahead. Despite his efforts, as soon as the sand shifted to green grass, Søren fell into a peaceful and careless slumber.

When he awoke, he was lying on a bed of thick grass. Looking up at the blue sky, he knew he didn't feel right. His heart felt thin and frail, as if he was being stretched away from himself. Having never felt such a feeling, he tried to ignore the sensation.

As he sat with his palms pressed against the grass, he tried to understand where he was. Did the beast carry him there, or was it all just a part of some dream? A rising panic swelled up as he yearned to be with Eirún. He never thought he would want to be back in the orphanage so bad. Suddenly, the thought of Mathios and the river rushed back to him, and he shook with a deep pain.

His back ached, but not nearly as it had the day before. Or maybe a week before? He didn't know. Rubbing his blistered and chapped lips together, he lifted his hand to his swollen jaw. It still throbbed, and he was afraid to move his mouth. He checked the burn on his arm. Although tender, the scab had grown smaller and softer from the saltwater. There was no sign of the beast or the hovering shadow.

Just ahead, a deep clear lake filled the heart of a vast green valley. Beyond, the horizon lay covered behind towering mountains of dark, rocky slopes. Except for a single weeping willow beside him, no tree grew. No birds chirped, and no insects crawled on the ground. The only sound came from the distant moaning wind. The sun was just rising in the east as the branches from the willow slowly rustled together in the breeze. He placed a hand on his stomach as it growled at him.

He lifted his heavy hand to his chest and felt something inside his shirt. Touching his neck, he pulled the leather strap and set the lens in his palm. Running his fingers over the cracked glass, he looked at it for a long while. He never got to tell Eirún, but even if the ring he had was from his real mother, he'd gladly lose it again to have this lens. He didn't want another mother. He wanted her. Remembering how angry she was with him, he, at last, buried his head in his knees and wept.

After some time, he lifted his face and let the wind cool his wet cheeks. Peering at the lake again, he lifted himself to his feet and walked forward, his numbing toes pressed into the cold sand. The water was clear and smooth. He could see all the way to the deep stony bottom, although he saw no fish. There was a purity about the land around him. He could almost feel its innocence—untouched by human hands as if he was the first soul to ever stand there. For a second, he wondered if he was even in Daecland anymore. He knelt and dipped his hands into the cold lake and took in a drink. The water flowed down and soothed his throat, and he sighed as the cool liquid eased the pain in his jaw.

A sudden howling wind bellowed from the jagged peaks. Startled, he looked up. On the far side of the lake, just before the roots of the mountains, lay a dark mound of brown and gray. Its colors felt uninviting within the beauty of the emerald landscape.

Curiosity took the best of him, and he walked along the beach. His footsteps echoed in the silence of the valley. Making his way around the lake, he neared the mound, and a sudden blast of wind rushed from the east, and he gagged as a familiar putrid smell of rotting earth and sulfur filled his nose and clung to his throat. Although he could remember some things, most of his thoughts were vague, like shifting shadows, and the familiarity of the smell was beyond his grasp. He lifted his shirt to cover his nose and squinted his burning eyes as he continued forward. A thick mass of flies began to swarm around his ears, clinging to his clothes and face. Søren swatted them away, spitting out as one crawled into his mouth.

Shielding his eyes from the sun, the mass now appeared to be a large creature. It was so still it appeared dead, but he couldn't be sure. A thought kept popping in his mind like a flashing light. He needed to run away. Stay safe. But something familiar about the creature kept him standing there.

Lying down, with its back toward Søren, its height reached three times himself. Still holding his nose, he walked along its length toward its rear, observing the matted gray fur. It had no tail, but its hind legs stretched out across the grass, where sharp ivory talons curled from its paws into the earth. A frisson rushed from Søren's jaw and down his chest as his balance wavered for a moment. He peered up toward the head, where its long mouth hung open, with a sagging, pink tongue. And teeth—rows of teeth, long and jagged like the mountain peaks.

He caught his breath. That couldn't have been the beast he had ridden earlier. It was too big. Too terrible. He cowered back as he shot glances around him. He slowly took a step back. But just as he did, a deep, rumbling growl echoed from the mouth of the beast, and its side raised and lowered with a heavy breath which snorted through its nose. A spark shot down Søren's spine, and he opened his mouth to cry out, ignoring his cracking jaw, but nothing came out. With legs quivering like rope, he turned and stumbled until he controlled himself, and then he ran—away from the lake and away from the beast. Over ledges, through ditches and bogs, he went on until his pulse started beating in his neck. His legs ached, and his bare feet bruised as they pounded over the rocks, but he never looked back.

Approaching the incline of a steep ridge, his legs grew numb, and his lungs burned. When he finally crested the peak, he leaned over and braced his hands on his knees. Across the landscape, the rugged mountains sloped down into gently rolling hills with sharp peaks still lightly scattered along the northern horizon. Far in the distance, a thin strand of smoke stretched into the air.

The Prisoner of Astford

Standing just north of Astford, beneath the crisp blue sky, Egbert tugged on the thin twine. The hog only grunted, digging its nose in the rich earth, snorting for truffles. Egbert sunk his chin into his neck and pulled down his shirt over his large belly with his free hand. He never could keep it down. Although the sun was high, he quivered in the chill of the autumn air. He was jerked forward as the hog moved on, forcing him to pick up his pace. "Blast it, Egbert! Take it easy!" he shouted at the hog as it neared a large, smooth-barked tree with broad leaves, just turning yellow.

The tree line, running along the hills of the eastern horizon, always reminded him of the old tales Henley used to tell him. Stories of hero's like Acton and Wrecan—always traveling into dark forests, rescuing damsels, or fighting off strange and mysterious beasts. Egbert wasn't too sure about fighting anything, but he always liked the idea of rescuing some maiden in distress.

Egbert picked his nose. He almost wiped the sticky end of his finger on his shirt, but something scurrying in the distance pulled his attention. He pulled his shirt down again, stretching it almost to the point of ripping. It was probably nothing, but what if the scurry was a maiden running through the fields? Maybe she was lost and needed a strong man to look after her? The last thing Egbert needed was to look ungentlemanly with his gut hanging all over the place. Looking over his left shoulder, Egbert's daydream dwindled. The figure of a small boy ran down a hill against the backdrop of the Great Fringe.

"Who goes there?" bellowed Egbert, followed by a grunt of disappointment.

The boy sped up until his legs wavered and buckled as he collapsed at the bottom of the hill. The hog trotted toward the boy, pulling Egbert behind. After a few steps, Egbert leaned over, pulling on the twine so he could catch his breath. It was further than he thought. The twine slipped through his hands. "Get back!" He picked up the twine as the hog shoved its nose on the boy's face.

The boy was breathing, but his eyes were closed. Scratches and bruises covered his body, with his left cheek looking almost vile as it protruded awkwardly out, swollen and discolored. His tattered clothes didn't look much better.

"Hello?" questioned Egbert, poking his finger against the boy's shoulder. The boy opened his eyes and startled with a hoarse scream, scooting away from the hog. Looking into the boy's eyes, Egbert gasped and took a step back. They were dark and empty—nothing like he had ever seen. His mouth went feeble, and his heart lurched. "Are you's . . ." he could barely get it out. "Are you's a hant?"

The boy narrowed his eyes. "Hant?"

"Don't you know what a hant is? A ghost?"

The boy shook his head.

Egbert dared to lean forward and poked the boy in the shoulder again, then he jumped back. "What happened to you, boy? You a'right?"

"What?" he asked.

"What you running from?"

"There's a—there's a monster." He pointed toward the north, still catching his breath. But nothing could be seen except the low-lying hills backdropped by the mountains. "It was by a lake."

Egbert noted his strange accent. "You hit your noggin or somethin'? There ain't no monsters round here. Just sheep, mostly." He shook his head. "Youngsters and their imagining's. You look famished. What's your name?"

The boy continued to stare at the hills, taking in quick, deep breaths. "I'm sorry?"

Egbert rolled his eyes. "I said, what's your name?"

"Søren," he finally said.

"Søren, mind telling me what town you's from?"

Søren looked at him oddly.

Was the boy really that dumb? "Where—is—you's—from?" Egbert drew out in a loud voice.

Søren didn't say anything.

"Now I know ye can talk, I jus' heard ye."

"M—Mr. Baulfr's orphanage," was all he said.

Egbert frowned. "Mr. who?"

Søren's gaze darted around. "I—I came from over there." He pointed north-eastward, toward the mountains.

Egbert looked toward the vastness of the mountain range. "Ain't nothing up there but the Great Fringe." He pondered for a moment. The Great Fringe? What would he be doing over there? And he sure did look peculiar, with that blonde hair. And what a strange accent. Suddenly, he let his mouth drop. With darting glances, he dropped the twine and left his hog while he grabbed Søren under the arms and, with a great grunt, threw him over his shoulder. Holding on to Søren with his right arm, he desperately tried to hold up his sagging trousers with his left hand as he trotted toward the outskirts of the town.

"Where are you taking me?" cried out Søren, beating Egbert's back.

"Sorry, but I got no choice! Can't have you being seen!" Egbert huffed and heaved until he finally dropped the boy to the ground and grabbed hold of his wrist before he could run off.

"Ow!" screamed Søren.

"Now, don't get cross! You wanna be seen?" Then Egbert lifted up Søren's arm and noticed the scab. "Oh, dear! Sorry," he said. "Here," he grabbed his other wrist. "Is that better?"

Søren raised an eyebrow at him.

"Now, you just be quiet, and no harm'll come to ye. Ye hear?"

Søren didn't say anything.

"Bugger, boy, don't look so wary. I ain't gonna hurt ye."

Søren gave a slight nod as Egbert struggled for a moment to lift himself back to his feet, and holding Søren by the hand, kept low as they walked to the town.

"They'll be so proud of me," Egbert said to himself with a grin. "They might even name me Corporal!" He laughed as he shouted, "Corporal Egbert!" He covered his mouth and looked around frantically, making sure no one heard him. "Quiet," he whispered.

Starting off once again, he led Søren through the backdoor of the old town hall. Built of dark wood, it was the only two-story building in all of Astford. In the days when the lords of the House of Denholm still ruled the area, it was the center of most of the village activities. But since the Daecish arrived, they built a new town hall on the eastern side of the village, leaving this one practically deserted.

Inside, he led the boy across the wooden floor, which matched the walls. Passing a table surrounded by several empty chairs, he came to a door that led down a set of stairs toward the cellar.

It was a small space, consisting of a single room built of stone, with two iron caged jail cells on the right side. Egbert set Søren on the straw-laden ground of the first cell and closed the door. Grabbing the brass key from a wall-mounted shelf, he locked the door shut. "Now, you jus' wait here, I'll be right back!" He ran up the stairs, grunting with a great racket as the wooden steps bowed beneath his feet. He shut the door behind him.

* * *

Bile roiled in Søren's stomach. A dark, ghost-like silence settled into the dank cellar, with only the occasional drip of water from some unseen corner. The thick scent of mold was almost too much. He tried to take in his surroundings, but a parched mouth and a growing fear of the darkness kept his mind distracted. He laid his face in his hands, hoping the room would stop spinning. The thin, stretched out feeling which had plagued him since he awoke in the valley had returned. A rattle in the cell echoed to his right, like the clanking of rusted iron. But as he peered into the shadows, only a rat made its way along the edge of the stone wall until it vanished into a dark crack.

Did the rat make that noise, or was he just hearing things? Maybe he was going mad? Søren closed his eyes as if doing so would make that terrible room go away. Part of him wanted to shout, but he only sat silently in his own disbelief. The monster. The shadow. Waking up in this strange land. It was all too much to take in.

After several minutes, a low commotion rustled from upstairs, and dust fell through the board cracks of the ceiling. The door to the cellar swung open as Egbert and two other men walked down, each of whom carried a lantern in their hand.

"Here he is, Burlan! I told you I got'm! Straight from the Great Fringe!"

The two men walked to the cell gate, peering at Søren. "Egbert, what have you done?" One of them asked, setting his lantern on a shelf. He must have been Burlan. Søren had never seen hair so dark— black and parted to the side. He didn't look mean, but there was a seriousness in his brown eyes. Almost like he'd lost something, or maybe something bad happened to him.

"Pardon, sire?" Egbert peered over Burlan's shoulder at Søren. His eyes were small and spread out, almost too far, giving him a fishy look. "I did what should have been done, right? Henley, you're proud of me, ain't ya?"

"Egbert, you can't just kidnap a child," Henley said with a sigh.

"Well . . ." Egbert trailed off, fiddling with his fingers. Even as he slumped his shoulders and sunk his wide chin into his neck, he stood nearly a foot taller than the other men. Søren didn't realize he'd ever meet someone fatter than Baulfr. Maybe Adis was. Both of them had more teeth than Egbert, though.

Henley leaned down, eyeing Søren. His expression seemed a little gentler than Burlan's. His hair was lighter, and his face square, with a short wide nose. But his clothes and accent were just as strange as the others. "He don't look Sunderian, that's for sure."

"He's got a Daecish look about him," Burlan said. "Certainly pale enough. Maybe Egbert's right?"

"Reckon he might be a half-breed?" Henley offered.

"Don't think so," Burlan replied. "They never live long. One side or the other would've killed him out of shame by now. Besides, look at him. He ain't got an ounce of Sunder blood in him." He paused. "Henley, take a look."

Henley peered at Søren's jaw. "Looks broken."

"Not the jaw. His eyes, they're . . ."

Both men looked at Søren for a long while, occasionally glancing at one another, but said nothing. Søren looked away in embarrassment but kept shifting his eyes toward them. Despite his fear, he was intrigued by the oddness of these men.

"Egbert," said Henley. "If you don't mind waiting upstairs, I'd like to talk with Burlan in private."

Egbert slumped his shoulders even lower, if possible, and nodded as he moped up the stairs. As he shut the door, Søren heard no more footsteps, only heavy breathing through the door crack.

"Egbert?" Burlan rolled his eyes. "You're not eavesdropping, are you?"

"No, sire, Mr. Burlan!" His voice sounded muffled but loud. "Jus' goin' on my way!"

Burlan quietly laughed. "What are we gonna do with him?"

"He's gone too far this time," Henley said in a darker tone.

Burlan motioned for Henley to step back from the cage, but Søren could still hear their words. At first, he hardly understood them. It was as though their sentences were so slurred together they sounded like one jumbled word. But when he listened carefully, he could make out most of what they were saying.

"You're right," Burlan said, "but Egbert's just a dolt. He only wants to do something to make us proud."

"I understand your kin and all, but kidnapping? Really? If he don't mind himself, one day he'll—"

"I know, I know," Burlan said. "But—"

"But what?"

"What if some use could come out of this?"

"What do you mean?"

"Well . . ." Burlan paused.

Søren looked behind him at a small opening near the top of the stone wall, barred with iron rods. It gave no light, and it was too high for him to look out of. It didn't take long for his fingers and toes to grow cold as the chill penetrated through the dirt floor. Looking higher up, he could just make out the glow of warm light on the floor above, spilling through the cracks of the ceiling.

"If the boy's really Daecish," Burlan went on, "that's worth something, ain't it? Maybe the—" He eyed Søren and cupped his hand around Henley's ear, mumbling some inaudible words.

"I don't know," Henley replied. "Sounds too risky for my blood."

"Well, what about the Fringe? What if perchance he came through 'em? What if he knows of a pass?"

"A pass? Sunder's been sending out people to look for a pass for ages, and none's ever been found. Besides, what are we gonna do with a pass through the Fringe? March into Daecland and wave hello?"

Burlan threw a hand in the air. "What have you got in mind, then? What are we supposed to do with the poor lad?"

Henley turned to Søren and crossed his arms. A strange chill ran through the cellar, and goosebumps rose on his arms and legs. "I don't know. Egbert didn't just kidnap anyone. What if he's really Daecish? Egbert'll be hanged, and if we get involved, we'll be right there with him."

"Which is why we got to protect him. He's got the mind of a child. He's stupid, but he don't deserve to go to the gallows." Burlan set his hands on his hips, meeting Henley's gaze. "Let's have a meeting with Abbot. Perhaps he can shed some light on this."

There was a short silence. Søren shivered as he gazed at both men. They both looked so big. What were they going to do with him?

"You sure about this?" Henley asked.

"It's the best option we've got. In the meantime, he can stay in the cellar. No soldiers will find him here." Henley didn't seem to listen as he still looked toward Søren. "Those eyes," he said. "They look so heavy and—"

"I know what you mean," Burlan replied. He walked over to Søren and knelt down. "You just relax. We ain't gonna hurt you. What's your name?"

Søren swallowed as he glanced back and forth between them. Another chill ran through the cellar, but this time it sank into Søren's bones. With a deep quiver, he rubbed his arms. Strange—the other men didn't seem to feel the coldness at all.

"Poor feller," said Henley.

"He sure got a look of wary on him, don't he?"

Henley reached an arm through the bar and patted Søren's foot. "It's all right. You don't have to be afeared. What's your name?"

Søren's chin trembled. "Søren," he said in a feeble voice.

"You hear that accent?" Henley whispered. "He's from Daecland all right."

"What about your clan?" Burlan went on.

"I don't—I don't understand."

91

"Where you are from, lad?" Henley asked.

He tried to think, but fog filled his mind. "I can't remember the name of my town."

"You at least know if you are from Daecland?"

Søren nodded.

"You sure?"

"I—I think so."

"How'd you get here, Søren. Can you remember that?"

Søren thought until his head hurt. "I was on a beach, and," he shuddered at the thought of the monster. "I rode on something, some animal. Then I ran here."

Burlan rubbed his head. "You rode on an animal?"

"I think so."

"Like a horse?"

Søren shook his head. "Like a . . ." He tried to think of how to describe it, but his memory didn't seem to work very well.

"You said you woke up on a beach," Henley interrupted. "A shipwreck, maybe?"

Søren shook his head again. "I was in a river, and after that, I woke up by the beach."

Burlan leaned into Henley's ear—the light from Henley's lantern flickered against his face, creating ghastly shadows. "Impossible. Those currents would've only drifted him further out. He would've drowned and been long dead."

"Maybe you're right," said Henley. "Maybe he found a way through the mountains?"

Søren swallowed. "I didn't go through any mountains. At least," he looked down, holding his fingers, "I don't think so."

"You sure?"

Søren nodded again.

Henley gave a sudden, peculiar look. He pointed at Søren's chest. "What have you got there?"

Søren grabbed the lens from outside his shirt. "Eirún gave it to me," he said. "Please d—don't take it."

"Whose Eirún?" Henley asked.

He sniffed, looking down again. "My mother."

"For Theos' sake." Henley sank back on the dirt floor. "The poor lad."

"Listen," Burlan replied, reaching his hand through the iron bars, "we aren't gonna take it. We wanna help. Can we just have a look?"

Søren continued to stare at them, pressing himself a little further back.

"Just for a spell," Burlan reassured him. "We'll give it right back."

Not trusting the men, he only shook his head.

"Here," Burlan said. He pulled something from his pocket and slipped his hand back through the iron bars. "This was my pa's, and I promised to never part with it. How 'bout we trade for just a minute? You keep that 'til I give your trinket back. That way, you know you can trust me."

Søren held out his hand, and something small but heavy fell into his palm. It was a ring. Unlike the one he lost, it was gray, dull, and slightly misshapen, but on the inside was an imprint of a horse. Seeing it reminded him of being at the orphanage. And with Eirún.

Feeling more comfortable, he slowly lifted the necklace and handed it to Burlan.

Burlan's eyes narrowed. "What is it?"

Henley, peering over his shoulder, poked at the glass with a finger. "Is that glass?"

"It's certainly Daecish," Burlan replied. "I ain't never seen fine glasswork like this."

Taking it from Burlan's hand, Henley moved over to the lantern sitting on the shelf, peering at the glasswork and brass in the dancing light. "The craftsmanship is incredible." He placed the back end of the lens to his eye but quickly took it away. "Burlan," he said with a laugh. "Look here."

Burlan took the lens from Henley, peering through it. He blinked several times and moved it away from his face. "Ain't that peculiar," he said. "Everything's wrong way up." He flipped the lens over, looking through the dome end of the glass. "I can't think of a single forge in Sunder that could fashion brass like this." He turned to Søren. "What is this?"

"I—I think it's called a lens."

"What's it for?"

"It's used t—to make pictures."

"What you mean by pictures?" Henley asked. "Like paintings?"

"I don't know. But if you p—p—put it somewhere long enough, I think, it will make a c—" He closed his eyes, trying to force the word out— "capture the image of the room. But it needs more parts."

With a swallow, Burlan set the lens on the shelf and took a step back. Henley picked it back up and peered through it again, waving his hand in front of it. "I don't know. That sounds a bit too odd for my liking."

They both walked over to Søren, and Henley handed it back to him as Søren handed him the ring.

"Whatever it be," Burlan said, taking the ring from Henley, "we don't need to share this with anyone yet."

"Thank goodness Egbert ain't seen it."

"You're right." Burlan laughed. "He'd store it in that box o' junk he has and never let anyone close to it."

Henley looked back at Søren with a furrowed brow. He almost seemed sad. "You thirsty?"

"A little," Søren barely got out. But truthfully, his throat burned.

"I'll be back." He stood up, grabbed the lantern, and walked up the stairs. He opened the door and shouted with a startle. "Egbert!"

"I's sorry, sire! I wasn't eavesdroppin', I's uh—I's uh—"

"Come on," he said, as both of their footsteps pounded the ceiling, raining down dust.

Burlan peered up the stairs, then turned back to Søren. "Don't look so heartbroken," he said. "Theos knows you're here, and it ain't by accident. Sometimes, it helps to know that."

"Who's Theos?" Søren looked around the room.

Burlan ran his hand through his hair as if to make sure it was parted. Then he crossed his arms and leaned back. "Perhaps you really are Daecish. Theos is the creator of this world. The name is older than the Sunderian language. Older than even the Sarig."

Søren didn't respond. He didn't really understand what he was talking about.

"Well," Burlan grunted as he stood up. "Henley will be back shortly. Just try to get some shuteye. We'll try to find you some warm blankets before too long." Leaving his own lantern on the shelf, he walked up the stairs and closed the door behind him.

Sitting alone, Søren slunk back into a corner and slipped the lens over his neck. His stomach felt as if a massive rock had just formed in it. Having never spent a single night away from the orphanage, he first longed for something familiar. Something that felt like home. But he knew that if Eirún were just there with him in that cell, he'd be happy. With raised knees, he buried his face in his arms, imagining himself sitting next to her as she hummed a soft tune.

Hearing the sudden rattle of a chain, Søren jerked up, glaring at the cell next to him. At first, he didn't see anything, but he knew the sound wasn't in his head. He peered harder into the darkness until a shape came into view. Sitting in the shadow of the far wall was a man, with his feet bound to the ground, his hands shackled together by a single chain.

The man grunted as he awoke, his wild hair covering much of his face. But his eyes caught Søren's. Just then, the upstairs door swung open, and Henley walked down the steps with a plate and mug in his hands. "Here's some bread for you," he said. He set the plate and a mug of warm milk on the floor. "Eat and get some rest. I'll bring you a nice thick blanket tonight." He turned and walked back up the stairs and shut the door.

Søren crawled over and first drank the milk, which was thicker and creamier than he was used to. But it was sweet with an almost nutty aftertaste. Afterward, he attempted a small bite of bread, but he winced as a sharp pain shot through the left side of his broken jaw. He attempted another bite, but his stomach still felt heavy with homesickness. He slid the plate away and glanced uneasily to the prisoner. "Are—are you hungry, sir?" Søren mumbled.

The prisoner twisted his mouth into a wry grin.

An uncanny feeling stirred in Søren's heart toward the strange appearance of that man. Despite his ragged clothing and thin frame with a bloated stomach, his eyes were silver and sharp, as if full of thought and intention. Søren split his bread in half and, stretching his arm between two bars, tossed it to the prisoner. His throw fell short, however, and the bread landed just at the prisoner's feet, out of his reach. The prisoner continued to stare at Søren curiously as he reached for the second half of his bread, and giving more thought for aim, tossed it; this time, it landed on the prisoner's lap. Without saying a word, the prisoner grabbed the bread with his hand and, with a strain, bent over and ate.

Søren, though wary, felt drawn to the prisoner's eyes as if he was being invited into the vastness of his knowledge. And yet, there was a cold emptiness in them. As if the beauty of the eyes was a mirage or something worse. Something deceptive. Nevertheless, he worked up the courage to ask, "Do you have a name?"

"Do I have a name?" replied the prisoner in a hoarse laugh, revealing his rotting teeth. Søren blushed with embarrassment. The prisoner struggled to swallow the last bit of bread down his throat. Coughing, he spat out a glob of a thick black mass across the dirt floor.

"All men have a name," he said. A thin trail of blood dripped down his chin. "But mine, well, that depends on who you ask."

"What do people call you?"

The prisoner closed his eyes with a wide grin. "Some call me Murderer, others call me Lord. I have been called Defender, and I have been called Deserter—Savior and Enslaver. But no one has ever called me Child. What is your name?"

Taken aback by the oddness of his reply, Søren could not help but remain silent as he stared into the prisoner's eyes. He seemed to never blink. At last, Søren spoke. "Søren. My name is Søren."

"Ah, Søren," he said. "Why are you here, Søren?"

"I don't know."

"Where are you going?"

"I—I don't know."

"So, what purpose do you have?" The prisoner tilted his head.

Søren didn't reply. The words came to him like a punch to his soul. He stared through the prisoner into some great distance. What was his purpose? "To be with Eirún," he said in a quiet voice.

"Where is she?"

With furrowing eyebrows, a tear ran down his cheek. "I don't know," he said, looking down.

For a while, the prisoner sat in silence as if observing him. "Tell me," he finally said. "Where do you come from?"

Søren slowly lifted his head, not bothering to wipe his cheeks. At first, he didn't say anything as his mind escaped from the cell and wandered into past memories. Though much of his memory seemed distant and vague, other thoughts were perfectly clear. He sat back and studied his dirty, shivering palms. He couldn't say why, but he felt compelled to spill out all he could remember. From broken memories, he recollected the orphanage, the boys, and Eirún, whom he told the prisoner was his mother. He shared how Mathios had struck him and dragged him into the river. He even talked about the hovering shadow and the beast-like monster that carried him to the valley.

The prisoner remained quiet the entire time, never blinking until Søren finally finished.

"A shadow," the prisoner said, his gaze fixed on the ground. Then the prisoner looked up. "You have seen more than few will even hear tales of. You were cast into the sea and are now alive to tell about it."

His dark, unnerving words snaked around Søren, and he tried to shake the thought.

"Yet you are far from home. Far from Eirún."

Søren's throat tightened.

"What of your mother and father? You didn't tell me about them."

"But I t—told you, Eirún's my mother."

"No, she isn't."

Søren's heart ached. "But she is. She told me I could call her—"

"Tell me about your real parents."

The question prompted him to recall memories he'd long abandoned. "I—I can't remember much about my father. I remember holding his hand when he took me t—to the orphanage. I also remember sitting beside him, riding in a carriage. I could see trees and fields. But my mother—" just calling someone other than Eirún that made him feel sick again. All he knew of his real mother was what Baulfr once told him. She didn't want children, so she gave him away. But he didn't feel like saying that. "She died when I was very young." His eyes broke from the prisoner's.

"Abandoned," the prisoner replied.

Søren didn't say anything, but he knew he was right. No one loved him. No one cared about him.

"First your parents, now Eirún."

"Eirún hasn't abandoned me," Søren defended.

"Where is she then?"

Søren's eyes watered again. He couldn't give an answer. Was she even looking for him? Maybe she didn't care about him. The last time she really talked to him, she did say he could no longer call her his mother. He gripped the lens in his hand. "No!" he suddenly shouted, refusing to believe it.

The prisoner tilted his head but remained silent for a moment. "You should be careful," he said at last as he peered at the stairwell.

"What d—do you mean?"

"You cannot trust these men. They'll send another for you, but if you go with him, you will never go home again."

A lump rose in Søren's throat.

"He will lead you far away into darkness."

Just as Søren was about to speak, several footsteps trembled the floorboards above.

* * *

Slouched in the corner, Egbert patted his fingers together. What were they looking at in the cellar? A lens? Why didn't they want him to see it? He just wanted to look at it. Maybe get a chance to touch it.

"Let's make this quick," stated Lord Abbot, stepping into the room. Even with thin hair and a pear-shaped body, Abbot often held himself straighter and more proper than other Sunderians. Which made sense. He was a lord once. But even with that title, he was now as poor as Egbert himself—and he smelled it too.

Abbot cocked an eye and stared hard at Egbert. "What have you gotten yourself into this time?"

Egbert slunk his face into his neck and hung out his bottom lip. Why did everyone have to get on to him? "Well, Lord Abbot, Egbert tracked the boy's scent. It's a good hog, my Egbert is."

Burlan covered his face with his hand. "Egbert, why do you call that stupid pig by your own name?"

Egbert turned to Burlan with a slight frown. "My own mother named that hog." Actually, it was the hog's father she named Egbert. But after she died from the plague, along with the rest of his family, save Burlan, he thought he should keep the name going in her honor.

Burlan didn't respond as he looked at Abbot. "Thank you for coming."

"No problem, Burlan," he said with a half-smile, but his face looked shaken with worry. "Now, let's be quick about it."

"Right you are," Burlan replied, grabbing a seat for Abbot as they all sat at the single table.

The setting sun sent thin strands of light beaming through the cracks of the gray barn wood walls. Egbert shivered as a cool breeze crept in from the outside. He glanced back and forth between the men.

"As you now know," Burlan continued, "Egbert, though kind as he is, has taken it upon himself to apprehend a lad he found wandering north of the town."

"And you think he's from Daecland?"

"Aye," Burlan replied. "He's as Daecish as they come."

"Just a half-breed." Abbot dismissed with his hand.

"Pardon, sire," Henley butted in, "but we don't think so. His accent is strong. And he seemed to have a hard time understanding our dialect."

Abbot sat stiff with no response.

"And," Henley continued as he glanced at Burlan, "his clothes are a bit weathered. If I had to guess, he's traveled for a very long time."

"If you'd like, we can take you down to see him," Burlan offered.

Abbot shook his head sternly. "As I said when you first came to me, I'll have no part in this. I'll only give my advice. It's my best understanding that there's no boy at all. This is only a conversation. Understand?"

"We very much understand," said Burlan, running his hand through his hair. "So, as you see, it seems very possible that he, perchance, is from Daecland. And if he is, well—"

Henley made a gesture for Burlan to pause. "Sire," he interrupted. "Firstly, we know that this is a terrible situation we're in. Our chief concern is protecting Egbert. If it gets out that he captured this boy, especially if he's of Daecish blood, he'll be hanged."

Egbert tried to stop his knees from shaking as he pictured hanging from the gallows.

"However," Burlan added, "the boy said he washed up on the beach from a river in Daecland, which we know is impossible. So, how'd he get here? As far as we reckon, Daecland's never brought families to colonize, but only military and political officials. If this boy's from Daecland, he must have come through those mountains." He leaned forward. "Who knows what possibilities that could open up?"

"I already said that ain't gonna—" Henley began.

"I've heard enough," Abbot interrupted, waving a dismissive hand. "Neither of your opinions matter. And this whole thing's nonsense. I don't know where this boy's from, but the moment we start piddling around for some mountain pass or using one of their own for that purpose, we'll be marked as partakers in the Silent Hither. I'll not risk it!"

Burlan's face went red as Henley stared at him. Then Henley turned to Abbot. "So, what's your advice then?"

"I suggest," Abbot replied, interlocking his fingers on the table, "you throw the lad back into the hills and pretend you never found him!" He pointed at Egbert. "And make sure he stays quiet! For his own sake!" He stood up. "Now, if you'll excuse me, I've been here too long. I'm headed home." With a raised eyebrow, he looked sternly at the two men. "I was never here. Understand?"

As Abbot walked out the door, the room was left in awkward silence until Henley sighed. "You shouldn't have mentioned the mountain pass," he said. "You're the only one who thinks anything of it."

Burlan didn't respond. Egbert wasn't sure what to think. But his stomach was growling. And couldn't he just see the lens once? Just once?

"Maybe we ought'a just turn him over to the Daecish," Henley went on. "Say we found him wandering 'round or something. If he's their kin, they'll treat him well enough, I imagine."

"I ain't giving them the boy," Burlan retorted. 'They'd question him and find out we hid him." He moaned and rubbed his head. "I wish I could just start this day over."

"We're in a tight spot, that's for sure," said Henley as his eyes stared blankly into the floor. "One thing I find peculiar, though."

"What's that?"

"The boy said he rode on an animal from the beach. I took it as some tall tale, but the closest shore is days away. And he would've had to pass through some pretty steep terrain or even the Amyrran Forest to get here. Ain't no way he did all that on his own. Especially dressed as he is."

Burlan squinted. "You're right. He must've ridden something, but he said it wasn't a horse."

Henley blurted out a laugh. "Sounds like something out of Hælend's Ballad."

Burlan chuckled, but the creases around his eyes tightened. "You don't think?"

"Of course not. Don't be ridiculous. Besides, the ballad says it'll be a man, not some runt of a boy."

"I don't know," Burlan said slowly. "His story. Those dark eyes. It's like he's dead or a hant or something. What if he rode an alphyn?"

The color in Henley's cheeks drained. "You don't actually think that, do you?"

Egbert's stomach suddenly turned nauseous. He wasn't sure if it was from the hunger or the idea of that boy riding an alphyn. Maybe both.

"Probably not," Burlan mumbled. "But either way, we're in over our heads. There's others smarter than us who ought'a talk to him."

"What do you mean?" Henley asked.

"Abbot ain't gonna help. We can't abandon the boy. We can't keep him here. Maybe we should send word to Everwind."

"You mean the Dark Horses?" Henley asked in barely a whisper.

"Why not? We don't know what to do with the boy, but they've got experienced men. It'll get him off our hands, at least."

"You don't think they'll mistreat him, do you?"

"Of course not. They're good men. They'll look after him as their own kin."

Henley looked across the room for a minute. Egbert thought he looked tired. Henley was probably as hungry as he was. "Maybe you're right," Henley said. "But we'd need to send a dispatch to ride quick. The longer that boy's here, the more likely we get hanged. And what about Abbot?"

"We'll send Finley. He's looking for work, and he's got the fastest horse in Astford. And I'm not worried about Abbot. You heard him yourself. He won't say a thing."

"But did you hear him? He's against the Silent Hither. His own son was sent to the mines, and he don't seem to care. He jus' might hand us over to the Daecish to save his own skin." He gave a deep groan.

"I don't care," Burlan replied coolly. "I'm tired of living in fear. We can hide the boy somewhere else for now. But what else can we do?"

* * *

"Did you hear that?" the prisoner asked.

"A little," Søren replied

"It's already begun. They're going to send for a man to come get you."

It suddenly hit Søren. Where was the man going to take him? Maybe he could escape? But where would he go? He didn't even know where he was. He ground his teeth. "Where am I?"

"You are in Sunder." The prisoner gave another large grin. "I imagine you've never heard that name before?"

Søren shook his head.

"Well, that makes sense."

"What do you mean?" Søren asked.

The prisoner stretched his neck as he looked up toward the ceiling. "That's the irony of it, isn't it? Your own people kept from the truth. I bet you never heard of the War of the Wisps either?"

Søren could only ponder the names the prisoner spoke of. Then out of nowhere, he remembered the name of his town. "Folkbjörn," he whispered to himself. "How far away is Folkbjörn?"

"Very far," the prisoner replied.

"How—how long have I been away from home?" he asked himself.

"Probably longer than you realize."

"But I couldn't have survived. Not in the water."

The prisoner narrowed his eyes as if he knew something, but he said nothing.

Eirún

The muffled noise of scrimmaging and cursing echoed from downstairs through the shallow floorboards. Eirún sat in front of a narrow table beside her dresser, gazing at her bedroom door. Holding her breath, she could only hope she wouldn't hear footsteps coming up the stairs.

When the noise quieted, Eirún released a relieving breath. She opened the small drawer beneath the tabletop and pulled out a letter. Cutting behind the wax seal with a letter opener, she unfolded the crisp seams of the paper beneath the light of a half-melted candle:

Eirún,

Yrsa and I are doing as well as we can. Not much has changed since you left for Scathwold last month. I still can't believe Mr. Solveig refused to take you on after Søren passed! I understand he needed an apprentice, but what a heartless man! Though I can't say I expected any different from a man in Vagholme. And I dare say, Mr. Audin doesn't sound any better. We greatly worry about you and the conditions there. Over the past few weeks, your letters have become more discomforting. Doesn't he have a home to go to? It doesn't seem right, him sleeping in the shop all of a sudden. I cannot see why you bear it any longer. It would please us to see you leave that place and come back. Mr. Baulfr has told us that he is willing to give you your old position back, and Yrsa and I both would feel far better if you were away from that dreadful man.

Has he hurt you? If so, please don't hesitate to report him to the constable. They'll take care of him. If not, I'll just have to head over there myself and do him in!

Write back as quickly as you can!

Adis

No. Mr. Audin hadn't had his way with her the way he wanted to. Maybe it was fear that held him back, or maybe it was some sick form of savoring the anticipation. Either way, it was only a matter of time. She folded the letter and slid it back into the drawer, pulling out a fresh piece of paper. She convinced herself that she wasn't depressed, but like a storm on the horizon, she could feel it coming.

Staring at the paper, she thought about burning it in the candle and setting it down on the ground. Maybe under the bed, just to see what might happen. Instead, she picked up a pen and dipped it in the ink jar:

Dear Adis,

Thank you for your kind words and comfort. And you are right, I cannot stay here any longer. I wish I had gone ahead to Vagholme and looked for work elsewhere. It would have been better than here. Nevertheless, I will take my chances and leave, but the details will have to wait until I can write you from another place. Please do not worry about me. I am doing fine.

She paused for a moment, her hand shaking as she glanced at a fading bruise on her right forearm. She continued:

I do regret to say that I will not return to the orphanage. I could not bear to walk within those walls again. I am sure you understand. To be truthful, I have been afraid to leave this place. Afraid he might look for me. He has threatened me with it before, but I cannot take it any longer, or else I'll take my own life.

Suddenly the pen fell from her grip, and she placed her hands on the sides of her head and closed her eyes. She tried to come up with something to absorb her thoughts, but just as a moth flutters toward a flame, her mind drew to Søren. She could see his face. The first day she met him, as he reached up to her apron with his tiny hands. She could hear his voice. But worst of all was the expression on his face when she had yelled at him in the kitchen. He looked so scared, and yet she cut him to pieces with her words. The guilt weighed on her like a headstone, crushing the life out of her.

A sudden image of Søren's back floating down the river flashed in her mind, and she burst out into a loud sob. Leaning off the chair, she fell to her knees and pressed her mouth into her hands, hoping to not be heard.

"Wha's going on up there?" came the drowsy voice of Audin from downstairs.

Eirún choked and caught her breath. "N—nothing, sir!"

She waited for a response, but only subdued snoring drifted up.

Laying her head down, she let herself whimper into her arm. She lay there for longer than she probably knew. When she finally crawled to bed, she stared endlessly through the arched ceiling of rough-cut timber. The untimely patter of rain on the tin roof soon turned into heavy drumming. Was some fate guiding her life? Why did it hate her so much? She rolled over and closed her eyes.

The next morning, she awoke, though very little light spilled through the closed shutters of the mostly empty room. Chalky green walls, cracked and water-stained, with no trim, save what wrapped around the shallow fireplace, which had long stained the ceiling above black, gave the room a lifeless feeling. Like a prison. The muffled voices of customers roamed around the shop downstairs. She opened the shutters and gazed across the gray sky with the town square just in front of her. Shops with glass front windows lined every side. A boy skipped along the cobblestone, spinning a toy wisp through the air in his hand. But it was still early, and customers were just now making their way down the streets.

After getting dressed, she fixed her hair up with a pin and glanced at the table, noticing her unfinished letter. She balled it up and threw it in the fireplace.

Walking down the stairs into the shop, she noticed that Audin worked his usual charm by showing several customers his new line of steam-powered pumps.

New oak shelves that lined the walls, all filled with various parts and components, revealed that the shop did well. Two large windows were set in the front wall, giving customers a glance into the store before committing to an hour-long conversation about why they needed to purchase a pump. Most of them didn't need one, but they usually bought one anyway. One of the older female customers, too fat for her calico dress, chirped with joy.

"Oh, Mr. Audin!" She winked. "You truly are a great man! It's wonderful. My husband will dearly love this, and it is so beautiful and shiny! Is it made of gold?"

"It's brass, but thank you, my lady," Audin replied, tipping his hat and revealing his greased back light-brown hair. "This pump is top of the line. Built with the same quality and craftsmanship of the Norfrost line. I do hope you will enjoy it. Now, remember," he pushed his thin spectacles back up his bird-beaked nose, "keep the components properly oiled, and she'll last you many happy years."

The lady blushed as she turned her cheek. "Of course, of course, Mr. Audin. My husband wouldn't dream of neglecting such an investment. Now how much do I owe you?"

Audin walked over to the counter and grabbed a thin stack of papers. "I've already got your down payment, so," he flipped through the pages, "two-hundred and eighty aracs, I believe."

The lady opened a small pouch. "Do you take notes?"

"No, ma'am, I apologize. Paper money's too fickle for use, in my opinion. I take all coinage—brass, silver, and gold, as well as credit."

"Of course, of course; I had to ask, you know. I've tried to get rid of these notes for some time. It seems most places are afraid to take them." The lady handed him three gold coins from her pouch.

"Three-hundred? Very good, ma'am." He went back to the counter to get her change. "You might try taking the notes back to the bank where they may exchange them for coins. For a small fee, of course." He handed her four silver coins.

"Thank you, Mr. Audin," she said, turning away. "I'll keep that in mind! And a good day to you!"

"Good day, ma'am!" He turned to Eirún. "Ah! Eirún, good morning. I hope you slept well?"

Eirún nodded but kept her eyes away. "Yes, sir."

"Good, good," he replied cheerfully.

Eirún continued to a cramped room in the back, which Audin had given her as an office. Closing the door to a crack, she sat in a wooden chair and stared blankly at a pile of budgeting sheets stacked beside her typographer, where a blank paper was still rolled into the platen. She felt like sinking into the floor, but instead, she straightened herself, and a sternness grew in her heart. She'd go to Norfrost. Start over. But how? Maybe she could get Baulfr to wire a recommendation. Surely, Adis could talk him into it.

She reached beneath her chair and pulled out a hidden sack. Unlatching the buckle, she opened it and rummaged her hand through the mess of clothes and a loaf of bread wrapped in cloth. Finding the bottom, she pulled out a book, glancing at its cover. She ran her fingers along the gold etching before pulling out her feather bookmark from between its pages. Lifting it to her nose, she breathed in the familiar smell of aged leather and paper. She buried it back in. Stealing a glance through the crack of her door, Audin worked a sales pitch with another customer. She hurried to the window, where she opened the shutters and dropped her sack into an empty crate in the alleyway.

Back at her desk, her heart pounded against her chest, and her palms sweat as she tried to control her growing nervousness. She opened her desk cabinet and pulled out a heavy pouch of coins. She eyed it for a moment, wrestling with her own conscience. Then she pulled out a dozen gold coins worth twelve-hundred aracs. It would be easy enough. She could re-write the budgeting sheet, add a few items to the expense reports. It would take him months to notice. She stood up and walked over to the window. Opening her sack, she pulled out a dark leather purse and hesitated for a moment. This wasn't right. It was theft. But it was the only way. Biting her bottom lip, she glanced to her office door before pouring the coins into the purse and stuffing it back into the sack.

Quickly she returned to her desk and made the appropriate changes to the reports. Grabbing the pouch holding the rest of the coins, she walked over to a coat hanger mounted on the wall and slid on her jacket, and walked out of her office.

"Yes, yes! Have a good day," said Audin to the leaving customer, another man in a black suit and top hat. Audin turned as Eirún approached.

"Where are you off to, dear?" he asked.

"Just to the bank to make a deposit," she replied, holding up the pouch.

As she walked toward the front entrance, Audin took hold of her arm as he snatched the pouch from her hand. From behind his spectacles, his beady black eyes bore into hers. "I'll take it later this afternoon. I need you here today." He glanced at the entrance, then leaned into her, whispering in her ear, "Don't think I don't know what you're up to. I've got more connections in this town than the mayor. You so much as even try to escape or snitch me out, I'll have you dead and buried by nightfall." He squeezed her arm, almost making her cry out. His warm breath reeked like molded cheese. "No one will care, no one will question, easy as that." He took a snort, followed by the nauseating sound of swallowing mucus, and released his grip. "Now, get back to your office and stay there until I say otherwise."

Just then, another customer rounded the front entrance.

"Welcome, sir!" said Audin, stepping away from Eirún.

"Good day, Mr. Audin!" said the customer, a young man with a thin cane. "I'm in need of repairing my pump. I know it's out of warranty, but it seems the piston may be jammed. Could you take a look?"

The customer looked nice enough. All she had to do was cry out for help.

"Of course, of course," Audin replied. "And don't bother with the warranty nonsense. I stand behind my products a hundred percent. Now let's step outside and take a look." He fired a stern glance at Eirún as he followed the young man out the door.

Eirún tightened her throat and hurried back into her office and closed the door. Sliding against the wall with her back, she covered her face as she held back the tears. "Stop!" she said aloud, trying to compose herself. "Stop!" She took in a deep breath and wiped her eyes. The depression crept upon her, but she shook it off. "Tonight. No matter what, you will leave tonight."

That evening, Audin had kept to his own business and never so much as even spoke to her. She laid in her bed, staring up at the arched ceiling just like every night. Her body shivered in a cold sweat as she waited until he had been long asleep.

As the minutes turned to what felt like hours, she slowly sat up, fearing dawn would come too soon. She quietly got dressed, pausing periodically to listen. Throwing on a light coat, she snuck to the door, being sure to not step on the boards that creaked—something she had put to memory over the past two weeks.

The brass knob turned in her hand, and she pushed the door open. The long narrow stairway descended directly in front of her. It was so dark, she could only make out the first few wooden steps. Setting a foot on the first stair, she carefully set her other foot on the one below. She paused, waiting for her eyes to adjust as she tried to ignore the sound of her own pulse through her ears. The blackness gave way to dark-gray shadows. She went down a few more steps.

She froze.

She thought she saw a shadow, but as she stared longer, it appeared to be nothing. Resuming her way down, her chest ached as she tried to not exhale too loudly. Making her way into the shop, Audin's door was slightly ajar, and all was black in his room. She could hear his muffled snoring.

Now moving swiftly, she made her way to the front door and turned the knob.

It had been locked with a latch on the inside.

Sweat dripped down her temple, and her fingers trembled. Did he know she would try to escape? She looked back at his bedroom. Where was the key? Glancing around the room, she tried to recall where she had seen him hide it—beneath the flowerpot. That's where it was.

She hurried over and lifted the pot. Nothing. Frantically patting the area, she had to fight the tremble in her arms. She was sure it'd be there. But then . . . had he moved it? She couldn't be sure. Tears began to fill her eyes. She swore she would never stay another night there, even if she had to break through a window. She wiped her eyes and tried to think how she could escape. Then it dawned on her.

He had moved the key the other day. She walked over and stretched her hand above the frame as she pressed herself against the glass window of the door. Running her fingertips along the thick dust, she felt the key and quickly slipped it into the latch. There was a click, and she turned the knob. The door swung open, and the cool breeze of the night air brushed against her face.

But just as she took one step out, something hard clawed into the back of her scalp as she was pulled backward.

She tried to scream, but no sound came out. Her trembling legs went out beneath her as she was dragged back by the hair, banging her left elbow against a shelf.

She desperately tried to get to her feet as bruises marred her legs. Even if it meant her death, she would not stay here. She gripped Audin's hand with both of hers, trying to relieve the pain that shot through her head.

"Where were you going?" he shouted as he threw her down at the bottom of the stairway.

Eirún fell on her knees, and finding her voice, cried out as she climbed up the steps.

"I warned you about trying to leave!"

Feeling the grasp of his hand gripping her left leg, the memory of his many salacious threats flashed in her mind. She turned and repeatedly kicked at his face with her right foot. His nails dug into her skin as he held on tight, reaching for her with his other hand as he shouted some insult. In a panic, Eirún's fear turned to anger as she bent her right knee back. Letting out a shout, she kicked forward, landing her heel directly into his nose. The blow was so hard, Audin's upper body bowed backward, and he lost his balance, tumbling down the steps. He landed at the bottom with a thud. Without a second thought, Eirún ran back into the bedroom and slammed the door, bracing it with her back. Dizziness swamped her as she tried to control her gasps.

Finally, she settled down, and a haunting silence fell around her. From the bottom of the stairway behind the closed door, nothing stirred. On the edge of her desk sat the letter opener. She grabbed it with her shaking hand. For a long time, she stood, pointing the letter opener at the door. Hair was strewn across her face. Sweat dripped down her temples and back.

At last, she took a step toward the door.

Once she was close enough, she slowly reached out her hand and turned the knob. With only a crack between the door and the frame, she peered down the stairway. Once again, dark shadows melted together into blackness at the bottom. There seemed to be a shape. Maybe it was Audin's body. Maybe it was just her eyes playing tricks on her. All around, the silence seemed to tear at her nerves.

She placed one foot on the top step. After a minute, she took another. Soon she could just make out the shape of a leg awkwardly lying up the steps. She gripped the letter opener tight until her fingertips dug into her tingling palms. Audin's foot was now only one step below her. With clenched teeth, tears streamed down her face as fear riveted within her. She hesitated, too afraid to go any further. Should she go back upstairs and climb through the window? No. It was too high.

Still pointing the letter opener at the body, she slowly lifted her foot over his leg and placed it on the next step below. Her shoe stepped in something wet. She held in her gasp and lifted her other foot, but as she leaned forward to bring it down, she slipped off the step and fell hard on her elbows, letting out a painful cry.

Audin didn't move.

With a scream, she planted her hand on the step to lift herself up, smearing her hand in the sticky puddle. Dropping the letter opener, she ran out of the stairway, pushed open the front door, and bolted through the town square. The moon was hidden in the darkness of the early morning, with an insipid light rising in the east. No one could be seen. She suddenly stopped, remembering her sack. Racing back to the side of the shop, she gasped as the light of a street lantern revealed the bright blood staining her hands and shoes. Frantically, she examined her surroundings. A shallow puddle of water gathered along the backside of the building. She fell on her knees, washing away the blood.

Grabbing her sack from beneath her office window, she ran back toward the square. Beneath the distant lantern lights, a single black carriage, pulled by two horses, idly rolled west out of town. She slowed her pace and checked her hands, then waved toward the carriage. "Excuse me!" she said in a tone louder than she meant.

"Dear me!" an elderly lady in the carriage gasped, holding her hand to her chest. "Miss, you mustn't run up to people like that."

"I'm—I'm sorry ma'am," Eirún replied. She glanced over her shoulder to Audin's shop. "But if you please, I need a ride."

Sitting beside the lady, an elderly man with sagging jowls met Eirún's gaze with a slight frown on his face. The carriage driver in the front only raised an eyebrow at her from beneath his top hat. "Where are you going at such an early hour?" the man asked. "And why do you look so frightened?"

Eirún thought for a second as she held her coat tight against the bitter wind. "I'm trying to get to Norfrost to see some friends," she replied. "It's an emergency, and I have no way. Please, sir."

The man seemed to probe her mind with his glare. "What were you running for?"

The lady swatted at him. "Have some manners, Geirleif! Can't you see she's freezing?"

Geirleif straightened up. "I'm only looking out for us, Eilis. It's good to question strangers. Especially before dawn,"

Eilis rolled her eyes. "You forget that we are out in the early morning as well, and no one is questioning." She turned to Eirún. "Of course, you can ride with us, dear. We are headed to Norfrost ourselves. But I hope you aren't in a hurry. We are slow travelers, and we must stop in Folkbjörn overnight, I'm afraid."

Eirún strained a smile. "That isn't a problem at all. Thank you." She walked to the back of the carriage and opened the door, taking a seat on the row behind them. Geirleif gave Eilis a concerned look, then called out to the carriage driver to continue on. As they left the town, Eirún kept her eyes fixed on Audin's shop until it slowly rolled out of view.

An Incident in the Western Plains

A s the wind blew from the Mountains of Einarr, the putrid smell of death, seeping from the bloated corpses, filled Eilívur's nostrils. Tethering his horse to the maple tree, he wiped the dust from his nose. A private and a corporal, both swordsmen, drew their swords as they followed two officers into the house, which sat nestled at the bottom of a low ridge.

A crow fluttered away from the carcass with the broken skull. Eilívur removed his helmet as he walked toward the body and took a knee. He gently placed his hand on the stomach. Ulnleif.

Not far was a fist-sized stone, covered in dried blood. Eilívur held his composure, but his insides ached. They had come to arrest a man who had willfully plotted and participated in rebellious uprisings. And they were brutally murdered for it, including his own brother. But he didn't expect anything less from Sunderian insurgents. They hated the Daecish occupation, but for no other reason than their own pride. They protested and complained of mines and slums, yet they turned a blind eye to the reality that the Daecish had arrived just in time to save their kingdom from falling into disarray and economic depression. Limited monarchies, such as in Daecland, were one thing, but corrupt absolute monarchies were never able to sustain a kingdom for long, and with the madness of their own King Albern, Sunder was at the end of its days. If it wasn't for Eilívur's own people, this Silent Hither wouldn't have even had a country left to fight back for.

Ulnleif was barely seventeen. Still a child in Eilívur's eyes. But he couldn't let the sorrow get to him now. Not in front of his men. He swallowed the lump in his throat and tried not to think about how he would have to write up the death certificate.

Second Lieutenant Rhett walked back outside. With overly thick, brown hair, he looked much younger than he actually was. "I'm terribly sorry for your loss, sir."

Eilívur stood up, back rigid. "What have you seen inside?"

"There are two bodies near the back bedroom," Rhett replied. "One's Commander Jótham. But no sign of Lombard. He looked down at Ulnleif with a grimace. "This was a bloody massacre. Must have been an ambush of at least half a dozen men."

Eilívur's boots kicked up dust as he walked around the bodies. The footprints had long been swept away by the wind. Near a patch of dried grass, he picked up the broken ends of an arrow, covered in dried blood, then threw them back on the ground. Entering the house, he covered his nose. The private stood to his left, peering out of the hole in the wall.

"What did this?" he asked as he picked up a clump of daub. "You don't suppose Lombard had explosives with him?".

"Don't be foolish," replied Eilívur as he made his way across the room. "Other than wisp canons, there is no gunpowder in Sunder."

Working his way past the bloated bodies, he entered the bedroom and walked over to the open window on the northern wall. Unlike everywhere else, the outside ground, just below the window, was caked solid, as if it had once been damp. Probably from where they dumped water. He noticed a series of cluttered footprints molded into the earth and followed them with his eyes, where they faded away from the house. He paused. A trail rose north along the ridgeline. Glancing back into the bedroom floor, he took note of the dried mud footprints, hardly visible, coming in from the window.

As he headed back into the family room, several of his men gathered together. A puddle of blood stagnated on the dining table. Two arrows, stained a brownish-red, lay scattered on the floor.

"Looks like they were in the middle of dinner," said the corporal eyeing a clay pot, which had apparently been moved to a chair from the table. It was still half-filled with old, coagulating stew, with mold growing up the edges.

"Almost makes you feel sorry for them," said the private, rubbing his thin mustache.

"Sorry?" replied the corporal. "It's our men that's dead. And did you see the sergeant's face in the bedroom? Or the commander's brother outside?" He glanced at Eilívur with a startle, apparently not realizing he was there.

One of the officers picked up the clay pot and sniffed. He coughed fitfully. "That's foul," he said, dropping it back on the chair. He wiped his hands off on his uniform.

"Sir, if you don't mind me asking," asked the private, "what do you make of the scene? All our men dead, Lombard and his family are gone. Something's not right."

"Must have had a gathering that night of some sort," suggested the corporal. "Something our men didn't expect. How many do you think there were?"

"One, maybe two," Eilívur replied, running his fingers through several hanging herbs. He huffed out his nose, trying to remove the scent of the rotting venison.

The men looked at one another and laughed nervously.

"One or two?" asked an officer with a smirk.

"Certainly not," whispered the corporal.

Ignoring their comments, Eilívur examined the two arrows before dropping them again. Then he walked out the front door.

Outside, he lifted his hand and traced the scar below his right ear. His brother joined the Army of his own will. Death was just a part of the career. But Eilívur still couldn't shake the sorrow welling up in him. He should have never brought the boy to Sunder.

"Sir," came the voice of Rhett. He let out a low cough. "Sir, I've been under you for six years, and I would trust you with my life, but with all due respect, you've got us all stumped here. How have you come up with only one person? Our men are very skilled in combat. I just see it as—"

"I said most likely one, maybe two," Eilívur corrected.

"My apologies, sir."

"It's all in the manner of how they died," Eilívur explained. They were killed in a sequence. Two of the bodies were killed with weapons—one with an ax, one with a sword. Two were killed primitively." He pointed to the ground. "It's hard to tell with the wind stirring all the dirt around, but the only sign of a body being moved is one that is no longer here, which would add up to five bodies. If there were more men, there should be evidence—wounds, weapons, something. But all we have is this spot here and a dried puddle of blood inside. There are three arrows, two whole and one broken, but they're all of Daecish make."

Rubbing his chin, Eilívur peered through the hole in the wall as the other men came outside. "One of the archers was gored by a Daecish sword. The sergeant inside is missing his. It makes sense that the same person that killed the archer likely killed the sergeant beforehand, then took his sword. But again, it's possible there were two killers.

"If you notice the sergeant's face, he was beaten to death: no blade wounds, no ax wounds. The killer likely had had no weapons. I'd say he was killed either after the ax was broken or before he had one. But in either case, killing the sergeant explains how he got the sword."

"Why wouldn't he just use the ax?" asked Rhett. "Even if it was broken?"

"You're assuming he had time to think about it. Commander Jótham and the sergeant could have attacked at the same time."

There was a look of almost disbelief among his men. He knelt down by the archer near the broken wall, brushing off bits of twigs and dried mud from his chest. He stood back up. "Someone gored him and drove him through the wall."

"Through the wall?" The corporal smirked.

"Get your head back in Sunder, Corporal. These aren't brick walls." He picked up a clump from the wall remains, crumbling it in his hands. "It's just clay and twigs braced by a few rotting beams."

"Clay and twigs or not," an officer confessed. "I've never seen a man do something like this."

"A man can do anything if it means survival," Rhett replied. He grinned. "Maybe we should throw the corporal through one of the walls to test the theory?"

The corporal gave a half-hearted laugh, but Eilívur ignored the comment. "Then our last victim," he continued, intentionally keeping his eyes from Ulnleif, "was beaten to death by that stone." He pointed to it.

"Why do you think he died last?" Rhett asked.

Eilívur sighed and rolled Ulnleif's body over. "Because his body is lying over the debris from the wall. He died after the crash occurred. And the sword was still in the other archer, which explains why a stone was used."

"What about Lombard?" Rhett asked. "You think he survived?"

"Maybe."

"Where do you think he would have headed?"

"Can't say for sure."

The men all looked toward the east as if they thought they might see a man running in that direction.

"Maybe Llynhithe?" the corporal suggested.

"Doubtful," Rhett butted in. "I don't think that whoever killed our men would be foolish enough to head toward a city, especially if it was Lombard. His face is posted all over this kingdom."

Eilívur glanced toward Rhett, curling up the corner of his mouth. "Good observation, but we have to remember one thing."

"What is that, sir?"

"Whether it was Lombard or someone else, there's a family to look after, and a city is the best place to do that."

"Sir?" Rhett questioned.

"Lombard had a wife and three children—two girls, fairly young, the third, a boy. If you would have done your research, you would have known that." Rhett's eyes fell as if he was disappointed in himself. Eilívur hid his smile and pointed toward the house. "In the bedroom, there were tracks below the window at the back of the house; a whole mess of them."

"The wind didn't blow away the tracks?"

"They were molded into the earth. I imagine they must've dumped water out that window at some point. It seems much of the family headed north. But a pair of larger prints entered the bedroom the same time the other prints were leaving. I imagine that's who killed Jótham and the sergeant. If you remember the position of the bodies, they were going into the bedroom when they were killed."

Rhett looked around. "I don't see a well around here. Where do you think they got their water?"

Eilívur set his hands on his hips. "That's a good question."

"You also mentioned a boy. Is there any information on him?"

"Arnon," Eilívur replied. "Lombard's oldest child; sources said he is near adulthood. I imagine it was either him or Lombard who entered that bedroom door."

Rhett frowned. "So where do we go from here?"

Eilívur nodded to the bundle of wood that had been collected. "Let's give a proper service first. You know the order. Jótham first, then the enlisted together. Take off their armor—any belongings we'll ship back to the families."

"What of your brother?"

Eilívur's jaw went weak for a moment as the question forced his mind from his work. "The same. It's the way he would have wanted it."

As the men burned the bodies, Eilívur made sure the ceremony was out of sight and spoke privately to Rhett. "You will all go back to Llynhithe."

"Not you, sir?"

"It's possible a survivor could have headed there, but most likely Denhurst."

"Is that where you are headed, sir?"

"I think so."

"What about the family?"

"I'm not concerned with women and children," he replied. "If they are still out there, they won't be any trouble. If they made it to a city, well, we know what happens to orphans and widows." But as he spoke the words, the thought of the trail came back to him. He should check it out.

Rhett kicked his foot across the desiccated ground. He bent over, picking up a small slab of dried clay. "Not sure they would survive for long out here anyway." He crumbled the slab in his hand, with the fine dust wafting through the air. He shook his hand and wiped it on his coat.

"They've made it well enough so far," Eilívur replied.

Rhett grimaced. "I heard they started the first phase of the draft in Everwind. Next will be Denhurst."

Eilívur gave no response. The draft was as much of a surprise to him as it was for Rhett.

"What do you think of it?" Rhett continued crossing his arms. "We haven't even been told what we're drafting them for. Are we at war with Varghoss again?" He scrunched his eyebrows. "I've got family near the border."

"If we are at war, they haven't informed us. But rest easy, Lieutenant. It's nothing to be shaken about."

Rhett's expression didn't change. "If we are at war, do you think it's wise sending Sunderians to fight for us? It's not like they're our allies. Won't they just rebel?"

"Orders are orders; we simply obey. Go gather the men. It's a two-and-half day ride to Llynhithe. I spotted a trail heading up the ridge behind the house. I'm going to see where it leads. I'll catch back up shortly."

"You're going alone, sir?"

Eilívur walked toward his horse without looking back. "I'll be fine, Lieutenant."

Galloping along the ridgeline, Eilívur caught sight of a small foot trail, which he followed for nearly three leagues until he rounded a hill. The cabin, nestled at the bottom of a shallow valley, looked deserted as its front door sagged open against the wooden hinges. Eilívur dismounted his horse and pulled his sword from its sheath. He slowly made his way through the front door. The single-room house was empty.

Keeping his sword drawn, he headed around the fire pit, eyeing his surroundings carefully. A few chairs. A single table. Nothing of importance. He stirred the tip of the blade in the ashes. Whoever had stayed there knew how to cover their tracks. He walked back onto the front porch and worked his way around the cabin. On the left side of the house, two long, wavering imprints which pressed into the earth ran south. Knowing the marks came from wheels, he followed them until they were lost in the grass.

He mounted his horse and rode to the top of the eastern side of the valley. At the bottom, on the far side, sat a well. He rode down and dismounted, kicking his boot through dried horse manure scattered around the stone base. The droppings continued for a short stretch north.

Eilívur glanced in the direction he imagined the horse going. "If the wagon was heading south," he asked himself. "Then who was heading north?"

Riding south toward Lombard's home once again, he caught sight of another path, which veered west and eventually led to a pile of rocks lying awkwardly at the side of a barren hill. He pulled back the reins of his horse. "I did not see you before," he said, dismounting.

He approached what was now an evident grave. Gray and white stones were stacked across the surface, with a single large stone at the head. Getting down on his hands and knees, he lifted the stones one by one and began to dig through the loose dirt. It was a shallow grave, and soon he uncovered a face he recognized. Lombard. He removed the rest of the stones and examined the body. He had two arrow wounds—one in his shoulder, the other in the left side of his breast. In the center of his chest was a deep cavity stuffed with cloth—one of the oddest traditions he had ever seen in Sunder. Separating the heart from the body.

Eilívur sat for a moment, wiping his hand on the dried grass. Lombard's body accounted for the two whole arrows inside, but the broken arrow he found in the yard still needed a body to account for.

With his bare hands, Eilívur slid the dirt back over Lombard and returned the stones the way they were before. "Lombard," he said, standing back up, "I hope all of your rebellions were worth the price of your son."

The Flags of Everwind

Bringing his father's horse to a halt, Arnon peered across the expanse of the Swelling Sea. Hovering gray clouds curled along the dark horizon as the warm air currents from the south collided with the bitter winds from the Great Fringe. There was something haunting about those dark waters. Storms were one thing, but his father, and just about everyone else from the older generations, told tales of great serpents dwelling in the deep underwater caverns. Wyrms, they were called in Hælend's Ballad and other ancient poems. But as far as he knew, no one's ever seen one. It was said in the Acwellen Chronicles that they wouldn't come out of the sea until the end of the world, at which point they would devour everything in their path until all was dead and the sun itself went out. His neck tingled with uneasiness, and he quickly gave Ansel a kick. He hoped to reach the Western gate of Everwind before the storm approached.

The city walls, built centuries ago by the Earlonians, rose in the distance. An immediate sense of familiarity washed over him, and yet, his heart sank. Behind the walls ascended numerous elaborate structures and spire towers, glistening like clear water as the high sun, threatened by the encompassing dark clouds, dashed its rays upon the stone. Although astonishing to look at, the black flags reminded him that, other than the Spire, they were all built by Daecish hands. Even much of the castle had been altered and added on to.

The breeze from the sea cooled his face, and he closed his eyes. He could still picture the flags of Sunder fluttering in the wind, bearing the image of a black warhorse, backdropped with crimson red. When he opened them again, he observed the green hills to his left. This place was as good as any. Dismounting Ansel, Arnon pulled a wooden shovel from the satchel and took hold of his father's heart, still wrapped in cloth. He walked through the dew-laden grass, and at the top of a high hill, he dug a small but deep hole and buried it there. Even though it was just his heart, it helped Arnon not feel so alone.

He wiped his hands and carefully rubbed his sore shoulder. Not far away, Ansel chomped on the grass, and Arnon furrowed his brow; it was rare for common folk to own a horse, and he needed to disappear among the people of the city. He remounted and headed south. He soon changed his bearing slightly to the west and galloped toward a port village, less than a league from the city.

Approaching the front entry to the stable, Arnon glanced across the mud street, which was worn down and sunken from years of travel. A group of men in mud-stained tunics bickered at one another on the edge of a grassy field, just beside a larder, situated on the western side of a meager cottage. They shoveled manure from one pile to another with shouts and various insults. One of the men, an elderly one with a hunched back, pointed to an imaginary line between the piles.

Arnon snickered to himself. In just about every village he could think of, no one owned the land. And what once belonged to the lord of the manor now belonged to the Daecish. But even with the change of official ownership, men took whichever plot of land they had to grow their food on with pride. And piling one's manure on another man's borrowed portion was not only an insult, but it was also punishable with a hefty fine.

Across the road, Arnon entered the village stable, where he made stowing arrangements for Ansel. Although he gave the stable keeper fifteen aracs to keep and feed his father's horse, he knew he'd probably need that money later. But he didn't have a choice.

"Thirty days," the stable keeper told him. "Or hereby, the horse is property of the stables." He pointed to a scroll. "You sign here at the bottom."

Arnon gripped the goose-feather pen awkwardly and scribbled an illegible mark.

"Good enough."

The walk along the Western Road faired easier than he had thought. He blended well enough into the crowds as they bustled to and from the port. Before he realized it, he could already see the city walls not far in the distance.

Passing beneath the shadow of the main gate, he arrived at the first crossroads of the Western District. Last he remembered, the cobblestone streets were just being laid down over the old mud roads, but what stood before him, on the north side of the road, was a different city altogether. New shops, homes, even factories had been erected. Most were built of brown brick and mounted with broad chimneys, but some were more elegant. Tall arched entryways, braced by ivory columns, gave the street a regal feel. A Daecish feel. Arnon swallowed the bad taste that just formed in his mouth.

Although most of the people in the streets still wore jerkins and tunics, a crowd of men, passing by the front entrance of a refurbished inn, wore dark suits over flared sleeved shirts. Adorned with tall hats and canes, they walked hand-in-hand with women outfitted in glittering dresses which belled out below their waists, careful to keep their laced ends from touching the dirty ground.

But even with the recent renovations of the city, their proud expressions boasted of a prosperity Everwind hadn't quite reached yet. On the southern side of the road, a flock of ducks waddled in front of several wooden stands, built from limbs and rough-cut boards, lined up between two alleyways where the cobblestone turned to mud. Tailors, potters, cobblers, and other craftsmen, all in tarnished attire, worked diligently, along with their wives and children, to sell their handcrafted items to passing customers. Sometimes to the point of harassing the poor passersby.

"Nearly a hundred, I'd reckon," Arnon overheard a short, bald man talking to several others.

"Still can't believe them pale-faced dastards think they can just take our brothers in the night like that," replied another man.

"Well," replied the bald man as he spat into the mud, "the Daecish been meaning to clean out the slums for some time. I fear we might be next."

Arnon turned south down one of the alleyways as he tried to piece together their words. Taken in the night by the Daecish? Was that the draft Porter was talking about?

On either side ran low half-timber homes, topped with thatched roofs. The scent of burnt wood and earth filled his nostrils, then he caught a hint of something foul. Up ahead, on the right, stood a butcher's stand, where puddles of old thickening blood steamed beneath hordes of flies. His stomach grew unsettled, not from the smell but from the familiarity. Memories of his father, mother, and sisters swept over him. With the recent unfolding events, he felt disconnected from his memories, as if they were apart of another life— one that he could never go back to.

When he approached the corner of the Fire and Water Tavern, built of stacked stone and rough-cut logs, a woman, in a blue tunic and a white wimple, stood in the street at a crossroads, hollering to a passing crowd of men. "Their war ain't ours! Bring our husbands home!"

Several others shouted, but the presence of oncoming Daecish soldiers brought them all to silence. Arnon suddenly felt exposed. He threw the hood of his father's bearskin cloak over his head and slipped inside the tavern.

Arnon blinked until his eyes adjusted to the dim light glowing from the lanterns, situated on about half of the dozen or so round tables. A few men sat in a back corner, drinking and playing some sort of game with dice. Heat crept from the hearth to his left, smoldering as the earthy scent of burning peat hung in the air. Other than the mounted wolf's head on the wall behind the hearth, Arnon was surprised at how little he remembered the tavern. He pulled back his hood and walked across the straw-laden floor to the bar.

Just then, Drake pushed through the swinging kitchen door, situated behind the long wooden bar, wiping his hands with an old, brown rag, revealing dark scabs on the knuckles of his right hand. With a bald head and thick mustache and beard, save his chin, which he kept clean, he looked more like a blacksmith than a tavern owner.

"Well! If it ain't—" He paused and peered with a cocked eyebrow at the men as they played their game. He motioned for Arnon to go with him into the kitchen, shutting the door. "I can't believe it. Arnon!" he said, gripping Arnon in his thick, muscled arms. "Is that hair on that chin of yours?"

Arnon tried not to frown. He knew it wasn't much yet, but he was proud of it. "Drake, it's good to see—"

"You've grown, ain't you?" He gave a hearty laugh, gripping Arnon's shoulders.

Arnon gasped as a sharp pain shot from his arrow wound.

"You look just like your father." Drake winked and put his hands on his hips.

Arnon exhaled a sigh of relief.

"Just not quite as big, yet. But we'll thicken you right up!"

"Really?" Glancing down at himself, Arnon didn't think he was that small. Maybe compared to Drake or his father. But who wasn't?

Drake took a step back. "What the other men'll say when they see you!" He grinned, shaking his head.

Arnon opened his mouth to speak.

"Oh," Drake interrupted again. He peered through the kitchen almost nervously and spoke in a low voice. "You and the kin ain't been here in ages. You can't stay here during the day. Daecish been too common as of late. Been performing inspections, you understand?"

"Yes, Sire." They were only second cousins or something like that, but Arnon could hear his own father's voice in Drake's. A vivid image of burying his heart flashed in his mind, and he felt a tremble in his jaw.

"Now, I think it best you walk out the back. Come back after sunset; we've got a meeting then. But be careful. We don't want you being seen. The Fire and Water Tavern's been one of the best-kept secrets of the Silent Hither for the past ten years." He pushed Arnon gently through the backdoor. "Now, you tell your father I said welcome back, and I'll see you both tonight."

"Drake?"

"Yes, boy?" he replied, holding the door handle.

"My father," Arnon hesitated for a moment. "He passed."

Drake tilted his head as if he didn't hear him right. But as Arnon only looked at him, his face grew dim as his hand dropped to his side. "How dreadful, boy. How?"

Arnon briefly told him his family's situation as Drake took a seat on a crate on the edge of the alleyway. When Drake asked how they escaped, he mentioned that he had killed the Daecish soldiers but left out the details. He slightly leaned forward as if his aching bones weighed a hundred pounds.

"That cursed land," Drake said, rubbing his hands on his face. He didn't seem to notice Arnon's uneasiness. "The Daecish have brought nothing but grief on us all. We've lost a good man, a good man indeed." His expression fell into a deep frown. "It's always hardest when you lose your own kin."

Arnon didn't say anything.

"Did you bury his heart in Everwind?"

"Just north of the city," Arnon managed to get out as he attempted to collect himself.

"Good, lad. That's where he always said he wanted to wake up again, at the end of all things."

Arnon imagined a day when he would see his father again, and the burdens of this world would vanish. Maybe he would be like a child again. Innocent. Maybe even ignorant of some things.

"Well," Drake said, standing up with another sigh. He placed a hand on Arnon's shoulder. "I'm glad you're back. You've been missed."

"Thank you, Drake."

"Your father was better than any man in all of Sunder." He turned to head back to the kitchen.

"Drake?" Arnon asked.

Drake turned around.

"Porter mentioned that a draft may be coming. Has it already happened?"

"It has. They were taken in the night; rumor has it that there'll be more. Took a toll on the Silent Hither, too." His nostrils flared, and his throat turned red. "They won't even tell us why they're drafting us."

"How bad was the Silent Hither affected?"

Drake stepped toward Arnon and peered down the alley at the distant Western Road. "It wasn't good. But I imagine the draft'll ignite a new fire in our people. Let's hope so anyway." He walked back to the kitchen and grabbed the door. "Keep your head up. There's still hope. I'll see you tonight."

Arnon stared helplessly ahead as Drake closed the door.

* * *

With the sun long set behind the dark clouds, Geoffrey sat at the kitchen table, staring at the cold brick oven. Sarah walked down from their bedroom and sat in front of him. "Are you nervous?" she asked.

Geoffrey regained his focus. "You ask that so calmly. If you mean me going to the meeting, well, not really. It's you and Lilly I'm worried about." Terrified would be more like it.

Sarah grabbed Geoffrey's hand and looked at him with those deep green eyes. "I don't like it, either. But it's the right thing."

"Taking care of you, our baby girl, and our child in your womb, that's the right thing."

"Going through with this *is* taking care of us," Sarah replied. "You have a good heart, and if there's any man who is capable of this, it's you."

An uneasy silence filled the kitchen, and Geoffrey wasn't so sure he agreed with his wife. He ran his finger along the wood grain of the table. "I'm having second thoughts about going."

Sarah's expression grew stern, and she let go of his hand. "You think I don't want a simple life?" she asked. "To just be happy? I dream of that day. But have you already forgotten the husbands and fathers who were just taken from their homes? From their own children?"

"But Sarah, I could be hanged."

She looked around as if to find the right words. "You once told me that it is just as evil to watch evil happen while doing nothing about it."

"I don't remember saying that."

She gave him a cold stare.

"Okay, maybe I did. But if something were to happen to me, or if the Capital Guard or even the Daecish found out I was involved, what would happen to you and Lilly?"

"I married a man who loves mercy and justice," Sarah replied. "A man who will stand by it, no matter the cost. We have enough money to sustain ourselves. You need to do this. You don't sleep. You hardly eat. You can't think of anything else."

Geoffrey squirmed. It was as if she had just opened a closet of secrets.

"It haunts you, Geoffrey, I see it. If there was ever a man with a calling, it is here, now. I would rather us die for what is right than to continue living in the shadows of the suffering people out there."

For a long while, Geoffrey didn't respond but only looked at her. She wasn't just beautiful; she was strong-willed and confident. For eleven years, she'd been there for him, always supporting him but also keeping him in check. In many ways, he wished he was more like her. "You're right," he said, and he gently squeezed her hand.

She smiled. "Good thing, I was just getting started."

Geoffrey laughed. "I sure did marry the finest woman in Sunder, didn't I?" He wiped his hand down his beard. "Well, if I'm gonna go, it's time."

He gave Sarah a long hug, then walked upstairs and kissed Lilly on her head, who was fast asleep. Walking down to the front door, he put on his coat and turned to Sarah. "I love you more than you'll ever know."

"I love you, too," she replied.

"I'll be back soon." He closed the door behind him.

It didn't take long to get to the Southern District. The streets were empty, and drizzle fell as he approached the back entrance of the Fire and Water Tavern. There was only one young man waiting under a wooden awning. "Still early?" Geoffrey asked.

The young man looked up. His hair was a disheveled mess, and he looked like he hadn't slept in a couple of days. "Drake said he'd come get us when it was time."

Geoffrey looked around for a moment before walking over and reaching out his hand. "I'm Geoffrey."

"Arnon," the other man replied, shaking his hand.

Drawing his hand back, Geoffrey crossed his arms, trying to keep dry what little he could with the soft rain trickling down his coat. He glanced back at the door as they both waited in awkward silence.

"Is this your first time to a meeting?" Arnon asked.

Geoffrey glanced back with a nod. "Well, in a way. I've met with Wesley and the Court before."

Arnon pointed to the ring on his finger. "I noticed you were married."

Holding up his hand, he smiled. "Eleven years. Yourself?"

"Not yet." His eyes looked worried for a moment. "Maybe when I'm older."

Geoffrey chuckled. "I know many men who have married young." He sat on a low crate next to Arnon, hoping to get some relief from the rain.

"Yes, but probably not with a future in the Silent Hither."

Geoffrey cupped his hands in front of his mouth and blew into them.

"You have any children?" Arnon asked.

"I have a two-year-old girl, Lilly, and another on the way in about a month or so."

"Is it hard?"

Geoffrey almost laughed. "Having children?"

"Well, I mean having a family while you do this." Arnon motioned his hand toward the tavern.

Geoffrey thought before he answered. "You're Lombard's son, aren't you?"

A sudden glint sparked in Arnon's eyes. "You knew my father?"

"Not personally, but his name is pretty well known around here. Including the names of his family." He glanced at Arnon. "I'm an investigator for the Capital Guard." He lifted his finger. "Not for Ónarr. I prefer to say I work directly under King Albern."

"But doesn't King Albern technically work for King Ónarr?"

"Well, in a way, but my job mostly deals with the city issues— crimes, break-ins, that sort of thing. Ónarr doesn't have time for that, which is why he still uses Everwind's Capital Guard."

"I'm surprised the Court doesn't think you're a spy," Arnon said with a half sneer.

Geoffrey laughed. "Maybe they're getting desperate."

Arnon bent down and picked up a splinter of wood, which he rolled in his fingertips. "If you'd like to know, my father just recently passed."

Geoffrey raised his eyes in surprise but settled his expression. "I'm sorry to hear that. I'm sure you miss him."

Arnon didn't respond.

Geoffrey took in a deep breath, taking in the night air. Puddles began to form in the depressions of the muddy alley. "You asked if it was difficult for me, getting involved while having a family. Can I ask you a question?"

"Sure," Arnon replied.

"What did you think of your father leading the Silent Hither as a Dark Horse?"

Arnon grinned. "I was proud of him. He did what he thought was right." He paused again as if he was taken back to a memory. "And he wasn't afraid."

"And I'm sure he did it because he loved his family," Geoffrey replied. "And that's why I want to help the cause. I know it'll be hard, but it's the right thing." He sniffed and wiped rain droplets from his sleeve. "The most selfish thing a man can do is to live his life without regards to the world his children will grow up in. I don't want to be that kind of man."

Arnon studied Geoffrey as if trying to read his thoughts. "It's only getting worse," he said at last. "It's not just the Daecish. It's the people themselves. I haven't been here in five years, and it's so different. It's like there's a division growing between our own people."

Geoffrey knew Arnon was right, but just as he was thinking of how to respond, the sound of distant footsteps caused them both to look up as several men and women made their way down the alley. At the same time, the back door to the tavern swung open, and Drake's head peered around the corner.

"It's time," he said.

A Meeting in the Dark

Arnon shivered in the cold dampness of the tavern's cellar. At first, it was too dark to see until Drake lit several other lanterns hanging from the face of dark wooden shelves, lining three of the stone walls. A single shelf on the back wall was stacked full of hard rind cheeses, which still looked early in their aging process. Arnon's stomach growled. Two other shelves were deep-set with many cubbies, all filled with bottles of various ales, elixirs, and spirits. There were even a few bottles of spiced wine Arnon recognized.

Before long, another group of men and women came down the stairs, chatting quietly to themselves. Among them, Arnon recognized Wesley, who had just looked at him from across the room. Wesley's mouth fell open as he walked past the other men and embraced Arnon.

"Arnon!" he said in a voice that always sounded a little too shrill for any man. He held Arnon by the shoulders to look at him. There was a hint of distress in his eyes. "I can't believe it. Drake told me you was here, but I just can't believe it."

Arnon half-heartedly smiled. Wesley's face had grown solemn. He also looked thinner than Arnon remembered, with sunken cheeks and a sparse, scraggly beard. Deep scars ran down the side of his right jaw to his throat. Arnon wasn't sure, but he assumed they were from the abuses of Wesley's father from when he was young.

"Drake has," Wesley began but hesitated, glancing at Drake behind him. "He let us know about Lombard." His eyes glistened in the torchlight.

Arnon barely nodded. The others in the room, mostly older, hard-looking men, went solemn and quiet. Arnon hardly recognized any of them. The ones he did, he couldn't remember their names.

"I'm so sorry for your loss," Wesley continued. "It was a loss to us all. Your father will be missed by more men than the death of any king. I reckon we'll give a ceremony first thing in the morn'."

"Thank you, Wesley," Arnon replied. "Father loved you like a brother and always spoke well of you. My mother and sisters also send their love." His own words sounded so formal, he felt like he was speaking at his father's funeral.

"Myla! How is she? And the girls?"

"They're doing well. They went with Porter to stay with Galvin in Denhurst."

"I'd have loved to have seen her again," Wesley replied. "But I guess that's best. Things are faring well in Denhurst. Myla, Fleta, Hazel. They'll be well taken care of, I don't doubt."

A shiver shook in Arnon's chest. Just the way Wesley mentioned their names, and the expressions of the men around him, made him realize that even though his mother and sisters were far away, he was in the company of family.

"Well," said Wesley. "It's good to have a member of the Greystrom family here once again." With that, several men came and patted Arnon on the back.

"Welcome home!"

"Ye' look jus' like yer father," said one old man with a lazy eye.

"It's an honor," said another, shaking Arnon's hand far tighter than he would have liked.

Wesley handed Arnon a wooden chair. "We got much we can discuss and catch up on later. For now, let's get on with business."

Grabbing chairs, stools, and crates piled in the corner, the men and women, as if in routine, set them all in several rows facing Wesley. Geoffrey sat with his arms crossed and eyes narrowed. His hair and brown beard, peppered with patches of gray, looked clean and well-cut compared to the rest of the men. It was obvious he'd been around the Daecish for a few years. Arnon wiped his damp, cold palms on his thighs. He wished he had something to fiddle with.

"Fellow Dark Horses," Wesley began, "I'd like to first introduce both Arnon and Geoffrey. Geoffrey here, as I mentioned to you before, has met with the court—Drake, Morgan, myself—and has been approved to join the Dark Horse leadership. Given his role in the Capital Guard, I don't doubt he'll prove a great asset to the Silent Hither." Wesley stretched his hand open to Arnon. "And as many of you know, Arnon's the son of the late Lombard Greystrom."

There was sudden applause as many eyes turned in Arnon's direction, nodding in affirmation and shaking his hand again. Wesley waited for their attention before he continued. "Arnon's certainly had a long journey, and I expect everyone to show him due respect. Now, as we're aware, times have been dim as of late. The first phase of the draft is still clear in our minds, and we've lost some good men because of it."

"How many?" interrupted a girl sitting two seats beside Arnon.

Wesley raised his eyes. "It's difficult to say, Adelyne. No Dark Horses, but the Silent Hither will feel the effects."

"But ain't some joining the Silent Hither 'cause they's angry over the draft?" asked a man.

"Yes," Wesley replied. "But the numbers are still not in our favor. We will need to work diligently to fix that."

"Go ahead and read that letter we received," Drake spoke up.

Wesley lifted his hand. "Don't worry, Drake, I'll get to that."

As the discussion continued, Arnon couldn't help but occasionally shift his eyes toward the girl, Adelyne. He liked that name. Although the room was dim, he could easily make out her sharp blue eyes and curly chestnut hair, hinted with shades of auburn, which reached down to just below her shoulders. He tried, more than once, to shift his eyes back to Wesley, but each time he found his gaze drawn right back to her. He was almost baffled at how beautiful she was. It didn't take long for him to give up, and he just stared for a moment. When she ran her fingers through her hair to behind her ear, he noticed a dark bruise on the side of her left cheek.

She suddenly shot a stern glare at him. He quickly turned his face as it burned hot, not daring to look at her again. "Idiot," he mouthed to himself.

Able to finally focus, the conversation continued as Wesley listed off a few of the names of the men drafted. Apparently, there was concern over the future of their wives and children. Geoffrey raised a hand.

"Geoffrey?" Wesley asked.

"What's our plan to recover the numbers we lost in the draft?"

"Excellent question," Wesley replied. "As of now—"

"If I may," spoke up an elderly man, with a thick white beard, which he trimmed, but not very well. Arnon recognized him from his childhood but forgot the name.

Wesley swallowed with that look he always gave when he got upset or nervous—wide eyes, like a young child about to cry. His bucked teeth and droopy face only exemplified the expression, but he motioned to the man anyway. "Of course, Morgan, go ahead."

Standing up, Morgan presented himself very formally, despite his stained, worn garments. "As you're all aware, for the past eight months, we've established a dozen teams across the city, mostly the slums. Awareness, training, that sort of thing." He let out a sigh that sounded more like a grunt as he clasped his hands behind his back. "Our issue is reaching folks beyond the lower-class. The poor make up the majority of those who join, and it ain't enough."

"How many do we have?" Arnon asked.

"We don't have an exact number right now, but prior to the draft, we were just under two-hundred . . ."

141

Morgan kept talking, but Arnon couldn't hear another word as he sank back in his seat. Two-hundred? What were they going to do with so few people? He should have gone to Denhurst.

"If I may," Geoffrey spoke up. "I understand I'm new here, so I'm just trying to figure out the big picture."

"You're fine," Wesley added.

"I've admired the men in the Silent Hither for a long time," Geoffrey continued, "if, for no other reason, because of their courage to stand up against unjust tyranny. However, I can't help but ask a pressing question. How exactly does Everwind plan to succeed? Let's say we get a thousand men to join. Then what? Are we going to fight the Daecish? Take back the city? If we do, won't more Daecish come?"

Drake stood up and raised a hand. "See, the Silent Hither's an idea. As of now, it's in the hearts of the families who've lost everything. It remains in the dark alleyways and cellars. The key to its success is getting the rest to join it. Only then can we rise against the Daecish. And yes, we'll fight, and most likely, they'll send more troops and fight back. But we'll never quit. The Silent Hither's a testimony that the pale-faces will never fully conquer us. We'll fight for our home 'til none of us are left. You can be sure of that."

Arnon sunk further into his chair. So few numbers, yet so many Daecish. Was this a lost cause? No. His father would have never believed in something so strongly if there were no hope.

"In the meantime," Wesley added. "We've got to continue what we're doing. Strengthening the teams, training the men, spreading awareness."

"In my experience," Geoffrey added. Arnon was surprised that his expression looked so calm and collected. As if Drake's words didn't even phase him. "The people need to see that the Silent Hither cares for her own. Is that not the heart of why we exist?"

"Hear, hear!" Morgan exclaimed, along with several others.

"Many of them are starving," Geoffrey continued. "We need to get out there in the slums. Get our hands dirty. We can hand out clothing, food, whatever we can. I've got connections with several who are doing that now. I can get bread, wine, water—"

"My tavern's always open," spoke up Drake.

"Yes!" Several applauded.

The scent of mold and cheese started to mix with the sweaty men around Arnon. A sharp pain began to form between his eyebrows, and he rubbed his forehead.

"We've already looked into it," Morgan added, "which is one of the reasons I was so eager to bring you on. Our teams would be the perfect avenue. When they go out recruiting the people, we'll put them to work. Each team could focus on the care for their part of the city."

"And they can inform the people if another draft's coming," Drake added. "We won't let them be caught off guard again. We'll fight next time if we have to!"

There was another applause as several men and women whistled.

"Why wasn't that done before the first draft?" Arnon asked. "Even I knew it was coming. Were the people not informed?"

"The information our spies gathered was very little," Wesley answered. "We didn't know when or where it was going to take place, or even who exactly was going to be drafted."

Maybe it was the thought of doing something more exciting than sitting here all night, but the mention of spies sent Arnon's blood running with excitement. He wanted to know more. "Did the spies find anything else?" he asked.

"Letters, mostly."

"What about the Palace of Ingvar?" spoke up Morgan again. "We've approved the next assignment. Should we not discuss it?"

Wesley motioned his hand toward Adelyne. Arnon wished there was a little more light as he glanced at the profile of her face. "You're scheduled for another mission next week, isn't that correct?"

"Four nights from tonight," she replied. "Murdock and Quinn already have the map and gear."

"Good. Now about your viewpoint," Wesley continued.

"Viewpoint, sire?" She raised an eyebrow.

"Your lookout."

"Sire, I've never used a viewpoint yet, I'm sure—"

"I understand," Wesley interrupted, "but the board's agreed that given the higher number of guards lately, a viewpoint is needed."

Adelyne gave a slight nod but said nothing.

"So, we got to decide who'll be that viewpoint. Murdock and Quinn will already be occupied, and Darby, Kenneth, Elric—they've all been taken in the draft."

There was a low commotion as the crowd conversed with one another. Several men shook their heads with frowns.

"Who we got that's qualified?" Wesley spoke over them.

The crowd went silent, but no one raised a hand. Arnon wanted to raise his, but he hesitated. Maybe he should just listen for a while. Besides, the last thing he wanted to do was volunteer and fail. What would they think of him then? What would his father think?

"We may have to recruit someone else," suggested a man. "We aren't qualified for such a mission."

"Nonsense," replied Wesley. "You're telling me there ain't one man willing to stand as viewpoint?"

"We aren't holding back 'cause of fear," continued the man defensively. "We just aren't as qualified as Darby or Elric were. We can't take no chance in a mission failing. It may be better to hire from outside."

Arnon bounced his knee nervously until he finally raised his hand.

"Yes, Arnon," said Wesley.

"I've—" he cleared his throat and gazed at all the eyes now staring at him, "not done anything officially, but ever since I was young, my father taught me how to hunt, to stalk, and escape when I needed to. I can be the viewpoint if you need one."

Several gave nods, but others shook their heads. Adelyne did not seem impressed.

"I have no doubt," Wesley replied, "that he raised you in a manner that will prove to exceed even the most capable men." He swept his eyes across the crowd. "Have we any objections?"

The crowd remained silent, but Adelyne stirred in her seat.

"Well, that settles it, then."

Suddenly, Adelyne turned toward Arnon. "Can you read?" she asked.

"I'm sorry," Arnon replied, as his ears warmed. "What?"

"Can you read?"

What did that have to do with anything? Arnon scarcely shook his head. Was she really that upset that he looked at her earlier?

"Then how can he possibly do this mission?" she asked, looking back to Wesley. "How can he know which documents to steal?"

"Besides you, myself, and Morgan," Wesley replied, "I don't think anyone else here can read, and you know that. Besides, he'll be a viewpoint. He doesn't have to read."

Adelyne only glared at the floor.

"Anyway," Wesley continued, "we will go over the details in the evening on the 'morrow. Let us move on."

Arnon shook the embarrassment away. She may have been pretty, but he wasn't growing too fond of her attitude.

"Now what about this letter Drake spoke of?" a man asked.

"Yes, yes," Wesley replied, pulling a letter from his pocket. "The court and I received a letter from a dispatch from Astford early this morn'. Signed by Burlan Dunhaven." He paused as if he didn't know what to say next.

"Well, tell them what it said!" Morgan hollered.

"Well . . ." Wesley hesitated. There was a stillness in the cellar, and Arnon suddenly felt how humid and sour the air was. But at least his headache was fading. "Apparently, a boy's been found near Astford. And, well," he laughed, "Burlan believes he came from Daecland."

A sudden commotion broke out. "How old?" one asked.

"When did they start bringing families over?" questioned another.

Wesley motioned his hands for everyone to calm down. "Please, please," he said. "First of all, if this is true, this boy would be too young to be a Daecish soldier, and as far as we know, the Daecish haven't brought over anyone but government officials and military units."

"Just a half-breed!" shouted a man. "A bastard product of them pale-faces and our own loose women!"

Several men grumbled and Adelyne visibly stiffened.

"Burlan reckoned the same thing at first," Drake responded, "but says he's certain the boy's not."

Arnon thought the whole idea seemed ridiculous and not even important. How would a boy from Daecland help with anything?

"How'd he get here?" someone asked.

Wesley laughed again as he started scratching at a red and scabbed part of his forearm. He had done that for as long as Arnon could remember, and he knew it was the scratching itself that caused the scabbing. "The letter's not very clear. One possibility is that he found a pass through the mountains."

Several men grumbled. Even Arnon knew that a search for a path through the Great Fringe had left a dark and terrible memory in the minds of the Sunderian people.

"Impossible!" shouted one man.

"What were the other possibilities?" asked another.

Drake turned over his shoulder and looked at the crowd. "The letter mentioned that the boy claimed he washed up on the shore and rode some large animal to Astford."

"What kind of animal?" asked one.

Wesley shrugged. "Probably a horse or something."

"But in the letter," added Morgan, eyeing Wesley with a stern glare, "Burlan said he questioned the boy, and he said it wasn't a horse, but a monster."

An old man sitting beside Arnon leaned toward him. "Sunder's Bane is upon us. It's the sign of Hælend's Ballad."

"It was an alphyn!" shouted another man.

Despite a shiver running down Arnon's arms, he laughed.

"Absurd!" shouted another.

"I always thought the Bane would at least be a man, not some child still suckling from his mother's breast!" shouted another as he made a crude impersonation.

The crowd erupted into laughter, but Adelyne rolled her eyes.

"Quiet!" Wesley exclaimed. "We're jumping to conclusions! And absurd ones at that! In fact, now that we're all aware of it, I think we can all agree that this is not worth our efforts."

Morgan stood up and slammed his fist on a barrel top. "I don't agree!" he shouted coldly. "You may not think this important, but Drake and I both say it's worth an investigation."

Wesley wiped the sweat from his forehead, but he didn't say anything. Arnon stiffened. He couldn't believe Morgan talked to him in such a tone. Wesley was supposed to be the leader.

"How do we know for sure that this boy's actually from Daecland?" asked a man. "Did he have blonde hair? Did he sound Daecish?"

"According to Burlan, both," Morgan replied, "but he—"

"But that don't mean anything for certain," interrupted an older woman. Her eyes were bright in the dim light, but her dark wrinkled skin blended into the shadows. Arnon recognized her as Bell, though he couldn't recall how.

"Burlan did say the boy had some sort of Daecish gadget on him," Drake added. "Something which could not have been made in Sunder, unless it was by a Daecish forge. He called it a lens, but he didn't say what it's used for."

"I've never heard such a thing," said Bell.

"This whole thing here's absurd," said another.

Arnon felt his headache coming back. He looked at Adelyne, who seemed to be in her own world as she focused on the ground. Another man glanced in her direction, and Arnon hoped he didn't look that creepy when he had stared at her.

"Now, now, let's at least consider this," said a man behind Arnon. "We might at least send a few men to question the lad."

"Agreed!" several shouted.

Wesley leaned forward with a stern expression. "What if this is all a trap? Have you thought about that? We have so few volunteers as it is. Can we really afford to send a team across the kingdom to learn about some petty boy? No, we need to meet about this further and wait."

Drake waved a hand as if to ignore Wesley's comments.

"But Burlan's a trusted man," said someone in the front.

"What little we know of him, yes, he seems trustworthy." Wesley's voice shook. "But how do we know this was even written by Burlan? Or that he isn't just excited over nothing? Men have grown desperate lately. And men in Astford, as you all know, have a long history of being overly superstitious."

Several men's faces went red. One man even gripped a small skinning knife, sticking out of his left boot.

"That's too Daecish for my hearing'," Drake spoke up. "Long have we held to our legends, and calling our own people superstitious ain't warranted in my tavern."

Wesley lifted his hands. "I didn't mean it that way." He kept glancing to the ground as if he was afraid to look at Drake in the eyes. "You know I hold our own history dearly. I simply meant that there are some folk, especially in Astford, who tend to stretch the truth in order to give others false hope. And in our fragile state, we can't afford that."

The crowd went to silence. Arnon understood why Wesley gave resistance to the idea, but he was beginning to think that it should be looked into.

"I'll go," said Geoffrey suddenly. He stood up to the left of Arnon as the men gazed up at him.

"Geoffrey?" questioned Wesley.

"I joined this cause to help. And if I'm seeing this correctly, this is a mission perfect for my credentials. I investigate for a living, I can go alone, and it'll cost you nothing. Nothing may come of it, but it can't hurt to try."

Wesley furrowed his eyes as if he was worried. "We were hoping you would be *here*."

"I can be there and back in two weeks."

"But how can you go alone? What about spies in your work? Wouldn't your superiors question it?"

"I often train investigators in other towns. My job frequently sends me abroad, and, in fact, I schedule the trainings. I'll simply schedule one for the guard in Astford within the week—short notice, but not out of the ordinary. I'll be well equipped with a carriage and supplies."

"Hear, hear!" called out several other men.

"If that is the wish of those present," Wesley replied. "Of course, we will need court approval."

Several let out exaggerated sighs.

"Approved," both Drake and Morgan said at the same time.

"All right then," Wesley said, throwing his hands in the air. "I thought we would meet about it privately, but since you all insist, we'll work on Geoffrey's departure immediately." He looked at Geoffrey. "Just be careful. It was going abroad alone, and getting caught, that caused Porter, one of our best men, to go into hiding six years ago."

The meeting went on for a little longer but ended earlier than Arnon would have expected. After Fellhouse, it seemed no one felt very comfortable staying together in one place for too long. Yet as early as it was, his traveling had brought him to the point where he could barely keep his eyes open. Drake was talking to Adelyne about something, but he couldn't hear.

"Arnon?" asked Wesley, coming to his side. "You have to forget your family name."

Arnon tilted his head. "Forget my family name?" But even as he asked it, he knew that would be the best way to stay unnoticed by the Daecish.

"I mean it, Arnon." He placed both hands on his shoulders and narrowed his eyes. "Trust me on this. Never use it. And as much as you can, stay out of sight."

"I will."

After Wesley left, Arnon found Drake piling the stools and chairs back in the corner.

"Drake," he said sheepishly.

"Aye?" He replied without looking at him.

Arnon waited until more people went up the steps. "Is there somewhere I can, um . . ."

Drake smirked. "You need a place to stay, don't you?"

"Yea, I think so."

"You can stay here if you like. Though it ain't much." He wiped off his hands on his apron and crossed his arms. "Just be sure to never stay at your old family home. It's safe enough to visit if you're careful. But the moment you move in, the Daecish'll get suspicious."

Arnon hadn't even thought of his family home. He tried to hide the homesickness that suddenly welled up in him. "Don't worry, Drake. I won't."

* * *

The light drizzle had picked up to a steady rain with soft thunder rumbling in the far distance over the sea. But for his entire walk home, all Geoffrey could think about was whether he'd be back from Astford in time for the baby to be born. He soon walked past the Tea House— the official name for the hall of the Merchant's Guild. He glanced through the window, which was just barely opened to let in the breeze. Lester sat at a table next to a large fireplace in the warm, lit room. Geoffrey didn't really want to stay out in the rain, but he couldn't resist. Standing in the shadow of the outside corner, he peered in and listened.

"A toast I raise to your good fortunes!" exclaimed a Daecish officer as he stood with one hand on the fireplace mantle, his other holding a goblet of red wine. The large room was filled with mostly wealthy Sunderian merchants and landowners, with a few other Daecish officials and officers. "And may these gifts from the king do you well. Never again will you require the sun to tell your time."

Another cheer and much discussion commenced as tiny brass contraptions were handed out to the Sunderians, although Geoffrey couldn't tell what they were.

"I've never seen such handsome craftsmanship!" exclaimed a man, eyeing the piece in his hand. Several of the Daecish officers helped the Sunderians twist tiny knobs on the top of the brass plates, which looked as if they opened. Lester was shown how to wear it in his new waistcoat pocket as the officer ran a thin chain through the middle button.

Lester cleared his throat and held his goblet high. "And now let us toast to your good fortunes and our thanks for your work here in our splendid city. May we always be in debt to His Majesty's throne in Daecland!"

Geoffrey rolled his eyes.

There was another loud cheer as Lester brought down his goblet and drunk half the wine, wiping the dribble from his chin. After the men all drank, another man stood up. "Lords and gentlemen!" he called out. "Just a reminder that the symphony, which our Daecish friends have graciously invited from their homeland, will be next month at the Barrow Theater." He nodded his head in appreciation to the Daecish officer standing by the mantle. Geoffrey recognized this one as Commander Veurðr. He only saw him on occasion at City Hall, but he knew enough about him that he was a respectable man, at least as far as Daecish officers went.

The commander grinned and nodded back. "Do mark your calendars, for it is a symphony in honor of our alliance and friendship." There was another loud cheer. "But now, let us not waste any more time." He motioned for a man in a fine black tailcoat and top hat to come forward, now standing in front of an object covered in a black sheet. A quick silence fell among the crowd. "It is our honor and duty to afford you the best in this land," he continued. "From one ally to another. Therefore, I present to you the promise of a new future!"

Commander Veurðr then gave a dramatic pull as he lifted the sheet into the air. Sitting upon a stone slab was a brass mechanism, roughly the size of an ale barrel. Several pipes ran from the top to bottom with a thin rod protruding from its side, ending in a small circular device, all mounted on a long, wide cylinder.

There was weak clapping from some, accompanied by a few raised eyebrows and low murmuring. "What exactly is it?" asked one of the Sunderians.

A great roar of laughter burst out from the Daecish.

"My apologies," said Commander Veurðr. "This, gentlemen, is the model of a steam engine." He pointed to several components, explaining their purposes.

Even Geoffrey couldn't help but be impressed as he heard about boilers, steam pressure, and pistons. It made his heart race as if it was too much, too fast. Sixteen years ago, such a thing would have been unimaginable in Sunder.

"This is our future," he continued, "and our hope. For this steam engine is what produces the essential power to build Sunder into the greatest kingdom the world has ever seen!"

If Geoffrey hadn't caught himself, he would have laughed. The confused look on the faces of the Sunderians made it obvious they didn't understand even the most basic concept of what Commander Veurðr was trying to explain. But, apparently, that didn't matter since they all clapped anyway. Commander Veurðr waved his hands in the air. "And by next week, we will be taking full investments for your business expansions."

The men embraced hands with one another, their faces red with fervor.

"A cause for more wine!" one finally yelled. "More wine!"

Geoffrey shook his head to himself and hurried home.

The Tinder of Denhurst

I t's your turn." Hazel snickered, sitting beneath the shadow of the wagon.

With her chin resting on her palm, Fleta moaned and moved an owl piece across the board. She wished she could be more like Arnon, but this was the dumbest game she had ever played.

"Too bad." Hazel snickered. "You lost."

Fleta exhaled in relief and stretched her arms. Nestled in a wide holler, surrounded by several tall, dark pines, which creaked and swayed against the high winds, the camp felt secure and safe from the barren countryside. This was the first time she had seen so many trees in six years, but she would have preferred seeing hardwoods. Pine trees, especially this kind, with their thick, scaly bark and thin, scraggly limbs, looked pitiful and ugly compared to the broad beeches and elms outside of Everwind.

Beside her, Porter pulled the kettle off the fire and sat down on an old stump. After soaking his face with a hot, wet rag, he pulled out a long knife with a cream-colored bone handle. He once told her that the knife had been passed to him from his grandpa, who got it from his grandpa before that. The story was that it was originally forged in Earlon and made its way to Sunder by way of the Isen Road. If that were true, the knife was as old as Llynhithe since trading ceased between the two kingdoms nearly three-hundred years ago. At least, that's what her father had taught her.

Fleta continued to gaze at the marbled gray blade as he scraped his chin. It reminded her of the hunting knife her father had made for Arnon. Just the thought of it made her look away. All her life, she had her father to look after her. If ever he was away, Arnon was there. But now, they were both gone.

"Why would you do that?" asked Hazel, watching Porter scrape the sharp knife up his cheek. "Don't that hurt?"

Porter laughed.

"Don't ask such silly questions," Fleta retorted. Most of the time, her nose felt clogged, and even *she* could hear the nasally sound in her own voice.

"Fleta," Myla said as she tied two canvas flaps together, enclosing the wagon. "Use kinder words toward your sister."

Fleta rolled her eyes but caught Myla's stern glare and looked away. "Sorry, Hazel." But she didn't mean it. Hazel was six now, but Myla still treated her like a baby.

Porter rubbed his chin. "I haven't shaved my face clean in twenty years."

Myla looked toward Porter with a smile. "Does this have to do with going into Denhurst?"

"Can't be too careful." Putting away his knife, Porter loaded his wool blanket back into the wagon. Afterward, he grabbed the entrails of the hare they ate the previous night and threw them into the fire, which gave a loud pop as sap burst from the inner grain of the pine logs.

Fleta didn't mind eating meat, but she couldn't stand the thought of killing. The first time she helped her father clean the organs out of a deer, she was seven years old. The moment she looked into its large dark eyes, she burst into tears. Lombard hugged her and explained that none of the deer would go to waste, and one day, there would be a new world, and death would vanish. She wasn't sure exactly what all that meant, but the look in her father's eyes told her that it was worth waiting for. Maybe he was already there, waiting for them.

"All right, girls," said Myla. "Time to get in the wagon."

"When will we be in Denhurst?" Fleta asked.

"An hour or so," replied Porter, pointing south through the grove. "That way."

Across the wagon, Myla gazed at the floor with a furled brow and heavy eyes. A single bead of sunlight streaked down her face. She must have felt the same way as Fleta did. Hazel, who was wrapped in her arm, looked up at her. "Mama?"

"Yes, Hazel?"

"I miss Arnon."

She smiled, giving Hazel a gentle squeeze with her arm. "I know you do."

"When will we see him again?"

"Before too long."

There was a short pause.

"I miss Papa, too," said Hazel in a softer tone.

She looked into Hazel's eyes and rubbed her fingers through her hair. "I miss him, too," she told her.

Fleta's gaze momentarily dropped to the wooden floor of the wagon. Why didn't her mother ever look at her that way?

Hazel took Myla's hands and pressed her fingertips against hers as if to compare the size of their hands. "When will we see Papa again?" she asked.

Myla sighed softly, but Fleta could hear the shake in her lungs. "One day, Hazel. One day we'll see him again."

Fleta turned her face away and laid her cheek down on her arms.

The ridge faded into the earth, and the winding Fellmoore River soon rolled into view on their left side. Its water ran brown and deep, flowing gently through the countryside—a few large, white fowl perched along the muddy banks. As the wagon drew near, they lifted their long wings and fluttered upstream behind them. Fixed beside the river, not far in the distance, tall palisades, cut from thick, rough-barked pines, arose into the air, encircling the city of Denhurst.

Fleta peered over her shoulder through a crack in the canvas. Although she was born in Everwind, her memory was vague, and the dark walls and rising buildings seemed so big. Almost overbearing. As they neared the gate, several guards halted the wagon and stood beside Porter.

"I'll have your papers," said a Daecish officer, placing his hand on the neck yolk.

Porter reached into his pocket and pulled out a folded piece of paper, and handed it to the officer, who opened it and scanned through its contents. Two other guards in black uniforms encircled the wagon and pulled back the bonnet cover, peering at the girls. Hazel grabbed Myla's arm. Fleta tightened her muscles as her shoulders trembled. She had seen Daecish officers her whole childhood, but now that they had killed her father, a hatred began to grow in her.

"Mr. Rupert Keegan," inquired the officer, "you checked out from Everwind six days ago?"

"Yes, sire."

Fleta quickly wiped a tear from her cheek but kept her eyes on the officers.

"You have any relations here?" the officer continued.

"Just my cousin, Kent Burnwall."

"And what matter are you visiting him for?"

"Small reunion," Porter replied, motioning his hand back to the girls.

"How long will you be staying?"

Porter scratched his face and looked up with a squinted eye. "Three weeks to a month. Not heading back too soon. The travel's hard on the girls."

Fleta didn't think she could spend more than a day surrounded by those terrible people. But calming her nervousness, she relaxed her muscles. Now was not the time to react. Arnon told her to look after her family, and that is what she would do.

After eyeing Porter for a moment, the officer made some markings on his papers then handed them back. "Fifteen aracs."

Porter handed the officer several notes. The officer waved for them to continue through the gate. As the wagon rolled into the city, Myla went to the front and sat beside Porter. "When did we have to start having papers to go anywhere?"

"It's only for wagons going betwixt Everwind and Denhurst, and I think maybe Llynhithe now. Galvin said it started about five months ago to keep track of who's coming and going. Several weeks ago, he sent me all the paperwork and aracs I needed to get in; all I had to do was give it a date of departure."

"Is Kent really your cousin?"

Porter chuckled. "No, but we'll be staying at his place. He bought up an old inn a few years ago." He faced her mother with a strange smile, but she didn't seem to notice.

Watching from behind, Fleta was old enough to know that he smiled longer than he should have, especially since her mother's gaze was fixed ahead. The only other time she saw a man look at her like that was her father. The thought made her want to spit as if she just ate something rotten.

Continuing through the city, Myla came back into the wagon and sat next to Hazel. Fleta had pulled back the canvas and gazed at the passing buildings. Most were built of wattle and daub, framed with pine logs, though a few were built of stone. All the roofs were thatched, but unlike the heather which covered her own home in the Western Plains, most of the homes here seemed to be covered with reeds or rushes. Smoke slithered from the windows, and the streets were all mud. Mosquitoes buzzed in the air, and a few made their way into the tent as Hazel tried to swat them away.

Porter pushed out a long breath. "Denhurst," he said, looking back. "Daecish architecture ain't touched her yet." He faced forward again, and a grunt mingled with a faint laugh spilled out. "Makes you wonder what all them tolls and taxes are for."

Crowds of people buzzed around the market where a jester imitated chopping someone's head off. He threw a spiraling red ribbon into a group of small children, resembling the blood spewing from the man's neck. They laughed as a girl picked it up and ran off.

They soon approached a large two-story building with two balconies lining the front, its back situated against the city wall. Porter guided the mules behind the building, beneath a low overhang.

"We made it," said Myla, taking a deep breath.

Fleta examined the log siding and windows. Would this be her new home? The idea of living in such a nice building should have excited her, but with her father and Arnon gone, a strange emptiness filled her. Like a hole that was slowly filling up with sorrow and loneliness.

Following the others, Fleta stepped down with her cow skin boots sinking in the mud. She awkwardly bowed her legs, trying to swat away the mosquitoes while at the same time trying to step out onto a dry patch without getting mud on her brown dress. Porter tied up the mules as he moved an empty trough in front of them, filling it with feed from a small barrel.

Each of them grabbed a satchel or bag, except Hazel, who held her ragdoll in one hand and grabbed Fleta's hand with the other. They walked through a back door and ascended a set of wooden stairs. Porter motioned for the girls to pause as he opened a door and peered into the well-lit room filled with tables and chairs. He smiled and swung the door open.

"Galvin!" Porter called out.

Galvin turned with a startle as Porter wrapped him in his arms. Myla rushed toward him with her hands over her mouth while Hazel and Fleta remained in the doorway.

"Myla?" Galvin continued as he hugged her. "I didn't expect you!" He laughed with a large grin. "Come in! Make yourself comfortable."

He grabbed their satchels, setting them beside some chairs near a large hearth. He peered at Hazel, then Fleta. "You both sure have grown. What's your mother been feeding you?"

Both Hazel and Fleta awkwardly smiled, but after he turned to talk to Myla again, Hazel leaned over. "Who's that man?" she whispered.

"I think it's Galvin," Fleta replied. She thought she recognized him, but for some reason, she thought he would have looked different. He had short brown hair, with just a hint of gray, and a tight reddish beard, almost like a younger version of Porter. His eyebrows were strong and straight, but his left eye was grayed, and it wandered as if he could never keep it focused.

From a dark hall on the right, two men walked in, one taller than the other.

Porter glanced at them uneasily as Hazel stepped over and wrapped her arms around Myla's waist.

"Don't worry about them," Galvin said with a smile. "They're friends. Kent let them stay the night. Hugo. Oliver." He motioned his hands toward them, respectively. "This is Porter and Myla."

Hugo, the tall one, pulled his thumbs from behind his leather belt, wrapped around his brown tunic, and shook hands with Porter. Afterward, Oliver kissed Myla's hand and patted Hazel on the head with a smile. Fleta couldn't seem to keep her eyes off of his thick dark hair and gray eyes. They were beautiful and sharp, like iron. Sure, he was probably five years older than her, but she didn't think that mattered. She wanted to lift her hand, so he would kiss it, but after he glanced in her direction, he walked out with Hugo through another door. Did he think she was ugly, too? Was it because of her nose? Back in Everwind, a boy once told her that her nose looked like a bird's beak. Arnon even once told her she looked like a horse. She knew he said it in anger, and so she forgave him, but she also knew he wouldn't have said it if it wasn't true.

She held her composure, but for some reason, she felt like crying.

"Where's Lombard and Arnon?" Galvin asked Myla.

Myla's eyes watered. Porter drew in a deep breath. "Let's let the girls take their stuff to the bedroom upstairs," he said. "They've had a hard journey." As he gave a slight motion to Fleta and Hazel, Galvin's face went grave.

Fleta took Hazel's hand as she followed her mother and two elderly women, dressed in wool gowns with cream-colored bonnets covering their hair, across the room. Everything inside was wooden; floors, walls, and furniture. Although nothing about it felt Daecish, she figured this was the nicest place she had ever been in. Like a large, lively tavern, only empty, as if they had the whole thing to themselves. One of the women pointed to a door on the right side of a long hallway. "Here's where you'll be sleeping," she said, setting their sacks beside low beds of straw, which made the room smell like a stable. "There's a bathing room just down the hall."

The other woman laid a stack of towels on the floor. "We'll get the fire going shortly, so you'll have hot water." They both disappeared out of the room.

Fleta widened her eyes. She had once heard about the Daecish bringing in private bath basins, but she had never had the opportunity to use one. In Everwind, unless you were wealthy or Daecish, there was only one public bathhouse which you had to pay for; otherwise, you washed yourself like everyone else did—in a shallow foot tub with a rag.

"Mama?" she asked.

"I know, dear. You go ahead. I think I'm going to get some rest." Her eyes looked swollen as she laid herself down on the bed. Hazel laid down beside her.

"Are you sure you don't want me to stay with you?"

"I'll be fine, Fleta. You go ahead."

Grabbing a towel, she hurried after the women down the hall.

* * *

"I can't believe it," Galvin said, sitting on a tall wooden stool, barely holding on to the mug resting on his leg. The smoldering coals from the hearth warmed his face as the smoke rose and swirled around the ceiling like thin spiraling streams. "Lombard's gone." He took in a deep, shaking breath, watching the glowing embers. "I assumed he'd be around long after us. But, I guess I assume too much." He leaned over and rubbed his forehead.

"Still getting headaches?" Porter asked, slumped back in a wooden armchair.

"Since Fellhouse."

"Think you'll ever get your sight back?

"The left eye's shot," he replied. "All it's good for is keeping me awake at night."

"It hurts that bad?"

"Aye," Galvin said, taking a drink. "I reckon my right eye's got to work twice as hard, and it lets me know it."

Porter tapped his mug on the chair arm. "Arnon took the long way to Everwind, but I reckon he's been there for almost a week by now. I hope Wesley hasn't buggered things up too much."

Galvin slightly smiled. "Wesley ain't too good at anything, even buggering things up. And Arnon has his father's spirit in him; he'll be a good help to 'em all, I don't doubt."

"We went by Lombard's homestead on the way down," Porter said, "just to get a couple of supplies. I kept the wagon far enough, so the girls wouldn't see, but," he sank his chin into his palm with a look of surprise on his face, "the bodies. Four Daecish men were dead." He looked at Galvin and chuckled. "I think Arnon killed them all himself."

Galvin raised an eyebrow. "Surely Lombard helped."

"Based on Myla's account, Lombard was killed early on. She said she didn't actually see it, but she heard some shouts and, apparently, he was shot. Arnon didn't talk about it at all, but Galvin, some of them pale-faces looked like they were beaten to death with his own fists. And Arnon's got the injuries and bruises to prove it. One looked like he was thrown through a wall."

Galvin wasn't sure what to say, but he was Lombard's boy after all.

"I just don't know how he did it," Porter admitted.

"If he's anything like us, or his father, it's hatred. It can drive a man to do anything without a second thought. Arnon just may prove to be the leader Everwind needs. And it couldn't come soon enough. If all goes according to plan, we'll be marching there before winter."

Porter dropped his arm. "March toward Everwind?"

Lifting his mug again, Galvin stopped halfway and smirked. "I done told you a dozen times. We're gonna take Denhurst."

"Your numbers are that good?"

Galvin took another gulp before setting his mug on the floor. "They're good enough that if the draft starts here, which rumor has it'll be soon, I don't think the Daecish will be prepared for what's coming for 'em."

Porter didn't say anything, but his eyes raced in thought.

"Ever since Kent joined our movement," Galvin continued, "the people have multiplied. They aren't as fickle and cowardly as the folk in Everwind. These lowlanders are prouder of their country than anyone I ever met. Pure Earlonian blood still flows through their veins. They're the ones that first rebelled against the Daecish before there was ever a Silent Hither if you remember."

"And I also remember the pale-faces executing the rebels," Porter replied.

"Aye, but that only motivated the people to push harder. It's been growing for the past four years, and now, with Kent's reputation, it's exploded."

"The Daecish haven't caught onto him yet?"

Galvin laughed. "Of course not. He's far too cunning. They think they have him wrapped around their fingers like they have with the blubbering rich fools in Llynhithe and Everwind. I mean, look around you. We are in one of the nicest inns in Denhurst, and not a single Daecish soldier has set foot in here for two years."

"Is it still open?" Porter asked.

"Not really. At least not lately. Some people stay here and there, but Kent mostly uses it for us." He leaned toward Porter and pointed upstairs. "Kent did manage to get one of those copper bath basins installed."

Porter raised a single eyebrow.

"I know, I know," he replied, lifting a hand. "It's Daecish. But when you sit in one of those with the water piping hot..." he let out a long sigh. "There's nothing like it."

"Sitting with your whole body in hot water like that," Porter replied, shaking his head. "It can't be good for you. Makes you bleed more, you know?"

"Well, it's worth it."

A short silence followed as both men stared into the fire.

"We're either going to have to get the girls out of this place or at least somewhere safe," Galvin said, breaking the silence. Porter met his gaze as he continued. "When that draft comes, Denhurst will be a battlefield."

Porter chuckled. "I told Arnon I'd send word to Drake as soon as I had a better idea of our situation here. Guess I ought'a send it sooner than later."

"Don't send anything yet," Galvin replied. "Wait 'til the battle's over. If we lose, it won't matter anyway. But if we win, then he'll be in for a pleasant surprise."

Folkbjörn

Eirún opened her eyes. Despite the occasional breeze of cold air seeping through the cracks of the guest cottage, the early morning sun warmed her arms as its rays gleamed through the windowpanes. She sat up, straightening herself on the large, thick mattress. Behind her, the cherry headboard swirled in elegantly carved patterns, matching the rising posts on each corner of the bedframe. It took her a moment to remember where she was.

As she stood up, steam pipes rattled beneath the floorboards while the large clock, mounted on the left wall, ticked by as the pendulum swung in front of the hanging weights. Just before her, she could see herself in a looking glass, situated above a washing basin. Her blonde hair was in a tousled mess, with dark bags below her eyes as if she hadn't slept in weeks. Even she could notice the stark juxtaposition between herself and the room around her. She may have been a wreck on the inside, but she knew she needed to at least fix her appearance.

The shape of Audin's body lying at the bottom of the steps wouldn't leave her memory. She closed her eyes for a minute. One day at a time. That's all she could do.

After getting dressed, she grabbed a white headdress which she fitted low, just over her brow.

Satisfied with her concealment, she stepped outside. The cobblestone streets of Folkbjörn already bustled with crowds of merchants and traders. A steam carriage rolled by as the pistons clinked and hissed. The driver lifted his top hat to Eirún with a grin. She stood for a moment as the smell of soot and horse manure filled her nostrils. To the east, just on the edge of town, the chimneys of Gunborg

Orphanage barely peaked above the brown-shingled roofs of the other buildings. She was thankful she had slept through the passing over the Finnvard River the previous night.

Although the thought of Adis and Yrsa filled her with a desire to see them, she wished to not remain in Folkbjörn any longer than she had to and decided it was best if no one knew she was there. Although she was pretty sure Audin was dead, she couldn't help but wonder if he might have survived. Neither scenario made her feel any better.

To the north, several merchant stands were propped up along the sidewalk. Hanging from the wooden supports of the cloth awnings and filling makeshift tables and shelves, dozens of metal trinkets and contraptions buzzed and popped with whistling steam—cheap and useless novelties. But the sweeping effects of consumerism enchanted the crowds into a blind stupor. Taking out loans of credit, with interest rates usually higher than a week's worth of income, they threw their aracs away for junk as if they were heirs to princes and kings.

"Ladies and gentlemen!" A merchant pointed to a gathering crowd. Eirún was surprised that he didn't seem to be selling anything. "Feast your eyes on the future!" He bent down and pushed away a black curtain that hung beneath the stand and fumbled with a small brass steam engine, smaller than Eirún had ever seen. After he turned a valve, there came a low rumble, then a whistle as the engine began to vibrate. Standing back up, the merchant pointed at the table above the engine, where a glass orb sat with a thin copper wire running from its base. Beside it was another orb, with wool padding pressed against it. Several men and women smiled at one another.

"Are you ready?" asked the merchant, holding a finger in the air. Then he flipped a switch, and the first orb began to glow a dim yellow. Several in the crowd gasped. "This, ladies and gentlemen, is the future! Voltaic lighting!" An exaggerated grin spread across his face. "Already being installed in Norfrost and Fingate. It will soon stretch as far east as Vagholme!"

"How does it work?" asked a man. Like just about every other man, he wore a black top hat with a black cane in his right hand.

The merchant grinned. "I was hoping you would ask that." He pointed at the wooden posts along the streets, where wire cables, insulated by glass bottles at each post, ran through the city. "Much the same way as the telegraph!"

It had barely been a year since they were installed, and all Eirún knew, since voltaic power was still a recent phenomenon in eastern Daecland, was that telegrams were somehow sent and received through them.

The merchant turned another set of valves on the engine until the second orb began to spin against the wool padding. After a moment, he bent down and turned back a valve, and the orb came to a stop. "Quick!" he said. "I need a volunteer. How about you, sir?"

A large, fat man with a fuzzy mustache cleared his throat and took a step forward.

"Very good! Very good! Now, everyone, look very carefully. Sir, all I want you to do is to touch this glass."

The man peered at him and twitched his mustache. "What will it do?"

"Well," said the merchant with a chuckle, "it will feel strange at first, but I assure you it's harmless."

The man laughed uneasily. "But what will it do?"

The merchant put a finger to his chin. "It will give a small shock, but it's harmless, I promise. Much like when you touch a doorknob on a dry winter day."

Several in the crowd tried to encourage the man, who only held an uncertain expression on his face. But after glancing at two attractive women who motioned for him to go on, he took a deep breath, tried to suck in his gut, and slowly pointed his finger toward the glass globe. He hesitated for a second then touched it. There came a pop, and the crowd laughed. Eirún startled at the sound. She eyed the glass but noticed nothing out of the ordinary. The man's eyes went wide as he shrunk back his hand, shaking it.

The merchant laughed. "What you just felt, sir, is the power of a voltaic-static generator. Of course, this model is only a simple example, but it illustrates the force which powers this very light. Think beyond telegrams, even beyond lights! Soon voltaic power will energize wisps and the very steam carriages you drive!"

He went on for a while longer, but catching sight of Geirleif in the distance, Eirún left the crowds behind and continued north. The merchant's words, however, pressed on her too easily. The world was changing far quicker than she liked. Having been raised in the country, she preferred things to be simpler.

Approaching the carriage, Geirleif attempted to pick up a large suitcase and grabbed his back. "Oh!" he blurted as he stood hunched over with a purpling face. Dressed in a black tailcoat suit, his hair was thick and white, matching his bushy mustache.

"Let me help!" Eirún said, placing a hand on his back.

"Oh, no, no," he replied, shaking his head. "I cannot allow a lady to bother with loading luggage."

Eirún ignored him and grabbed one end of the suitcase. Geirleif reluctantly lifted the other end as they slid it into the back of the carriage. "Well, I do thank you very much," he said with a slight laugh. "Did you sleep well in the guest cottage?" He spoke with a certain sophistication Eirún had not yet noticed.

"I did, thank you."

He looked at her with a probing eye and a half-smile as if he didn't believe her, then closed the carriage door. "Oh! And forgive me," he continued raising a hand, "I wanted to apologize about my attitude in Scathwold yesterday morning."

Eirún smiled. "I understand; you don't have to apologize."

"Well, I should have been more polite." He walked around to the side door. "And for the life of me, I don't recall your name."

Eirún hesitated for a second. What if Audin was still alive and looking for her? "Kari," she said.

"Well, Kari, I am sure we will all enjoy your company on our trip to Norfrost."

"And likewise," she replied.

Geirleif searched around his pockets for a minute. "Blast it!" he said. "I left my watch at the bakery." He glanced at the carriage, then back to the townhome. "I am terribly sorry to bother you with this, but would you mind fetching it for me? I've got to finish loading this carriage, and if I don't—"

"I don't mind at all," Eirún replied.

Geirleif wiped his brow again. "That is very kind of you. I'll let Eilis know. I imagine we'll be leaving as soon as you return."

Geirleif turned to go back into the house while Eirún walked down the cobblestone street. It was not a long walk, and despite her inner turmoil, she found herself enjoying the cool air as the sights distracted her from her thoughts. Cheese shops, wine shops, artisans, and cobblers—all built of brick with shingled rooftops. Their doors swung open and shut with busy customers as the mounted bells jingled on the upper doorframes. Coming to a small crossway, she glanced down an alley to her right. Lying on the damp ground, beside a pile of broken crates, was a dark bundled blanket, which concealed some mass beneath it. Thinking no more of it, she continued to the bakery and walked through the entrance. Sitting on the counter was Geirleif's watch.

"Sir?" she asked politely. "I've been sent to fetch Mr. Geirleif's watch."

The baker looked up from the oven and blushed.

"Mr. Geirleif? Oh, yes, yes! Lord Beron! Pardon me, pardon me!" He wiped off his hands and straightened his short, thinning hair. "That's right, he must have left it." A bashful smile turned up the corner of his lips. "Well, you best take that back to its rightful owner, then."

Lord Beron? Was Geirleif a lord? Sudden anxiety welled up in her. She took the watch. "Thank you," she replied.

"My pleasure, my pleasure," he said, and Eirún turned to walk out the door. "You look awfully familiar, madam," he continued as he pulled a loaf of bread from a brick oven. "Have you been in here before?"

On one occasion, she had been sent by Adis to that bakery to fetch flour, but the last thing she wanted was to be recognized. She turned. "Can't say I have, sir."

"Ah, well, my mistake. Have a good day!"

"As do you," she replied and quickly stepped out the door.

Hurrying back, she darted her eyes across the faces of the crowds. If Audin wasn't alive, surely the police were now aware, and they'd likely be looking for her. Of course, they were. She knew she couldn't get away with this. Twice she sighted an officer and did her best to hide her face. Approaching the alleyway, she decided to turn down it and continue the rest of the way from behind the main road, away from prying eyes. But just as she gazed between the two buildings, there was the same bundled blanket. Only this time, whatever was beneath it had shifted.

She peered closer, squinting her eyes. Suddenly she gasped. Barely visible from beneath the covers was the unmistakable thick red hair of Mathios.

Eirún dropped the watch and held her breath in her throat as her mind instantly filled with thoughts of Søren. His smile. His young face. His body floating lifelessly down the Finnvard. As if possessed, she walked toward Mathios with clenched fists and snatched the tainted wool blanket from his body. Everything in her wanted to lash out at him, but instead, her jaw dropped, and her heart sank.

Leaning back until her body fell against the brick wall, she gazed at the scabbing boils spotted along Mathios's thinning frame. With a sallow face, his crusted eyes wandered, unfixed on the world. Grime filled his long fingernails, and his clothes were ragged and thick with mud and bodily fluids which saturated the ground around him. Eirún covered her nose against the strong scent of urine.

Unable to speak, she stared at his shivering body. After a long while, she hesitantly leaned forward and placed her hand over his forehead; the heat rose into her fingers like a steaming kettle. Against her own will, tears began to swell, and she cringed, ripping her headdress off. Tightening her fists against her head, she let out several loud sobs. Though a few people peered down the alleyway, no one stopped or offered help.

Soon Eirún calmed her quivering chest and wiped her nose. Mathios was asleep. Or dying. She wasn't sure. His face looked mournful with his lips curled down. Almost, she thought, she could hear a slight whimper. Her anger lessened to sorrow, and even sympathy, toward his pitiful state.

She took his blanket and wrapped it back around him. Still wiping her nose, she peered across the alley. She didn't know why, but she couldn't leave him. With a strain, she lifted him up from beneath his arms and dragged his motionless body out of the alley and into a back street. Slowly she pulled him around piles of garbage, which filled the air with a fermented smell of rotting food, pausing several times to catch her breath until she finally reached the townhome from behind. Dragging Mathios along the side of the house and toward the front, she pulled him up the steps and carefully laid him down by the front door. A passing group of women gave her a strange look but kept their distance.

"Dear me!" exclaimed a man dressed in a black servant's suit, walking toward the door from inside the house. "What has happened to this boy?"

Geirleif stepped around the man. "Curses, it's that boy!"

"What boy?" came the voice of Eilis. She wore a dark scarlet dress, with a wide-brimmed hat set above her short curly gray hair.

Geirleif turned to Eilis, pointing at Mathios. "You know, the one that murdered that boy at the orphanage!"

"Oh my!" Eilis set a hand against her chest. "How did he get here?"

By that time, a few bystanders had stopped at the bottom of the steps. Geirleif and Eilis both looked at Eirún for an explanation. She turned her back to the crowd.

"Kari?" Geirleif asked. "Why did you bring him here?"

She only looked down, trying to hide her flustered red eyes. What was she doing? Even she didn't really know.

"You know this boy, don't you?" he asked.

Eirún nodded. "Mr. Geirleif," she said, shaking. "I think he is dying. I found him in an alley, and—" She held back another onset of tears. "I couldn't just leave him."

The servant stepped forward, leaning over Mathios as he held his nose. "I guess that's what happens when you are legally too young for prison and yet banned from the community."

Geirleif shook his head, almost sympathetically. "Too shameful. This country's pitiful excuse for a justice system. Sending juveniles to the streets. Too shameful!"

"They didn't send him to the streets," replied the servant, still looking at Mathios. "They just didn't know what to do with him. No one would take him." He crossed his arms. "I imagine there aren't too many minors convicted for murder for them to worry about it." He wiped his balding head with a handkerchief. "What will happen next?" he mumbled as he walked back inside, clicking his tongue.

There was a silence as they all glared at Mathios. Eirún thought she should say something, but she didn't know what.

"I can see it troubles you greatly," Geirleif said to Eirún. "We've got room in the carriage. I'll have our chauffeur grab some blankets.

We'll bundle him up and take him with us. Perhaps we can get him some medical attention in Norfrost. That is if he lives long enough."

Thieves in the Palace of Ingvar

It didn't take long for Arnon to make his way to the outer palace wall, which ran west toward the main entrance. Murdock and Quinn had explained the basics—get to the high vantage point on the northern wall, keep an eye out for Adelyne as she slipped into the Eastern Storehouse in the hopes of finding any documentation of value, and if something should happen to threaten her safety, he was to cause a distraction. They didn't really explain to him how he was to cause a distraction, and Adelyne still wasn't too happy about him tagging along, but he didn't care. He wanted to prove himself, but he wished they would have been more thorough on his job. Was this how all their missions went?

After climbing the ivy, which crept into the ancient stacked stone, he perched himself beneath the shadow of the northern tower to his right. Satisfied with his concealment, he took a moment to catch his breath and rotated his left shoulder. The arrow wound was healing well by now.

From the top of the wall, he was able to get a clear view of the lawn and the area where Adelyne was to cross over. Of all the Daecish renovations in Everwind, the Palace of Ingvar proved to be the most exquisite. Both storehouses had been rebuilt of fine stonework, which curved inward toward the front walkway, creating two half circles that faced one another. Across the landscape stood tall marble statues of Daecish heroes and figures he didn't recognize. The house itself sat behind the storehouses, with high-reaching towers and balconies built into its elaborate framework. Many torches and lanterns lit the roadway and every door. But other than two windows lit on the bottom floor, all was dark within the house itself.

It had been several minutes, and there was no sign of Adelyne yet. Although he was in the shadow, Arnon didn't like being so high. He was too open. Directly below the other side of the wall grew a cluster of small trees and bushes. From that angle, he could see just as well and be better hidden. He crept over the edge and began the descent. Lowering himself between two fir trees, he squatted as soldiers continually patrolled the storehouse.

How Adelyne was going to pull this off without being seen was beyond him. Maybe he should just sneak into the Eastern Storehouse himself, grab some important documents, and race back to Murdock and Quinn before she even had the chance to climb the wall. Of course, he wouldn't actually do that. He couldn't read. But based on the way she treated him, she could definitely use a little humility.

Soon, his legs began to ache. Why hadn't he seen her cross over yet? Or maybe she already did, and he was too late. The last thing he wanted to do was blunder his first mission. It didn't take long for his instincts, or maybe it was his ego, to overrule the instructions he was given.

Thick green hedges ran south along the eastern wall. They would hide him easily enough, and he could probably get an even better vantage point. Keeping low, he crept between the hedges and wall, pausing only when a soldier passed by. The sensation of stalking a deer rushed back to him, and he couldn't help but hold a grin as he continued stealthily along. Peering over the hedge, the northern tower now seemed small and distant, and the back entrance to the storehouse, where Adelyne would enter, stood about twenty yards ahead.

Now sitting, he watched intently until a shadow slipped over the edge of the wall and dropped behind the hedge several yards in front of him. Arnon crept forward. Adelyne glanced over her shoulder and startled as he lifted a finger to his lips. Her expression shifted to a stern frown, and she crawled toward him.

"What are you doing here?" she said in a hoarse whisper. "You're supposed to be by the north tower!"

"I was," Arnon replied. "And I waited for what felt like half the night. What took you so long?"

Adelyne motioned toward the Eastern Storehouse. "Several guards and soldiers went into the back door. They still haven't come out."

Now Arnon was sure this wasn't planned out very well. "I thought Quinn said they didn't go in there this late at night."

"So did I." She gave a leering smile. "I don't think they were going inside to work."

"What do you mean?"

"I saw two soldiers carrying a barrel of ale. A third came afterward and looked around to make sure no one was following."

"You mean they were sneaking away to drink?"

Adelyne shrugged. "Seems like it, but either way, we for sure can't go in the storehouse." She peered south at the back end of the house where the Administrative Office stood high, capped with a dome roof of dark shingles. "But there are other options."

Arnon peeked over the hedge. "I thought Murdock said to stay away from there."

"You can leave empty-handed if you want to, but I don't plan on leaving here with nothing."

"Third shift," commanded a distant guard across the lawn, "turn in your logs."

Both Adelyne and Arnon hunkered down and waited in silence. After a moment, nothing else was heard.

"All right," he said, "but I'm not going to just sit here and wait on you."

Adelyne held in a breath and shook her head. She was obviously irritated. "This is going to be a lot more difficult with two people."

"No, it won't. My father and I use to hunt together all the time. You just have to know how to do it correctly."

Adelyne tilted her head. "Well, master of burglary, enlighten me."

Arnon grinned. "First, we'll cover more ground. It'll quicken the time we need to find anything. Second, it'll provide another set of eyes. For example, if I was picking a lock, you could stand behind and watch my back."

"Except I would be picking the lock," Adelyne replied. "You can stand watch."

"Either way." Arnon sighed. "If we both work together and stay quiet, we can do this."

Adelyne thought for a while. "Fine, but if you get caught, I'm leaving you behind." She began to turn around, but Arnon grabbed her shoulder.

"I have a lot of experience working in pairs," he said. "Let me take the lead."

"Why can't you just follow me?"

"I would just rather be in the front."

"We don't have time for this," she retorted. "Why do you have to be so stubborn?"

Arnon's jaw dropped. "I'm stubborn? You're the one that's—"

Adelyne ignored his comment and turned, crawling south without him. Arnon's face turned hot. But holding his temper, he followed her closely until they arrived at the southern city wall, its height reaching nearly twenty feet. There the path ended along with the hedge. Their only option was to head across an open lawn toward the back entrance to the administrative office.

Wrapping around its circular frame sat many dark windows. Although the main entrance was inside where the office connected to the eastern wing of the house, there was an outside door, which stood in shadow. It had an appearance of long neglect. Vines crept up its length, intertwining within the iron hinges. Surrounding the door were several tall fir trees and a single water fountain, no longer in use. From here on, the darkness would have to serve as their only concealment.

They both sat low, waiting and watching in silence as the guards patrolled.

"There," said Adelyne as she curled her dark hair behind her ear. "As soon as that guard passes, that gives us—"

"About a four-second window," Arnon replied.

She glared.

"Sorry, I didn't mean to interrupt."

"It's fine," she said. "You're right."

As they waited for the guard to make his way back around, Arnon shifted his weight on his tiring ankles. "What are we looking for, anyway?"

"I'll look for notes and documents," she replied. "You can look for anything else of value. Anything that may be useful."

Arnon wasn't sure what that meant, but he nodded.

"But only what we can fit in my satchel," she continued. "Anything more, and we'll be overburdened." She squinted through the hedge. "Our window's about to open up. You ready?"

"To the fir trees?"

"To the fir trees."

In the darkness, they lurked across the dew-strewn lawn, holding their breath and keeping their eyes fixed on the back of the guard heading north. For a brief moment, they passed through the glimmer of distant torch lights from the back of the eastern wing before darting behind the fir trees on either side of the door with their backs to the stone wall. Barely a dozen feet away, a guard passed by, taking no notice as they stood behind the trees, shrouded in shadow.

After he passed, Adelyne slipped the leather wallet from her satchel and removed two picks. Waiting for another guard to pass them by, she quickly stepped in front of the door, digging the picks into the iron lock. Although she was in the shadow, Arnon grew nervous that she was too exposed. He kept his eyes ahead on the lawn as best as he could between the branches, thick with short needles. Adelyne pulled the picks out of the lock and drew back behind the tree. Arnon raised his eyes, but she shook her head. "It's rusted," she said with barely a whisper leaving her lips. "I'll try again."

After waiting for another guard to pass, she stepped in front of the door again. Arnon held his breath, hearing the pins click as the lock finally opened. Adelyne rejoined him, storing the picks back in the wallet. At the next opportunity, she stepped in front of the door and effortlessly removed the lock, pushing the door open. Arnon followed, and they both slipped into the darkness. With great care, Adelyne closed the door behind them. They stood frozen, listening.

All was silent, and they both breathed a sigh of relief, relaxing their tense postures.

"Let's make this short," Adelyne whispered.

Creeping through a dark, narrow hallway, Arnon sniffed in the dank mold. Dust and cobwebs caught in his fingertips as he guided his hands along the walls of stacked brick. Ahead, the hall opened to what appeared to be a small storage room. The moon shone through high windows, casting a silver light over piles of books and crates, littered along the floor, which created a winding path to another door on the far end. Having never seen so many books in his life, Arnon took in the sight for a moment. Stepping lightly along the uneven floorboards, Adelyne took the lead. The room was so quiet that Arnon could occasionally hear the scurry of mice.

"That must be the office on the other side," whispered Adelyne, pointing to the door.

"Let's look around here first," Arnon replied.

Adelyne nodded, and they both took different directions. Lifting up a few books, Adelyne waved her hand to clear the air of the thick dust. Arnon crept to a stack of two chests and slowly lifted the lid of the top one, reaching his hand inside, but found nothing. He gently removed the chest and set it on the ground, then opened the lid to the bottom one.

A muffled voice came from the other side of the door leading to the office. Adelyne shot a wide-eyed glance at him, and Arnon felt his insides tighten into knots. They both hurried behind a large stack of crates in the back corner with their eyes fixed on the door. A soft glowing light swept beneath the door crack, revealing thick layers of dust and rat droppings inside the storage room. The light flickered brighter as it neared the door. The voices of two, maybe three, men could now be heard just on the other side. Arnon took a deep breath, holding it in.

After a moment, the light grew dim and vanished along with the voices.

"We should wait," said Arnon. "We don't want to take any chances." They both sat with their backs against a wooden crate. Arnon kept his eyes on the door. After several minutes, he situated to a more comfortable position. "Can I ask you something?" he asked in a quiet voice.

"Sure," Adelyne replied.

"At the meeting in Drake's cellar, did you think it strange that Wesley never mentioned the draft? I mean, they at least knew about it, but no one else did. They were all caught by surprise."

"I'm pretty sure it was agreed among the Dark Horses to not cause any unnecessary panic. They didn't have enough information to really go off of either. They didn't know when or where it was going to happen."

"I guess that makes sense."

"What about the boy?" Adelyne asked. "You think Geoffrey's in Astford yet?"

"He should be, but I still don't know what to think about it."

"I think the people are desperate for anything that might give hope."

Arnon thought about the low numbers of the Silent Hither. It still made him feel distraught, but there wasn't anything he could do about it. Morgan, Drake, and the rest seemed as if they knew what they were doing. Maybe things would change soon. Adelyne visibly shivered as a cold draft crept in from some unknown open crevice within the walls. The room grew darker. Several clouds must have passed over the moon.

"There's talk, you know," said Adelyne, breaking the silence, "being your father's son, that you may take Wesley's place one day."

Arnon remained quiet, not sure how to respond. He liked the idea of being a Dark Horse, but rumors that he would replace Wesley on the Court only bothered him. "Wesley isn't very respected, is he?"

"I don't know about that," she replied. "Folks give him a hard time, but Wesley's family."

"Well, my father wanted me to be a Dark Horse, but I don't think I'm ready for the Court."

She only nodded, and Arnon glanced at her as she looked ahead. She still had a bruise, though it had faded some. "How'd you get that?" he asked, pointing to her cheek.

She swallowed and lifted her hand, touching the bruise.

Though he wasn't sure why, he thought he may have upset her.

"Just an accident. I hit it walking out a door."

"Looks like it hurt."

"It did." Adelyne glanced back over the crates. "You ready to get back to work?"

"I guess so."

They both stood up and again proceeded across the room, carefully winding their way around stacks of dark crates and furniture. Arnon found his way back to the bottom chest. Slowly, he lifted the lid and reached his hand inside, feeling the cool touch of a small box. Lifting it out of the chest, he gave a soft blow, scattering dust across the room.

In the darkness, it was hard to make out its features. He walked to Adelyne.

"What is it?" she asked.

"I'm not sure," Arnon replied. "It's locked."

Adelyne took the box from Arnon and examined the hinges and lock. Then looking at the door, she risked giving the lockbox a shake. They couldn't hear anything. "I'm not sure if it's anything useful," she said, "but we should take it anyway."

"Are you sure it'll be worth it?"

Adelyne peered at the box. "This is no ordinary lock on here. Either this is a lock reserved for the king's personal belongings or otherwise something valuable. I can't figure why something like this is in some old storage room."

"Maybe somebody thought this was the best hiding place."

"Maybe," replied Adelyne as she slipped the lockbox into her satchel. "It sure is heavy, though."

"Do you want me to carry it for you?" Arnon smirked.

Adelyne faintly snorted through her nose. "Let's just go into the office."

"Just trying to help."

He caught her trying to hide a smile. "Do you want to lead?" she asked.

Did she really say that? Of course he would. He stepped in front of her toward the door. He took in a quivering breath and placed his ear next to the keyhole. Then he nodded at Adelyne and gripped the handle, giving it a slight turn. Locked. "We need to pick it," he whispered.

A curling smile bent Adelyne's lips. "Would you like to try?" She offered him the wallet.

"Sure, I mean, if you're okay with that."

"You know how to pick locks? You know the different kinds and how the pins work?"

"Of course, I do," he said more sternly, reaching for the wallet. Of course, he had never done it before, but he couldn't let her know that. Besides, how hard could it be? He opened it up, looking through the assortment of picks. Some were straight. Some had flat ends. Others bent in sharper points. He had no idea what he was looking at. He picked up the first one to the right and handed the wallet back to her. "My father taught me all sorts of things," he began to say as he poked the lockpick around the inside of the keyhole. It wasn't working. He turned around and noticed Adelyne holding her hands over her mouth as she held in her laughs. "What?" he asked. "What's so funny?"

Adelyne shook her face as she reached just above the doorknob and turned a small latch.

He dropped his head. "It was locked from this side?"

Adelyne finally let out a whimper but quickly covered her mouth again. "I'm sorry," she said. "Just, when you said it needed to be picked, I couldn't resist."

Why did he have to be such an idiot? "I think you should take the lead now."

Adelyne patted his shoulder. She turned the knob, pushing the door forward. At about halfway, the old iron hinges creaked, and Adelyne's hand froze. They stood motionless for a moment until they were sure it was safe to move on. Then they both slipped between the door and the frame, careful to not push it any further out.

Inside the administrative office, Arnon almost lost his breath. Around the circular room were many tall windows, outlined with thick curtains which stretched from the ceiling to the floor. The moon once again shimmered from the parting clouds, shedding the room in a colorless blue light, which revealed the checkered black and white floor, lined with many fine rugs. Several desks sat to his left, with three deep-set bookshelves rising between the windows. On the far end of the room stood a large, double doorway that was propped open. Beyond, the marble floor continued into what looked like a long hallway, but nothing else could be seen. Arnon was at once filled with both wonder and anger. Although it was beautiful, it felt foreign and invasive.

Adelyne pointed toward the open doorway. Although they appeared to be alone, the sheer openness made him feel exposed. His heart pounded through his chest as he pictured his head on a stump with a swift ax swinging down to meet it. Adelyne took another step forward, and he reluctantly followed.

With each step, Arnon's boot sank softly into the thick oval rug below him. Adelyne pointed at a desk. It was larger than the others and accompanied by a large, eloquent leather chair. The bookcase behind it lay riddled with unorganized piles of books and scrolls. The desk must have belonged to either the king himself or at least some high-level secretary.

Adelyne went on toward the bookcase while Arnon paused at the desk, glancing among the papers before him. He picked up a stack of sheets. He had no idea what they said, but it probably wasn't important. At least it made him feel better to think so. Setting the sheets down, he aimlessly observed the room again, quietly patting his hand against his thighs. Adelyne pulled out a few papers from a shelf, her fingers flipping nimbly through the leaves, never making a sound. Setting them down, she walked over to the desk where Arnon stood. She flipped through the pages he had tossed aside and then pulled out a single leaf.

After a moment, her eyes grew wide as they danced across the page. She looked up at Arnon, then slipped the page into her satchel. She motioned for him to head back toward the storage room. Arnon looked peculiarly at her but turned and led the way.

Upon entering the storage room, Adelyne gently shut the door, and they waited in silence until they were sure no one had heard them. At last, Adelyne walked toward the narrow hall, which led outside.

"What did you find?" Arnon whispered.

"A letter from Eirik to Ónarr."

"Who?"

Adelyne narrowed her eyes. "Really? Eirik? King of Daecland?"

"Oh, that Eirik."

"What do you mean, that Eirik? What other Eirik do you—" She took in a deep breath. "Never mind." She pointed to the letter. "This is a signed letter from Eirik telling Ónarr that they are temporarily ceasing funds to Sunder. On top of that, he's calling in certain debts."

"Does it say why?"

Adelyne re-scanned the letter. "It's a little vague, but it does mention something about mining expenses in Daecland. Apparently, there are certain issues going on, and funds need to be diverted elsewhere." She squinted as if something caught her attention. She held the letter up to the moonlight. "The letters. They're so strange, almost perfect."

"What?"

"This could be a really big deal."

Arnon raised his eyebrows with a blank stare.

"You don't know why this is a big deal, do you?"

"I do. I'm just thinking."

"About?"

Arnon wasn't sure what he was thinking.

Adelyne rolled her eyes. "If Daecland calls in their debts, this could bring financial problems. We're talking about an economic crisis." She pointed to the letter. "This could cause potential chaos in Everwind, possibly all of Sunder."

Arnon folded his arms. "You sure about this?"

"All I know is what the letter says."

Arnon scratched his head. "But all the merchants think it's only getting better. Business, renovations, it's all growing."

"Exactly." Her eyes went wide. "This might be just what we need to push the upper-classes against the Daecish. If they knew that this was going to happen, it could change everything."

He wasn't sure it was as big of a deal as she made it out to be, but even he couldn't help getting excited at the possibility. "We have to tell the Court."

"Wait," Adelyne replied. "We have to be careful. We can't let something like this get into the wrong hands."

He glanced over his shoulder at the door behind him. "I agree, but we can figure that out later. Let's get out of here first."

The Wine Cellar

Geoffrey stepped up to the log inn adorned with oiled parchment windows and lined with ivy, which had grown all the way up to the thatched roof. To the left of the front door grew a garden of herbs clustered with thick weeds, on which either side stood two mighty oaks; their leaves painted gold, blended with copper and a red so brilliant, they looked like burning scarlet. The bleating of goats and the clucking of chickens echoed from the croft behind the inn.

He took in a deep breath. Surely, he had time before the baby was born. But what if she gave birth before he got back? Or what if she didn't survive it? It wasn't uncommon. Even his own mother died giving birth to his younger sister. They were both buried in the old Everwind cemetery, now hidden beneath the Daecish Military Quarters. "Only two days," he told himself. "Then I'll head back."

Geoffrey opened the wooden door, which barely moved on the thick hinges.

"Geoffrey!" said Bartholomew. "Haven't seen you in almost two years."

"How are you, Bartholomew? Has it been that long?"

Inside, the aromatic scent of cinnamon and cloves floated in the air, which Bartholomew, the innkeeper, always hung in the front entry. The smell of rotting heather seeped from the thatched roof. He could even hear the chirping of baby birds nestled somewhere above him, with white droppings on the floor to prove it. It reminded him of better times. A single wooden desk sat on the far back wall, and on either side stood two wooden doors, leading to the only two rooms in the inn.

"Aye, it has." Bartholomew stepped around the desk to shake Geoffrey's hand. He was well dressed for a Sunderian. He must have had it in pretty good with the Daecish. "And I'm well, thanks for asking."

"The place hasn't changed a bit," Geoffrey said, situating the heavy satchel on his shoulder.

"I imagine we got a bit more luck than the folk over in Everwind."

"It's changing every day."

Bartholomew rubbed his jet-black beard. "Which is why I stay here in the hills."

Two years Bartholomew's senior, Geoffrey was jealous he didn't have any gray hairs like he did. "How's Langleigh?"

"Just fine," Bartholomew replied. "She and Cyril finally got married."

"That's wonderful to hear. Is she still singing?"

"Once or twice a week up at the tavern, but not like she used to." He took the satchel from Geoffrey's shoulder. "But you look tired." He unlocked the latch as he let the door swing open. "The trip must have worn you plum out. You rest right in here, and I'll get you some bread and wine."

Like the front entry, the room was dark, with a single lantern flickering on a barrel remade into a small table beside a straw bed. The walls were built of logs, lined with clay. It felt a little bit dirtier than last time he had stayed, but he didn't mind. "Thank you, but I'll eat later. I start training this evening."

"Already?"

"I've only got two days before I have to head back."

"Two days?" Bartholomew said with a grumble. "It must've taken at least a week to get here. The Daecish these days—they expect you to do a month's work in a day! I don't see how you do it."

Geoffrey chuckled and took out a set of clothes from his satchel. "It's not so bad. At least I don't ever have to worry about feeding the family."

"Well, you can't ask for more than that." Bartholomew turned to walk back through the door. "You just holler when you want something to eat."

"Thank you."

When Bartholomew left, Geoffrey grabbed a white rag. He walked over to the window and stuffed the corner of it into a crack between the logs on the outside of the building. In the letter to Wesley and the court, it was the only instruction given on what he was supposed to do. He could only hope Burlan knew what he was doing.

After his training course, Geoffrey walked back across the village. He soon realized that he had no indication of how he was supposed to meet this Burlan character or what he even looked like. Hopefully, he would meet him at the inn.

Upon entering his room, he turned up the lantern wick. A pewter plate of old bread and cheese sat on the side table by the window; beside it perched a neatly folded letter. He sat down and read:

Meet me in the Alcouv Tahvern ahfter sunset.
I'll be at the bar eatyng lark. Wayt amowment
ahfter I leave, then fallow me out the door.

Burlan Dunhaven

"Another tavern?" he asked himself. His job had him spending most evenings in taverns. It would have been nice to meet somewhere else. And what was he to make of this man-eating lark? That's not much to go on. Although it was signed by Burlan, he had no idea what he looked like. But he was impressed. Not many in Sunder could write, especially those raised in Astford.

Stuffing the letter in his pocket, he took a quick bite of the bread and cheese before heading back outside. Realizing that the sun had now set, Geoffrey picked up his pace as he trotted across the village. Up the road on the right, by the community well, hung the swinging sign of the Alcove Tavern.

A quick-paced melody accompanied by loud singing flowed through the glowing open windows, giving the tavern a lively feel. There was nothing like good old mountain music. Through the windows, a thick blanket of smoke hovered around crowded tables of men who chatted too loud, drank too much, and played too many games, while their wives were probably busy at home keeping the house clean and putting the children to bed.

Stepping inside, the aroma of a large boar, slowly roasting on a spit over the hot fire, made Geoffrey wish he hadn't eaten the old bread and cheese back at the inn. To his right, within a crudely built wooden enclosure, stood a brown and white heifer, chewing on dried straw; each time it bent down, the misshapen cowbell clanked from its neck. Beside the fire, near the front corner, sat three old men, two with a fiddle each, one with a fife, playing an upbeat melody while several in the crowd clapped on their knees. Two couples were even dancing in circles with interlocked arms. It had been years since he had seen anything like that in Everwind.

And there was Abbot, slouching at a table in the back corner. With a greasy patchy beard and thin strands of hair on his mostly bald head, he looked drunker and fatter than the last time Geoffrey saw him. And if it wasn't for his half-open eyes, he would have sworn the old forgotten Lord of Astford was asleep. Despite his shameful state, Abbot still managed to wear the moth-eaten cloak, with the fading yellow-threaded emblem of the House of Denholm barely visible on the left shoulder. Geoffrey shook his head. He gave Abbot another year before he'd drink himself to death.

At the bar, Geoffrey took one of only two empty seats, both of which were on the far-right end. Looking back to the crowds, he became increasingly aware of how many Daecish officers were in the tavern. Though he didn't count, there were enough to make him sweat. Trying to remain as inconspicuous as possible, he waved at the barman. "A porter, please."

"Right 'way, sire," the barman replied.

Most of the other men at the bar had red eyes, sunk deep behind dark bags. Many had scars and missing teeth. The harsh environment of living in the country was far different than the life Geoffrey was growing accustomed to. He hadn't realized Everwind changed that much since he was a child.

It was then that he locked his eyes on the men's plates at the bar. There wasn't a single man eating lark—there were three. Trying to make himself a little more obvious, he eyed the men, waiting for one to meet his gaze, but none of them looked up. Suddenly, a Daecish officer took the empty seat next to him, blocking his view.

Swallowing, a sudden cold sweat came upon Geoffrey. His head went light, and he feebly gripped the mug with both hands. His heart pounded as he envisioned the officer reading his mind. Maybe he ought to just get up and leave. Just go back to Everwind, abandon the whole thing. Probably not worth it anyway.

At that moment, one of the men who had been eating lark stood up from the bar and walked out the door. He never as so much as gave a glance at Geoffrey. Geoffrey cursed in his head, having no idea if that was Burlan or not.

"I haven't seen the likes of you before in this tavern."

Geoffrey looked up as the officer gave him a half-smile.

"I noticed your uniform," he continued. "An officer of the Capital Guard? What brings you here from Everwind?"

"Yes, sir," Geoffrey said, hoping it was the right response. "I came up for a couple of days to lead a training course for the Town Guard."

"That's right." The officer rubbed his blonde mustache. So many of them looked the same to Geoffrey. "We were told you had arrived this afternoon. Officer Arkwright, correct?"

"Yes, sir," Geoffrey replied again. He would have probably thought of something else to say, but the idea of the Daecish knowing his name brought an uneasy feeling in his stomach.

"Very good," was all the officer said.

The gentle strum of strings brought a quietness to the tavern as both Geoffrey and the officer looked behind them. The string band had left, and on a high stool sat Langleigh, Bartholomew's daughter. Her head was low as her long black hair curled over her shoulders. She wore a simple pastel yellow dress, and in her hands, she held an old dulcimer, carved from black walnut, fitted with four wired strings. It looked well made, like the fiddles he saw earlier. Other than in Astford, that was a rare sight. Few men still retained the knowledge from the south country on how to make instruments of such quality. Most in Everwind and in other places were made out of gourds and gut string. Geoffrey couldn't help but smile. He even once bought himself a cherrywood psaltery from the local luthier here in Astford. He never could figure out how to play it, though.

Langleigh soon slowed her strumming and plucked the strings softly with her fingertips, ringing out a high and haunting melody. In a rich Sunderian accent, she began to sing in a cool, clear voice like running water:

Long ago in forests deep
At the foot of mountains, steep
When Amyrran spread wild
The land yet undefiled
An alphyn stirred from its sleep

When fair Wrecan was still young

Full of mirth, yet bold and strong
He left behind Earlonian thrones
Desire seeped from his bones
To hear the old Sarig song

At the brink of Amyrran Wood
In awe and fear, yet he stood
Through tangled thorn, he pushed forth
Hoping in the hidden north
The Sarig dwelled, fair and good

Days went by, and sleepless nights
No sign of hope came in sight
Then at dusk, he paused in step
From below arose and crept
An alphyn, his foe, and blight

With sword in hand, he leaped out
Leaves shuddered above his shout
Iron met flesh, red blood spilled
Gashes deep, his foe he killed
Yet his life he held in doubt

With an open bleeding side
He crawled north until he died
Of the Sarig, he saw none
For they passed like a setting sun
Their tale hath faded in the night

As the strumming of her fingers ceased, a heavy silence filled the room. Long had the fate of the Sarig people haunted the Sunderians, and no one in the tavern, not even the Daecish, dared to speak, as if they refused to stir from their own deep thoughts.

At last, a large, full-bearded man lifted a mug. "Our fathers arrived in this here land, fleeing an unknown act of wickedness, and how did we start anew? By an act of malice, perhaps even greater than the one before. We cannot escape our past, but we can honor the dead."

At that, Geoffrey and many other men raised their mugs, except for the Daecish.

"To the Sarig of old," the man said.

"To the Sarig of old," they all returned.

"May the ghosts of that ancient race find peace."

One of the Daecish officers stood. "That'll be enough," he said, and he motioned for Langleigh to depart.

Soon conversations crept back up, and Geoffrey remembered his task. The two men were still eating lark, but before long, one stood up and left. Fearing he had already missed his opportunity when the first one departed, he was just about to stand up when the officer spoke, staring into his mug. "Training the Guard in investigations, was it?"

"I'm sorry?" Geoffrey asked, halfway out of his seat.

"Why you're here. They said you would be training the men in criminal investigations."

"Ah, yes, sir," he replied, glancing back to the front door. "That's correct."

"Good, we need those men trained top-notch." He took in a gulp of beer. "There are too many folks in this town that can't be trusted. Men getting themselves in the wrong kinds of affairs." He looked behind his shoulder at several men sitting at a table as he continued. "Men acting like proper citizens in the daytime, but in the night, they whisper rebellion. But we'll get rid of them." He took in another swig. "Or execute them."

Geoffrey's palms turned wet and cold. His mug was still mostly full, but he didn't think he could have another drop. He decided he had been there long enough. "Well, sir," he said. "It was a pleasure, but I must be off."

"You do that, Mr. Arkwright," the officer replied, drinking down another gulp.

Geoffrey set an arac note on the bar, not bothering to wait for any change. He was careful to remain casual as he walked toward the front door and out into the cold night.

Stuffing his hands into his coat pockets, he peered into the darkness. Across the street, the vague outline of a man stood in the shadow of a tall stone building. Looking around for any signs of a soldier, Geoffrey walked across the dirt road, keeping his eyes on the man.

"Arkwright?" the man whispered from the shadows.

Geoffrey snuck into the alley, now recognizing him as the first man that had left the bar. Even in the shadow, he could see his black hair, neatly parted to one side. "Burlan Dunhaven?" he asked.

Burlan nodded.

"How did you know my name?" Geoffrey asked.

"I saw the rag out the window, and Bartholomew let me slip the note into your room." As he spoke, he looked at Geoffrey's uniform with narrowed eyes.

"Don't let the uniform throw you off. I work for the Capital Guard."

Burlan's eyes darted back and forth between Geoffrey and the alleyway.

"You have my word," Geoffrey continued. "Wesley himself sent me."

At last, Burlan nodded and motioned for Geoffrey to follow him around the back of the building, where they walked along an overgrown path that wound its way north from the village. Feeling a cold tingle on his nose, Geoffrey gazed up to the dark clouds above. It couldn't have been snow. Far too early.

Although no moon could be seen, there was just enough light to make out the shadow of a small patch of oaks standing idly in the midst of the open landscape. As Geoffrey stepped beneath the leafy boughs, he swept his eyes back toward the village, half-expecting to see a whole raid of soldiers following close behind.

They came upon an old stone foundation, the building having long been gone. On the eastern side, behind the stump of a felled beech tree, sat the entrance to a wine cellar barricaded by two wooden doors.

Burlan glanced over his shoulder. "Everything all right?"

Geoffrey wanted to be polite, but he could hardly keep his wits. "Could we have not arranged an easier way to meet? Like at the inn?"

"Did something go wrong?"

Geoffrey rubbed his forehead. "Besides half the men at the bar eating lark, being in a room full of Daecish soldiers, one of which I had a wonderful conversation with about executing rebels, I would say it went rather well."

Burlan breathed in through his teeth as if he could feel Geoffrey's tension. "I see. Next time I'll make better arrangements." He opened the door, motioning for Geoffrey to go first.

"Next time, we'll request you come to us instead," Geoffrey replied with a smirk as he walked down the stone steps into the cellar below.

Bowing his head beneath the low wooden ceiling, Geoffrey was surprised at how welcoming the room felt. Upon a table sat a lantern. The flickering light danced across several empty barrels in the left corner. The stone floor was strewn with dried straw, with a rug laid out below the table. It wasn't even damp. On the far wall stood an empty wooden case, looking as if it once housed wine and ale.

Beside the case sat a man in a chair, his hands clasped together and head back, his chest rising and falling in what would have looked like an uncomfortable slumber, but his open mouth and drool on his chin showed otherwise. In the back-right corner laid the thin figure of a boy, wrapped in several thick blankets.

Burlan walked toward the man in the chair. "Henley," he said, placing a hand on his shoulder. "He's here."

Henley awoke with a slight startle, immediately wiping his chin.

"You all right?" Burlan asked with a laugh.

"Of course," Henley replied. "Just ah—" He paused to yawn, then motioned toward the boy. "The lad don't ever get tired of stories. I've told him just about all I know."

Burlan slid two empty barrels around the table. "Has he eaten?"

"Quite a lot," replied Henley, sliding his own chair over.

As they all sat, Burlan pulled out a clay pipe, which he filled with tobacco. Lifting the glass from the lantern, he lit a piece of straw, which he brought down into the pipe bowl. Geoffrey smiled at Burlan's pipe and the glass lantern. It was interesting how Sunderians resisted so much of the Daecish ways and yet seemed completely oblivious to the influence they had on their everyday life.

"I know it's late," Burlan said, taking a slow draw from the pipe, "let's get started."

Geoffrey glanced over at the boy but could not make out his features hidden beneath the covers. He clasped his hands and looked at Burlan and Henley. "So, what have you got for me?"

"We've attempted to question the boy further since we sent the letter," Burlan replied. "But we've spent most of our time fostering him back to health."

Geoffrey nodded in understanding.

"However," spoke up Henley. "His story never changes. He's convinced that he was thrown in a river in Daecland and somehow came by sea. He also mentioned seeing some shadow mist, and afterward, he rode some sort of beast until he woke up in a valley just north of the village."

"And what do you think?" Geoffrey asked.

Henley glanced over at Burlan.

"Honestly," Burlan said, "I reckon he's from Daecland. He looks it. Sounds it. He recounts details, names, places." He sighed through his sharp, pointed nose. "And his description of this animal he rode . . . it's eerie." He stared hard at Geoffrey. "There's no lying in his face. Perchance," he lowered his voice, "perchance he's telling the truth?"

"Or maybe the boy ain't right in the head," added Henley as he pointed a finger to his thick tuft of hair. "It's possible he just fell off a ship and made up some of this stuff, but it's awfully strange."

Geoffrey sat back for a moment and adjusted his belt buckle. "What about this lens? Can I have a look?"

Burlan motioned to Henley, who walked over to the boy and carefully took a small object from his loose fingers. He handed it to Geoffrey.

Geoffrey turned the cold, heavy brass component over in his hand. "Careful," Burlan said.

"Fine workmanship," Geoffrey observed. "Certainly not from around here. What did the boy say its purpose was?"

"It captures things," replied Burlan.

"Well, not quite," butted in Henley. "Søren said it captures an image. When we questioned him further, he mentioned a painting of people or something of the sort, that was made from this here lens. But other than that, your guess is as good as ours."

Burlan leaned forward, pointing to the glass. "Here," he said. "Look through this." He flipped it over, and Geoffrey brought it to his eye. "Hold it out at arm's reach and look through it. Do you see? Everything's wrong-way up."

Burlan was so close, he breathed on Geoffrey's nose. Geoffrey leaned back, handing the lens back to him. "I've heard about this effect before in one of the Earlonian Chronicles. In it, there's a story about a man who ventured into a cave. Coming to a dark chamber, he saw a small hole that was broken in the rock with light beaming through it.

On the far side of the wall, there reflected the world outside the cave—trees, grass, and sky, but everything was upside-down."

Burlan and Henley only stared at Geoffrey.

"Light," Geoffrey continued, "travels in a straight line. So, if the light from the sky is coming down through a hole at an angle, it'll appear on the bottom of the wall."

Henley shook his head, and Burlan raised an eyebrow. "I can't figure why that would make it wrong-way up," Burlan said.

Geoffrey sighed. "Well, in any case, you're right. This is certainly Daecish. I'd imagine, given the grooves cut into the back, that this is part of a larger contraption."

"That's what Søren said," Henley replied. "He said it was part of a camera or something like that."

Burlan shook his head. "You ever wonder what it's like? Daecland?"

Geoffrey slowly nodded. "Often." He kept his mind from wandering too far and interlocked his fingers. The night was getting late. "Aside from this lens, what about this boy?"

Burlan took the pipe from his mouth. "He's clearly Daecish, and he got here somehow. Maybe he found a path?" He lowered his voice again and peered at the boy, still sleeping in the corner. "Or maybe he's what the old chronicles spoke of. I know he's a boy and all, but what if he's Sunder's Bane?"

Geoffrey was beginning to see why Wesley thought some in Astford might be overly superstitious. "This draft has taken a toll on those of us in Everwind. The Silent Hither's still there, but it's fragile. What we need right now is something solid. Something useful. I'm not sure I would go around telling people that some boy is Sunder's Bane." He snickered under his breath. "It's a bold claim. And even if he did come through the Fringe, what then? Are we just going to walk into Daecland?"

"That's what I was saying," Henley mumbled.

Burlan's jaw clenched. He was clearly irritated by his comment. "What about the animal he rode?"

"A boy riding some animal hardly means he's Sunder's Bane," Geoffrey replied. "Besides, the ballad records a man riding an alphyn."

"But there's something different about this lad," Burlan argued. "He's not—" He hesitated. "He's not like everyone else. And the description he gave of this animal . . ." He looked at Henley and rubbed the black stubble on the front of his neck. "I think it best we just show Geoffrey ourselves. Why don't you wake him?"

"All right," Henley said. "But before you talk to him, I should add that we ain't mentioned why the Daecish are here. He knows there are Daecish soldiers around, but he don't know why. We just thought it would be best not to share something like that yet. It might scare him."

"I understand," Geoffrey replied.

Taking the lens, Henley stood up, headed over to the dark corner, and after gently setting the lens back in the boy's palm, he placed his hand on his shoulder. "Søren," he said.

Burlan leaned toward Geoffrey. "Perhaps if you talk with the boy, you might think differently."

Geoffrey peered into the shadow as the boy slowly sat up, rubbing his eyes and yawning. Henley helped him get to his feet, and they walked toward the table.

"Who's here?" the boy whispered in Henley's ear as he slipped the lens around his neck.

Stepping into the lantern light, Geoffrey caught his breath as the boy looked up at him. At first, his eyes seemed solid black, but as he continued to stare, the hazel color barely peeked through. But even so, there was something that troubled Geoffrey. It was like looking into the eyes of someone who had seen a thousand years of life, yet there was no life left in him—almost as if his soul was lost and his spirit gone.

"Søren, would you like some water?" Burlan asked.

Søren shook his head and looked up at Henley. "Is he here to take me away?"

Henley smiled. "You don't worry about a thing. Whatever happens, we won't let any harm come to you."

Holding his hands together in his lap, Søren glanced at Geoffrey, but his eyes occasionally danced away as he fidgeted in his seat.

Geoffrey cleared his throat. "Your name is Søren?" he asked.

Søren nodded.

"I'm Geoffrey."

Søren only looked down, occasionally glancing up.

"Søren, if you don't mind," Geoffrey continued, "I would like to hear your story. How you got here. Could you tell me that?"

Søren looked up at Henley and then Burlan.

"Go ahead," said Burlan. "He's here to help."

There was a certain look of worry in Søren's expression as if he was battling with himself. But at last, he told Geoffrey about the orphanage, the drowning, and even about the hovering shadow and the animal in the valley. But mostly, he talked about Eirún, who was apparently his mother.

When Søren had finished, Geoffrey leaned back in thought. "What did this animal look like? The one you saw sleeping in the valley."

"It was hard to t—tell. It was really big. It had big teeth and lots of gray hair, like a monster."

"How big?"

Søren looked around the cellar. "As big as this room, maybe?"

Geoffrey narrowed his eyes. "Did it have a long snout, sort of like a wolf's?"

Søren's eyes went wide. "Yes! Really long, like this." He stretched out his arms as wide as he could.

Trying to take in a slow breath, Geoffrey's jaw went weak. "And you said," he had to force the words out, "this was the animal which you rode on from the beach?"

Søren nodded.

Geoffrey's back broke out in a sweat, and he eyed Burlan and Henley. This had to be a joke. "Did you tell the boy to say that?"

Burlan raised his hands defensively. "Of course not. It's just as he told us."

"Sounds just like the description in the Acwellen Chronicles," responded Henley, "don't it?"

"And Lord Aberthorn's account," Geoffrey added in barely a mumble. He peered into Søren's dark, hollow eyes.

"What is it?" Søren asked.

"Nothing. It's um," Geoffrey stumbled over his words. "It's possible you rode an alphyn."

"That's what Mr. Burlan t—told me." Søren slunk back "Is it dangerous?"

"No, no. It's just a big animal." He said the words, but his head went light, and he struggled to keep his mind focused. Burlan stood up and waved at Geoffrey to follow him up the stairs.

Outside, Geoffrey shivered once again in the chill of the night air. Beyond the trees and black hills, a harvest moon now sat on the edge of the horizon, like a large glowing eye.

"What you think?" Burlan asked.

Geoffrey couldn't get Søren's eyes out of his head. And those stories. A hovering shadow. The alphyn. It was too much. "I haven't the slightest idea what to think." He crossed his arms and kicked at the grass with his boot. The moon was rising fast and was as red as blood. It seemed to peer at him like a warning presage—an indication that something terrible would soon come to pass. "But there's something not natural about the whole thing." He forced his eyes away from the horizon. "Do you really think he could be Sunder's Bane?"

"I got no idea, but it creeps me out."

There was a long silence, and they both gazed at the horizon again as dark clouds swiftly passed over the moon. Geoffrey tapped his thigh. Just because the boy said he rode something that looked like an alphyn didn't mean he did. But his eyes, the cave-ins, and the smells showing up in Everwind—it all just seemed to go together. But it was probably in his head. The mind was notorious for making connections where there were none.

"Whatever the case is," Burlan said, breaking the silence. "The boy can't stay here. We're not the only ones who know about him. There are others, some of whom I dearly wish did not."

"Who?"

Burlan looked as if he didn't want to answer. "A cousin of mine." He hesitated. "And Abbot."

Geoffrey smacked his hand against his forehead. "You don't mean Abbot Ridley?"

Burlan groaned and barely nodded.

How could they have let a knucklehead like that know? Geoffrey just knew he was going to get caught and hanged. He closed his eyes and counted to five in his mind. "What are they saying?"

"Nothing," Burlan replied. "As far as I know."

"Nothing?"

"Abbot thinks we took him and left him in the wilderness."

"What about your cousin?"

"You don't have to worry about him. He's not all there in the head."

That didn't make Geoffrey feel any better. "So, what's your plan?"

Burlan breathed into his hands, then rubbed them together. "I ain't sure; I thought you might help me with that."

Geoffrey thought hard about the situation unfolding before him. Maybe he should just leave, forget he ever came here. But the more he thought about it, the heavier his heart grew. Whether or not Søren was Sunder's Bane or even Daecish, he was helpless and alone. If Sarah were here, she would have taken him home and probably even adopted

203

him. She was a better person than he was. He grunted at himself. "Would you like me to take him?"

Burlan let out a long breath and slacked his shoulders. "I was hoping you'd say that. But what would you do if you did?"

"I have no idea. But the first plan would be to get him away from anyone who knows anything about him. Whether he will be a help to us or not, I don't know. Maybe we might help him find his way back home to his mother if it's true. What was her name?"

"Eirún," Burlan replied.

Geoffrey scratched his chin. It was curious that Søren said he grew up in an orphanage. Did his mother not want to raise him for some reason? He peered back at the open cellar door, just able to make out the murky voices of Henley and Søren. "So how do we get him out of here? We can't have a blonde-haired boy with eyes like that walking around town."

"I've already thought of that. When you're ready to leave, I'll make sure you won't part without a couple of barrels of ale to take back. We'll keep one empty."

Geoffrey faked a smile, but inside he hoped he wasn't making a mistake.

The Old Greystrom Home

Taking in a slow breath, Arnon looked upon his old home. It was strange to realize that it was his by inheritance since his father had died. He was the oldest child and the only son. But with Daecish occupation, he didn't want to spend more time in that house than he had to. A couple of hours would be long enough.

At least from the backside, the house seemed to have been maintained over the years. The thatched roof stood strong, and the old shutters still covered the open-air windows. Even the wood trim held fast. A musty scent of mold lingered in the air, and the gray sky above had momentarily held back the chilling rain. Just as Drake had said, not a single Daecish soldier was in sight. Along the Western side of the house ran an alleyway where rotting wood and debris piled up against the outer wall; mostly the remains of chairs and a table, but a few of his father's animal traps were piled on the bottom. It would have been nice to have had those in the Western Plains.

Stepping up to the back door, he turned, catching something in the corner of his eye. Across the street, by a butcher's shop, Adelyne stood, looking in his direction. She startled as he noticed her and hurried toward him. As she crossed the street, a young man paused in his step, eyeing her as she passed. She glanced at him but continued on.

"How do you deal with that?" Arnon asked.

"Deal with what?"

Arnon motioned to the man. "Everywhere you go, men always look at you."

Adelyne avoided eye contact. "You get used to it."

"Must be annoying," Arnon said, now studying the house again. He glanced back at her with a grin. "So, why were you staring at me from across the street?"

Adelyne lifted an eyebrow. "You think I'd stare at you?"

"Maybe." He crossed his arms and leaned against the wall.

"If you want to know, I was a little early, and I noticed you looking at the house, and I don't know, I just stopped."

"And then stared at me?"

"No."

"No?" He still smiled.

"No," she said more sternly.

Arnon laughed. "Just making sure."

She squinted her eyes with a slight leer. "Are Drake and the others here yet?"

"They'll be here soon."

"I wonder what they'll think about the letter."

Arnon stretched a kink out of his neck. "We'll find out, I guess. What about the lockbox? Did you hide it?"

"Exactly where you said to. But I can't open it 'til I get my tools back from Murdock."

A splash of water made them both turn. A mother led her four young children along the road; her two youngest ran ahead to jump in a puddle. Arnon drew his attention back to the house.

"So, this is your home?" Adelyne asked.

"Used to be." He pushed open the door with a loud creak as the musty smell of an old abandoned house filled his nostrils. "We might as well wait inside," he said, stepping in. Adelyne followed behind.

It took a moment for his eyes to adjust as he stood on the straw-laden floor, still damp from the leaking thatched roof. Since it had just quit raining, it would likely still drip for another few hours. The single-room home stood entirely empty, with only a small pile of firewood in the corner. The upper ceiling of straw and twigs, braced by thick beams, had been stained black from a hearth that was no longer there. A ghostly smell of old wood and smoke still hung in the air, mingling with the mold.

He could still see Fleta rushing around to help his mother load the cart outside. His father had just grabbed Hazel from the loft. Barely a year old at the time, she woke up from her sleep with a loud cry. It all went so fast. Before he knew it, they were outside the city, heading to the Western Plains.

Arnon took a few steps, imagining where the table and chairs would have been. On the far wall, the front door had been barred shut from the inside. On the left, a ladder led to the loft. Built of hand-hewn wood with the bark still running along its length, it was the first time he helped his father make anything. He even remembered his father helping him make the Burrow Hunt game for Fleta and him to play. She never liked it the way Hazel did, though.

Whenever friends came over for dancing and food, Arnon would always find some excuse to hide up in that loft; he hated dancing because he knew he wasn't any good at it. When he was still young enough, Drake would sometimes pull him back down and make him do a jig with him or help clap to keep beat. Despite the embarrassment, Arnon deeply missed those days. There was so much laughter and joy. And tales, lots of tales were told during those long nights. But now, all of that seemed so long ago it was like a hazy dream, almost forgotten.

With a sigh, Arnon sat on the floor with his back against the wall. Adelyne stood for a while but didn't say anything. Then she walked over and sat beside him.

"Of all the memories," he said after a long silence, "the stories my father used to tell us around the dinner table have stuck with me the most."

"You must miss him very much," she replied. "We all do."

"You knew my father?"

"I was too young to know him, but when my family was hurting for money, he gave my father work and helped keep us out of the slums." She picked at the frayed leather at the bottom of her tunic. "It wasn't long after my mother died that we were forced back into the slums, though." There was a look on her face, almost painful. "Please don't share that with anyone. I just wanted you to know that your father was loved."

"You shouldn't feel embarrassed," Arnon replied. "My family has relied on others as well. Especially on Drake."

Adelyne parted a strand of hair that fell over her eye. "For as long as I can remember, Drake's been there for me."

"I'm surprised we never met before," Arnon said. "We've been around the same people for so long."

"I actually remember you," Adelyne replied. "But I was probably ten or eleven, last I saw you."

"Really?" Arnon tried to recall ever meeting her, but most of his memories of Everwind were a blur.

There was another awkward silence.

"Do you think we'll ever actually get the Daecish out of Sunder?" she asked at last.

Arnon chuckled quietly. "Already losing your faith in the letter?"

"Not at all!" she continued. "I just—I mean, Geoffrey said even if we take Everwind one day, they'll just send more. Their numbers, their technology, it all just seems too much. And . . ." She hesitated. "What if we do win somehow, and it doesn't get any better?"

Arnon wasn't sure he heard her right. "Doesn't get any better?"

"You've heard the way some of the Dark Horses talk, haven't you? Don't they sometimes seem a little cruel? What if Sunder only gets worse after the Daecish leave?"

Cruel? What on earth did she mean by that? All Arnon could do was shrug. "I don't know what you're talking about. Do you mean like Drake?"

"Of course not," Adelyne replied. She shook her head. "Never mind, they're just silly rumors I've heard. And men get rowdy when they're drunk. Probably means nothing."

Arnon frowned.

"I guess I just wonder if we have what it takes. Even if this letter got out and thousands joined us, do you still think we could take on the Daecish and drive them out?"

It seemed like she was changing the subject, but Arnon thought about her last question and didn't know what to make of it. Resting his chin on his arms, he puffed out a heavy breath. That very thought had left him with more doubt than he cared to admit.

"Honestly," he said. "This letter might be our only hope, but even then, we might not have what it takes."

Adelyne sank back. "Then don't you feel like you're wasting your time?"

Picking up a thin splinter of wood off the ground, Arnon snapped it between his fingers and tossed it into the pile of wood in the corner beside him. What could he say? Sometimes he did feel like it was a waste of time. Maybe they should just quit and go about their lives as best as they could. He grunted. Just the fact that he thought that turned his stomach. Suddenly, a memory of his father came to him so vividly, it was as if he could hear his voice in his head. "It's not about doing something simply because we know we'll succeed," he told Adelyne. "It's about standing for what's right, what's good, even if we lose."

As he spoke, calmness washed over Adelyne's face.

"If there was anything my father gave me," he continued, "it was a conscience. Some will choose whichever side benefits them the most, ignoring what's right or wrong. But my conscience would torment me if I did that." He stood up and walked over to an open window, looking out into the alleyway at the same pile of rubble he had seen earlier.

"But how do you know we're on the good side?" Adelyne asked, joining him. "How do you know what is truly right?"

"Sometimes I don't," he said. "But fighting for those who can't help themselves, who are starving in the streets or being sent to the mines, that seems right to me." Arnon mustered a smile. "You're a lot different from what I thought."

Adelyne raised her eyebrows. "What do you mean?"

"You know, at the meeting at Drake's place. You seemed pretty upset when I volunteered for the viewpoint."

"Well," she said with a smirk, "I wasn't angry with you for volunteering. I just wasn't so sure you were up for the task. Besides, that was a very important meeting. And if I recall, you wouldn't stop glancing over at me."

Arnon blushed. Adelyne laughed, covering her mouth. Peering at the pile of wood outside, he narrowed his eyes. Was that what he thought it was? He walked out the front door and around into the alleyway.

"I didn't mean to embarrass you!" Adelyne called out, still chuckling. "Are you really leaving?"

Standing in front of the pile, Arnon bent down and picked up a small yellow owl figurine, lying in stark contrast against the dark charred wood. For a fleeting second, he felt as if he was back in time, as if his family were just inside, on the other side of that wall. His chest felt heavy as the reality dawned on him that his family would never be whole again.

Adelyne walked over and stood beside him. "Arnon?" she asked. "Is everything—"

"What are y'all doin'?" hollered Drake and Morgan together from just outside the alleyway. Both Adelyne and Arnon jumped as the men let out deep-bellied laughs. "Youngsters these days," Drake said. "Come on, let's go!" He and Morgan marched to the back of the house.

Arnon stuffed the owl in his pocket as they both followed after them. The gray sky had once again thickened as a steady cold rain began to fall. "Why don't the Daecish patrol around here?" he asked.

"Oh, they do," Drake replied, rubbing a hand across his bald head. "Just mostly out front along Fellhouse Street. Usually, at this time of day, though, they're not searching for secret meetings, if you catch me."

Arnon followed them into the house, but their location didn't sound very safe to him.

Drake set his thick hands on his hips and looked around the room. "I ain't been here in years." He sighed and turned to face Arnon. "I appreciate you willing to meet here. I know it must be hard, being your family home and all, but meeting in the tavern during the day ain't wise."

"It's fine," Arnon replied. "But where's Wesley?"

Drake looked at Morgan, who only shook his head as he pulled out a short pipe from his pocket and began to pack the black tobacco he had pulled from a small leather pouch. "We haven't seen him since before you gave us the letter."

Adelyne eyed his pipe.

Morgan winked. "Stole it from a pale-face who left it on a table at Drake's tavern." He looked around, and Arnon figured he just now realized there was nothing to light it with. With a sigh, he shoved the pipe back in his pocket.

Drake rubbed his chin. "Perhaps after this, we ought'a go to Wesley's home, see what he's been up to. But anyway," he pulled out the letter from his pocket, "we can't wait for him forever. Morgan and I've got some good news."

Adelyne and Arnon glanced at one another.

"After you showed us the letter, Morgan here worked some magic, and I think we can use it to our advantage."

Morgan raised his chin with a sense of pride. "You ever heard of a printing press?"

Adelyne wrinkled her nose in thought.

"A what?" asked Arnon.

"That's what I thought." He reached out, and Drake handed him the letter. "The Daecish are a bit more advanced than you probably think."

"That's not hard to imagine," Arnon replied.

Morgan held the letter out for them to read. "Did you notice anything different about the writing?"

"I did," replied Adelyne. "All the letters and spacing were perfect."

"Yea, I think I noticed that too," Arnon added.

Adelyne rolled her eyes.

"I did," he replied shortly.

"Okay."

"Anyway," Drake interrupted. "This wasn't written by hand. See, they invented this contraption thing—"

"It's called a typographer," said Morgan.

"Yes, anyway, but this letter," Drake pointed at it, "was made with it. And it's actually a copy. You can tell by the little lines. See here? This was copied from a printing press."

"How do you know all that?" Adelyne asked. "You can't even read."

"How do I? Now, listen here," Drake instructed with a waving finger. "I may not know how to read, but I've got plenty of knowledge in this here head of mine."

"Drake's got nothing up there," butted in Morgan. "He learned it from me."

Drake waved a hand to dismiss him.

"If you remember," Morgan continued, "I was a secretary for King Albern when the Daecish first came. I only managed to last a few months, but after we moved from the castle to City Hall, I got to use one of them typographers. And I saw a printing press."

"What does it do again?" Adelyne asked.

"Like Drake said, it makes copies of documents. You just arrange these blocks of letters together on a big iron plate. Press it down on parchment, and there you have it—a copy. You can make as many as you want. It's a bit more complicated than that, but you get the point."

Arnon scratched his head, but Adelyne's eyes lit up. "That's incredible," she said. "What else did you see when you worked there?"

"A great question for another time," Drake interrupted. "But let's keep to the point."

"How's this going to help us?" Arnon asked.

"Well," said Morgan clearing his throat. "we had an idea that might help persuade the merchants and other upper-class folks to join our cause. We could use one of them typographers to make more copies of the letter, enough for 'em all to see. But as you can probably guess, we can't very well walk up to any ol' store owner and show him. We'd risk exposing the Silent Hither. So," he eyed Adelyne, "we get Adelyne to type up a new letter and—"

"Why Adelyne?" Arnon interrupted.

"Because my eyes aren't as good as they used to be," he snapped at Arnon. "And *she* can read. Now don't interrupt. Anyway, we type up a letter that looks just like this one, but instead of being addressed from Eirik to Ónarr, it'll be addressed to the Merchants Guild."

"And we'll tweak it a bit," added Drake. "You know, add some horrible details that'll really upset 'em."

"Yes," Morgan continued with a nod. "We'll tell them that all loans are called in, all funding's ceased, raised taxes, whatever. The key is, we can make our letter look just as official as this one. And once we write it up, we'll use a printing press to make two or so dozen copies."

Arnon felt like everyone else in the room was smarter than him. Even Drake. He raised a hand.

Morgan sighed. "What is it?"

"Sorry, but where are we going to get this printing press and type thingy?"

Morgan raised his chin. "I just happen to know where we can find both. When Drake, Wesley, and myself met Geoffrey for the first time,

I asked him if they still use them in City Hall. He said they did and that in the basement below there are several just sitting there."

"So, we have to break into the basement of City Hall and steal them?"

"Steal them? No, no, you can't just steal a printing press. It's far too big. We'll just use them there."

"But won't we get caught?"

Morgan crossed his arms. "Get caught? I imagine if you can sneak around the Administrative Office, we can survive in an old basement for a few hours."

"If you say so," Arnon said.

Morgan scowled. "Now, where was I? Oh yes. So, we make up two or so dozen copies, put them by the front doors of the shops in the middle of the night, so no one will know they're from us, then the next morning they'll read them and," he caught his breath, "hopefully they'll riot, join our cause, and get the Daecish out of here."

There was a short pause as Arnon tried to process it all. The smell of rotting straw in the ceiling kept drawing back old memories of his father re-stuffing their bedding. "This sounds crazy," he said at last.

"Yea, but it's a good idea," added Adelyne, leaning against the ladder to the loft. "This could actually work."

"But what if it doesn't? What if they know it's fake?"

"We ain't making up this letter outta thin air," Drake responded. "It's based on a real letter you found. All we got to do is add a little fuel to the fire and hope for the worst."

"And of course," added Morgan, "it may not work out. It's possible they'll discover it's a fraud, and they'll assume the Silent Hither is the most likely culprit."

"At which point they'll increase their investigation efforts, we get caught, and most likely executed," Drake finished.

"Wow," said Arnon. "That's definitely a risk."

"It's worth a try, though," said Adelyne.

"It certainly is," replied Drake.

Arnon rubbed his face. It didn't sound like a good idea, but then again, he didn't think he understood it all. He wished he was out in a field hunting somewhere. "Well," he slapped his hands on his sides, "when do we go to City Hall?"

* * *

Wesley stood at the entrance of a large office. The ceiling, braced by thick, decorative molding, must have towered at least twenty feet from the floor. From its center, a grand chandelier hung low. The walls were a dark blue, with white wainscoting running along its base around the room. The thick rug sprawled across the marble floor as his boots sunk in with each step. Having never seen such grandeur, he almost forgot why he was there. He focused his attention back in front of him and overheard a secretary talk with an officer of the Capital Guard—an old chubby fellow with Daecish spectacles on his nose.

Glancing back at him from across the room, with a large smile on his face, the officer waved the secretary away and motioned for Wesley to walk over and have a seat. "I apologize about the wait. We were caught up talking about the symphony coming up."

"Symphony?"

The officer puffed out his chest. "I've been invited to a symphony. Something I hear is popular in Daecland. A musical entertainment of sorts, with many instruments, I'm told. They say the instruments of the Daecish produce the most beautiful sounds that ever have fallen on the ears of man."

Wesley wasn't interested.

"Anyway," the officer continued, clearing his throat and pushing his spectacles back up his round nose. "What did you say your name was again?"

"Wesley Gladestone," he replied, sitting across from the desk. He couldn't help but occasionally eye the two Daecish soldiers who stood on either end of the room.

"Ah, Mr. Gladestone. I'm officer Ogden, but you can just call me Barnaby. Now, you said you had some information for us on the Silent Hither. May I ask how you came about this information?"

Wesley eyed the Daecish again with a shaking breath, praying he knew what he was doing. He had thought long and hard about this for a couple of years now. Considering the consequences. Pondering the executions that would likely take place. Those thoughts had always held him back. But now, there was no changing his mind. He was angry. Tired of being mistreated. Tired of being ridiculed. His whole life was a joke. Besides, in his heart, he knew the Silent Hither would never succeed against the Daecish. It had always been a fool's hope. It was just a matter of time before someone else ratted the Dark Horses out. If he didn't do it, someone else would. Then he'd be executed. He was just looking out for himself. It's what any sensible person would do. "I'm a Dark Horse." His mouth barely moved, and he wasn't even sure if he actually said the words.

Barnaby froze. "A Dark Horse, you say?" He glanced over his shoulder as one of the soldiers hurried out of the room. The other walked over and stood behind Wesley. "Hold that thought for just a moment," Barnaby said with a raised finger. Wesley swallowed as the first soldier walked back into the room, followed by three Daecish officers. Barnaby stood up. "Excuse me, Sir." He motioned for one of the officers to take his seat and then stood off to the side.

The officer sat down. He was taller than other Daecish men Wesley had seen, but as with other Daecish officers, his uniform was blue and in perfect condition. He also had typical short hair, a clean face, save a long blonde mustache waxed out to the sides. It was as if they all got together one day and decided to try and look as much alike as possible.

"You told Officer Ogden that you were a Dark Horse. Am I correct?" the officer asked.

"Y—Yes, sire."

"I am Commander Gunnar Veurðr. If what you say is true, at this moment, you are under arrest." He unrolled a scroll. "By command of the king, as written in Article Forty-Three, all citizens of Sunder, participating, exchanging, or assisting in the Silent Hither are hereby declared traitors of Sunder and Daecland, and have forfeited their rights as citizens, unto payment of death for high treason." He rolled up the scroll. "How do you respond?"

Wesley stiffened in his chair as cold sweat dripped down his back. "I'm here to offer my services, sire." He already couldn't remember the officer's name. I—" His chest shook so uncontrollably that he couldn't continue.

"I suggest you speak."

Keep it together. Wesley drew in a long breath, scratching at his arm again. It was as if an underlying itch was always there, and he could never get at it. Keep it together. "You may put me to death, sire," he said. "But if you do, you might regret it. I want to help you stop the Silent Hither."

The commander looked up at the other officers with a cocky sneer. "Why would we need the services of a peasant?"

"I'm not only a Dark Horse, but I'm a part of the leading court. I help make all the major decisions, I facilitate all our meetings, and I'm in close contact with Dark Horse folk in other cities."

Tapping his finger on the table, the commander eyed him for a moment. "Why would you betray your people so easily?"

Wesley looked down at his lap before he answered. Your people? He had no family. Morgan, Drake? Galvin or Porter? Was that supposed to be his family? Lombard was a good man, but Lombard was dead. "I . . ." he began, but he couldn't find the words. It was truly sinking in that he would be the cause of all their deaths.

He strengthened himself. Whether it was him or someone else, it was going to happen anyway. And really, it wouldn't be him at all. It would be the Daecish that killed them. He was only doing what he thought was right. At least, that's what he told himself. "Truthfully," he said at last, "I wanted the Silent Hither to succeed. I wanted to be free of Daecish oppression. But as the years have gone on, I reckon . . ." He tried to think of a good answer. "I reckon I've made a mistake. I don't like the slums. I don't like the mines. But you've helped our cities. I see it. You gave us a new start. Better homes, medicine, a future. If I continue, I fear I'll be doing the wrong thing."

It was the first time those words ever came out of his mouth, but as he said them, they made sense. Many other Sunderians felt the same way. He wasn't alone. Yes. He was doing the right thing.

"Then why not just quit? Why come to us?"

"Because I think it should stop. They mean well, but in the end, they'll cause more harm than good." He believed his words enough, but at that moment, he really wanted to save himself.

The commander leaned back in his chair. "I appreciate your change of heart, but that doesn't change the fact that you're still a traitor. If what you say is true, we cannot pretend your past doesn't exist. There is still a law we must maintain."

"Then I ain't telling you nothing." He tried to hold his posture but never had he felt so small and vulnerable. "But if you let me go, I'll tell you everything I can to help stop the Silent Hither."

"Mr. Gladestone, first of all, this movement you speak of, this Silent Hither, is nothing more than an irritation. You don't seem to realize that the position you have put yourself in does not go very well in your favor. If we wanted information, we could just torture you, then kill you afterward."

This was it. He was done for. A sudden flashback of his father clubbing him in the side of the head with a switch because he shut the front door too loudly raced through his mind.

The commander laughed as he slapped the desk. "You've put yourself in a peculiar position, have you not? I'll tell you what, you give us one piece of information so we can know you are who you say you are, and we'll consider what to do from there."

The uncertainty sent his whole body trembling. He needed to know he would live through this. "But can you not guarantee my—"

"This is your only option," the commander replied. "Tell us something; otherwise we'll have you executed for treason by morning."

Wesley looked into the commander's eyes. Sharp as swords, they pierced into him. He wasn't bluffing. "Just recently," Wesley swallowed, "an official of City Hall joined the Dark Horses. Officer Geoffrey Arkwright."

All three officers turned to Barnaby.

"Officer Ogden?" the commander asked. "You were close to Arkwright, were you not?"

"I—I had no idea," he raised his hands and took a step back. "I swear!"

"Where is this Officer Arkwright now?" the commander asked Wesley.

"He volunteered to go on some foolish mission to Astford. He should be back in a week."

Barnaby frantically shook his head as his chubby cheeks jiggled. "He just rescheduled his assignments before he left! He was sent to go there on a training assignment. But none of us knew. You have my word!"

The commander rolled his eyes. "Relax, Officer Ogden. You've let enough things slip under that fat nose. I don't doubt that you had no idea. You have no fear of my suspicion." He looked at the officer standing to his right. "Write up an investigation warrant and send a dispatch to Astford immediately. We need to locate Officer Arkwright and find out who's been in correspondence with him in Astford."

"Wait," Barnaby said with a flustered face. "What will happen to him? Will—" He hesitated. "Will he be executed?"

"That is not your concern." The commander stood up. "Arrest him," he said, pointing to Wesley. "We'll get the information we want and then decide what to do with him later."

Along the Road to Norfrost

The carriage rocked along the rough road, but the journey toward Norfrost had been easier than Eirún had expected. She sat in the rear with her back against a large wooden trunk, her arms wrapped around her knees, pressed against her chest. They had been traveling for nearly a week, and low-lying mountains behind her had long covered her view of Folkbjörn, and for the moment, concealed her fear of what had become of Audin or what might become of her.

"Kari?" came Geirleif's voice from near the front. Eirún looked up at him. "Take a look ahead."

Eirún shifted herself to see where Geirleif was pointing his finger. Along the southern horizon rose dark mountains backed by a pale blue sky. Adorned in blankets of ice and snow, their peaks towered high above the clouds.

"The mountains of Einarr," said Geirleif. "The tallest peaks in all of Daecland, marking our southern border."

Eirún was at a loss for words. As a child, she had seen the mountains many times, but they had lost none of their magnificence in her growing age. A view of such majesty couldn't help but make one wonder if it was made by something outside of this world. Her own people had always wondered what lay to the south, and she loved the idea of some unexplored country, teeming with untouched forests and rivers. Since the invention of the wisp, the government was finally sending voyages across, but very little was still known to the common people. Some spoke of distant colonies being established, but such things were not yet in the books, and most of what she had heard she had taken for rumors.

Beside her, Mathios lay wrapped in a gray wool blanket, with only his face visible. Eirún placed her hand on him, feeling the slow rise and fall of his chest. She touched his head; it was still warm. The skin on his face was bruised yellow, and his eyes seemed to sink deep behind his pink eyelids. Lifting her hand from his forehead, Mathios slowly opened his eyes. He moved his lips, but no sound came out as he stared blankly toward the top of the carriage. His glazed eyes wandered before finally catching hers, but he quickly looked away. He shifted his hands, and a groan escaped his lips, but Eirún placed her hand over his and gently ran her fingers through his hair. "It's all right," she said. But as soon as she said the words, she knew that was a lie. It wasn't all right. She was caring for the boy who took away her greatest joy.

Eilis turned around from the front of the carriage. "Geirleif," she said. "The boy is awake."

"Here," said Geirleif as he stretched his arm back to hand Eirún a flask. Taking it, she lifted Mathios's head in her lap, allowing him to drink. He took in a small sip but immediately coughed it out. After his chest relaxed, he tried to take in another drink, but Eirún pulled the flask away. She wanted to help him. She wanted him to get better. But at the same time, she didn't. His eyes wandered for a moment longer but soon closed as he fell back asleep.

Eirún spent the rest of the afternoon gazing into the rugged countryside, where shallow drapes of snow gathered in the crevices and valleys, lying hidden from the sun. In the course of the passing days, grays and browns began to dominate what was once a green and rocky landscape. Mines had become more common. Large pumps breathed out steam and cried a loud and terrible sound as they lifted coal and precious metals from the deep caverns below the earth. Mounted above these contraptions stood tall bar structures, parching the landscape of life and beauty.

"That's steel," Geirleif said, pointing to the structures. "A wonderful invention. Much stronger than iron."

"Goodness," Eilis said. "We never stop, do we?"

"No, my darling. Our world is changing every day." He gazed across the landscape. "Marvelous, isn't it?"

All Eirún could see was a wasteland. A bleak and scarred earth, broken beneath the rise of industrial expansion. She found herself missing the views from earlier in their trip and began to daydream of a time long ago, before mines and steam engines. When the world was slower and yet filled with more wonder—a time when a vast and wild land of dark forests and hidden valleys remained untamed and shrouded in mystery. Her heart sank as she watched it all disappear.

The carriage came to a halt. Eirún peered between Eilis and Geirleif. Up ahead, several other carriages were parked in front of a blockade, where a few officers in black uniforms, covered in thick blue wool coats, stood. One held a sheet in his hand, walking along the row, inspecting the carriages one by one. Eirún tried to listen to what he was saying, but his words were muffled and distant.

They were looking for her, weren't they?

With a rising heartbeat, she quickly examined the surrounding luggage. Despite how foolish she felt, she buried herself between two chests before setting a leather case on top of her. There was just enough space for her to peer ahead from the darkness. Geirleif and Eilis turned around.

"Kari?" Geirleif asked.

"Good evening," came the sound of the officer as he stepped up to the carriage. He was talking to the driver, but Geirleif poked his head through the open window.

"Good evening, sir," he said.

The officer unfolded a sheet of paper, holding it in front of Geirleif. "Have you seen this girl?"

Eirún held her breath. Although she couldn't see the paper, she just knew it was a sketch of herself. Suddenly the tight space within the chests became cramped and hot.

"I—" Geirleif stuttered. He peered at Eilis. Her eyes widened as she vaguely glanced in Eirún's direction.

The officer narrowed his gaze. "Have either of you seen this girl?" he questioned more sternly. "She goes by the name Eirún Brynhildr."

Eirún's stomach raised into her throat.

"I, uh, I don't think so," said Geirleif. He swapped glances with Eilis, his eyes still wide. "Eilis, have you?"

"No," she said in a trembling voice. "I can't say I have."

The officer raised an eyebrow as if unconvinced. "Where are you heading to?"

Geirleif's voice quivered. "To Norfrost."

"And what brings you there?" continued the officer, now motioning for another officer to join him.

All Eirún could do was wait for them to search the back. They were going to find her. She would be arrested. Her chest relaxed, and a sudden calmness came over her as she pictured herself being dragged away and thrown into some prison. Did it really matter? Where was she going anyway? For a second, she even considered sitting up and just getting it over with. But something held her back.

"Well, uh—" Geirleif mumbled, with sweat forming around his temple. "We were just returning to our estate at Beron Manor. After visiting family just outside of Vagholme."

The officer paused. "Beron Manor?"

Geirleif reached into a leather satchel, pulled out some papers, and handed them to the officer. The officer shuffled through the leaves. "Lord Beron, I apologize," he exclaimed, standing at attention. "I wasn't aware you were on the road!"

"Oh no, it's—it's quite all right," Geirleif said. "You were simply doing your job."

The officer ordered his men to move the other carriages to either side of the road. "Make way for Lord Beron!" he commanded.

Geirleif waved his hand toward the officer. "Please don't let me stop your search of the other carriages."

"They've already been searched, sir."

"Very well," Geirleif replied as the driver picked up the reins. His tone suddenly calmed. "If you don't mind me asking . . ."

"Sir?"

"What is that girl wanted for?"

"For the murder of Syrkell Audin, Sir. A merchant in Scathwold."

Geirleif gave an obviously fake cough. "I hope you find her."

"Sir!" replied the officer as he saluted.

When the officer disappeared, Geirleif let out a loud sigh but Eilis still sat frozen as they rode around a bend, with the blockade now disappearing behind them.

Even now, Eirún was too afraid to move. They both knew.

"What are we doing, Geirleif?" Eilis asked in a hoarse whisper.

Geirleif looked straight ahead without turning. "I—I don't know. But I knew picking her up was a bad idea. I just knew it!"

"Why didn't you tell the officer she was in the carriage?"

"I don't know!"

Eirún sank into the floorboards as guilt consumed her. She tried to control herself, but she burst into a sudden sob as a suitcase slid off her back, thudding against the carriage floor. Eilis gave a startled scream. The driver steered the horses to the side of the road, bringing them to a halt. After giving a quick glance at Eilis, Geirleif stepped out and walked to the back, opening the rear door. Balling into her hands, she could barely keep her eyes on him.

Geirleif looked at her for a moment. "You're a murderer?" he asked.

Eirún shook her head.

"Then why was your face sketched on that paper?"

With tears pouring off the tip of her nose, she continued to shake her head. "I didn't mean to." She sniffed, trying to control herself. "He was coming to hurt me, and—"

"And what?"

"And I tried to fight him," she continued, barely able to catch her breath, "but I didn't mean to kill him." She continuously wiped her cheeks and mouth.

Geirleif turned his attention to the horizon, breathing heavily through his nose as his chest rose and fell. He slid his fingers into his waistcoat pockets. "Now, try and calm down." He lowered his eyes to meet hers. "I think you better tell me everything."

Eirún nodded, and after a moment, managed to control herself. With her hands hidden in her lap and her face down, she told Geirleif and the others all she could remember. About the orphanage. Søren. Even how Mathios had murdered him.

After explaining how she came to work for Audin, Geirleif groaned a deep sigh. "Wait here, and don't go anywhere." He walked over to Eilis and the driver, but Eirún could still hear them.

"Lord Beron," the driver said, taking off his top hat and running a hand across his bald head. He stepped out of the carriage. "Are you sure you can believe her? It might be wise to turn around and hand her over to the authorities."

Geirleif ran his fingers down his cheeks while he repeatedly shook his head as if arguing with himself in his mind. "I don't think she's dangerous, and her eyes seem truthful enough, but we also cannot put ourselves at unnecessary risk."

"We're already at risk," said Eilis. "We just lied to those officers!"

"I understand that, but we must do something."

"Like what?" Eilis replied. "Just leave her and that boy on the street?"

"If I may advise," the driver said, "a man of your status ought not to meddle in such affairs."

"I know, I know," Geirleif replied, still shaking his head.

"Perhaps we might drop her and the boy off at the next inn?" the driver offered.

Eilis' worried expression began to look more irritated as she stared at the driver with a half-open mouth. "If I may!" she exclaimed. "Leaving a helpless boy and girl in some inn is not an option!" She glared at Geirleif.

As if he could read her mind, Geirleif motioned for the driver to return to the carriage. A cold chill caused goosebumps to rise over Eirún's arms. She bundled them together.

"What if she is telling the truth?" Eilis asked at last. "Geirleif, you know how dreadful those shop owners can be to their servants. I don't know why the law allows a girl to work for men like that in the first place. They're just asking for disaster." She peered back toward the carriage and met Eirún's gaze. "That poor girl. Her life sounds so tragic."

The wind picked up as snow swirled across the rocky landscape like fine dust in the dry air. Geirleif glanced up at the sky and shook his head as if in disbelief with himself. "All right," he said. "When we come to the next inn, we'll decide what to do."

By nightfall, the carriage came to a halt. To Eirún's left stood a tall wooden building, capped with many gables and lined with thin windows. A wooden sign, reading 'The Clocktower Inn,' hung above the front door. Geirleif opened the back door to the carriage, giving Eirún a hand to let her out. The moon shone high in the clear sky, and Eirún did her best to not make any eye contact as she grabbed her satchel. The driver helped Geirleif carry Mathios out and into the inn, but all she could do was follow from behind, wondering what their thoughts were about her.

Inside, the sound of ticking and the whistling of steam from the kitchen welcomed her. Several clocks adorned the walls, and a large coal furnace sat in the left corner beside the desk. The floor was wooden, save a cobblestone slab beneath the furnace. Iron pipes ran through the roof and across the ceiling. The warm glow in the room quickly made Eirún realize how tired she was.

Geirleif talked with the innkeeper by the desk. Taking three skeleton keys, he handed one to the driver and another to Eirún. "Your room is upstairs to the left," he told her. "I want to help you, and I trust you will still be here in the morning?"

"Yes, Lord Beron. And thank you."

"Please, call me Geirleif." He motioned up the stairs. "You can go on up. We'll bring Mathios up shortly."

The tick of the clocks faded as Eirún made her way up the winding stairway. At the top, wall-mounted lanterns had been turned down low, and the hallway lay in shadow. She turned the knob, and the door swung open, revealing a small room. Through the closed window to her right, the moon shone a blue light on the landscape, which contrasted with the yellow glow casting out onto the bedroom walls from the lantern. Sitting at the foot of the sturdy bed, lined with many pillows and thick quilts, she set her sack down and breathed in the seasoned aroma of the cedar furniture. Despite the occasional outside gust of wind, the room lay quiet.

As much as she wanted to resist it, the darkness was coming over her—that terrible feeling of misery and worthlessness with no end. And yet, as much as she hated it, fighting it was like trying to fight off sleep in the late hours of the night. It was so easy to just give in.

The door pushed open, and Geirleif and the driver walked in, carrying Mathios on a small cot. "We'll see you bright and early," said Geirleif as he quietly shut the door.

With her hands in her lap, Eirún had a difficult time looking at the frail body lying before her. For the first time since they left Folkbjörn, the blanket was no longer wrapped around his body and head but only draped across from his lower chest down. And the carriage must have been in more shadow than she realized, for she had never seen him so clearly. Below his long matted hair, the skin on his face had cracked dry and wrinkled around his hollow eyes like bleached worn leather. His collarbone and shoulder blades stuck out from his yellowed skin— gaunt and skeletal. Still thirteen, he looked like an old man, starved and withered of life. She wasn't even sure how she had recognized him in the alleyway.

She wanted to feel pity like she did when she first found him. She tried to search for that feeling again, but the coldness set in. He was helpless and unwanted. Dying. Why didn't she feel sorry for him? Suddenly, a thin trace of guilt stole into her heart. She realized that the only reason she kept watch over him was that he was the closest thing she had to Søren.

Walking around the room, she blew out the candles. When she went to blow out the last lantern on the bedside table, she stopped and turned as Mathios let out a low moan. He slid open his eyes and looked up at her, trying to move his cracked lips.

"Eirún," he said in barely a whisper.

She bit down on her teeth behind her closed mouth.

"Eirún," he whispered again. His eyes watered, and his mouth fell into a frown.

Ignoring him, she blew out the lantern and lay down on the bed, and hid beneath the blanket. But under the veil of darkness, all she could picture was Søren. His tearing eyes as he helplessly wept on the cot in the kitchen as she yelled at him. His body floating down the river.

Gritting her teeth, she ground out a low wail. With a clenched fist, she hit herself in the side of the head. She just wanted it all to go away.

The Flames of Denhurst

Galvin stood in the cellar doorway, looking at Myla and the girls huddled beside the now mostly empty shelves, which were tipped uneasily against the walls. All that was left were scattered piles of rotten cabbage on the dirt floor. The whole room looked distraught, matching the expression on the girl's faces. "You'll be safe in here," he tried to encourage them. "If something happens, go out the trap door beneath the back pantry. It stays locked from the inside." He pointed to the far side of the cellar. "There, you'll find a gap in the city wall. You can escape into the country there." He gazed at Myla intently. "Only leave if you feel you have no other choice. I fear the walls will be guarded on the outside."

Myla nodded as the girls huddled near the pantry. Galvin closed the cellar door behind him and ran back up the stairs. Kent looked out a window toward the north end of town. His reddish hair and clean-shaven face always made him look more Daecish than Sunderian. Maybe that's why they always liked him so much.

"How much time we got?" Galvin asked as he stood beside him. To the east rose a red sun, shrouded behind low clouds which choked the city in a dense fog.

"It's hard to tell," Kent replied. "But the carriages are making their way through the gate now. It'll be five, maybe ten minutes before they approach the houses."

"And everyone is in their positions?"

Kent shrugged slightly but still looked hopeful. "The draft came earlier than expected, but we got the word out as quickly as we could. We should be ready, I don't doubt."

Galvin walked over to Porter, who sat in front of the hearth, wiping the leather handle to his two-handed war hammer.

"We should have gotten the girls out of here," Porter said.

"I know," Galvin replied. "We thought we had more time." He peered toward the staircase leading to the cellar. "They should be safe. It's locked from the inside, and Kent will be here."

"And we've gone over the plan with all the leaders?"

"Yes, Porter, we are more than prepared."

Porter nodded but looked unsure. "We got to give this everything we've got."

"We will."

Porter managed a smile. "But you're not as young as you used to be."

Galvin laughed. "Your hair is whiter than mine."

"That's not from old age; that's from wisdom."

"Well, I'm sure it'll do you well in this battle."

"How 'bout your eye?" Porter asked.

"Don't worry about me."

Kent stepped away from the window and drew his sword. "They're heading toward the houses," he said. "Six are coming this way."

Galvin sat up and grabbed a shield off the mantle. "You ready?"

"We don't stop 'til we take Denhurst."

* * *

Nearly two-hundred-and-fifty Daecish soldiers marched through Denhurst, breaking off toward various houses and buildings; several large iron carriages rolled behind. Officers waved hands and barked off orders as the soldiers carried open shackles, swords, and crossbows. Corporal Sigurðr stood in the back of a group heading toward a two-story timber-framed house on the west side of town. The rising sun evaporated the fog and blazed across the rooftops. He raised a hand in front of his face, trying to shield the light. Being his first draft, the anticipation sent his blood pumping.

"Remember," said a sergeant next to him. "Most of these men are still in their beds. We catch them off guard, shackle them, and bring them to the carriages. We can fit twelve in a carriage before we load up another one."

Sigurðr nodded.

"Don't hesitate to draw your sword. It makes them cower. But don't strike anyone. Our orders are to harm no one unless they use violence against us first." He tapped his crossbow. "Pointing this at their head does the trick, too."

Sigurðr nodded again. The muscles in his neck stiffened.

"You look nervous. Don't be nervous. What's your name?"

"Corporal Sigurðr," he replied.

"How old are you?" The sergeant looked barely any older than himself, but there was a hardness in his posture that made him seem more like a commander.

"Sixteen last week," Sigurðr answered with a thin crack in his voice. He straightened his own posture, hoping to seem taller than he was.

"I didn't think they sent soldiers that young over the mountains. Anyway, I'm Sergeant Alric. You're going to be fine. Most of the men should come out on first command."

Sigurðr nodded for the third time, but their conversation fell short as they came to the house. An officer walked up the wooden steps, which sagged beneath his weight. Beside the front door, he peered through a side window with his hands cupped around his face, but even Sigurðr knew it was no use trying to look through that warped glass, paper, or whatever it was. The officer looked back at four lieutenants, who stood at the center of a wide crossroads. Behind them, houses lined the streets on all sides except where the jousting field stretched on the far end.

"He's waiting for the lieutenant's call," Alric said. "We all go in at the same time. I did this in Everwind, and it's still just as exciting the second time."

A deep, resonating sound reverberated throughout the city, and both Sigurðr and Alric looked over their shoulder as a lieutenant blew a dark horn.

With it came an unexpected crash.

Nearly jumping into the air, Sigurðr turned back around as the front door was kicked open from the inside. More than a dozen armed men poured out of the house as soldiers stumbled back, falling over one another with shouts and screams. One soldier tripped backward from the stairway, and his steel-plated brigandine slammed into Sigurðr's face. As his head threw back, blood streamed from his nose. White spots blurred his vision. Blinking, he drew the sword from his hilt and went to wipe at his nose but shuddered when a soldier screamed as a man swung an ax down, splitting his head in two. Sigurðr's throat tightened as he looked away.

The entire city had now erupted into chaos as soldiers and men intertwined with one another—swords, pitchforks, and clubs waved in the air. A Sunderian man charged at Alric. They exchanged blows, and almost without thought, Sigurðr heaved his sword into the man's ribs. The man turned to Sigurðr with a face twisted in pain. For a second, Sigurðr actually reached out his hand to help the man. To offer some sort of kindness in response to the terrible thing he had just done to him. But the rising mix of emotions caused Sigurðr's mind to go numb. He stumbled back and let the tip of his sword fall to the ground.

"Don't stop, Corporal!" yelled Alric before charging into a skirmish.

Sigurðr's head grew dizzy as the blood ran down his blade. His heart pounded so hard it hurt his chest. Heaps of men crawled over one another, fighting both within and outside the buildings. Blood sprayed from heavy blows as bodies collapsed, splattering mud into the air. Tears began to run down Sigurðr's cheeks as he backed away from the closest skirmish. If he could just hide beneath a carriage, he'd live through this. He glanced to his right. A man charged toward him with an ax raised high. As the ax thrust down, Sigurðr froze and only turned, sinking his head into his neck as the ax embedded into his left shoulder.

He opened his mouth and fell to his knees, but no words came out. His breath was gone, and the sudden warm flow of blood poured down to his fingers. He fell over on his back. The man wearily lifted his ax again to finish the job, but an arrow suddenly pierced through his throat. The ax fell from his hands, and he collapsed into the mud.

Sigurðr reached his right hand over his shoulder; his left arm hung lifeless by his side. Shock had kept him from fully realizing that only a few strands of muscle kept his arm attached. Leaning up on his right side, he dragged himself toward a carriage, just thirty feet away. His hand slipped into the wet earth as blood continued to flow down his chest and arm, mixing with the muddy water.

Black smoke rose in the air as buildings ignited and screams fell from their windows. The smell of burning wood and flesh crawled into his nose. Bodies of soldiers began to pile up as throngs of men moved from one house to another. As his mind cleared, a pain-like fire throbbed from his shoulder to the rest of his body. The carriage wasn't far now, but his head wouldn't quit spinning. He lifted himself to his knees, then to his feet; his arm hung like nothing more than a rope dangling from a limb. He took one step at a time, his feet faltering as his upper body grew heavier with each step. Everything wavered in and out of focus. The desire to just lie down and fall asleep pressed his eyelids down, but he fought the temptation.

Almost to the carriage.

Deliriousness took the better of him. Up felt down, and left felt right. Warm urine ran down his leg. He continued to stagger toward a crowd as the world spun in circles. They looked Daecish, but he couldn't be sure. He lifted a hand to call out, but just then, a white-haired man charged at him with fierceness in his eyes. Wielding a large war hammer, the man lifted it behind his shoulder and brought it forth with a mighty heave.

A crack of horrible pain shot through Sigurðr's head as an immense pressure crushed the left side of his skull. A high, piercing sound rang in his ears and then faded to silence.

* * *

Smoke slithered beneath the cellar door. Wrapped tight in Myla's embrace, Hazel buried her face in her mother's chest as Fleta listened to the shouts of men behind them from somewhere outside. Myla's eyes gazed intently at the latch of the trapdoor. A loud thud against the outer wall made them jump.

"Listen," Myla said in a quivering voice. "I'm going to check on Kent. I want you to wait inside the pantry. Stay away from the trapdoor."

"No, please!" cried Hazel.

"It'll be fine," Myla said, rubbing Hazel's hair. "I'll be right back. Now, go on."

Every instinct told Fleta to grab on to her mother. To not let her go, but instead, she took her sister's hand as they went into the pantry. She pulled the door closed, leaving only a small crack as she watched her mother walk to the front of the cellar.

Her mother peered into the stairwell from between the cellar door and the frame. "Kent?" she asked in a loud whisper. "Kent?" She brushed her hand against the iron latch before unlocking it. When she pushed the oak door open, a thin wave of smoke whipped into the cellar. She turned back to the girls and lifted her finger to her lips.

Fleta shook her head. "No!" she said in a hoarse whisper.

Myla motioned for her to stay back and inspected the room above the staircase. The heat from the room above, which emanated an orange glow, warmed Fleta's face. Myla grabbed the upper part of her dress and covered her mouth and nose and headed up the steps and out of sight.

Sweat dripped down Fleta's temple, and arms as the voices of men and clashing metal continued from outside. Although a wall stood between them, she felt exposed and vulnerable, as if the men somehow knew exactly where they were. A sudden scream cried out from upstairs, and both girls jolted. Something had happened to her mother. Fleta pushed the pantry door open and ran toward the stairway.

"Fleta!" cried Hazel. "Don't leave me!"

"Stay there!" Fleta shouted, running up the stairs. The thick smoke instantly choked her, and she took a step back, almost losing her balance on the edge of the step. Holding her arm to her mouth, she crouched low to the ground and looked around with squinted eyes. The roaring fire and crackling wood drowned out all other noises. Smoke poured through cracks in the ceiling, fogging the room so that she could only see a few feet in front of her. She crept toward the nearest light, which came from the open front door. There laid Kent's body with blood puddled beneath him. Her first thought was to run back down to the cellar. But she needed to find her mother. She grabbed his sword.

The sound of beating against wood came from the other side of the room, followed by a loud whimper.

Fleta examined the room in the sound's direction, but the smoke concealed her vision. Gripping the sword with both hands, she pointed the blade forward and snuck toward the sound. After a few steps, the silhouette of a man in black Daecish armor came into view. He turned over chairs and tables as if he was desperately in search of something.

Her legs froze. Barely able to open her watering eyes, she crouched and backed away until the silhouette of the man vanished. Still sweeping the floor for any signs of her mother, she prayed she wouldn't find her dead body. The smoke thickened, and although she attempted to maintain a calm breath, an uncontrollable cough overcame her. Afraid the Daecish man would hear her, she hurried to a window to her right and pushed the wooden shutters open, taking in several deep breaths. With the open window came a gust which channeled through the house and out another window on the other side of the room, somewhat clearing the air.

A loud voice called through the smoke. "Drop your sword!"

An unexpected blade swung down from the smoke to her right. Fleta fell back against the wall with a scream as her sword was hammered from her hand. Crumpling to the ground, she scurried on all fours toward a table to her left.

"I'm not going to hurt you!" the voice called out.

At first, she wondered if it was Galvin or Porter, but the accent was clearly Daecish. Patting the ground, her hands met with the tip of her sword's blade, and she picked it back up.

The breeze had ceased, and smoke filled the room once again. The man was nowhere in sight.

Flames now licked high through the floorboards on the western end of the room. The roar of the fire grew so loud, almost nothing else could be heard. Where was her mother?

Suddenly, the shadow of the man came into view. His back was to her as he searched the ground below the window. Slowly raising herself up, she tried to control her coughs as she wiped her watering eyes.

Despite her trembling hands, she repositioned her grip of the sword for a downward stab. Then, with all of her strength, she gritted her teeth and thrust the blade into his upper back. The man cried out a muffled scream behind the black cloth wrapped around his mouth and nose. Reaching for his back, he spun around and stumbled toward her, mumbling inaudible words. Then he fell backward into the table with a dull thud.

The room around Fleta went gray and distant, along with all sound. Losing her sense of balance, she dropped her sword and lifted her hand to lean against a wall that wasn't there. She stumbled over until she managed to grab hold of the back of a chair. Closing her eyes, she tried to erase the terrible feeling coursing through her veins.

She looked at the body. Was he actually dead? Forcing herself to look away, she scrubbed at her cheeks. She needed to find Mother.

From the man's face, she grabbed the cloth and ran back to the window to catch her breath. Leaning over the seal, she coughed out the smoke from her lungs and her eyes soon adjusted to the cityscape, a bleak wasteland of smoldering ruin. There were little to no Daecish left fighting, but the ground was riddled with their lacerated bodies, wallowing in mud and pools of blood as if the wet earth was too full to drink it all in. She caught a glimpse of Porter just beneath the window, lifting his war hammer over his shoulder. Lying at his feet was the lifeless body of a Daecish soldier. Although the top of his head was crushed into a soggy dark-red mess, there was still a wide-eyed expression of fear frozen over his pale face. He barely looked any older than her.

Galvin ran up beside Porter. In that moment, Fleta doubted what her eyes witnessed. First, Porter stripped the soldier's clothing and embarrassment swept over her frozen body for seeing a naked grown man. But when he, along with Galvin, began to dismember the soldier, her mind went into shock. Their blood covered hands moved swiftly, cutting and pulling apart. The body of the young man had been reduced to nothing more than butchered meat.

Guilt smothered Fleta for simply witnessing such an act and she looked away, locking her eyes as tight as she could, hoping to squeeze out the image pounding in her mind. But disbelief that Galvin and Porter could do such a thing forced her to look back just in time to see them carry the body up a set of stairs to a high balcony. From there, they threw what was left of the young man onto the palisades as the rough-cut point of a pine log gored him through his stomach.

Acid burned Fleta's throat.

The bare bodies of the Daecish were piled along the entire eastern wall as blood dripped from their severed limbs. Some still had their heads; others had been sawn off and stuck on the palisade points. A few others were barely alive, unclothed and crawling along the base of the walls as they bled out from their dismemberments.

Fleta leaned over and gripped her stomach. Her bowels heaved, and she threw up on the inside floor. An unintentional wail escaped her lungs as she lifted her shaking hands to cover her mouth—the images would not go away. "Mama!" she shouted. "Mama!"

In her desperate cries, she remembered that her mother was still missing. She made herself calm down and wrapped the cloth around her face. Wiping her eyes, she ran back into the smoke. Staying low, she weaved around tables and swept her eyes across the floor. "Mama!" she cried out.

Unable to remain inside any longer, she stumbled over toward the front door. But as she did, she saw what looked like a body lying near the eastern sidewall, just below a window, with the shutters still closed. "Mama!" she cried out, running toward her. She shook her shoulders, but Myla didn't move.

Across the room, flaming timbers of wood broke through the ceiling with a loud crash, hurling ash and sparks into the air. Fleta grabbed Myla beneath the arms and began to drag her toward the front door, which was no more than ten steps away. With a slip, she stumbled over a broken chair and fell hard on her elbows. She clenched her teeth and got back up, lifting Myla once again. Tables and chairs continued to block her way, and she screamed in frustration until she finally threw herself backward through the front doorway and into the mud outside. On her hands and knees, she scrambled over her mother and pressed her ear against her chest. She wasn't breathing.

"Mama! Wake up!" Tears dripped from her own nose onto her mother's face.

"Fleta!" came the sudden voice of Galvin rounding the corner.

At the sight of him, she fell back. "Stay away!" she screamed.

But Galvin only kneeled beside her mother. "Myla!" he yelled. "Myla!"

Fleta was so afraid all she could do was watch. "She isn't breathing!"

The burning of the building gave a deafening roar.

He shook Myla's shoulders. "Myla!" He turned to Fleta. "Where's Hazel!"

Fleta stared at her lifeless mother.

"Where's Hazel?" he hollered again.

Fleta looked at the building as a horrifying realization enveloped her. She stood up and burst back into the building.

"Fleta!" Galvin called after her.

Flames reached at her from all directions, and the room filled with black smoke. Keeping her hand on the wall, she ran toward the stairs, but all she could see through her stinging eyes was fire and smoke. She cried out and ran back outside. Running past Galvin and her mother, she rounded the house toward the trapdoor at the back of the cellar. She pulled the iron handle. It didn't move. It had been locked from inside. She kicked at the door as tears ran down her face. She screamed out, beating her fists against the thick wood. "Hazel!"

Galvin ran up from behind and moved Fleta aside as he kicked at the door, which jarred against the iron hinges. Several times he kicked, but the bolts held fast. Fleta fell back against the city wall, covering her face in her hands with violent sobs.

Galvin shouted and continued to kick, but the bolt seemed to give no further.

Assembly of the Gales

Eilívur grunted as he bundled his arms and raised his collar to shield himself from the freezing rain and wind. He wasn't in Norfrost anymore. He was in Everwind. Wasn't Sunder supposed to be warmer? At least he never had to guess how this city got its name. Hurrying west through the main courtyard of the Northern District, he kept his gaze down.

As he passed into the Western District, a peculiar sulfur-like smell caught his nose, but he thought nothing more of it. Through the thick mist, City Hall finally came into view. He stepped inside and walked over to the Capital Guard office.

"Yes, sir, I'll get those files right away," said a secretary, walking out of the office. Officer Barnaby Ogden looked up as she departed. He hurried to his feet, standing straight with his nose high and large belly protruding forward.

"At ease, Ogden," said Eilívur, sitting at the front of his desk. "Please, have a seat."

"Commander Tyr," Ogden said in an uncomfortable tone as Eilívur grabbed an apple from a small basket on the desk. "Back from Llynhithe already?"

"I have a warrant out for a man. Arnon Greystrom, son of Lombard Greystrom."

"Oh, w—well, of course," Ogden replied, wrestling through papers on his desk.

"Have we hired a sketch artist yet?"

Ogden shook his head, jiggling the loose skin hanging from his neck. "We're still working on it, but I'll write up the warrant right away."

Eilívur grunted. That was one thing Llynhithe had that Everwind didn't. Someone skilled in criminal sketch portraits. It made the whole process easier. Why this office hadn't hired one was beyond him.

"But you may like to know we have a man in custody who, um," Ogden cleared his throat, "is a Dark Horse."

"Name?"

"He goes by the name Wesley Gladestone. Says he's a court leader."

"Explain."

"Something like a leader of the Dark Horses, if you will." He wiped the sweat off his brow. "He turned himself in just yesterday."

"A court for the Dark Horses?" Eilívur laughed to himself as he gazed across the room for a moment. The smell of fresh paint and the blue tapestry on the eastern wall reminded him of home. "Maybe they're more organized than we thought. Has he told us anything?"

"As far as I'm aware, he's kept his mouth shut on most matters until we agree to forgive him of his past treason."

"Who ran the arrest orders?"

"Commander Veurðr, sir."

"Good. Where is he?"

"I believe he said he was going to the Tea House."

Eilívur looked through the window across the room. He couldn't see the Tea House, but just the thought of that place annoyed him. "You mentioned that this Dark Horse was silent on most matters. What has he spoken of?"

"Well, uh—" Ogden fumbled with his fingers, then slid his spectacles back up his nose. "He reported that a man within our division has had correspondence with the Silent Hither, a—and he will be charged with execution, I believe."

Eilívur chuckled. "In this division?"

"Yes, sir."

"Is nothing left untainted? And the name?"

"O—Officer Arkwright, sir. Geoffrey Arkwright."

Eilívur scratched the back of his head, feeling where the ends of his short blonde hair began to curl. He needed to get it trimmed again. "Rewrite that order and tell Gunnar," he cleared his throat, "I mean Commander Veurðr to have him drafted, not executed."

"Sir?"

"Orders have come in to draft all prisoners."

"What of those with capital offenses?"

"All of them," Eilívur replied shortly. "Just be sure to change the order."

"Yes, sir, I'll get on it right away."

Keeping his eyes away, Ogden's face fell into a frown. "You know this Officer Arkwright, don't you?" Eilívur asked.

Ogden looked up with swollen eyes. "Since he was a boy."

"Ogden, I understand your sorrow, but he's not a boy anymore. He's made his own decision."

"I know."

Eilívur stood up. Ogden's feelings would not sway him on maintaining justice for the sake of peace, but he could not help but have pity for the old man. "Take the rest of the day off."

Back outside, he strolled over to the Tea House. He peered into the window and sighed. Lester just had to be dining at the table next to Gunnar's. He wasn't sure which annoyed him more, the Silent Hither or the Merchant's Guild.

He pushed open the door and walked in. Gunnar waved, and Eilívur slid a chair across the light oak floors and sat across from him. Just behind Gunnar, set beneath a wide decorative mantle, the deep fireplace smoldered.

"Why do you always eat here?" he asked.

Gunnar took a sip from his teacup. "Closest thing to home we've got."

Eilívur gazed around the multi-faceted room, filled with bays and nooks. The imported white tile ceiling, framed in crown molding, rose high above their heads, and numerous candles had been mounted on the burnt sienna walls. To his left, the large window of diamond-shaped panes, framed in glazed iron, looked out onto Old Birchton Way.

A chair scraped across the floor, and he glanced across his shoulder. Lester stood up as another man entered. Eilívur couldn't help but stare at his overly protruding gut and thick legs.

"Mr. Claude," Lester said, wiping his face with a napkin.

"Good afternoon, Mr. Lester." Claude shivered. "Wind's picked up. I hear it is going to be a bad winter."

"That's what they always say," Lester replied. He took a step back, examining Claude's new-looking suit. "Daecish cotton-linen and silk. They certainly tailored you just right, didn't they?"

Claude held the open ends of his black tailcoat with a grin. "You think it fits all right?"

Eilívur tried not to laugh, but the buttons to his waistcoat strained against his bulging mass.

"You look exquisite, Mr. Claude. Like a new man." Putting on his top hat, Lester looked in Eilívur's direction. "Good evening Commander Tyr. Commander Veurðr."

Eilívur nodded back as Lester and Claude stepped outside.

"Why do they try to talk like us? Forcing the accents," he asked Gunnar in a low voice.

Gunnar chuckled in his throat. "Just trying to fit in."

"All merchants care about is money. And this place reeks of the hypocrisy."

"Yea, well, where else are you going to get tea in Sunder?"

"Military Quarters. Infirmary. City Hall."

Eilívur looked at the room again. "But why'd we put so much work into this place? It's for the Merchant's Guild. City Hall doesn't even look this nice."

"You know King Ónarr wants the people's loyalty. Make them feel Daecish. Treat them as one of our own." Gunnar leaned forward. "Anyway, you should have heard the conversation I just overheard from Lester and his friend."

"Who?"

"The man left before you got here. I think his name was Miles." Setting his teacup on the table, Gunnar leaned back against the chair. "Just small talk mostly. The upcoming symphony, steam engine investments. Lester's managed to undercut and buy out several specialty shops in the Eastern District, giving himself a virtual monopoly on certain items. To top it off, he's reworking some of his factories for coal shipping to Daecland."

"How's he going to get it there? Through Llynhithe?"

"Runevast."

"Runevast is only for military personnel."

Gunnar rolled an end of his long blond mustache. "He seems to think it will open up to commercial shipments by next year."

"I doubt it," Eilívur replied dryly. "We would have heard something first."

"Unless King Ónarr's officials are in talks with the Merchant's Guild."

"Bypassing us?"

Gunnar crossed one leg over the other and fiddled with the handle of his teacup. "I wouldn't put it past him. Anyway, that Miles, though, he's got a curious sense about him. He didn't seem to think things were going as well as Lester did. The economy, I mean. Apparently, he ran some numbers and saw demand dropping by the end of the year."

"Why?"

"I don't know. But if Lester and the other merchants keep at their pace, there'll be excess supply. Either prices will plummet, or they'll have to decrease their products. Either way, shops will go out of business. Not to mention the debt being racked up in Sunder right now. There's not enough coal in this land to power a single wisp."

"Copper's doing well, though."

"Yea, but King Ónarr doesn't get a single arac for it. Norfrost controls it."

Eilívur laughed. "How do they expect us to pay off debts if they take our only valuable resource?"

"Your guess is as good as mine. But Lester was optimistic. Thinks the draft will boost the economy back up." He took a sip of tea. "War is always good for the economy."

Eilívur picked at his fingernails. He hated talking about economics. "Have you heard from your family?"

A glint appeared in Gunnar's eyes. "Hilde gave birth to a boy."

Eilívur grinned. "When?"

"Six months ago. He's strong and healthy."

"Have you named him?"

"Balder."

"That's a good name. I'm sorry you missed it."

Gunnar looked down between his clasped hands. "It's just a part of the job, isn't it?"

Eilívur nodded thoughtfully, but Gunnar's eyes reddened.

"How about you?" Gunnar asked. "Have you heard from your mother?"

Eilívur sent Ulnleif's death certificate to Runevast just before he left Llynhithe. She had probably read it by now. "Not since last summer."

"You should write to her."

Eilívur unconsciously ran his finger down the scar below his ear.

"How'd you get that scar, anyway?" Gunnar asked as he motioned toward his own ear.

Eilívur wiped a streak of dust off of his sleeve. "My mother."

Gunnar chuckled and waved a dismissing hand.

Eilívur faked a small grin. It wasn't a lie, but he didn't feel like talking about it, so he let it pass.

Of Mines and Wisps

For the past two weeks, it's happening all over," said the innkeeper behind the counter. His thinning blonde hair had been slicked back with so much oil, you could see straight to his scalp. "Norfrost is in chaos."

"Norfrost? By the love of—what could be causing it?" Geirleif asked, rubbing his chin. He had heard that the mining industry had some difficulties, but nothing to this extent. He threw a hand in the air. "I thought with all the money going into it, mining was increasing!"

The innkeeper shrugged. "Your guess is as good as mine, but one by one, the mines are shutting down."

"The world is getting ahead of themselves—advancing too quickly," said a man who sat in a corner drinking coffee. By the look of his outdated beige suit and worn shoe tips, he obviously thought higher of himself than he ought to. "Everyone gets in a hurry and has to have the best thing." His last remark was accompanied by his glance at the clocks around the room.

The innkeeper didn't seem impressed. "Well, sir," he replied. "The world's advancing, and nothing's going to stop that. And it's because of my clocks that you will leave on time."

The man raised an eyebrow, taking another sip from his cup. "Nothing against your clocks. I just find the whole mining scenario amusing."

"How so?" the innkeeper asked, propping his bony elbow on the counter.

Geirleif wanted to say something, but he held it in. The last thing he wanted to do was sound like this know-it-all in the corner. Geirleif was a lord of the General Assembly, after all. His job was to be the example to the common people. Lead Daecland into a bright future with dignity and self-respect.

"Everyone's always talking about the progression of society as if technology's going fix all our problems," the man replied. "But these mines are just the start."

Geirleif rolled his eyes. He couldn't hold it in. "I don't know where you heard that nonsense from, but I've never heard anyone suggest that technology's going to fix every problem."

"Lord Thorsen from the General Assembly said something like that at a dinner party once," added Eilis.

Did his own wife just accuse the General Assembly of mumbling such drivel? "Eilis, dear, I have been on the General Assembly for twenty-seven years. I've known Lord Thorsen nearly half of that time, and never have I heard such words come from his mouth. Our country thrives on the voice of the people themselves, not the stuff we make." He stared at the man in the corner. "But if you mean to critique the methods of Norfrost's progressive measures, then I will gladly retort. If we continue progressing technology, education, worker's rights, then yes, we will fix many, if not most, of society's issues. It's been proven."

"That's based on an assumption that everyone will always cooperate," the man responded with a mocking finesse in his tone. "What about corruption? Those who commit crimes?"

Geirleif's chest tightened. "Statistics have proven again and again that the majority of crimes are committed by those in society who are less fortunate, often ignorant. It is a social issue, not an individual one." He jabbed a finger forward.

Eilis stepped over and patted Geirleif on the back. He relaxed the tension in his neck.

The man calmly took another sip of coffee. "So, the wealthy and educated don't commit crimes?"

"I'm not saying that," Geirleif replied, but he was sure to soften his tone.

The innkeeper waved a hand. "None of that makes a difference to what I'm saying. It isn't the worker's rights or education that's causing trouble in the mines. It's something else." He leaned forward almost as if to whisper to Geirleif. "There's a rumor going around of monsters."

Geirleif stared at the innkeeper, baffled. "Did you just say monsters?"

"Monsters," the innkeeper said, nodding. "From the depths. They've been disturbed, and now they're waking up."

The man in the corner chuckled, but Geirleif shook his head. "Utter nonsense," he said. "Sir, have you gone mad?"

The innkeeper leaned back and grabbed a book as if to busy himself again. "Believe what you like, but that's the rumor that's going around."

Geirleif turned at the sound of Eirún walking down the steps. Thank goodness. Perhaps this ridiculous conversation would end. "Ei—" he began to say her name but quickly realized that might not be wise to say publicly. "Kari," he said instead. "How did you sleep?"

"Fine. I was just coming down to grab some milk for Mathios," she said, still standing at the bottom of the stairs. She held her hands together in front of her, and by the looks of the bags under her eyes, it didn't seem she slept at all.

Early that morning, he and Eilis had agreed that Eirún would stay at the manor. At least until they figured out how to sort out this situation. "How is the boy feeling?" he asked, conscious of keeping a kind tone.

Eirún half-smiled. "He seems to be doing better."

"Very good, then." He turned toward the innkeeper. "Will you get her some warm milk?"

Setting his book down with a thud, the innkeeper walked into the kitchen.

Geirleif grumbled. "The service here has declined in recent years. No respect whatsoever."

After breakfast, it didn't take long for everyone to load the belongings into the carriage. Eirún and Mathios were already situated inside, and the driver was following behind. Despite the reasons, Geirleif could not help but wonder what kind of impact the shutting down of so many mines would have.

Eilis approached him. "Do you trust her?" she asked in a soft voice, keeping her eyes on the closed door of the carriage.

Did he? He didn't know. But something in him told him he should. "To tell you the truth," he replied, "I don't know if I should, but I'm going to. I can't see a lie in her eyes."

"Me neither," Eilis replied. "But I'm afraid. I know we agreed to let her stay for a while, but she *is* wanted by the authorities." She glanced at the driver and whispered. "And what about our chauffeur? He knows about her. What if he says something?"

"He won't," Geirleif replied. "I talked to him this morning. I made it clear that despite the complexities of the situation, we are within the law."

"But we aren't Geirleif," she replied with worry-stricken eyes. "You know that."

"I . . ." He didn't know what to say. She was right. They weren't within the law. "I don't know. But how can I just hand her over to the authorities? You know she'll be found guilty."

"I know," she said quietly.

"And Mathios," he continued as he peered at him through the carriage window. "He killed the only boy she loved, and think of the way she now cares for him. I don't think you or I could have done something so selfless." He looked back at his wife. "We have to do what we can."

Eilis kissed him on the cheek. "I think you're right."

* * *

As the morning mist vanished beneath the high sun, they continued west toward Norfrost, the landscape growing more rugged with each passing hour. Mines began to grow more frequently, dotting the landscape, though many were uninhabited. A gust of wind brought a strange scent, foul and thick, to Eirún's nose. Geirleif and Eilis mentioned it as well, but soon their conversation stopped as Geirleif pointed toward a mine, where a large wooden vessel was tipped on its side, coal scattered across the barren ground. No one could be seen around it.

Soon, they passed another mine, where a few workers stood idly, shoveling coal. Their wool pants and white shirts were long worn out and stained black and gray. Geirleif stopped the carriage and stepped out, approaching the workers. From the carriage, Eirún heard only the distant voices of the men outside. That same sour smell once again lingered in the air.

Geirleif sat back in the carriage, groaning heavily as he rubbed his face.

"What is it?" asked Eilis.

"I don't bloody know," he said. His frustration could be easily felt. "Half the men have quit this mine, saying they've heard noises."

"They quit because of noises?"

"Not just noises," replied Geirleif. "Several men have disappeared." He threw his hand in the air. Apparently, half the mines on this side of Norfrost have been abandoned or caved-in."

Eilis put her hand to her mouth. "How terrible!"

"I always said mining was dangerous work," the driver said, looking over his shoulder.

"From the sound of it," Geirleif added, "no one thinks these are natural cave-ins. They say they're something else. Evidently what our innkeeper got his story of monsters from."

An immediate silence fell in the carriage, but as Geirleif rubbed his fingers on his forehead, it seemed there was more worry going on in his mind than he was letting out. The collapsing of mines was an unnerving thought, but Eirún couldn't even imagine what could be causing it all. Her biggest worry was what would happen to her once she arrived in Norfrost. She had no family or friends there. Knowing there was a warrant out for her arrest, she assumed her picture would be in Norfrost before long, if not already. She couldn't stay there. She couldn't get a job. Maybe she would find another ride and go as far west as Fingate.

"We need to head on," Geirleif said, interrupting her thoughts. "I've been gone for far too long. I fear what state Norfrost may be in." He flicked the reins.

By midday, snow covered most of the ground, and their road rose until deep ravines dropped off on either side. They soon curved around the base of a wide, towering mountain littered with firs and pines. When they turned north, now facing the mountain, the clouds parted, and her eyes opened for the first time to the city of Norfrost.

The city looked as if it had been carved into the rock, creating three levels, almost cone-shaped, which rose into the air. Arriving near the bottom level, they passed through a large steel gate. Beyond lay streets and avenues, crowded with brick and marble buildings—all decorated with ornate windows and thick hand-cut trim. Every road was paved and lined with tall streetlamps—none of which flickered with flame but glowed, steady and bright from voltaic-power.

The carriage jolted as they rode over two tracks of iron, which ran around the lower level's base. Following the tracks with her eyes to the western side of the city, a steam-powered locomotive circled the lower level until it spiraled up to the second. Some of the carriages carried passengers, but most seemed to haul coal. Near the back of the lower level, Eirún marveled at a great staircase, where thick crowds of people made their way up and down as if their very lives depended on making it to their next appointment.

Up the stairway toward the second level, many wisps were leaving and landing into great bays with circular doors, glimmering like polished brass. High above, jutting from the center of the second level, sat the third tier, where Norfrost Castle, home of King Eirik, rose high above the rim of the world.

Such a sight sent Eirún's heart pumping. To come into such splendor, and yet not know what would even happen to her tomorrow, filled her with both excitement and fear.

Geirleif turned toward her. "Be sure to stay low until we are further in the city."

Eirún slouched but maintained a clear view of the outside. A boy, wearing a short-brimmed hat and dark worker's pants, supported by thin bracers, stood on a corner, holding a newspaper and calling out to bystanders, "One arac per issue! One arac per issue! All you need to know about the mines!"

Before long, Eirún's view was blocked by great throngs of men and women who marched in front and behind their carriage as they held signs in the air. The mob soon encircled a large brick building to her left, where others were already throwing stones and crying out inaudible protests. Geirleif looked restless in the front seat. The driver flicked the reins, hurrying the carriage through.

Through the Fields of Everwind

With only a hint of light breaking through the thin joints of the lid above, Søren strained his eyes to see outside. A sudden clanking of a hammer echoed in his ears. Then the splintering of wood as an iron ring was pried up and over the barrel.

"Hold your ears and watch your head," Geoffrey said. Søren covered his ears as Geoffrey broke the lid with his hammer, removing it in several pieces. "Give me your hand."

Søren was lifted out of the barrel and into the sunlight. Squinting, he watched Geoffrey put a hammer away in a chest near the rear of the carriage.

"Come have a seat up front," he said as he reached a hand toward Søren. "We're far enough from Astford where we won't be seen by anyone."

Just as he was about to follow Geoffrey to the front, Søren instinctively reached down to feel the lens that hung around his neck. He caught his breath as he patted his chest. "Where is it?" His heart pounded in his ears. "What happened to it?

"What's the matter?" Geoffrey asked.

"M—my necklace!" exclaimed Søren. "It's gone!" He peered into the empty barrel. Nothing. He swept his eyes across the floor. "Where is it? I—I thought, thought I had—"

"Now, now." Geoffrey placed his hands on his shoulders. "Take it easy. I'm sure it's around here somewhere. Let's think for a minute."

Søren nodded quickly but looked in the barrel again. Geoffrey walked around the carriage, sweeping the floor with his eyes. He dropped to the road. "Maybe it fell off after you climbed out? It could have slipped through the floorboards of the carriage."

Søren peered down as Geoffrey crawled on his hands and knees, brushing his fingers through the thin grass that ran through the middle of the road. "Any luck?" Geoffrey called out.

Falling on his rear, Søren gazed at the grain of the wooden floor. He wanted to cry, but all he felt was anger. Why was he so careless?

Geoffrey climbed back onto the carriage. "Maybe you left it in the cellar. Is that possible?"

Søren only shook his head. It's the only thing from Eirún he still had. She would be so upset if she knew he lost it. "It's all I have. I c— can't lose it!" He balled up his fists.

Geoffrey wrapped an arm around his back; his big hand weighed heavy on his shoulder. At first, Søren shrunk down in bitterness, but when Geoffrey gently hugged him against his side, Søren felt a comfort he hadn't had since he was with Eirún. His clenched teeth softened to a quivering chin and his eyes blurred with tears.

"I'm so sorry," Geoffrey said. "We're too far out now, or else I'd turn back." He paused as he rubbed his short beard. "I have to get back to Everwind. But when we return, I'll send a letter to Burlan. Perhaps he can write back and let us know he still has it. Then we'll arrange a way for you to get it back. Does that sound okay?"

Søren slightly nodded. Geoffrey's accent was a little different than Burlan's or Henley's. It was similar but not as thick.

"I know how important it is to you," Geoffrey continued. "I'll do everything I can to get it back."

Søren nodded again.

Geoffrey climbed to the front of the carriage, and Søren wiped his tears and followed him.

"Not as cold as it has been," Geoffrey said as they both climbed into the carriage, but Søren barely heard him as he was busy looking off into the distance toward several large animals grazing in the grassy hills.

"What are those animals called?" he asked.

Geoffrey flicked the reins as the two horses began to trot forward. "Hillock Cattle, or sometimes we call them Dunbeasts."

"Dunbeast," Søren said to himself, taking notice of their long, rust-colored fur, which feathered in the wind. White horns grew from the sides of their head and curved upwards. Søren thought back to the monster he had ridden. Maybe that was a Dunbeast, only larger and uglier? But his memory was still somewhat fickle and hazy. He lifted his hand to his chest.

"Are you okay?" Geoffrey asked.

Lowering his hand, Søren took in a shivering breath. "My heart feels . . ." he began to say but trailed off, not able to find the correct words in his mind. Some late autumn flower must have been in bloom, for the wind carried thousands of white petals that swirled and danced through the cool breeze.

Geoffrey scrunched his eyebrows as if he was thinking too hard. "Your heart feels like what?"

"Like it's weak," Søren replied. "Or empty." He shook his head. "B—But that's not right. It just feels different."

"Does it hurt?"

"No."

"How long has it felt like this?"

"Ever since I woke up in the valley."

"Where the alphyn carried you?"

Søren nodded.

"Are you sure it wasn't a horse?"

Søren shook his head. "It was much bigger than a horse."

Geoffrey occasionally glanced at Søren, but he remained quiet as the carriage rocked along the dirt road. Dark birds soared high above in wide sweeping circles. Søren reached over and touched the hem of Geoffrey's jacket sleeve. "You aren't dressed like the others."

"The others?" Geoffrey asked.

"Mr. Henley and um . . ."

"Burlan?"

"Yes, Mr. Burlan. And there was another one, but I c—can't remember his name. But they wore strange clothes."

Geoffrey smiled. "You mean their tunics. Yes, I guess you would find that strange."

"Your clothes look like the ones at home," said Søren. "Are you from Daecland?"

Geoffrey laughed. "No, no, I'm not. This is my uniform, which the Daecish issued us to wear. But when I am not working, you'll also find me in a strange outfit too." He smiled and pointed to Søren. "But I imagine you won't find them any stranger than what you're wearing."

Søren examined his brown tunic and dark green pants, not really having noticed the clothes Henley had given him. He smacked his lips. "Do you have something to drink?"

Geoffrey handed him a leather skin. "It's all we've got 'til we come to the next inn."

When Søren pulled out the quark, he noticed the water seemed dark and smelled a little like sour bread. With a hint of cinnamon and clove. He took a sip but coughed it out.

"Sorry," Geoffrey said. "We don't really have anything else." He tilted his head. "I bet you'd like some tea, wouldn't you?"

Søren raised his eyes with a quick nod. He loved tea, at least whenever Eirún managed to get him a cup.

"I brought some leaves from home. When we get to the inn, I'll brew a pot. How does that sound?"

Søren nodded again.

"You sure do nod a lot," Geoffrey said with a chuckle.

The road slowly descended as the landscape opened before them, with patches of old-looking trees and scraggly bushes scattered along the hills. The sun sat just above the horizon with its broad rays covering the landscape in a golden yellow. A cool gentle wind sighed through the rippling tall grass. Geoffrey straightened his back and rubbed a hand through his hair. "So," he said with a yawn, "what do you think of Sunder?"

Søren thought for a moment. "It's warmer than home." He sniffed. "And it has a different smell."

"How's that?"

Although Søren couldn't keep his eyes off the landscape, he reached for his shirt as if he could still feel the necklace around his neck. His stomach sank, and he dropped his hand.

"How's that?" Geoffrey asked again.

Søren blinked a few times. "Um, back home smells—" he wrinkled his nose.

"Sour?" Geoffrey asked.

"No. More like the cellar."

"Like the cellar? You mean musty?"

"Yes. It smells musty at home."

"Daecland smells musty?"

"The orphanage always did."

Geoffrey laughed. "I'm sure not all of Daecland smells so bad."

"Maybe," Søren replied, "but I never said it was bad. I kind of miss the smell."

"Tell me about your mother, Eirún," Geoffrey then said. "What is she like?"

Søren kept silent for a moment; the only sound came from the turning of the wheels squeaking along the axles. A fluttering white petal, caught in the wind, landed on Søren's lap. He picked it up, pressing it between his finger and thumb. It released a pungent odor.

His last memory of her was when she was angry with him. He wished he could tell her he was sorry. "She was nice," was all he said.

"Just nice?" Geoffrey asked. "What does she look like?"

Søren slowly smiled. "She has long hair, but she always wears it up. Her eyes are greenish, maybe bluish. No, they're mostly green. She's t—tall, like all grownups. She always wears dresses with an apron." He paused to stop his chin from quivering. He felt the prisoner's words sink into his heart. That little thought that she didn't care about him. That she probably found some other boy to call her son. But as he did before, he blocked the thoughts out of his mind. "She was the first person that was ever nice to me. She would take care of me and t—teach me how to read. She told me I wasn't alone and that she wouldn't leave me . . . I hope she misses me."

"I'm sure she misses you very much."

The words of the prisoner suddenly overcame him, forcing him to face that terrible question. Did she really abandon him? "Do you think she's looking for me?"

Geoffrey swallowed and didn't reply right away. "I'm sure she'd give anything to find you." He pulled on the reins, bringing the carriage to a stop.

The sun sank below the horizon, and golden yellows deepened into pink and crimson. In the distance, a small cottage sat perched on a grassy hill with a thin trail of smoke rising from its chimney. Beside the cottage rested a single gray tree with heavy boughs, most of which had now lost their leaves, save the few branches which still held onto faint bands of red.

Søren looked at Geoffrey as their eyes met. "You have nothing to fear," Geoffrey said, lifting Søren's chin. "You'll be taken care of, and I'll do everything I can to get you back to your mother."

Søren didn't say anything, but the words meant more to him than Geoffrey could have known.

"All will be made right; you'll see."

With a growing smile, Søren remembered when Eirún once told him that. Watching Geoffrey as he smiled back, the prisoner's words came back to him once again, as if they were bent on making him think of nothing else. Was Geoffrey the man the prisoner warned him about? The one who would take him away and lead him into darkness? But Søren didn't take any heed to it. He really liked Geoffrey.

Over the course of the next three days, they lodged in small inns and encountered few travelers, but no one paid any particular interest in Søren. By evening on the third day, the towers of Everwind Castle peaked over the rolling hills. Søren looked on in awe.

"That looks like Folkbjörn!" he exclaimed. "Well, sort of."

"Much of what you see has been built by the Daecish," Geoffrey replied, "so I would imagine it does look more like home than Astford."

"But what about that thin one? The one that looks like a t— tower?"

"That's the Spire of Earlon."

"That looks different. Did your people build that one?"

"Sort of," he pointed to the city. "You see the castle?"

Søren nodded.

"My people originally built that about a thousand years ago. And when they did, they rebuilt the Spire of Earlon to match it. Of course, the two look nothing alike now that the castle has been renovated by the Daecish."

"If your people didn't build the tower, then who did?"

"Long before my people came here, there was another people who lived here. My ancestors called them the Sarig, but I don't know what they called themselves. They lived all over this land and built the most beautiful villages. One of those is where Everwind is now. The Spire's all that's left of what they built."

Søren straightened himself as a rush of excitement flooded his mind. He always loved stories, especially ones about people from the past, but he rarely heard any in Daecland. "There's no more?"

"Some say there are still some standing ruins in the Amyrran Forest, maybe in the mountains, but few people travel in there these days. I've never been, so I don't know."

"What are your people like?"

Geoffrey chuckled under his breath. "We're interesting, I would say. Certainly interesting." With his eyes on the road, he leaned toward Søren with a smile. "We love old stories and songs."

Søren's heart leaped. "D—Do you know any?"

"The most famous of our stories is probably Hælend's Ballad." A troubled expression came over his face.

"Can you tell it to me?"

Geoffrey swallowed. "Um, sure, but I must warn you that it's a little . . ." he thought for a minute. "It's a little strange and scary."

"That's okay."

"And it has to be sung." He looked at Søren with a half-smile. "And I'm not a very good singer."

"That's okay," Søren said again.

Geoffrey gave a hesitant cough. Then he began to sing the ballad:

Beneath the world's dark rim
At the dusk of kingdom's age
When land and sky grow dim
All men will give their wage

From waters deep and cold
From below, the earth and rock
Wyrms will arise from old
Alphyns awake and walk

Listen closely to their wail
Their pride and courage undone
It'll arrive on the blowing gale
After the setting sun

A man shall awaken
From seas of bitter cold
His guilt and shame be taken
Made pure in the shadow's fold

As Sunder's Bane, he'll come
With eyes as dark as shadow
Those in his fate succumb
Waters will cease their flow

Listen closely to their wail
Their pride and courage undone
It'll arrive on the blowing gale
After the setting sun

Upon an alphyn wild
The Bane shall lead the horde
All that man's defiled
Will fall beneath his sword

A feast for birds is given
The flesh of beasts and men
The warmth of the sun be hidden
All souls exposed within

Listen closely to their wail
Their pride and courage undone

It'll arrive on the blowing gale
After the setting sun

Dark and long the season
The days of great reckoning
Bitter tears from treason
Death arrives beckoning

The wage of all be paid
The desert spreads out wide
Life and tree will fade
None beneath will hide

Listen closely to their wail
Their pride and courage undone
It'll arrive on the blowing gale
After the setting sun

In the dark will arise a light
A dawn of joy is given
Many will raise with open eyes
Their treasons now forgiven

The sun will bring a chorus
For One has paid the cost
Anew will arise a forest
A fount put down by Theos

Listen closely to their cheers
For the Giver of life has won
He's wiped away all their tears
After the rising sun

When Geoffrey ended, he looked at Søren. "What did you think?"

"The story or your singing?"

Geoffrey laughed. "The story."

"I'm not sure I understood all of it, but it felt sad and, like you said, a little scary."

"It is a sad song, but there's hope in it as well."

"What kind of hope?"

"Hope of a restored world. And a resurrection after death. There are more stanzas at the end, but they've been lost now for many years."

Søren shifted his weight as the wooden seat beneath him made the back of his legs sore. "But why would someone write a song about so many scary things happening t—to his own people?"

Geoffrey gazed ahead. "Our people have always had a sense of judgment coming upon us."

"What do you mean?"

A sudden look fell upon Geoffrey's face. Søren always gave that look when he felt guilty. "We haven't always done what is right."

Søren was about to ask another question, but rounding a curve, the city came upon them. The stone wall seemed much higher now, but it still did little to hide the dominating buildings behind it.

"Would you like to stay with me and my family?" Geoffrey asked.

Søren pulled his eyes from the view. "What work will I do?" he asked.

"Work?" Geoffrey replied. "Goodness, no. You won't be doing any work. Lots of eating, maybe. And, of course, you may have to play with my little girl. She is only two, you know."

Søren said nothing, watching a bluebird dart in front of the carriage.

"My wife, Sarah, is a very good cook," he continued, patting his stomach. "She makes the best cobbler in all of Everwind. And I'm not just saying that because she's my wife. Really, it is."

"What is she like?" Søren asked.

"Well, how about we go home and see her. I'm sure she'd love to meet you."

Just the thought made Søren want to clap his hands and jump. "I'm sure I will like her, too."

At that moment, a northern gust brought a whiff of a foul smell. Søren thought it smelled familiar, but he couldn't recall where. Geoffrey sniffed the air and looked around earnestly as if he was expecting to find something. But the smell left as fast as it came. "Søren," he said. "Go ahead and put your hood on. And when we come to the gate, I want you to look down, all right? Don't look at the guards."

Søren nodded.

"In fact, if you ever happen to come across a guard from your country, don't ever talk to them and don't ever give them your name. Do you understand?"

Søren nodded, but Geoffrey's instructions made his stomach churn. "But what if they ask me my name?"

Geoffrey seemed puzzled for a moment. "What if we gave you another name?"

Søren wasn't sure what he thought about that.

"Just for now. A Sunderian name."

"Like what?"

"Well . . . How about Roane? That's a strong name."

"Roane," Søren said quietly. He liked the sound of it and nodded.

"Then Roane it is," Geoffrey replied.

The carriage drew up toward the Eastern Gate, which was two large wooden doors framed in iron, with one of the doors partly braced open. Geoffrey pulled out several papers from his jacket pocket. A Daecish officer stepped over and took the papers. He walked over to a small stand where several other officers huddled together. Søren couldn't help but notice all the buildings. Although some of them looked like home, others were smaller and had an older feel. More than anything, he couldn't believe how many people there were—carriages, shop stands, and crowds everywhere.

"Geoffrey Arkwright?" said the officer, coming back to the carriage.

"Yes, that's right," Geoffrey replied. "Is there something wrong?"

The officer drew a sword as three other guards and an officer surrounded the carriage. Søren slunk into the seat and covered his face, barely peeking through the cracks in his fingers.

"What is this about?" Geoffrey asked.

Two officers grabbed Geoffrey and bound his hands.

"I demand to know what this is about!" he shouted.

Søren shuddered as one of the officers wrapped his hand around his upper arm, sinking his fingers into his skin. He smelled sour, and his cheeks were spotted with small scars that made his face look like it was made of cheese.

"Keep your hands off him!" Geoffrey yelled.

"Under command of King Ónarr," said the other officer, "you have been found guilty of treason." He unrolled a scroll. "'As written in Article Forty-Three, all citizens of Sunder, participating, exchanging, or assisting in the Silent Hither are hereby declared traitors of Sunder and Daecland and have forfeited their rights as citizens.'"

Geoffrey's eyes grew wide. Søren wanted to cry out, but he couldn't say anything. Were they going to take Geoffrey away? Was he not going to go home with him?

The officer rolled up the scroll. "Put him on the carriage to Runevast."

"Let the boy go!" Geoffrey shouted, straining his arms against the soldier's grip.

The officer who held Søren by the arm looked at the other officer. "The boy?"

Leaning forward, the officer stared at Søren's face, and a shudder overcame him, which shifted into a look of disgust. He waved his hand. "Send him to the mines."

A Symphony of Sorts

Arnon sat on the edge of a marble fountain, carved into the shape of a great wolf. Water poured from its mouth, bubbling into the pool below. In his hands, he split a blade of grass down its length. Behind him ascended the steep gray towers and gables of Everwind Castle, with the main hall centered in the front, braced on either side by flying buttresses. Although it was called a castle, before all the recent renovations, it was technically the keep, and in the days when King Albern still ruled, lords and ladies, who clearly had nothing else better to do, would attend the hall several times a year, and try to marry off their sons and daughters to wealthier noble families. At least, that's what his father used to tell him.

"Am I late?"

Adelyne strolled toward him through the courtyard. The breeze gently blew strands of her hair across her face. Just above her left ear, she had braided in three white flowers. Arnon forced his mouth closed and tried his best to not stare. "I've only been here for a few minutes." He kept glancing at the ground.

She looked up at the heavy clouds. "We sure did meet early; we still have some time before we pass all these out." She partially opened a satchel, which hung at her side, revealing a stack of folded letters.

Arnon stood up, letting the blade of grass fall from his hand. "I'll get too nervous just sitting around in a tavern. I gotta walk around or do something to get my mind off of it." He pointed at her flowers. "Where did you get those?"

Adelyne reached her hand up to her hair as she softly grinned. "Iberis," she said. "They bloomed last week, but they don't last long, especially when it's this cold, so I wanted to wear them while I could."

Together, they walked around the courtyard along the stone paths, which went off in different directions—one toward the eastern tower and another finding its end at an entrance to the northern wall, lined with thin lancet windows, above which ran a low parapet. Scattered among the courtyard stood ancient broadleaf trees, mostly oak, chestnut, and elm; their heavy limbs were now empty, and their leaves littered the cobblestone and grass.

Ever since their meeting in his family home, he had spent just about every day with her. Granted, it hadn't been that long, but he had never spent this much time with a girl before, and he quickly forgot about the initial dislike he'd had for her when they first met. In fact, it was his time with her he began to look forward to the most. But he'd never actually admit that to her.

"It's pretty remarkable how easy it all was," Adelyne said.

"I know," Arnon replied. "Not only did we get the printing press going, but there was everything we needed down there." He kept his voice low. "Right down to the Daecish wax seals."

Adelyne laughed. "Like it was meant to be."

"I just hope we don't get caught setting these out tonight."

"At least we've got Murdock and Quinn helping. That should get it done quicker."

Arnon nodded but didn't respond.

Up ahead, several older men, 'scholars' as they were called, walked out of the Spire of Earlon, carrying with them a handful of the few books Sunder possessed. Arnon peered at the rising vine-laden tower. At its peak sat a great bell, which once rung during the celebration of the Creation of the World.

"You think they'll ever allow us to celebrate again?" Adelyne asked, motioning to the tower.

"The Daecish don't care for our stories. They say the celebrations are too costly and impractical. It seems most of the people are all right with that these days."

"What do you think?"

"I think it's a shame that people so easily give up what they once cherished all their lives." But not his father. He refused to sacrifice principle with popularity. To his dying day, he held the past, and Theos, with deep reverence.

"What do you think of the alphyn rumors?" she asked.

Alphyn rumors? With everything going on, that was the last thing on his mind. "I don't know. I heard someone saying it had to do with the smells, but Everwind's always smelled bad."

Adelyne laughed. "You know," she said, looking at the castle, "I used to come here as a little girl."

"Really?"

"My dad used to work in the castle, and I'd visit him with my mother. Sometimes we'd walk around the courtyard. It sure looks a lot different now." She paused for a moment, then pointed to an arched Daecish building, supported by numerous white columns. "There used to be a small grassy clearing where that building now stands. I'd always run and hide from her behind the hedges to see if she could find me. Those were always the best hiding spots."

"Where are your parents now?"

Adelyne glanced at her feet as they walked around a large marble statue of a horse raised on its hind legs. "My mother died about eight years ago. She caught a fever."

"I'm sorry."

"After that," she hesitated, "my father and I were forced to move back to the slums. Your family had already left. But Drake did whatever he could."

"Where's your father now?"

She was quiet for a moment. "I haven't seen him since the draft."

Arnon slowed his steps. He wasn't sure what to say. He thought back to their first meeting. The draft had happened barely a week before he had gotten there. Was that why she seemed so upset?

A gust of wind swirled several leaves into the air and across the stone pathway until they were caught in the grass. "That must be very hard," he said at last. "But you must hope that you'll see him again."

"Maybe."

There was a sorrowful look on her face, but there was also a hardness to it.

"What's his name?"

Adelyne bundled her arms. "Darragh," she said in a quiet voice.

Arnon thought that name sounded familiar, but he wasn't sure if he had ever met him or not. "And your family name?"

"We're part of the Morley clan."

"Adelyne Morley," he said to himself.

"What about you?" she asked. "Do you have any other family in Everwind?"

"Not really. Drake's a second cousin or something like that."

"What?" Adelyne said with raised eyebrows. "He's a Greystrom?"

"You didn't know that?"

"No!" She laughed. "I can't believe it." She pulled her hair back, which had blown across her face.

"Why'd he never tell me?"

"Not sure. I guess he doesn't really announce it." He thought of his mother and sisters. He knew Fleta could take care of herself, but he really hoped Hazel was doing all right. He unconsciously pulled out the yellow owl from his outer jerkin pocket and fiddled with it in his hand.

"What's that for?" she asked.

Arnon looked up at her.

"That," she said, pointing to his hand. "I saw you grab it out of the alley the other day."

"Oh," he said. "This was from a game I used to play with my youngest sister, Hazel." He suddenly felt a little childish. "It's not a very good game. We just made it up one day."

"Well, I'm sure you play fairly, 'cause she's how old?"

"She's six," Arnon replied, curling up just the corner of his mouth, "but if anyone needs to learn how to play fair, it's her."

"She's your sister," Adelyne smirked, "you should always let her win."

"Don't worry, I do."

Approaching the far eastern side of the courtyard, the wind began to die down, and the dark clouds looked as if they were going to sink to the earth. Two men walked in their direction from around the corner of a castle tower. One of them looked Adelyne up and down. Arnon surprised himself when he fixed the man with a hard stare.

Adelyne glanced over her shoulder at Arnon, and he quickly straightened his face. She faced forward again, but he could tell she was smiling.

How embarrassing.

Ahead, Merchant Street grew busy with a dark mass of crowds, apparently heading toward the Barrow Theater—a large circular building built of brown brick. It even had glass windows.

"I wonder what's going on there," Adelyne asked.

"I'm not sure, but maybe we should head the other direction." He barely heard his own words.

"I agree," she said, as they both turned the other way. "You know," she continued, "you shouldn't go by your name anymore."

"I haven't given my family name since I've been here. Wesley already warned me about that."

"I don't just mean your clan name," she said. "Your first name as well. It isn't very common, you know?"

"What name would you suggest?"

Adelyne tapped her pursed lips. "How about Hubert?"

"Hubert? That sounds like a horrible—"

"Careful. I had a dog named Hubert."

"You thought of a dog's name for me?" He opened his mouth and scrunched his eyebrows. "And who names a dog anyway?"

Adelyne burst into laughter. Her crystal blue eyes shimmered in the outside light. Did she look this pretty earlier today? Maybe it was the clouds. His stomach began to flutter.

"I did! And it was a good name."

"I don't know."

"If you don't like it, then you think of a better one."

Arnon chuckled. "If Hubert's my only option, I'll have to." The wind picked up again. Brown leaves fell from the trees like slow and steady rain. Arnon shivered as an oncoming dark winter choked out the last couple of weeks of autumn. The gust left as soon as it came, and Arnon peered south. "You know, I still haven't seen Wesley, have you?"

"I haven't, now that you mention it."

Arnon thought for a while. "I should go ask Drake if he's seen him. Besides, Geoffrey should've been back by yesterday. Maybe he's at the tavern. What about the lockbox? You get that open yet?"

"Still working on it. I got the tools, but it's well made. It'll take a few picks and a lot of patience to crack it open."

"Sounds like whatever's inside may be worth it, then."

* * *

Inside City Hall, Eilívur stood by a large window, through which the overcast sky brought in the only light. He watched one of the puniest Sunderians he had ever seen stumble through the shadows. His thin wrists were bound in chain, his arms held firmly by two Daecish soldiers. His eyes were so heavy they seemed to sag into his dimwitted-looking face. Even his hair stuck out in a wild mess. Was this Wesley Gladestone really one of the leaders of the Silent Hither?

"Please," said Eilívur, trying not to chuckle. "Have a seat." He motioned to an empty chair in front of the desk.

Wesley sat down as the wood creaked beneath him.

"Commander Veurðr tells me that you are willing to work with us," Eilívur said as he sat down and clasped his hands together on his chest. "Yet, you require your past crimes to be pardoned, am I correct?"

"That is correct, sire."

"Now Commander Veurðr has tried, on more than one occasion, to persuade me to just force the information out of you before we either have you executed or drafted."

Wesley gave no expression.

Eilívur rested a finger on his cheek. "But that is not the way I do things. No, Mr. Gladestone, I think we can work something out."

A slight glint came across Wesley's eyes. "Sire, I'm willing to do whatever you ask."

Eilívur straightened himself and looked hard at Wesley. "I am willing to forgive your past crimes, but you must do two things. First, tell me all you know. Who are the active Dark Horses? Where do they meet? Second, I want you to go back, as their leader, and report to us every week their current activities."

Wesley's leg visibly twitched. "You want me to go back as a spy, sire?"

"Yes."

"But, if I told you everything I knew, then you could just go in right now and end it. Why would I need to continue?"

"Mr. Gladestone, you know a great deal, no doubt. But do you know everything?"

"What do you mean?"

"Can you tell me exactly how many people have joined the Silent Hither? Can you tell me where they live? Do you know how the movement is growing in Llynhithe, Denhurst, or Astford?"

"Well, not entirely, but I do know a lot."

"Exactly. If I raid the Dark Horses now, others will join again. It's happened before. I'm sure you remember Fellhouse Cellar?"

Wesley looked down.

"If I am going to act," Eilívur continued, "I mean to end it once and for all. Commander Veurðr informed me that you are in contact with Dark Horses in other cities. I need you to keep up communications with them and keep me updated once a week. I'll also need you to update me on numbers, plans, anything you can on the movement here in Everwind." He paused. "You look confused."

"It's just," Wesley replied. "I ain't no spy. I can tell you what I know, but I'm not sure I can—"

"This is your only choice. If you value your freedom, this is my offer."

"What if I get caught?"

"That'll be your concern, not ours."

There followed a short silence until Wesley gave a hesitant nod. "I'll do all I can."

"Good," Eilívur said, standing up. "Oh, and one more thing."

"Yes, sire?"

"What do you know of an Arnon Greystrom?"

Wesley swallowed, and his face paled. "Arnon, sire?"

Eilívur raised his eyebrows. "You do know who Arnon is, correct?"

"Yes, sire, I do."

"Do you know where he is?"

"Not at the moment."

"But you have seen him here? In Everwind?"

Wesley looked up at the soldiers standing behind Eilívur. He barely nodded.

"We have a warrant out for his arrest."

"For what crime?"

Eilívur planted his hands down on the desk. For a moment, the sun peeked from behind the clouds and sent a ray of light into the room. Tiny specks of dust hovered in front of Wesley's weathered face. "On suspicion for the murder of four men—a sergeant, two lieutenants, and one commander."

Wesley's focus wandered away as if he was lost in thought.

"The look on your face tells me you know something."

Wesley didn't respond.

"I have good reason to believe Arnon is guilty." Eilívur hardened his tone. "If you know something, I expect you to tell me."

"Arnon," he began to say slowly, "did mention to one of our men about killing some Daecish soldiers. After they killed his father."

Eilívur leaned back. He knew it. "Tell me, what does he look like? I'll need a description for our investigations."

Wesley's eyes danced in thought. "Dark brown hair."

"How long?"

"Down to his neck, maybe?"

"What does he wear?"

"Jerkins, mostly."

"His eyes? How tall is he?"

Wesley shrugged and raised his hand as if to measure Arnon's height. He seemed about average. "He has brown eyes."

Eilívur carped under his breath. This wasn't helpful at all. "That sounds like every other Sunderian in Everwind."

"I don't know what else to say."

Wesley must be hiding something. Maybe he was trying to make it vague on purpose. "Does he have any unique features? A scar? Something?"

"Not that I know of."

Wesley must certainly be lying. "Fine. As soon as you see Arnon or learn of his whereabouts, I trust you'll inform me."

Wesley nodded.

"Good." He cleared his throat and motioned for the soldiers to unshackle Wesley. "You are free to go, but don't try anything foolish. I will see you in a week. Now, if you'll excuse me, I have a symphony to attend."

Outside, Eilívur took in a long breath, feeling the crispness of the cold air in his lungs. Was Arnon really worth all the attention? It seems the boy was only protecting his family. And wouldn't he have done the same thing? Across the street, a mother held the hands of two of her children as they walked past the Tea House. A third child tarried behind them, kicking a stone along the ground. Eilívur scowled. It wasn't just about the death of his brother. Arnon had unlawfully killed four men. He deserved the death penalty.

Eilívur hurried down the steps and began the long trek across the city.

By the time he made it to the Barrow Theater, he found himself entangled in a mass of merchants and self-proclaimed lords, all dressed in newly acquired black coats and top hats. Seeing several other Daecish soldiers near the theater entrance, Eilívur walked over.

Men swarmed from all directions, displaying their new wardrobes with great pride. They lifted their chins high and twisted their freshly grown mustaches. Smoke billowed from their pipes while they bowed at the feet of women arrayed in multi-layered dresses of pastel colors.

"They must feel like true Daecish lords now," said a young soldier standing next to Eilívur.

"I'm sure they do," he said. "But what you wear does not define who you are."

The doors of the theater swung open, and the crowds began to tighten around the entrance. Eilívur followed after them.

Inside, the men and women gasped. A renovation from Daecland had brought jewels, stonework, and an endless amount of décor embedded into the vaulted ceiling. Bows and ribbons twirled around the handrails and banisters. Glassworks of spectacular craftsmanship were displayed on every table. Clocks of many shapes and sizes chimed and rang along the walls. Along the floor stretched a rich, red carpet. At the center of the gallery, on a large stone pedestal, sat the model of a steam engine.

Everyone swarmed as they eyed and contemplated the gadgets and decorations. Soon a man in a black suit and white gloves walked over and stood in the center of the gallery. Despite his short stature, he held his chin high. "Ladies and gentlemen!" he said in a raised voice. "If you would please find your seats. Our symphony will begin shortly!"

The crowd reluctantly parted from their newfound idols and dispersed down two rows of stairs on either side of the far end of the gallery. Eilívur waited for the crowd to make their way to the theater before following. He found a place to stand at the bottom of one of the stairways. Gunnar arrived and stood beside him.

"Commander Veurðr," said Eilívur, giving a nod. "I didn't expect to see your presence in such a madhouse as this."

Gunnar crossed his arms. "A madhouse it is, but I wouldn't want to miss it."

"Why's that?"

"Well, it isn't every day you get to see a look of such wonder among people." He waved his hand around the room. "This is all new to them."

Eilívur sighed. "It probably won't last, though."

"You heard the rumors, too, then?"

"Yesterday. Norfrost plans on decreasing our pay by as much as thirty percent." He gazed across the crowd as they all took their seats; their faces gleamed, and their voices rang shrill with laughter. "And King Ónarr owes more debt than this entire city's worth."

"A Colonel just came in this morning from Runevast," said Gunnar. "Said he heard rumors that Daecland is in a rough state—something about the mining industry struggling, rise in coal prices. Maybe that's why they're cutting pay?"

"Let's hope they're just rumors. All our money's in coal mines, and we've got nothing to show for it yet."

Gunnar laughed through his nose. "You think when we invaded Sunder, we got too ahead of ourselves?"

"Perhaps," Eilívur replied as he leaned his shoulder against the wall. "Cost too much and gave too little reward. But that's all politics, and I don't care to go there. What I do know is that if Daecland is hurting, then Sunder will hurt too, and apparently, it's going to start with our pay decrease."

"What do they expect us to do? Find other work as well?"

"We'll do whatever we have to, but things will get ugly. This economy went up on a dream that never happened. We may lose thirty percent, but if these rumors are true, everyone in this room will be in financial ruin one day."

There was a long silence as the symphony began to play. Oboes and flutes accompanied by a strumming harp filled the room with a sense of warmth and life—a feeling reminiscent of taking in the first scent of a flowering garden on an early spring day. Ironic, given the current situation.

"What do you think this will mean for us in the long run?" Gunnar asked at last.

Eilívur scrapped a piece of mud from his boot onto the carpet. "I'm not sure what to think right now."

Thus Wrought Death and Ruin

The following dawn, the rising sun brought a dull light into the Northern District as Eilívur peered out of the frost-etched window of his home. Thin traces of snow lined the rooftops and dark alleyways, and frozen puddles dotted across the road.

Eilívur knew the frost would have already arrived in Daecland, but not in this forsaken place. Wasn't it supposed to still be autumn? Gazing at the cool ashes in his fireplace, he shivered. The fires in that thing never kept him very warm; all the heat went straight up the flue. In his childhood country home, his family had a wood-burning stove that kept the whole house warm, even in the coldest months. But Norfrost was even better. About six years after he transferred from the Nautical Armada to the Army, he was put into military housing—tiny townhomes crammed side-by-side and one on top of the other, like fine brickwork. They were all even painted that same dull, liver red, outlined in cheap white trim. But for every half-dozen homes or so, a single boiler was installed, which sent heat through vents into every room. Eilívur sighed. He only got to enjoy it for four months before he had been sent to this undeveloped frontier.

Someone pounded on Eilívur's door. Buttoning the top of his black shirt, he threw on his blue overcoat and hurried to the door and opened it.

Gunnar stood before him, his face tight. "Eilívur," he said. "Grab your sword."

Marching down Merchants Street, Eilívur made sure to keep his distance from a gathering crowd who gazed at the owner of a dyer's shop, standing in his front doorway. His face grimaced a burning red as a letter fell from his hand. He slammed his shop door shut and locked it from within. A sudden wail echoed from another shop across the street. Shouts erupted from the other direction.

Eilívur glanced over his shoulder to the two squadrons following him. "Bolts in the crossbows!" he shouted. Beside him, Gunnar kept up his pace with a stern expression. "How many are at the treasury?"

Gunnar wiped his nose. "Mobs or soldiers?"

"Soldiers."

"Don't know. Half a dozen?"

Eilívur grunted. "They'll be dead before we get there."

To his left came the sound of shattering glass and a shriek, which sounded more painful than angry. On the sidewalk to his right, a man with curly black hair frantically reached out his arms toward an older man. The old man paced back and forth in a torn black tailcoat. Gripping his hair in his hands, the pacing man shouted inaudible words to himself, all the while cackling hysterically.

"Mr. Lester!" the first man shouted. "Please control yourself!"

Eilívur and Gunnar peered at one another.

Lester looked up, and his and Eilívur's eyes met. "You!" He sneered, walking in their direction. He threw a crumpled letter to the ground. "You've brought this upon us!" He kept up his pace beside Gunnar and jabbed his finger. Claw marks marred his face, and his eyes were a wild mess. "You can't just call in our loans!"

"Back off, Lester," Eilívur replied. "We're doing everything we can!"

Lester's wrinkled face twisted into a scowl as he raised back his hand. Gunnar let a fist loose and knocked Lester to the ground.

"Bind him!" Eilívur shouted. "Keep him off the streets!"

Continuing on, crowds hurried in and out of alleyways. The treasury wasn't far now. "Have you read the letters yet?"

"Only briefly," Gunnar replied. "But it seems the rumors are true. Debts called in, funding temporarily ceased. They even added a tariff to all imports."

"What on earth possessed King Ónarr to send a letter to every merchant?" Heat rose in his face. "Was he trying to bring ruin?"

"Your guess is as good as mine."

Turning a corner, one of the soldiers behind shouted something, but his voice was drowned in a storming sea of men and women swarming the treasury building. Pressing against its outer wall, men threw stones through a large window.

"Cease your entry!" the guards hollered out from inside. "Cease, or we will use force!"

The crowd continued to press forward until a group of men laid their tailcoat jackets over the broken glass. Eilívur's pulse throbbed in his neck as the crowd began to crawl through. The guards on the inside brought down their swords as they hacked at the heads and shoulders of the men, but like a horde blind with fury, the crowd continued to press through until the window clogged with a bloody heap of lifeless bodies.

The true nature of the Sunderian man was coming out. Wild beasts cloaked in gentlemen's clothing. Eilívur saw it coming all along.

He ordered the squadrons to surround the mob. Shields were braced against their chests with crossbows pointed forward. The mob quickly turned and began throwing stones in their direction. He nodded to Gunnar.

"Attack!" Gunnar shouted to their men.

* * *

Sarah peered through her window, holding Lilly's hand. Small crowds moved up and down the streets and alleyways. Several soldiers scampered in uncertain directions, following the crowds as they shifted from one building to another.

"What's going on?" Sarah asked herself. She turned to Lilly. "And where's your father? He should've been back two days ago."

Lilly looked up but said nothing.

Walking toward the wooden table, Sarah exhaled several quick breaths as she braced her hands beneath her belly and eased herself into the chair. Lilly was now crawling beneath the table with a small wooden horse in her hands. Sarah glanced down and smiled, remembering how many blocks of wood it took Geoffrey to finally carve one out last summer.

The house lay quiet, save the neighing of Lilly, scampering her horse across the floor. The brick oven sat cold and barely used, with a small stack of dishes that still needed cleaning. Unable to shake the loneliness that came over her, Sarah continually tapped her finger on the table and stirred in her seat, glancing toward the window. She forced her eyes back to the table and stared at a half-woven basket.

Why hasn't he come back yet? He didn't come home and not tell her, did he? A sudden thought hit her like a punch to the heart. Was he cheating on her? It was because she was overweight and pregnant, wasn't it? She tried to think about every girl they knew, wondering if he'd ever glanced at them before. Of course he had. Soon, she convinced herself that he was secretly in love with one of them. That's probably why he said he liked to go to the tavern so much. She felt sick. But then, in a strange sort of way, she laughed and cried at the same time. She had no reason to think such foolish things. Her mind did this on occasion when she was with child. It was as if an insecure version of herself had momentarily taken over, yet there was nothing she could do about it.

With a deep breath, she knew he would never cheat on her. His struggles were of a different kind. And although he had changed over the years, he wasn't perfect, but it wasn't perfection she wanted from him. It was honesty and the willingness to fight temptations in order to do what was right. And he was better at that than any other man she knew.

Pulling the basket toward her, she half-heartedly weaved the dried stems through one another. But just as she started, she shoved the basket away and looked one last time through the window. He still should have been back by now. She stood up, pushed her chair back, and called for Lilly.

She opened the front door and peered outside. Several soldiers headed away through the alleyways, following the small crowds eastward. Sarah put a hand to her mouth when she noticed a thick black smoke rise in the distance ahead. Grabbing a scarf, she wrapped it around her neck, and taking Lilly's hand, she headed toward City Hall.

* * *

Looking down from the balcony of his one-room lodge, Barnaby sat in his chair, watching as Sarah and her daughter Lilly hurried along the road. Lilly tugged at her mother's hand as they walked up the stairs to City Hall and disappeared inside. It was pointless. Geoffrey wasn't there. Sent to the mines. Drafted. Maybe even executed. Who knew?

Stepping into the silent room, a bottle of whiskey hung loosely in Barnaby's right hand. His eyes weighed heavy, and his posture sunk low. Thin wisps of smoke flowed from the blown-out candle on his desk, littered with many papers. On the top of a short stack laid a letter he received that morning. He still couldn't wrap his mind around all the consequences that would soon follow. But he didn't want to.

Beside the letter sat a coiled rope. Not too long ago, he liked to fancy the idea of one day living in Daecland. Sometimes that was why he kept papers out on his desk. That seemed like a Daecish thing to do. Diplomats and scholars. They were all so smart.

Outside, several small birds circled around one of the spire towers of City Hall; the black flags of Daecland fluttered in the wind. The clouds hung low, moving swiftly from the west. Barnaby closed his eyes, and a shaking sigh escaped his mouth. He threw back the bottle and took a long draught; the sweet notes of oak and vanilla now tasted bitter to his tongue and soul. Above his desk, he stared at the rope until the room around him began to fade in shadow. His heart raced and his fingertips went numb.

How long he fixed his eyes upon the rope, he didn't really know, but before he knew it, he was already standing on a chair and wrapping it around a crossbeam fastened to the arched wooden ceiling. His vision blurred, and his head felt light as he tied a crude snare on the hanging end of the rope; his eyes blankly stared into the world beyond his balcony.

As he slipped the snare around his neck, Sarah stumbled back out of City Hall with two guards following behind. The last thing he heard was her deep-throated cry before he kicked the chair over.

The Lens

E gbert peered through the crack of his bedroom door, hoping Henley was still in his room on the other end of the dark hallway. He inched the door closed and walked over, sitting at a small table, where a low-lit candle, mostly melted to its base, gave the only light.

From his pocket, he pulled out the leather cord, the lens dangling from its end. His eyes went wide as he gently set it on the table. "So pretty," he said to himself in a slow drawl. He tapped the glass end with his finger, poking it like an insect, wondering what it might do. Then, by some wicked irony, he glanced at the edge of the table, where it butted up against the daub wall. A black beetle crawled across the wooden top—its hard-shelled body lightly bounced as it made its way over each wooden grain. Egbert quickly hammered the beetle with the lens until only a creamy smudge remained on the table. Wiping drool from his mouth, he roared a deep-bellied laugh.

A knock came from the door, and Henley stepped in.

"Would you like some supper?" he asked.

Egbert stumbled out of his seat, trying to conceal the lens.

"Egbert," he said sternly. "Where did you get that?"

"Nowhere," Egbert said, trying to stand straight.

"Egbert," Henley repeated, taking a step forward.

Egbert looked down with his shoulders quivering. "I—I jus' wanted to touch it," he said. "I didn't steal it. Promise!"

"Then how did you get it?"

Egbert sniffed hard and wiped his nose, his other hand holding the lens behind his back. "I's walking 'round, and I saw you and Burlan

and that man putting Søren in a carriage, and this fell to the ground."
He lifted his hand to show Henley the lens. The two ends of the leather
cord were undone.

Henley crossed his arms. "You were walking at sunrise? Egbert,
you are never up that early."

Truly he never did wake up that early. But maybe he did? He
couldn't remember. "I was. I was."

"You were spying on us, weren't you? You know that is a bad thing
to do."

Egbert burst into a sob. It was a real sob, one full of sorrow and
guilt. He didn't mean to steal the lens. It was just so pretty. And why
did he kill that poor beetle? "I's sorry," he managed to get out through
his wheezing. "I didn't mean to. I mean, I mean, I did, but I's sorry! I
just wanted to touch it."

"It's all right," Henley waved a hand. "But I think it's time to give
it back now." Henley took another step toward Egbert and reached his
hand out.

Egbert closed his hand around the lens. "Give it back?" he asked.
"Now? But—but I just—" It was so shiny and round.

"It ain't yours, Egbert. It's Søren's, and we got to get it back to
him. Can you help me with that? You said you were sorry."

Egbert closed his eyes, his lips curled down in a deep frown.
Henley just wanted it for himself. "I just want it," he retorted. "I found
the boy, and I want to keep it!"

Henley took in a deep breath. "Egbert." He took another step.
"You can't keep it. That ain't right. Now give it here."

Egbert gritted his teeth. What gave Henley the right to take the
lens? Was it because they thought he was stupid? Some dolt? "No,
Henley!" he bellowed. "You always talk to me like I's stupid. You never
appreciate me. Not you, not Burlan. And all I want is to keep this here
lens. Since I found that boy, I get to."

Henley scowled. "You're not yourself. Now you just give it back!"

He grabbed at the lens as Egbert pulled back. Heat rushed into Egbert's head, and everything blurred. Before he knew it, he was grappling with Henley as he pulled at his collar. "No!" Egbert cried out. "No!"

"It's okay," Henley shouted as he went to back off, but Egbert grabbed at his throat with his other hand, dropping the lens to the floor.

"Egbert!" Henley cried. "What—What are you doing!"

Now gripping both hands around his neck, Egbert cried out, shaking Henley's shoulders as his head flung back and forth. "You're just a stupid beetle!"

Henley gasped, helplessly trying to pry Egbert's hands away.

Egbert threw Henley's head back and forth until there was a snap. With clenched teeth and foam spitting out of his mouth, he continued to shake until Henley's body went limp and his head hung loose. His eyes were wide and still. Egbert let go, and Henley fell over onto the table and slid to the ground.

Egbert took a step back, shaking his head. What had he done? Not Henley. He loved Henley. "Henley," he whispered. "I's sorry. I didn't mean it!" He bent down and laid a hand on Henley's back. "Please, Henley. Please get back up."

Weeping, he shook Henley's shoulder as a throbbing ache twisted through his chest. For a second, he found it hard to breathe. He nudged Henley's shoulder and let out a whimper, snorting in the fluids which dripped from his nose.

Henley didn't move, and Egbert couldn't bear to look at him anymore. Forcing his eyes away, he spotted the lens lying on the floor. He looked back at Henley, then to the lens again. He grabbed it and stuffed it into his pocket. No one needed to know he had it. But poor Henley. And what would Burlan have to say? Just the thought terrified him. He'd probably take away his dinner, maybe even breakfast. He'd better get a bite before Burlan got back home. With a great heave, he climbed to his feet, pulled up his sagging trousers, and left the room.

The Sundering of the Arkwrights

Adelyne hurried alongside Murdock as they headed to Birchton. For such a thickset man, she had a hard time keeping up with him. Distant shouts arose from the east. The day was dark; clouds continued to lower, threatening to bring freezing rain. The western wind shifted as a gust rushed across the street, bringing with it a haze and the thick odor of smoke.

"Not sure I expected the people to react so quickly," Murdock said in his deep voice.

"Or violently," added Adelyne.

"I sure hope this turns to our favor. The way the merchants are acting, it'd make you think the Day of Reckoning was here."

"Maybe it is."

"Don't tease too much about that," Murdock replied, scratching at his head through his dark red hair.

"You might be right."

"I wasn't teasing." She firmly believed that she feared the end more than anyone else. The judgment of Hælend's Ballad afflicted her with a constant throbbing sickness. At times it felt subtle, but it never truly went away. "Quinn said he saw more carriages outside the city this morning."

"They gonna draft in the middle of this? Ain't that a hoot."

"We'll see."

"Let's hurry up. Morgan's waiting for us in Birchton, and I don't want to stay in these streets any longer than I have to." He looked behind him as if he thought someone was following. "I still can't believe Geoffrey ain't back yet. Two days late. Can't be good. And where's Wesley been? He left town or something?"

Adelyne suddenly stopped, peering at a scroll nailed to a lantern post.

"What's it say?" he asked.

"Arnon Greystrom," she said as a knot twisted in her stomach. "Wanted on account of murder."

"Arnon? How'd he get himself in this mess?"

Adelyne didn't say anything. Distant shouts suddenly grew louder.

"You hear that?" he asked.

She gave a terse nod, and they both continued on with a quickened pace. But a loud cry to their left stopped them. On the steps of City Hall sat a woman on her knees. A little girl stood beside her, sobbing as she rubbed her eyes. Two Daecish soldiers stood at the top of the steps, arguing with one another. Glancing at Murdock, Adelyne headed across the street toward the woman.

"Miss," said Adelyne, gently laying a hand on her back as she knelt beside her. The woman seemed not to notice as she clenched her stomach in pain. She looked as if she was ready to give birth. "Are you all right?"

Murdock stood a short distance away, hesitantly eyeing the soldiers—their argument distracting them from their presence. The shouting crowds in the distance continued to draw nearer.

"Stay clear!" came the sudden shout of one of the soldiers, now turning from his counterpart. "This woman is under arrest!"

"Mama!" the little girl cried out.

"On what charge?" bellowed Murdock.

"For conspiring in the Silent Hither! Now back away!" The soldier stomped down the steps, carrying a set of iron cuffs in his hands. Adelyne took a step back as the other soldier looked sympathetically at the little girl.

The woman cried out in pain as she continued to grip her belly. "They took my husband!" She wept. "They took Geoffrey!"

Murdock and Adelyne turned and glared at one another. The soldier with the cuffs stood by the woman and turned to the other soldier. "Grab that wailing girl!" he said.

"Please!" the woman continued. She turned and grabbed hold of the little girl. "Please don't take me from my baby!"

Murdock swelled his barrel chest. He stepped up toward the soldier with the cuffs. "You'd dare take this mother from her child?"

The soldier gave Murdock a sharp glare, but the woman broke out in another scream, gripping her stomach again. At that moment, echoing shouts caught everyone's attention. Marching between the buildings and through the alleyways, a crowd approached with a loud chant, but their words were inaudible. A smaller band broke off from the crowd and began throwing rocks through the large window of the Tea House. One man kicked the door down, and the others followed inside. The soldier tossed his cuffs to the other one and ran up the steps. "I'm getting reinforcements," he shouted. "Arrest her and get them out of here!" He disappeared into City Hall.

Loud commands echoed from inside, and the remaining soldier held the cuffs loosely in his hand, looking at the woman, desperation rising in his large eyes. He frantically glanced back at the front entrance, then to the oncoming crowd. Cursing at himself, he ran down the stairs, dropped the cuffs, and approached Murdock. "I don't have it in me to arrest her. You'll have to hit me," he said.

Murdock cocked an eyebrow, and Adelyne's jaw dropped, but the guard's expression remained stern and unchanging.

"What?" Murdock asked.

"It can't look like I just let her go." The guard glanced back up the steps. "Now! But make sure you hit me hard; very hard."

Murdock only stood there. After glancing back to the crowd, Adelyne rolled her eyes and stepped in front of Murdock. With a clenched fist, she struck the Daecish guard just above the ear. Murdock startled as the guard fell over with a thud.

"You just punched a Daecish—"

"Let's get out of here!" Adelyne yelled. "She's in labor!" She picked up the little girl, who screamed and flung her little arms at her.

"You can't be serious." Murdock picked up the woman in his arms as they both ran south.

"We need to get to Drake's tavern!"

The oncoming crowds had now flooded the streets. "No more Ónarr!" some cried out. "End the Tariff!" others shouted.

Before they knew it, Adelyne and Murdock were caught within the throngs. Few were willing to allow Adelyne through, and she soon lost sight of Murdock. The little girl gripped onto Adelyne, too afraid to open her eyes.

"Murdock!" Adelyne yelled, but her voice was drowned in the sea of roaring commotion.

She bumped into a grim-faced man with a cleft lip and greasy hair. He turned and gave her a sneer. Turning her gaze away, she continued to struggle forward while the little girl cried into her neck.

Making no ground, Adelyne's frustration sent a heatwave through her. She tensed her shoulders and took a deep breath. With narrowed eyes, she mustered her strength and heaved through, bumping and shoving men and woman out of the way. "Move!" she hollered out.

Several cursed at her, but she ignored their empty threats.

At last, she crossed south of the Western Road and came into the Southern District. There, the crowds began to thin as they continued marching northward. Adelyne looked around but saw no signs of Murdock. Holding on to the girl tightly, she raced to the tavern.

Rushing to the back entrance, she pounded on the door. Drake swung it open, motioning for her to hurry. There in the kitchen, the woman lay over a cot that had been laid out. Murdock, Morgan, and Bell knelt beside her.

"What's your name?" asked Morgan, holding the woman's hand. With clenched teeth, she gripped his hand and pushed out deep, quick breaths.

"S—Sarah," she said. Her lips and chin trembled as she closed her tearing eyes.

The look of pain on her face made Adelyne feel nauseous. Why would any woman want to go through that?

"They—" Sarah gasped for air, then tensed her body so hard her face turned purple. "They took my husband from me!"

"Sarah," said Bell, running a hand down her cheek. "My name is Bell. Now don't you worry, we're gonna take care of you. But right now, we need you to breathe and push, all right?"

"Mama!" came the sudden cry of the little girl, squirming to get out of Adelyne's grip.

"It's all right, it's all right," said Drake, coming to stand between the girl and Sarah. "Your mother's gonna be fine. What's your name?"

The girl curled out her bottom lip with a heavy pout. "Lilly."

"Lilly." Drake smiled. "Your mother is about to have a baby. Why don't you come into the tavern with me and get you a nice, warm glass of milk?"

Lilly drew a shaking breath from her little lungs and nodded.

Carrying her through the kitchen door, Adelyne followed Drake into the empty tavern, with Morgan following after.

"Not a soul's been in here today," said Drake glancing back. "Since these riots broke out."

"I thought you were in Birchton?" Adelyne asked Morgan.

"I was," Morgan replied. "At least, for a short time."

"What happened?"

Morgan eyed Drake for a moment. "Birchton was peaceful enough, but mobs were marching through to storm the Northern District walls. Drake got me out before I got caught up in the riots, or worse, clubbed to death."

"Is there any sign of people wanting to join the Silent Hither?"

"It's far too early to tell," spoke up Drake. "Everyone's still reacting. They just want their money."

"I've heard mixed things," Morgan added as he rested his arm on a stack of crates. "Some spoke well of the Silent Hither, but others were blaming it."

Adelyne stared at Morgan. Why would they blame it? "Do you think they know we wrote the letters?"

"No, they believe them all right. They just think the Silent Hither's to blame."

"But how could they—"

"Maybe 'cause the merchants never liked us, to begin with," Morgan suggested with a brief chuckle.

"Everyone's just reacting," interrupted Drake. "Folk's gonna blame anyone they can right now. We got to just wait it out 'til things cool off. I'm stiff hopeful, and so should the both of you."

Adelyne wasn't so sure. What if this backfired on them? What if everyone turned against the Silent Hither rather than join it? She clamped her lips closed. Glancing at the cellar door, she startled. Arnon leaned against the wall with his arms crossed. He looked as if he was lost in his own thoughts.

She let Lilly down, who reached for Drake's hand as he took her over to a tall wooden shelf lined with drinks and sauces. On the bottom rack were several corked bottles of milk. Morgan walked back into the kitchen.

"You two," said Drake, pointing a finger. "Don't stay out here long. Best kept secret, this place. Don't want to ruin it. Go back to the kitchen or down to the cellar."

"On our way out now, Drake," replied Adelyne. She turned back to Arnon. She knew he was aware of their presence, but he looked down, almost solemnly. Did he really murder people? He didn't look like that kind of a person. "How's the Southern Squalor?" she asked.

Arnon shifted his eyes up at her. "Rioting was too much to stay for long."

Rioting. It was terrifying to think that, in a way, she started this when she found the letter. What if innocent people died? Would she be guilty? No. Thinking like that would only drive her mad. "That's Geoffrey's wife in there, isn't it?"

"That's what Drake said."

"She said they took him. I wonder where?"

Arnon squinted. "I don't know."

For a moment, they both stood silent as they uneasily listened to another loud scream from the kitchen.

"Where'd you find her?" Arnon asked.

"Murdock and I were heading to Birchton, and we saw her lying on the steps of City Hall. These two soldiers were going to arrest her. Then the mobs came, and we took her and ran here."

Arnon only nodded, but she wasn't sure if he was listening. "I wonder where Wesley is," he said at last.

"Who knows," Adelyne replied, "but apparently, there's going to be another draft. Possibly tonight or on the 'morrow."

Arnon only looked down as he bumped his boot against the stone wall.

Adelyne lowered her head to try to catch his eyes. Something was wrong. She cleared her throat. "I saw arrest warrants posted all over Everwind."

He still didn't look up at her.

"They were for you."

Arnon quit tapping his boot against the wall. "I know."

Adelyne crossed her arms. "How?"

"Morgan told me this morning."

"It says you're wanted for murder. Is that true?"

Arnon rubbed his face with his hands. "Wesley told me to stay out of sight; maybe he was right. I wonder how the Daecish know I'm here?"

Adelyne felt like throwing up. Why did she care so much? "Who'd you murder?" she asked bluntly.

Arnon finally looked up with red eyes. When his gaze met hers, his expression softened, and he sighed. "The men who came to our home—after they killed my father, I thought they were going to come after the rest of us. My mother. My sisters. I did what I thought I had to." His expression almost looked fearful as his eyes darted in some memory.

Adelyne relaxed her arms, and she sat on a barrel of ale, laid on its side. She stared at the mug stains on the bar in front of her, which had long penetrated the cedarwood, leaving dark rings along the bar top. It seemed like it was just yesterday when the tables and chairs were pushed against the wall as the tavern came alive with everyone playing music and dancing together. She could still picture her mother and father swinging in each other's arms. As a little girl, she had always assumed days like that would go on forever. But it all just ended one day. Some people died; others changed. She would have given anything to feel like that innocent little girl again.

Adelyne sighed the memory away. Arnon was just protecting his family. How could she judge him? If he knew about her, he'd probably never talk to her again. Her bones suddenly ached beneath her guilt, and her eyes drifted to the floor. "I'm sorry," she said.

"It's okay." In the corner of her eye, she saw him tilt his head. "What happened to your hand? It looks swollen."

She tried to shake the soreness out. "I punched a Daecish soldier."

Arnon's eyes went wide. "You did what?"

"He told Murdock to hit him, but he wouldn't do it. So, I did instead."

"Wait." He gave a cocky smile. "A guard said to hit him?"

Adelyne laughed. "I'm serious. Ask Murdock!"

He squinted as if he was thinking of some smart reply, but after a moment, his face relaxed. "I'll just take your word for it." He continued to gaze at her. At first, she thought he wanted to tell her something, but he only remained silent. His brown eyes looked deep and caring. No one had ever looked at her like that before. She suddenly became conscious of how she looked. Her hair wasn't parted weird, was it?

The door swung open, and Drake walked back in with Lilly. "I done told you two not to stay here too long," he said with a scowl.

Adelyne startled.

"Sorry, sire," Arnon replied.

Drake only grunted. Lilly held his hand as she carried a wooden tankard in the other, splashing milk onto the floor with each step. At that moment, the front door to the tavern creaked open, and a man stepped in. He had a dark, thin beard, with sparse black hair to match. His clothing looked weathered, and his boots tracked in mud as he walked over to the bar. Adelyne didn't like the look of him.

"You looking for a drink, sire?" Drake asked.

The man eyed his surroundings. "I be lookin' fer the owner."

Drake crossed his arms. "I be the owner."

The man whispered something in Drake's ear.

Drake grunted as he lifted the backside of his shirt, showing the man a thick scar on his lower back. The man pulled out a letter and handed it to Drake over the bar. "I's told to give this to you." He then spat a brown glob of tobacco on the ground and walked back out.

Drake eyed the letter for a moment.

"Do you want me to read it?" Adelyne asked.

At first, Drake didn't say anything. Then he looked up at the front door. "It's got the seal of the House of Emsworth on the front.'

Arnon stepped forward. "From Denhurst?"

Just then, the kitchen door swung open, and Murdock peered through with a smile. "It's a boy!"

* * *

Geoffrey sat with his back against the cold iron bars of the empty carriage. His wrists ached in the iron clasps, and his parched mouth was filled with sores. Swallowing, he grimaced as his throat burned. A gentle patter tapped on the carriage roof as the heavy clouds gave into freezing rain. Several guards and soldiers stood in the road; the Northern Gate of Everwind was about half a league to the south. Black smoke emerged from somewhere within the city.

Before long, another carriage rolled into view. The soldiers cleared off the road while the commanding officer stood firm, waving his hand for the carriage to come to a stop. Geoffrey lowered his head, but he listened to two of the soldiers conversing in front of him.

"Two more on the way," said the soldier to the right.

"Where's the wisp scheduled to land?" asked the other, who sounded as if he hadn't yet reached manhood.

The first soldier scanned a piece of paper in his hands. "Looks like Fingate."

"How did you all draft anyone with all this chaos going on?"

"We skipped the slums and took the rioters instead. Well, as many as we could fit."

"Will this be all of them?"

"Pretty much," replied the soldier to the right. "Except for a few carriages from Astford. They'll be in Runevast before we are, I imagine."

Geoffrey looked up at the other carriage, which stopped just ahead. The men inside were battered and bruised, but almost all of them were dressed in fine suits and coats. One man still wore his top hat.

"We figured if the men want some action, we'll give them some," the first soldier continued as he walked toward the iron cage and pulled his sword from its sheath. He banged the broad side of the blade against the iron bars with a loud clank. "You hear that, recruits! You're off to Fingate!"

Most of the men inside bowed their heads in obvious regret, but others held a fierce look in their gaze. The man with the top hat lashed his arm out, grabbing at the soldier's collar. "You pale-faced slags!" he hollered.

The soldier shouted and brought his sword across, thrusting a deep gash in the man's arm. Crying out, the man pulled his arm back, gripping it in his shirt.

"You! Stop there!" shouted a commander. He pointed to the soldier, who now stood at attention. "Go grab a bandage for the recruit. And if I so much as see you act in a disorderly conduct again, I'll have your right hand!"

"Sir!" replied the soldier who hurried toward a supply cart at the northern end of the road.

Riots in Everwind. Mobs. Geoffrey's stomach twisted at the words. The smoke from the city stretched into the sky, thick and black. "Theos protect them," he said to himself. He fought back tears as he thought about Lilly and Sarah wondering where he might be.

The rain had now picked up to a steady downpour, sending cold water down Geoffrey's back. The threads of snow from the night before, nestled in the crevices of the hills, all but vanished. A hoarse cough caught at his throat. From the south, he heard a commotion down the road. Fog had now concealed the sight of Everwind's Northern Gate, but not far in the distance, the dusky outline of men marching toward him came into view. There were two rows of them, all clasped in chains that bound their feet and hands. They, too, were dressed in fine clothes, although mostly torn and unkempt. Several had welts on their heads, and one had a black eye and a bloody mouth with missing teeth.

The soldiers ordered them toward Geoffrey's carriage.

"You stay put," said a soldier to Geoffrey as he unlocked the iron door, which shrieked as it swung open. One by one, the men were stuffed in, sitting nearly atop of one another. They attempted to shift their legs and hands but soon gave up as the iron cuffs dug into their ankles and wrists. Several men had wedding bands on their fingers. No one spoke a word, but the confusion in their eyes spoke loud enough. An older man near the back of the carriage suddenly broke the silence with loud wails.

"Please!" he said, looking at a soldier just outside the carriage. "This is a mistake! I'm not supposed to be here! I wasn't rioting. I'm a proper citizen!"

The soldier looked the man up and down and only half-sneered before he walked off. The man's eyes grew wide as he glanced to the other men in the carriage as if waiting for them to defend him. Geoffrey then realized that the man was Lester.

There was a shout, and several men lifted their heads. The wheels of the carriage suddenly turned, and they all staggered and toppled against one another as several men moaned. Geoffrey's heart began to race as the walls of Everwind disappeared from his sight.

* * *

Arnon sat at the bottom of the steps trying to comprehend the words he just heard.

"Are you sure that's all it says?" Drake asked with his hands on his hips.

Morgan, who sat on a stool, looked over the letter again. "They've taken Denhurst and began marching north as soon as this dispatch was sent."

Drake paced the floor and rubbed the top of his bald head. "I knew they were strong enough, but this is faster than I can handle. And all it said was to be prepared for their arrival?"

Morgan raised a finger. "And that they'd send another dispatch when their army was outside Everwind."

"But they don't say how many they've got?"

Morgan shook his head.

"Or when they'll be here?"

Morgan shrugged. "They said they'd send another dispatch when they're here."

"You sure you're reading it right?" Drake questioned. "You said yourself your eyes ain't as good as they used to be."

"I know what I read!" Morgan shot back.

Although excitement filled Arnon, like Drake, he couldn't help but feel overwhelmed. "So they're coming here to take Everwind?"

"That's what it looks like," Morgan replied, wiping his nose with the back of his hand.

"What else can we do?" Arnon asked Drake. "The city's in chaos."

"And Wesley's been gone for over a week," Drake grunted as he leaned back against a shelf. A dangling cobweb brushed the top of his bald head, and he startled as he quickly wiped it away. "He needs to be here."

"Look," Morgan said, "if Galvin is really leading an army to Everwind, all of this disorder could work to our advantage. The Daecish are so occupied with stopping the riots, it may just give us a chance to prepare, take them by surprise, and take the city."

"You think so?" Drake asked. "But they've got thousands of armed men."

"Aye." Morgan stood up. "Nearly four-thousand if your estimates are correct. But who knows what we've got from Denhurst?"

Drake blew out a deep breath and sat on Morgan's stool. "We've got a few hundred in the city. It'll never happen."

"Don't say that yet—these riots. Everything's changing. We just got to wait and see."

"So, we should just keep doing what we're doing?" Arnon asked, but he could barely get the words out. His deflating confidence in the Silent Hither didn't matter now. This was their only opportunity, for better or worse, and he felt like he should do more than just carry on.

"I think so. We add to our number as best we can. Increase training, store whatever weapons we can."

"Strategize the best places to attack from within this city," Drake added.

"But most importantly," Morgan pointed to Drake and Arnon, "we can't tell anyone 'bout this. If this letter gets leaked out, we'll never stand a chance."

"So I can't tell Adelyne?" Arnon asked.

Drake gave him a sharp look.

"Just making sure."

"No one," Morgan added.

"But how can we prepare if we don't tell them?"

"Carefully," Morgan said. "Everyone in the Silent Hither knows that we aim to take back Sunder. Preparing for war is something we do. We keep doing what we're doing, but with more vigilance. We just can't let them know about that army. The surpise'll be critical to our victory."

"What about Wesley?" Arnon asked. "He's on the court with both of you."

Morgan frowned. "He does need to know, but he's been gone for so long." He folded up the letter. "Let's see if he shows up first. Then, we'll go from there."

The Depths of the Lower Quarry

Bound in chains at the rear of a line of four boys and two women, Søren continued through the rugged landscape. Every step weighed more than the last as his feet sunk into the wet earth. The freezing rain fell fast and heavy with a trembling roar. Water rushed down his hair and face, forcing him to keep his eyes squinted. Although the trek was difficult, he thought it better than the cell he had been locked in for the past several days.

The boy walking directly in front of him stood nearly a head higher and blocked most of his view of what lay ahead. To his right, the green grass had now faded to a dull black and gray, as if all life had fled. Mounds of rock, gravel, and mud rose high to his left, with water flowing down their crest, bringing swift streams that rushed over his feet.

The line came to a sudden stop. A bustle of commotion broke out, but Søren could see nothing. Soon, two men appeared in thick dark gray pants and over-shirts. With stained black faces and goggles situated over their brows, they examined each of the boys and women. One woman cursed and wept, but Søren couldn't see why.

One of the men stepped up to Søren. Looking down at him, a sneer formed on his face as if he smelled something nasty. Water continually dripped down his goggles and nose. On his upper right sleeve was sown a patch of Daecland's flag.

The man bent over and peered into Søren's eyes. Søren turned his gaze away, but as he did, the man's jaw dropped open as he caught a glimpse of his eyes. The man blinked a few times. He waved for the other man to walk over. "Take a look at this boy," he said.

"You mean the blonde-headed one?" replied the other man.

"Peculiar, isn't it?"

The man nodded. "I thought the same thing. I've never seen a half-breed this old."

"No, not that. His eyes. They're—" He looked at Søren again, a hint of awe in his expression. "Looks like a ghost or something."

The other man laughed. "You've been stuck out here too long. This one will go to the lower quarry." He turned and ordered the line to continue forward.

Drudging up a muddy, steep slope, the same smell Søren caught just outside Everwind began to rise in the air, but Søren still could not remember where he had smelled it before. As the line passed over a deep rut, his foot slipped beneath him across the gray mud, and the iron cuff around his ankle dug into his lower shin. He clenched his teeth and tried to get up, but the others in line, having not noticed, continued forward, dragging him through the gravel. The boy in front turned, noticing the dead weight. He helped Søren up but remained silent.

The roar of the rain ceased, and the gray sky fell into darkness as they entered the mouth of a mine. Dark wooden beams ran along a rock ceiling, braced by support columns. A strange stillness pervaded the dark and humid cavern, and an eerie warmth clothed Søren like a thick blanket. At first, he found it hard to breathe, but then a sudden strong whiff of that familiar sour smell rushed from somewhere in the darkness and caught Søren off guard, making him gag. Where had he smelled it before? He tried to think, but his mind just went blank.

The others in front coughed. They halted, and the men who had brought them disappeared deeper into the darkness. Everyone covered their nose with their hands, but no one spoke.

Soon, two torches wavered in the distance, and with them returned the two men. Their voices and footsteps echoed against the walls. One of them carried a key as he set the torch in a hold on the wall near the front of the line. Approaching a young woman, they released her cuffs. Even in the dim torchlight, Søren could make out her pastel yellow dress. But her eyes were hidden behind strands of her wet black hair strewn across her face.

The man walked toward Søren. "Put your hands down," he said.

Søren slipped his hands from his nose, and the man released his chain from the line. Ordering Søren to move to the front, the man bound his cuffs to a chain connected to the girl's so that they were now fastened to each other.

"Take these two to the lower chamber," said the man with the key. "I'll take the rest to section four across the ridge."

As he walked down a dark, uneasy slope, the narrow walls and low ceiling pressed in on Søren. He imagined himself crawling until he got stuck. He feared he would suffocate, just like the boy in the chimney back at the orphanage. But to his relief, the passage broadened. Occasionally, another tunnel would appear to his left, leading further and deeper into the earth. As he tried not to breathe through his nose, Søren's head started to throb, and his stomach went queasy. A crude wooden handrail had been built on his left, but the cuffs prevented him from reaching out to them for balance. The girl never looked behind her.

They soon approached a more open space with several passages leading in different directions. The smell faded, and Søren took in a deep relieving breath. A cold draft crept from a dark passageway on his right. But all of the passageways were dark, save one straight ahead, which brought forth an orange glow and the clank of distant hammering and shouts.

He stepped into a large open chamber with an uneven ceiling. Golden torches and lanterns lined the walls. An iron track ran around the chamber's length before exiting through another passage on the northern end, where two mules stood uneasily in a cramped corner. Along the left wall arose a single ledge, upon which workers of men, women, and children slaved over the broken rock. Some heaved picks against the walls while others passed tin pails, full of coal, up and down ladders and along rows of lines, until they were dumped in wooden carts on the track. Armed guards, bearing the Daecish flag on their sleeves, were posted in various locations. The worn and ragged clothing, stained black, made everyone seem as if they had been trapped in there for years.

The man sneered. "Welcome to your new home," he said before disappearing through the black tunnel they had entered from.

Søren's breath quivered. Was this his new home? Since he had awoken on the beach, his senses seemed numbed, as if he was watching strange and uncanny events unfold before him, but he was not really a part of it. He half believed Burlan, Geoffrey, and the others were all part of a dream, and he would soon wake up in the orphanage.

But now, he felt awake. This was it. This is where he would be for a long time.

Just ahead, several guards in Daecish uniforms conversed; one stood with his arms crossed as he pointed to one of the lines of men and women. "Which one you think, Algöter?" he asked.

One of the guards, apparently Algöter, peered along the line of people, then glanced toward the girl, standing beside Søren.

"That one?" the other guard asked.

Algöter leaned into the other guard's ear. Their conversation became quiet, mumbling words Søren could not understand. The girl trembled in her chains. She glanced behind her to the tunnel but didn't seem to notice him. Despite the dirt on her face, she looked kind like Eirún, but younger. Maybe if they didn't put her in chains, she would feel better. But her eyes were filled with water.

Søren's legs began to ache. It was like standing in the dining hall at the orphanage all over again, waiting for Baulfr's orders. He could see the burning coals in the fireplace, and he sniffed as if he could smell the scent of mold lingering in the air. That would have been a nicer place to stand in.

An image of Eirún smiling at him rushed to his mind. A lump formed in his throat, and he closed his eyes, hoping to drown away the sounds of hammering and breaking coal. He lifted his hand to his chest and reached for the lens he knew wasn't there.

Algöter walked over and unshackled both Søren and the girl. For a grown man, his neck looked overly thin, with sunken cheeks and round ears that stuck out. He ordered the girl back through the tunnel as the other guard led her away. Then Algöter motioned for Søren to follow him toward the ledge along the left wall. After climbing a ladder, Algöter pulled him to the front end of a line where the black rock was picked and broken.

"There," said Algöter. He shoved a woman over within the line. With brilliant red hair, she had green eyes and wore a brown dress, stained with what looked like soot. It was obvious she had been in the mines long enough to age her beyond her years. "You fit in here," Algöter continued, pulling Søren next to the woman. He peered at Søren for a moment and winced. "When the coal comes to you, pass it down. Any questions and you lose your meal. Got it?"

Søren nodded, and Algöter went back down the ladder.

"It's not as bad as you think," the red-haired woman said in a weak voice that matched her thin lips and tired face. She wasn't as pretty as Eirún, but she reminded him a little of Yrsa. And he liked that. "Be glad you didn't start as a breaker or a door boy," she continued, "them are lonely jobs. You'll fit in here just fine. Soon, I'll hand you a pail, and you just pass it right along. Once we start, we don't stop. It gets heavy after a while, but in a few more hours, we'll have dinner."

He didn't say anything but nodded. At the bottom of the ledge, Algöter talked with other guards as they pointed to him. For some reason, it made him feel afraid as if they were planning to hurt him. What were they saying?

A thick, gristly cough came from a man in the line to his left. He had a frail body and bulging stomach and long, wiry, unkempt hair. As the man grinned with a gleam in his silver eyes, Søren recognized him.

"I—I met you in—"

"In Astford," replied the prisoner. His black teeth glistened in the torchlight.

Søren only stood with his mouth half-open. "How did you get here?"

The prisoner laughed, shaking the chains around his hands. "I was tried. If you can call it a trial. And I was condemned to life. But I have been condemned to worse before. How did you get here?"

Søren peered at the deep bruises already forming around his wrists and ankles. "I was taken."

The prisoner didn't say anything.

"I wasn't supposed to be here, though. A man came and rescued me."

"Rescued you?"

Søren nodded. "He said I could live with him, and I would eat lots of food, and I would get t—to play."

"And yet he left you?"

Søren's chest tightened. Geoffrey didn't leave him. "He was taken from me."

"How?"

"These men came. They said they were going to d—d—" He thought for a moment.

"Draft?"

"Yes! Draft him. But I don't know what that means."

"Interesting," the prisoner replied. "They will be taking him to Fingate, I imagine."

"Fingate?"

"In Daecland."

Søren's heart sank. He thought Geoffrey would come for him. The prisoner placed a hand on Søren's shoulder, and he shivered as the cold fingers penetrated his damp shirt. "I told you not to trust him. I warned you, but you have not listened. Now look where you are. In darkness, just as I said."

It felt like a brick fell onto Søren's chest.

"Things are already beginning to turn for the worse."

Søren's breath quickened, but he startled as the woman to his right nudged him in the shoulder. She went to hand him a pail of coal. Trying to process the prisoner's words, he reached for it, but the woman held a look of concern in her eyes. An older man, with light gray hair and an overgrown beard, peered from behind her shoulder, sharing the same expression.

Søren handed the heavy pail to the prisoner, who lifted his hand from Søren's shoulder and reached for it. But he paused before he spoke. "Geoffrey will not come to you," he said. "He has forgotten you, just as Eirún has, and everyone else."

A sudden sorrow welled up in Søren's throat. He often told himself that she had forgotten him, but he refused to believe it. "But she loves me."

"Boy?" came the sudden voice of the woman to his right.

Søren startled and turned.

"Who are you talking to?"

Søren peered at her. "I'm talking to—" he began to say, turning around. Then his voice cut short. The prisoner was gone.

The Darkness

Søren stood motionless with his mouth hanging open. In the prisoner's place stood a boy slightly taller than himself with thick black hair. His face was long and thin—almost pale beneath the black dust. But more so, his eyes were wide with worry.

"That boy sounds Daecish," the older man whispered to the red-haired woman.

Søren couldn't respond as he frantically searched for the prisoner. Dropping the pail of coal from his grip with a loud crash, he peered down the ledge along the floor, and he even looked up. "Where has he gone?" he asked out loud.

"What's going on up there?" shouted Algöter.

With shaking arms, the woman picked the pail off the ground, refilling it with the spilled coal. She handed it to the boy on Søren's other side.

"I said, what is going on up there?"

The woman grabbed another pail as it was handed to her and tried to pass it to Søren. "Quick, take it!" she said.

Where was the prisoner? He was just there. An image of the cell in Astford flashed in his mind.

"Take it!" she shouted.

Søren startled. His eyes darted around. He almost forgot where he was. The woman once again slipped past Søren, handing the pail to the boy. Algöter marched toward the bottom of the ladder, a scowl upon his face. "If I have to come up there, it will be the last time you draw breath!"

Søren startled again and nodded. At that moment, he finally realized he had been speaking aloud in front of the guards. He disobeyed Geoffrey, and he could only hope no one heard him. The woman handed him another pail. He gripped the thick iron rings on either side, the weight once again catching him off guard. He passed it to the boy.

That night Søren and the other workers were shackled once again and sent out of the chamber through the passage he had entered that morning. Heading toward the entrance of the mine, he passed where the foul stench still seeped from the deep caverns and finally stumbled into the night sky, where the cold earth once again felt wet. But the sky was clear, with only a few passing clouds occasionally blocking the starlight from his view. His arms shivered as he watched as each breath condensed from his mouth, billowing out into the air.

The woman who had handed him the pails was chained in front of him with the black-haired boy behind him. They climbed up a large hillside, but the darkness made it difficult to see far into any distance. A throbbing pain had swelled in Søren's right knee, and he winced as it shot pain down his leg. When they crested over the top of the hill, a shallow valley below lay beyond where a camp of many tents sat, surrounded by glowing torches. Steam arose on the eastern side from a long canvas-like pavilion, which stood higher than the tents, braced by many ropes pegged into the ground. Other workers gathered in small crowds. Most were lined on the north side of the pavilion, while others walked out of the south side with bowls curling with steam in their hands. Surrounding the camp, several towers, built from long beams of cut timber, stretched into the sky, where guards perched at their tops with crossbows in their hands. Around the edge of the camp patrolled many more.

Walking down the hill, thick with dried bushes that scraped across Søren's legs, they arrived at the pavilion. There a guard unshackled their hands, tossing the long chain of cuffs into a pile. In a false sense of freedom, everyone departed in different directions.

Standing alone, Søren fiddled with his fingers. What was he supposed to do now? He felt very small among the many workers passing by, apparently taking no notice of his presence. Everyone was blackened from the mines. Søren looked down, seeing the black within the lines of his own palms. A gentle hand laid on his back, and the red-haired woman who had been working next to him smiled. "It's best to get in line," she said. "Before the soup runs out."

Søren nodded, noticing several scars wrapped around her wrists.

"I'm Agatha, by the way," she continued. "You can eat with me if you'd like."

Søren nodded again, but seeing Daecish guards around, he didn't speak.

He followed her along a line of workers, which stretched through the camp until it was hidden behind several tents. Following Agatha with quick steps, he weaved between men and women, trying to keep up. Many worn faces passed by him with faded eyes as if they wandered aimlessly with no purpose. Everything from the people, the tents, and the ground looked gray in the dim torchlight as if all the color had been sapped out.

Reaching the end of the line, he stood quietly, hearing only the heavy, congested coughing from all directions. Occasionally, he took a step as the line continued forward, but with a growling stomach, it wasn't as quick as he would have liked.

Søren felt a bump from behind. Turning around, a large man motioned his hands for Søren to walk. Looking forward, Søren realized that Agatha was already at the entrance of the pavilion, a few yards ahead. He must have zoned out again. She half-smiled as he rushed toward her.

Following Agatha out of the pavilion, Søren looked down to his bowl and took in a long sniff. It looked and smelled just like the soup from the orphanage. Old salty broth with a hint of sour milk. He never thought he'd be so excited to drink it again.

Agatha led him to a tent. There was a blanket on the inside, but a man already slept on it. Imitating Agatha, he sat down in the mud and sipped his soup. Although the murky scent of wet earth and rain filled his nose, he could almost feel the warmth of the orphanage as the broth ran down his throat. Just beside him sat another tent, which looked larger and sturdier than the others. Beside its entrance were two mounted torches, blazing in the night.

Although he could only see through the open flap from the side, a large cot and even a dresser sat near the inside front corner. A Daecish guard stepped out, buttoning up the top of his uniform. It was Algöter. His eyebrows scrunched, and there was an aimless gaze in his eyes as if he was thinking of something deeply sorrowful. Algöter glanced back in the tent, murmuring something Søren couldn't understand. Soon, the girl in the pastel yellow dress, whom he had seen earlier that day, walked out with her head low and her arms folded across her chest. Her long black hair covered her face. From another part of the camp, another guard approached the tent.

"Colonel," the guard said with a casual salute. Despite being almost a head shorter than Algöter, his clean uniform and stiff posture gave him a more regal feel.

Algöter kept his eyes away from the girl. "Lieutenant."

"Reports are in for today," he said, glancing at the girl. She kept her gaze to herself.

"And?" replied Algöter.

The lieutenant shot his eyes back to him. "Four dead—three men, a woman."

"Any blood?"

"Only from the woman, just before she died."

Søren shuddered. Blood from what?

"Was she coughing before she died?"

"They all were, sir."

Algöter rubbed his face. "Burn the bodies east of camp. The wind's been steady from the west; don't want to add more to the stench that already saturates this depressing wasteland." He hacked out a heavy cough, then cleared his throat. "How much coal did we bring in today?"

"Just shy of sixty loads, sir. Most of it dirty."

Algöter sighed. "I should have put in for the copper mines." He rubbed his chin. Søren caught sight of several scars—thin lines running along the inside of his wrist caught in the torchlight. On his other wrist, he wore a bandage, tainted with blood. "That isn't enough. We need to up our production if this mine is going to make any profit."

"Anything else for me, sir?"

Algöter waved his hand toward the girl. "Find her a tent."

"Yes, sir." He walked toward her, but she turned her face away; her damp cheek glistened in the light. Almost timidly, he took her by the arm and guided her along the muddy ground in Søren's direction. Algöter walked back into his tent.

"We'll take her," spoke up Agatha as the lieutenant was about to pass. He glanced over and guided the girl through the mud, helping her sit next to Agatha.

"Thank you," the Lieutenant said. Sadness clouded his features as he peered at the girl. "I'm sorry," he whispered, just before he stood up and walked off.

Agatha handed the girl her soup. "If you can, you need to drink."

The girl didn't take it. She didn't even look up. Although she was quiet, her back shook with each cry. In the orphanage, he would do that sometimes at night, when he didn't want the other boys to hear.

Agatha set the bowl down beside her. "What's your name, darling?"

The girl didn't respond.

Agatha rested her hand on the girl's back. "I'm Agatha, and this is
. . ." she looked at Søren.

Geoffrey told him he wasn't supposed to share his real name, yet
as hard as he tried, he couldn't remember the new name he was given.
But Agatha wasn't a Daecish guard. Maybe it would be okay to tell her.
"Søren," he whispered.

Agatha held a peculiar look on her face, but then she smiled. After
a moment, the girl mumbled something.

"What was it?" Agatha asked.

"Langleigh," the girl said.

Agatha rubbed her back. "You'll stay with us, Langleigh. We'll look
out for each other."

Runevast Port

Geoffrey awoke as the carriage stopped, and a strong scent of human sweat filled his nose. The air howled as a blast of wind rushed down, biting through his bones. Darkness began to break, and the starlight faded into the rising morning light as a gentle rain pattered once again on the wooden roof of the carriage. Before him, loomed the tall gnarled peaks of the Great Fringe. They appeared menacing and angry as if they threatened to kill anyone who attempted to cross through their dark passes.

The night before, he had dreamt that he was at home, watching Lilly play by a warm fire. Sarah was holding a baby. But his hopes of ever seeing them again washed away with the rain. He wondered if Sarah had given birth yet, or if she had even survived it. He pictured Lilly all alone in the dark house. What if the Daecish arrested her too? With a throbbing head and a stomach that shifted like sloshing water, Geoffrey let out a deep, quiet sob.

A soldier walked over, taking a drink of rainwater which he collected in a large flask. He observed the men with a crooked jeering smile. When he stepped forward, the recruits scrambled toward the carriage bars. Shouts and moans broke through the pile as men were trampled and stepped on. All sense of moral duty was strangled by the sheer will to survive. The soldier laughed as the men pressed themselves against the bars, sticking their tongues out like rabid dogs. Based on their clothing, Geoffrey thought it strange, even unnerving, to think that just a few days ago, most of these men were some of the wealthiest Sunderians in Everwind.

Tipping over the flask, the soldier let water dribble down their faces. "Drink up, recruits!" he shouted, throwing the flask into the carriage. "We've got a long flight ahead of us." The men dove over one another, grasping for the mostly empty flask as water poured out of its opening and through the boards of the carriage floor.

Geoffrey never moved; his attention caught on Lester. With red eyes and drooping gray hair, he hung his mouth open with a swollen white tongue. Like a ragged doll, he slumped over, looking as if he was dead, except for the feeble rise and fall in his chest.

The iron door unlocked.

"All right, recruits," said a commander. "Listen carefully! We will exit the carriage one by one in the order we tell you. If anyone dares to escape, resist, or takes too long in following orders, your head will be severed on the spot." Two other soldiers walked over and stood by the carriage door, gripping a single-handed sword with a leaf-shaped blade in their right hands. The commander continued. "When we are all out of the carriage, there will be a single line. There you will each get a flagon of water and bread. Be quick about it! We will be boarding the wisp shortly."

Lester was dragged out first as his feet stumbled along the ground. The commander pointed to another man, then Geoffrey. Geoffrey stood up, his ankles sore and his legs numb. With each step, he felt unsure if he'd be able to take another. But when he set his feet on the soft grass below, a sense of relief to be outside of the bars swept over him.

A sudden, loud roar startled the men. Geoffrey glanced to his left as the wind rushed against him, blowing his hair back. Situated at the foot of a great mountain sat a wooden ship on dry land. Its forecastle and aft looked just like any other ship he had seen, but attached above it, by many ropes, as if it was the mast and sails itself, hung a great golden-brown inflated balloon. The balloon was not round but of a misshapen long oval shape, with several cables wrapping around its breadth, tightening into it so that it bulged out as if it was going to burst. Two great propellers spun into a blur on either side of the ship, producing a deep hum that echoed off the face of the towering rock walls.

Such a sight brought back nerve-racking memories of when the Daecish first invaded.

While all the recruits stared at the wisp, several soldiers came by and passed out the flagons and bread. It was then that Geoffrey noticed four other carriages ahead, where many more recruits of men stood in various lines. For a moment, he thought he recognized Burlan, but he couldn't be sure. As a soldier handed Geoffrey his food and water, he took a quick drink and rushed to fill his groaning stomach. At the first bite, a sharp pain shot through his throat, and he gagged, throwing it up. Slowly, he took another small bite and washed it down with water. He glanced to his right. Lester didn't seem to eat at all. Instead, his hands barely held onto the bread and brown leather flagon, which hung at his side. He looked at the nearest soldier.

"Please," Lester said in a half mumble.

A recruit standing next to him turned. "Be quiet and drink your water! Do you want to be killed?"

"Please," said Lester again, but the sound of the propellers kept the soldier from hearing him.

What was he doing? "Lester!" Geoffrey tried to whisper as loud as he could. Lester glanced at him, his eyes lost and desperate. "They'll kill you if you don't hurry and eat. Don't talk to them!"

A soldier looked in their direction. Geoffrey shot his gaze ahead and continued drinking and eating, painfully swallowing the bread down. Lester let his bread and flagon fall to the ground.

With his hand on his sword hilt, the soldier walked over. Lester lifted his shaking hands up as if to plea. The soldier raised a cocked eye. "Please, sire," said Lester. "I—I'm not supposed to be here. I'm the head of the Merchant's Guild. I wasn't part of the mob. I've always been faithful to your lordship." He took a step forward out of line. "Please, sire."

Geoffrey held his breath, and his heart quickened, but he remained still. The soldier turned back to a commander, who had been observing the situation. The commander gave a single nod. Lester looked at the commander, then the soldier, who now stepped up to him and grabbed the chain between the two shackles on Lester's wrists. Stumbling over his feet, Lester was pulled out of the line.

"Thank you, sire," Lester said with a new glint in his eye. "I assure you the commander will understand. I will pay whatever is asked."

"Get on your knees, recruit."

Lester's eyes went wide. He looked at the commander, who stood motionless, then back to the soldier. "Of course," he said in a quivering voice. He peered back toward the other men in the line with such fear on his face; it was as if he knew he was going to die. Attempting to kneel-down, his knees trembled so violently, Geoffrey could see it.

"Look down," said the soldier.

Lester looked down. "Theos have mercy."

The soldier pulled his sword from the sheath.

"Theos have—"

The blade swung down across Lester's neck, and his head fell from his body. It rolled on the ground with a hideous thud. Dark red blood poured out from his body as it soaked into the green grass.

A man who had stood next to Lester bent down and grabbed his bread and flagon of water off the ground. He drank down the water as it dribbled down his chin and neck. Then, taking a mouthful of bread, he shoved the rest in his pocket.

"Theos, help us," Geoffrey whispered to himself.

"Let that be a lesson to every one of you," the commander shouted. "If you disobey, you will pay with your life."

Within the hour, the soldiers had several lines of recruits trudging around a low rocky hill southeast of the wisp. As they veered around its base, several buildings of brick and wood came into view, perched along the foot of the mountain. From their roofs, steam whistled through piping which ran in and out of each building. On the western side sat three other wisps across a flat plateau. Their balloons hung lifeless and deflated behind them.

As the recruits continued toward the running wisp, the wind from the propellers blew strong and howled. Steam spewed from beneath the hull. Ducking through a low door built into the side of its wooden hull, all was black until Geoffrey's eyes adjusted. A plain space soon revealed itself, with round open windows and several wooden beams rising from the deck to the overhead. Two feet below the iron mesh floor, another floor slanted inward toward small openings on the far side of the ship.

Being second to front now, Geoffrey was led to the far-right corner beside a round window.

"Stay put," said a soldier. "And if I were you, I wouldn't turn around."

Geoffrey said nothing but only looked through the window at the green grass, which rose until it faded to bare rock upon the steep slopes of the mountains.

He glanced back, feeling the shove of a man press against his body. Another man came and then another as they were packed in, one by one, pushing Geoffrey against the hull. Hot breath brushed his neck and ears. Soon he could no longer move to lift his hands. Despite the window, Geoffrey found it difficult to breathe. His head throbbed, and the smell of the tight space quickly went sour.

After a few moments, his knees buckled beneath his weight as the wisp lifted from the ground. Men throughout the lower level gave out murmurs of uneasiness. Geoffrey felt queasy as if his organs had sunk into his stomach. It didn't take long for several recruits to start hurling; Geoffrey could only hope the man directly behind him held a strong stomach.

The grass below drifted further away. His ears popped, and in the far distance, he could just make out Astford. His heart pounded. Sarah. Lilly. Would he ever see them again?

He closed his eyes and prayed silently.

A Rupture in the Earth

E ilívur sat at his desk in the Office of Foreign Jurisdiction. He tried to keep his official composure, but the words of the lieutenant made it difficult to do so. "Let me see the letter," he said. The lieutenant handed Eilívur the letter, and he read over it. After a moment, he set the letter down. "Denhurst is taken," he said to himself. "Where is the man who delivered this message?"

"Sergeant Alric, sir. He's still in the infirmary."

"I must see him at once."

Eilívur went to stand up but paused as a soldier came to his door behind the lieutenant. "Sir, I was sent to deliver this." Walking over, he set a wooden box on Eilívur's desk and left the room.

Eilívur peeled off the Vagholme stamp and gazed at the outline of the Daecish flag etched into the wooden lid. "Wait for me outside," he said to the lieutenant.

The lieutenant saluted and walked out, closing the door behind him.

Eilívur sat back down and slid the box toward himself, letting out a deep sigh as he lifted the lid. Resting on top of a few other items was Ulnleif's Sunderian Expedition medal. All soldiers sent over the mountains got one—it was his only decoration. Eilívur picked up a silver clasp of a shield. It was his father's, but after he had died in Kalestrond, at the Battle of the Rime Fields, his mother had given it to him. When Ulnleif joined the Army, Eilívur then gave it to him as a gift.

Once again, Eilívur found himself feeling the scar below his ear. He had already been in the Nautical Armada for seven years when his father died. Ulnleif had been only two. Since then, whenever Eilívur was home from deployment, he would spend every day with the young boy, teaching him and raising him up to be a man. In every practical sense, Ulnleif was his own son. Of course, Ulnleif knew Eilívur was his brother, but he never remembered his real father, and that was probably for the best. Like many other life-long commanders, their father was a hard, unforgiving, and controlling man who often mistook abuse for justice.

An ache hit his chest. He could feel the same kind of man in himself.

About six months before Eilívur transferred from the Nautical Armada to the Army, Ulnleif had stolen a few aracs from their neighbor. The boy was only seven at the time, and he hadn't stolen enough to put a dent in anyone's pocket. But it wasn't the amount that troubled Eilívur. Ulnleif had stolen it from a lady with a loudmouth and a bitter disposition. She spread rumors that he wasn't raising Ulnleif properly, and she even whispered the audacious lie that the boy may not even be the son of his real father, which cast a promiscuous light on their mother. Of course, the rumors died as quickly as they came, but Eilívur couldn't shake his hurting pride. If Ulnleif hadn't of been so foolish, none of this would have happened.

One night, he had too much to drink, and in a fit of anger, he shoved Ulnleif to the ground, bent over and smacked his face with the back of his hand. Just as the poor boy cried out, his own mother, who was stronger than many men he knew, shoved him off of Ulnleif, and his face hit the corner of the rough-cut dining table. He ended up with a nasty cut below his ear and a heart full of regret.

Eilívur wasn't sure what had come over him. Perhaps he had acted out by the only example he knew. But from that moment on, he vowed to be a better man than his father. He would look after Ulnleif and never lay another finger on him. Even when he was transferred to Sunder, he made sure his brother was transferred with him.

With a heavy sigh, Eilívur closed the box. He should have sent Ulnleif's body home. Standing up, he pinned the shield clasp through his uniform over his left breast, wondering if there was anything else he could have done to protect his brother. Probably a lot of things. But now wasn't the time to doubt. Straightening his jacket, he walked out of the room.

The lieutenant hurried to keep up with Eilívur's pace as they walked through the bitter wind, rushing across the center courts of the Northern District. The gray sky laid low, and a foul smell lingered in the air. Traces of snowflakes began to drift slowly to the earth.

"Feels like I haven't seen the sun in months," said the lieutenant.

Eilívur didn't feel like responding. The district seemed to be in a constant state of confusion as officers continually hurried from one office to another. Ulnleif soon faded from his mind as current dilemmas began to consume him once again. Other than a rumor that some guy, who may or may not have been Arnon Greystrom, had been spotted a few days ago with a girl in the Eastern District, there was nothing. No leads. No hints. Even Wesley's description of the young man was useless. It didn't help that the moment he stepped back into that cursed city, the economy crashed. Paired with this Denhurst fiasco, there were now infinitely more pressing matters which demanded his attention. But he wouldn't give up. Sooner or later, he would continue his investigations. And justice would come.

"Commander," the lieutenant said, "how many have we lost so far?"

"Since the pay decrease?"

"Yes, sir."

"We don't have a solid number of deserters yet, but when they're caught, we'll have to build several more gallows to be sure." Riots, deserters, Denhurst. It was as if some fate forced everything to fall apart at once.

Arriving at the infirmary near the southeastern entrance, shouting crowds could still be heard through the bolted doors leading to the rest of the city.

"Will it ever end?" the lieutenant asked.

"Not without reinforcements. With minimal transportation, we could only draft so many."

"You would have thought that would have been enough to scare them." The lieutenant remarked as his thick eyebrows dipped viciously. "What about the prostitutes? Men are saying they're spreading out from the slums. I've heard rumors that even some of our soldiers are taking part in their, um, services."

Despite strict laws forbidding Daecish soldiers from sleeping with Sunderian women, Eilívur knew it was impossible to control completely. Women in poverty would do what they needed to survive, and men would do whatever it took to satisfy their appetites. Still, half-bred children were incredibly rare. Whether that was because the women managed to keep themselves from getting pregnant or if they simply disposed of the infants at birth, he wasn't sure. "One thing at a time, Lieutenant. For now, send a dispatch for Commander Dagr in Llynhithe. Inform him of Denhurst and request reinforcements."

"Without approval from King Ónarr?"

"I'll inform the king. You have your orders."

"Yes, sir," the lieutenant replied and then departed.

Walking inside the infirmary, the smell of alcohol and various pungent remedies filled Eilívur's nostrils. Cots lined the open room with many lanterns hanging along the walls. A wide fireplace burned behind Gunnar, who stood beside Halvard. At twenty-six, Halvard was young for a commander, and his babyface only exemplified his age. But he had led enough regiments to prove his worth. Beside the two commanders sat a sergeant, wearing his torn and stained uniform. He held a posture as if he sat as proudly as he could.

"Commander Tyr," said Gunnar, taking a step forward. "I assume you've heard?"

"The sack of Denhurst?" Eilívur replied. "Unfortunately, yes."

"Everwind in chaos, Denhurst taken, what next?" Gunnar asked.

Eilívur didn't respond but eyed the man sitting on the cot; the sergeant badge on his left shoulder was still covered in dried blood. "Tell me your name, sergeant," he said.

"Einhoth Alric," the sergeant replied.

"Tell me, Sergeant Alric, what exactly happened in Denhurst."

Alric glanced at the other commanders, then back at Eilívur. "Sir, as I have told Commander Veurðr and Commander Halvard, we were going through our scheduled draft. It was dawn, we had the carriages, everything we needed—weapons and shackles. I was equipped with a crossbow. We were told to use force only if needed." Alric paused for a second as if trying to recount the events. "We thought it would take an hour at the most. But as we came to the doors . . ." He trailed off and shook his head. "None of us saw it coming."

"Saw what coming?"

"The whole town was armed; swords, axes, picks, hammers, shovels, you name it. They came out of the doors and alleyways. The house I was at held twenty, maybe more, men. The whole city turned against us. There was no way for us to know." He gazed across the room. "And then . . ."

"And then what?"

Alric lowered his head. "The bodies. I saw them."

"Speak up," Eilívur said in a stern tone.

"They stripped off their clothes and hung them on the palisades. Sometimes their whole bodies, sometimes just their heads. To some of them," he said with a shiver, "they did unspeakable things before impaling them alive." He shook his head as a tear dripped to the ground. "I heard them scream."

"Monsters," spoke up Gunnar.

"How did you escape?"

Alric looked up at Eilívur as his body tensed. "I swear I didn't desert. I stayed until I saw no more alive. But I couldn't take it. I thought if I could just make it to Everwind, I could at least give a report. So, I backed into an alleyway and snuck along the city wall until I reached the main gate. There I found an officer's horse, and I rode as quickly as I could."

Eilívur studied the commanders.

"The horse is in our stable," said Halvard.

"This is not the place for such discussions," Eilívur said, "but we have no time. We must get the news to our regiment officers. Who knows the plans of those in Denhurst? They could be marching here for an attack, as far as we know. We must be ready." He went to turn but held back and lifted a finger. "Everyone in this room is sworn to secrecy. If any of this gets out to the public, it could shift the Sunderians further against us, and we—"

An abrupt rumble came from outside, and the earth beneath the infirmary trembled. Lanterns wavered against the walls, and one collapsed to the floor, shattering glass across the room. The commanders faltered and grabbed on to whatever they could.

"What was that?" shouted Halvard.

Eilívur's eyes widened as he caught his balance and walked toward the door; the others rushed behind.

The ground shook again.

Several other officers and men stumbled outside from surrounding buildings, bracing themselves on door frames, barrels, or anything they could find. A sudden eruption exploded in the distance, and everyone covered their ears. Several men threw themselves to the ground.

"Over there!" hollered Eilívur as he pointed north. "Toward the courtyards!" He ran north along the road, stopping just shy of a thick cloud of dust that billowed into the air. The central courtyard, which once stood green with fine-cut stone pathways running through its length, was now a sunken pile of rubble and earth. Only a few statues remained, tilted and half-sunken into the ground. The foul smell of death and sulfur penetrated the air. Eilívur covered his nose with his hand.

Everyone stared in awe, not yet daring to take a step. Then, as if something stirred beneath the ground, the depression of broken rock throbbed. Several soldiers stumbled backward, drawing their swords from their sheaths. There was a short silence.

Eilívur breathed heavily, not daring to move. Even with his talents, he could not fathom what this was. Then, what remained of the stone pathways suddenly upheaved like rippling water. Whatever was beneath ran southward. Stones and dirt flung into the air as shouting men dove out of the way.

Then as quick as it came, it ceased.

With their trembling swords pointed forward, no one said a word. All that remained was dust in the air and a path of overturned cobblestones and earth.

* * *

Arnon and Adelyne stood at the window of her home in the Southern Squalor, looking north. Like his own family home, Adelyne's house was a simple cottage with a dirt floor and a large hearth. On the left wall ran a set of wooden steps leading to an upstairs attic, which had been converted to a bedroom. As they peered north, nothing could be seen, but a low, distant quake rumbled beneath their feet.

"What was that?" Arnon asked.

"I'm not sure," Adelyne replied. "Maybe another riot?"

Arnon thought about the army marching from Everwind. He hoped they didn't miss the dispatch. "I wonder when the riots will stop."

"I don't know," she replied. "But our numbers are growing. Drake and Morgan seemed to have been working harder than ever." She turned to him. "Have you seen the cellar lately? It's stacked full of supplies. Murdock thinks something's up."

Arnon smiled.

"Do you know anything?"

"Me?" He wished he could tell her about Denhurst, but Drake would kill him.

Adelyne narrowed her eyes.

"All I know is that we need to be ready. Something's gonna happen soon." He leaned forward against the window seal and tapped his foot against the floor. Was his family with the army? Were they even okay?

"We're getting as ready as we can be." She gazed through the window. "There's so much poverty, though. So much disorder."

"And poor Drake," Arnon added.

"What do you mean?"

"Aracs have just about gone worthless. No one wants to spend their money on taverns."

"You can't blame them. So many families have lost so much, and in such a short amount of time."

"It's a good thing we're already poor." Arnon chuckled.

With only a half-smile, Adelyne continued to peer back through the window, and Arnon took the opportunity to steal a glance. Her dark auburn hair fell into slender curls just below her shoulders. Beneath her brown tunic, which reached to her knees, her olive skin was smooth. He couldn't help the captivation which fell upon him. He longed to kiss her, but he barely knew her.

"Arnon?"

"Huh?" he said with a startle.

She tilted her head, and the corner of her mouth curled up. Arnon wished he could just disappear. Suddenly, she leaned forward and kissed him on the cheek. Arnon's face burned. Raising a hand to cover her mouth, she giggled. Arnon finally swallowed, and his head went light.

"Come on," she said, grabbing his hand. "Let's try to get this lockbox open again."

In a daze, Arnon followed her to the back of the room. Light broke through several holes in the thatched roof, the walls having long needed repairing. They both sat down in front of a wooden table, upon which sat the lockbox with several picks lying beside it over a small rag. Adelyne lifted the box, so the lock faced upwards. With a lock pick in each hand, she slid them one at a time into the keyhole.

"Hand me that pick," she instructed Arnon.

Trying to settle his heartbeat, he reached for a pick, his palms in a cold sweat.

"No, the one closest to me." She smirked at him. "I thought you were an expert at lockpicking."

"Very funny. This one?"

She laughed. "Yes."

He picked it up, but it immediately slipped out of his hand and fell on the floor.

Adelyne rolled her eyes.

"It was heavier than it looked," he protested as he got on his knees, fumbling his hands along the straw.

Adelyne busted out in laughter. "What kind of excuse is that?"

"Found it," he said as he sat back in the chair. He blew out a breath. "Didn't think I was going to find it in that mess."

"That's nice, now hand it to me." Reaching her index and middle fingers up, she now held both picks with one hand and took the third pick from Arnon. With great care, she slid the pick into the lock. Arnon held his breath. A sudden click sounded. Groaning in frustration, Adelyne pulled the picks out.

"You were a lot closer that time," he said, trying to encourage her.

"After nearly two hours, I should hope so!"

She shook her hands out, and with a deep breath, she started again. She slid the two picks into the keyhole with both hands. She motioned them up and down, and then carefully, she lifted her middle and index fingers. She reached for the third pick with the tips of her fingers. Click. With a loud grunt, she pulled the picks out and threw them on the table.

* * *

Wesley sat on a stool in the dark cellar, picking at a scab on his left arm. The blood dripped wet against his fingertips, but he couldn't stop scratching. The talk with Drake and Morgan earlier that day didn't go as well as he hoped. He should've acted sicker. That would have been better. Various scenarios and plans ran through his head, but nothing satisfied him. They would catch on. He had been gone too long. He glanced back at a stack of shields and hauberks. He never noticed that before. To the right of the stairwell, in the corner, sat a pile of straw, with a wool blanket thrown over it.

The door upstairs swung open, and Drake walked down, carrying two tankards. Setting them on the steps, he walked over to the straw pile and picked up several tipped-over mugs and a moldy piece of bread lying on the blanket. "Going to bring rats in here if he can't clean up after himself."

"Who?"

"Arnon!" He pointed to the bed. "I'm trying to keep the knucklehead outta sight, but he's got to learn to pick up his mess."

Wesley only nodded. He was so nervous he wasn't sure if that was a natural response or not.

Wiping his hands on his stained apron, Drake pulled out a stool and sat down.

"Morgan not coming back?" Wesley managed to ask.

"No." Drake placed his hands on his knees. "He's headed to Birchton. It's getting ugly out there."

"The riots?"

"That and the prostitutes. Girls used to sell themselves in the slums, now they're coming out in the open streets. Apparently, Old Bale up at Three Rivers is only encouraging it."

"Bale? I've never known him to do that."

"Apparently, he started housing some in his rooms. Sells 'em off, makes a profit." He spat on the floor with a look of disgust. "This chaos is bringin' out the worst in people. They'll do just 'bout anything for a profit."

Wesley didn't respond. Was he just like Bale? Turning for the worst in desperate times?

"I still can't believe you had a fever that long." Drake handed him a tankard of mead and eyed him up and down. "You certainly look rough enough."

Wesley sputtered a weak cough. His lungs felt fine. "I'm not sure how I survived, to be honest."

"Well, the important thing is you're back." Drake rubbed his forehead and took in a long drink, keeping his eye on Wesley. "Who took care of you, if you don't mind me askin'? I'm just surprised no one told us. We even sent someone to your home to check on you."

He knows something, doesn't he? Could Drake tell he was lying? "You remember that old maid, Dabria?"

"Aye." He took another drink.

"She kept me at her place in Birchton, but she's so old, I'm not even sure she recognized me. And I was too delirious to tell her anything." He hadn't seen Dabria in two years. He kept looking away. "As soon as the fever broke," Wesley continued, "I came to. That's when I went out and saw the riots and ran to you as quick as I could."

With a grunt, Drake stood up, setting his tankard on a shelf.

"What's all that for?" Wesley asked, pointing to the shields.

"Not much, we found 'em in the crawlspace. Figured I'd polish 'em up."

"They look old."

"Aye." Drake pulled down a thick cobweb from the top of a shelf. "Geoffrey's gone, by the way. In case you ain't heard."

"Not back from Astford?" Hopefully, that sounded believable enough.

"Arrested, most likely drafted. At least that's what Sarah heard when she went to go see her husband, just before she gave birth."

He didn't know she was pregnant, but maybe he did. Come to think of it, Geoffrey did mention it when he first met him. She was probably in the slums by now. Maybe even at Old Bale's place. "That's terrible," he said. "Do you know what happened to her?"

"She's up at Adelyne's place. She's helping her look after the little ones."

That made Wesley feel better. "How bad did the draft hit the rest of us? I know you already explained to me the letters y'all wrote up, but the draft had to mess that up a little bit."

"Actually, the draft took mostly merchants. In fact, it only helped raise our numbers."

"More people are joining?" Wesley tried to hide the shock in his tone.

"For now," Drake said as he pulled out two full bottles of wine from a high shelf and set them in cubbies. "When the draft took place, that sealed the merchant's anger against the Daecish." He picked up his tankard, drinking the rest down. "So, they began to join us. Or rather us them."

"What do you mean?"

"A whole mob of merchants marched right into the Southern Squalor and were recruiting any man they could find to help storm the Northern District. Many of 'em were members of the Silent Hither. So now we've got our members joining merchants, merchants joining us. It's all a bit chaotic right now."

"And the Daecish aren't stopping them?"

"How can they? They can't even take control of the city. Matter fact, rumor's gone 'round that some of the Daecish are deserting." A deep laugh rumbled from Drake's chest. "They're so busy stopping riots and protecting the Northern District, we've hardly seen 'em in Birchton or the Southern Squalor."

Wesley heaved a deep breath of disbelief. Everything seemed to be working in the opposite way he had anticipated. Had he made a mistake? "Do you know where Arnon has gone to?" he finally asked.

"Not sure," Drake replied. Then he narrowed his eyes. "Probably off gallivanting with Adelyne somewhere. I can't seem to ever find 'em when I need 'em." He grunted and shook his head. "Just a couple of youngsters."

"That's funny. Last I saw Adelyne, she didn't seem to care for Arnon. They're together often then?"

"Aye," Drake chuckled, but his face quickly went somber. "Theos knows she deserves it. I just hope she don't break his heart."

Wesley gave no response. Every question he asked felt so mechanical like he was interviewing Drake. He hated being a spy. "Have you heard word from Llynhithe or Astford since I've been gone?"

"We haven't heard anything from Astford since Burlan wrote. And Llynhithe . . ." Drake rolled his eyes. "They're a pitiful group. You know we don't ever hear much from them. All they ever do is talk. No work. No effort; just a bunch of cowards."

"What about Denhurst?"

Drake repeatedly wiped something from his trouser leg as if thinking to himself. "Nothing as of yet. But we're hopeful. Galvin and Porter are strong men. They know what they're doing." He looked at Wesley with hard eyes.

Wesley looked at the ground, suddenly feeling uncomfortable. "I think I'm going to go rest for a while. Is it okay if I lie here?"

"Make yourself at home," Drake replied. He stood up and walked up the steps. "Just holler if you need a drink," he said before closing the door.

Wesley sat there for the better part of an hour, running events and scenarios through his head. His stomach churned. Not three days ago, he was sure he was right, but now he began to worry. The Silent Hither seemed to be going well. Should he confess to Drake? Maybe they would take him back if he gave them information on the Daecish. He shook his head. He didn't have anything on the Daecish.

His whole life was unfair. His own mother didn't stick up for him when he was beaten by his father. But she got a fair share of beatings as well. When he was eight, his father finally died, and his mother left him at one of his sister's houses. She said it was his sister, but he knew they had different mothers. Only Theos knew how many kids his father really had around the city. But after a few years, his sister and her own children didn't want him either. They used to stick out their teeth and mock his voice. They finally sent him to Lord Hornsby, a distant cousin to King Albern's father, where he was made a squire. Unfortunately, he barely lasted a month before he was deemed too weak—he could hardly even carry the knight's shield. But it didn't matter anyway. The knights may have been employed under the House of Burgess, but the years leading up to Daecish arrival, they had become barely more than an honorary title. And when the Daecish arrived and did away with the houses, the knights went away with them. They even executed every relative of King Albern's, leaving virtually no possible heir.

By the time he was fifteen, Wesley found himself barely surviving as an apothecary apprentice. He was barely fed, but he made it through into his adult years. He knew he was ugly enough that girls never so much as glanced at him, and so as much as he wanted to, he never courted or married. When the Silent Hither started, he had already made acquaintances with Lombard and Landon. Through them, he met Drake. But Drake always looked down his nose at him. Just like Morgan. Just like Galvin and Porter. His life was one failure after another.

He prayed that Theos would judge every single person who was ever cruel to him. They deserved it. Maybe except for Lombard. He and his family were the only ones who were kind to him. But now Wesley had betrayed them. He had turned in Lombard's only son.

In a sudden rage, Wesley clenched his fists and gritted his teeth. His eyes welled up, and the veins in his throat throbbed. Whether it was from conscience or cowardice, he wasn't even sure, but he wept violently into his hands. All he knew was that he was a defeated man. Maybe he should just take his life and end it all.

* * *

Arnon watched Adelyne slip the third pick into the keyhole. There was no sound. He would have noticed the excitement in her eyes, but standing over her, he was too busy taking in the smell of her hair. Almost a subtle jasmine—a glimpse of spring in the darkness of the approaching winter. His palms sweated once again. Letting out a slight shivering breath, he wiped his hands on his jerkin.

"I'm nervous too," she said, keeping her eyes on the keyhole. "But I'm so close."

Arnon froze his hands on his knees, realizing he was more obvious than he thought. "Yeah," he said, clearing his throat.

"Shh!"

"Sorry," he whispered.

Holding her breath, Adelyne steadily turned the third pick counterclockwise as the other two picks pivoted in her right hand. A click and the keyhole turned to the left.

"Got it," she said.

Arnon let out a deep sigh and sat down in the chair beside her. "How do your hands feel?"

She laughed as she withdrew the picks and waved her hands in the air. "Cramped."

They both stared at the box.

"Do you want to open it?" she asked.

"No, no," he replied. "You did all the work."

"All right, then." She placed her hands on either side of the lid. "Here goes nothing." She slowly began to lift it as it shifted upon its back hinges. She peered inside.

"What is it?" Arnon asked.

"I'm not sure," she replied. "A painting of some sort?"

Arnon leaned over and looked in the box with an unimpressed grunt. "A what?"

Adelyne lifted a small piece of stiff paper out of the box and cradled it gently in her palm. It was of a family—a man, a woman, and four small children.

Arnon squinted. "Definitely not a painting. There's no color. It has to be a sketch."

"But look at it," Adelyne replied. "I've never seen a drawing with detail like this."

Their clothing looked regal, royal even—definitely Daecish. None of them smiled but only held firm expressions. Though most of the picture was dark and worn, with an almost burnt and tattered look, the family could be seen clearly—except for the smallest child on the left, whose figure lay hidden behind the darkened edge.

"They're obviously, Daecish," Adelyne said, then she put her hand to her mouth. "I think this is Ónarr and his family!"

"It sure does look like him," Arnon replied.

Adelyne slightly scrunched her eyebrows together as if she was sad. "What's wrong?"

Adelyne studied the picture quietly for a moment. "It's just, it's odd to think of the Daecish in this way. Ónarr having a family, I mean." She gasped. "Look!" She pointed to one of the small children, whose left arm was blurred and somewhat transparent. "Why does it look like that?"

Arnon's head prickled with fear, and his mouth went dry. He leaned back up in the chair. "I don't know—looks like a hant or something. Let's put it back."

Adelyne didn't seem to pay attention as she gazed into their faces. "Or we could not."

"Their eyes," she said. "They look so real."

"Yes, yes, very interesting." He stood up. "But this picture's completely useless. It was a waste of time."

Adelyne turned the picture over. Her face grew solemn.

"Now what is it?"

She gently set the picture in the box. "There was a note on the back." She looked up at Arnon, and he almost thought he could see redness in her eyes. "This photo was a gift from his wife." She paused. "In memory of their children."

Arnon sat back down. "'In memory of their children could mean anything."

Adelyne closed the lid to the box. "What if it means they died? And we stole this picture from him."

"Yea, but," Arnon started to say, but he wasn't sure where he was going with it. "Do you actually feel guilty?"

"Of course, I do. Ónarr had this picture locked away for a reason. It obviously meant something to him."

Arnon raised his eyes. "You can't be serious? We went in there to steal documents in the hopes of destroying everything he stands for because, if you remember, he's our enemy. And you feel guilty for stealing a picture?"

"For talking about principles so much, you sure aren't showing it now."

Arnon clenched his jaw. He was angry, but more so at himself. He could feel that same hatred he had when he killed those men crawl over him. He should have been proud of protecting his family, but it only made him sick.

"I'm sorry," she said.

Arnon swallowed.

"It's just—I want to free Sunder, and I want Ónarr gone, but taking this, it doesn't feel right."

"I guess all I can see in Ónarr is the man who's trying to destroy everything I care for. He and all the Daecish; they're the enemy."

"They're people too, though. They have families they love."

Her words cut to his heart as he wondered whether the men he had killed had their own families. No. It didn't matter. "While they steal and kill ours," he snapped. "Have you already forgotten that they drafted your father?"

Adelyne gave him a sharp glare as water welled in her eyes. "Why are you so unpleasant all of a sudden?"

Like a veil being lifted from his face, Arnon suddenly checked himself. This was not the way his father taught him. And the last thing he wanted to do was upset her. "I'm sorry."

Adelyne stared down at her lap. "It's okay."

Her voice sounded pitiful, and Arnon felt ashamed of himself. "I mean it. I'm really sorry I said that about your father." She didn't look up. "It's hard, losing someone so close. My father was my best friend. My whole life, really."

She only shrugged.

He really wanted to hold her hand, but just the thought made his own hands tingle. "I, um," he cleared his throat. "I can say things without thinking sometimes, but I would never intentionally upset you." Shaking off his nervousness, he took her hand in his. Her fingers felt soft and delicate against his rough skin.

She looked up at him. Those eyes. They drew him in like a beckoning trance. He wanted to lean forward and kiss her. But what if she didn't want him to? That would be terribly awkward. But maybe she wanted him to kiss her? Then if he didn't, she might wonder . . . He should quit thinking. He leaned forward. She leaned away.

Arnon quickly turned. Theos, just take him now. "Sorry!" he stammered.

"It's okay," she replied. "I just wasn't expecting . . ." Her words trailed off. Then she tilted her head to the side. "You've never kissed anyone, have you?"

His cheeks tingled. He really didn't want to say no. "Not really."

Adelyne nodded with a growing smile, then scooted her chair toward him. His entire body stiffened to the point that he couldn't even swallow. Relax, he tried to tell himself, but it wasn't working. Still holding his hand, she leaned forward, letting her nose brush his own, and his heart skipped a beat. He never thought being this close to her would make him so . . . afraid. She closed her eyes, her breath on his. Then, her delicate lips gently laid against his, and his head swirled with dizziness. Breathing in her aroma, a subtle earthy scent mingled with the jasmine from her hair. He tried to ground himself, but it was no use—his entire body tingled, inching ever closer to hers. Her fingers slipped from his hand, and she stroked his neck.

Lifting his own hand, he caressed her soft cheek with the back of his fingers, then ran them down her bare shoulder, feeling the smoothness of her skin. She slowly opened her eyes and her gaze danced back and forth between his before she kissed him again, this time lightly placing her hand against his chest. Arnon felt his heartbeat against her palm, and all at once, he felt euphoric in ways he had never experienced, and yet his body trembled with anxiousness.

The faint cry of a baby broke from the upstairs bedroom. Adelyne leaned back. Arnon suddenly found it difficult to breathe. He could barely think straight. Part of him wanted to kiss her again; the other part felt like he was doing something wrong. It was all so new to him.

"I should probably get going," he barely said.

Adelyne stood up and pulled her hand back. "You're right." She nervously straightened her hair. "I need to go upstairs and check on Sarah anyway. Sounds like she could use some help."

"Sounds good," he said. Sounds good? Who says that?

They walked to the front of the room, and Adelyne opened the door. Arnon stepped outside. The breeze cooled his hot skin.

"Will I see you tonight?" she asked.

"At the tavern," he managed to get out.

"Make sure you go straight there."

"Yea, I know." He took a step back, but his foot slipped on a loose rock. Catching himself, he gave an awkward chuckle and could only hope she didn't notice his blushing face.

She smiled but pointed a finger at him. "Riots are still going on, and your name is still posted all over the city!"

"I know," he said, his head still spinning. "I'll be careful, I promise!" Reluctantly, he turned and headed down the road.

Beron Manor

Eirún leaned her arms against the decorative marble railing. Below the third-floor balcony, a green lawn of nearly a hundred acres stretched before the manor, finding its end at a tall iron fence, encircling the entire property. Beyond, she could just make out the eastern edge of Norfrost, nestled behind the face of the mountain. High above, a thick cloud rolled down the rocky slopes until it curled and misted over the city, merging with the smoke and steam. As far as she was, the faint hum of crowds, steam carriages, and locomotives still reached her ears. The wisps in the sky seemed to soar less frequently than they had in the previous days.

In the courtyard below, maids, coachmen, and servants hurried around, carrying trays, trimming bushes, and brushing horses in preparation for some great feast that evening. She had heard that all but King Eirik himself would be present. Taking in a deep breath, she walked back through the double doors of ornamental glass and delicate trim.

A draft of warm air, scented with some floral fragrance, welcomed her as she sat on a cushioned chair situated in front of cream-painted vanity with an oval glass. The ceiling was lined with white molding, and from its center hung a bronze fixture, where thin filaments glowed a golden yellow from within the glass orb. Bare copper wires ran across the ceiling and into the walls, which were a pastel pink. How did she ever end up in such a grand place?

Staring blankly into the looking glass, she ran her fingers along the threads of her satin dress and situated the pearl pin which held her hair up. On the vanity lay a silver bracelet inlaid with many stones.

Behind her sat at a trunk in front of her bed, where her old clothes had been packed in and locked away. Upon a side table in the corner sat an empty birdcage. They treated her like royalty. They even introduced her to the staff as a distant cousin, but it felt like an act. It was any day now, and she'd be handed over to the authorities.

She closed her eyes and took in a shallow breath. By now, she had accepted the darkness clouding her mind. She hated her misery, and yet she clung to it, afraid to let it go.

There came a knock, and Sylvi peered her head around the corner of the partially opened door. With a plump rosy face and hair as light as snow, she looked as young as a teenager, but Eilis said she was already in her mid-thirties.

Eirún smiled. There was something about Sylvi that reminded her of Søren—a look in her bright blue eyes as if she was innocent but lost. Sylvi sheepishly bowed her head and stretched out her arm with a note sticking out of her hand.

Eirún walked over and gently took it from her.

Sylvi peered up at Eirún through a crack in her long hair.

"Thank you," Eirún said.

Sylvi nodded with a wide smile, revealing her crooked teeth, then she hurried away, thumping her feet loudly down the hall.

Eirún opened the note and sighed. The doctor had arrived and wanted her to meet in him the library. She glanced back to the vanity, then to her bed, which was covered in more pillows than she could count. She could just pretend she wasn't feeling well and wanted to take a nap. But she knew it wasn't polite to keep someone waiting.

Approaching the winding staircase, which descended three levels, she peered up at the lofty dome ceiling, which was painted like a large canvas depicting sieges of the Northern Sea. Great long, narrow ships arose on either side until, at the heart of the ceiling, coiled a great serpent from the deep blues and grays, frothed with white. From the serpent's mouth hung a broad chandelier with many lights, which cast the room in a warm glow.

Cracks ran through the painting, and in some places, the plaster broke through as if the image was a distant memory the Daecish no longer cared to honor.

Reaching the bottom of the stairs, she strolled past the drawing room as her shoes tapped on the marble floor with each step. At the library entrance, she paused as an officer stepped to the side and extended a low bow, allowing her to pass. Eirún nodded awkwardly, still uncertain of her proper responses. The officer smiled and continued on his way.

The moment she entered the library, she could not help but notice a large map, hanging between two bookshelves, stuffed with volumes of books. Weaving her way around tables and cushioned chairs, she gazed at all the cities and rivers she had never heard of.

"That's Sunder," Geirleif said from behind her.

Not expecting his voice, Eirún startled.

Geirleif pointed to the map as he held a glass of brandy in his other hand. "We have not discovered what lies further south, but of Sunder, we have just about every mile surveyed, save of course the sources to some of the rivers flowing out of the Mountains of Einarr."

Eirún took notice of the names on the map. "Have you been there?" she asked.

"Only once." He took a sip from his glass. "To Runevast port. Daecland is quite peculiar about who they send over the mountains."

"What was it like?"

"Green and a good deal warmer. We estimate within the next fifty years we'll colonize families."

Eirún's eyes drifted along the map from Runevast to Everwind. "Are there natives already living there?"

"There are." Geirleif set his glass down. "But I hear we get along with them well enough."

As she continued observing the various towns and features, she noticed a slim side table in front of the window to the right of the map. On it was laid a smaller map, framed in dark wood and encased in glass. She picked it up. It revealed both Daecland and Sunder, but there were no cities. Forests covered most of the land, and odd markings dotted the landscape. Most were in Sunder, though a few were in Daecland. "Why does this one look different?"

Geirleif leaned over and examined it. "That is a very old map from before we arrived. Of course, the map itself isn't that old, and it's likely not entirely accurate. But based on archaeology and exploration," he pointed to the markings, "those are the locations of the ancient cities of the Astyrians. I believe they call them the Sarig in Sunder."

Eirún tilted her head. Although the Astyrians once lived in Daecland, very little was known about them. "They must have been a great people to have lived in such a large area," she said.

"As far as we can tell, they didn't cover it all at the same time. Their earliest settlements have been found in Varghoss. It's believed they were largely nomadic then. It wasn't until they migrated to Daecland that they began building permanent settlements. Unfortunately, almost everything we've found is little more than simple foundations buried beneath the earth. But in Sunder, that's a different story."

"How did they get to Sunder? They couldn't have had wisps."

Geirleif raised his eyebrows. "You're right. The only way would have been by ship, but there's no evidence of any seaside dwellings or that they were ever mariners. It's a baffling mystery. All we know is that they were in Sunder a long time. Thousands of years even. And that's where they remained." He pointed to the few settlements along the southern face of the mountains of Einarr. "Our research and digs in Sunder are still minimal, but what we've found," he gave a short laugh, "is enough to keep one in wonder for a lifetime. Their architecture and craftsmanship's like no other."

Eirún had so many questions about Sunder but didn't know where to begin.

"My lady," came the voice of a well-dressed man, stepping into the library. "You arrived earlier than I expected."

"Doctor Reorik," said Geirleif as he grabbed his brandy. "Good to see you. Now, if you'll excuse me, I will leave you with Eirún. I have some matters which need tending to."

Reorik smiled beneath his gray mustache and offered Eirún a seat. "Would you care for some tea?" he asked.

"No, thank you," Eirún replied, sitting down.

"Well, if you don't mind," he said as he walked to the wall and pulled the rope. "I haven't had a cup yet this morning."

A moment later, a footman entered the library. "Sir?" he asked.

"Tea, please."

"Very good, sir."

Reorik sat beside Eirún, and his expression grew somber. "Do you know why I called you here?"

Mathios would die soon. She already knew that. "How is Mathios?"

"I wanted you to know first." Reorik clasped his hands together, clearing his throat.

"Mathios awoke early this morning. However, he is still a bit delirious, and his body is failing. He will not be with us much longer. It's a miracle he made it this far."

"How long do you think?"

"It's hard to say. It could be a day, a week, maybe longer."

Eirún pitied him and was glad that his suffering would soon end. But terrible feelings still lingered in her heart. On the one hand, he was the last thing she had of Søren, and she didn't want to lose that. On the other hand, she still felt anger toward him. A hatred. Both emotions made her feel like a terrible person. Why couldn't she forgive him?

Reorik glanced through the door and into the entry hall. "I'm sorry to cut this short, but we ought to leave the library. The guests will be arriving before long." He leaned forward. "He is able to communicate a little, and he's asked to see you. Would you like me to take you to him?"

She knew she should. It would be the right thing. "Maybe another time," she replied.

* * *

Sitting straight in his seat, Geirleif looked across the long mahogany table, surrounded by diplomats and department heads, including nine members of the General Assembly. He hated the rose-painted walls in that dining hall. Forty-five years ago, his mother had them painted that color, and he never had the heart to change it. At least Eilis didn't mind the color. For a second, he wondered what Sylvi was up to. Probably with Eilis. A scenario he often thought nerve-wracking. He took his mind off it, and it quickly wandered to Eirún. He tried to hide any concern in his eyes. The economy and condition of the mines were enough to give a man in his position a stroke.

"Chancellor Thialfi," said Hrunting as he took a sip of white wine. His first name was Kjell, but he never was too fond of it. Despite his clean-shaven face and darker hair, he was a Daecish lord in the fullest sense. And he had always been a good friend. "What news do we have of our mining industry?"

Geirleif raised an eyebrow. This would be interesting.

"Excellent question, Lord Hrunting," replied Thialfi, one of the younger men at the table, with a thin mustache to prove it. Though he had only been chancellor for two years, he had proven his worth in administering the affairs of Daecland. Essentially, he did everything the public probably assumed the king did. "Unfortunately, we are still in the very early stages of our investigation. But given the high demand for coal and the near standstill in excavation, the damages are extensive. I fear we have only seen the beginning of the repercussions."

"But we've temporarily limited steam engine production and air traffic," Geirleif added. "That will at least help conserve what coal we have for the time."

Several men mumbled to one another at the table.

"What about the employment of the miners?" asked Thialfi's wife, Lady Embla. Well before her years of wisdom, she held a firm posture and wore a black dress with a flamboyant black hat. "Is there any plan in act for their reimbursement?"

Thialfi slid his glass to the side, indicating for more wine. The head butler, Ulfr, hurried over and filled it nearly to the brim. "I was in a meeting two days ago, and as you already know, darling, we have agreed that we're in no obligation to reimburse workers who quit their jobs, no matter the reason." He took a sip of wine.

"Agreed!" said Geirleif. "Excuses of monsters and such! I wouldn't be surprised if they weren't all collaborating with one another. We all remember the labor unions last year. And protests are already popping up in Fingate and here in Norfrost."

"True," said Hrunting, "but to be fair, the unions formed last year were due to work ethics. Many of the miners were treated inhumanly, and it was our duty to support them. But this," he motioned his hand forward, "is like nothing we've seen. Too many people from too great distances apart are reporting the same sounds and smells. The accounts are very similar. We've experienced collapses in a mine here and there before, but not like this. The miners are truly afraid."

"Lord Beron," interrupted Embla. "You mentioned a trip from the east, and you smelled the strange odor yourself?"

"I did," Geirleif reluctantly admitted. "A scent of sulfur. But I cannot testify where it came from."

"Either way," butted in Thialfi, "it is being investigated. In the meantime, we must look into alternative incomes. With the drop in our coal production, prices have skyrocketed, and not just in coal, but in all products coal related. That, in turn, is affecting our shipments—"

"Of just about everything else," Geirleif interrupted.

"Yes," Thialfi continued. "Wisps and all other modes of transportation powered by steam will be impacted. I fear if we do not act quickly, we will face a depression. Alternative incomes must be given. I believe we have a few proposals? Is that correct, Mr. Hodur?"

Geirleif could feel the weight of endless meetings and budget cuts sinking on his shoulders. This was going to be a long year.

Hodur, the Secretary of Economic Affairs, flipped open a thin leather-bound book and pulled out several leaves of paper, glaring at them through his round spectacles. "That is correct, Chancellor. We have several options as of now, all of which will take much time to put into effect."

An immediate chuckle worked its way around the table.

"Certainly, there isn't that much paperwork when passing a bill?" added Hrunting sarcastically. "Just a few signatures!"

Several broke into laughter, but Hodur did not look impressed. "Our first proposal and the one for discussion this evening," Hodur continued, "is our foreign investments."

"You mean Sunder?" asked Geirleif.

"And Varghoss, but yes, to begin with, Sunder. As you are aware, we've temporarily halted a large sum of money going into Sunder and have asked King Ónarr to procure fifty percent of owed debts. With the tariff and temporary pay decrease, that should at least give us a momentary relief as we sort out this mess."

Hrunting laughed. "Ónarr will never pay it."

"Perhaps," Hodur replied.

"What of this rumor that we are going to pull out of Sunder altogether?" asked Embla.

Several men sniggered.

"And this is why we don't trust anything that comes out of the drawing room when women are conversing!" spoke up one man.

The table burst into laughter.

Embla blushed, and Thialfi patted her hand. "Dear," he said aloud, "I understand that there is worry about their limited coal production, but our empire would collapse before we pulled out of Sunder. Besides, I believe Mr. Hodur was just about to inform us of alternative sources of income and energy."

"Yes, thank you," Hodur said. "As I was saying, we cannot depend on coal alone. But as most of you are aware, we don't have to. Several expeditions have returned from Sunder and the southern borders of Daecland, near the oil fields. Some gold has been discovered, but more importantly, an abundance of copper is being excavated, particularly from the western regions of Sunder."

The table broke into a low conversation.

"For voltaic power stations?" asked Hrunting as he rested his sharp chin on his fist

"For voltaic power stations, telegraph communications, alloys, printing, you name it. The discovery of voltaic-magnetic induction has revolutionized our kingdom, as your house bears witness, Lord Beron."

Everyone looked up, eyeing the lights hanging from the ceiling. Revolutionized the kingdom was true enough, but coal was still a necessity. "But do we not need coal to generate such power?" Geirleif asked.

"For now, yes, but as you are aware, hydro-voltaic power research in Fingate has already proven to be an effective means for energy. Although we will always need coal, soon, we will have alternatives. Within the decade, voltaic power will spread as far east as Vagholme, possibly even Sunder."

Geirleif knew well enough about hydro-voltaic dams, but he doubted water could provide enough power for the whole of

Daecland. Especially since stations could only be placed near flowing rivers.

"Speaking of Fingate," added Hrunting, "Lord Beron, are there any more recruit shipments heading to the dilution sites?"

As his mind jumped to the shipments, remorse threatened to grow in his stomach, but he shook such silly feelings away. "I have authorized the shipment of one more this month," he replied with a raised chin, "scheduled in three phases. However, I believe given our economic circumstances, I will wait to authorize any more for the time being."

"And the experiments are going well?" asked Embla.

Geirleif would rather not talk about the experiments. "As far as I am aware, they are. Muskets should be in already, and the psychoanalysis testing has given us positive results. I haven't been there myself." For some reason, it made him feel better to say that. "But our researchers have been hard at work, and with our technological advancements, Varghoss has kept to our peace treaties. Now, if we can just keep Kalestrond on the other side of the North Sea." He grinned at Thialfi. "But I'm not so sure we shouldn't go to war; it just might boost the economy."

Several men laughed.

Thialfi returned the smile, causing his thin mustache to part in the middle, but he replied in a serious tone. "I cannot speak of Kalestrond at the moment. They are as fickle as the Daecish weather, but Emperor Skyr of Varghoss has kept true to his word for three decades, and so will we. Those peace treaties serve to do more than keeping one another at bay. They form an alliance."

The conversation came to a pause when several footmen walked into the dining hall carrying silver bowls of salmon soup and platters of whole sheep's head, which they set on the table. On the smaller platters were many hard rind cheeses and rye bread served with honey and cream. Geirleif took in the savory smell. This was his favorite time of the day. "Well," Geirleif said, "let us take a rest of such ill tidings and enjoy our dinner!"

"Not before I offer a gift," butted in Thialfi.

All at the table looked in his direction as the footmen left.

"Our alliance with Varghoss," he continued, "has proven to be a most valuable asset. As you all know, our exports of natural resources have increased their gunpowder production." He pulled out a small wooden case from beneath the table and stood up. "And as such, they have given a small token of their gratitude."

Several men whispered to one another, keeping their gaze on the case.

"Lord Beron," Thialfi said, now looking at him, "I offer you a gift."

"Chancellor, you really did not have to—"

"Please, Lord Beron, it is my pleasure." He walked over to Geirleif, setting the wooden case in front of him. He placed his hand over it as he continued. "Now, I would be lying if I said it was solely from me, when in fact this is indeed a gift from King Eirik himself."

Geirleif examined the swirling cut-ins etched into the cedarwood lid. The border was laced with gold, with the red crest of King Eirik embedded in the center.

"On behalf of myself, King Eirik, and all of Daecland, we want to bestow this gift to you in thanks for your many years of commitment and service to your country."

"And an added thanks for the wine tonight!" interrupted Hrunting raising a glass.

There was an immediate laugh and applause as Geirleif lifted the lid. Inside sat a small firearm set into a fitted recess, lined in purple cloth. Fitted with a wooden grip, a brass frame, and a barrel of refined steel, the weapon looked more like a piece of art than a weapon. Geirleif eyed the various components, all decorated with gold inlays. Eight round iron balls, a glass vessel, and a short, thin rod lay inside the case as well. Geirleif picked up the firearm, almost in awe. "This is beautiful workmanship," he said, holding the gift delicately in his hands. "Though I've seen their name on paperwork, I've never held a Varghossian Matchlock."

"Not a matchlock," Thialfi replied. "A wheellock." He took the firearm from Geirleif, gripping it by the handle. "Unlike the matchlock, it doesn't require a match. There is a piece of pirate which produces a spark, thus igniting the gunpowder." He pointed to the back of the firearm. "You rotate the arm here, then push the priming pan open." He pulled out the glass vessel, filled with coarse black powder. "Then you fill the powder, stuff the ball, just like with a matchlock." He set the firearm down. "But I'll show you how that is all done later."

"That is remarkable!" exclaimed Geirleif.

"Indeed," replied Thialfi. He pointed to Hrunting. "Your friend, Lord Hrunting, even worked alongside the Varghossians in its design."

Geirleif smirked. "Varghoss cannot take all the credit then, can they?"

"We will let them have it," Hrunting replied with a chuckle. "Although they aren't as accurate as the muskets, they'll prove to be a great asset to our interests. Modeling their barrel design has also improved our canons. Stronger. More efficient."

"And if I am correct, this is not the first of its kind?" Thialfi asked.

"That is correct," Hrunting replied. "Varghoss has an earlier model which they've been using for a few years. This one is a significant upgrade, however."

"We look forward to seeing how they work once the shipment is sent to the Dilution Sites," Thialfi said.

"A shipment?" Geirleif asked.

"For combat testing," Thialfi chuckled. "You signed the papers yourself!"

"Oh, yes, yes!" Geirleif replied, rolling his eyes at himself. "You must remember that I see papers all day, but rarely do I set my eyes on the real thing. I knew the muskets were arriving, but not something of this quality."

"Well, as you may have guessed, Commander-in-Chief Asger has requested both muskets and wheellocks issued for the military by the end of this winter."

Geirleif shook his head. "Just remarkable. This will change warfare as we know it. I'll have to ask for a report as soon they're finished testing."

"I'm anxious for that myself," Thialfi replied.

Geirleif lifted the wheellock from its case once again, a smile still on his face. Thialfi went back to his seat. "Thank you," said Geirleif to the entire table. "This is a kingly gift."

Shifting Shadows

The chill of the morning air was left behind as Søren plunged into the earth once again. The march to the lower quarry had been a task of repetition by now. Before him marched Agatha, just as she had the previous days. He saw Langleigh in the evenings at the camp but never in the mines. She never seemed to talk, but she always smiled kindly toward him. On more than one occasion, when he tried to sleep in the tent, several of the mineworkers would peer through the flap, mumbling amongst themselves about his accent and Daecish appearance. Several mentioned his eyes with looks of horror on their faces. The guards seemed to ignore him for the most part. Yesterday, the black-haired boy, who had always marched behind him, developed a heavy cough, and today, Søren did not see him. Instead, a thin man with brown hair marched in his place.

Continuing through the dark tunnels in silence, Søren's stomach constantly rumbled. But through the course of the days, he had learned to ignore his natural instincts. Rubbing his hands together, he felt the calloused skin that had built up along his fingers and palms. He wagged his head, attempting to shift his lengthening hair out of his eyes. His heart still pattered dimly as if it was the distant echo of what it was meant to be.

When he reached the chamber, workers were already picking the rock and dumping the coal into bins in a mechanical rhythm. Søren caught a glance of two guards hauling the body of a large man into the dark passage on the northern end of the chamber; his shackled feet dragged across the broken rock like dead weight. Algöter walked up to the line, ordering men and women in one direction or another. Søren and Agatha were sent once again up the ladder to the ledge along the left wall. Twice, Søren had picked the rock from the wall, but today, he would haul pails again. Through the mindless work, he had found the resistance to bear on, though whether he was growing stronger in his small arms or only in his mind, he wasn't sure.

Hauling coal, his thoughts wandered as they often did. His dream last night was still vivid in his mind. With a thin smile, the prisoner crawled to him like a phantom, whispering inaudible words in his ear. Then the prisoner gripped his hands like the cuffs around his wrists, holding him tight with long fingernails cutting into his skin. Søren kicked and screamed, but the prisoner only laughed.

He grabbed a pail, passed it along, then grabbed another.

Eirún came to his mind. Once, he had wandered through the back door of the kitchen. Stepping outside, he could see Eirún pulling weeds from the garden. Walking up to her, she opened her hand and revealed a large strawberry she plucked from the patch. "Try this," she had said. Søren could still taste the fresh, sweet fruit as it watered his mouth. He wished he still had his lens, but more so, he wished she was there to tell him that she loved him. He couldn't shake off the prisoner's words, and yet he somehow wanted to hear it. Just to prove that no one ever actually loved him.

He grabbed another pail and passed it along. The mundane sound of coughing and the breaking of coal barely registered in his ears anymore. Thick dust hovered in the air, making it difficult to make out the details on the far side of the room.

The backyard of the orphanage was so green and bright beneath the warm sun. Clear and breezy. It reminded him of the fields outside Everwind. The Dunbeasts and the white petals, so unique against the autumn backdrop, swirling in the wind, he thought he could still smell the pungent fragrance. For a moment, he pictured Eirún and Geoffrey there with him. Maybe Geoffrey would marry her, and then he could be his father. But he knew that would never happen.

A sudden shift appeared in his peripheral vision, near the far side of the chamber. It had happened for only a second as if all shadow and light had altered in the blink of an eye. He focused on the shift but saw nothing, only dancing torchlight among the blackened walls and floor. Did anyone else see it? Gazing around the room, lines of men, women, and children still sluggishly passed the pails along, or swung iron picks against the rock.

A small boy on the bottom floor bent over with a loud cough, fighting for breath. His coughing grew harder, and he took in a last struggling breath before falling over. Algöter walked toward him, wielding a short whip with several throngs. He lashed against the boy, but the boy didn't move. A crowd huddled around, blocking the boy from Søren's view.

"Out of the way!" Algöter yelled. "Back to work!" He slashed his whip against the onlookers while other guards shoved them aside.

When the crowd dispersed, a guard picked up the boy's limp body in his arms and carried him into the darkness of the northern passageway. The other guards went back to their posts, and the men and women continued hauling coal. Søren was handed a pail. Another flickering shadow passed in Søren's peripheral vision, and he froze with the pail in his hand. He passed the pail along and focused his gaze directly toward the flicker but again saw nothing. Shifting his gaze away, the flicker reappeared in his peripheral vision as it continued shifting the light.

Søren held his breath, keeping his eyes fixed forward. Another pail was handed to him, and he mindlessly passed it along. From the corner of his eye, a thick shapeless shadow emerged from the wall itself, swallowing the torchlight. No one else seemed to notice. Søren tried to look at it, but just as with the flicker, as soon as he did, it disappeared.

Gazing at the far wall, it came back into his vision. Within the hovering shadow slowly walked a large creature, like a dark silhouette.

The memory of the smell from the mine entrance—and from outside of Everwind—came back to him. It was the same monster he had met once before. An alphyn, Geoffrey had called it.

Its four legs stepped silently as its head and body lay low as if it was a great wolf stalking its prey. Prowling through the lines of men and women, light was continuously being drawn into the shadow's form around it, like a smooth stream of flowing water. Once, a man turned as if he felt or saw the alphyn behind him, but he went back to work, paying no more attention.

The beast paused before several guards. Søren's heart began to pound. He was continually tempted to look directly at it, but it always vanished within the shadow. Then he heard a scream.

A woman dropped her pail as she stared across the chamber, pointing her finger. Glancing back toward the alphyn, Søren startled as the shadow had completely disappeared, but the alphyn came into full view. The lights from the torches brightened, revealing thick wooly hide and its hideous face. The chamber shattered into an uproar as everyone stumbled back against the walls. The two mules whinnied and rose on their hind legs before they bolted through the northern passage, dragging the tipped-over wagon behind them. Women and children dashed behind carts and piles of rock. Several men attempted to stand their ground, but within a few seconds, they cowered back with the rest.

With a trembling hand, one guard pulled his sword from his sheath. The alphyn lowered itself to the ground as if ready to pounce. A low growl thundered through the chamber, sending tremors through the rock as dust quaked from the ceiling and floor. Torches throbbed with pulsating light. Then the alphyn leaped upon the guard.

Letting out a horrid scream, the guard fell beneath the weight of the beast as his sword was flung into the air. Except for Algöter, who hid behind a crevice cut into the rock, the other guards stumbled through the southern passageway, shouting out indecipherable words.

Several women cried as the alphyn scooped up the guard with its jagged teeth and his body folded in half, spilling blood onto the ground from either side of its mouth.

Søren's eyes went wide, and he shrunk back. Agatha wrapped her arms around him, forcing him to the ground. "Don't look at it!" she yelled. "Just stay with me, and I'll protect you!" But Søren couldn't help but keep his eyes open as the alphyn peered at the others with small beady eyes. The entire chamber fell silent except for low whimpers.

The sound of a deep, moaning wind picked up. It didn't seem to come from the tunnels but from all around.

"Theos, don't leave us," Agatha cried. "Please protect us!"

The alphyn turned its head up to the ceiling as thick saliva dripped from its jagged teeth. Black streams of shadow seeped from the walls and rushed into the alphyn like tentacles, penetrating its hide. The chamber once again erupted into shouts as the alphyn transformed into a black, deathlike monster of swirling wind and shadow. Its small eyes now glowed like blue fire, and it looked up at Søren.

The alphyn leaped upon the ledge in front of Søren as he scooted against the wall. His heart beat so hard against his lungs, it was difficult to breathe. Men and women threw themselves into corners, and one girl jumped off the ledge. Agatha turned her back to the alphyn, covering Søren.

"Go away!" she cried out, but the alphyn stood motionless.

Its body continued shifting, like swirling black wind that sighed from somewhere in its body. Slowly, it took a step toward Søren and opened its mouth, revealing darkness so deep it sent tremors down Søren's skin. A low resonating rumble then came from its throat, like nothing he had ever heard before. It was not a fearful sound but a beckoning one. It wanted him.

Søren's shoulders and chest quivered, and he relaxed his grip on Agatha, but she only clung to him harder. Then the alphyn took another silent step; its head was now only inches from him. The cool wind brushed against his face as its glowing blue eyes flickered in the shadow.

"Please," Agatha pleaded in a trembling voice. Her face was hidden in her arms. "Leave us alone!"

Looking into those eyes, Søren never felt so small. But not of the alphyn itself, but rather the shadow which now filled it. It was terrifying and powerful, yet at the same time, beautiful and mesmerizing, as if it was a growing tempest, swallowing up the atmosphere around it. Somehow, Søren knew that because of the shadow, the alphyn would not hurt him. He reached out his hand, resting it on its head. With a deep satisfying breath, Søren's heart leaped in his chest. The thin feeling that had consumed him since the valley vanished and a new strength swelled within his depths.

The shadow beast lowered its back to the ground, and Søren slowly stood up.

Agatha sat speechless as she lowered her arm. "Your eyes . . ." was all she got out.

As if enchanted, Søren lifted his leg over the alphyn and sat on its back. Gripping his hands into it, all he felt was a firm, cool wind. He wasn't sure if he was even holding on to anything. The alphyn turned and faced the ledge. Unsure of his grip, Søren wrapped his arms around its neck just before it leaped onto the bottom floor. Screams once again broke into the silence. Several men and women now cautiously stood. The alphyn straightened itself, and its muscles flexed. Then its body began to tremble, like a droning vibration.

What was happening? Søren lifted his hands, not knowing what he should do. Dust began to fall from the ceiling, and the sound of cracking rock echoed through the chamber. Søren suddenly sunk his head into his shoulders as the ceiling of the southern passageway collapsed behind him with a great thunder, blocking the entrance from the front of the mine. Everyone in the chamber shuddered and cried out, hiding once again.

Black dust filled the chamber with a thick haze, and Søren coughed as he lowered his head and covered his mouth. On the ground lay a guard's sword. Instinctively, he leaned over and picked it up, wielding it awkwardly in his hand. The alphyn strode toward the northern tunnel while several of the workers stumbled backward and ran through the passage.

Inside the tunnel, all was dark, except for a single lantern that hung from an iron spike on the right wall. The alphyn quickened its pace to a lope. Soon, far on the other end, a single glint of light came into view. Despite the chaos of the moment, Søren could not help but see the light as freedom. Was he leaving that terrible place behind? But where was the beast taking him? Such a thought sent a new kind of fear through him. Would it eat him like it did the guard?

Workers flung themselves against the wall as the alphyn passed them. Then, bolting through the low ceiling and into the open, a blast of cold wind rushed across Søren's face. He closed his eyes as he adjusted to the light outside.

Blinking with a squint, the iron tracks below him curved to the right until they lay hidden behind several large mounds of coal. To his left ran a low bluff, in front of which sat a wooden cart, where two lifeless bodies lay. There were no guards. Despite the fact that snow was falling, hills of deep green rolled in the distance. On the northern horizon emerged the white peaks of the mountains.

The alphyn quickened to a sprint, and Søren jolted, almost dropping his sword. He gripped the alphyn as best he could but risked glancing over his shoulder. Workers poured out of the northern passage as they frantically looked about them in the open air. He thought he could see Agatha, but he wasn't sure.

For what felt the better part of an hour, Søren rode eastward with the setting sun hiding behind gray clouds. The snow turned to freezing rain, and though it fell sparse, it stung across his face as the shadow beast hurtled through the undulating landscape. Now bearing north, they began to rise along a ridgeline while the sky went dark, quickened by the heavy clouds.

The cold penetrated through his drenched clothing and sent continuous trembles through his arms and back. His legs and rear soon began to ache. Would they be riding through this all night?

A sudden flash of lightning raced across the sky, and Søren sank into the back of the alphyn. He didn't know how much longer he could take this.

Looking over his right shoulder, the falling landscape opened to the east. He squinted and thought he could make out many tiny lights in the distance below him. Another bolt of lightning ran across the sky, and hundreds of black dots briefly illuminated in the heart of a valley. With another flash of lightning, he could make out tents and horses.

He kept his eyes fixed on the valley, waiting for another flash, but none came. The alphyn continued northward.

Sixteen and Forty-Seven

A resounding roar echoed into Geoffrey's ears as he awoke with a loud gasp. He lifted his hands to cover his ears, but they were stopped by the grip of an iron chain around his wrists. Cold sweat drenched his entire body, and his blurred vision kept him from looking around. He blinked several times until his eyes adjusted.

Dressed in a long, gray-knit shirt, his bare legs and feet stretched out in front of him on what looked like a stone floor, but the rough flat surface was seamless and gray, like dull marble. Everything felt damp, and he could barely flex his ice-cold fingers. The roar began to ease. As it slowed, the sound of rushing water soon broke into a gentle stream.

A loud snap made Geoffrey's muscles jolt. Several sparks, as if from a fire, hung in the air before they quickly faded. Men, wearing strange masks and tan coveralls, stood around a tall table, concealing whatever it was that lay upon it. Occasionally a man would lay a small instrument on a shelf against the wall, only to grab a different one. Above them hung a strange light from the ceiling, not like fire, but one which neither wavered nor flickered inside a glass orb. The light strained Geoffrey's eyes, and he looked away. On the left wall, several glass windows were propped open, bringing in sunlight from outside. Iron pipes, handwheels, and brass levers filled the ceiling and other walls—all damp with moisture.

Filled with a sense of abnormality, as if he was taken to a foreign land in a different time, Geoffrey only sat staring. Nothing in the room felt or looked familiar. Beside him sat several other men in gray shirts, also bound in chains. Two he recognized from the wisp, but the others he wasn't sure. One of the men lay lifeless on the ground. The others hung their heads low.

Geoffrey turned his gaze to his own lap. The last memory he could recall was the wisp and the pass through the mountains. He had felt feverish and weak, then nothing. Where was he? Fingate? Was that in Daecland or somewhere else? It all felt so strange; maybe he *was* in the Day of Reckoning. An image of Søren riding an alphyn flashed through his mind, but he quickly tried to shake it away. It was a ridiculous thought. He could only hope the poor boy was okay.

"He's stabilized for now," said one of the men in a thick Daecish accent.

Geoffrey turned his focus to the table they stood around. Two of the men stepped away with their hands in the air in front of them, dripping in something red. They disappeared into another room.

Geoffrey's spine trembled. Lying on the table was the body of a man. His chest had been pried open, and some metal contraptions protruded from his exposed insides. Several dark-looking ropes, or maybe something else, hung from the ceiling, finding their end somewhere inside the man's body. His lips flinched once or twice and, for a second, Geoffrey thought he heard a gurgle from his mouth. But his eyes remained wide, pried open by thin metal clamps.

Tearing his face away, Geoffrey tried to control his breathing, hoping he would awake from this nightmare. Just then, two other men walked toward him from some unseen doorway. One of them placed a hand across his forehead.

"We thought we might lose this one," he said to the other man. "But looks like he broke the fever." He lifted his hand beneath Geoffrey's arm. "Come on, let's move him to Section Three."

The other man gripped Geoffrey's right arm as they dragged him across the floor. Now in a dark hall, pipes ran along the ceiling, connecting a series of lanterns. Like the one in the room, they shone bright with no flicker to be seen. From their base ran long, copper-toned string, joining together with one another.

Light suddenly burst forth as a door swung open. Geoffrey closed his eyes against the high sun. A cold gust rushed upon him as his back and legs scraped across the dirt. He squinted at a wall of salmon-colored sandstone to his right. To his left ran a handrail, with the landscape opening beyond. He caught only a glimpse of barren flat sand before he was taken around a corner.

They propped him against another wall of sandstone beside two-dozen other men locked in chains. About eight or so over to his right sat Burlan with his face down. Geoffrey dared not call out to him yet. They all wore gray-knitted shirts like his, which went down to their knees, each with a number sewn upon their right sleeve. Geoffrey glanced at his own sleeve, reading two pairs of numbers—sixteen and forty-seven. Two other men in tan coveralls walked toward them.

"That one," said the one on the left. "Number Forty-Two."

"Let's go, gray-shirt," said the other.

They picked up a man who sat at the front, four down from Geoffrey. His head was bald, and his large stomach hung out beneath his shirt. Geoffrey recognized him as Claude, one of Lester's associates. Lifting him up, they guided him through an iron gate that led into a tall circular fence, forming a ring. They closed the gate behind him. Claude glanced back toward the others through the iron bars, his fearful eyes briefly meeting Geoffrey's.

A second gate, on the opposite end of the circular fence, swung open. Another gray-shirt was brought inside opposite of Claude. Apparently, the numbers four and thirty-three were stitched on his sleeve, as a guard called them out. The two men in tan coveralls walked back over and stood in front of Geoffrey, leaning against the outside of the fence. Geoffrey repositioned himself to get a better view.

"What are we testing today?" said the man on the right. His skin was so burnt and leathered, he looked as if he'd spent his whole life in this desert.

The one on the left read over a sheet of paper. "Symptoms Testing—Battle Derangement Disorder. Thirty-Three just spent twelve days in a mock field."

"With the explosives?"

"The trenches are taking a tougher toll on our men than we expected." He pointed to Claude. "The fat one just came in three days ago. We figured he'd be a good test run for Thirty-Three."

Inside the fence, both Claude and the other man staggered in the sand, glancing around as if they were madmen who had never seen daylight.

"We ready?" said the man to Geoffrey's left.

The other waved his hand in the air.

A small hammer was thrown into the middle of the ring, and a sudden loud shriek began to wail, high and sharp. Geoffrey covered his ears as the sound pierced into his skull. He couldn't tell where it came from.

Thirty-Three fell to the ground. Screaming, he held his ears and clenched his eyes closed.

The sound stopped briefly, then blasted again. Still covering his ears, Thirty-Three continued to scream, lying on the sand. The sound eased, and Claude stepped around the ring, his stomach jiggling while his back slid against the fence. Several of the men in coveralls laughed while two others approached the fence and attentively scribbled down notes in leather-bound books.

The sound continued once again, and Geoffrey winced. From behind the fence, several men began to shout at Thirty-Three. The Daecish man to the right of Geoffrey raised his sunburned hand in the air, and the sound stopped again. He gave a signal to another man in coveralls, who walked to the iron gate. Swinging it open, he stepped toward the hammer and picked it up off the ground. He walked forward as Claude fell back, raising his arms to shield himself.

"Please!" he cried. "No!"

With his left hand, the man tried to move Claude's arms out of the way as he rocked the hammer up and down in his right hand. He finally brought it down on Claude's head, but not hard enough. Claude wailed as blood spilled down his head, seeping into his gray shirt below the right side of his neck. The man swung the hammer down again, and Claude's arms went limp.

He tossed the hammer back in the center of the ring and stared at Thirty-Three, who only sat on his knees with his gaze down.

"That's how you do it!" he shouted.

Two other men ran in and dragged the lifeless body of Claude out of the fence, leaving a trail of blood behind.

Geoffrey hung his face in his hands. Poor Claude. This must be it. They were all being punished for all the wrong they had done. Wiping his eyes, he stopped his mind from digging out memories he had long suppressed. He knew he wasn't good, but he also believed in mercy. Why would Theos allow this?

One of the men in coveralls now stood beside him and scanned down a sheet of paper. He glanced at Geoffrey's arm sleeve. "Let's do this one," he said. "Number forty-seven."

Two men ran over, and Geoffrey was pulled to his feet. His cuffs were unshackled from his wrists. Flexing his fingers, the infected scabs trailing around his red, swollen wrists stung against the breeze. The gate swung open, and he was pushed through. Stepping inside the ring, he heard the gate close behind with a dull clank. Number Thirty-Three still sat on his knees.

The sound wailed again, and Geoffrey covered his ears but kept his eyes on the hammer. Thirty-Three looked around frantically as men once again began shouting behind him. Letting out a scream, he ran for the hammer.

Geoffrey sprang forward, but Thirty-Three took the hammer and swung it down. It grazed Geoffrey's left shoulder. Letting out a grunt, the warm blood dripping from his lacerated skin was a lurid warning that if he didn't kill this man, the man would kill him.

With his other hand, Thirty-Three shoved his palm against Geoffrey's chin, bowing his head back. Gripping his arm in both of his hands, spit foamed from his mouth as his neck muscles strained. He released his left hand, pushing Thirty-Three's palm away, and both of them collapsed to the ground as the hammer bounced across the sand. Entangled in one another's arms, Geoffrey screamed as Thirty-Three bit into his forearm. With blood running down his arm, Geoffrey let go and clutched the wound. All humanity had left this man as if years of torment had twisted him into a savage animal.

Thirty-Three scampered toward the hammer and grabbed it.

Still holding his forearm in his right hand, Geoffrey straightened himself. He charged toward Thirty-Three, who raised his hammer in the air. But before he could bring it down, Geoffrey pummeled him against the fence. The hammer fell from the man's hand as the air shot out of his lungs in a hollow gasp.

Geoffrey picked the hammer up in his left hand and raised it up as Thirty-Three heaved and coughed. Geoffrey's stomach churned with sickness and shame as he held his arm in hesitation. But just as Thirty-Three leaped toward him, Geoffrey brought the hammer down just above his forehead. A sudden flow of blood spurted down Thirty-Three's face. His eyes rolled up, and for a brief moment, his hands feebly continued to grip at Geoffrey's shirt until he collapsed. Dropping the hammer, Geoffrey staggered backward and fell to the ground.

The gate swung open, and a man in coveralls pulled him out of the ring and back to where he had sat before. They clasped the chains back around his wrists. A man walked over and stood above the body of Thirty-Three and scribbled notes in his leather-bound book.

The Letter that Broke the Clouds

Eilívur sat in his office, flipping through papers. Regiments. Divisions. The numbers were outdated. Commander Dagr and Gunnar sat across his desk.

"I still don't understand your concern," spoke up Dagr.

Eilívur looked up. "Bodies are still lining the streets in front of the treasury. Half of the Eastern District is in ruin with smoke still rising from the ashes." He pointed out the window. "I've got two gallows being erected as we speak to deal with the rioters and deserters. I asked for reinforcements! Not two squadrons who won't be here for three weeks!"

Dagr raised his hand in the air. "It's all we can afford to give up right now."

"What am I going to do with thirty men?"

"Our soldiers cannot abandon Llynhithe for the sake of Everwind."

"If we are not prepared, Everwind may very well be taken."

"By who?" Dagr wrinkled his face. "The mobs?" He let out a loud sneeze.

Eilívur let the papers fall back to his desk. "If Wesley's report is correct—"

"Wesley?" he asked, wiping his sharp nose with his handkerchief.

"A mole. But if he is correct, these mobs are now the size of a small army. And if the Silent Hither took over Denhurst. Took over Denhurst," he said louder, "then what is to stop them from taking over Everwind?"

Dagr titled his head. "I received your list of Dark Horses here in Everwind. It's minimal, and it's nothing we can't handle. We simply—"

"I'm not finished," Eilívur interrupted. "Our city is at its frailest. Because of this forsaken pay decrease, soldiers are deserting every day."

It seemed as if the air began to thicken in Eilívur's office. Sweat dampened the inside of his uniform, and he loosened his collar.

"Llynhithe has also suffered a decrease in—"

Eilívur slammed a hand on the desk. "We have not the organization nor the strength to retake Denhurst and hold Everwind without Llynhithe!"

"I understand your concern, and I have two squadrons who will arrive within the next three—"

"That is not enough!"

"What if those in Denhurst decide to march toward Llynhithe instead of Everwind?" Dagr asked. "Have you considered that?"

Eilívur bit down on his teeth and focused his gaze on the far wall where a crack in the plaster ran from the floor to the ceiling. Keep it together. "Llynhithe is stable, the Silent Hither there is almost non-existent. They would never be so foolish as to march on Llynhithe," he raised a finger, "yet. But if they possess Denhurst and Everwind, then they have a chance."

"They won't take Everwind."

The heat in Eilívur's veins rose, but he controlled his tone. "King Ónarr expects these reinforcements, and we are going to have to give him an answer today. And it'll be on your head, not ours."

"If I may," butted in Gunnar.

Eilívur leaned back with his hands clasped across his chest.

"It's too late. If all we get are two squadrons, then that's all we get. We can send another request. But in the meantime, let us double the sentries outside the city wall, focusing our efforts along the southern and eastern borders since that is most likely where our enemies will march from. We have catapults, we have a strong cavalry, and we're in a well-fortified city. We can inform King Ónarr that reinforcements are at least coming, and we are doing all that we can in the meantime."

Eilívur feared Commander-in-Chief Asger would be called in from Norfrost before the end of this, and he'd probably get decommissioned. "What other choice do we have? But we must act quickly. War will be upon us before we realize it."

"I seriously doubt an uprising of primitive farmers merits the term 'war,'" added Dagr.

"These primitive farmers happened to take the third-largest city in Sunder," Eilívur replied. "You clearly do not understand the gravity of the situation."

* * *

Arnon tried to catch his breath as he crossed onto the Western Road toward Fellhouse Street. Not ten minutes before, Murdock sent him to get Adelyne. "A dispatch brought a letter," he had said. "Drake wanted Adelyne there for it." Arnon took in a deep breath, a stitch lancing his side. Was the letter from Denhurst? The thought sent a shiver of excitement mingled with fear down his back.

Besides the occasional person walking alone, the street felt empty, like a ghost town. Most of the buildings in the Western District still held intact, but the shouts from the north reminded him that the city still rumbled beneath the anger and confusion.

Up ahead, a rioting crowd rushed south from one alleyway to another—several held clubs, which they gripped tight in their hands. One man, clearly a Sunderian merchant, wielded a Daecish sword. There was a hard anger frozen on his face. Arnon moved to the other side of the street and continued on.

Approaching the junction where the Western Road turned into Fellhouse Street, Arnon turned south. His boots cracked on frozen mud. About two blocks down stood a group of people at the corner of a building, just on the edge of the Southern Squalor. Arnon halted beneath the shadow of a low overhang. Three young men gathered around Adelyne, chatting. They appeared to be about Arnon's own age and were dressed in traditional Sunderian attire. But one man, the one standing closest to Adelyne, sported a black jacket and top hat over his worn tunic. He held a cocky grin. By the look of him, Arnon figured he wore the outfit as a mockery. He probably either stole the jacket and hat or pulled them off of a dead body.

The man said something, and Adelyne laughed. He reached a finger over and brushed it against the front of her tunic in a grossly inappropriate manner. Adelyne didn't stop him but only smiled.

Arnon immediately felt like he was going to throw up. A wave of heat swelled up in him like a steaming kettle. For a second, he considered running at the man, but by some deep convicting conscience, or perhaps by an act of grace, he remained still. The men soon departed and disappeared down an alleyway. Adelyne walked away from Arnon's direction, apparently to her house.

He stood there for what felt like an hour. What were they talking about? Why did she let him touch her in that way? Arnon would have never done that. He thought back to her question about whether he had kissed anyone. How many men has she kissed? Had she ever kissed the man in the top hat? Arnon never cried. He didn't cry when his family left for Denhurst. He didn't cry when his father died. But for some reason, a pain shot through his stomach, and all he wanted to do was ball up and weep.

"Arnon!"

Startled, he turned as Drake marched toward him.

"What are you doing?"

What was he doing? Arnon only shook his head. "I'm sorry . . ." he trailed off.

Drake crossed his arms. "You should've been at the tavern half-an-hour ago! I'll get Adelyne; you hurry on!"

The walk back passed in a blur. By the time he made it to the tavern, Arnon wasn't even sure which way he took to get there. He opened the door and stepped inside. The room lay in darkness; all the tables and chairs stood empty. In the far corner, the cellar door was propped open.

Downstairs, the lanterns were already lit, but no one was there. Several maps had been stretched across a long table, with rusted swords and old shields bearing the black horse of Sunder leaning against a corner. Stacked beside them were cuirasses, hauberks, chest plates, and helms. It looked more like an armory than a cellar.

Arnon stood by the steps and rubbed his face. He ran his hands through his hair until he felt like he was going to pull it out. All he could picture was Adelyne kissing some other man. He clenched his fists and thought about punching something, but the cellar door swung open. Drake walked down, followed by Adelyne. Arnon quickly blinked, trying to calm himself.

Adelyne smiled at him, then looked at the floor as Drake stepped over to Arnon's sleeping area. They both looked back up at him.

"What is it?" Arnon asked.

Adelyne kicked at a tipped-over tankard. "It looks like a trash heap down here."

Drake blew out an exaggerated sigh and picked up the tankard. "I done told you, you're gonna bring in rats!" He handed the tankard to Arnon and peered at him oddly. "What did you do to your hair?"

Adelyne chuckled and stepped over to Arnon. "It's all over the place." She reached out her hand to lay it down, but Arnon stepped back and tightened his jaw.

"It's fine," he said. He wanted it to sound cold, and he hoped she noticed.

She let her hand drop, and she tilted her head. "Is . . . is everything all right?"

Drake rolled his eyes. "He's fine. Now, if you two are finished," he pulled out a letter from his pocket and leaned toward Arnon with a whisper, "a dispatch came in this morning with a letter from Denhurst, you hear? It's time we have a meeting."

Arnon checked himself. This was it. At that moment, loud footsteps hurried down the staircase, and Morgan, Murdock, and Wesley came into view.

"We ready?" Morgan asked, wiping the sweat from his forehead with his sleeve.

"Aye," Drake replied. He handed Morgan the letter and walked across the cellar to grab a few extra stools.

"Brothers," Morgan said as he sat down. "And Adelyne." He smiled. "We received a dispatch this morn' from Galvin Barclay of Denhurst. I don't know the best way to prepare you for this, so I'll just be blunt. As we speak, there's an army encamped in the Keld Valley." He paused, eyeing everyone in the room. "The Free Sunderian Army."

Wesley stiffened.

"From Denhurst?" Murdock asked.

"They sacked Denhurst a couple of weeks ago," Morgan replied, "and began marching north."

"How many?"

"Roughly twelve-hundred," Drake added.

Murdock gasped. "Twelve-hundred?"

Adelyne cupped her hands over her mouth.

Arnon's body froze, and his mind raced. A Sunderian army coming toward Everwind was exhilarating. Everything they could have hoped for. And yet, how could they be ready? Was he ready?

Wesley's eyes flicked from side to side. "Denhurst taken?" he asked. "And they're here, outside of Everwind?" He looked up to Drake, his pitch heightening. "How long've you known about this?"

Drake eyed Morgan, then looked back to Wesley. "We received the first letter about two weeks ago."

"Why didn't I know about this?" he suddenly shouted as he slammed a hand on a stool top.

Everyone in the room startled, and Drake narrowed his eyes and took a step forward. "'Cause, you ain't been around as of late!"

Sinking back, a scowl formed on Wesley's face. "I should've known. I'm a Dark Horse. Matter of fact, I'm on the court. I should've known."

Arnon couldn't help but feel sorry for Wesley. Of course, he should've known. But just as his father had always said. He was an outcast.

"And I'm sorry for that," Drake said in a calmer tone. "But I've barely seen you, and the secrecy of their march was too critical."

"You don't trust me?"

Drake's neck went red.

Wesley huffed a quiet laugh. "I see how it is."

"Please," Morgan interrupted, "we can deal with this later. I'm sorry, Wesley. I stood by Drake on this decision. It may not have been the wisest, but it's done. We'll settle this matter as soon as we can, but in the meantime," he motioned a hand up the stairs, "we've got an army outside the city, ready to invade."

Wesley sat back on the stool and rubbed his forehead but didn't say anything.

"I knew something peculiar was going on." Murdock grinned through his red beard as he examined the stacked shields and cuirasses. "Every available corner in Birchton and the Southern Squalor's stacked with 'em."

"And we need more," Drake added. "We've been preparing for this day for a long time, but now it's upon us, and quick."

"There's a few more things the letter mentioned," Morgan added, "which are important. The army's wearing mostly Daecish armor, but they've painted red horses on the front and backs for our clarification."

"That's good to know," said Murdock.

"They've asked for a dispatch to meet them by tonight," Morgan continued. "They plan on invading by the 'morrow.'"

"By the 'morrow?" Murdock hollered. "That don't give us any time!"

"We'll make it work," Drake added.

"I can go to them," spoke up Wesley.

Morgan glanced at Arnon. "They've requested Arnon specifically."

Arnon accidentally breathed in his spit and coughed out loud. They wanted him to go? What if he messed something up? What if the Daecish caught him? For a second, he imagined his father gazing at him from across their kitchen in the Western Plains. What if his father could see him right now? Relaxing his tense shoulders, he gave a small nod. "All right," he said.

Wesley covered his eyes as his face turned so purple a vein bulged along his temple.

"You better go quick," Drake said to Arnon.

"I'll head out now," Arnon replied, but he kept his eyes on Wesley, whose face only darkened. Something was wrong with him, but Arnon wasn't sure what to do. With the events unfolding before him, he could barely think straight as it was.

"And be careful!" Morgan folded up the letter. "There's no keeping this a secret no more, but we need to take every precaution we can to keep the Daecish from learning about it. In the meantime," he peered at Adelyne and Murdock, "we'll need messengers to head to Birchton and the Southern Squalor. Adelyne, can you gather the teams?"

"Of course," she replied.

"If you'll take the Southern Squalor," added Murdock, "I'll grab Quinn and head straight to Birchton."

"Afterward," Drake said, looking to Adelyne, "go stay with Sarah, make sure her and the little ones are safe."

"I will."

Murdock laid a hand on Arnon's shoulder. "Are you sure you can handle this?"

After today he wasn't so sure. "If I leave now, I can grab Ansel and be there by nightfall."

"After we leave here," Drake said. "I'm gonna take you another way out the city. It's safer than the gates and quick enough."

"You may not return before the army invades," added Morgan. "Tell Galvin we've got lookouts posted around the city. We'll be prepared to attack when they do."

"I will." His heart began to beat faster.

With a large grin, Drake wrapped a thick arm around Arnon, squeezing him tight. "You're gonna do just fine!" he said. "Just like your father!"

Arnon forced an awkward smile. "Thanks," was all he could grunt.

After Drake let him go, Arnon looked back to Wesley. He felt bad for him. He had been sick all this time and practically left out of all the decisions. "Are you okay with this plan?" he asked.

Wesley didn't answer. His left hand still rubbed his temple, and his eyes had glazed over. The room went silent as they all stared at him.

"Something's wrong," Wesley finally spoke up in a sluggish tone. "Something popped . . . in my head. Maybe?" His words were drawn out. "We should talk to the court about it first."

Arnon glanced at Drake and Adelyne. "But the court's all here. Morgan, Drake."

"You all right?" Morgan asked.

Wesley suddenly looked up. "I'm . . . I'll just . . ." He turned and ran up the stairs, his body occasionally slamming against the wall until he shut the door behind him.

Drake peered up, following the sound of Wesley's footsteps above them.

"You think the fever's back?" Arnon asked.

"Not sure," Drake replied. "But something ain't right."

"We don't got much time to waste ourselves," Morgan said as he approached the steps. "I'll find Wesley and meet back with you," he told Murdock.

"See you there," Murdock replied, and they both left. Adelyne soon followed after them, but halfway up the steps, she paused and looked at Arnon as their gaze met. Her eyes looked sorrowful. She turned and walked up, and Arnon's heart quivered. As soon as he was about to run after her, a hand rested on his shoulder. "How're you doing, boy?"

Arnon frowned at Drake. He felt terrible. "I'm doing all right."

Drake cackled. "You've the look of a man with a broken heart."

Arnon felt his blood rise to his cheeks.

"She's a good girl, you know?" Drake said, peering up after Adelyne.

Arnon didn't respond.

Drake met Arnon's gaze. "So what's got you down?"

It was like hearing his own father's voice. "I don't know, Drake. I can't help the way I'm starting to feel about her."

Drake grinned.

"But," he continued, "and I know this is going to sound stupid, but men are always staring at her and today she was talking to this creep," he grunted, "and she smiled at him."

"She's a pretty girl. If girls smiled at you all day, you'd smile back on occasion, I'd imagine."

A short laugh burst out Arnon's nose. "Sure, but this guy," he hesitated, "he touched her like . . ." He didn't even want to say it. "He basically grabbed her, if you understand what I mean. And she didn't stop him. She smiled back as if she liked it."

Drake leaned his back against the stair railing and crossed his arms. His eyes narrowed in thought. "I've known Adelyne since she was a little girl. And there are some things . . ." There was a hesitation. "Her father," he started to say but paused.

"Her father?"

"She ain't had the easiest life." He looked at Arnon like he knew something but wouldn't dare to say. "She's a good girl, and I love her like a daughter, but she's got a hole in her heart." He sighed. "A brokenness. And she's trying to fix it, you understand? She's trying to fill that hole."

Arnon peered at Drake but didn't say anything.

"She looks differently at you, though. You should know that. When you're 'round, there's a gleam in her eyes I ain't seen in a long time." He stretched his back and stuck his hands on his hips. "Anyway, we best get going. Time's running short."

Arnon crawled through the small opening of the city wall. He eyed Drake on the other side, who was already restacking the stone. "How come I never knew about this?" he asked.

"Shh!" Drake hissed. "Been a secret since I's a boy. You don't tell no one 'bout it, you hear?"

"Don't worry," he tried to reply, but Drake had already sealed the hole shut.

Arnon kept low by the wall until no one else was around. Then he hurried to the Western Road, ensuring he was far enough to not be seen by any Daecish guards along the gate. The clouds up above swirled, dark and heavy. It looked like it might snow. To his surprise, there were no crowds along the road. Maybe it had something to do with the riots.

Within the hour, he arrived at the once bustling fishing village on the shores of the Swelling Sea, which now sat empty and ghostlike. Only a few buildings of daubed wattle and thatched roofs remained untouched. Most were either broken into or burned to the ground.

Only a handful of people were in sight as they rummaged through the remains of a destroyed cottage.

A blast of wind rushed from the sea and cut straight through his jerkin. Bundling his arms, he set his gaze on the stable, trying to control his rising panic. It looked as if it had long been abandoned. Nearby, a short man stacked some small chests onto the back of a wagon with two horses mounted in the front.

"Sire?" Arnon asked, his voice drowning in the rushing wind. "Sire!" he spoke louder. The man turned. "Have you seen the stable keeper around the village?"

"The stable keeper? You mean Thomas?"

Arnon paused, trying to remember if he knew his name. "He was holding a horse of mine—a bay horse. Went by the name Ansel, if that means anything."

The man thought for a moment. "Yes, I know the horse. Thomas spoke of selling him off. Said he ain't received no payments. Times were rough, he said, and he needed the money."

The blood drained from Arnon's face. He had completely lost track of time. He said in a loud and anxious tone, "Do you know who he sold it to?"

"Matter of fact, I don't know if he ever got 'round to it," the man replied. "Last I saw him was the day before the riots came, I reckon." He glanced toward one of the burned-down buildings. "I left for the countryside until things calmed down. When I got back, his stable was empty. I reckoned Thomas up and left."

Arnon gaped at the man in disbelief. He felt like a fool stepping into his worst nightmare.

"Sorry I couldn't be of more help," the man finished as he went back to loading chests.

Arnon's chest felt heavy above his shaking legs. He was supposed to ride to meet the army. Fight a battle. But he had no horse. With a throbbing headache, he made his way to the stable. On the porch, he peered through the front door window of hand-blown glass. All was dark and empty. The worst part was that he lost his father's horse. His family would be so disappointed in him, they'd probably never speak to him. He pictured his father lying dead on the ground. A sudden surge of anger erupted out of him. With clenched teeth, he balled his hands into white fists. Abruptly, he began to kick against the door as it rattled against its hinges. With a loud scream, he swung his right hand through the window, shattering the glass.

With panting breaths, he pulled his fist out; a clean, open cut ran just above his knuckles. Warm red blood trickled out and poured between his fingers onto the floor. Gripping his hand in his jerkin, he cursed. Nothing on the wooden porch looked of any use. He reached his left arm through the broken glass and unlocked the door, which easily swung open. Inside, it lay empty, except for a single chair tipped over on its side. He stepped over to another door on the right, leading to the horse stalls, and pulled it open.

A whiff of manure and feed caught his nose. Four empty stalls, two on either side, lined the straw-laden hall. The gray sky outside dimly lit up the sparse wooden boards of the ceiling and walls. Picks, shovels, and reaping tools leaned against the far wall, with a brown rag hanging on the end of one of the handles. He took the rag and wrapped it around his hand, tightening it down until the bleeding stopped. Stepping back outside, all he could do was stand there and peer across the village in hopelessness. The man had now left with his wagon, and the wind died down. Thick flakes of snow lazily drifted to the earth, making soft, quiet patters in the stillness of the air.

Winter had begun.

His mind reluctantly went back to Adelyne, and he imagined her kissing other men. But then he recalled the look on her face at the top of the stairs and the words Drake had shared with him. He wished he could have talked to her before he left.

Across the way, two other men were repairing the clay walls of a small fish market. Beside it, a tall gray mule had been roped to a stunted tree. He had to get to Galvin and the others. He had to think of something. But what? He knew he couldn't walk to their camp, and he certainly wouldn't go back to Everwind.

Taking a deep breath, Arnon walked over to the two men working on the building. As he crossed the dirt road, the older of the two, who was holding a bucket of wet clay, looked up at him with a brown, leathery face and thin gray hair.

"Sire," Arnon said, holding his wounded hand against his chest. The other man, younger and with more hair, cocked an eyebrow as his eyes followed the blood that streaked down his jerkin and trousers. Arnon looked around awkwardly. The older man seemed to be chewing something, though he never swallowed. "You, uh," Arnon said with a cough. "You don't happen to know if I can borrow that mule?"

The younger man squinted. "How much you got?"

"Well," Arnon reached for a money pouch on his belt, which he knew wasn't there. "I don't actually have any with me, at the moment, but I'd pay you once I came back with . . ." His words trailed off into a mumble. They'd never let him have it.

Both men stared at him.

"With the mule," Arnon finally got out.

The younger man shook his head. "Don't think that'll work."

Arnon stood for a moment as both men walked into the empty market, going back to their repairs. Then he turned and walked back across the street with his head down. He didn't know where he was going. He was a failure.

He felt his lungs deflate, but just as he did, he paused in his step. "No," he told himself. That would be a terrible idea. He continued on but stopped again. He slowly looked back at the mule tied to the tree. The two men were inside.

"Don't be a fool," he muttered.

In the Valley of Shame

The steps creaked as Adelyne carried a clay pot full of hot stones. The smoke from the downstairs hearth billowed against her as she pushed open the door, made of crudely framed limbs. She set the pot down and picked up a cloth. Sarah sat in the far corner, covered in a thin blanket as she nursed the baby. Beside the back wall, Lilly slept soundly on a straw pallet just below a small open window, covered only by a tattered sheet. A cold breeze occasionally made its way into the room, blowing the sheet back.

"I think the smell's been bothering Acton," Sarah said in a dry voice. Beneath her disheveled hair, her cheeks had lost color. "Every time a gust comes in, he starts crying." She eyed Lilly with a half-smile. "She doesn't seem to mind, though."

With the cloth in her hand, Adelyne set the stones beneath the wool blanket beside Lilly and a few beside Sarah. "Acton," she said. "I like that name."

A gentle laugh made Sarah's eyes crinkle at the sides. It was the first time Adelyne had heard her do so.

"What is it?" Adelyne asked as she sat down beside her.

"Nothing, it just reminded me of . . ." Her eyes dimmed, and her smile faded. She resituated herself to lay Acton down on her lap, who was now fast asleep. "I don't know what to do," she admitted. "I don't know how we'll make it without Geoffrey."

"You don't have to worry about that right now," Adelyne replied. "You'll be taken care of, and one day Geoffrey will be back. You've still got hope."

"How?" Sarah looked up with red eyes. "If he isn't already executed, he's what? Drafted to Daecland? How's he ever going to come back? Are they just going to let him go? Is he just going to walk back home?"

Adelyne thought hard for an answer, but she found her own self getting discouraged. She was a Dark Horse. She was supposed to help win back Sunder. But even she knew that not all Sunderians meant well. What if the wrong person took control afterward? No. She couldn't think like that. She needed to focus on the good. "If we win back Everwind, there's hope that we'll get the Daecish out of Sunder for good."

Lines formed across Sarah's forehead as if she was only getting more upset. "You don't understand. If we fight the Daecish, that'll only seal his fate from us." She closed her eyes. "Our actions are probably going to kill him and everyone else they've taken."

Adelyne held in her breath. She'd never thought of the consequences of their actions for those who were drafted. If they took back Everwind or even all of Sunder, those in Daecland would be lost. Would her father be killed? Part of her hoped so, but the other part hated herself for even thinking it.

Sarah broke into a sudden loud sob. "Geoffrey's not coming back," she cried. "And our fate's as good as his. I've seen the widows and their children in the slums." She sniffed as tears dripped from her nose. She stroked Acton's thin, dark hair. "So many of them don't make it. And the ones that do . . . they do unthinkable things just to feed their kids."

Wrapping her arms around her knees, Adelyne wanted to say something, but Sarah's words made her suddenly feel filthy. She stared across the other side of the room where the jarred-open door sagged on its old wooden hinges. She could still remember, not long after her mother died, when she would lay awake in fear, staring at that same door. Then, late in the night, her father would walk in, closing the door behind him. Her eyes welled up. Why did Arnon act like that in the cellar? Did he find out about her?

"Are you okay?" Sarah asked, wiping her nose.

She blinked and glanced around the gray and empty room. "We'll just have to survive," she said in a cold voice. "I've had to do it for a long time."

Sarah barely tilted her head as if she was carefully taking in every word she said.

"I'm sorry," Adelyne said. "I didn't mean to say it like that."

"Is there something you'd like to talk about?"

Tears unexpectedly welled up. Surprised at herself, she chuckled and wiped them. She'd wanted someone to ask her that question her whole life. "I'm supposed to be here for you, not the other way around."

"And you have been. Now, what's wrong?"

Her lungs shivered, and her hands fell into her lap. "You have so much to deal with."

Sarah smiled. "I'm okay."

Her heart desperately wanted to spill it all out. Just to get it over with. But then what? Everyone would look at her like a whore. But that's who she was, wasn't it? Adelyne hated herself, but she didn't want them to hate her too. "What's the point of living?" she confessed but was shocked that she actually said it out loud. "We're all going to die anyway."

Sarah looked at her in such a way that Adelyne felt as if she could see right through her. Sarah lifted her chin. "You know that death isn't the end, don't you? Things will get better."

"But what if I want it to end?" She picked at the thin crack at the bottom of her leather tunic. "Even if everything gets better after we die. Why must we be tortured until then?"

"I don't know why some things are allowed," Sarah replied in a gentle voice. "But I once asked my father the same thing when my mother died."

"How old were you?"

"I was seven."

A lot of children lost their parents at young ages. It was just a part of life. But for some reason, the fact that they had both lost their mothers made her feel more comfortable around Sarah. "I was ten when my mother died."

Sarah held Adelyne's hand. "When I asked my father why she had to die and why we had to suffer through it, he said there are some things worth suffering for. I didn't really understand what he meant, so he put a mug in front of me and said, 'If I had a drink right now, I'd be thankful, but I'm not very thirsty, and so I could only enjoy it so much. But if I were put in a desert for a day or two, and I had nothing to drink—if my throat burned, and I suffered because of it—imagine how I'd feel if I stumbled on a fountain of cool water.'" Sarah paused as if she was thinking. Lilly whimpered from some dream but remained asleep. "It may not be the best answer," she continued, "but I've never forgotten it. I believe that, somehow, we will enjoy the next life more because of the suffering we go through now. I don't know how it will all work, but I imagine we'll look back to our pain and know that it was all worth it."

Her illustration only disheartened Adelyne. Her own suffering was different. Sure, her mother died, and her father had abused her afterward, but she had done wrong things herself. Terrible things. "What if you caused your own suffering? What if it's because you've . . ." she couldn't finish her sentence.

"I think there are some things we cannot experience apart from suffering," Sarah replied. "Even when it's because we've done things that are wrong."

It was like she read her mind. "Experience things like what?"

"Like a certain kind of love. Not a shallow, selfish love. But the kind of love that's real." She brushed aside a few strands of brown hair that had fallen down her cheek. "If I hurt someone terribly, and even though they didn't have to, they forgave me, and so I was freed from my guilt, that's a kind of love that could only be experienced by the suffering of my own wrongdoing."

Adelyne's chin trembled. She could never forgive her father, neither could she forgive herself. She wished Arnon was there.

Sarah pulled Adelyne toward her and hugged her. "Now you listen here. I know you've got something going on that you don't want to talk about."

Adelyne tightened her jaw but didn't say anything.

"I've seen that same look in others," Sarah continued. "You don't have to tell me, but you must trust Theos. He's merciful. He'll turn your sorrow into joy."

But Theos knew everything about her—everything she'd done. If she couldn't forgive herself, why would he? She sniffed and wiped her nose. "You sound like my mother whenever she talked about Hælend's Ballad."

"Geoffrey used to sing that song to himself at night." She laughed. "But he was a terrible singer!"

Adelyne couldn't help but smile. "Did he know he was?"

"Of course, he did. I told him!"

Adelyne gasped and covered her mouth. "You did?"

"He didn't mind. He knew I liked his voice anyway." Sarah sighed and continued to rub Acton's hair. "You're right about one thing, though," she said. "We're going to have to work hard just to survive." She scrunched her eyebrows as if remembering a painful memory. "I keep seeing girls out in the streets at night. Showing off themselves. Some of them are mothers. Others are too young to be. We wouldn't have made it if you hadn't taken care of us. You've been very kind and generous to open up your home."

"I'm just doing what I can," Adelyne replied. "I know it isn't much, but the others will help too. Drake, Morgan, Murdock. We've always looked after one another."

"I'm sure you're doing more than enough."

"For now." Adelyne glanced out the window as a cold breeze crept in. "But it's only going to get colder."

"I'm afraid you're right," she replied.

"We'll find you someplace warmer as soon as we can."

A sparkle lit Sarah's eyes. "I've got an idea. When this is all over if we survive it, why don't you come stay with me at my home?"

"But what about the Daecish?"

"If what you say about this army is true, I don't think the Daecish will be looking for me anymore. Besides, my house is warm, it has an indoor kitchen and," she looked at Lilly, "she needs to be home."

Overwhelmed by the gesture, Adelyne wasn't sure how to respond.

"And we could house others," she added. "Those who need a place."

"From the slums?"

"I'm not sure if there's much of a difference between the slums and everywhere else now."

"But there's so many who need a place."

"We have room," Sarah continued. "Servant bedrooms upstairs, several rooms downstairs. We have glass windows, a fireplace. It's perfect for taking in others."

Adelyne's interest piqued. "How will you decide who to house?"

"What about the widows and girls in the streets? They've got no families, no one to look after them. If anyone needs a safe place, they do."

"I know Drake would be willing to help," Adelyne offered. "As much as he could at least. He's got connections with several farmers south of the city. I'm sure they've got more than enough grain stored for winter."

Lilly suddenly awoke with a loud wail. She sat up, reaching out her arms. Adelyne rushed over and brought her to Sarah.

"Honey? What's wrong?" she asked as Lilly continued crying.

She rubbed an eye. "I . . . I heard you talking." She cried. "And, and, and . . ." She took in a quick breath. "I thought daddy was home." She whimpered and sniffled her nose. "But he's not."

Sarah's eyes welled up as she held her close.

* * *

Arnon braced the mule with his legs and grabbed a fistful of mane at the base of its neck. He never liked riding bareback or without reins, but today he was thankful his father had taught him how to do it. He glanced back toward the port village. "Just for a couple of days," he justified to himself. "I'll return the mule and send a few aracs back with it."

Bearing northwest, he galloped toward the Keld Valley, being sure to stay clear of mines and any roads. Cresting over a low, sloping hill, a sudden gust of wind rushed upon him, flapping his clothes against his body. He wished he hadn't left his father's bear cloak at Drake's tavern. The snow now began to fall heavy and fast, leaving the rolling hills shrouded in white, with thin streaks of deep green and brown barely breaking through along the ridges and bluffs.

Scattered around the base of many hills sank several depressions, deep and dark, like the mouths of great caves. Passing them by, a rank odor crawled into his nose, and he gagged. He had smelled that scent before, but never this pungent. For a second, he thought back to the rumors of the Day of Reckoning drawing near. He shook off his nerves and reminded himself that rumors of those days had been around since Hælend's Ballad was first penned.

By sunset, the landscape eased into gentle slopes. Arnon turned southeast and rode on until a shadow appeared in the distance where the earth lowered into the Keld Valley. He brought the mule to a slow trot. He never knew why it was called a valley. It was more like a gorge. The Western side was practically a cliff, jutting down a thousand feet, and although out of sight, he knew that on the northern and eastern ends of the valley ran several paths, but the steep ravines, riddled with boulders and hemlock trees, would be impossible to descend on the mule. He decided to ride to the southern end of the valley, where a slope ran beside great jagged rocks swelling from the earth into sharp points; The Mouth, it was called by many. Although it took longer than other routes, it followed a shallow holler which descended easily enough for riding.

Approaching the first set of rock outcroppings, he rounded a sharp gray boulder, covered in moss and ice. Ahead, the earth ran down into the dark of the valley where many tents and wagons clustered in a clearing within the surrounding trees. Torches moved around like small yellow dots as everyone seemed to move around busily.

"Hold there!" shouted a voice behind Arnon.

He turned.

A middle-aged man holding back an arrow notched into a yew cut bow stepped around Arnon, keeping his eyes fixed on him. "What's your business?" he demanded.

Arnon slowly reached into the opening of his upper jerkin and pulled out the folded letter. "I'm Arnon Greystrom, with the Dark Horses of Everwind. I received this letter from Galvin Barclay."

The man looked at Arnon for a moment. "There anyone else with you?"

"No one."

The man stepped around the mule and glanced west behind his shoulder, his arrow still pointed at Arnon. The sun now sank beyond the western horizon, casting long dark shadows along the rim of the valley walls. The man let his left hand leave the bow and reached for a curved, cream-colored horn that hung at his waist. Placing the horn to his lips, he blew a reverberating, deep howl into the valley below. The entire camp seemed to halt in their tracks. Several shadows ran toward horses, and they soon galloped up the southern crest. The first of the horsemen rode up beside the man. The horse whinnied as he brought it to a halt.

"Colin," the newcomer said, "lower your arrow." He dismounted his horse.

Arnon's mouth dropped. He lowered himself down and stood as the man came forward. "Galvin?" he asked.

Galvin bellowed a large laugh as Porter followed up from behind.

"Arnon Greystrom!" Galvin shouted as he wrapped his arms around him. "Can't believe it." He stepped back. "And you're even taller than me!"

"It's good to see you, Galvin," Arnon said with a laugh.

Porter tussled Arnon's hair. "No welcome for me?"

Arnon clasped arms with Porter and smirked. "I'm glad to see you're still alive."

Porter chuckled and slapped Arnon on the back, but Arnon kept glancing at Galvin. The gray traces in his brown hair made him look older than he last remembered. He was also slightly heavier. And there was something wrong with his eye. His father had mentioned that it got damaged in the Fellhouse incident, but Arnon couldn't remember how. He tried not to stare at it. "How's my family?" he asked Porter.

"Why don't you see for yourself?"

"They're here?"

"Aye, and I'm sure you all got lots to talk about."

Arnon followed behind as they led their horses down the sloping pass. The events that had wrecked his day began to fade as he thought about his family once again. It was strange to feel the satisfying comfort of being with his mother and sisters after so long, and yet the absence of his father left an overwhelming void that seemed to spoil any lasting peace he might have.

As they continued to the camp, he explained the situation in Everwind, including the letters they had made and the riots. Neither Porter nor Galvin spoke until he finished.

"The letters caused all that?" Porter asked.

"I think it had more to do with the timing," Arnon added. "Apparently, the Daecish received a pay decrease just before we passed out the letters."

"I reckon in the midst of the riots and chaos," Porter suggested, "no one paused to ask where they came from?"

"I ain't sure if I'm more surprised that the letters worked or that you were able to snoop around Ónarr's office without getting caught," Galvin added with a sly grin.

Porter let out a deep-bellied laugh.

As they continued to descend, Arnon peered north to the dark line of the valley's edge. "Did either of you notice the ground when you marched from Denhurst?"

"You mean the sinkholes?" asked Galvin.

"Yea, but some looked like trenches. Long and deep."

"We saw a few."

"Alphyns," added Porter gazing ahead.

Galvin rolled his eyes. "Every time the weather changes, you blame it on alphyns or wyrms or something else."

"This time, it's different."

"Yea, well, that's what people've been saying for hundreds of years. I'll believe it when I see it."

Arnon wasn't sure what he thought. But if alphyns really did come, that was supposed to mean the end. The ancient chronicles described them like massive wolves, only they had larger mouths and they crawled out of the ground. The sudden thought of those things eating his family made his gut feel nauseous.

Reaching the bottom of the valley, the sun now slept, and the stars awoke, glimmering like small white jewels. The clouds had temporarily broken, and the valley slopes, veiled beneath drifts of snow, shone silver beneath the high moon. Arnon was surprised that he could see his own shadow.

After they crossed through patches of hemlock tree and briar, they arrived at the edge of the camp, made up of scattered tents and wagons.

"Where's Ansel?" Porter asked, glancing at the mule.

Arnon looked at him in silence. "I don't know," he said at last.

Porter pulled out a rope from his satchel. "Here," he said, tossing it to him. After wrapping the rope around the mule's neck, Arnon tied it to the wooden brace with the other horses and closed his eyes, and let out a quiet moan. Porter patted Arnon on the back before walking toward the camp.

"I'm sorry," Arnon said to himself, but half wondered if his father could hear him.

Stepping through sheets of ice, broken only by tall, brown clumps of dead weeds and thistle, men and women looked busy as they hauled swords, armor, and shields inside the large clearing within the hemlock forest. The neighs of horses and shouting orders echoed through the valley. Arnon's eyes stayed sharp as he glanced among the crowds.

Then, as if he had awoken from a long dream, he watched as his mother and Fleta stepped out from behind the flap of a tent. In the torchlight, the smile on their faces gleamed full of life. As Fleta ran forward, Myla stopped and turned back. She called out, and from beneath the flap of the tent, Hazel stepped out in her nightgown, holding a thin doll in her hands. When she caught sight of Arnon, her doll fell to the ground, and she ran across the lawn in her bare feet, shouting out his name.

Arnon lowered to his knees and opened his arms as she leaped toward him. Picking her up, he held her tight, feeling her soft hair against his face. He took in a deep breath through his nose. Kissing her on the head, Fleta and Myla embraced him.

"I've missed you all so much," he said.

"I missed you more," Hazel replied.

Myla hugged him tighter, but Fleta kept her face down and slowly dropped her arms as if ashamed to hug him.

The night grew late as Arnon and his family sat in the tent. He listened to their stories of Denhurst, paying close attention to how Galvin tried to kick down the door to rescue Hazel, but it wasn't until Porter had shown up with his hammer that they could break it from the hinges. The whole thing made Arnon shudder. Often, Myla and Fleta went quiet, as if something dwelled on in their mind which they wished not to talk about. Arnon could only imagine the reality of warfare must have been hard for them to experience.

But when Myla spoke of Fleta and how she had killed a Daecish officer and rescued her, a deep sense of respect filled Arnon. He was the firstborn, and Hazel was the youngest, and he knew that Fleta felt like something in between—never quite fitting in, so she mostly kept to herself. But there was something different about her now. As she sat in the corner of the tent, she looked older and darker in the eyes. A look he understood all too well. When Myla laid Hazel down to sleep, Arnon asked Fleta to join him outside.

Stepping into the night air, the moon was once again hidden by clouds, and snow fell in heavy drifts, pilling up in the depressions. Arnon reached down and picked up a small twig, poking it through the blanket of snow. He broke it in half and rolled a small end between his finger and thumb. "I want you to know you did the right thing," he said at last.

Fleta only stared down at her feet.

"When father was murdered." He paused, his own words coming out with a terrible reality. "Afterwards, Fleta, I killed those men."

She didn't say anything. Even now, she looked barely older than a child, with a look on her face as if she was forced to experience something her mind could not yet handle.

"I felt so terrible," he continued, "but I knew I had to protect you, just like you had to protect Hazel and Mother. Father would be so proud of you." He was disgusted at himself for saying it like that. Was he trying to make himself sound like a hero? That was the last thing he was.

She nodded, but Arnon heard a whimper as she set herself on the ground, resting her chin on her raised knees. "I feel wrong," she confessed in a trembling voice. "I killed that man, Arnon."

He sat down and wrapped his arm around her.

"What if he had a family? What if he had children?" She sniffed. "And Hazel. I just left her!"

"You couldn't have known—"

"No," she interrupted. "I left her, Arnon. She'd have died if Porter hadn't shown up." She continued looking at Arnon with her large eyes and quivering lips. "And Mother. Until she started coughing, I thought she was already dead."

Arnon let out a sorrowful sigh. "But she didn't die because you pulled her out of the house."

She turned her face away.

He didn't know what else he could say. He continued to hold her close. Suddenly, she buried her face in her knees, and her back shook hard. "And I can't," she cried out. "I can't get the images out of my head!"

Arnon lifted his hand from her back. "Images of what?"

"Of the bodies." She bawled into her hands.

Arnon narrowed his eyes. She must have seen the battle. He wanted to say something else, but she was crying so hard, she could hardly breathe. When she began to calm, Arnon laid his hand back down. "I know it's—" he began to say, but Galvin and Porter walked over to the tent.

"Sorry to interrupt," said Galvin. "Should we come back?"

"No, no," Arnon replied. "I know we've got a lot to do tonight." Fleta suddenly stood up and stepped back into the tent. Arnon watched her as she laid herself down on a thick bearskin rug. He turned to Galvin. What else could he do?

"The whole thing's been hard on us all," Galvin said. "Come on, we've got a lot to go over."

Arnon followed them as they walked toward the center of the camp.

"Don't get too nervous at the meeting," Galvin said at Arnon. "Just be yourself. We've already informed the others about the situation in Everwind, so I won't make you say too much." He ended with a smirk.

"Look 'round, Arnon," Porter said. "We're done hiding. There's no more Silent Hither or Dark Horses." He pointed at a group of footmen exercising with their swords. "We're the Free Sunderian Army."

"All of our lives are about to change," added Galvin.

Arnon continued looking at the footmen exchanging blows. "How'd you even manage to get an army this far north without being seen?"

"Very carefully and only at night," Galvin replied.

"Honestly," Porter added, 'I didn't think we could make it unseen, either."

"But in the end," Galvin butted in, "it was a march of the like which hasn't been seen since our forefathers arrived from the Southern Kingdoms! The Houses of Emsworth and Burgess will be reunited again. Now come, let's keep moving."

"How's Wesley?" Porter asked as they approached a large octagon-shaped tent. From its sides were many ropes pegged into the ground. The entrance flaps hung closed, concealing the inside.

"Honestly," Arnon replied, "he's acting a little strange. When we got your letter, he looked almost as if he lost his mind. He was saying things, but nothing made sense."

Galvin and Porter eyed one another.

"Well," Porter said, "he's a good man, and though your father always believed in him, I knew he wasn't fit for leadership. He gets himself overwhelmed at times." He stepped through the tent flap, casting a golden glow on the outside ground. "But we can talk about that later."

Inside, large lanterns lined a long wooden table. Around it sat several men in Sunderian officer's attire—burgundy tunics, though some look faded to nothing more than tans and browns. On their left sleeves were stitched a black horse, on their right, the crest of the House of Emsworth.

"Brothers," spoke up Galvin. All the men stood up and saluted him. "I'd like to introduce to you, Commander Greystrom."

Arnon's eyes went unintentionally wide. *He's a what?*

"He's here to represent the House of Burgess in Everwind," Galvin continued.

All the men shifted their position toward Arnon, saluting him. He awkwardly lifted his left hand to his head.

"Right hand," whispered Porter into his ear.

Arnon switched hands.

"Take your seats," said Galvin, grinning at Arnon.

Arnon sat in a tall wooden chair. He felt like a child compared to the older and more experienced-looking men as they laughed and passed around a decorative jug of what Arnon assumed to be spiced wine. Observing their thick beards, he touched his face. Besides a few hairs on his chin, it was completely clean. *Maybe one day.*

"Brothers," Galvin said in a raised voice as he unrolled a map of Everwind before him. "As you all know, we plan to march at first light of the morn'. We've informed Everwind of our coming, and they've responded. As some of you are already aware, Everwind's in a moment of crisis. Riots, economic depression. However, Commander Greystrom has informed us that numbers have risen, and the cause seems to be in our favor."

"If Everwind's experienced such chaos," asked a brigadier whose uniform looked too tight, "then won't the other cities be affected too?"

"We are not yet aware of the situation in other cities," Galvin answered. "But we got to keep our focus on Everwind for now. Future events depend on whether we take this city or not. And based on Commander Greystrom's estimate, the city's more breakable than we had anticipated. It seems Theos may be in our favor."

Despite the cold air, the back of Arnon's neck suddenly felt hot. The numbers certainly appeared better, but he wasn't sure they were that good. He prayed he didn't give the wrong impression.

"How's the organization of the Silent Hither inside the city?" Porter asked.

Arnon wasn't really sure. It kind of felt like a big mess. "Although we've been given considerably short notice, we are acting quickly. Drake, Morgan, and others are getting into position as we speak. We'll have watches posted throughout the city, so they'll know when the attacks begin. Unfortunately, there's no way for us to organize or time it any better."

Several men nodded. At least they seemed to understand.

"Our three main positions are here," Arnon continued as he pointed to the map. "Fire and Water Tavern, the Southern Squalor, Birchton."

"Do you think it best we invade from the south?" asked the brigadier with the tight uniform. Even his sleeves barely touched his wrists. "Since most of them are already on that side?"

"I would think it wise," replied Porter.

"Actually," added Arnon, "I think we should stay clear of the south and focus instead on the eastern and northern walls."

"From the north?" asked the brigadier.

"Riots have been attacking the Northern District. The Daecish'll be weak there."

"Also," added Galvin, "if the Daecish are aware of our victory in Denhurst. They'll be looking south, no doubt."

"You got any information on Daecish reports?" asked another brigadier with a missing eye and teeth so rotten they looked as if black oil had been splattered upon them. "The areas of concentration in the city?"

A sudden gust of wind whipped through the tent, sending the lantern flames into a frenzy. "Other than stopping the riots in the Northern District," Arnon replied, tightening his muscles against the cold, "the Daecish are mostly operating in squadrons and regiments in the Eastern District, stopping uprisings where they can. Quinn estimated about four Daecish legions in the Northern District."

"What of your numbers?" Galvin asked Arnon. "How many have you got?"

For Theos' sake, Arnon had no idea. Last he knew, they didn't even reach two-hundred. But with the chaos going on and the Merchant's rebelling, who could know? He only prayed Drake and Morgan had it all together. "It depends," he finally answered. "The Silent Hither here has never been big, but our numbers have grown, and we've got merchants and others on our side now." He swallowed. At least that's what Drake told him. Should he overestimate a number? They probably needed the confidence. "Probably close to a thousand or so."

Several of them men grumbled to one another with shaking heads.

Galvin clasped his hands and looked to one of the brigadiers—the oldest looking one at the table. "What about our battalions?"

"We got twelve hundred men," he answered. "Five companies of just over two-hundred a piece. Each divided between four to five bands. The ratio we agreed on," he eyed another brigadier who nodded, "is one archer to four footmen, along with four horsemen, for each band."

Galvin looked across the men at the table. "Brigadiers," he said. "You each have your companies managed? Chiefs and sergeants established?"

"Since we arrived," replied the older man.

Taking in a long breath through the nose, Galvin eyed the men. "We knew the Daecish numbers would be greater," he said, though not solemnly. "We also knew that they had the advantage of supplies and protected walls."

Arnon's heart pounded.

"But we've got two advantages," Galvin continued. "If we divide into two battalions, one coming from the north and the other east, they'll be fighting a three-front war. I'm confident the House of Burgess will not fail us from within."

"And the other advantage?" one asked.

"Our strength ain't in numbers, but here . . ." He struck his chest. "This is our home, not theirs. There's a fire that burns in us, which the Daecish in Everwind never tasted. One of our men's worth three of theirs."

Several men beat the table with their fists. "Hear, hear!"

"For the House of Emsworth!" exclaimed others.

"May Theos damn 'em all!" shouted one.

"And all of Daecland!"

The crowd of men erupted with fervor as the old brigadier, to Arnon's right, leaned toward him and cackled with black teeth. "I hope every one of their wives dies in childbirth. And the youngsters with 'em." His face suddenly twisted into a frown as he shifted his gaze to the table in front of him. "As my own daughter did when she labored in their coal mines." He looked up at the rest of the men and raised his voice as theirs quieted. "They threw her body and my grandchild's in a ditch." His eyes swelled, and he stood up. "But we paid 'em back. If we don't kill every one of them pale-faces, we'll send 'em bleeding to their wives. Remember the walls of Denhurst!"

Whatever courage Arnon had, it vanished like a vapor.

"Remember the walls of Denhurst!" several others chanted as they stood with raised drinks. "Remember the walls of Denhurst!"

What happened in Denhurst? When Galvin and Porter smiled as one brigadier mimed a castrating gesture, which Arnon took to mean something they had done to their conquered enemies in Denhurst, his stomach lurched. The old man's story revealed the darkness of the Daecish all too well, but he feared that same darkness was in the tent with him. These were the men he had looked up to all his life—his father's men. And they were not the kind of men he imagined.

The Silence before the Storm

In the shadow of the early morning, everyone had either long been awake or hadn't slept at all as they formed their ranks to march west. At the command of the brigadiers, horses and men trudged through the thick blankets of snow, making their way along the southern pass, which ran through a steep, wooded holler. Everything was white.

At the top of the valley crest, Arnon stood beside a long line of wagons. Although most of the families stayed back in Denhurst, about two-dozen women and children came with the army. They were to ride out to the Green Carrick Inn at Crossroads until Everwind was safe enough for them to return.

Myla and Hazel stood before him. A few feet away stood Fleta, her gaze caught on another boy, who occasionally glanced back at her. With short black hair, he looked about her age, maybe sixteen at the oldest. Arnon was surprised that he wasn't in armor. Maybe he had to look after his family.

Myla stepped forward, and she gave Arnon a hug. "I know there's nothing I can say to keep you here," she said, taking a step back. She grabbed his hand, cupping it in both of hers. She looked older and more tired than when he last saw her in the Western Plains. "Be careful. Stay alert."

"I will," Arnon replied.

She gripped his hand tighter. "Do what's right. No matter what others do. You hear me?"

Did she mean what happened in Denhurst? He wasn't exactly sure what happened, but Fleta's sobs the night before, and the look in his mother's eyes as she stood before him, caused a sharp pain to shoot through his gut. If nothing else, he was furious that his family had been exposed to something so debasing. "Of course, I will," he answered.

"I love you." She kissed him on the head and walked to the wagon, with Hazel following her.

Fleta walked over and stood before Arnon, looking up at him. "Thank you for what you said last night."

Arnon hugged her. "I love you."

"I know," she replied.

He glanced to the young man who now clambered into the back of a wagon. "So, who's that?"

Fleta looked over her shoulder and blushed. "Beckett."

Arnon's eyes crinkled. "Is he decent?"

She let out a laugh. "What is that supposed to mean?"

"Is he kind to you?"

She nodded with a growing smile.

"Good," Arnon replied, hugging her again. "You deserve it."

She didn't say anything.

"I need you to take care of Hazel and mother while I'm gone."

"When will you be back?"

"I don't know, but soon."

Fleta kissed his cheek. "Make sure it's soon." She walked toward the wagon.

Arnon looked ahead at Hazel, who stood off in the distance, her light brown hair brushing across her face in the breeze. She held her rag doll loosely in her hands, and a scowl formed on her face. Arnon walked up and kneeled in front of her.

"I know this is hard," he said. "But I'll be back."

"But that's what you said last time," she replied.

"I know, and here we are again."

"For only a day."

He lifted her chin with his finger. "Don't lose hope," he said. "I'll be back soon. I mean it."

Without saying goodbye, she turned and walked off.

Arnon's stomach weighed heavy. "I love you," he called out.

He barely heard her words in return as she disappeared behind the canvas at the back of the wagon.

Galvin had ridden up the slope and joined Arnon as the wagons rode east toward the blazing sun, gleaming yellow across the white horizon. Galvin raised his hand, shielding his eyes. "It's a bitter life we got," he said. "We must appreciate every moment of it."

"After this battle," replied Arnon in a cold tone, "I'm going to do whatever it takes to be with my family."

Galvin didn't respond.

Although Arnon did everything he could to hide his emotion, he couldn't shake the grief growing in him. "What happened in Denhurst?" he asked, hearing the tremble in his own voice.

Galvin met his gaze. "What do you mean? We won."

Arnon tried to calm his breathing. "My mother and the girls, they . . ." He paused. "They acted like something was wrong. And then the men last night, the things they were saying about the bodies. It just—"

"War ain't ever easy," Galvin responded coolly. "It brings out the best of men and the worst."

"But that doesn't justify the hatred or the—"

"Your father understood, and so will you."

Arnon's head went hot, and he peered hard at Galvin. "My father would have never done that!"

Galvin looked ahead with a deep sigh. "Tell me, Arnon, what drove you to kill those men at your home?"

Losing his breath, Arnon clenched his fists. It was like Galvin just pulled out the darkness in his heart and set it before his face. "I was protecting my family."

Galvin stared off into the horizon. "Just don't make the mistake of thinking you're better than these men. The same hatred that runs in their hearts runs in yours, and I think you know it."

Was this the cruelty Adelyne hinted at in his family home? Would these men be the future leaders of Everwind? Arnon tried to think of something to say, but all he could do was wonder if he really was the same. He walked off.

With the sun now peeking over the mountains, the Free Sunderian Army headed west in the long formation of two battalions—one of three companies in the front and the other of two companies in the rear. Arnon rode alongside Galvin while Porter commanded the rear battalion. He couldn't shake the weight of Galvin's words.

Glancing at the men around him, he felt somewhat out of place with the other officers dressed in full uniform. Almost all the men, in fact, were in full armor—clothed in black Daecish brigandines, bearing a Sunderian horse upon their chests and backs. Several had various helms, burgonets, and bassinets mounted over their faces.

Although a round wooden shield was slung over his back, he grimaced at his leather chest plate, where a long gash cut across the breast. His leather wrist guards above each hand didn't feel much more protective. He was more like a volunteer than a commander. And it didn't help that he was the only one riding a mule. He was at least thankful that it now had a saddle and reins. Trotting through the snowy hills, Arnon looked to his right as Porter rode toward them.

"We're ready to depart," he said to Galvin.

"Go ahead as planned. But be sure to stay clear away from the city, and don't advance until we attack. Keep the sentries in sight of us so they can keep you informed."

"We wait for your advance!" hollered Porter. He kicked at his horse, and it sent him galloping.

Arnon heard him shout out commands for the rear battalion to march toward the northern gate. As they broke from the rest of the army, a single brigadier on horseback led the way, followed by the cavalry. Behind marched rows of footmen carrying long wooden ladders and two battering rams.

It didn't take long for the ride to strike an ache in Arnon's legs and rear. He always kept his eyes ahead and never spoke to Galvin. Several men to his left prayed aloud as they rode. For the first time in his life, he didn't want to pray. Theos would just mock him anyway. He'd lost his father, then he carelessly lost his horse. Galvin and Porter were different men. And then Adelyne. He knew he was a fool for caring so much, but he couldn't stop thinking about her. He couldn't eat. He had hardly slept. He knew he should just move on, but he couldn't. He wanted to be with her more than anything.

The thought of that man touching her the way he did brought up a well of emotions he had never felt before. It was like being angry, heartbroken, and ridiculous all at the same time. But more than anything, he was angry with himself for giving her such a cold look afterward. And he never even told her why. For all he knew, he had pushed her away, and she was with that man at that very moment. Terrible thoughts came to his mind, and he unintentionally moaned.

He forced himself to focus again. Feeling for his father's sword, which was sheathed at his side, he glanced at the plain silver crossbar shimmering in the sunlight. Mounted on the side of the mule in a leather sleeve hung an unstrung bow and quiver of cedar arrows. Slid into his right boot was his hunting knife.

He consciously held his chin high and kept his breath calm but could only hope the others riding beside him didn't notice the trembling in his legs and back. With each cresting hill, he expected the walls of Everwind to rise into view—the anticipation threatened to kill him before he even drew his sword. But he swore to himself that if he would survive this, the first thing he'd do was talk to Adelyne.

* * *

Walking through the front entrance of the Office of Foreign Jurisdiction, Eilívur glanced toward a full suit of armor hanging against the plaster wall. It brought back memories of the invasion into Sunder, and he hoped he didn't have to feel the burden of war again. He stepped into his office and found Commander Dagr sitting in a chair with a calm expression on his face, hiding well whatever aggravating nonsense he wanted to discuss. "Commander Tyr," he said, giving a half-honest salute. "Or should I say Commander-in-Chief?"

"Only if war breaks out," Eilívur added, returning the salute.

Dagr leaned back in his chair as he twiddled his thumbs. "I wonder why you got the position over the other commanders?"

Eilívur sat down with a raised eyebrow. Whoever commissioned this idiot? "If by other commanders, you mean Second Commanders. Last I checked, I've earned my First Commander rank, which I believe is the only one in Everwind."

Dagr waved a hand. "I'm sure it had nothing to do with your experience in both the Army and the Nautical Armada? You were a—"

"Captain," Eilívur replied shortly.

"Oh, forgive me," he continued. "I thought it was boatswain. I thought captains were only a part of the Airborne Armada, not the nautical branch."

Eilívur frustratingly let his hand fall to the desk. "The ranks are the same in both branches, and you know that. Why are you here?"

Dagr sat up, interlocking his fingers. "Oh, nothing really," he said. "Well, actually, two things."

Eilívur's face burned hot. He was hoping this would be a short encounter.

"First," Dagr said, now picking at a loose thread on the armchair. "One of your sentinel guards from mine—" He looked up in thought. "Mine six, I believe? Maybe five? Either way, one of your mines out here. He's a colonel and is in our infirmary at the moment. Actually, several are in the infirmary, but he seems to be the most interesting of the bunch. Anyway, they have all reported that a mine collapsed, and they show the injuries to prove it." Dagr paused as his lips curled up.

"We've had mine collapses before."

"No," he continued. "This is the interesting part. All of the guards have been rambling on about this animal of a sort. Some wolf-bear-like creature, but quite different. Larger and uglier. At least, that's what they said. Another mentioned some shadowy darkness coming over it and changing it into some black monster." His eyes went sarcastically wide at his last word. "And further, they all claimed that this monster ate a guard. A full-grown man!" He paused and leaned forward. "Ate him. Gobbled him up. Like something from a story!"

Eilívur remained silent for a moment, trying to process the account. They must be going mad down there from all the coal dust. "What about this colonel you mentioned?"

"Ah, yes. Well, if you can believe it, the story gets more interesting. The other guards said they ran and fled. But this colonel, Algöter, I believe is his name, stayed behind. He said this animal went up to one of the workers, a small boy, who apparently looked rather Daecish. And the boy . . ." He hesitated as he laughed at himself. "The boy climbed on top of the animal, and they both rode out of the mine."

Who could believe such a thing? Was Dagr playing some sort of foolish prank?

Dagr lifted both hands in the air and slapped them on the arm of the chair. "So, there you have it!" Dagr said. "The tale is spreading like wildfire through the infirmary. Your men are losing their minds."

Eilívur took in a deep breath. He'd heard the name Algöter before. Just before he left for Llynhithe, a complaint was put in about his treatment of mineworkers—particularly women. Maybe this Algöter was playing like he lost his mind to get out of the charges? He had seen it before. But what about the other accounts of this creature? Eilívur closed his eyes and rubbed his fingers against his forehead. "This whole country's insane," he mumbled to himself.

"Say again?" Dagr asked.

"Nothing," Eilívur replied, opening his eyes. "What about the workers? What happened to them?"

"I asked several guards, but no clear answers. One said he saw some rough-looking men and women stumble back into the city, but he wasn't sure if they were from a mine or not. Others assumed they ran off or were eaten."

"Are there any workers remaining in the mine?"

"Not in that quarry. Whether they have fled from the other chambers, I don't know."

Eilívur let out a sigh. "As bizarre as this is, I've got other things to deal with first." He paused. "What else did you have for me?"

Dagr leaned back, his expression growing more serious. "I heard you've made a request to King Ónarr for troops from Llynhithe without speaking to me."

"And Astford," Eilívur replied. "I've also requested King Ónarr to write to Commander-in-Chief Asger in Daecland, informing him of our situation and need."

"Why wasn't this discussed with me? It's why I'm here, is it not?"

"And look what good it did me," he replied shortly.

"Be careful, Commander," Dagr added.

Eilívur cocked his head. "If I remember correctly, Second Commander, I, not you, have been entrusted with the safety of Everwind. It is my duty to look out for her best interests."

Just as Dagr lifted a finger in protest, Commander Halvard walked up to the door, followed by a lieutenant.

"Gentlemen," Halvard said, maintaining a stern expression, despite his young face.

Eilívur eyed both men. "What is it?"

"This morning, Lieutenant Cael found the mole in City Hall."

"Wesley?"

"Yes," the Lieutenant answered. "He was a mess, sitting in a back corner. His breath reeked of alcohol."

"What did he say?"

"Mostly nonsense," Halvard said. "But when I arrived, we were able to make some sense out of him. He mentioned a Sunderian army and the name Arnon Greystrom, here in Everwind."

Eilívur stood up. "Greystrom or the army?"

"We think Greystrom, but he was hard to understand."

Dagr looked up at Eilívur from his leather chair but didn't move. "That name," he said, snapping a finger. "He's the one they've been talking about in Llynhithe. The one that killed a dozen of your men."

"Did he give a location?" Eilívur asked, ignoring Dagr's comment.

"Not that we're aware of," Halvard replied.

"Where is Wesley now?"

"I went ahead and ordered him to be locked up. Until he sobers up."

"After that, I want—" Eilívur began but was interrupted when a sergeant approached the door.

His eyes were wide, and he stuttered. "T—Troops in full formation have been sighted marching east of Everwind!"

Eilívur stiffened. "Our troops?"

He eyed the men. "We're . . . we're not," he stuttered. "We're not sure, sir. They look Daecish, but their armor's painted red."

He knew it. "Denhurst," Eilívur said in a low voice. "How many are there?"

"The sentry estimated six-hundred."

"That's it?" Dagr laughed.

"That's not including from within the city," Eilívur said in a raised voice. "Sergeant, inform Commander Veurðr at once! We need archers along all the walls and battlements. Get the women and children inside all buildings. Lieutenant, make sure King Ónarr is informed." He began to walk out the door but turned back at Halvard. "Send a squadron to Runevast. We must send word to King Eirik!"

"Shouldn't we go through King Ónarr first?" Halvard replied as he wiped the perspiration forming on his brow.

"We do not have time for written approvals!"

Dagr raised his hands in the air. "And that's how things work around here, it seems."

Halfway out the door, Eilívur jabbed a finger back at Dagr. "I relieve you of your command. Go back to Llynhithe!" He walked out of the room.

Within the hour, soldiers and officers were already scrambling from one building to another. Colonels and lieutenants assembled soldiers, while others ordered men to mount braces against the city gates. Taking in the scene, Eilívur cursed himself for being caught so soon. He marched toward the stable. "Rally your men!" he shouted to a sergeant. "Send them to the Eastern Gate!"

A gust of wind blew from the north, and Eilívur took in a breath through his nose and let out a gagging cough. "What's that horrid stench?" he asked aloud, but no one seemed to hear him.

* * *

Drake leaned out through the tavern window, watching as a commander rode on horseback along the Western road. The stomp of soldiers marching east rang along the cobblestones. In his right hand, he gripped his hammer, with a sharp point forged on one end. It was his father's hammer, and he always kept it close. In his other hand, he held a short single-edged ax. Sniffing the air, his face turned sour, and he leaned back into the tavern.

"The Daecish are moving," he said to the many armed men who stood before him. The room was dark, and all the tables and chairs had been piled into one corner. Men stood in every free space, even on the bar top. Most held a shield and some sort of weapon, mostly swords or maces. Several wore rusted cuirasses, while others were fortunate enough to have the addition of faulds hanging below their hips and helms. A tap sounded against the open window. Murdock and Quinn stood outside. "Any news?" Drake asked.

Quinn leaned over to catch his breath, then coughed, clearing his throat. Drake never could get over how small his chin was compared to his wide face. And those eyebrows. There were as thick as a forest. "The soldiers have spotted the army east of the city. Our sentries reported that the Northern gate's barred, and the Southern will be soon, I reckon. Most of the Daecish, however, are focusing the legions along the eastern wall." He looked past Murdock toward the street. "I can't hardly handle that smell. What is it?"

"Don't know," Drake replied. "But if it's alphyns, let's hope they're on our side."

Quinn laughed.

"But more importantly," Drake continued. "No one advances until Galvin's army attacks first."

"Just as planned," Murdock said, blowing something from his nose onto the ground in the alleyway.

Quinn kept tapping his thigh with one hand and anxiously bounced on his feet as his eyes kept darting back down the alley.

"You ready to fight?" Drake asked.

Quinn caught himself and let out a breath. "I'm just a farmer, but I'll give it everything I got."

Drake smiled, but he feared Quinn wouldn't make it. "That's the spirit." He motioned to Murdock. "Is Wesley with you guys?"

Murdock looked at Quinn. "I ain't seen him.".

"Maybe he's with Morgan in Birchton?" Quinn asked.

"Maybe," Drake said. "Is Adelyne with Sarah?"

"Since last night," Quinn replied.

"And our final count?"

"All men ready," replied Murdock. "We have nearly four-hundred betwixt Quinn's and mine. Last I heard, Morgan's got just shy of three-hundred in Birchton."

"Including ours, that's close to eight-hundred. That's . . ." Drake paused. "That's better than I thought."

"The numbers are a lot better," said Murdock, rubbing his nose. "But it may not be enough. Many of these men ain't never fought."

"Well," Drake replied, gripping tight his hammer and ax. "They got courage, and that's what I'm looking for."

"Let's hope so," Murdock replied. Then he slapped the windowsill. "Let's get back before we're seen."

Quinn nodded, and they both disappeared into the alley.

Drake turned and faced the men in the tavern. Their faces were hard and determined. They may all die that day, but he wouldn't trade this moment for any other. "We ready?" he asked.

Four men by the bar each handed out a large tankard of spiced wine. Drake had been saving it for such a day as this. As it was passed along the room, every man took a quick drink. Drake took the final sip of one of the tankards and held it in the air. Together, in a low reverberating voice, all the men chanted:

With swords sheathed on side
And tankards raised up high
We'll sing our last farewell
At the ringing of our death knell

With brothers, we march this day
For Theos, we shout and pray
Our hearts will kindle and burn
Though few of us return

Our daughters and maidens shall weep

Hælend's Ballad

When sorrow of loss runs deep
We'll sing our last farewell
At the ringing of our death knell

After the Setting Sun

E verwind rose up in the distance as the sun began to crest over the western horizon. By now, Arnon's rear was numb, and he longed for something to happen. This silent wait was like a cruel joke reminding him that death was on its way. He prayed for the sun to cease in its place before the day passed into night.

Shouts echoed from behind the city walls. Just before him, in the rolling hills, several crevices had appeared beneath the snow in various areas, making horse riding treacherous. He thought back to the similar depressions he had seen the previous day; the same smell whipped like rot in the air as other men coughed and complained over it. He glanced to his right as a brigadier galloped over.

"The cavalry's ready for advancement," he said in a stern voice. "The archers ready?"

Galvin scanned his battalion, raising a hand. Two other brigadiers raised theirs in return. "Ready," he replied.

The brigadier pulled the reins of the horse to face toward the city. "Do we send in surrender demands?"

"The Daecish?" Galvin laughed. "They'll never surrender. Besides, we'll only give them more time to prepare if we do so. Remember our meeting," he said with his eyes on Arnon. "This is your first battle. Don't worry about giving commands. You stick with me, fight your heart out, and stay alive!"

Arnon nodded but kept his eyes on the city. Behind the battlements, small black figures moved along the stone wall.

"They're forming their defenses," said Galvin. He turned toward the brigadier. "Porter should be nearing the Northern Gate. Let's not waste any more time."

The eastern gate of Everwind let out a sudden thundering creak as the two mighty oak doors pushed open. A loud blow of a horn sounded, and it seemed as if an entire army poured through the open gate, marching in dense rows like black ink, slowly spilling across the white landscape.

Arnon's heart felt as if it was going to burst through his chest. He tried to keep his breathing calm, but he couldn't keep his back from shivering. All around was silent, save the blowing wind and the occasional neigh of a horse. He could only hope Drake and the others were ready within the city.

He startled when a large horn throbbed through the fields. Galvin raised a hand. Imitating the other archers around him, Arnon notched an arrow. He kept his eyes fixed on Galvin, and his bandaged left hand shook as it strained against the bow; the scab cracked, and a thin stream of blood trickled down to his wrist. Galvin brought his arm down.

Arnon released the bowstring. A sea of arrows soared high, wavering in the air. Shouts echoed from across the field. Clanking and screaming resounded as the arrows fell upon the Daecish.

"Again!" hollered Galvin as he raised his hand.

The distance between the two armies gave Arnon a false sense of safety. And the archers had done more damage to the Daecish than he'd expected. Without hesitation, he notched another arrow. Galvin lowered his arm, and the arrows were loosed.

After they fell, a commander across the field bellowed out, "Archers!"

Galvin looked back toward the battalion. "Raise your shields!"

Fumbling the shield off his back, Arnon held it above his head. He looked at his legs and tightened their grip against the mule. Many twangs reverberated, and Arnon clenched his eyes shut, picturing the arrows flying toward him. He tightened his chest as sweat poured down his arms and back despite the freezing wind. Time felt as if it had stopped.

Whistles and thuds fell all around the field, followed by cries. Daring to open his eyes, he watched several men slide off their horses with deep groans. He slowly lowered his own shield to his side. Another sudden twang from across the field sang out.

"Shields!" Galvin cried.

Arnon flung his shield up once again, but he accidentally knocked himself just above the brow, and his head flew back. Scrambling, he ducked beneath the shield, clenching his throbbing right eye. He jolted as the impact of an arrow slammed against his shield, trembling against his arm. He let out a gasp for air and waited for the others to lower their shields before lowering his. Barely a finger-breadth from the edge, a cedar arrow protruded out of the oak; its iron head barely poking through the other side. Galvin glanced at him with a smiling nod. Arnon couldn't even force one in return.

Raising his sword, Galvin turned to the cavalry and footmen. The archers stepped to the side, allowing the footmen to move forward. Arnon slung his shield on his back. He unstrung the bow and slid it into the leather sheath on the side of the mule, and pulled out his father's sword.

Galvin nodded toward each brigadier of the three legions. "Brigadiers!" he commanded.

Arnon tightened his grip. This was it.

"Charge!"

An eruption of neighs and whinnying broke out as the army galloped forward. Holding on to the reins with his left hand, his sword in his right, Arnon continued kicking at the side of the mule. The field rumbled beneath the thundering army as the horses foamed at their mouths. To his left, a large red Sunderian flag beat violently against the wind.

All nervousness disappeared from Arnon as a rush of strength and urgency surged through his body. He let out a shout, and a sudden, loud crash of swords and armor hit him. Horses collapsed forward against the Daecish phalanx as men were flown to the ground, their ribs and backs breaking beneath the weight of hooves and armored boots. Nearly in shock from the chaos, Arnon swung his sword down upon helms and shoulders around him. Each blow trembled the hilt in his hands. The Daecish moved swiftly as they swung at the legs of the horses, causing them to collapse forward.

Dirt, snow, and blood flung into the air within the sea of men. Arnon could barely pick out the red paint of his own people. The sharp clashing of iron and shouts pierced at his ears. If commands were given, he couldn't hear them.

Continually striking his sword down, he caught a glance of a Daecish soldier thrusting his blade into the breast of a horse as it reared up on its hind legs. Another Daecish soldier stumbled back, and Arnon raised his sword to bring it down upon his head, but his mule was pierced with an arrow. Its legs buckled as Arnon was thrown off its side, collapsing onto the ground.

Delirious, he lifted himself up and wiped the snow from his throbbing right cheek. The Daecish soldier raised his sword, but a colliding mass of men suddenly pressed between them. Arnon tried to swing his own blade, but the crowds were so thick he could barely move.

For a split second, there was a small gap, and Arnon instinctively swung his sword against the face of a Daecish soldier, hitting him in the mouth and shattering his teeth. The soldier hunched over and grabbed his face just as a horse galloped through, trampling him and several others along the ground.

Beside Arnon, a man was stabbed through the neck, and blood splattered into his eyes. He frantically wiped them, but his dirt-sodden hands only made it worse. Bodies continually slammed against him as he desperately tried to see. Wracked with fear, all he could do was peer through his squinted eyes and scream as he brought his sword down on another soldier.

* * *

Eilívur's throat burned as he shouted from the eastern wall. Blood poured from the bodies of the clashing armies, dyeing the snow a deep crimson, which made the entire field look like a giant pulsing wound. He turned to Gunnar. "Send out the second cavalry!"

Gunnar raised a hand, motioning toward the gate. Six men heaved as they swung the gate open, and nearly two-hundred Daecish soldiers and officers on horseback crowded the eastern road as they galloped forward.

Eilívur ran south along the wall to pass a building that blocked his view. He held his breath as three large masses of men ran through the alleyways, charging toward the horses. Two groups approached from the rear as one poured along the city wall, cutting off the horses near the front.

"Where are our city defenses?" he screamed.

Gunnar looked north at a young lieutenant who looked across the field with childlike awe as if he had never seen a battle before. "Sound the horn!" he hollered.

The lieutenant startled and lifted the horn. He blew it high and loud.

Eilívur hurried to the archers. "Shoot them!" he yelled as he pointed toward the oncoming raid. "Shoot them!"

Arrows shot into the streets, impaling both Daecish and Sunderians. Eilívur looked on helplessly as half of his Daecish cavalry was caught in the onslaught. Catching his attention, two lieutenants and a colonel ran toward him along the city wall.

"Commander!" shouted the colonel as he covered the stump of his bleeding ear with his hand. "The Northern District has been breached! They've broken the gate and are climbing the walls! We need more men. Now!"

* * *

Wielding both weapons in his blood-soaked arms, Drake ran toward a soldier who had fallen from his horse. He swung his hammer, and it glanced across the soldier's helm but quickly brought down the ax with his other hand, and it sunk into the soldier's collarbone. The young man collapsed with a shriek.

"Don't let the cavalry through the gate!" Drake hollered. "Do not let them through!"

He searched for Murdock, but the mass of horses blocked any possible view. With a glance, he caught sight of Morgan thrusting his sword down on a fallen man. Archers continually shot from the walls where they either gored the men or the arrows shattered along the city streets. One arrow pierced a horse's upper thigh, and it reared back with a loud neigh. Another suddenly bored into Morgan's back. Just as he reached behind with a gasp, another arrow pierced his stomach, and he fell over, lost in the crowd.

Every limb on Drake's body went heavy. But Morgan didn't die for nothing. Several shouts distracted him as he glanced to his right. Daecish soldiers charged from the south. They rushed toward the skirmish with a loud crash as men collided together in a tangle of iron and blood. Suddenly, the sharp pierce of an arrow burrowed into Drake's left shoulder. His left knee collapsed, but he caught himself and remained standing. He hardened his face, and he ran, hooking one soldier in the side with his ax, then bringing the hammer down onto his face.

Another arrow pierced into his left thigh. He let out a deep-throated gasp, and his muscles knotted while a sharp pain shot up his body. Gritting his teeth, he held his hammer in the air and took a step back as his foot slid across the slush on the cobblestone. Ahead in the distance, a soldier caught sight of Drake and charged toward him.

A fiery heat surged within Drake's veins. Gripping the ax at the bottom of the handle, he arched his arm back and slung it forward, sending it spinning through the air until the back end slammed into the face of the soldier. The man fell backward onto the mud at the edge of the cobblestone street. Narrowing his eyes, Drake marched toward the fallen man and thrust his hammer down into the crown of his head. Now separated from the crowd, he dropped the hammer and gripped the shaft of the arrow in his thigh with both hands, breaking it at half point. He attempted to reach for the arrow in his shoulder but couldn't get a solid grip.

He picked up both the hammer and ax and marched back into the battle.

* * *

With the sun entirely set behind the city wall, the sky fell into darkness. Although his eyelids were still sticky with blood, Arnon could see clearly again, but it did him little good. Darting his gaze around the battlefield, the horrible sensation of losing his perception in the darkness came over him. The clanks of clashing armor and screams now became muddled and their direction uncertain. Gripping his sword in front of him, he felt the bump or shove of a man, but they all appeared as shadows.

The battle seemed to be thinning, but scattered crowds could still be heard fighting in the chaos. Shadows of men now trickled out of the Eastern Gate with torches in their hands; he could only hope they were Sunderians. He tried to make his way toward the city, walking and stumbling over dead men. Bodies were piled everywhere. His hands and feet sloshed through the blood and gore which seemed to seep from the ground itself. Although little detail could be seen in the darkness, his imagination filled in the gaps.

An ache formed in his stomach as the horrors of the carnage around him sunk in. Men butchering one another with little or no thought to the lives they were ending. Children without working fathers would starve. Even more wives would be driven into the streets. For the first time since he killed those men at his house, he thought of the Daecish. He had no idea what life was like in Daecland, but if it was anything like Sunder, more than just the lives of men on that battlefield would be ruined. And his own hands were red with their blood.

He numbed the thoughts from his mind and continued across the field. Two men exchanged blows just ahead, their armor glimmering in the dim light of a nearby torch.

Trying to perceive who was on which side, a sudden strong gale blew from the west, bringing once again the foul stench. His hair blew hard behind him as loose armor clanked and toppled over the bodies all around. Then the wind stopped as suddenly as it came, and a tremor rumbled from the ground. His knees gave away as he leaned against the dead body, his eyes searching the dark earth. The two men before him paused as one held his sword in mid-swing. They looked toward the ground, both taking a step back. Another soldier rushed within the darkness, goring the soldier that was holding his sword in the air. Arnon quickly laid low.

Another quake throbbed. Another soldier fell over in front of him as Arnon held onto the body, holding his breath. It seemed as if the entire battlefield slowly went quiet; the clashing of swords grew distant and far between. Then, as if the earth itself was breaking, a large eruption exploded in the field. The thud of dirt and rock flinging into the air was followed by the shouts of men. With trembling legs, Arnon slowly stood up and backed away, peering at the dim shadows in front of him.

When the eruption died down, a haunting silence once again fell on the field until a great and terrible roar, like the sound of many beasts within loud rushing waters, thundered in the darkness. The hair on Arnon's arms stood on end, and he gripped his ears.

"Alphyns!" several cried in the darkness.

"Run!"

Alphyns? Arnon glanced in all directions. His heart pounded, but he still couldn't see anything. A man screaming rang in his ears before the cries rose high as if the man were slung into the air, followed by the ghastly muffled sound of crunching armor and bones.

At the same time, near the city wall, a torchlight bobbed up and down in the air as whoever was carrying it ran with all his might. From behind charged a towering form, whose long gray, woolly hide fluttered in the torchlight. It opened its mouth, and the flash of long white teeth glistened before they snapped back down around the man, engulfing the flame of his torch.

Arnon ran, tripping and stumbling over bodies. Dark silhouettes bumped and slammed against Arnon as the battlefield turned into a jumbled confusion. He caught another sudden putrid smell, like a mixture of sulfur and burning flesh, so thick it clung to his skin. His stomach churned, and he vomited, but he never stopped running.

The Passing of Mathios

Geirleif sat across from Eilis as they both picked at their dinner. Occasionally, he glanced up but remained silent. Behind him, standing beside the dining hall door, Ulfr glared at a footman who had just started working at the Manor a few weeks ago. As hard as he tried, Geirleif couldn't remember the young man's name.

"Bring his lordship some more tea," Ulfr told him.

The footman left the room.

Geirleif looked up at Eilis. "You think she'll be all right?"

Eilis lightly patted down the side of her curly gray hair. "I'm sure Eirún will be fine, Geirleif. Of course, it will be hard for her."

"Well, at least she'll have a chance to say goodbye to the poor boy," he said almost to himself. He took a sip of tea. The doctor said Mathios may make it two more days if he was lucky.

"Is everything all right, dear?" she asked as she fiddled with the clasp at the end of her necklace. It had been fourteen years since he had given that to her. The photograph inside the clasp had long worn out, and yet she still wore it every day, despite the occasion. Such a thought made him lose his appetite.

Geirleif set his cup down and looked at Ulfr. His black suit bulged tighter every week. His obsession with baked goods was beginning to take a toll on his professional appearance. "Would you leave us for a moment, if you please?"

Ulfr bowed. "Yes, your lordship." He stepped through the tall double doors, closing them behind him.

Geirleif waited for a moment, then looked back to Ellis. "How do you think Eirún is faring? Here, I mean."

"You think about her quite a lot, don't you?" she replied curtly.

Why would she have to say something like that?

"She seems to be doing fine," Eilis went on. "I imagine this lifestyle isn't easy for her." She let out a quick chuckle. "All the servants, official dinners, politicians walking in and out. I'm sure it's overwhelming. For goodness sake, I haven't even gotten used to it!"

Geirleif tapped his fork on his plate. "You think she'll stay?"

"Will she stay?" Eilis replied. "I think the better question is, is it safe for her stay? For her or for us?"

"You mean she ought to leave?"

"No, but she is a wanted woman. For murder, I might remind you."

"But it wasn't murder," Geirleif interrupted.

"And I agree with you," Eilis continued. "But the law doesn't. Sooner or later, this will come out in the open. I'm just saying, for her sake and ours, we must think of the future."

Geirleif sat in thought. "You think I still did the right thing?"

Eilis let out a sigh. "I wasn't sure at first, but yes, Geirleif, I do think you did the right thing. I don't know if others will see it that way, but in my heart, I wouldn't have it any other way." She set her fork down on the gold-edged plate.

A sudden muffle started up outside the door, which sounded like an argument.

"I'll take it to him!" Ulfr spat at someone, the voices becoming louder. Most likely that poor footman. Geirleif pitied the poor man. He was a good footman, but he was simple, and Ulfr seemed to not like him at all. Geirleif grunted as a thought came to him. Was Ulfr standing just behind the door the whole time?

The door pushed open, and Ulfr walked in. He looked a little flustered as he straightened his tailcoat over his fat rear-end. The footman stood back in the hall with eyes as nervous as a cat cowering before a hound.

Ulfr cleared his throat. "This telegram came in for you this afternoon, your lordship." He set the envelope beside Geirleif's plate.

"Thank you, Ulfr." He gave him an eye as Ulfr bowed and walked back out, closing the door behind him.

Eilis sipped her tea. Geirleif opened the envelope and read through its contents.

"Well?" Eilis asked after a moment.

Heat rose into Geirleif's head as his vision momentarily blurred. His mouth wouldn't even move.

"Geirleif?"

"It's nothing," he finally got out.

* * *

After having dinner on her own, Eirún found herself strolling through the winter garden at the end of the eastern wing. Many white columns ran around the smooth, cut-stone floor. From the tiled ceiling hung several black lanterns, flickering a soft, glowing light. Rosemary, thyme, and basil filled her nose as she bent down, sniffing each one. Arching over the rows of potted plants, long copper pipes occasionally released steam, keeping the garden warm and full of life.

The garden was only a small part to the grandeur of the manor, but the longer she remained, even that felt more like a prison, camouflaged in marble and wainscoting. She was stuck with nowhere to go. All of her life, she had a purpose. She took care of her mother. Then she took care of orphans. She took care of Søren. Now she was just existing for the sake of existing, all the while a heavy cloud hung over her, reminding her that at any moment, this exquisite prison could be replaced with one of brick and iron bars. But was there really a difference?

Footsteps echoed from the hall and a maid, carrying silver knives in one hand and a cloth in the other, stepped into the garden.

"Do you know the time?" Eirún asked.

The maid briefly looked back in the hall at a large grandfather clock. "Just after seven."

Eirún nodded and walked into the hall. The maid bowed as Eirún passed her. She could smell the polish that had tainted the maid's hands.

In the hallway, voltaic lights had been mounted along the plastered walls, which were painted a dark forest green. Passing a side table, she picked up the book she had placed there earlier that evening. She headed on.

Geirleif was chatting with another man as she walked through the library. They both held pipes in their hands while thick smoke wreathed around their heads.

In a corner leather chair, Sylvi played with her pup as it wrapped its little gray paws around her hand. Her condition continued to intrigue Eirún. Eilis had told her that when Sylvi was still young, she got terribly sick. After the fever broke, she could still hear well enough, but she couldn't speak, and her mind always remained like a small child's.

Sylvi let out a hysterical laugh and caught sight of Eirún. She often followed her around the house, but Eirún wasn't in the mood tonight. When Geirleif turned toward her and smiled with a nod, Eirún silently bowed her head and smiled back but continued through the entry hall.

Her fake smile quickly disappeared as she approached the drawing room. She had refused to see Mathios since they arrived. And as much as she knew she should, she had no feelings for him. She had tried to pity him the way she did when she found him in the alleyway. But instead, her misery toward herself only grew.

A nurse walked up the steps from the basement.

"Is Mathios asleep yet?" Eirún asked.

"Haven't checked yet, my lady," said the maid, setting her sheets down on a long wooden bar. "But usually, he is awake around this time. If you would like to go down and see him, you may."

"Thank you." She glanced back through the hall. Sylvi was already looking for her as she peered into different rooms.

Hurrying down the stairs, she sniffed as the air in the dark hallway below thickened with lantern oil. The walls were built of gray stacked stone; the thick wooden floorboards felt sturdy below her feet. She grabbed a lantern from the wall and turned the wick up, sending out more light. She often explored the basement. She enjoyed it more than the upper manor. It felt older and simpler as if time slowed within its halls. Yet it was also large, with many rooms, as if it had once been a great hall in ages past.

Several maids and footmen dressed in aprons and tailcoats walked by her, carrying trays. As always, they would pause and step to the side, bowing their heads. Eirún nodded and continued on. Coming near the end of the hall, she stopped in front of a thick oak door to the left, painted a creamy white. She placed her hand on the glass knob but hesitated. She tried to remember back to when Mathios was young and still innocent in her eyes. Abused and neglected like the rest of them. But it didn't help. She was still just using him to satisfy her longing for Søren. It sounded absurd, even in her own mind. Was she going mad? She didn't care.

She pushed open the door.

A tall wooden dresser stood against the far wall, and in the corner sat a small bed with Mathios beneath the sheets. Eirún gently set the lantern on the dresser and, with the book still in her hand, walked over and grabbed a chair in the far corner. As she slid it across the wooden floor, the trimming of her dress kept getting caught beneath its leg. Sooner or later, she was going to throw these absurd clothes away and put on her old ones again despite what anyone else thought.

Finally, situating herself, she opened the book in her lap and pulled out the feather. She took in a long smell of the familiar scent. Images of reading to Søren popped in her head. She turned the pages to the back of the book. She ran her finger down a list of root words and their meanings. She cleared her throat and looked up at Mathios sleeping under his sheets. She lifted her hand and placed it gently on his shoulder.

"Mathios?" she whispered.

She waited a moment.

"Mathios?" His shoulder felt stiff, and she lifted her hand in hesitation. Slowly, she placed the book on the ground, stood up, and leaned over the bed. She slowly lowered the sheet from his face. His eyes were half open and still; a trail of blood ran from his mouth, staining the pillowcase. She took a step back.

It had happened. He was dead.

Part of her wanted to cry. Part of her was numb. She pulled the sheet back over his face and sunk back into her chair. She sat for a long while, staring at the outline of his body. He was usually a large boy for thirteen, but the sickness had wracked his body so badly that he looked barely bigger than Søren. Taller still, but possibly even thinner. She pulled the sheet down again and made herself look into his eyes. Even in death, there was grief on his face.

Suddenly, her obsession with Søren faded for a moment, and she saw Mathios as he was many years ago. Lost and confused, trying to figure out why he even existed. At the Inn, along the road to Norfrost, he had called her name. That night, she could see it in his eyes that he wanted forgiveness. When they got to the Manor, he had even asked to see her. But she never forgave him. He wept for it, and she ignored him.

Eirún sunk her face into her hands and broke into a loud sob.

* * *

Geirleif tapped the stem of his pipe against his teeth, aimlessly looking across the library into the halls beyond. Eirún had just passed by, and although Hrunting hid it well, Geirleif caught him occasionally glancing up from his newspaper toward her. But could he blame him? With that long blonde hair and fair skin, she was a stunning girl.

Eventually, Sylvi, still in her nightgown, left the library and wandered through the hall. He never could figure out how she could see through her long thick hair, which covered her face. She disappeared down the stairway to the basement.

Sylvi's mother was one of the best maids he had. When she passed away, taking care of her asinine daughter was the least he and Eilis could do. Geirleif moaned beneath his breath. The telegram had his stomach in knots. But he needed to think through this rationally. Certainly, there was a solution.

Hrunting tossed the newspaper onto the floor beside his chair. "It's all nonsense," he grumbled.

"What is?" Geirleif asked.

"The news. All it ever talks about are scandals, murders, and corruption. I mean, really? What's wrong with people?"

"Reporting scandals is what sells."

Hrunting raised an eyebrow. He was forty-three, and yet he looked thirty. Geirleif wished he looked that young when he was that age. "Which only makes it more disturbing," Hrunting went on. "Murders, thefts, and whatnot. It's almost as if people wished they could do these things themselves, but since they can't get away with it, they just have to placate their cravings by reading about it instead." He held his hands in the air. "Why do people want to read about how a person hung himself?" He pointed at the newspaper. "That's the headline on the front page. It even quotes a personal letter this poor man wrote to his daughter before he did it."

If it wasn't for the telegram, Geirleif would have been far more entertained by Hrunting's rant. He could go like this for hours. "They probably keep writing that stuff because people like you keep buying the papers."

Ignoring his statement, which he often did, Hrunting grabbed his cup and held it out. The footman walked over and filled it with black tea. Setting it down, he picked up his pipe and cradled it loosely in his other hand. "Thank you," he said to the footman. He looked at Geirleif. "Anyway, forgive my tirade. What were we talking about earlier?"

Geirleif blew out a puff of smoke from his pipe. "But you were just getting started," he said, hoping Hrunting wouldn't notice the anxiousness welling up in him. "Besides, I don't think anyone much cares what I am blabbering about."

"Oh, no," Hrunting replied. "I find it very interesting. There is much going on, especially in Fingate that I am not aware of."

"Well, truthfully, there is much I don't know of either."

Hrunting laughed. "But do you not approve all the experimental trials within the dilution sites?"

Geirleif sat back in his chair with a frustrated sigh and glanced at a maid dusting off a stack of books.

"Is everything all right?"

"Yes, yes," Geirleif said shortly. He set his pipe on the table beside him. "But as you were asking, yes, I do approve of the trials, but it's all paperwork. I sign here, sign there." He waved a hand in the air. "And I'm not the only one. I only sign for Section Three."

"I'm not familiar with Section Three," replied Hrunting. He picked up his cup of tea again, taking a sip.

"Sites pertaining to combat advancements," Geirleif continued. "We run a series of tests determining how we can improve anything from soldiers, military equipment, battle derangement disorder, physical injuries . . ." He trailed off. He didn't like to think about it very much. "Things like that."

Hrunting wiped his hand down his clean-shaven face. "You ever wonder about it?"

Geirleif raised his eyebrow. "Wonder about it?"

"The Dilution Sites. What goes on there?"

"No, Lord Hrunting," he said. "I try not to mix my conscience with my work. Ethics have their place, but I work for the king. I don't have the luxury of dealing with ethical questions."

Hrunting set his pipe down beside the teacup. His mouth and nose twisted as if he wrestled with his next question. He leaned back. "But do you think that makes it right? Just because it's classified as work?"

Was Hrunting accusing him of something? "Neither you nor I know precisely what goes on in the Dilution Sites—"

"There's likely a reason for that," Hrunting interrupted.

"Perhaps, but if we want to delve into ethics, then we must consider the greater good of the society as a whole, not merely the individuals. If we want to better this world through medicine or defense systems, there are certain processes we must take in order to get there."

"But is not society made up of individuals? Do they not have personal rights?"

"Hrunting, my dear friend, I have too much on my mind tonight to go into another debate with you about political theories." He waved a finger. "And if you ask me, you read too much controversial material for your own good. One of these days, you're going to say the wrong thing to the wrong person and get yourself in trouble."

"Then let me ask it another way if you don't mind."

Geirleif let out a sigh. Did Hrunting not hear a word he said?

"What do you think is the duty of man?" he asked, narrowing his eyes in thought.

"I think man's duty is to better society."

"What about for himself? Has he any purpose to his own self, or is it to society alone?"

This was going to take all night. He scanned his eyes across the dark floor-to-ceiling shelves. Certainly, of all the hundreds of books filling this library, there was at least one he could give Hrunting to satisfy his constant badgering. "I think every man owes it to himself to pursue happiness, to live a full life in a way that he sees fit."

"That's what I don't understand," Hrunting said. "To say that man's purpose is to better society, and yet at the same time he is to pursue his own happiness, is a contradiction of values."

For goodness sake, what has Hrunting been reading? "How do you mean?"

"What if what makes a man happy is to do the opposite of what society demands of him?"

"Of course, a man's pursuit of happiness must be in accord with society. Society is made up of the *people* who govern for the common good. If an individual goes against that, he is overruled."

"Then do you believe that society determines what is right and wrong?" Hrunting asked. "Ethically?"

"What else could? The natural world? What an absurd question."

Hrunting didn't seem offended. Even Geirleif knew he had a stronger spine than most men. "What if society said it was good to murder an innocent person for no reason other than it wanted to? Would it then be okay to do so?"

Geirleif looked ahead to the entrance of the library and thought for a moment. He wanted to say no, but then Hrunting would think he won the argument. "I don't know," he said.

"I'm going to assume you would say no. Is it possible then that our conviction of right and wrong comes from something higher than society?"

"Like what?"

Hrunting shrugged. "A personal mind, a god, I don't know."

"My lord," came the voice of a maid, stepping into the library. "You have been requested to Mathios's quarters."

Geirleif let out a long sigh of relief. Perfect timing. "I'll be there right away."

In the downstairs basement, Geirleif hurried through the dark hall, following the maid, who carried a lantern as dancing light wavered upon the stone walls. Ulfr came out of his office with an obviously fake smile. "Pleasure seeing you down here, my Lord!"

Geirleif passed by him. "Ulfr," was all he said. He didn't know why, but something about Ulfr's attitude had been rubbing him the wrong way lately. He could have sworn he was listening in on his conversation at dinner.

Now standing at the doorway of Mathios's quarters, he tried to see Eirún's face, but she looked down as she sat on her knees before the now-empty bed. Mathios must have already been taken away. At her side sat Sylvi in the chair with one hand on Eirún's shoulder, the other holding her pup as it tried to escape from her grip.

"I apologize, your Lordship!" Ulfr spoke up from behind Geirleif. "No maid is to place a hand on a lady's shoulder!"

Sylvi glanced up, removing her hand, and she let her face fall into a frown.

"It's all right," Eirún said. "I was here alone, and she was only making sure I was okay." She looked at Sylvi. "Thank you."

Sylvi's mouth trembled as she ran out of the room.

Geirleif glared at Ulfr.

"It's not respectable, sir," Ulfr mumbled.

"I do not care about proper respect! Never speak to that child like that again!"

Ulfr looked down resentfully. "I beg your pardon, but she's not a—"

"Leave us!"

With a red face, Ulfr bowed and stepped out of the room. Geirleif closed the door, leaving only a thin crack, and walked over to Eirún. He let out a sigh and stood awkwardly above her for a moment. Should he sit in the chair? Should he stand? He quietly sighed again and took off his tailcoat. He ineffectively dusted off the wooden floor and sat next to Eirún. The room was silent as she stared at the empty bed.

"I don't think I was ready," she said at last.

Despite her wet cheeks beneath her blonde hair, and tired green eyes, she still had a youthful appearance, as if she was still too young to experience the miseries of this world. If he had ever had a daughter, Geirleif would have liked to think she would have been like Eirún. A small pebble was stuck between two boards, and he picked at it with his fingers.

"We never are," he replied.

Eirún sobbed. "I don't even know why I'm here."

Geirleif found himself holding back his own watering eyes. "Mathios was lucky to have you. You gave him many happy days in the end."

Eirún kept her gaze down. Geirleif thought his words fell short of how he really felt, and he wished he had something better to say.

"I just . . ." she said with a sniff. "I almost wish I hadn't found him."

Geirleif placed a hand on her back. "Now, don't say that. I know you miss him, and I know this is hard, but it will pass."

Eirún closed her eyes, shaking her head. "It's not that. I feel—I feel guilty." She glanced at the bed again, letting out another sniffling. "I want Søren back."

Patting her back gently, Geirleif tried to understand the pain she must feel. Other than losing his parents, who were well into their old age, he had never experienced anything like this.

"I only wanted Søren," she continued. "And Mathios was the closest thing I had to him." She laid her face in her hands. "I miss him so much."

Geirleif drew in a deep breath, his mind blank for words. Then, after a moment, he took his hand and turned her cheek toward him. "Now listen to me," he said gently. "You cannot help what you feel, but I know that isn't the whole story. The harm he's done to you is just unthinkable, and yet I've seen how you care for him, the forgiveness you've shown him. That's something I could have never done. But you did. And forgiveness . . ." he thought for words. "It's the most powerful thing. It set him free from the burden of guilt."

Eirún's eyes darkened, and she slunk low as if something forced her to the ground.

Geirleif's chest tightened. Did he say something wrong?

She lowered herself until she laid on the ground, weeping onto the floorboards. Geirleif straightened himself. What was he supposed to do now?

He patted her on the back again. "It's all right," he tried to encourage her.

She never looked toward him but only mumbled in a cold, emotionless tone, "I'd like to be alone for a while."

Walking up the stairs, Geirleif wiped the sweat from his brow and untied the cravat around his neck, letting it hang loosely from his shoulders. He walked through the drawing room and into the entry hall.

"Everything all right?" came the voice of Hrunting near the front entrance.

Geirleif joined Hrunting as they both stepped outside. The snow looked like a sea of liquid silver in the moonlight. A few lanterns moved up and down the front lawn as men patrolled the grounds.

"Yes, yes, everything is as fine as it can be." But that was a lie. He felt terrible. "We knew the boy would pass, but it's still a shame watching such a young life go lost."

"You mean the boy who was with your . . .?"

If he hadn't been so troubled, he would have laughed at Hrunting. He acted as if he had no idea who Eirún was, and yet every time she passed by him, he would briefly lose focus of whatever they were talking about.

"Just a distant cousin," Geirleif said at last. "And the boy's name was Mathios."

Hrunting held his hands behind his back and drug a line through the snow with the toe of his shoe. "I can't imagine it would be easy for anyone," he said.

"It's more than that for her, though. I've told her this many times, and I'll say it again—I have never known such a selfless girl. That boy Mathios had hurt her in a terrible way."

Hrunting looked at Geirleif.

"A terrible way," he continued, "and she has only shown him mercy."

"What did he do? If you don't mind me asking?"

Thick snowflakes drifted silently to the earth. Geirleif glanced back to the door. "If I tell you something, will you swear to secrecy?"

"Of course."

"I mean it."

"Geirleif, we've been friends for many years. I promise."

He took in a deep breath. "Eirún isn't my cousin."

Hrunting's eyes piqued in interest.

"A while back," he continued, "Mathios had killed a boy in an orphanage Eirún was working at. For a while, it stirred up quite a bit of controversy in Folkbjörn. But the point is, Eirún cared deeply for the boy he killed. He was like a son to her."

"You're joking?"

"I wish I were. After Mathios had killed the boy, Eirún found work in Scathwold, but things didn't go very well. I don't know all the details, but apparently, she worked for a merchant who had a darker side to his character." Geirleif hesitated for a moment, his own mind conjuring up faded memories of his own personal life, but he quickly forgot it. "As far I can collect," he continued, "he attempted some terrible things."

Hrunting didn't say anything but only lowered his eyebrows.

"And in self-defense," Geirleif went on, "Eirún knocked him down a set of stairs, killing him."

Hrunting slightly shifted his head back. "She did that?"

As the chill of the night air crept into Geirleif's stiffening fingers, he interlocked his hands and leaned an elbow on the marble railing. "Unfortunately."

The corner of Hrunting's mouth curled up. "That's a tough girl."

"I didn't expect that response!" Geirleif laughed.

"Then what happened?"

Geirleif explained how she stumbled upon his carriage in Scathwold and how she had taken care of Mathios since finding him in the alley.

"Incredible," Hrunting said at last. "You don't find many people like that these days."

"There's a problem, though. The body of this man has been found, and Eirún is now wanted for murder."

Hrunting stiffened.

"And I just received a telegram this evening asking for my presence at the Norfrost Precinct in three weeks. I'm wanted for questioning regarding my connection with her."

"They know she's with you?"

"It appears so," he said. He rubbed his temples. "Over and over again, I worked through my memory, and the only thing I can figure is that when we were in Folkbjörn, I had left my pocket watch in a bakery. I foolishly asked her to get it for me. Perhaps the investigators found out that she was there asking for my watch."

Hrunting didn't say anything at first. He slid his hands into his pocket. "Does Eilis know?"

Geirleif pursed his lips. The last thing on his mind was Eilis. He shook his head and tried to control his growing fear. The full reality of his situation began to sink in. "I don't know what to do, Hrunting. The worst part is, at one point, we were stopped on the road. Officers had a sketch of her face. I lied to them. I told them I'd never seen her." He paused and looked hard at Hrunting. "She was in the back of the carriage as I said those very words. And what's more, they knew who I was. One of the officers even called me by my title."

"But surely—"

"There is no way around this, Hrunting. I am an accomplice. It's only a matter of time before I'm arrested."

"But you're a lord, a member of the General Assembly. Perhaps they'll—"

"That won't help anything!" he said in a hoarse whisper. "Nothing's above the law, not even the king."

Hrunting looked back through the front door as a footman walked from one hall to another. "What are you going to do?"

Geirleif laid a hand over his eyes. "I don't know. I can't turn her in. I can't just throw her out. I don't have the heart for it. I'll . . ." He had no idea what to do. "I'll run or something."

"Don't be foolish."

Geirleif gave a short laugh, his hand still over his eyes. "You're right. That's a terrible idea."

"Not to mention you're Lord Beron. Everyone knows who you are. You're too old to be running—"

"Yes, yes! I already said it was a bad idea."

"What if you tell them you saw her in Folkbjörn, but you didn't know she was wanted? You could say you didn't recognize her in the picture. That happens at times, and there's no reason they won't believe you."

Wiping his cheeks, Geirleif sniffed in the cold air. "You have no idea how bad of a liar I really am. That officer on the road, when he stopped us, I thought he could see right through me. Besides, even if they did believe me, what am I going to do with Eirún? They know what she looks like. She can't hide here forever."

"And you haven't hidden her very well *here* either," Hrunting added, shaking off half-melted snow from his shoe. "All it takes is an investigator to show up with another picture of her face."

"Which may happen sooner than later, especially now that they know there's a connection."

"Geirleif, I don't know what to tell you. But it seems to me that your first step is to get her out of here."

"I already said I'm not going to throw her out."

"I didn't say throw her out. Send her somewhere safe."

"Where? Another city? They'll just find her again. That'll only make things worse."

A tiny black shadow fluttered above them and landed at the top of one of the manor columns. Maybe a bird, but probably a bat. Geirleif wouldn't have minded being either one at the moment. No problems. No worries. All he'd have to worry about would be food and shelter.

"What about another country?" Hrunting asked.

"Another country?" What a foolish idea. "Varghoss has been entirely closed off since last year. And with the current political atmosphere, neither Kalestrond nor the Steinfjell isles are even remotely a possibility." A fog of air billowed from his lungs. "No. I'd get caught if I did something so foolish, and I'd only further doom myself and my family. I'll just have to go to the precinct and see if I can't pull some strings."

Hrunting crossed his arms.

"I've got no other choice," Geirleif continued with a shrug.

"You may pull some strings for yourself, but not for Eirún. Besides, the northern countries may not be open, but I bet you could get her into Sunder."

"You know that the only people they ever allow are deployed military personnel and diplomats. And the moment I walked her on a wisp, they'd recognize her immediately."

"First of all, I seriously doubt they'd recognize her here in Norfrost. She killed a merchant, not King Eirik. Second, you don't just walk her on a wisp, you sneak her on."

"Good grief, Hrunting, who do you think I am? The special operatives?"

And why was he so quick to advise him to do such drastic things? But, of course, Hrunting was always like that. It was like he got bored with life and always needed to find something to stir things up a bit. He didn't know how Hrunting had lasted so long in the General Assembly without getting himself arrested for something foolish.

"Besides," Geirleif continued, "there's no scheduled wisps going to Sunder right now. Not until this whole mining crisis settles down."

"There's some going to Fingate," Hrunting said. "And you have control of when they leave and what they ship out. I bet you could even make a personal visit. Get her on board. Then you could just steer it on over to Sunder yourself."

Steer it himself? Hrunting was out of his mind. "Your ideas are going to get me killed. I don't even know how to fly a wisp."

"It's not that difficult. I've done it. Just steer her over, drop her off, and bring yourself back. It'll take you a week at most. You would be back in plenty of time before you have to go to the precinct."

Geirleif rolled his eyes. He already knew he wouldn't do something this foolish. "If I turn myself in, I'll likely get a few years in prison. If I steal a wisp, I'll likely get executed. Besides, it wouldn't be that easy. They'd recognize her in Sunder and—"

"They're not going to have a warrant out for her in Sunder."

"If they find out she sailed in a stolen wisp, they might."

"Well, if you really believe she is innocent, and you don't want to see her in prison, you're going to have to do something."

There was a long, uneasy silence as both men looked out across the stretched-out lawn. A cloud had covered the moon, veiling the landscape in darkness. Geirleif didn't know what to do. But it didn't really matter, did it? He was doomed to lose his title. Terrible desperation only continued to assault him.

"Do you hear that?" Hrunting asked.

"Hear what?"

Hrunting looked toward the city. Geirleif held his breath. Faint shouts lifted up in the distance. Screams even.

"Is it coming from the city?"

"I can't tell," Hrunting replied. "But whatever it is, it doesn't sound good."

A rogue gust brought a familiar foul stench to Geirleif. What in the world could be going on?

Rise of the Free Sunderian Army

Through the ruined gate, bodies lay strewn across the earth. To Porter's left and right stood many men gripping their weapons. Quietly breathing, and yet a look of fear remained in their eyes. Not a single living Daecish soldier could be seen within the Northern District.

Porter blew hard out of his nose and stole a quick glance over his shoulder. The large monster, which once stood as high as the city wall, now lay in a lifeless pile of contorted gore and gray fur. Hanging over its jagged teeth, its long tongue dripped red onto the snow. White eyes rolled back in its head and armed on each of its front feet, long black talons, nearly the length of a man's arm, curved into sharp points. Such a sight was enough to give him nightmares for the rest of his life.

Porter turned back around as the ground shook with a heavy step. Another alphyn. He kept his eyes on the city wall. The creak of tightening leather and the clanking of armor and swords told him the men were getting in position.

"Don't let it through the gate," he said in a low voice. He hoped the alphyn would move on, but his gut told him it would come for them.

To his dread, its head appeared behind the open gate. It sniffed the ground with a loud snarl and glanced up at the men, letting out a thundering roar. It positioned itself to charge into the city.

Porter forced his panicking mouth to open. "Attack!" he yelled as the men all bolted forward.

The alphyn leaped from its hind legs at a great speed, severing between the men like a sword through water. Its talons slashed across the air as several men fell, dismembered in two; blood splattered and poured as screams echoed through the streets.

"Aim for the head and behind the shoulder!" Porter screamed, swinging his war hammer against its hide.

The alphyn continued roaring as the men fought against it. One thrust his sword into its hind leg but quickly lost his entire upper body as the creature whipped around and sank its teeth into his flesh. With frantic shouts, several men lunged their spears into its side until, at last, it faltered in its steps. It spun around, flinging three men across the broken cobblestone ground. The others stumbled out of the way. With a raised head, the alphyn let out another roar and pounced toward the broken earth in the middle of the courtyard. Viciously, it clawed at the earth in its attempt to burrow into the ground.

"Don't let it go!" Porter charged forward. "Kill it before it escapes!"

The men continued piercing its lower side. Several went to hacking at its hind legs until, at last, the monster lay still, half-buried in the earth. Porter wiped his nose on his arm. The heavy breathing of the other men condensed in the chill air around him.

From the corner of his eye, he caught sight of several girls hiding behind a partially opened door. By their dress, he knew them to be prostitutes. He didn't have too many aracs, but he had also been alone in the Western Plains for a long time. Sunderian culture had always frowned on fornication. The old chronicles even threatened divine judgment. But in his own mind, whores didn't count. They were already forsaken. A shameful blemish to society. Besides, he'd be paying for their next meal, and they sure looked like they needed it.

"Commander Ulwick," came a voice behind him. A brigadier walked over with long leather cords and straps in one hand. Iron hooks in the other. "Found these in a building over yonder. There's about two dozen more if we want it."

Porter took a leather cord and pulled it, testing its strength. He peered at the wall. "That'll do. Let's hang the bodies on the outside. It'll give a nice welcome to any Daecish trying to walk in."

* * *

Arnon awoke with a startle. Over his feet laid the open torso of a dead Daecish soldier. Beneath his head rested the legs of someone else. He cringed as his whole body ached beneath his blood-soaked jerkin and armor. He placed his hands on the ground, lifting himself up, but felt something awkward with his left hand. Lifting it up, he blinked, disbelieving his own eyes. All that remained of his little finger was a short, bloody stub. He examined it for a moment, then glanced along the ground, almost expecting to find his finger lying there.

Just ahead of him was the body of a young Daecish soldier with a pale face. Staring into his lifeless eyes, death felt more strange than sad. As if it was unnatural and invasive. Like something that was never supposed to be. For a second, the bodies in front of his home flashed into his mind, but he ignored the thought.

Shifting the torso from off his legs, he eyed his right boot, noticing his hunting knife was missing. His posture sank. His father made that knife, and he would never find it in this field. Then he felt for his sword and felt his temperature rise. Where was it? He glanced around frantically. By sheer chance, he saw the end of the silver pommel just beside him under the body of a Sunderian. With a grunt, he pulled the sword from beneath the corpse. Blood and mud lined the hilt and blade. It would rust soon if he didn't clean it.

Shouting dimly echoed across the field. Several Sunderian men battled a creature in the far distance. Its girth and grotesque form would have normally caused him to shudder, but it all seemed so surreal. Were they really alphyns? It was one thing to sing songs about them. It was another thing to see them. Three large carcasses slumped not far in the distance; one looked as if it had a hundred arrows protruding from its back and sides.

What was left of his finger began to throb, and his daze faded while reality sank in. Were the alphyns a sign of the end? The words of Hælend's Ballad rushed to his mind. Although there was no other explanation he could come up with, he couldn't even begin to imagine what that meant. All he knew was that the ballad never sounded like something he wanted to live through. With a grunt, he lifted himself up on his feet but had to pause as a rush of blood ran into his head.

At last, the alphyn roared while the men climbed on its back, thrusting swords and spears into its flesh. Near the city gate, several older men paced around the battlefield, looking around the bodies as if they were searching for someone earnestly.

Besides the men cheering at the now-dead alphyn, the air around him reeked with the smell of death. The field that lay white only a day before was now ridden with an endless sea of bodies and horses covering the sloping hills of churned earth and red snow. Many were older men, but some looked younger than himself.

Crows crowded in on the field. High above, vultures soared, their wings fluttering in their broad circular flight. The copper smell of blood mixed with alphyn filled his nose, and he shivered as a cold breeze kicked up. He wished he had his bearskin cloak.

Wiping off his father's blade as best as he could, he sheathed it beneath his belt and looked around to see if he could find the mule lying somewhere. Of course, he'd never find it in this mess. Wondering what the current prices for mules were, he reckoned it was likely more than he had.

Despite the destruction of the earth, with endless trenches and sinkholes, there were very few alphyns. By the cheerful looks of the Sunderian men walking to the city gate, it even seemed the Daecish had been defeated.

Did they actually win? He stumbled toward the gate, but his aching body, with a sharp pain shooting up his left leg, forced him to waddle. It didn't help that every limb in his body felt frozen from the cold. Twice he tripped over a body, but as he finally made it to the gate, a Sunderian soldier walked out.

"Excuse me!" Arnon shouted.

Even with the bandage wrapped around his head and one arm in a sling, Arnon recognized him as the archer who had stopped him at the crest of the valley two nights before. But he wasn't sure if the shades of red on his brigandine were paint or blood. Maybe both.

"Commander Greystrom?" the man asked.

"Ah, yes," Arnon replied, straightening himself. He shivered again. "Colin, correct?"

"Yes, sire," he replied.

"Do you know where General Barclay is?"

Colin pointed toward the city. "They have the remaining Daecish cornered at the Palace of Ingvar, I believe."

"We've won the battle?" Arnon asked eagerly.

Colin held a peculiar look on his face. "Well, commander, if you can call it winning." He gazed across the field. "These monsters have all but devastated the land." He motioned toward the gate. "Luckily, only a few came up inside the city."

Arnon peered through the gate as if expecting to see an alphyn standing there. Only horses and men scattered the Eastern road; blood still seeped into the cracks of the cobblestones. Another gust of wind blew through the gate, and Colin slouched his shoulders as Arnon rubbed his arms. Suddenly a fear crept into his heart. Only a few alphyns came into the city, but was Adelyne okay?

"But since sunrise," Colin continued, "most went back underground."

Arnon was ready to leave and look for Adelyne, but he checked himself. He needed to know what was going on. "Underground?"

"All at once. As soon as the sun rose up. 'Course, we got several troops of our men hunting any stragglers still left. Better keep an eye out just in case." Arnon couldn't wait any longer. He thanked Colin and hurried into the city.

* * *

Gunnar stood silent beside two officials, their bodies tense as they watched King Ónarr toss a stack of books against the brick wall. Dust clung to the sleeves of his blue uniform; the golden aiguillette on his left shoulder was spotted with brown dirt. Great drops of sweat dripped down his flustered face from his thin hair as he lifted open chests and crates.

"Your Majesty," said one of the officials with a crack in his voice. He cleared his throat. "What is our plan of action?"

The king pointed his finger to the floor of the room. "Where is it?" he asked. "Where is it!"

The official shook his head with an open mouth. "We could not find it, your Majesty."

The king placed his hands on his soaking head as he set his heavy frame on an emptied chest that had been tipped on its side. "It was the only thing I specifically asked for, and yet you cannot find it!"

The room lay in a thick silence. Gunnar wasn't sure how he felt. The Daecish were defeated in Everwind. But what could that mean? Eilívur would probably get demoted. And either he'd be stuck in Sunder longer than he ever wanted to be, or he'd be sent home. He missed his wife, Hilde, and wished more than anything that he could see his newborn son.

"We've lost Everwind," the king said to himself. "To peasants." He looked up at the officials with purple rings around his eyes. "And now I cannot find the only thing dear to me."

"Your Majesty . . ." said the official, but his voice trailed off into silence.

The king said nothing.

With worry in his eyes, one official turned to the other and whispered in his ear. "We must retreat to Llynhithe and get the king out of here. Even if we must bind him to do so. These monsters are everywhere."

The other official nodded and did well to maintain his posture, but his constantly bouncing heels revealed that he was as anxious to leave as the others.

Gunnar took in a calm breath with his hands clasped in front of him. "Your Majesty," he said. The king didn't look up. "Your Majesty," he continued. "Commander Tyr is here with the remaining troops. He requests your plan for further action."

The officials glanced uneasily at one another as the king remained silent. Thick particles of dust floated around the lanterns before disappearing into shadow. Gunnar felt the sudden need to sneeze, but he held it in as best he could.

"Further action?" the king finally asked. He slowly straightened himself. Whether his face was wet from sweat or tears, Gunnar couldn't tell. His own nose tickled, and he suddenly let out a loud, high-pitched sneeze. He knew it was higher than most men's, but no one in that room seemed to care in the tension of the moment.

The king stood up and walked forward with a slight limp. "I've lost two of the greatest cities in Sunder, and others will likely follow." He released a long groan, inappropriate for any king, and then placed a hand over his brow. "By some witchery or conspiracy against me, I must depart. But what does it matter?" He walked past Gunner, who could smell the sweat on the king's face as he entered the administration office. "Take me to Commander Tyr."

Ahead of the king, Gunnar stepped into the upstairs room. Beside Halvard and Dagr, Eilívur stood at perfect attention, stilled clothed in his tattered uniform and seemingly unaware that the abrasion above his right brow still bled down the side of his face. Gunnar gave him a hard stare while barely shaking his head in the off chance that Eilívur could read his mind and know that the king was losing it. But as Gunnar stood beside him, Eilívur never seemed to notice him as his unblinking gaze remained fixed on the opposite wall.

Hearing the king holler as he followed his two officials up the stairs, Gunnar held his breath.

"Commander-in-Chief, Eilívur Tyr." The king locked his eyes on him as he walked toward the desk. "So, this is the man of the hour. Our commander who has lost our city. What say you?"

Eilívur remained unmoved. He always did handle himself well in the worst of moments. "Your Majesty, our men did their best to serve you. Our conditions were not optimal, and we were not prepared. We failed to hold the Northern Gate, and their numbers were more than we anticipated."

The king waved a hand. "We outnumbered them three-to-one!"

"Your Majesty, there were unexpected—"

"Silence! We have lost our capital to these. . . to these peasants! Albern is nowhere to be found, likely hiding in some passage in the castle. I'll have his head before the end of this!" He slammed a fist on the desk and peered across the room in a hot temper. "We can no longer hold our ground in Everwind. We must retreat to Llynhithe."

"What of the creatures?" spoke up Gunnar.

"Kill them!" he spat. "Unless you're afraid of animals, Commander Veurðr?" He paced the floor. "We must go to Llynhithe, then we'll send a dispatch to Runevast. He scowled at an official standing behind him. "Are you writing this down?"

The official hurried to the desk and wrestled his hands through some documents.

"A dispatch has already been sent, Your Majesty," Eilívur added.

The king paused in his step and glared at Eilívur. "When was this sent?"

"Yesterday, Your Majesty."

The king swelled his chest and stepped forward. "By what authority did you send a dispatch to Runevast if it wasn't mine?"

Dagr gave a faint smile.

"Your Majesty," Eilívur replied. "We were in a state-of-emergency. I was acting Commander-in-Chief, and we needed reinforcements. If Llynhithe would've sent what we needed, we may have been able to save the—"

"Do not blame Llynhithe! The only reason this city was ill prepared was because neither you nor your commanders," he shot a stern glance at Halvard and Gunnar, "dealt with these riots in an efficient manner."

"Your Majesty," Halvard defended, "we did—"

"I don't want to hear it!" The king interrupted.

Halvard visibly swallowed. He wasn't used to being chastised like this. But even Gunnar felt the growing tension. The cluttered office seemed to only get smaller, and he desperately wanted to loosen his collar. But he dared not move.

"The dispatch you sent was before the city fell!" the king continued. "We must send another informing King Eirik of our current situation." He raised an eyebrow at Gunnar. "Commander Veurðr, you will leave this morning for Runevast. Report to Commander-in-Chief Asger as soon as you arrive in Norfrost."

"Yes, Your Majesty." He tried to not smile, but he was actually going home.

The king shot his gaze back to Eilívur. "I hold you responsible for the loss of this city, Commander!" His face suddenly went red, almost purple. "But do you know who Norfrost will blame? They'll hold me accountable for your folly!"

Even Gunnar felt the king's spit spray on his face. Poor Eilívur.

Taking a step back, the king drew in a long breath with closed eyes as if he was attempting to collect himself. "We depart today for Llynhithe. But as for you, Commander-in-Chief Tyr, as protector of this city, you shall stay behind until you have negotiated the treatment and release of our prisoners of war!"

"Yes, Your Majesty."

"Your Majesty," spoke up Halvard again, though in a calmer, bold tone. "Must we surrender all of Everwind so easily? Surely we haven't reached—"

The king's stature and motions looked as if a gust of wind threatened to push him over. "No one said anything about surrendering. I speak only of a momentary retreat. King Eirik will respond as he sees fit, and you will all do as I command!"

* * *

Outside the Palace of Ingvar, Drake leaned against a walking staff he grabbed from the tavern and peered across the lawn. Wrapped around his shoulders was Arnon's bearskin cloak. It was the coldest morning of the season so far. Certainly, Arnon wouldn't mind. Besides, he made sure to sear and wrap his wounds first, so he wouldn't get any blood on it.

Statues lay toppled and broken across the piles of white snow. All was dark behind the many windows, and not a Daecish soul could be seen. They were probably hiding like cowards in the storehouses. Behind, men moved eagerly around, positioning themselves at vantage points. Although no alphyns could be seen, tremors ran through his heart at the thought of their appearance. He didn't doubt for a second that this was the end. A sudden pain shot up his body, and he grimaced. Blood still managed to run down the wound in his leg. He hiked up the cloak and double-checked that it was clean.

"Part of me's overjoyed, and part of me's terrified," Galvin said, coming up beside him.

"I hear you," Drake replied. "I ain't heard any since dawn, but they're comin'. It's the sign. This's a bitter victory indeed."

Galvin raised his chin. "I won't say that yet. Alphyns may've come, but they've been here in Sunder before."

"Maybe a thousand years ago, and even then, it was only a handful here and there. But what we saw last night . . ." His voice trembled.

"We'll keep going. We're still breathing, and our city still stands, don't it? We're not stopping now. Not 'til Sunder's Bane."

"Aye," Drake replied. "Or wyrms." He glanced behind his shoulder. Over the crowd of men, the streets lay empty. "I just pray Arnon's alive."

"We'll go out there and look as soon as we can," Galvin replied.

Just then, Quinn ran over. "Overlooked the entire eastern road," he said, panting. "Still haven't found Murdock. He hasn't shown up here?"

Drake shook his head. "Once we're through here, we'll look through the bodies again. With Morgan gone, I can't imagine losing Murdock and Arnon."

Both Drake and Quinn looked at the palace. Despite its elegant design, it was Daecish. And he always thought it was ugly. Yet, Drake couldn't stop his smile. Now that it was about to be Sunder's again, it didn't look so bad.

"You think Daecish will keep holding off?" Quinn asked.

"It depends on what Ónarr orders them to do."

Galvin turned toward three rows of men on his left. Many had long tossed their axes and rusted swords for Daecish weapons, with an entire row wielding crossbows.

"At my command," Galvin shouted, "we march forward! Do not stop until the Daecish surrender, or they're killed!" He lifted a hand for them to begin their march.

"Wait, wait!" Drake shouted, pointing toward the house.

Both Quinn and Galvin looked up. A door at one of the ivy-laden balconies swung open. An officer walked toward the white railing.

"Hold your positions!" Galvin called out.

"By the request of King Ónarr," the officer hollered with his chin held high. "We ask for the presence of your leader and two witnesses for the arrangement for the prisoners of war and the retreat and protection of His Majesty and his commanding officers!"

An eruption of cheers broke through the crowd of men.

"Victory!" they screamed out. "Victory! For the House of Burgess!"

Quinn slapped Drake across the back, and he let out a howl from the pain.

"Sorry!" shouted Quinn with a laugh.

But Drake didn't care. This was it. They took back Everwind. Everyone in the crowd embraced one another. Galvin held a wide grin upon his face; the cheers rose high and echoed through the city streets.

Drake suddenly caught sight of Arnon approaching between the stone walls. He pointed across the rows of men. "Galvin!" he shouted. "Arnon's here!"

Galvin peered above the crowds and pushed through the men, with Drake following close behind. A surprised smile formed on Arnon's face as Galvin embraced him.

"We weren't sure you made it," Galvin hollered in a loud voice above the cheers. He pointed toward the palace. "They've surrendered! We got Everwind!"

Arnon shouted with joy and hugged Galvin again. He then turned toward Drake. "I see you survived the battle!" he said with a laugh.

"And the cold!" Drake replied. "Thanks to your father's bearskin!"

Arnon smiled, but he looked almost blue.

"Here," Drake said as he took off the cloak and wrapped it around him. Then he brushed his hand against the dried blood on Arnon's head. "It seems you barely made it!"

The crowds of men continued shouting out and singing songs. They even broke out into dances and jigs—something Drake hadn't seen in the public streets since the Daecish first arrived. Several men were lifted up on shoulders while one waved the red flag of Sunder high in the air, the black horse fluttering against the wind. A warmth filled his heart, and he took in a deep breath.

"Where's Adelyne?" Arnon asked in Drake's ear.

Drake thought for a second. "Now that you mention it—"

"What?" Arnon asked, cupping his hand around his ear.

"I said, now that you mention it," Drake shouted again. "I ain't seen her since the night before the battle. I imagine she's still at her place with Sarah."

Arnon darted his eyes around the crowd. Drake grabbed Quinn by the shoulder and hollered in his ear. "Have you seen Adelyne?"

"Not since yesterday!"

Drake turned back to Arnon, but he was already gone.

The House of Good Hope

Wet snow and mud seeped through Arnon's leather boots as he marched south. Despite his anxiousness to find Adelyne, he could not have been more thankful that Drake handed him his father's cloak. It wasn't just that it kept him warm—after losing his horse and his hunting knife, it was quickly becoming one of the last of his father's heirlooms he still possessed. And what would his father think of him now? He helped reclaim Everwind. He actually did it. His face stretched into a wide grin. He hoped his father could see him from wherever he was.

Although the smell had somewhat faded since the alphyns went below ground, the stench still hung in various pockets of the city. He veered east as the wall of the Palace of Ingvar disappeared behind a line of buildings running south. As he approached the Southern Squalor, a ruined house, piled high with stone slabs and thatched roofing, blocked his way. He hurried on until he came to the city wall. His pulse pounded through the veins in his neck. He tried to block out images of Adelyne's body laying lifeless somewhere, and he prayed once again to Theos that she was still alive—to let her be okay.

Rounding a corner, he stopped in his tracks. About ten yards ahead, an alphyn lay with its back against the wall and its legs sprawled out in front of it. Fear filled Arnon's mind and he sprinted past the alphyn until piles of rubble and earth arose to his left, stretching into the heart of the slum.

His gaze darted along the broken half-timber and shattered walls of wattle and daub. Other than a large clay pot and some iron fittings, Arnon couldn't see much of the contents of the houses. He kept expecting to see an arm or a body, but to his relief, he saw none. Somewhere in the distance, a baby cried. He paused.

"Sarah?" he called aloud.

The sound grew louder, and before long, a mother stepped out from an alleyway, carrying a small bundle in her arms. She eyed Arnon for a second but hurried into another alleyway, disappearing out of sight. With a groan, Arnon picked up his pace until Adelyne's house came into view. Although some of the timber in the back corner had been broken in, the house otherwise appeared untouched. He sniffed hard as the smell grew stronger.

"Sarah!" he hollered out. "Adelyne!"

There was no sound.

Arnon raced through the back door.

"Adelyne!" he called out.

He hurried up the steps to the attic. The door already stood ajar, but inside was only a chair and a ragged curtain hanging limp in front of the open window.

Arnon ran back downstairs, and through the front door, hundreds of scenarios raced through his mind. Sprinting through the alleyways, he darted his gaze left and right but saw no sign of Adelyne or Sarah. Where were they?

A sudden rustle from around the corner of a small neighboring home brought him to a skidding halt. "Hello?" Arnon called out.

The rustling stopped, and Arnon drew his sword. He crept to the edge of the alley and listened—quick, shallow breaths. Gripping the hilt of his sword tight, he peeked around the corner.

He faltered. A young man, probably younger than himself, stood with a pair of brown trousers half-way on. Pale, freckled skin and hair as yellow as the sun. Daecish.

Piled in the snow beside him lay a discarded Daecish uniform. Arnon glanced to the open window beside the young man, where a tunic and a pair of leather shoes sat on the window sill. "Where did you get those clothes?" he asked, pointing his blade toward him.

"Please," the Daecish man replied, pulling the trousers up. "I'm not armed. I—I—" He pointed to the window. "I found these inside. No one was home. I just . . ." He looked at Arnon as if at a loss for words. "Please don't kill me."

Here was a Daecish soldier, stealing clothes from Arnon's own people. He was a deserter, running away like a coward. He deserved to die.

Arnon stepped toward the soldier as he thought back to the death of his father. He thought of the draft, the slums, the mines. His blood simmered. But then Adelyne's words came back to him. The Daecish were people too. There was probably a family somewhere that loved this young man. Then he pictured the brigadiers around the table in the Keld Valley, and he lowered his sword. "Go," he said.

The Daecish soldier grabbed the shirt and shoes and shuffled around Arnon, keeping his gaze down. Before he passed around the corner, Arnon turned. "Wait," he said, and he took off his bearskin cloak. As it slipped from his shoulders, he was in disbelief with himself. Of what little he had left of his father, how could he give this away? Much less to a Daecish man. "If you walk out of here in just that, you'll freeze to death. That's if you're not seen and killed before then." He handed him the cloak.

The Daecish soldier glanced at the bearskin, eyeing Arnon intently. Then he took it and wrapped it around his body and head. "Thank you," he said before disappearing around the corner.

Approaching Fellhouse Street, Arnon turned left and crossed over onto the Western Road, and hurried toward the Fire and Water Tavern. Crowds of men from the Free Sunderian Army still gathered in front of the Palace of Ingvar, dancing and playing music. Peering into the crowds, Arnon searched for Galvin, Drake, or anyone he knew. Balling his fists, he continued to the tavern.

Just outside, Drake limped towards the front door.

"Drake!" he hollered.

Turning over his shoulder, Drake leaned against the door frame.

"Have you seen Adelyne or Sarah yet?"

Drake situated himself with a grunt. "Can't say so. Did you check Adelyne's place like I told you?"

"I just came from there," he said, gritting his teeth. "It was empty."

Drake let out another groan as he opened the door. "What about Sarah's?"

"Where's that?"

A cheering crowd passed by the tavern as one man played a fief, shrill and sharp.

"Just below City Hall," Drake replied when the crowd passed. He walked inside, and Arnon followed.

The tavern sat in darkness. Chairs were piled in the corner, and tables tipped on their side. Drake winced, his jaw clenched in pain, and Arnon felt like he should help, but he desperately wanted to find Adelyne. "You okay?" he managed to ask.

Hobbling to the bar, Drake went to pick up a chair. "I'll be fine. I just need to get off this leg."

Arnon hurried over and set the chair over for him.

"What happened to your cloak?" Drake asked. He sat down and propped his leg on the base of a tipped-over table, letting out a long sigh.

"I let someone borrow it," Arnon answered. He went to grab two other chairs to resituate the room, but he couldn't hide his worried face.

"Get outta here," Drake said, apparently seeing the anxiousness in his face. "You can help me fix the place up after you've found the girls."

Arnon dropped the chairs, his face lighting up. "Don't worry!" he shouted as he ran out the door. "I'll be back!"

* * *

Holding a bundle of wool blankets and a basket, Adelyne stood in the doorway behind Sarah, who held Acton in her arms; Lilly ran from her side into another room on the right. Sarah stared across the empty entry hall as some memory raced through her mind. Adelyne expected her to burst into tears at any moment, but she only stood stiff with glazed, frozen eyes.

Adelyne glanced outside and shut the door. Though she didn't talk about it, the look of the alphyn, just outside her home, wouldn't leave her mind.

"Last time I was here," Sarah said, "was when I went to go find Geoffrey."

Adelyne bit down on her lip. Despite knowing her for such a short amount of time, Sarah seemed to be one of the strongest women she had ever met.

Sarah reached over to a mounted peg, where an officer's coat hung on the wall. She patted the sleeve for a moment before letting it fall back. "I think we'll be safe here."

"I wonder what the rest of the city looks like," Adelyne said.

"Can't know for sure," Sarah replied. "Not 'til we get out there."

"You think the others are all right?"

Sarah had a somber look in her eyes. "We'll hope so."

A brief thought of Drake and Morgan passed through Adelyne's mind—wondering if they were alive or not. But mostly, her thoughts dwelled on Arnon. Why did he seem angry with her in the cellar? The thought of him being dead made her stomach drop.

"Okay," Sarah said. "We've got a lot of work to do."

Adelyne barely paid attention to her words as she looked at the front door. She almost contemplated going back out there to search for him but knowing there was nothing she could do at that moment, she took in a breath, trying to forget her fears. She peered at the brick fireplace and the thick oak frames and crossbeams lining the smooth walls. "This place is beautiful."

Sarah grabbed the wool blankets from Adelyne and set them on a tall side table. "Once we get all the rooms set, it'll be perfect for what we need. Do you know how to cook?"

Adelyne set the basket on the floor. She was a terrible cook, but she could survive. "I've cooked before, but I may need to re-learn a few things."

With a smile, Sarah glanced into the kitchen to check on Lilly. "That'll be fine. Can you garden?"

She couldn't remember the last time she even held a spade, but she didn't want to sound completely useless. "Of course."

"In a few weeks, we can go ahead and start seeding for spring. We've got a garden and a few chickens out back." She set her hand on her hips. "Don't know if they've made it though, without being fed. In the meantime, we've got grain, lentils, onions, dried corn, and some salted meat. We'll see if we can't get more by the end of the week."

A loud knock on the door startled Adelyne with a shout. Sarah stared at the door as Adelyne backed away.

"Hello?" Sarah called.

The doorknob turned, and the door creaked open. At first, Adelyne let out a sigh of relief as Arnon's head peeked around the corner, but as he let the door swing open, her jaw dropped. Dirt and dried blood stained his face dark—a startling contrast from the white in his eyes. His clothes were torn and soiled, and his left hand, especially, was dark with blood. He took a step in, staring at Adelyne.

He looked like he was going to cry. And to her own surprise, Adelyne felt her own chin quiver as he stumbled forward and wrapped her in his arms. He buried his face in her hair, and she let herself sink into him. She couldn't explain why, but he felt more like a home than any place she had ever lived. After a moment, probably longer than either of them thought, Sarah cleared her throat. Adelyne smiled and lowered her arms.

Sarah scanned Arnon up and down with raised eyebrows. "You need to get cleaned up if you're going to walk in this house."

Adelyne stood in the hall beside Sarah, just outside the bathing room. Sarah had just filled the copper basin with steaming hot water.

"You sure about this?" Arnon hollered from the other side of the door.

"You'll be fine!" Sarah said. She laughed at Adelyne. "He'll get used to it."

Adelyne smiled, but she understood. She liked to feel clean, but she had never taken a bath in hot water before and likely never would.

"Is it safe?" Arnon yelled back. Sarah waved for Adelyne to follow her to the kitchen. "Don't come out 'til your clean!" was all she said.

Adelyne sat at the table, holding Acton in her lap, while Sarah began cooking. Not long afterward, Arnon stepped into the kitchen with his dark, wet hair brushed behind his ears—their long tips still dripping onto Geoffrey's old tunic and trousers. He'd rolled his sleeves up to his wrists, and the legs of his trousers piled over his feet. Adelyne covered her mouth but couldn't help laughing out loud. Arnon frowned at his clothes.

"Don't worry," Sarah said. "I'll clean and mend your clothes by the 'morrow."

"Thank you," Arnon replied as he walked to the table and sat down across from Adelyne.

Rubbing Acton's hair, she couldn't help but notice the red stump of what used to be Arnon's little finger. "Did you get a scratch?" she asked with a smirk.

Arnon widened his eyes. "A scratch? This is a wound."

Adelyne laughed.

"I'm serious," he replied. "Look at it!" He shoved his hand in front of her face.

"Poor thing. How will you ever move on?"

Arnon rolled his eyes. "Do you know how hard it is to hold things? This will affect how I do everything."

"I'm sorry," she conceded, still holding a smirk. "But don't worry too much. You'll have me to help."

Arnon smiled.

"I was thinking," Sarah said from across the room as she kneaded a mound of dough with her elbows. Lilly sat on the floor beside her, playing with a wooden horse. "What do you think of the name, 'House of Good Hope?'"

"I like it," Adelyne replied.

"What's it for?" Arnon asked.

"After things settle down, Sarah and I are going to bring in some of the girls. Give them a place to stay."

"Girls?" he asked again.

"The ones in the streets."

Arnon looked confused. Did she have to spell out everything? "The prostitutes."

"Oh," Arnon replied with reddening cheeks. He turned his gaze away and cleared his throat. "That sounds like a good idea."

"I think we can house around ten," Sarah added. "Maybe a dozen at the most."

Arnon fiddled with his hurt hand, which slightly trembled. He held it as if trying to make it stop. Adelyne wished she could know what he was thinking.

"I wonder what's going to happen next," he said at last. "We actually won, but it's not what I expected."

"What do you mean?" Sarah asked as she sat down at the table.

"I don't know. The whole city's a mess. There's no structure. I just have to trust that Galvin and Porter know what they're doing."

"It seems they did with Denhurst," Adelyne added. She looked through the window. The sun was still high, but everything looked gray.

Arnon sighed. "But the alphyns. They're actually here."

Sarah reached over and grabbed Acton, who was now sleeping in Adelyne's lap. He pouted but soon fell back asleep on Sarah's shoulder. She remained quiet for a while, seemingly in deep thought. "If Geoffrey were here," she said at last. "He'd say it's the end. And I think I'd believe him. The Daecish, the alphyns. There's just too much."

Arnon didn't say anything, and Adelyne's guilt rolled over her and suffocated the fleeting moment of happiness she just had. Hælend's Ballad spoke of everyone paying for the evil they had done. She had so much in her own life, she could hardly see clearly. Looking at Arnon, she wished more than anything that she was the kind of person he thought she was.

The Great Fringe

S øren awoke, lying on a bed of green moss, which grew thick and soft beneath a tall rock outcropping. Just beyond the ledge, the shining sun glistened against the snowy mountains, which swelled and rippled until they opened up into hills of rolling green and white.

Before him lay the broken body of a large brown hare. He picked it up by its ears, and with a grimace, grabbed his sword. With the edge of the blade, he cut into the fur and split the body, just as he did the fox the day before and the fowl before that. He peeled back the skin as he bit into the warm meat. With a gag, he swallowed; its tasteless texture felt like a mix of moist gristle and rubber.

Licking off his greasy fingers, he glanced up to the top of the outcropping. There stood the alphyn in its dark swirling form. As if caught in its own breeze, its body blew against the wind that came in long gusts from the mountain peaks above. It calmly stared back at Søren with its deep glowing blue eyes.

The alphyn leaped from the outcropping, landing silently before Søren. It peered northward and up along the mountainside before it lowered its back. Almost instinctively, Søren slid the sword through his tunic belt and sat on the alphyn. Though it neither spoke nor gave any physical motions of communication, Søren felt as if the beast could read his thoughts. He became conscious of his own thinking, often feeling embarrassed by what came up in his mind.

Without warning, the alphyn sprinted forward along the mossy rock. Søren leaned forward and gripped his hand tighter into the swirling wind as it began its ascent up a near-vertical slope.

Through the course of the day, the alphyn carried Søren through wide caverns and along steep crags, stopping only to allow him to rest for brief moments. He caught glimpses of several arched entranceways, intricately carved out of the weathered rock, like doorways into places too dark and foreboding for even the bravest of explorers. Perhaps they led to a realm of spirits and ghosts and other things he dared not think of.

Ruined pillars lay scattered along the ground, and even a large stone bridge connected two crumbling peaks high above him. It was all so surreal, as if he had entered into an ancient world that had long been forgotten. For a moment, it awoke something in him. A desire—almost a determination—to step into one of the dark tunnels, just to see what lay beyond. But soon, the ruins passed, and as the terrain turned bare and gray, save the white snowdrifts that piled high at the base of cliffs and precipices, his mind wandered once again to the beast and the mystery of where it was taking him.

Ahead, Søren caught sight of a disfigured mass of some creature, huddled against a rock wall. Within the tangle of old flesh and bones hung traces of wool rags. Realizing it was the body of a man, he looked away, but at the same time, he was shocked that the sight didn't horrify him more. He stared back at the body until the alphyn passed it by. Maybe a spirit had killed this man for trying to walk through one of the arched doorways.

Crossing into the shadow of a high cliff, which towered to his right, a few sparse rays of sunlight broke through cracks along the high edges. Sharp jagged boulders piled high at the base of the cliff, forming shallow caverns and hollows. The alphyn slowed its pace, and Søren peered into the dark tunnels, waiting for something to pop out of them.

Strange rodent-like critters occasionally darted from one rock to another. At times one would perch upon a rock, peering curiously toward him and the alphyn. He marveled at the sheen of their silvery-blue fur, almost shifting in color, depending on how they moved in the light. If he was in any other situation, he would have tried to catch one, so he could pet it.

The alphyn came to a halt, and Søren unintentionally slumped forward. Up high, the occasional howl of wind echoed into his ears, but no breeze brushed his skin. Becoming conscious of the sound of his own breathing, he wondered why they stopped. Then, like the rumbling of distant thunder breaking through a quiet night, a low growl rumbled from within the deep hollows of piled rock. The critters scurried and hid from sight.

Søren pulled his sword from his belt. Though it was relatively short, it weighed long and heavy in his hands. Holding his breath, he looked earnestly along the pile. He saw nothing, but the growling grew again.

"Why are you stopping here?" he asked aloud.

He darted his eyes around, stirring himself uneasily. The alphyn only remained still. At the howl of wind above, Søren caught motion from the top of one of the great boulders. A tall gray wolf stared down at him with a calm face, but its eyes were bright and yellow, piercing him with vicious intent.

Movement within the caverns soon began to stir as the form of several other wolves emerged into the light. Their large paws fell silently with each step. Their sides were sunken in, almost skeletal, and they fixed their gazes toward him.

"Please," he said, unsure if he meant to the alphyn or the wolves. He tapped his hand on the alphyn's head. "Please go!" he shouted.

Foam poured from their gnashing teeth as one of the wolves let out a ravenous snarl. Søren screamed as he fell backward behind the alphyn. He scrambled to his feet and gripped the sword in both hands. The wolves began encircling the alphyn in a slow prowl, their stomachs low to the ground. The alphyn remained still. Soon, a single wolf, with fur as black as midnight, moved away from the pack toward Søren.

"Help!" he cried out with the sword trembling in his hand, trying to see through the tears blurring his vision. The wolf crept slow and steady. Foam dripped from its long white teeth.

The wolf pounced with a snap of its jaws, but it kept a short distance. Søren fell backward, and his back hammered against a rock as he let out a gasp. His sword whipped up just as the wolf came at him again. The blade stuck the wolf in the side of the mouth, and it lashed back with a snarl. Søren tried to get his feet below him, but the wolf pounced again. He held his arm out as a shield, and the wolf bit into his flesh above the wrist. Searing pain lanced through him and Søren let out a loud cry, dropping the sword, as the wolf shook its head. His senses blurred as he frantically grabbed at the wolf's face.

The wolf fell back with a yelp. Søren blinked several times, clearing his vision. Pawing at its own face, the wolf tried to stand on its wobbling legs. But as it took another step, it fell over, still and lifeless.

Søren stared at the wolf, then his hands, in disbelief. The other wolves lay on the ground, still and quiet, their eyes locked on the alphyn, which looked as if it had never moved. One by one, they crept back into the darkness of the tunnels.

Peering at his wrist, he observed two deep puncture wounds as warm blood dripped from his fingers onto the rocky ground. Fear seized him and he panicked. Curling his arm into his chest, he wept aloud.

He was just a young lost child, wounded, with no one to care for him. He was alone. That is what he told himself. But as his tears soaked his face, an awareness slipped into his heart. There was no one there to pity him—no one to bind his arm. Crying had always made him feel better, and yet he grew ashamed of himself this time. Even though the bravest of boys would be just as scared in his position, something else nagged at him. He cried out not from pain, but because he wanted someone to feel sorry for him. He wanted someone to pick him up. But there was no one there, and he felt like a fool.

Søren straightened himself, and a hardness came upon him. Not a cold one, but a strength and courage from deep in his soul. The alphyn stepped toward him. Søren wiped his tears and felt a drawing captivation as he looked into its glowing blue eyes, until all around him seemed to go dark. There was something primal about this beast, as if it had been around since ancient times, if not the beginning of time itself.

The alphyn lowered its head, and Søren blinked as he came back to. His arm began to ache and throb. Getting to his feet, he picked up his sword, sliding its blade through his tunic belt, with his other arm still curled in his chest. As he straddled his legs over the alphyn's back, it raised itself and walked over and gripped the slain wolf in its mouth and continued north through the base of the cliff and back into the light.

No birds chirped. No trace of life could be found. The alphyn followed a high pass where wind gusts howled like violent gales, but they seemed to pass across Søren barely any stronger than a breeze. At times, Søren's head would hurt, and his breath would thin. But the spells would come and go until they came far between, eventually passing altogether. To their left, the ground dropped into a dark pit, too deep to see the bottom. A shiver ran up his spine.

As the sun began to fall behind the western mountains, they came to a shallow natural cave. The alphyn dropped the body of the wolf and stooped, lowering Søren to the ground. Pulling out his sword, Søren leaned it against the wall and looked at his arm again. The bleeding had stopped, as well as the pain, but its mutilated appearance caused him to look away. He would have felt better if he could wrap it.

Ducking his head, he walked inside the cave but turned to watch the alphyn pace northward and out of sight. Exhaustion and fatigue had long sapped him of his strength, and he did not hesitate to lay down on the hard rock. He did not even remember closing his eyes before he fell fast asleep.

At some point in the middle of the night, Søren awoke in a cold sweat. He darted his eyes around, trying to see the walls of the orphanage. At first, all was dark, save the dim moonlight which barely revealed the shape of the mouth of the cave. He sat up, cross-legged, and rubbed his eyes, wiping the sweat from his face. He knew that the temperature was far below freezing, but warmth seemed to flood his veins. With adjusting eyes, he suddenly startled and pressed his back against the rock. Sitting near the mouth of the cave was the prisoner, who, leaning against his bent knees, gazed ahead into the moonlight. With a gaping mouth, Søren said nothing.

The prisoner turned to him with a smile. "Have you been sleeping well?"

Søren didn't respond.

The prisoner looked back outside. "That is a pretty gash you've got," he continued.

Søren's arm twitched, but he kept his eyes fixed on him. Although the prisoner's figure was largely hidden in the shadow, Søren could tell that his clothes were still tattered, and shackles still bound his wrists. The prisoner turned toward him again and tossed over a thin cloth. It fell a few feet in front of Søren.

"This should help with the wound," he said.

"How—How did you get here?" Søren asked. He took a quick glance outside the cave. The alphyn was nowhere to be seen.

"A shadow is not the only thing that can pass through the Fringe," he replied.

"A shadow? Do you mean the alphyn?"

"The alphyn is nothing but a dumb beast. I mean the shadow that fills it." The prisoner stretched his legs out and shifted his position, now facing Søren's direction. "You must be careful, though. A shadow cannot be trusted."

A howl echoed across the mouth of the cave.

"It saved me from the mines. And—And from the beach."

The prisoner picked up a handful of dust and pebbles from the ground. Then raising his hand, he parted his fingers as it slipped through. "Nothing good ever happens when a shadow appears," he said. "Like everyone else, it'll only betray you."

His last sentence lingered like a returning nightmare. Eirún didn't save him in the river. Burlan and Henley had locked him away and then just handed him off to someone else. Everyone pretended to love him, but no one really did.

"I understand your pain," the prisoner said. "Always ignored, beneath the shadow of everyone else. They say they're there for you, but whenever you need them most, they're gone."

Søren let the words sink in. Maybe the prisoner did understand him. But he still cared for Eirún, and more than anything else, he wanted to be with her.

"Now you're beginning to understand your doom." The prisoner smiled.

"Doom?"

"The shadow has cursed you and all that care for you. Do you not see?"

Søren shook his head. "That's not true."

"Has the shadow ever so much as talked to you? Told you where you are going? What is it going to do with you?"

Søren sat silent for a moment. "It's never spoken to me."

"Ah," replied the prisoner with a nod. He then peered back outside, both hands mounted on the ground. "I'll tell you where it's taking you. To a fate worse than death. It's going to use you to destroy everything you hold dear. All whom you meet are wrought within it. Henley's already dead. Soon the others will follow. Even Geoffrey.

Even Eirún. It will spread like tangling roots, infecting all those around them. Eventually, you too will perish."

His words sank into Søren's soul like poison.

"If you continue with the shadow, your doom will work its full course."

"But what can I do?"

"I have seen the foundations of the earth and of time," said the prisoner in a sudden haunting tone. "If you want to end your misery, you have but one choice."

Søren felt his head go light and his breathing go heavy.

"You must end your life. And end it now."

To die. That was a word that had often passed through his mind. But since he had awoken in this strange land, death seemed to be a part of him, and yet always fleeing from him. He still wasn't sure if he was even truly alive. But the thought of really dying, to never see Eirún again, shook him to his core.

Søren wavered for a moment as if his body had taken a sudden blow. He fell forward on his hands, and his back trembled as violent sobs quaked from within. He wanted to shout, but all he could do was weep.

The prisoner gazed ahead to the other end of the cave.

Søren awoke with a shout. He sat up, wiping tears and dust from his sore cheek. Leaning on his hands, he looked across the cave, panting. The wind was quiet, and outside was white. There was a relief as he realized it was a dream, but then he caught sight of the thin cloth the prisoner had tossed to him. His heart sank, and for the next hour, he only sat and stared.

Eventually, he stood up and grabbed the cloth, rubbing the silky fabric in his fingers. He thought about the prisoner's words, but something caught his attention. Peering at the rock wall to his left, as if he could see through it, he tried to listen. Although there was no sound, he thought he could hear, or maybe he felt, the presence of the shadow on the other side.

He went to wrap the cloth around his wounded arm, but only dried blood smeared across his smooth skin. No puncture wounds could be seen. He wiped the blood on his tunic and looked at his arm in awe. There weren't even any scars. Instinctively he felt his other arm, where he had been burned by Mathios, which now seemed like a lifetime ago. When he was in the mines, it was scarred red, but now all traces were gone.

Stepping outside, his feet sunk into the deep snow, and he grabbed his sword. He walked over to the wolf carcass and cut off a portion of meat. After only a few bites, he was already full. He wiped the blood from his mouth. When the thought of water came to his mind, he realized he hadn't had anything to drink since yesterday, and even then, he had to melt handfuls of snow in his mouth.

The thought of it made his throat burn, and he glanced back to the entrance of the cave. Disbelieving his own eyes, he caught sight of a small pool of water, more like a puddle, just beside the cave entrance. Regardless of how it got there, he hurried over and dipped his hand. The water was surprisingly warm as he took in long sips. When he stood up, he saw the footprints of the alphyn heading north. With no other sign of it, he followed the tracks, wielding the sword in his hand.

When Søren finally approached the northern side of the mountain, the wind died down, and he lifted his eyes. Before him, the alphyn lay before a large, sharp boulder. It looked normal once again, gray and hideous, with sharp teeth and beady eyes. On either side of the boulder, behind the alphyn, the pass split into two forks, where the mountains seemed to unfold before the open land. Hundreds of peaks cascaded downward until they fell into many valleys, thick with strands of fog, finding their end in other great ranges of mountains further north.

"Where am I?" Søren asked himself. He stepped toward the edge, overlooking the land beyond. He strained his eyes, hoping to see something in the distance.

"That is Daecland," came a deep, throbbing voice.

Søren startled and turned. Swirling above the mountain peak hovered a thick, dark shadow, like a black storm cloud, with glowing blue light occasionally streaking through it. A massive force pressed against Søren's chest, and his knees turned to water as he fell to the ground.

"D—Did you speak?" he managed to ask.

But despite his question, his mind was consumed with hundreds of shameful memories of his life. It was as if he felt filthy and offensive in the presence of something so pure and grand. If he could have moved at that moment, he would've buried himself beneath the snow.

"I did," came the same voice, which was so low the earth trembled beneath Søren's hands.

In shame, Søren kept his gaze down. "Are you taking me back to Daecland?"

"Not in the same way you are hoping."

A lump swelled in Søren's throat. "But—But I thought you might take me to Eirún." The shadow gave no response, but Søren felt something lift his chin. He looked upon the shadow once again. Despite the silence, he thought he could feel sorrow, perhaps even pity, seep into his soul from the shadow. "Then, where are you taking me?"

"You cannot yet see things as you ought to," said the shadow, shifting closer to Søren. "Greater things are at work through you."

The sound of the shadow's voice rolled like thunder through his body. In one sense, it filled him with terror, but in another, it soothed his bones to the point where his eyes became heavy. "Then," his voice drifted as he strained to open his eyes, "then why did you bring me here?"

"Look to the lands beyond."

Søren looked over his shoulder, only to see the same shrouded valleys and peaks stretch out below him.

"The end of the kingdoms of the world draws nigh."

Søren turned his attention back toward the shadow but kept his gaze on the snow in front of him. "What do you mean? What will happen t—to the people?"

"They will die."

Søren's chin trembled. "But why?"

The shadow didn't give an answer.

"I don't—I don't—" He clenched his eyes, trying to get the sentence out. "I don't understand! Why are you t—telling me this?"

"It is not for you to know why, but to know who. And he will work the end through you."

"What does that mean?" he shouted. "Is this what the prisoner was trying to tell me?"

The shadow moved closer to Søren as rays of sunlight streamed into its darkness from the clouded sky above. "The prisoner knows only what is given. And from his mouth, knowledge is corrupted."

"He was lying?"

"Behind the prisoner's words lay a hidden strand of truth. But he cannot see the end, but only ruin. You are Sunder's Bane and Daecland's Blight. From you will come forth the Day of Reckoning."

Søren clenched his teeth as he sought to end the madness welling up in his mind. He had so many questions, but only darkness filled his thoughts. "Why?" he pleaded again. "Why must everyone die?" His heart pounded as the thought of Eirún came to him.

The shadow didn't respond.

"Why must they die?" he shouted.

"Death is not an end." The shadow continued to hover closer as streaks of blue light flashed through the darkness, and rays from the sun seeped into it like slow-moving water.

"But they're good people," he barely got out. "They don't deserve to die."

"Not all who breathe are alive, and not all who die are dead. Do not be quick to assume what you do not yet understand."

As if defeated, Søren sank into the snow. "Why are you doing this to me? Why can't I just be with Eirún?" Tears blurred his vision. "Please," he begged. "Please just take me to her!"

"What you look for in Eirún," the shadow said in a softer voice, "you will never find."

With a broken heart, Søren's tears dripped off his nose.

"She cannot be what you want her to be," the shadow continued. "That is only found in one greater than herself."

Søren looked up, sniffing in his tears. "Do you mean my real mother?"

"No. Although your real mother has abandoned you, Eirún has adopted you in her heart. But I mean one even greater."

Søren didn't care about one greater.

"You cannot go to her now."

Søren tilted his head down and saw a deep chasm run down the side of the mountain. He thought of the prisoner's command, and he pictured himself falling to the bottom. "Then just k—kill me," he whimpered. "I don't want to live."

The shadow had now come so close it was only inches from Søren's face, and the soft winds cooled his burning mind. "It is not your life you wish to end, but the misery you mistake it for. There is life beyond the suffering you endure. There is resurrection and reunion."

"I don't understand."

"There are some things that run deeper than death. Although the fate of many will be wrought through you, so will something greater, which you cannot yet see."

Despite the shadow's words, Søren found himself not wanting to believe in any such thing. Instead, the words of the prisoner and his own self-pity threatened to consume his mind. As much as he hated that thought of not being loved or wanted, he also wanted to think of himself as the victim while everyone else was to blame. But as he continued looking into the shadow, as the cool winds brushed against his face, deep brokenness welled up. The prisoner's words and his self-pity soon dissolved, and once again, all he could feel was his own need to be cleansed from his wrongness.

His heart deeply regretted the way he talked to Eirún at times. He knew he made her sad by always trying to make her feel sorry for him. She was kind to him, and all he ever thought about was his own happiness. He suddenly broke into another sob, but of a different kind. It wasn't because he felt sorry for himself, but because he wanted to be different. He covered his face with his hands. "I'm sorry," he confessed.

Suddenly, a peace filled his soul, and when he looked up, the shadow began to spread out like a thin mist being chased away by the sun. Søren glanced around, but like a strong gust of wind, the mist rushed toward him and filled his lungs. With a loud gasp, his eyes were opened, and blood rushed through his veins in a way he had never felt before.

Before the Executioner

Across the barren yard of the camp, dust stirred with the cold breeze. Geoffrey's head felt light and his eyes heavy. His strength had long left him. Several men walked or staggered mindlessly along the yard littered with rags. More than a few rotting bodies scattered the ground, bringing the sour stench of death to those who were barely surviving. Occasionally, a man would peer up at the tall iron fence, which ran around the yard in a wide circle, within which Geoffrey and the rest of the gray-shirts were enclosed. Guards, dressed in traditional blue uniforms and dark head caps with a short brim in the front, roamed around the outside of the yard and always kept their eyes on the prisoners.

On the other side of the fence sat a series of brick and salmon-colored buildings, two of which were connected by a single underpass. In front of the buildings ran a road to the east; it disappeared behind a brown hill. Despite how much he pondered, Geoffrey could not figure out the purpose of the ropes, which stretched from building to building, constantly giving off a hum like the distant swarm of bees. It all felt Daecish, but on a level he had never experienced in Sunder.

He glanced behind him. Only an endless desert stretched out until it stopped at the low rise of distant gray mountains—an empty, hopeless land that seemed to mimic the state of his soul.

Men in tan coveralls approached the camp occasionally, but only for short moments to take notes of the decaying men. One man, who sat beside Geoffrey, looked seconds away from death. His skin stretched across his bones, and his long legs were as thin as his arms. Staring ahead, he slowly closed and opened his eyes as if he lost the strength to blink. Another man rocked back and forth as he habitually picked at brown and yellow bandaging, which covered the stump of his left arm, cut off just below the elbow. Others lay motionless. Sometimes it was hard to tell who was still alive.

The first few days, Geoffrey couldn't help but fall into a depression from the sights around him, wishing there was something he could do to relieve their pain. But soon, it became familiar. Death became routine, and his own heart slowly grew numb.

At various times during the day, a loud horn was blown, and several guards would call out numbers. Usually, they took two dozen or more gray-shirts with them. Most of the time, less than half would return, and all Geoffrey could do was wait for his turn.

Since he arrived, he received very little water and no food. His throat burned, and his tongue felt dry against the roof of his mouth. He glanced toward a long shallow trough lined against the fence, which the guards would occasionally fill with water, though they only poured enough for less than a third of those in the camp. Geoffrey could never seem to get to it before the others licked it dry. In the bunkhouse behind him, several men moaned in their sleep.

A loud creak of iron drew Geoffrey's attention. He glanced over to see the gate swinging open. Several guards and men in tan coveralls walked over; four of them carried bundles of wooden cases in their arms. One of the men in coveralls, who had a distinct thin mustache stretching below either side of his nose, held a horn in his left hand, which he lifted to his mouth.

In an amplified voice, he spoke across the camp. "Division sixteen! Numbers thirty through thirty-nine!" he shouted, looking down at an opened leather-bound book. "Thirty through thirty-nine!" he shouted again. "Report to the gate!"

Geoffrey let out a sigh of relief as he double-checked that his number was forty-seven.

After a while, only six men came to the front. Several guards griped, now marching toward the bunkhouses. They walked back out, dragging men out of their cots. One guard grabbed the man with the missing forearm.

"This is only nine," another man in tan coveralls said.

A guard to the far left motioned toward a bunkhouse where another guard was walking out.

"Number thirty-two is already dead!" he shouted across the camp.

Throwing a hand in the air, the man with the mustache looked back at his page. "All right, bring me twenty-nine instead." He looked up. "Twenty-nine! Come forward!"

Though most of the men could barely stand, an older man limped over and stood before the guards. Another gray-shirt, who stood in the line, fell over as dust billowed beneath his body.

"Strip their clothes and bind them to the fence," said one of the guards, taking the horn from the man in coveralls. "Listen up, gray-shirts!" he hollered, looking across the camp to a crowd of nearly a hundred ragged and starving men. Small scars dotted his cheeks and nose. His right eye was dull and hazed over with a thin red circle trailing around his iris. His left leg, below the knee, was missing, with the pant leg folded up. In its place were two brass-colored rods, with several tubes. At the bottom was a boot, matching the one on his other foot.

"News from Norfrost informs us that budgets have been cut this year!" He began pacing back and forth as he spoke. With each step, he limped as the rods shifted against his weight in a mechanical and unnatural way. How each rod pushed into the man's flesh, flexing the leg muscles, made Geoffrey feel nauseous.

"What does that mean for you, you might ask?" the guard continued. He glanced back to the line of men with his good eye. The men were stripped naked and shoved against the fence as their arms were raised high and wrists tied to the thin iron rods like animals ready to be skinned. He faced forward again; his short blonde hair lay mostly hidden beneath his dark cap. "Some of you might see it as freedom. Freedom from this wasteland. Freedom from pain. But it depends on how you look at it, I guess. Others may see it as . . ." he trailed off. "Well . . ." He lowered the horn as if he suddenly got bored with what he was saying. He mumbled something to himself, but Geoffrey couldn't make out the words.

He motioned for the other guards to bring over the wooden cases. Setting them on the ground, the guard bent over and lifted the lid to one of the cases and pulled out a small contraption. He held it out to the onlooking crowd. "If you're wondering what this is, don't worry. You will find out soon. Today you have all been honored to partake in weapons advancements!" He eyed the contraption in his hand, then looked at a man in coveralls with a laugh. "What are these called again?"

"Wheellocks," the man replied.

"What about the muskets?"

"Next week."

Several other guards began loading around thirty wheellocks with a dark coarse powder. Nine of the wheellocks were handed to men in coveralls. The main guard held the tenth wheellock as he raised it up, pointing it at the man with the missing arm. The man only looked ahead in a daze, with his single arm awkwardly tied above him.

The guard glanced to the others beside him. "Are we ready?"

"You first," said one.

The guard stretched out his arm, and a loud boom broke through the camp as smoke exploded from the wheellock. The guard jolted back on his mechanical leg as if even he was unprepared for the power in his hand. Geoffrey shuddered and covered his ears. Many men fell to the ground with a look of shock on their faces. The armless man shook and wavered against the fence, his eyes rolling in the back of his head as blood flowed out like a steady stream from a single hole in his lower left side. Several men ran into the bunkhouses, closing the doors behind them, but the doors swung freely back open.

When the Daecish first invaded Sunder, Geoffrey had seen distant canons firing from the wisps. But this was something completely different.

Another loud boom sounded, then another. Geoffrey winced and covered his ears again. He glanced toward the men in coveralls, who shot off the other wheellocks. Several of them laughed as the victims cried out and convulsed against the fences, helplessly bleeding out. For several minutes they did this, setting down one wheellock and grabbing another until all the men hung lifeless by their wrists. The guard turned to the man with the mustache and leather-bound book.

"How many more are we getting rid of?" he asked.

The man scanned his book. "Budget requires fifty to dispose of. However, we need to save the wheellocks for actual training purposes."

Several of the other Daecish grumbled with their apparent disappointment.

"What's the plan, then?" asked the guard. "How do we get rid of them?"

Looking up, the man rubbed his mustache and pointed toward the bunkhouses. "We'll just quit giving them water until enough die. It's cheap and efficient."

The guard placed his hands on his hip, peering across the camp. Whenever he blinked, his right eye never seemed to close all the way. "Ought to be able to use the wheellocks on them. If we have to cut budget, at least let's enjoy it."

"You don't cut budget by wasting gunpowder," the man with the mustache replied.

The guard walked away as he stood beside another guard, not far from Geoffrey. "At least we can save our food and water for the next few days."

"We weren't feeding them anyway," the other guard snickered.

"You didn't have to say that. I at least like to think I did something."

As the crowd dispersed, Geoffrey lifted himself from his trembling legs. The reality of the destruction he witnessed barely sank into his mind as if it was nothing more than a bad dream—one which he imagined he would wake up from at any moment. He watched his feet as he walked to the bunkhouse. Just before he stepped inside, he glanced north at the iron gate as it swung open once again. Around two dozen gray-shirts were pushed through as the gate shut behind them. Paying no more attention, he went inside the bunkhouse. He laid himself down on the hard wood of a bunk, situated beneath an open window. His stomach groaned, and he rolled over to his side. A hand hung down from the bunk above him. Closing his eyes, he prayed that the man wasn't dead, but the smell filling his nose told him otherwise.

Never had he been so tired, and yet he could never sleep. Lazily, he lifted his eyes, observing the men around the room. Most sat in silence; others mumbled to themselves. One man held a small ragged doll in his hand. Geoffrey thought it must have been his little girl's. The man broke into a low sob.

"Theos," he mumbled. "Free us from this place."

"Theos ain't here," said a young man with a baby face and small chin, two bunks down from Geoffrey. He laid on his back, staring at the bunk above him. "He don't care 'bout us or anything else in this forsaken place."

"No, he's here," the man with the doll replied. "And he'll come for us soon."

"Maybe the Daecish are right," said another man, sitting in the far back corner in shadow. Like several of the others, he had a bloated stomach. But his long greasy hair and thin beard made him look as if he'd been there for a few years. He even had iron shackles around his wrists. "Maybe there is no Theos."

"That ain't true," replied the man with the doll.

"You ever see a dead man?" the man in the back corner asked, propping his elbows on his knees. "You know what happens to him? He rots. He goes back into the earth. And that's all that ever happens. Neither you or I have ever seen anything beyond that. You don't know if Theos is real any more than if you're going to live two more days."

"Maybe all this is part of his plan," the man defended, but his own eyes looked doubtful.

The man in the back corner let out a gristly laugh. "You really think if Theos were real, he would let this happen to people? Watch them starve and be killed off like animals? It's all just made-up stories." He tapped his head. "It's psychological. Men make up things to make themselves feel better, and after a while, they begin to believe it." He let his bound hands rest on the floor. "If Theos were real, he really messed up in making this world."

Geoffrey wished he could think of something to say, but the man's words pierced into his heart.

The young man, two bunks down, let out a loud, unexpected cry. The rest of the bunk went silent as he rolled over onto his side.

The wooden door swung open, and several gray-shirts stepped inside. They looked a little healthier than the rest of the crowd.

"Out!" shouted a gray-shirt by the door as he pointed behind him. "Other bunk! This one's already full!"

"There's more room in this one," replied one of the men as he walked across the room and sat with his back against the wall. As they flooded in, Geoffrey recognized Burlan. A flicker of joy leaped in his heart as he sat up.

"Burlan!" he called, but barely a rasp came out.

Burlan darted his eyes around the room until they met Geoffrey's. He hurried over, and they embraced. As Geoffrey leaned back. "How'd you get drafted?" he asked.

Burlan shook his head. "It's all a mess." He looked to the ground as if trying to collect his thoughts. "Egbert," he said in a sorrowful tone. "Something went wrong with him." He sniffed with a quiet whimper. "He killed Henley. I don't think he meant to, but he killed him."

Geoffrey's mouth hung open.

"The Daecish were only getting worse in Astford, and when rumors of a draft came 'round, people spoke of leaving for good. Not long after you left, it came. I didn't think I'd be taken, but as soon as I stepped outside, two of them were headed toward the house and called me out by name. They didn't even let me speak before they took me to the carriage." He furrowed his brows. "I bet Abbot turned me in. I know I shouldn't have told that fat sluggard anything."

Geoffrey looked over Burlan's shoulder in a blank stare. "What about Egbert?"

"Don't know. I found Henley's body on the evening of the draft. I confronted Egbert, but by the time I got it out of him, the draft had started. I went outside to see what was going on, and that was it. They took me, and I haven't seen Egbert since."

"Theos have mercy," Geoffrey said to himself.

"How 'bout you?" Burlan asked.

"As soon as I arrived in Everwind, they arrested me. I don't know how they found out."

"What about Søren?"

Geoffrey let his face fall. He was either dead or dying somewhere in the mines for all he knew. "I don't know. They mentioned the mines, but other than that . . ." he trailed off.

Burlan's eyes filled with sorrow. "That poor boy," he said. "I reckon we killed him, didn't we?"

Geoffrey didn't say anything. He didn't even want to think about it anymore.

Burlan sat beside him. "You know, Bartholomew's in the other bunk. I saw him walk in as I came over here."

"Why would they take Bartholomew?"

"Who knows?" Burlan replied. "When they bring the water, we'll go see him."

Geoffrey grunted. "They're not bringing any more. Not 'til enough of us have died off."

A look of defeat fell upon Burlan as his shoulders slumped. Besides a few men murmuring to one another and the occasional moan, the room sat in silence. Between Geoffrey's feet crawled a small spider. Someone would probably step on it. He lowered his hand as it crawled on his fingernail, and he set it on the window seal. It soon scurried onto the outside wall and disappeared from Geoffrey's sight.

A man on the bunk across from Geoffrey looked at him with a troubled look. "I would've eaten that if I were you."

Egbert

As he prodded through the thick blankets of wet snow, Egbert's stomach bounced and jiggled beneath his short olive-browned shirt. At the base of a tall hill, he stopped, breathing heavily with his hands on his knees. With shaking legs, he leaned back, flopping onto his rear. He let out several gasps for air. After a moment, he breathed into his hands and rubbed his cold nose. All around was white, except the pastel blue sky above.

After several minutes, he heaved and grunted, turning himself over and climbed to his feet. Slowly taking one step at a time, the hill was so steep his nose seemed only a few feet from the ground. The weight of the lens hung against the inside of his shirt. He tried to block out the memories of Henley. It was too painful. All he could do was start over. Make new friends in Everwind. That Geoffrey feller brought that boy, Søren, there. Maybe they could be friends. But what if Søren tried to take the lens back? He gripped it in his hand as he continued up the slope.

Just as the sun began to descend on the western horizon, he, at last, reached the peak and paused for another rest. But as he looked for the others who had come from Astford, his heart leaped into his throat. A large gray monster lay dead at the bottom of the other side of the hill. Large teeth gaped open from a frozen mouth. Beyond lay heaps of bodies—people, horses, and more gray monsters. The ground was stained red and black all the way to the walls of Everwind.

Stumbling backward, Egbert tripped over his feet and tumbled over his head and down the hill once again. Collapsing at the base, he sat up and shook the snow from his hair. He felt for the lens. Praise Theos; it was still there.

"Don't you be 'fraid, Egbert," he said to himself. "You get back up! Make you a corporal they will!" He kissed the lens, tucked it back in his shirt, and climbed back to his feet.

Egbert eventually caught up with the crowd as they neared the city. Several men were lifting naked bodies along the outer wall, hanging them from what looked like meat hooks. With a shudder, he hurried through the city gate. Taking in several deep gasps, he discarded the thought and pulled up his sagging trousers. Then he re-gripped the lens. With his other hand, he held his brown leather sack, slumped over his shoulder. Inside the city, several walls and buildings lay in ruin, and men, women, and children begged for warm drink and food along the wet sidewalks.

Egbert struggled to pull down his shirt over his belly as the blowing wind cut through his bones with sharp pain. Struggling to pull harder, he tore a rip across the middle of his shirt. Sinking his chin into his chest, he let out an exaggerated sigh and flopped his hands against his sides—his leather sack thumping into the wet snow.

Loud commands came to Egbert's ears, and he looked up at several armored men handing out wool blankets. One man led a few families into a half-ruined building. Still holding the lens, Egbert picked up his sack and cautiously walked across the courtyard, careful to not step onto the piles of over-turned cobblestone. Sneezing from the pungent smell of freshly churned earth and something else he could not imagine, he risked letting go of his lens so that he could cover his nose with the top of his shirt. In the center of the courtyard lay a large sinkhole, partially filled with loose rock, and the bloody back end of a monster sticking awkwardly out. Egbert kept as close to the buildings as he could, keeping a safe distance. Although people were around, the city felt so silent he could hear the snowflakes land on the ground.

Approaching a back alley to his right, he glanced inside a ruined building but startled and fell back as he tripped over his feet.

"Monster!" he belted out as his feet slipped on the ice.

Twice he tried to get up but gave into crawling so that he could quickly remove himself from the sight. Several men who had been gathering piles of various bits of debris glanced toward him.

"M—More of 'em in here!" Egbert called out.

One of the men pointed to the building. "It's dead," was all he said before going back to rummaging through a pile of rock and wood. Egbert let out a sigh of relief but continued to sit where he was, with his back against the front stone wall of the building. The window just above his head had been shattered, with broken glass scattered around where he sat. He continually rubbed his hands together and breathed warm air into his palms.

On the other side of the courtyard, a woman looked at Egbert as she handed a pile of wood to a man beside her. She walked over.

"Are you all right?" she asked. "Do you need help?"

Egbert staggered to his feet and glanced over his shoulder. He pointed his finger to his chest. "Me?"

The woman turned her half-smile into a grin. Her sharp green eyes glinted, and the red hair around her face curled down below her neck. "You seem lost," she said.

Egbert pulled his shirt down to cover his hanging gut. She sure was a pretty maiden. Then he gripped the lens in his hand. "Maybe," he said, digging his wet boot into the snow.

She pointed to his hand. "What's that?"

Egbert tensed. "It was a gift! I swear it!"

"It's all right, dear. I only asked what it was."

Egbert took a step back. "It's mine," he said. "And it's a, it's a—" His mind went blank, and he couldn't remember what it was called. The woman gave him a strange look.

"It's a magical medallion," he said at last.

"Magical?"

"And only I can use it."

The woman looked at him as if he was a small child. "Well," she said. "You be sure to keep it well hidden then. Now, what's your name?"

"E—Egbert."

She reached out her hand. Egbert hesitantly reached out his and shook it, feeling the warmth of her delicate fingers.

"I'm Agatha," she replied. "You hungry?" She glanced back to the small crowd. "We haven't got much, but if you'd like some soup, you're welcome to it."

Egbert nodded. Lens. That's what it was called. But he liked the idea of a magical medallion, so he didn't say anything. As they walked across the courtyard, a look of deep concern rested in her eyes.

"Did my medallion scare you?" he asked.

Agatha smiled. "Not at all."

"Then why'd you look 'fraid like that?"

She frowned at the upheaved cobblestone where the dead creature was still barely visible. "We're in strange times," she said. "Alphyns have come and . . ." she trailed off, now gazing at the northern wall. Although the bodies hung on the outside, Egbert figured that's what she was picturing.

"And what?"

"Other things," she said almost to herself. "Things I can't describe."

Egbert didn't understand her, but it sounded scary.

Agatha laid a hand on his shoulder. "But we don't have to worry about that right now."

Approaching the crowd, Egbert kept his distance as Agatha grabbed a shallow bowl of soup and brought it back to him. The steam warmed his face, and he took in a long draught but let out a burning cough as broth splattered on his hands.

"Careful!" she said. "It's a little hot."

Egbert wiped his hand and occasionally took a careful sip.

"Did you come with the others from Astford?" she asked.

He nodded, taking another sip.

"I'm surprised y'all made it through the country with all the alphyns."

Egbert glanced back to the rolling countryside beyond the gate. "It was pretty rough going, but we didn't hear none 'til last night. Even then, we only heard 'em. It wasn't 'til this evening we saw the dead ones."

"What brought you from Astford?"

Egbert tried not to think about that. But he knew why most came. "After the Daecish brought the draft, we lost too many men. Not enough to farm, you see? So, a bunch of us left for Everwind." But even with that excuse, his stomach ached. He didn't know what he would do without Burlan or Henley.

He let out an unexpected sob. "Poor Henley," he barely mumbled. "I's so sorry."

"Egbert?" Agatha asked. "Are you okay?"

Egbert wiped the snot from his nose. "I miss my family." He pointed in the direction he imagined Astford to be. "They took my cousin Burlan," he said in a low voice. "And they took Henley, too."

"I'm so sorry. Do you have a place to stay here?" Her voice was soothing, like a gentle mother's.

He shook his head.

"That man over there," she said, pointing to a short man in black trousers and a faded brown tunic. Although the top of his head was bald, there remained a thick black band of hair around his head, peaking down to a full beard. "He's offered a few of us some work and a place to stay. Why don't you come with us?"

"Come with you?" Egbert replied in a sheepish voice.

"Yes." She looked peculiarly at his torn shirt and soaked shoes. Then she took his hand, and he suddenly felt warm on the inside. "You won't last the night out here like this."

Egbert peered at the man in the midst of the crowd with squinted eyes. "What's his name?"

"Blaine, I think. At least that's what I heard one of the girls call him."

Egbert looked at the city gate. Astford sure was far away. And he had no idea where he was going or even what he was doing, but he really liked the way her hand felt. He nodded. "Okay."

"Good." She gave him an encouraging smile and walked him over to the crowd. She looked at Blaine. "Sire," she said in a quiet voice.

Blaine turned with a preoccupied look on his face.

"Sire," she said again. "This is Egbert, and he needs a place to stay, and I was hoping—"

"Now look here, there's lots of people who need a place to stay." He eyed Egbert with a grimace. "I got no time to take in everyone."

Slumping his shoulders, Egbert looked down at his belly.

"But, sire, he doesn't have anyone. No family. I'm sure he could be useful."

Blaine eyed her up and down, his expression hard. "You're coming with him?"

"Of course," Agatha replied.

"As long you stay, he can stay. Just keep him outta sight." He turned his back to them and continued talking to several others in the crowd.

Egbert followed the small crowd west down a broad road. They were mostly women, with Agatha and another dark-haired girl following behind him. Everything was so big and grand compared to Astford, but there was also darkness, which made him feel sad. Piles of rubble scattered along the streets, and black smoke rose into the low-lying clouds. On one street corner, a large group of people huddled around a fire too small to warm a single man. Soldiers, some dressed in burgundy uniforms, but most in normal attire, except for olive sashes over their tunics, ran and marched in all directions carrying food and blankets. Egbert wondered, more than once, why no Daecish were around. From behind, several men marched through the streets shouting out to nearby pedestrians. "At dawn on the 'morrow!" they hollered. "At Everwind Castle! Hear the future for our city!"

"What's that all about?" Egbert asked, pulling his trousers up again.

"I'm not sure," came Agatha's voice, trailing behind him.

The men marched to a crossroads and disappeared down a southern road.

The crowd kept up a steady pace, and Egbert found it difficult to catch his breath, much less keep up with everyone else. Maybe if he could just keep those blasted trousers up.

It was the same with the trip from Astford. Often, he'd watch his feet and try to forget about how much further they had to go before they rested. But the worst parts were the long moments when no one talked. That's when he had time to think, and always, the reality of Henley came back to him. He was like a haunting ghost who stood behind his shoulder, always whispering "murderer" just to remind him in case he tried to forget. He would have felt better if he could've talked to somebody about it.

Egbert made himself quit thinking. "Where are you from?" he asked Agatha.

Agatha picked up her pace until they walked side-by-side. She held the dark-haired girl's hand, but she never spoke. "From here," Agatha said. "At least I was."

"What you mean?"

"I've been in the mines for three years."

"Mines? What was that like?"

She was quiet for a moment. "Hard and sad."

One of the women in front of them glanced back. "And strange," she said. "I heard there's a boy from the lower quarry who's riding one of them alphyns around. He'll eat you if he sees you. Some even say he's Sunder's Bane."

A shiver ran down Egbert's spine. "Sunder's Bane?"

Agatha looked troubled, but she whispered to him, "I don't think so."

"Said he's riding just outside the city," the girl spoke up again.

As the crowd turned west from the main road, they entered a dark alleyway where the cobblestone gave way to mud. On either side, thatched roofs hung low. A dim glow came from within a few of the windows, but most were covered by wooden shutters.

Several began to talk once again of the growing rumors of what happened in the lower quarry. Agatha patted Egbert on the shoulder. "Don't you fret about those stories. I was there in the mines, and something strange did happen. But I don't think he's dangerous."

Egbert nodded, but he was unconvinced.

Agatha motioned to several of the girls in the front. "Only a couple of them are from the same mine, but even they weren't in the chamber when it happened, so don't listen to them."

Egbert nodded again. "When did you get out of the mine?" he asked.

"Not long ago. It was a hard walk, but we managed to arrive just two days ago. Thankfully, before the battle began."

"The battle? Is that what I saw outside?"

"Probably. Some fighting went on in the Eastern and Northern Districts. But we hid in Birchton and were safe enough."

"What 'bout those monsters?" He glanced behind him, half expecting one to be following them.

"I didn't see any 'til this morning, but we could hear them."

The girl in front glanced back again. "Some came up in the southern parts. Cydney said she saw one."

The hair on Egbert's neck stood up. But Agatha patted him once again on the shoulder. "Don't let it scare you. Look," she said, pointing ahead. "We're almost to Three Rivers."

They reached a tavern soon after. Inside, a roaring fire blazed in the hearth near the left wall. As the warmth soothed his cold and dreary limbs, Egbert took in a long sniff of the scent of smoke, which hung in the air like a thick haze. To the left of the door, crowds of men sat around tables, while several women stood off to the right, near a back hallway, covered in shadow. Three young children chased chickens to and from the hallway. In the back ran a wooden bar, where a goat kept obnoxiously bleating.

"Alphyns," said an old man, sitting next to where Egbert stood. "They'll be comin' again tonight. Ye jus' wait and see."

Not a single man argued with him.

"Let's just hope they don't come in 'ere," said a man on the other side of the hearth.

"You think we really got the Daecish out?" asked another man, wiping down the bar. He wore an apron and had a thick black beard.

The old man took a sip of ale. "You got me Ol' Bale, but I reckon they're too many. We may have got 'em out of our town, but they be all over Sunder. What you think, Fletcher?"

"Pissed 'em off, that's all we did," Fletcher replied, sitting at a table next to the old man. He was young-looking and wore a faded brown tunic with a thick belt around the waist. But on his head, he wore a fine black Daecish top hat with a black coat thrown over the back of the chair behind him. Beside him sat a girl who didn't seem interested in the conversation. "Soon, they'll be coming with armies," he continued. "I bet we'll see wisps and canons before too long."

"That'd be our luck," said the man in the apron. Egbert figured him to be Old Bale. "Daecish and alphyns together."

"Led by Sunder's Bane," added the old man. He grimaced at himself. "Wyrms will be coming soon."

At that, the crowd went silent. Egbert realized that he was now standing alone at the entrance while the others had walked toward the back, standing between the end of the bar and the entry to the hall. Agatha was talking to Blaine with a troubled look on her face. Beside her stood several women, their faces rough and their clothes soiled and sparse. One looked to be in the last couple of months of her pregnancy.

"I ain't takin' no more aracs," Old Bale said to a young man. "Either you work fer the ale or pay with produce."

A young man shoved the paper notes back into his pocket. "I'll be goin' elsewhere then!"

"Ain't nobody using Daecish aracs no more. But good luck you!" Bale hollered as the man marched past Egbert and through the front door.

Fiddling with his fingers, Egbert wasn't sure what to do. Suddenly, Agatha grabbed the hand of the girl with dark hair and marched toward him. With a flustered face, she shot a glance back. "Let's go, Egbert," she said.

"So soon?" Fletcher asked from his chair. He raised the corner of his mouth, but his eyes were dark.

Agatha ignored his question as Egbert hesitated, glancing back to the hearth. It felt so warm in there. Did they have to leave?

"Egbert," Agatha said, now standing in the open doorway. "They won't let you stay without me, and I'm leaving. I'm sorry, but we have to go."

Dropping his eyes to the ground, Egbert walked through the door with heavy steps. The front door swung closed behind him. "Why'd we have to go?" he asked.

"All they wanted was to use us." There was a thin crack in her voice. "Sell ourselves for their own profit."

Egbert examined the other girl. She was shorter than Agatha, and she looked tired. Her dress was so marred in black soot, he could barely see the yellow beneath it. For a second, his heart fluttered at how pretty she was. If only he was more handsome.

"We'll ask if we can stay with them tonight," Agatha said, pointing to an alleyway where a family huddled by a fire.

They walked across the street, and a middle-aged man looked up. He had a patchy, sparse beard, and his hair didn't look much better. Beside him stood a woman and three small children. None of them were dressed much better than Egbert.

"May we join you?" Agatha asked.

The man moved over. "It ain't much, but you're welcome to it."

Although they sat outside, several crates piled high behind the family, and an overhang, braced against the northside of a large brick building, sat low and kept the heat in. With a grunt, Egbert sat down on the cold but dry ground.

"You folks just come from there?" the man asked, nodding to the tavern.

"We did," Agatha admitted.

The man shook his head. "It's turned for the worst lately. Nothing but shame now goes within those walls."

"We don't plan on going back," Agatha replied.

"Wise decision," the man said. "And what might your name be?"

"Agatha," she replied. "That's Egbert, and that's Langleigh."

"I'm Finlay." The man smiled. "This here's my wife, Kalyn, and my three boys, Aedic, Reed, and the oldest is Leon."

Kalyn took a wool blanket from around her shoulders and wrapped it around Langleigh. "You need to keep warm," she said. "Don't want to catch a fever." She touched a ring on Langleigh's finger. "Is your husband around?"

With her eyes cast down, Langleigh barely shook her head.

Kalyn rested her hand on her shoulder.

"We got separated in Astford," she said in a quiet voice. "When I was sent to the mines."

"Maybe when all this settles down," Kalyn continued, "he'll come for you."

"That's what I thought. But a group came from Astford today, and I didn't see him." Though her tone was sorrowful, Egbert thought it sounded lovely, like a singing bird. If only he was a dashing knight. Then he'd rescue her from all her sadness and marry her like a true hero.

Agatha gently laid a hand on Langleigh's back.

Everyone suddenly looked up as a low growl echoed in the far distance, beyond the city wall. The three young boys went wide-eyed and hid between their parents. Finlay glanced behind him as he listened. "It's happening."

"Wha's happening?" Egbert asked.

"The sun's down, and alphyns are coming back out."

"Are they coming here?"

"Don't know."

Agatha stepped out of the alleyway and looked up and down the road. Another distant growl rose up, almost like a howl. She looked back. "There's more than one, but I can't see any. Sounds like they're pretty far." She observed the low overhang. "I guess this place'll be as safe as any."

Glancing behind him, Egbert pulled himself to his feet. He wanted to be brave. To be a hero and impress Langleigh, but he just couldn't. Instead, he ran and hid behind the family. Maybe they'd get eaten instead.

A New Dawn

Quinn!" Galvin shouted with his back to the bottom of the steps. He strained his eyes over the amassing crowds flooding around the front courtyard of Everwind Castle. If Quinn hadn't been so short, he would've stuck out like a pig in a chicken coop. Other than Wesley, he was one of the ugliest men he had ever met.

With a sigh of relief, he caught sight of Quinn's wide face and tiny chin straining red as he shoved his way toward the steps. Galvin waved his hand in the air. "Over here! Hurry up!"

After a stumble, Quinn caught his balance and continued to push his way through the throngs of men and women. "I'm trying my best!" he shouted back.

From the roaring crowd, it became clear that the music and dancing of the previous day shifted into confusion and exhaustion. Dour faces marred the people. One man let out a curdling shout and raised up the gruesome end of a bloody talon. He looked half-mad beneath his dark green cloak. Galvin couldn't keep his eyes off the fleshy, bleeding end. As the man continued shouting inaudible words, Galvin made a point to not make eye contact.

Quinn finally made it to the bottom of the steps, and the crowds stepped away to either side and quieted down while two full detachments of soldiers from the Free Sunderian Army marched through, each detachment led by two Brigadiers in full burgundy uniform. The black horses stitched on their left shoulders held a new sense that day, and it seemed as if every eye that caught sight of it felt it.

Between the two detachments, several high-ranking Daecish officers and soldiers trudged along with their hands bound behind them. Many in the crowd sneered and spat at them. One dark-haired man threw a ball of snow, laced with ice and rock, toward a Daecish officer, hitting instead a Sunderian soldier in the cheek. As the soldier grabbed his face and stumbled over, two sergeants drew their swords and lifted him up. They continued forward, barking out at the dark-haired man. The detachments stopped just below the stairs.

With his back to the castle door, Galvin looked across the crowds, which ran thick all the way to the Spire. The cityscape beyond looked more like ruins than the Everwind he remembered, and the foul stench from the alphyns still drifted in the air. Several soldiers shouted for the crowds to quiet down.

Cold stiffened Galvin's fingers, and frost nipped at his ears and nose as he took in a deep breath. "Brothers and sisters of Sunder!" he shouted. "You're tired and weary. The night's been long, and the early winter has been bitter. But don't forget, over a thousand years ago, Burgess, Lord of Aberthorn, through many a hardship and loss, led our ancestors here from the Kingdoms of Earlon. Here they found breath and freedom from the lands in the south, which had long been stained with conflict. Here they found a land of peace and prosperity!"

The crowd fell silent, and all eyes fixed upon him.

"But as quickly as we had it," Galvin continued. "It was taken from us! Pale-faces stole our homes and our lives! Murdered our fathers and sons! And sent our women and children into the mines!"

Several men shouted and booed, raising swords high in the air. The Sunderian Army fought to hold their ground as several men gnashed their teeth and reached out their fists toward the Daecish prisoners. Galvin motioned his hands for them to quiet down.

"But alas, the sun has risen," he continued. "No longer are we in service to Daecland. No longer do you serve a king whose face you have never seen. Today marks the dawn of our freedom once again.

The House of Burgess and the House of Emsworth have united." He grinned. "And I heard word that many from Astford have traveled over, and so we welcome the House of Denholm with open arms. Together, we'll raise up the Statue of Lord Aberthorn, and the bells of Theos will ring clear once again!"

The crowd erupted into cheers.

"Hang 'em on the walls!" hollered a young man from the crowd, eyeing the prisoners.

"For the House of Burgess!" hollered another.

"Where's Albern?" shouted yet another.

With that last question, the anger and tension from the crowds quickened. Galvin looked at Quinn, who was shifting his gaze between Galvin and the captives.

"Nice speech!" he yelled in Galvin's ear, "but I think it's best we take the prisoners into the castle! Before a mob forms on us!"

Galvin raised his hands for the crowd to quiet down. "We'll look into the whereabouts of King Albern. You, the people, are our top priority. I know you've got many concerns. Assemble here once again, this time on the 'morrow, and we'll move forward with the plans for the city."

A loud booing broke out as the crowd demanded answers.

"Where's Albern?"

"Our homes and shops are destroyed!" screamed a woman. "Where will my children sleep tonight?"

Anxiety filled Galvin's gut, and as he looked toward his own people, a great burden for them overwhelmed him. "Madam!" he shouted. "I've fought for Sunder's freedom all my life. I've lost many a brother in that time. But none of them would have regretted giving their lives for this day. And if there is anything I'd give my life for, it's for this country and for her people. I've prayed to Theos day and night for her freedom." He eyed the women intently. "For your freedom. And now that we have it, neither I nor the Free Sunderian Army will leave you all to die in the streets. We'll rebuild this city a step at a time. We'll rebuild our homes and shops. We'll rebuild our families. By Theos, I'll die doing so if I must! And so good people of Sunder, let us act wisely. Let us take counsel on how best to repair our city. We'll meet again on the 'morrow with more answers. You have my word. Until then, the Free Sunderian Army will aid you in temporary lodgings and food."

"What about the alphyns?" one hollered. "They came back in the night!"

Galvin motioned his hands for them to calm themselves. "We've slaughtered all in our path and have driven them out of the city. But," he added hesitantly, "you're right. Many have gone beneath the ground, and it appears they return again at night."

Several gasped.

"It's the end!"

"It's not the end!" Galvin shouted in a harsh tone. "We will not be defeated!"

"But what are we to do when they come back?"

"Stay within the city walls," Galvin continued. "None, as far as we reckon, appeared in the city last night. You should be safe, so long as you don't go out into the country. Stay as warm as you can tonight. Find structure. All shop owners, I beg you to open your place for others to stay the night. I'll now depart and organize the soldiers to aid you."

With Galvin's final words, several broke out into cheers, though others seemed less thrilled. Galvin motioned to Quinn to bring up the captives. Then, opening the castle doors, he led the two detachments, along with the prisoners, inside, closing the doors behind him.

Quinn let out a deep breath. "Sure am glad that's over with."

Galvin barely heard as he peered across the long empty hall, built of rough-cut stone. The only light shone pale through the tall arched windows. It had been nearly twenty years since he had been inside the castle. "I need you to go find Porter. Find out where his prisoners of war are being held. Also, see if you can't find Drake and Arnon." Galvin rubbed his throbbing head. His eye was giving him trouble again. "We need an update on whether Murdock's been found or not."

"On it," Quinn said. He looked toward the front door as if he hesitated to face the crowds. He'd always been a bit on the timid side.

"Leave through the back entrance if it makes you feel better."

"I think I will," Quinn replied. He hurried through the great hall as his footsteps echoed beneath the high vaulted ceiling. Opening the second of three wooden doors on the far wall, he disappeared into the heart of the castle.

Two stone staircases, one on either side of the doors, led to balconies on the second level, which stretched back through the hall above where Galvin and the others still stood. Despite the outer renovations and some additional chambers added on, the castle still managed to hold on to its Earlonian roots.

He looked at the captives and motioned for Brigadier Bardsley to step forward. He was a young man but proved his worth in Denhurst. "Bring me the highest commanding officer. You," he pointed to the rest of the brigadiers, "send the rest of them into the dungeon for now."

"What about the deserters?" one of the brigadiers asked.

"Deserters?"

"There's been reports of some of the Daecish hiding out in the North District."

"Any Daecish you find are to be arrested immediately."

"Yes, General."

Galvin turned to the two detachments of soldiers. "I need two ensigns to lead twelve men in surveying the castle. Find Albern if he's here. Otherwise, make a list of anyone you see, as well as food, supplies, arms, armor, anything of importance. I'll also need twelve able men to take up rotating watch outside the castle. The rest of you are under command of Brigadier Abney. You will be divided into groups of six. Sergeants, you're in charge. You are to continue helping with food, clothing, whatever you can. But above all, keep the peace and maintain order."

"Sire," spoke up Abney with a salute. "We've already handed out all the blankets from the castle."

"Check the Northern District. Look in the Daecish quarters and abandoned homes. You should find plenty there."

After the soldiers had departed, the remaining two Brigadiers, Langston and Redfield, brought forward a first commander. His hair was short and blonde, and he held a faded scar beneath his right ear, which stretched half-way down his neck.

"Your name?" asked Galvin shortly.

"Commander Eilívur Tyr," he replied in a calm, collected tone.

"I've been told that your King Ónarr departed for Llynhithe along with his officials."

"They left this morning."

"And you've been appointed by your king to negotiate the treatment and release of your men?"

"Those were my orders."

Galvin began to pace around the commander. "Now see here, I got the power to hang you in the morn'. What's to stop me?"

"You will do what you feel you ought to do," the commander replied, staring through the stone walls of the great hall. "I have been given my orders, and I will do what I can with your permission."

Galvin didn't show it, but there was something intimidating about the commander. He was a prisoner, and yet he held confidence as if he was really the one in charge.

"I reckon we'll see how that works out for you." He looked to Langston. He had a large nose and beady eyes, but he was a lot smarter than he appeared. "Put him in the dungeon. But give him his own cell."

"Yes, sire," he replied, walking away with the commander.

"Send a dispatch to the Crossroads," he said to Redfield. "Bring back the families. But take no more than a dozen with you. We need all the men we can."

"What about the alphyns?"

"That's why we need to bring them back quickly. Travel only at day."

Redfield saluted, but his round freckled face held a hint of dread as he departed down the hall. Afterward, Galvin was left alone. He walked to the front entrance and peered through a thin crack between the two doors. Most of the crowd had dispersed, but several still stood with a look of misplacement as if they were trying to figure out how to put their lives back together. Did he have what it took to help build this city once again as the capital of Sunder? Denhurst was managed well, with the House of Emsworth fully reestablished, but Everwind was a different kind of city. But he loved his people, and he would do whatever it took.

Looking back across the hall, he let out a shaking breath. He hoped Arnon and the others were doing well out there in the city.

The Not So Perfect Plan

I don't know what's going to happen," Geirleif said as he looked out the carriage window. His own body heat rose into his face. "Thialfi didn't make sense. The whole meeting was a waste." He let out a sigh of frustration. "Eirik should've been there."

Hrunting leaned forward to the chauffeur. "Pick up the pace, will you?"

The chauffeur flicked the reins. As they rounded the Western face of the mountain, the city fell into the distance behind them. The sun had long been hidden, revealing a starry expanse over the eastern horizon.

"The entire city's in an uproar," Geirleif continued. "These," he grimaced and waved a hand, "these creatures are crawling up the southern road. If this city doesn't take precautions, they'll flood in before we know it."

"Let's hope that's not the case," Hrunting replied, looking out his own window. "Look at the bright side; at least we have a better idea of what caused the mining industry to collapse."

Geirleif turned to Hrunting. He must be joking. "Look at the bright side? These creatures are everywhere. You heard Thialfi. Telegrams from as far east as Vagholme are reporting them!" He moaned and balled his hands. "The mines are the least of our worries." He could sense an objection coming, so he lifted a finger. "And it'll be any moment before we get word from Fingate that the creatures are there too!"

"At least with all this going on, I doubt they'll be looking to arrest you now." Hrunting smiled. "That's a positive you can't deny."

Even though Geirleif didn't say anything, the thought did make him feel better.

Both men sat in silence. Geirleif listened to the sound of the squeaking axels and the trotting horse, backdropped by distant shouts and howls from the lower city, as the soldiers and guards were still likely keeping those horrid creatures at bay below the southern gate. There was a haunting feeling about it, and Geirleif felt ashamed of himself for being so afraid.

"You've been awfully kind to allow me to stay at your place," Hrunting finally said.

"Think nothing of it. I wouldn't feel safe in the lower level, and I wouldn't expect you to."

Hrunting tapped a finger on his leg. "How do you think this will affect Eirún?"

"I don't know," Geirleif replied, situating himself in the carriage seat. "I'm torn between waiting and seeing whether this chaos will continue. Like you said, it may be that it gets so bad, the case will be forgotten."

"Possible," Hrunting added.

"Yet on the other hand, if I wait, and it's not forgotten, then I'll be guilty of 'failing to appear.' So, it might be best to go ahead to the precinct."

"And just turn yourself in?"

"It could work to my advantage. If I appear now, in the midst of all this going on, they may be too busy to deal with it, and at the same time, take note of my cooperation."

"And drop the whole thing?"

"Maybe."

Hrunting chuckled as the carriage jerked over a pothole. "That's certainly a gamble."

"I don't see another option."

"And you haven't changed your mind about sending Eirún to Sunder?"

"Our best hope is to be honest and upfront."

"You better be sure. You yourself said the last wisp to Fingate leaves tomorrow."

"So, it does."

"After that, there's no turning back. You'll have to appear in court, and she'll be arrested and convicted."

"I'll vouch for her innocence."

"Vouch for her innocence? Geirleif, she's a woman." He laughed. "Who's murdered a man. A male! She'll never stand a chance."

"I've still got to try."

"But you're assuming they'd even let you testify. Most likely, you'll be on trial with her!"

Geirleif took in a deep breath but gave no response. He knew Hrunting was right, but no matter how desperate he became, he would never let himself be talked into something so foolish as stealing a wisp and sending her to some far-off country.

They rounded the west side of the mountain, and Beron Manor opened before them. The wide lawn stretched all the way to the large white house, which glowed from within its many lit windows. On either side of the front entry stood tall and intimidating white columns built of hand-cut marble. As always, several men walked the lawn with lanterns hanging from their hands.

"What's going on up there?" Hrunting asked, leaning forward.

Near the front entry sat a carriage, with a small crowd conversing at the foot of the steps.

Geirleif narrowed his eyes. "That looks like Ulfr."

Hrunting shot a look at Geirleif. "Talking to officers from the Norfrost Precinct."

"Stop the carriage!" Geirleif said suddenly. As the chauffeur pulled the reins, Geirleif kept his eyes on the crowd. "I knew it!" he whispered in a hoarse voice. "I knew that Ulfr was up to something. Curse that man! Always prying in business other than his own!" He looked at Hrunting. "You don't think he's turned in Eirún?"

"This can't be good," Hrunting said at the same time.

Geirleif's lungs tightened. "What am I going to do?" He ran his hands through his hair.

"Hold yourself, Geirleif. Let's just think for a minute."

"You think they can see us?"

Hrunting gazed across the shadowed landscape. "I don't know; it's pretty dark." He turned to Geirleif. "I've got an idea."

"What?"

Leaning forward, Hrunting patted the chauffeur on the shoulder. "Take us along the eastern path toward the back of the house."

"Right away, sir," the chauffeur replied.

"But take it slow!" Hrunting added.

"What are you doing?" Geirleif whispered as harshly as he could. "You'll get us caught!"

"No, I won't," Hrunting said as he continued to peer toward the passing crowd. "It's too dark, and we're far enough out of sight."

Geirleif sank into his seat. "You're going to get me hanged."

"Shh!"

The short time it took to ride around to the side of the house felt like an eternity. Lifting his head just enough to peer through the bottom of the door window, Geirleif glanced along the lawn, breathing steam onto the glass through his nose. Finally, he let out a breath as they passed out of view. He sat up and wiped the sweat from his face. "What now?"

Rubbing his forehead, Hrunting smiled. "I've got no idea."

"What!" he shouted.

"Just let me think."

"I can't believe—" he jabbed a finger at Hrunting. "Is this a game to you?"

"Calm down and listen. Go inside, get Eirún, and bring her back out here."

"Bring her out here?"

The carriage pulled under a large overhang, where a single door stood in the middle of the back of the house. Two footmen stood by the entryway, and the chauffeur attempted to walk over and open the door, but Geirleif waved him away.

"It's that or get arrested," Hrunting whispered.

"What if they already have Eirún?"

Hrunting thought for a second. "Let's just hope they don't. Now go!" He reached over Geirleif and pushed open the door.

Geirleif sat stiffly. "I'm not going."

Hrunting threw his hands into the air. "Fine, then get out, walk to the front door, and turn yourself in. You don't have the option to wait it out and see what happens anymore. It's now or never."

Pulling loose his cravat, Geirleif wondered if it was possible to sweat this much. "I feel light-headed," he said, trying to catch his breath. "I fear I may faint."

Hrunting patted him on the shoulder. "You're fine."

"What if I get caught?"

"The longer you sit in here, the more likely you will."

Geirleif peered at the footmen, then back to Hrunting. "I can't believe I'm doing this." He leaned out the door but hesitated. Then he slid himself out of the carriage and into the night air. He quickly leaned back in. "If I don't come back, I've probably been caught. Tell Eilis I love her!"

Hrunting rolled his eyes. "I'll tell her, now go!"

Hurrying through the back door, Geirleif attempted to straighten back his cravat, but his hands trembled too much to do any good. A footman passed him by.

"Your lordship," he bowed.

Geirleif motioned a half-nod but continued as he nervously twiddled his fingers. Sweat dripped down his arms. Approaching the back end of the entry hall, he stood in a corner beside the wide passageway. From the open front door came the sound of voices, but they seemed calm and unalarmed. Quickly, he stole to the left, passing through the servant halls. He peeked through a doorway leading to the library, but no one was in there. With a tsk, he looked down at his pocket watch.

"They'll all be in bed at this point!" he hissed at himself.

Taking the servant stairs, he hurried up. His legs grew heavy, and he quickly found it difficult to breathe. A maid approached from the top and startled.

"Your lordship!" she said. "What brings you in the servants' passage?"

"Say nothing of it! If you please!" He rushed past her until he reached another door. Opening it, he found himself in the main passageway on the third floor. He glanced to his right and jolted as he grabbed his chest.

"Geirleif?" said Eilis, tottering toward him in her nightgown. "What on earth?"

Eirún, dressed in a similar fashion, stood just behind her.

"No time to explain," he said, wiping his face again.

"You look like a wreck!"

"There are men downstairs," he said, setting his hands on Eilis' shoulders. He swallowed and strained for breath. "Men from the Norfrost Precinct."

Eilis tilted her head, and Eirún narrowed her eyes. Neither expression made it any easier to get his words out.

"I received a telegram the other day, and they know we have Eirún. I didn't tell you because I didn't know what to do."

A look of horror fell upon Eirún's face as she dropped her mouth and took a step back.

Eilis held a hand to her mouth. "Geirleif! What are we going to do?"

"I—I don't know." His lungs trembled. He looked at Eirún, and the look on her face made him feel as if he might weep. "But I won't let them take you. I promise!"

Eirún shook her head. "My lord, you can't—"

"It's already settled!" he said in a loud whisper. "You will not talk me out of it. I brought you here, and I will now get you out!"

"Where on earth are you going to take her?" Eilis asked with her hand still over her mouth.

Geirleif raised his eyebrows. "Sunder?"

"You've lost your mind!"

With a gulp, he nodded. "I think I might have."

"But . . ." She trailed off, apparently too dumbfounded to continue.

"Listen," he said, calming his tone. "We don't have much time. Eilis, you stay here. I'll take Eirún to the docks. There's a wisp going to Fingate. We'll get her on board and go to Sunder from there."

"And then what? You'll go with her?"

"I plan on coming back within the week."

"And then just pretend like everything is okay?" She scrunched up her eyebrows and peered down the shadowy hallway.

"They may know we let her stay here, but they won't know where she's gone or that we helped her. Other than you, myself, and Hrunting, no one knows where she's going."

"Hrunting!" Eilis narrowed her eyes. "He put you up to this, didn't he?"

"No," Geirleif cleared his throat. "Well, maybe a little—"

"Geirleif!"

"It's my decision, and it's already made!"

"But—"

"Now's not the time! We must go!"

Geirleif grabbed Eirún's hand and hurried to the door leading back to the servants' stairs. He glanced back to Eilis, who only stood frozen and confused. With a quick sigh, he walked back and kissed her. "I know this is madness, but I've done a lot of things in my life I regret. Let me do this one thing."

Her eyes began to water.

"If I don't come back," he said. "Go to your sister's townhome. She'll take care of you. I'm going to do whatever I can to keep us above water."

"Geirleif," she said, closing her eyes for a moment. "Do what you feel is right. Just be safe."

Holding her close, he kissed Eilis on the head, but she tensed under his grip. "I love you," he tried to comfort her.

When she didn't respond, he leaned back. There was a cold look in her eyes. Did she know something? Of course not. He grabbed Eirún's hand, and they disappeared down the servants' stairwell.

They rushed through the servants' passage as Eirún held her nightgown to keep it from dragging on the floor. Approaching the back door, he felt Eirún hold him back with her hand.

"Geirleif," she said.

He turned around. "We must be quick, my dear."

"I know, but . . ." She looked down. "You've already done so much for me. I can't let you do this. I'm willing to turn myself in."

He cupped her hand in both of his. "I will not let you do that. You have no idea what the prisons are like here, especially for women. It would be the death of you."

She didn't say anything, and as Geirleif peered into her eyes, a sudden sadness fell upon him. He couldn't say for sure, be she looked as if she didn't care.

"Please," he continued. "Let me take you. You can start a new life. There's nothing left here for you."

"What are you waiting for?" came the sudden voice of Hrunting, who was peering through the door. From the corner of his mouth hung a small briar pipe. "Let's go!"

Geirleif turned his gaze from Hrunting to Eirún. "Please, trust me."

Eirún nodded warily, and they hurried to the carriage.

Though he asked her to trust him, he wasn't sure he trusted himself at the moment. He would never forgive himself if he only made things worse for her. And what on earth was Hrunting doing with a pipe?

"Why are you smoking?" Geirleif snapped. "We don't have time for that!" He looked over the carriage. "Where's the chauffeur?"

"About that," Hrunting replied, sitting in the driver's seat. "I thought it best to send him away. We don't want more people than we need involved in this."

Geirleif lifted Eirún into the carriage and followed after, shutting the door. "Is he going to tell on us?"

Hrunting shrugged and blew out smoke through his nostrils. "I doubt it, but one thing's certain—I'm now caught in the middle of this with you." He glanced back. "Did you not grab her a bag or change of clothes?"

Geirleif slapped his thigh and grunted. "It didn't even cross my mind."

"So, she's going to Sunder in a nightgown?"

"You could have helped!" he retorted. He looked at Eirún and said with a calmer tone, "I'm terribly sorry. We'll see what we can do before we get to the wisp."

Eirún only held a blank stare as if she was still processing the whole thing.

"Don't worry," Hrunting said as he flicked the reins. "I've got her covered."

The moon did not show its face that night as they rode from Beron Manor to the lower level of Norfrost. An hour had passed with no interruptions, and Geirleif took in a sigh of relief, almost forgetting the plight that weighed over him. He wanted to talk to Eirún, but she never looked toward him and seemed to be in deep thought. He motioned for Hrunting to pause the carriage as he got out and sat in the front beside him. Flicking the reins again, the horses began their slow trot.

"How do you suggest we get Eirún out of Fingate to Sunder?"

Hrunting took in a deep breath. "I've thought about that."

"And?"

"You still got that wheellock in the back of the carriage? The one Thialfi gave you?"

He put it there yesterday for his trip to Norfrost, hoping Thialfii would show him how to work it properly. "I believe so." He eyed him. "Why do you ask?"

"No reason." He cleared his throat. "If we can get her to the wisp safely, I think you ought to go back home. I'll go with her."

Geirleif opened his mouth and caught his breath. He had a hunch that Hrunting was fond of her, but this was a bit excessive. "Absolutely not," he objected.

"Why? You've got a wife to look after." He paused to relight his pipe with a match. "And if you're here in Norfrost while she's going to Sunder, it'll look better for you."

"But you cannot possibly go with her."

"Geirleif." Hrunting chuckled. "I'm already a part of this. And I'm not married. I have no children."

"Obviously," Geirleif mumbled beneath his breath as he rolled his eyes.

"And!" Hrunting lifted a finger and gave him a stern look. "I'm an engineer. I can operate a wisp."

"I thought you said it was easy."

"More or less, but after the way you acted tonight." He let out a laugh. "I'm pretty sure you'd blunder the whole thing."

Geirleif raised his chin and narrowed his eyes. Hrunting was probably right, but he was still offended by the statement. "I can handle myself when the time calls for it."

Hrunting laughed again. "I don't doubt it, but we have no time for mistakes. Besides, there were a couple of things I didn't think about."

"What do you mean?"

"Well," Hrunting began as he repositioned himself in his seat, "the only way we can board a wisp to Fingate is if you give written authorization, correct?"

Geirleif glanced back at Eirún, who still seemed to stare at her feet. Although the clatter of the horse hooves likely kept her from making out their conversation, he kept his voice low. "Correct."

"So, your name will be on paper. They'll know you stole it. Even if you sail to Sunder."

"I thought you said we would be safe in Sunder?"

"I said they wouldn't have an arrest warrant for Eirún there. But if they know you stole a wisp and sailed for there, I'm sure they could make the connection themselves."

"Good grief, Hrunting."

"If, however, I take the wisp and you stay back, the blame can be utterly on me. You can simply say you asked me to acquire blueprints from the Dilution Sites for engineering purposes. You could even say you would have gone yourself, but since you were wanted at the Precinct, you thought it wise to stay in Norfrost."

Geirleif thought about Hrunting's solution as he looked east. The mountain dropped to the wide-open landscape where the land lay cloaked in darkness. Other than a few lights from distant towns, nothing else could be seen. The plan made good sense, but there was still a problem. "But whether it's you or me, won't they know you went to Sunder?"

"How're your navigation skills, Geirleif?"

"Navigation skills?"

"That's what I thought. And that's one other reason I should go instead. When we land at the sites, I'll take over the wisp. We'll steer it north a while. Once we're out of sight, we'll bear southeast. They'll think we went to Varghoss or somewhere else. They'll never track us."

"But how will you take over the wisp?" A thought he still hadn't worked out for himself if he was to take Eirún.

Hrunting waved his finger as if the words were on the tip of his mouth. "I haven't figured that part out yet."

"Of course you haven't because it's an absurd idea."

"You just get me and Eirún on board," Hrunting went on, apparently unbothered by his comment. "Inform the captain that I am to acquire the blueprints. Once that happens, you'll be done. Go home. Go to the Precinct. Don't worry about us. Eirún and I will be in Sunder in no time. We'll change our names and, hopefully, be forgotten."

Unsure of what to say, Geirleif only sat there. Then he looked Hrunting in the eyes. "You're going to do all this for a girl you barely even know?"

Hrunting smiled. "Well, I was a bit bored today. Sounded like a pretty good idea to me."

"You are a ridiculous man, but even I know you aren't that absurd." But even as Geirleif said the words, this was a way for him to get out of it, and it helped calm his nerves. Maybe he could reason with the Precinct and work his way out of this madness. But he was sorry that he may never see Eirún again. Or his best friend. "Okay," he replied.

Entering the eastern side of the city, the cobblestone gave away to a smooth paved road. To their right ran rows of tall brick buildings with dark windows, stacking up the mountain to the second level. Just as Hrunting veered the horses down a narrow road, running between two of the buildings, Geirleif caught a glimpse of the southern gate of the city. It was a wide-open space, where several roads met. Normally, it was a lively area with a small park of green grass and benches on the left, where entertainers and newsboys would often gather. But on this night, soldiers were posted at the gate, their attention fixed down the road beyond the city. Behind them stood a large crowd, especially for so late an hour. Occasionally, distant booms and pops sounded.

"Those muskets are already proving useful," Hrunting said as the view was lost behind them.

"Thank goodness we got them issued out when we did," Geirleif added.

Hrunting pulled the reins to a halt. He tapped out the ashes from his pipe, shoved it in his coat pocket, and stepped out of the carriage. "I'll be right back," he said as he ran into a building.

In front of the carriage, the road twisted and turned up the mountain to the second level. Some of the nicest homes in Norfrost were situated along that slope. Geirleif once lived there as a child, but he couldn't remember which house it was. He turned back to Eirún, who bundled her arms as a swift wind rushed into the carriage.

"Here," Geirleif said, handing her his coat. "I could use a good cooling down."

"Thank you," she said, wrapping it around her.

He had expected her to be afraid like he was, but instead, her expression remained downcast. He hoped he wasn't the cause of her grief.

"Eirún," he said as he patted her hand. "I'm realizing I didn't consider your own desire in all of this. I understand you were hesitant because you did not want to cause me any trouble, but I assure you that will not happen."

She allowed herself to smile.

"Tell me," he continued. "What's on your mind?"

She stared at her lap, holding her hands together.

Hrunting suddenly rushed back outside with two leather suitcases. He hurried to the other side of the carriage and opened the door, then he set one of the suitcases on the ground and unlatched it. "Go inside and change into these clothes," he said to Eirún. He held up a dress. "My sister's close to your size, I believe." He also handed her a hat and shoes.

Eirún grabbed the clothes and stepped out of the carriage. She frowned at Hrunting, then Geirleif, as if she was unsure. But she didn't say anything and walked inside.

"Where's the wheellock? Hrunting whispered.

Geirleif sighed. "Why must you have the wheellock?"

"If I'm going to steal a wisp and sail for Sunder, I'd like to have some sort of protection."

"But this was a gift from the king himself!"

"I'll give it back."

Geirleif laughed. "When you get back from your holiday in Sunder?"

Hrunting didn't respond, and Geirleif let out an intentional grunt as he walked to the back of the carriage. He pulled out a wooden case and handed it to Hrunting, who stuffed it in his suitcase.

"Do you know how to operate it?" Geirleif asked.

"Geirleif." He laughed. "I helped design it."

Eirún stepped back outside, wearing a silk dress of orange and cream. Although Geirleif thought she looked stunning, she hurried into the carriage as if she was dressed in something embarrassing.

Hrunting leaned toward her window and handed her a ring. "This is going to be awkward," he said, "but you will be going through a couple of name changes for your own safety. For now, you will be Mrs. Signy Hrunting, my wife."

She hesitated but slipped on the ring. "What's your first name?" she asked.

"Kjell," he replied, and he walked back to the front of the carriage.

By the time they reached the third level, Geirleif held a hand to his pounding heart and felt his head go light again. Riding along the smooth pavement, they rode around the wide circular base of the Norfrost docks, stretching high into the air. High above, centered in the front of the building, was a large round brass gate. Although it was shut, the low humming of wisps echoed from inside. Looking to his left, he watched the city fall below him like a long, deep staircase. From the eastern horizon, a gray light began to rise.

Following the winding road to the backside of the loading docks, Hrunting pulled the carriage to a halt. "We're here."

Eirún and Hrunting stepped out, but Geirleif couldn't move as he waved a hand to cool his face.

"Geirleif," Hrunting said. "Control yourself. You're our ticket in."

"I know," he replied, taking a deep breath. He stepped down from the front of the carriage.

Hrunting straightened Geirleif's cravat. "The wisp leaves in two hours. All you have to do is approve our passage to Fingate."

"Then what will you do?"

"You don't have to worry about that."

"What if they recognize Eirún?"

"They won't." Hrunting looked at her and held out his hand. She took it in hers. "As Mrs. Hrunting, she'll have no problem getting aboard."

Geirleif let out a loud breath. "Okay. Let's do this."

Thoughts of Escape

The guards threw one last body onto the wooden cart before pulling it back through the open gate, locking it from behind. Arms and legs bounced over the sides like lifeless rags. Beneath the rolling wheels, a trail of dust swirled in the wind until the cart was hidden from view. Geoffrey felt as if he had been in the camp for a year, but the reality was, he had no idea how long he had been there. Days seemed to drag on endlessly, but the cold nights felt even longer. A rumor had passed that morning that water would be brought in again, but Geoffrey didn't care. He wasn't sure if he wanted to prolong his life.

"Geoffrey," came a small voice.

He gazed at his feet stretched out in front of him, and his hands laid lifeless with the palms facing up. His mouth tasted like rot, and his tongue kept sticking to the roof of his mouth.

"Geoffrey." The voice grew louder.

Geoffrey dragged his eyes from his feet and looked to his right. Burlan was sitting next to him.

"You awake?" Burlan asked, his voice heavy with grit.

Geoffrey remained in a daze, and he hardly noticed that Burlan had stood up and walked off. Several minutes later, he returned and put a bowl in Geoffrey's lap.

"It's not much," Burlan said. "But it's something."

Geoffrey nudged the bowl, half-filled with a brown broth. Slowly, he picked it up, splashing a small amount on his lap. He bent over and took in a large gulp of what remained but let out a loud cough and spilled the bowl over.

"Easy!" Burlan said in a bitter tone. "You're gonna waste it!"

Geoffrey frowned at the bowl lying upside down on the ground. He lazily swung himself over on all fours and attempted to suck the broth from the dirt with his lips.

"Here," Burlan said. He took a few sips of his broth, then handed the bowl to Geoffrey. "Take the rest of mine."

He reached for the bowl, but Burlan grabbed his hand. "Drink slow," he said. "Small sips. Otherwise, you'll spit it out again."

That evening, the trough was filled with water, and another serving of broth was given. The next morning, they were each given a small portion of dark, stale bread. Although it wasn't much, Geoffrey felt his mind clear and a little strength return. Burlan sat beside him, their backs to the outside wall of the bunkhouse. Soon, Bartholomew walked over. Without saying anything, he sat down beside him.

"Geoffrey," he said.

"When did you get here?" Geoffrey asked.

"You've been out of it for a couple of days," Bartholomew replied. "I've seen you, but ain't so sure you've seen me."

Geoffrey barely chuckled at himself. "I think I'm coming to." He could barely move his lips as he spoke. "What happened? Why'd they take you?"

Bartholomew's gaze fixed on the ground between his legs. His heels sunk into the sandy dirt. "Can't say."

"They don't usually take innkeepers. Did you riot or something?"

Bartholomew shook his head. "It don't matter why we're here. We just are."

"Is Langleigh safe?" As soon as he asked, Geoffrey regretted it.

Bartholomew rubbed his hands habitually, and the veins in his neck stuck out. It was hard to tell if he was sad or angry. "They sent her to the mines. And her husband, Cyril . . . he didn't know 'til after they loaded her up. He tried to stop 'em, but she was already gone. They killed him right there in town."

Geoffrey's body tightened, threatening to shatter. He hadn't the slightest idea how his family was, but he figured he would rather it be that way than knowing as Bartholomew did.

With an arm propped on his knee, Burlan pointed to a series of buildings just beyond the iron gate. "Either of you been taken out yet? To work on the water?"

Geoffrey peered around the barren landscape. "Water?"

"Only once," Bartholomew replied, wiping his eyes.

"Where's water?" Geoffrey asked.

"On the other side of those buildings runs a river," Bartholomew said.

"But I thought it was all desert," Geoffrey replied.

"No," Burlan said as he stood up, raising his hand to shield the sun from his eyes. "We're on the edge." He pointed south but kept his voice low so the others around them wouldn't hear. "The desert goes that direction. And I ain't sure, but since that's south, I reckon that's the Great Fringe on the horizon. But just over there," he pointed back to the buildings and squatted back beside them, "it's pretty green. There's no trees or nothing, but there's a river rolling through a wide plain."

"You've seen it?" Geoffrey asked. "You've been out there?"

"A couple of times," Burlan replied.

A sudden desire to see something other than tan and brown came over Geoffrey. "How come I haven't been called to go out there?"

"I don't know."

"What did they have you do?"

Burlan sat back down. "They've diverted the river through this channel. It flows through these arched openings of one of the brick buildings in the back. Then it flows out the other side. I'm not sure why, but they've got some of us digging a channel to a second building; others are making brick from the clay."

Geoffrey thought back to the rushing water he'd heard when he had first woken up in that place. Was that where he was?

"What's got my interest, though," Burlan continued as he pointed again to the series of brick buildings, "is over there. You see that underpass between the two buildings?"

Both Geoffrey and Bartholomew squinted.

"Whenever we go out, we walk through there. There's a door on the right leading into that building. Last time I walked through, it was open."

"What was inside?" Bartholomew asked.

"It was pretty messy, and I only got a chance to glance in, but there was a lady in there folding guard uniforms."

"Why would that be of any—" Bartholomew began, but his words cut short when a low howl echoed from somewhere in the distance. "Did you hear that?"

"I think so," Burlan replied.

Geoffrey mustered the strength to stand, and they walked around the bunkhouse. Peering across the endless desert, they heard another howl. Deep and rumbling. Almost earthy.

"Sounds far away," Bartholomew said.

Geoffrey turned around. The entire camp, including the guards, gazed at the horizon. At first, no one moved, but the howls soon ceased, and most in the camp lost interest.

"There's a sound that'll keep you up at night," said Burlan as they sat back down. "What'd you think it was?"

"I don't know," Geoffrey replied. "A wolf?"

"That didn't sound like any wolf I've heard of."

"Maybe they have different kinds of wolves in Daecland," Bartholomew suggested.

Burlan picked up a rock and he fiddled with it. "I wonder if perchance, we could get those uniforms somehow and sneak outta here."

Bartholomew raised an eyebrow as he slowly turned to Burlan. "You aren't serious, are you?"

"I don't know." Burlan threw the rock down. "It could work."

"Now listen here," Bartholomew continued, "you've done lost your mind. How would we get in there? How would we change without getting caught? Guards are patrolling everywhere." He held out his hand and pointed to each finger. "We don't look Daecish, our beards are outgrown, we don't know where to go."

"I get your point; all I'm saying is that it's possible."

"Okay," Bartholomew said, half-laughing, "but incredibly unlikely."

"It's a good thought," Geoffrey added. "But they'd kill us on the spot."

"Well, as I see it," Burlan said, "we've got two options. We can die lying here doing nothing, or we can die trying to escape."

Bartholomew didn't respond, but Geoffrey couldn't argue with that. He just wasn't sure it would work.

"Don't sound like such a bad idea now, does it?" Burlan asked with a smirk.

"But where would we go?" Geoffrey asked. "We're in Daecland."

Burlan stood up and wiped the dust from his gray shirt. "Anywhere would be better than here."

The Kitchen Pantry

Arnon shuddered as he kicked at the wool blanket wrapped around his legs. Fleta and Myla stood helplessly before the alphyn, which snarled through its long teeth. Although he couldn't see her, Hazel cried out from some great distance. The alphyn pounced forward, and Arnon shouted as he reached for his sword at his hip, but he only rolled off the bed, hitting the wooden floor.

With a groan, he slid open his eyes and felt a rising knot in the back of his head. Only a thin light from the moon glowed through the window, leaving most of the room in thick shadow. The dark outlines of the dresser and chamber pot stood before him, and he rubbed his face. The thought of alphyns at the Crossroads terrified him. He didn't even know if his family was alive. The first thing he'd do when he got to the castle was make sure a band of men was sent to bring them back.

There was a knock. "Is everything all right?" Sarah asked through the door while she slowly cracked it open. Light from her lantern spilled across the floor. "I heard a thud."

Arnon pulled himself up, rubbing the back of his head. "I'm fine."

With Acton in one arm and Lilly by her feet, Sarah set the lantern on his dresser, stepped out, and walked back in with a mug of milk which she handed to Arnon.

"Thank you," he said, taking a large gulp. "I didn't mean to wake the children."

Sarah sat down beside him. "It's all right. The sun's almost up, and I think Adelyne's already getting ready."

"Where are you going?"

"There's girls all over the city now, but we thought we'd start in the Southern Squalor."

"It's pretty bad out there, isn't it?"

"It is." Her tone suddenly changed as she watched Lilly play with Acton's feet. "Sometimes, I wonder if we did the right thing."

"What do you mean?"

She sighed. "I'm probably impatient, but the city seems to have only been getting worse. We were concerned about the slums. Now all of a sudden, the whole city's one."

Hearing footsteps walking down the stairs, they both looked through the open door as Adelyne made her way down the hall. Dressed in her brown tunic, she held a stack of wool blankets. "I figured we'd get an early start," she said as she stepped into the room.

Sarah stood up and grabbed Lilly's hand.

Arnon set the mug down on the floor. "I need to head out as well. I told Galvin I'd go to this meeting they're having at the castle. Hopefully, he can tell me any news about Crossroads. I've got to make sure my family and everyone else there is safe. Who knows, alphyns could be there as well."

"I'm sure they've sent someone already," Sarah replied.

Arnon's stomach knotted up. "I hope so."

Sarah stepped out of the room, with Lilly following behind.

He looked at Adelyne as she raised an eyebrow at him. "What happened to your head?"

Arnon wished he had a better answer. "I fell off the bed."

She gently brushed his hair away from his face and smiled. He smiled back, but he could tell that there was an uneasiness in her. He was so overjoyed with seeing her again, he barely even thought about the man in the top hat. He deeply regretted giving her that awful look in the cellar just before he left for the battle. And he wanted to talk to her, but he knew they were about to leave. He gently grabbed her hand.

"Will you be back this evening?" he asked.

A glint appeared in her eyes. "Before dinner, if I can help it."

Arnon kissed her on the cheek and walked out of the room.

* * *

"Keep it at bay!" echoed a distant shout.

Across the dark horizon of the cityscape, all that could be made out were flickering lights and the splinter of the alphyn crashing into some building. Galvin held his breath and listened. Just as he was about to order more soldiers to their aid, he heard a thud and the soldier's shouts went to a low commotion.

He turned to Brigadier Langston behind him. "Send half a detachment to help clean up the mess."

Langston saluted and departed as Galvin walked back into the castle. By the left door on the far wall stood Quinn. "It's too early for this," he said with a yawn.

"You're telling me," Galvin replied. "Where's Drake and Porter?"

"They'll be here shortly."

"And Arnon?"

"Probably somewhere with Adelyne," Quinn answered. "But he said he'd be here for the meeting."

With the brigadiers all over the city, Galvin wasn't sure if the meeting shouldn't be postponed. But either way, he wanted to see Arnon. He never was good at showing his own emotions—or handling a conversation when someone else got emotional—and most people took him for being cold because of it. But the way Arnon looked at him just before the battle, when they stood outside the Keld Valley, cut to his heart. Wishing he had never said that about Arnon's father or even questioned Arnon's own character, he wanted to somehow mend the tension that developed between them. After all, he had loved Lombard like a brother, and Arnon was like family.

"Do you think he's really in there?" Quinn asked as they headed down a short passageway.

Galvin laughed. "Alphyns at night, half our city's homeless, prostitutes and bastards running around the streets . . ." He shook his head as they rounded a corner. Up ahead, several soldiers stood around the locked door to the kitchen pantry. "But this," he continued pointing to the door. "This here's just about the most ridiculous thing I've seen."

The soldiers stepped away from the door, allowing the two men to press their ears against its face.

"You hear that?" Quinn asked.

"Is that sobbing or laughing?" Galvin whispered.

"He's been doing that since before dawn," spoke up one of the soldiers. "We tried talking to him. We even ordered him to unlock the door, but he won't listen."

"Have you tried to break the door down?" Quinn suggested.

The soldiers looked at one another. "We thought it best to get permission first."

"Good man," said Galvin stepping away from the door. "But looks like it's our only option." He smacked his hand against the thick oak. "No foot'll break this thing down. We'll need a ram."

"There's one in the lower storage, sire," said a soldier with broad shoulders and a short neck. "I can get it right away."

"Very good."

Quinn put his ear back against the door. "You know Galvin, it may sound crazy, but I think he's laughing and crying."

Galvin chuckled. "I don't doubt it."

Quinn sniffed. "You smell that?"

Galvin breathed in through his nose. "Not really."

Quinn got down on all fours and sniffed below the crack of the door. He let out a gag. "For Theos' sake! It smells worse than a full chamber pot in there!"

Galvin squinted. "That's disgusting."

A few moments later and the soldiers hurried back with the battering ram. All four of them gripped the iron handholds and within three attempts, the door shattered from the lock. Dropping the ram, Galvin stood with his mouth agape. In the middle of the floor sat Albern, fat and naked, with his robe beside him—it used to be royal red, but now it looked soiled with . . . Galvin just shook his head.

All the shelves and cupboards had been emptied, and their contents now lay around the man in a rotting mess of half-eaten vegetables, raw meats, and unbaked dough. In various spots on the floor, reeked piles of bodily waste which seeped between the stone cracks. Smears of dark human sludge dripped off the walls, and his fingers looked the same color as if he had decided to paint with it.

"By Theos!" exclaimed one of the soldiers.

With a grimace, Galvin stepped into the room. "Mad King Albern," he said, eyeing the mess around him. "So, this is what the last member of the House of Burgess has fallen to?"

The king said nothing as he lifted a lazy eye up to Galvin. His greasy thin black hair smeared down the side of his face. He dropped his face with a low whimper mingled with laughter.

* * *

With a cane in his left hand, Drake followed Porter across the great hall, marveling at the vaulted ceilings and stone ribs. He didn't care how bad his leg hurt; he wanted to see the castle himself. Especially since Galvin had decided to re-establish the line of kings with the Free Sunderian Army acting as its force.

Behind him, the front door pushed open, and he and Porter turned as Arnon stepped inside. A soldier gave him a salute, and Arnon gave an awkward salute back. Drake grinned. There was an innocence, almost a childlike ignorance in Arnon that not even the battle could harden. He loved that boy like his own son.

"Arnon!" Porter shouted. As Arnon walked forward, he gave him a firm hug. "I heard you did well!"

"Galvin said he fought like a veteran," Drake added with a grin.

Porter looked at Arnon's bandaged hand. "I see you didn't finish without a few scars, though."

Arnon nudged Drake with his elbow. "But some came out of the battle worse than others."

"I got more spirit than the two of you combined," Drake replied, holding his chin high. "Don't care how crippled I get."

Porter let out a laugh.

"I noticed a lot of work going on in the city," Arnon said as he kept feeling the bandage around his hand. "People seem to be hard at work."

"Give Galvin the credit," Porter replied. "He's been working hard to heal the city, but it ain't easy. One step at a time."

"Has he said anything about the families in the Crossroads?" Arnon asked.

Porter slapped Arnon on the back. "Don't fret! A dispatch has already been sent out. They should be back in a week or two. But come! Let's go get Galvin before the meeting starts. I'm sure he'll want to see you."

Walking across the hall, they entered a long dark passageway, thick with smoke and oil. Drake ran his hand along the cool stone wall as he leaned on the cane. They soon approached a wide oak door which led to a set of stone stairs leading down. At the bottom, the air was cold and wet. A dozen cast-iron cells lined the wall to their right. Except for the last two on the end, each cell was filled with Daecish soldiers and officers. The smell of bodily fluids steamed into the air and caused Drake to let out a heavy cough as he covered his mouth with his arm. The men were thin, with dark and heavy eyes. One was stripped naked and bound in chains. Across his back were long lashes, caked in dried blood. Drake felt a growing sickness in his gut. With no room to sit and barely enough room to move, the men appeared tired and angry. Just outside the last cell stood Galvin and Quinn. Arnon pointed to the naked man in chains.

"Wouldn't quit yelling out," Porter said. "But we fixed that."

Drake locked eyes with Porter. "By treating them worse than animals?"

"Is it any different than the way they treated us?" Porter replied.

Drake didn't answer, but a long-hidden concern crept back into his heart.

"Arnon, Drake," Galvin said in a soft tone. "Good to see you both." He placed a hand on Arnon's shoulder and gave him a nod. "How you feeling?"

Arnon didn't respond as his gaze was fixed on the Daecish.

Galvin glanced over his shoulder. "I imagine this is a bit of a shock for you."

"It's a dungeon," was all Arnon said, but he looked uneasy.

"Is that who I think it is?" Drake asked, looking into the last cell. The old King of Sunder sat in his robe like a piled mess.

"Long before the battle started," Quinn answered, "he had locked himself in the kitchen. Even had all the food to himself."

Drake grunted. "Pitiful."

Galvin pointed to the officer sitting in the cell before them. "This is commander Eilívur Tyr. He's been assigned to handle all negotiations."

As Drake observed him, he took note that the officer peered up at Arnon with a calm expression, but his eyes looked as if they raced in thought. Arnon kept looking away as if it made him feel uncomfortable.

"They're going to negotiate with us?" Drake asked.

"We'll never negotiate with peasants!" shouted one of the Daecish from another cell.

"Quiet, pale-face!" Porter snapped as he kicked an iron bar.

"I'm not very hopeful," Galvin replied, "but we'll see."

"We should've beheaded Ónarr before he had a chance to flee," Porter added.

"What about the rest of them?" Arnon asked, surveying the other Daecish.

"We're running out of room," Galvin replied, "but I imagine it'll thin out before long."

Drake tightened his jaw. "You're gonna let them die in there?"

"I ain't decided yet." He motioned for them to go back up the stairs. "But let's continue this conversation away from prying ears."

As they began to walk away, they paused as Officer Tyr spoke up. "Arnon Greystrom?" he asked. He stared at him with keenness in his eyes. Drake glanced from him to Arnon, but Arnon didn't say anything. The officer laughed under his breath. "I've waited a long time to set my eyes on you. You're not as big as I would've thought."

"You keep your mouth shut!" Porter barked.

The officer remained calm as they continued up the stairs. Upon entering the upper passageway, Arnon stood off to himself, peering back at the dungeon door with a troubled look on his face.

Galvin leaned against the wall, crossing his arms. "I've only got a moment, but I wanted your minds on a few things. We got to think carefully about how to go forward. We not only have the alphyns to deal with, but the city is unstable. And it's any day before Ónarr comes back with an army from Llynhithe."

Drake never quite considered what would happen after the battle, but the political instability kept him up most nights. He wasn't the smartest of men, but he understood well enough that the condition of the city was prime for paving the way for tyrants and corruption. And with the high of the battle wearing off, he wondered what would happen if Daecland did come back in full force. What if they brought wisps?

"Not to mention the remaining Daecish in the mines, Astford, other places," added Quinn. "They probably don't even know we've taken Everwind yet."

"You think alphyns are there?" Porter asked. Standing in front of the only torch, it was hard to make out the features on his face. "Llynhithe, I mean. That whole city could be destroyed for all we know."

"It's possible," Galvin replied. "But we can't rely on it. Not 'til we know for sure."

"We can send a dispatch," Quinn suggested.

"I've already sent one brigadier with a dispatch to Crossroads. I can't afford to send any more out yet. When they get back, we'll consider it."

"Even if Llynhithe's in ruin," said Porter, "I bet a wisp is already on its way to Daecland."

Quinn's eyes widened. "What should we do?"

Galvin studied the stone floors for a while. Drake wasn't convinced that he nor anyone else in there had an answer. "Our main hope is they negotiate," he said at last. "With these alphyns tearing up everything, they may decide they don't even want Everwind anymore."

"Well, that's not very encouraging," Quinn replied.

"I don't care what condition she's in," added Drake. "I'd take a free Everwind over Daecish occupation any day." And he meant it. He'd fight for his country until his dying breath.

"All this talk is making me realize that we need to find a better way to communicate with the people," Porter said. "The whole city's a mess. No food. Most shops are closed down. We got to get 'em all on the same page. That's the only way we can move forward."

"You know what we could do," Drake suggested. "Morgan, Theos keep his spirit, showed me how to operate those printing presses in

City Hall. We could make leaflets to pass 'round the city. Inform the people of the work going on. Shops opening up. Food rations. Things of the like. It'll inform 'em and give a little bit of encouragement to boot."

"That's perfect," Galvin replied. "When can you do it?"

"As soon as you need me. But I can't read." He laughed. "I'll have to bring someone else along."

"I'll go," Quinn offered.

Everyone turned to him.

"When'd you learn to read?" Drake asked.

"Morgan taught me here and there, and," he blushed, "I've been studying on my own a bit."

Drake was impressed. Quinn was always a smart man, but he never took him for one who would commit to learning something so difficult. "We'll leave in the morn', then."

"We'll let Quinn know what to print by tonight," Galvin said. He wiped his nose and looked at Porter. "When you were in the Northern District, did you see any Daecish hiding out?"

Porter pressed his tongue against his cheek. "Maybe one or two. We did see some miners running in, though. Mostly women." He chuckled as he shook his head. "They were spreading a rumor that a man was riding an alphyn around. But some said it was a boy, so who knows? Either one's absurd."

Galvin raised an eyebrow. "Sunder's Bane?" He let out an uneasy laugh. "Sounds like they've either been in the mines too long, or they're taking Hælend's Ballad too literally."

Drake didn't say anything, but his skin crawled. Rumors or not, everything seemed to be falling into place, and he, for one, believed Hælend's Ballad wholeheartedly. Even the Acwellen Chronicles, for that matter. Before they knew it, the sun would go black too.

Galvin leaned off the wall, "All right, men, let's save the rest of this for the meeting on the 'morrow."

"I thought that was today," Quinn said.

"It was, but unfortunately, we've got to wait."

Drake grunted. He had walked halfway across the city for this stupid meeting. "Why?"

"I need the brigadiers present. And they're too busy tending to the people today. Besides," he sighed, looking down the hall. "I got to give a speech here shortly. I promised the people some answers."

Porter gave a cocky smile.

"What is it?" Galvin asked.

"I heard the speech you gave yesterday encouraged the people. Rumors are going 'round that you might be the new king. Be careful, or they may end up liking you."

Galvin as king? Drake respected the man, but the thought made him shudder. And with no heir left to King Albern, such a thing may just be possible in such tumultuous times. He wished Morgan were still alive. He was a good man who would have given wise council.

Drake frowned and turned to Arnon. "Will you help me to the tavern?"

By the time they made it to his place, Drake had lost himself in a sea of doubts. He forced himself to shake it off and to only focus on one day at a time.

"You gonna be okay on your own?" Arnon asked as Drake hobbled to the front door, his right arm around Arnon's shoulder.

"Everyone keeps askin' me that," he grumbled. "I'll be fine."

Arnon pushed the front door open. "You sure you don't want me to stay in the cellar?"

"I've got Bell, you go stay with Sarah. It's better there for you."

"All right, but just make sure you stay off that leg."

Patting Arnon on the back, Drake leaned against his cane and stepped inside. "Thanks for bringing me over. I got it from here."

"If you need anything, just holler." Arnon walked back down the road.

Inside, the tavern was empty, except for one old man who sat at the bar, with Bell wiping out a tankard from behind. Sitting down at a table near the smoldering hearth, Drake propped up his leg. With the tankard still in her hand, Bell walked over and sat across from him, brushing her gray hair from her face.

"Not much use in keeping the fire going," she said. "I ain't served a single meal all day."

With a heavy grunt, Drake leaned back against the hard chair as it stuck into his upper back. "It'll pick up. Once things calm down again in the city."

"You're gonna have to heal if you expect to keep this place going," she insisted.

Drake only crossed his arms.

"And quit walking on it! You just keep it propped up. I'll take care of you in the meantime."

The old man at the bar tipped over the tankard as beer dribbled down his yellowed beard. "It ain't the city that's hurtin' your business." He stood up, and letting out a ghastly cough, he walked across the room to the front door. "All the other taverns got girls. You want business, you gotta have supply to meet demand." He chuckled and walked outside.

Drake's face burned as anger rose up in him.

Bell looked down as if she was embarrassed.

"I don't care if I have to shut this place down," Drake mumbled. "I'll die before I take part in that. Weak men selling their souls for a few seconds of pleasure."

"And at the cost of those poor girls," Bell added. "Half of 'em are starving. The other half just want to feel loved."

"Well," Drake grunted as he rubbed his shoulder, "for the most part, I agree. But a few of 'em are guilty themselves. Seeking to trap men for their own vanity."

Bell's chin trembled for a moment, but she straightened her expression and stood up, walking back to the bar. "This world's such a broken place."

Music for the Soul

By the time Sarah and Adelyne reached Fellhouse Street, the sun was just peeking over the Western wall. With Acton in one arm and Lilly following closely behind, Sarah shielded her eyes as she watched the silhouette of two soldiers hauling up bundles of hay to patch in a shattered shingled roof. She only knew they were soldiers by the olive sashes. Otherwise, they dressed in normal tunics and jerkins like everyone else. At an old tanning shop, to her right, a boy in a woolen gown, apparently not old enough to have been breeched yet, hurried to an older gentleman and handed him a wooden mallet as he held up an oak board against a shattered door frame.

"I'm impressed," she marveled. "The city seems to be alive again."

Adelyne resituated the sack of wool blankets over her other shoulder. "I thought it'd be worse."

Sarah pointed down a side road that ran north. "That's where I grew up," she said. Paige and Chloe still lived in that area, but she hadn't seen them since before Geoffrey left. Granted, they were never very close friends, to begin with, but given the circumstances of the city, she worried for their safety. She glanced at Adelyne, who was watching her feet as they strolled along the street. "Have you heard from any of your friends? Since the battle?"

Adelyne shrugged. "Not really," she half-mumbled.

"Well, let's hope they're okay."

She shrugged again but didn't say anything.

Sarah figured her response was typical for girls her age. Normally she would have just let it go, but she really wanted to connect with her. After their conversation about suffering, she knew there was something wrong. The look on her face was one Sarah had seen on too many girls who had been terribly hurt. And they had both lost their mothers when they were young, so she understood what Adelyne was missing in her life. Maybe she could be there for her in a way that she needed. She took in a deep breath. "He seems like a good man."

Adelyne looked up. "I'm sorry, who?"

If Adelyne weren't looking straight at her, she would have chuckled at how awkward she suddenly felt. Was this what it was going to feel like when she tried to connect with Lilly when she grew to this age? "Arnon," she said.

"Oh," Adelyne replied. "He is."

"He reminds me of Geoffrey when he was young."

"In what way?"

Sarah thought for a second. "I guess it's kind of hard to explain. There's just something about him. He seems honest, strong-spirited, and . . ."

"Clumsy."

Sarah busted out into laughter. "He's clumsy?"

"You have no idea," she said with a grin. "Always stumbles over his feet, his words, his hands. I don't know how he gets anything done."

"Geoffrey wasn't quite like that, but he certainly had some quirks about him."

Sarah was about to say more, but she suddenly realized what she had just said. She'd talked about Geoffrey as if he was only in the past—a memory. Was she actually accepting the reality that he would never come home? An ache filled her heart, but she held it in.

At the crossing at King's Lane, two women, both of whose dresses were tarnished a dark gray, stood at the corner, near a crate full of clucking chickens, with a man sitting beside them. He sat in a heavy slouch, fiddling with his fingers.

"Should we ask them?" Adelyne suggested.

"Sounds like a good place to start," she replied. Although she was excited, a sudden nervous feeling about inviting people she didn't know into her home came over her. Was she sure this was a good idea? As ashamed as she was to even think about it, what if the girls had diseases? Or tried to secretly set up her own house as a brothel? She had her own kids to think about, after all. She rolled her shoulders. No, she was overthinking it.

As they approached, the man looked up. Sarah tried not to stare, but his eyes were further apart than most, giving him a fishy look. "Good morning," she said.

"Hello," said the taller girl. With the sun shining down, her hair looked as red as fire.

"I'm Sarah, and this Adelyne." She hesitated for a moment. "We just happened to notice you out here, and if you, or any girls you know, need a place, we're offering rooms at the House of Good Hope."

The red-haired girl cautiously observed them. "I appreciate the offer," she replied. "But we don't want to have anything to do with houses like that."

Sarah's back straightened. "Oh, no! That's not what we're doing. We're trying to help the girls get out of the streets, out of that business." She glanced up the road to her house. "We're offering rooms. You don't have to pay. We only ask the girls to help out. Gardening, cleaning around the house, or any other skills they may have. We're trying to help the city and give others a new start."

The red-haired girl smiled. "Your offer couldn't have come at a better time. I'm Agatha. This is Langleigh and Egbert. We just got back from a tavern." The lines around her lips tightened. "It was awful."

"Which tavern?" Sarah asked.

"Three Rivers, just that-a-way." She pointed north.

Sarah's chest went heavy. "Bale?" she asked herself. "He wouldn't."

"We could show it to you," Agatha continued. "There's lots of girls there, and they need help."

Sarah took a deep breath, feeling a shiver in her lungs. Geoffrey used to go to that tavern. But as far as she knew, it was a decent place then. "I think that's a good idea. Adelyne, are you okay if we head there first?"

"Of course," she replied.

"And you're all welcome to stay at our place," Sarah said to Agatha and Langleigh.

"Me too?" Egbert asked, picking at his nose.

"Well," Sarah started to say. She wasn't sure how comfortable she felt about taking in a man.

"He's harmless," Agatha insisted. "He and Langleigh both came from Astford. He's got no one." She leaned toward Sarah and spoke in a quiet voice. "He's simple like. He can't take care of himself, if you understand."

"I understand," Sarah replied. She tried to sound as kind as she could. "But this needs to be a safe place for the girls."

"No, you're right." Agatha looked at Egbert. His bottom lip stuck out like a small child's, and he grabbed Agatha's hand, lightly caressing it. "But I told him I'd care for him. Thank you for the offer, but he and myself will have to find a place somewhere else. I'm sure Langleigh would be grateful, though."

Adelyne glanced at Sarah. "What about Arnon?" she whispered.

Sarah sighed. Admittedly, Arnon was staying there, but she wasn't sure how much she liked that either. Not that she didn't trust him, she just thought it would be unwise. But she also hated telling Agatha no. Egbert really did look like he needed someone to care for him, and as far as she knew, there was nowhere in the city for him to go.

"All right, he can stay," she said at last. "I've got a room in the back where another man is lodging. He can stay in there with him."

Agatha smiled. "Thank you. You're very kind."

As they headed north along Old Birchton Way, Sarah glanced at City Hall. Even from the outside, it felt empty and abandoned. The front door stood slightly ajar, and the inside was dark. On their right, they approached Three Rivers, where hazes of smoke seeped through the open windows. The front door swung open, and a man and girl walked out. Dressed in a low-cut creamy dress, muddied at the bottom, her black hair was tied up with a faded blue ribbon. The man, who walked arm-in-arm with the girl, wore a top hat and black coat over a worn brown tunic.

"Adelyne?" the girl hollered from across the street. Adelyne hesitated in her step as the girl ran forward and hugged her.

"Cydney," Adelyne said in a frail voice.

"How long has it been? Two years?"

Sarah and Agatha looked peculiarly at one another.

"Something like that," Adelyne replied. It sounded as if she could barely get the words out.

The man stepped forward. "Who's your friends?" he said, peering at Langleigh.

Adelyne lowered her face. Sarah grew uncomfortable. There was an evil intent in this man's eyes. How did Adelyne know him?

"You remember Fletcher," Cydney asked, "don't you?"

Adelyne only looked up briefly.

"Well, do you want to come inside?" Cydney said in a cheerful tone.

"I don't think—" Adelyne began.

"We're actually here to offer a place for girls who are trying to start a new life," Sarah interrupted. She kept her eyes locked on Fletcher.

"A new life?" Cydney asked.

"From prostitution," she said bluntly.

A gleam appeared in Cydney's eyes but passed as quickly as it came.

"Why?" Fletcher asked. "They've got work and are doing just fine."

"Not all of them want to do that work," Agatha added in a cool tone. "Some only do it because they feel they have to."

Fletcher glanced back to the closed tavern door. "You start taking girls out of there, and you'll be taking business during tough times. Be careful. You may end up making more enemies than you realize." He studied Sarah for a moment. "What's your name?"

Sarah straightened herself. "Sarah Arkwright."

Fletcher rubbed his cheek. "You're the widow of that officer from the Capital Guard, ain't you?"

Sarah didn't respond.

With a nasty grin, Fletcher glanced back to the tavern. "There's quite a few men looking your way. Heard you was the cotenant to the home since you and your husband had no sons. It's an awfully nice house for a girl to lose to the crown, especially at your age. If you don't remarry soon, you just might find yourself in the brothel too."

Feeling her temperature rise, Sarah clenched her fists. "We have one son, and he is the heir." But even as she said those words, she feared the worst. She knew she couldn't keep up the cost of the home long enough for Acton to inherit it. Even if she did remarry, which she didn't have the heart to even think about yet, the turmoil in Everwind made any sense of security vanish.

Fletcher laughed under his breath. He looked at Egbert, who was looking down with his chin on his neck, fiddling with something beneath his torn shirt. "Let's go, Cydney." He gave one last glance to Adelyne before they walked away. "I'd just be careful trying to take away good business if I was you . . ." His voice trailed off.

"I don't care what he says," spoke up Sarah, trying to keep her voice calm. She shook off her cold, trembling hands. "If the girls want to leave, we'll help them."

"He's right, though," Agatha added. "It'll be dangerous."

"We must still try."

"But they'd never let us just go in."

Sarah let out a sigh of frustration.

"There's a back entrance," Langleigh spoke up. Everyone faced her, surprised at the sound of her voice—thin but sweet. "We could try to meet the girls in secret when they go out."

"That could work," Agatha replied. "But there's too many of us. Why don't I come back at night? I know several of the girls there."

"We could also try somewhere else," added Adelyne in a sullen tone. Her face looked pale.

Sarah looked gently at her for a moment. She wondered whether or not Fletcher had something to do with whatever was haunting her. "I think we should try to do whatever we can. Agatha, if you're willing, perhaps you can come by tonight and at least let the girls know that we are offering them a place. Adelyne and I can go to the Southern Squalor on the 'morrow."

"Of course," she replied.

* * *

That evening, Adelyne sat on the bottom steps inside the hall as Agatha and Langleigh prepared beds in the fireplace room to the right. In the kitchen, Sarah was preparing food, but as good as it smelled, it made her feel queasy. She should probably help, but she thought she might throw up if she moved. Why did Fletcher have to be there? Her arms and back occasionally trembled. If she didn't talk to Arnon, the guilt would kill her. Why did she care for him this way so much? Arnon probably just wanted to sleep with her like all the others anyway.

She shook her head. She knew he wasn't the same. She had to tell him. But how much should she share? Should she talk about her father? Maybe he'd pity her if she did. If she could just get it off her chest, maybe Arnon would love her as she was, and then she could start over. Have a whole new life.

Hearing the voice of Arnon outside, she wiped her eyes and hurried into the kitchen just as Sarah was pulling a loaf of bread from the oven. She sat at the table by the window and heard the front door open. Breaking into a cold sweat, her whole body shivered. He walked into the kitchen and smiled at her.

"How'd it go today?" he asked, sitting at the table.

Forcing a smile, she wasn't sure how to answer. Did it go well? Not really.

Sarah wiped her hands on her apron and sat at the table across from them. "It could've gone better."

"I noticed some girls are here," Arnon added. "That's good, isn't it?"

"It is," Sarah replied. "But it's going to be more difficult than we thought. We went to this tavern, and well . . ."

Adelyne tensed. She wasn't going to tell Arnon about Fletcher, was she?

"It's just a dark place," Sarah continued. "I fear some of the girls will want to leave but are too scared to."

"That's terrible." Arnon narrowed his eyes.

"What makes it worse," Sarah went on, "was that this tavern wasn't always like this. Bale, the owner, he's been a good man for as long as we've known him."

"What do you think happened?"

Sarah bit the side of her lip. "I don't know, but it's not just him. A lot of people have changed for the worse lately."

"I know what you mean," Arnon replied, sinking into his chair. "Sometimes you think you know someone, then one day, they're just different."

A lump rose in Adelyne's throat. It was as if he spoke straight to her.

"I think some people do the right thing only because they feel like they have to," Sarah said. "Because of the law or because it benefits them in some way. But as soon as things change, as soon as they feel like they can get away with it, their true character comes out. I'd never thought Bale would be like this, but apparently, he is."

Arnon smiled. "I can tell you're Geoffrey's wife."

She laughed. "I guess you end up sounding like the people you spend all your time with. Did you know him?"

"I only met him once, just before my first meeting at Drake's place. We sat outside in the rain and talked for a bit. But I remember something he said that stuck with me." He stared at the table, slowly rubbing his finger against the grain. "I can't remember exactly how he worded it, but he said that the most selfish thing someone can do is to live their life without concern to the kind of world their children will grow up in. And he told me that he didn't want to be that kind of man."

A tear ran down Sarah's cheek.

"I'm sorry," he said, looking at her. "I didn't mean to upset you."

"No." She wiped her eye with her apron. "Thank you. I needed to hear that." She stood up. "If you'll just excuse me for a moment." And she walked out of the kitchen.

"I probably shouldn't have said anything," Arnon admitted.

"I wouldn't worry," Adelyne replied. "I think you reminded her of what a good man he is."

Arnon didn't respond as he rubbed his forehead. "Was it hard going out there?"

"A little." Her head felt hot, and she thought she might pass out. She tried to say something, but she couldn't even begin to speak. At last, she took in a trembling breath. "Can I ask you something?"

"Sure."

"In the cellar, when we got that letter, you looked angry at me. Why?"

Arnon didn't answer at first as he gazed aimlessly in thought. "That day," he said at last, "I was told to find you and bring you back to the cellar." He paused, and his face went solemn. "I saw you down the road talking to this guy in a top hat."

Adelyne's heart sank. She knew it.

"When he, um . . ." Arnon fidgeted in his seat. "When he touched you the way he did, and you smiled back . . . I don't know. I just got upset."

Adelyne tightened her throat. She felt filthy and wanted to hide in a hole. In truth, she didn't know why she smiled at Fletcher. It was the first time she had seen him in a year, and although she despised the way he touched her, there was a part of her that was drawn to him and the way he treated her. It was as if she was attracted to the very thing she knew would ruin her. Her eyes blurred, and her jaw trembled. "I'm sorry," she said.

Arnon stood up and walked around the table, sitting next to her. She almost couldn't believe that he wrapped his arm around her and held her close. He didn't say anything, but a sense of relief fell over her. But she knew it would pass. He didn't know the whole truth. He didn't know who she really was. But as much as she wanted to, she couldn't bring herself to say anything else. She only closed her eyes and laid her head against his shoulder. Before long, the sound of Langleigh singing flowed from the room across the hall. Although Adelyne couldn't make out the words, the tune felt sad but beautiful, and it eased her mind.

"Music is so strange," Arnon said quietly. "We don't need it to survive, but yet we all yearn for it. It's almost like it taps into something deep inside of us. A longing for something. Like a dream that you want to go back to, but you can't quite remember."

Adelyne knew exactly what he meant. Whenever her mother sang to her, she felt as if it opened a new world. One she could only glimpse but never fully explore.

"Maybe music points to something greater," Arnon continued. "Something beyond ourselves."

Adelyne glanced up at him. Her life was a wreck, and she didn't know how long she could take it, but at that moment, there was nowhere else she would have rather been. She loved the way his mind worked and every word he spoke.

She loved *him*.

In the Court of King Eirik

Gunnar tried to keep his eyelids open as he sniffed his sour uniform. When was the last time he slept? Before him, Eirik sat in silence as he read through the papers. The office was just one reminder of how different Daecland was from Sunder. Three of the walls were painted a smoky-green, lined with white trim, and decorated with large paintings, except for the right wall, where a shallow fireplace burned. On the back wall ran wood paneling around two large windows, looking out from Norfrost Castle. Between the two windows sat a small desk, with three leather chairs, currently occupied by Thialfi, Houder, and himself, all facing toward Eirik. To the right of the king stood Commander Asger, dressed in full uniform, tailored and pressed to perfection.

Keeping a calm posture, Eirik kept his eyes on the paper. He had a wide, but strong clean-shaven face, with a large mole above his right eyebrow.

"I trust you slept well last night, Commander Veurðr?" Eirik asked.

Slept? He's been traveling since the day he left Everwind. And with all of those creatures roaming around Sunder, he barely thought he would make it alive to Runevast. His only hope was that he could see his wife and newborn by the end of the day. He was so close. Glancing out the window to his left, he thought he could even make out the roof of his house on the second level. "I have, Your Majesty."

"Commander Asger." Eirik looked up. "Are these numbers up to date?"

"Yes, Your Majesty." Asger rubbed his finger and thumb through his golden mustache. Gunnar was always jealous of men who had thicker mustaches than his. "But I fear we cannot take any action until our military has effectively put these creatures under control."

"How is that proceeding?" the king asked.

"We've contained Norfrost and Scathwold. Vagholme and Folkbjörn have been hit the hardest, but they are being contained as we speak."

"How bad are they?" Houdr whispered to Thialfi as he wiped a smudge off his spectacles.

Thialfi sighed through his nose. It was always hard for Gunner to remember that the chancellor was younger than himself. He was so put together and confident. "Our labs have dissected some of the carcasses. They think they're a migratory species."

"And Fingate?" Eirik asked.

"Not as many have appeared there," Asger continued. "And we are confident it'll be secured within a few days."

Dropping the papers, Eirik interlocked his fingers and looked at Gunnar. "Two days ago, a dispatch was sent to inform me that Denhurst was taken and an army has marched on Everwind. A day later, you arrive and tell me Everwind is taken, that these creatures are also roaming the lands of Sunder, and Ónarr is hiding in a hole in Llynhithe." He released a sour chuckle. "I should've put my little niece in charge of Sunder."

The king's expression was so calm, Gunnar almost believed he meant it.

"Commander, Asger," Eirik asked, "what if I told you I needed four fleets to be ready within two weeks? Could you make that happen?"

"Your Majesty," spoke up Thialfi, propping both elbows on the arms of the leather chair. He clasped his hands together. "If I may."

"Go ahead," Eirik replied.

"I understand that in our meeting this morning, it was suggested that we should take back Everwind as soon as possible. However, in our current state, can we really afford to send one-hundred and forty wisps across the mountains? Our economic condition is not optimal for such an invasion."

"Asger?" Eirik asked. "Do you comply?"

"Economically speaking," he replied, "I cannot give an answer. But from a militaristic perspective, we cannot afford to send that many. On top of dealing with these creatures, our northern fleet is not scheduled to return from Varghoss until the end of the year."

"Are we at war with Varghoss?" Gunnar asked, raising himself up.

"No, no," Thialfi replied. "We're just maintaining peaceful relations."

Gunnar relaxed his tense shoulders. For a second, he thought he'd be deployed again.

Hodur raised an eyebrow as he stared at Gunnar like a worried therapist.

Realizing he was too tired to think straight, Gunnar thought it best not to ask any more questions.

"Then what do you suggest?" Eirik asked Asger, who stroked his fingers once again through that thick, straight mustache. He must put oil in it.

"Four fleets would certainly quell any more rebellions, but for the sake of just taking Everwind and Denhurst, I believe one fleet is more than enough. If, of course, we first sail for Llynhithe, then we can take advantage of the fleet there as well."

"We may have the military strength," Thialfi said. "But invasions cost money."

"I understand," Eirik replied, "but if we don't take Sunder back, Varghoss might. Or worse, Kalestrond. And if we are ever to open trade with Earlon, maintaining a presence in Sunder is of vital importance."

Thialfi sank back in his chair as if defeated. "It must be approved by the General Assembly first."

"Then you best get started. You are dismissed."

Standing straight, Thialfi did well to hide his frustration, and he bowed like a true gentleman before he left the room.

"Tell me, Commander Veurðr, what is the condition of—" He paused, looking at his paper. "Commander Tyr?"

"He is being held as a prisoner of war in Everwind, as far as I know."

He raised his eyebrows. "Then who is acting commander under Ónarr?"

"Commander Halvard," your Majesty.

"Who on earth is that?"

"A Second Commander, Your Majesty."

He covered his face with his hands. "Does Ónarr understand nothing?" He let out an exaggerated grunt. "Gentlemen, this is what we'll do. I fear word of this will spread quickly, and we must regain our hold on Sunder as soon as we can. I want a fleet sent to Llynhithe in two weeks. Commander Veurðr, I now promote you to First Commander. You are to leave tonight for Llynhithe and take over as acting Commander-in-Chief in Sunder. Prepare the fleet as quickly as you can. You will have a stowage wisp following, with gunpowder and a legion's worth of wheellocks and muskets for issuing. Commander Asger will write up your orders, be sure to give them to Ónarr."

Gunnar did everything he could to keep a straight face. Most men never made it to First Commander, and as badly as he wanted it, he would have rather tended his garden. "Thank you, Your Majesty."

* * *

Eirún held her breath as she gazed at the distant landscape through the glass window. She had never been this high before, and the view made her lightheaded. Staring down at the world below, she thought of Søren. Still too young to understand the rules of the orphanage, he had once walked downstairs in the middle of the night. His hand barely reached the banister. She had just finished cleaning the kitchen when she walked into the dining hall and saw him from behind. Holding his hands together, he quietly called for her through the closed door, which led to the maid's quarters. She could still hear his voice.

"Eirún?" he whispered.

"Søren?" she asked, walking toward him.

He startled and turned around.

She picked him up in her arms. He was still so small. "What's wrong?"

"It's cold," he whimpered. "Can I sleep with you?"

Eirún almost chuckled. "It's not cold. If anything, the furnace keeps it too hot up there."

He fiddled with a small pendant pinned to the front of her dress. "Can I sleep with you anyway?"

Carrying him up the stairs, she kissed him on the forehead. "I wish I could, but you know it's not allowed."

The wisp lurched, and Eirún blinked. She'd give anything to take that moment back and let him stay with her. She'd even give her own life if she could just have the chance to tell him she was sorry. Sorry for yelling at him. Sorry that she wasn't able to save him.

Below, the world chugged by. It looked so small and reminded her she was leaving yet another person behind now, too. The last time she saw Geirleif was when they boarded. She hoped he was okay. And poor Sylvi. She never even got a chance to say goodbye. Part of Eirún felt bad for her disability, but really, she envied her. Sylvi had wonderful people who took care of her, and she didn't have a single care in this world. Eirún would have loved to be ignorantly happy like that.

"Incredible welding," Hrunting half mumbled while he ran his hand along the brass trim in the overhead. "How on earth did the machinists get the seams so perfect?"

The quartermaster, who stood behind him, seemed too busy reading over his log to hear the question.

The previous day Hrunting took the time to teach her all the terms and parts of the wisp and how they differed from sailing ships. She nodded and tried to smile, but most of it went over her head. Along both sides of the wooden hull, lined in riveted steel, were mounted several round thick-paned windows. On the port side ran a long leather bench. A rumbling engine piped and steamed on the starboard side. Paired with the humming of the propellers, Eirún wasn't sure how anyone could get used to the constant sound, much less sleep at night.

"This is a significant improvement from the earlier models." Hrunting knocked his hand against the window. The bottom of the sleeves to his white shirts barely peeked out of the gray tailored jacket, matching his pants. He always seemed to dress sharp. "How high can she go?"

The quartermaster looked up from his log, stroking his thick beard. His clear eyes and smooth skin made him look too young for such thick facial hair. "We still can't peak the Mountains of Einarr, but she'll go a good thousand feet higher than the previous models."

"And the steam?"

"We're still tweaking it. The older models—" He paused as the wisp jolted.

Eirún held on to the bulkhead as her heart lurched, but Hrunting laughed. "Just turbulence, darling." He let out a confident grin.

"Precisely right," the quartermaster added. "Nothing to fear. As I was saying, there is more to operate on the newer models as well."

"Very interesting," Hrunting replied. He walked over to a window and peered out. "How long until we arrive in Fingate?"

"By tonight." He flipped through a few pages. "It'll be another two days until we arrive in the Dilution Sites."

"Two days?" Hrunting turned.

"These animals," the quartermaster replied, "they've put us a bit behind schedule. But we'll make it work. Lord Beron stated that you are to acquire documentation in . . .," he flipped to another page, "Section Three?"

"Of the hydro-voltaic dam. Strictly for engineering purposes."

"Shouldn't be a problem." The quartermaster turned and walked back to the cockpit situated at the bow of the ship. Or maybe it was called the forecastle. Eirún couldn't remember.

Hrunting stepped over to her. "Everything is going just as well as we could have hoped. How you are feeling?"

"Better," she replied.

And that was the truth. Although she still couldn't shake the feeling of uselessness over the fact that everyone kept doing things for her, she had been able to put her cooking skills to use in the galley since they had been on the wisp. The familiar work sparked a new hope in her heart, and the cloud over her head began to thin. Maybe she really could start a new life in Sunder. Maybe she would find an orphanage she could work at.

Hrunting motioned for her to join him in the sleeping quarters in the aft of the ship. Stepping through the hatch, the room was compact but appeared well made. A single bed sat in the center and on the floor to the right; Hrunting had laid down a couple of blankets and a pillow for himself. She admired him for his integrity. For their entire trip, he had only been a gentleman to her. He walked over to a table and grabbed a map, and patted the bed as she sat next to him.

"Once we arrive in Runevast," he said in almost a whisper. "I think we should make for Everwind."

"But Astford looks closer."

"You're right, but Everwind is the capital. I imagine there will be more opportunities there."

Her guess was as good as his. "Everwind it is then."

He smiled and folded up the map. "So, tell me about yourself, Eirún. Tell me about your childhood."

"I grew up in the country," she said. "On a small farm in Fjellgard."

"Fjellgard?" Hrunting asked.

"It's too small of a town to be on the maps." She smiled. "I had a horse named Argo." She had nearly forgotten that she used to ride him every day. "My father traveled a lot, so I didn't get to see him much, but when he was home, he always brought me back gifts and spent nearly all his time with me."

That memory was always a double-edged sword for her. On the one hand, she cherished her father, but on the other, she knew the reason he spent more time with her was because of his past affair. Though her mother never left him, she had locked her heart from him. They always tried to keep it a secret from Eirún, but children always find these things out. For a second, Eirún wondered if that's why she never married. She never thought she could trust a man.

"He sounds like a good father," Hrunting said. "What work did he do?"

"He was a merchant and would follow the fairs around the cities. He even went to Varghoss once."

"Really?" He set his hand on his cheek.

Eirún blushed. Hrunting seemed genuinely intrigued.

"Did he bring you anything back?"

"From all of his trips, he would." She thought about the lens for a moment but quickly blocked it from her mind.

"What about from Varghoss?"

"Just a silly idol. I think it was of the moon goddess, but I lost it long ago."

"They've got over three hundred of them, you know."

"Three-hundred?"

"Gods," he said. "Of course, they've added more over the centuries."

Eirún never knew they had that many. Daecland had no official religion, and the cultures of other countries had very little influence, except for maybe a few towns on the western border. Her parents didn't believe in the gods of Varghoss, and nearly everyone she knew didn't either. Except for maybe Adis. But she would pray to anything if she thought it would help.

Hrunting's expression grew more serious as he leaned forward on the bed, resting his elbows on his knees. "You ever wonder if there's more to life than just," he motioned his hands around the room, "all of this?"

Eirún didn't really know what he meant. "Do you mean if there are gods?" She slightly laughed.

"Not quite. The gods of Varghoss are just manmade tales that reflect our own lust for violence and whatever else we crave." He snickered. "Don't get me wrong, the Varghossian myths are a good read, but not what I'm talking about. I mean something . . . something more real; something bigger than us, with a bit more mystery."

Eirún frowned. It was a subject she never liked to think about.

Hrunting fiddled with the clasp holding the end of the white sleeve of his shirt together. "When you've spent your whole life in Norfrost, you begin to notice people. Some are just surviving. Working day and night so they can feed their families. They go to bed, they wake up, they do it all over again. Other people are more prosperous. They work, and they make plenty of money. But what do they do with it? They buy more stuff. More clothes. Bigger houses. But really, we're all the same. Whether we're poor or rich, we're just existing from one day to the next until we die. Then what's left? Stuff? Memories?"

Eirún thought it was an interesting thought, but she wasn't sure she agreed. "Do you think that's really all life has to offer?" she asked. "Stuff and memories?"

Hrunting put his chin on his hand and twisted his lips in thought, "Perhaps not. I have always wanted children. Maybe a son."

Despite his comment reminding her of Søren, she began to grow fond of him. Certainly, it wasn't just because he was handsome. He had ideals. Or maybe it was virtue. Whatever it was, she enjoyed spending time with him.

"Anyway," Hrunting said. "If I don't stop now, I'll go on for hours." He stood up. "I'm going below to the mess decks. Would you like me to bring you some lunch?"

She was terribly hungry. "How about I go with you?" she asked.

He reached out his hand and helped her to her feet. "I'll always accept good company," he said with a smile.

The Future of Everwind

Drake stood at the entrance of City Hall, peering into the darkness of the partly cracked door as Quinn stepped up from behind with a lantern in his hand.

"You sure no one's in there?" Quinn asked.

"Aye," Drake replied. "'Course I can't know for sure, but it don't look like anyone's been in here for a long time." He pushed open the door.

His dropped jaw as his eyes drifted from the white marble floor to the tall red curtains rising thick to the arched wooden ceiling, masked in shadow. Even with the scattered papers and boxes along the winding staircase, it was the grandest room he had ever stepped in.

"You ever seen anything like it?" he asked.

Quinn shook his head. "It's beautiful. Looks like we ain't the first ones in here, though."

"I imagine rioters have come in and taken their share of things. Let's just hope the printing press is still intact."

"Where's it at?" Quinn asked.

"The basement. But I can't figure how to get there."

"I thought you've been here before?"

Drake turned to him with a smirk. Quinn's eyebrows were so thick they almost ran together. "We didn't walk through City Hall, you dolt. We crawled through the basement window in the back."

"Can't we take the same way?"

"We could, but I wanted to check this place out first. And I reckon there's an easier way than crawling through a window."

Stepping into a large room to the left, Drake felt his boot sink into the softness of the floral carpet. Like the rest of City Hall, the walls were dark blue and wrapped in white Daecish wainscoting. This room looked cozier than the one to the right of the entry hall. Instead of desks and chairs, it had a large fireplace, many rugs, and large leather seats and couches. He walked over to one couch with a curved back, covered in dark green silk, and sat down with a long sigh.

Quinn stood over him awkwardly.

"By Theos, if this ain't the softest thing I ever sat in." He patted the cushion. "Have a seat."

"I'm okay," Quinn replied. "The quicker we're outta here, the better."

Drake looked at the other couches. "I wonder if I can't get some of these in my tavern?"

Quinn laughed. "Let's get these leaflets made, then we can worry about that."

"You go on ahead. I don't think I can get up."

"I ain't leaving you up here alone." Quinn crossed his arms and puffed out his chest. Being shorter than most women, he was everything but intimidating. But Drake was glad to have him around. They had known each other since they were boys, and despite being younger than Drake, he always took the role of an older brother. Always trying to look after him. Drake wouldn't trade their friendship for anything. With a loud grunt, he reluctantly stood back up with Quinn's help. "If you insist." He leaned on his cane and pointed across the room to a dark hall. "I bet we'll find our door to the basement there."

Along the hall, several of the doors were locked. Others led to offices and storage rooms. But when he opened the door on the end of the hall, he smiled, seeing that it led to a set of stairs. However, an awful smell, like rotting meat, soon crept into his nostrils, and Drake began to worry about what he might find. He took Quinn's lantern and led the way.

Stepping onto the dirt floor, humidity seeped from the stone walls and clung to Drake's skin. The smell only grew stronger. Although Drake didn't say anything, he knew it wasn't an animal. He'd smelled rotting human corpses before, and there was no mistaking it. He could only hope it was a Daecish soldier.

When they entered a large, dark room with iron bars to the right, Drake could tell this part of City Hall was older than the Daecish, but for the life of him, he couldn't recall what stood here before they built over it.

Stepping over to the iron bars, he raised his lantern and squinted. "Must be a jail." He walked along the cell, which stretched to the other side of the room, as Quinn followed from behind. Drake paused as he caught sight of the outline of a body curled up in the corner. "Well, that's what the smell's coming from."

Quinn covered his nose and coughed.

Drake examined the room and found a set of skeleton keys on the wall. It took a few tries, but he found the right one, and the cell door screeched open. They stepped inside and walked to the body. A sickening feeling sank in Drake's stomach.

"Is that?" Quinn asked.

"Wesley," Drake said.

Some sort of liquid seeped from more parts of Wesley's swollen and yellowed body than Drake cared to think about. He wasn't even sure how they recognized him.

Quinn took a step back and turned, letting out another heavy cough. "Terrible fate," he said afterward. "What did they do, just leave him here to die?"

"Who knows. But I ain't gonna move him. He'll bust all over the place."

"I guess he got caught then? That's why we couldn't find him."

Drake had an itching suspicion that there was more to Wesley than either of them knew, but he didn't see the point in mentioning it. "He was a good man. Gave his life for the Silent Hither."

"Too bad he never got to see our victory," Quinn said. "You think we'll ever find Murdock?"

"At this point, he's likely done dead and gone. Must've been eaten by an alphyn or something. But come on," Drake walked out of the cell, "Let's find that printing press. We got to be back in time for the council."

* * *

Nearly two dozen men sat around the large wooden table with torches lining the bare stone walls. Iron rods, mounted near the ceiling, were all that was left of the Daecish tapestries, which had been torn down. The council chamber felt damp and smelled sour, and Arnon tried to keep his eyes open. That Egbert guy had slept in his room that night and snored so loud, he didn't sleep at all. And he was odd.

Across from him sat Porter, and to his right sat Quinn, who they just promoted to Ensign. Arnon glanced over toward Drake, leaning on his cane in the corner. Although Drake held a proud look on his face, he knew he felt rejected. All the chairs around the table were filled, but when he offered Drake his own seat, Galvin insisted that only military personnel be at the table. Apparently, it didn't matter that Drake was a Dark Horse. If that was even a thing anymore.

Arnon looked down at his new burgundy uniform with near reluctance. Other than what his father had taught him, he never had a moment of official military training, and the title of Commander felt more honorary than actual.

"Brigadiers," Galvin began, sitting at the head. He motioned to Drake. "Drake and Quinn have brought the leaflets. We're grateful for their hard work, and we're confident it'll help unify the people."

Arnon couldn't help but smile. He respected Galvin for being so positive in that statement. Although he couldn't read it himself, Arnon had heard that the leaflets were so badly misspelled the few people who could actually read in Everwind wouldn't even understand it. Poor Quinn. He was so proud of his work, too.

Galvin motioned to a brigadier at the other end of the table. He had long, light-colored hair, bald on the top, with a thin goatee. "Brigadier Abney has been leading the efforts in rebuilding the city. Do you care to update?"

Abney straightened himself, but his dark eyes looked weary. "Our men have been hard at work and, thanks be to Theos, nearly twenty shops have reopened their doors."

Several of the men nodded approvingly.

Arnon couldn't help but notice that most of the men in the chamber were from Denhurst. Why wasn't a native of Everwind put in charge of rebuilding the city?

"However," Abney continued, "winter is hard upon us, and our food stores are running low. Some have been slaughtering more livestock than needed for the meat—others are doing so because their cattle are starving anyway."

"That can't happen," Galvin stated. "We'll set up a fine for anyone slaughtering more than the limit. What about our grain reserves?"

"We've managed to store enough to sustain a hundred or so families for a few weeks."

Galvin looked at Drake. "What about the Merchant's Guild? Didn't they once pay duties to the House of Burgess? Could we not reinforce their dues and bring some temporary relief to the people?"

Drake cackled. "What Merchant's Guild? What the Daecish didn't draft, the rest were ruined by the economy."

Galvin huffed and tapped a finger on the table as he thought.

Arnon remembered his father's animal traps, piled up outside of his old family home. Maybe he should go set those and catch what he could. It wouldn't be much, but it could help.

"We've gained some rations from the bastard bonds," another brigadier said with a chuckle.

Galvin rolled his eyes. "Don't know if that's a good thing or not."

"Bastard bonds?" Arnon asked.

"Penalty to a man who gets prostitutes pregnant," Galvin answered. "We first thought we'd make 'em pay the mother so she could support the child, but we feared that may only increase the prostitution. So, instead, we make the men pay the city."

Arnon wasn't sure what to think about that. Penalizing the men was good, but some of the women were in the streets because they were literally starving.

"Our biggest concern," Abney continued, "are the alphyns and possible invasion of the Daecish."

Galvin clasped his hands together. "Brigadier Bardsley, how are our troops coming forth?"

"As expected," Bardsley replied. He had so few teeth Arnon could count them all with one hand. "Nearly four-hundred have joined the Army and are already being trained. The battlements, parapets, and gates should be fully armed and ready by the end of the week."

"Good," Galvin replied. "When Redfield returns from the Crossroads, we'll send a band to Denhurst, seek reinforcements, and re-establish trade." He looked at Abney. "And the alphyns?"

"Yes, sire. Many fear the alphyns, of course, but it's really the end they get sore over. Hælend's Ballad is being sung openly in the Southern District, as well as the Eastern. People are reacting in different ways."

"Some better than others," added another brigadier. He hacked something from his lungs into his arm and spit on the ground. "Just this morning, two footmen reported a murder-suicide in Birchton.

Apparently, a man stood in the middle of the street and shouted something about Sunder's Bane. Then he took a sword and slaughtered his wife and his own two youngsters. Afterward, he threw himself on his own blade."

"Murdering their own kin in the name of Theos," Galvin said, rubbing his head. "We need to get this under control."

Arnon's stomach churned. Sunder's Bane was meant to be the embodiment of innocence, taking vengeance against all evil. What this man did was a twisting mockery of that.

"What of Albern?" spoke up Porter. "The people still demand his beheading."

"I ain't decided yet," Galvin replied. "Let's see if the crowds pacify. I don't want the end of the House of Burgess on my hands just yet."

Arnon hoped Galvin had more of a reason for not beheading Albern than that. To kill a king, whether he was mad or not, was an offense of the worst kind.

Galvin propped his elbows on the table. "We need to move on to internal matters. . ." When he went on to explain how the council decided that all brigadiers were now the new official Free Sunderian Council, Arnon began to grow disillusioned. He had wanted to be a Dark Horse all of his life. Now, this council had done away with the Silent Hither and everything that went with it. It made sense now that they had taken Denhurst and Everwind, but his father had been preparing him his whole life for something that was now gone. Was this all really happening?

And would Galvin really consider killing the king? That, paired with the bodies in Denhurst and even the prisoners in the dungeon only added to his troubling conscience. But the more he thought about it, the more he knew he wasn't really any different. He'd done evil things, too. He wished his father was there. He'd know what to do.

When the council meeting had ended, Arnon stepped into the hall, and Drake placed a hand on his shoulder. "I got something I need to tell you. I wanted to bring it up in the council, but I thought it best we tell those who knew him first." He let out a sigh. "Wesley's body's been found. He didn't make it."

Arnon leaned against the wall. It would have been more of a shock to him, but he hadn't seen Wesley since he first got back. "Where was he found?"

From around the corner, Porter walked toward them carrying his war hammer.

"Grab your sword. A dispatch just requested soldiers in the Northern District. Apparently, some folk are causing a ruckus." He continued past them and disappeared through the door leading into the main hall.

Arnon turned to Drake.

"You go on, boy. We can talk about it later."

"You're not gonna go?"

"Nah, I'm headed for the tavern. My fighting days are over."

Arnon kept beside Quinn as they marched north along Merchant's Street behind the rest of the soldiers and brigadiers. Most of what remained of the gate were splinters and the leftovers of twisted iron bars.

"So, what is this Free Sunderian Council supposed to do anyway?" Arnon asked, trying to keep his breath.

Quinn blew warm air into his hands. "Govern the city, I guess. One feller said he thinks they'll vote on the next king, which will probably be Galvin."

"So that's the end of the House of Burgess, then?"

"I guess so."

"What do you think about it?"

Quinn scratched the back of his head. "I'm not a politician. I'm a farmer. I got no opinion on it. Besides, I figure once all this cools down, I'll ease my way out and go back to farming before too long. Get a place in the Western District if I can help it."

By the time they made it well into the Northern District, the soldiers in front came to a sudden stop. Standing on the southern end of the center courtyard were several women shouting out, with a group of men surrounding a Daecish looking building. Arnon hurried to the front where Porter stood.

"What's going on?" he asked.

Porter said nothing as several men in civilian dress dragged out four Daecish men from the front entrance. Tripping over the snow-laden ground, the Daecish staggered to their feet as the men gripped them by their shirt collars. Three were in their underclothing—white shirts with woolen trousers—but one was in full officer's attire.

"That's what's going on," Porter said, pointing forward. "Folks in the area must have found Daecish patients hiding out somewhere in the infirmary."

A dozen soldiers ran ahead and intervened between the men and the Daecish, forcing them to back away. A group of mostly women and a few men standing along the sidewalk cried out and cursed. One woman picked up a handful of stones and hurled them at the Daecish.

"Back off!" shouted a brigadier, shielding the flying rocks with his arm. He pulled the single officer in his grip away from the scene.

"I hope they all burn!" she shouted from a larger group on the other side of the courtyard.

Another woman screamed out and charged toward the Daecish officer. Her arms were stretched out in front of her with her fingers locked forward like claws as she knocked over the soldier and pummeled the Daecish officer. By the time the other soldiers ran over, her nails and teeth were already sinking into the face. He let out a scream, and it took three men to pull her off. "I hope you rot!" She burst out into a wail as she was dragged away from the officer. "You ruined me!" she cried. "You ruined me!"

"Nasty whores," Porter sneered. "Give themselves to men then blame 'em for their woes. She probably got herself pregnant."

Arnon looked at Porter as he remained gazing ahead. At that moment, there wasn't a single bone in his body that respected him.

"Don't let that wench go anywhere," Porter said to a brigadier, who had gray eyes and a large nose. "I want to know why she acted out like that. And question the witnesses. There might be more Daecish hiding." He walked off toward Galvin.

Arnon was left standing by himself, but he was glad to be away from Porter. Hesitantly, he walked toward the Daecish and caught a glimpse of the officer's mangled face. Deep gashes lined his cheeks and nose. One eye was covered with so much blood he wasn't sure if there was anything left. He glanced to the brigadier, who walked toward the girl, still being held by two soldiers. He knelt in front of her.

Making sure this brigadier didn't talk to her the way Porter would have, Arnon walked forward and squatted beside him.

"Madam," the brigadier said. She was sniffing in her sobs as tears and blood soaked her cheeks. Her light-brown hair smeared across her face. Her dress was gray and ragged. The brigadier brushed her hair aside. "I'm Brigadier Langston." He motioned to Arnon. "And this is Commander Greystrom. We're here to help you."

Arnon had never met him personally, but he already liked him. And in a quirky kind of way, his nose made him think of Fleta.

Langston glanced to the Daecish officer, about five yards to their left, now bound in chain. "I don't like the Daecish anymore than you do, but what you got against that man?"

"He—" She tried to control herself. "He's a terrible man! He's done harm to more girls than anyone's got a right!" She whimpered as she closed her eyes with more tears pouring out.

"Where did he do this?" Arnon asked.

"In the mines over yonder." She spluttered. "We was all there."

Langston stood up and walked over to another brigadier, standing in front of the Daecish officer. Arnon waited for a moment. He wanted to say something to comfort her, but he didn't know what. He wished

Sarah or Adelyne were there. They would know what to say. The girl kept her eyes closed, and he eventually walked over to Langston.

"What did you say his name was?" Langston asked the other brigadier.

"Algöter, or something like that. Not sure I'm pronouncing it right, though. Apparently, he was in charge of one of the mines."

"And took advantage of the workers, no doubt," Langston added.

Porter and Galvin stepped up to them, with Quinn following behind. "What did you get out of her?" Galvin asked Langston.

"I don't think she's a prostitute. She worked in the mines where this officer was stationed."

Porter rubbed his white-bearded chin. "I don't know about her, but the others admitted to whoring." He looked across the crowds to the girls, then back to the Daecish officer. "We'll throw the two younger pale-faces in the dungeon. But that's all we got room for." He pointed north to a set of gallows built near the northern wall. "We'll execute the third along with this feller. He's done enough wrongs for ten men."

"And the whores?" Porter asked.

"Bastard bonds ain't enough. We need 'em off the streets. There's some cells over in the old Daecish Military Quarters. We can lock 'em up there for now."

Porter picked something out of his teeth. "We ought'a shave the heads of the ones that gave their bodies to Daecish swine. It'll serve 'em right."

Arnon was dumbfounded. "Galvin," he could barely get the rest of the words out, "some of these girls are victims. Shouldn't we try to help them?"

"And we will. They'll serve their time, then we'll let 'em go. Don't look so surprised. It ain't a new law. For centuries prostitution's been punished. Besides, letting them sleep around while popping out bastard kids onto the streets is only going to make things worse."

573

Porter laughed.

"I understand that for some of the girls, it's a choice," Arnon tried to persuade, "but I really think some don't feel like they have one. Sarah's got a place, the House of Good Hope. She's helping girls get back on their feet. Can't we take them there?"

"I heard about the little house y'all got," Porter butted in. "All you're doing is fueling the problem. Those girls need to be punished."

Arnon didn't know what to say. He peered hard at Porter but only walked away. He tried to see from Galvin's perspective, but he couldn't understand it.

Quinn hurried up behind him. "You doing okay?" he asked. "You looked pretty red in the face back there."

"I'm fine," Arnon replied.

"I probably shouldn't tell you this, but it don't help my conscious none that some of the brigadiers were gossiping amongst themselves that Porter's been seen, more than once, coming back from one of them houses near the Southern Squalor. Just south of Merchant's Street."

Arnon stopped in his tracks and peered at him. "He's been sleeping with prostitutes?"

"Now don't share that. I'm just telling you, so you know that I'm as bothered as you are." He shook his head. "I wonder if Galvin makes him pay the bastard bonds."

Arnon couldn't even think straight. Porter was nothing but a hard-hearted coward. With a deep breath, he relaxed his tightening fists and walked toward King's Lane.

* * *

Drake looked up as Arnon stepped inside the tavern.

"How'd it go in the Northern District?" Drake asked as he took a drink of ale. This was his third that day. It helped with the pain and filled his stomach, but he hated the feeling of too much alcohol. Still nearly full to the brim, he slid the mug across the table. Arnon took a seat in front of him but didn't answer. With his sullen posture and glazed eyes, Drake figured Arnon had seen the bodies on the outside of the northern city wall. Drake hadn't seen them himself, but he heard just enough details from other people that he couldn't get the conjuring images out of his head. "You saw 'em, didn't you?" he asked.

Arnon scrunched his eyebrows. "You mean the prostitutes?"

"You didn't see anything on the walls?"

"On the walls?"

"Never mind. Just be sure if you're ever up in the Northern District again, you don't walk out that gate. There's things on them outer walls no man should see."

Arnon looked even more miserable than when he first walked in. Drake felt like a dolt for even bringing it up. "There's bodies out there, isn't there?" Arnon asked.

"How'd you know?"

"I just had a hunch."

There was a long silence as Arnon gazed at the table, fiddling with the stub of his little finger. Drake thought about bringing up Wesley but figured it wasn't the best time. "What's got you sore, boy? Adelyne again?"

Arnon chuckled at that. "Believe it or not, that might hurt less." He leaned back against the chair. "Everything is so different than I thought. I don't," he swallowed, "I don't trust Porter or Galvin. There's something wrong about them. They're not the same men I knew as a boy."

Drake knew this was coming. He respected both of those men for many years. They were the reason the Silent Hither did so well. But something always told him that if they had the power, they'd let it get to them. "Some men are tame when they're bridled, but once they're let loose, you've got to be careful. We'll just have to keep an eye on 'em."

"But can't you do something? They were just Dark Horses like you, Wesley, Quinn. Who made them the leaders?"

"Arnon, I'm a simple man. I ain't learned in the ways of Galvin and Porter. They're the Free Sunderian Army. We're peasants. Squatters and laborers. Things are gonna change quicker than you or I could imagine, I reckon."

Arnon held a firm expression as he narrowed his eyes. "My father used to tell me I would help lead one day." He pulled at a brass button on his collar. "But I hate this uniform. I feel like Galvin only gives it to me to honor my father, but I'm not leading anything. But honestly, I don't know if I could. I'm just a hunter . . ." his words trailed off. "At least I use to be."

"Your father was a good man." Drake wanted to encourage him.

Arnon vaguely nodded. "He used to talk about an Everwind, freed from the Daecish. But I don't think he believed it would look like this." Arnon's eyes were worn out. "If I ask you something, will you be truthful?"

"You know I will."

"You knew my father better than anyone. Was," he took in a shaking breath. "Was he like them at all?"

Drake thought for a moment. "I don't know what you mean."

Arnon kept his eyes on the table and mumbled his words as Drake leaned over to listen. "When I went to the Keld valley I heard about some things Galvin and his men did to the Daecish. My family didn't say anything, but they acted like they saw something from a nightmare. When I asked Galvin about it, he said my father would've understood. Do you know what he could've meant?"

Arnon didn't look up after his question, and Drake almost regretted he said he'd tell Arnon the truth. He loved Lombard like a brother, but like everyone else, he had some dark shadows in his life.

But didn't everyone? Drake still couldn't get Darragh's face out of his mind. "Your father," he said at last. "He was a good man. An honorable man, but—" he stopped as a surprised look came over Arnon at that last word. Drake promised he would tell the truth, but he dared not share all of it. "Like all men," he continued, "he wasn't perfect. But that don't mean you can't remember him as anything less than the father you knew. He loved you with all his heart. I swear it."

Arnon sat for a while. "You're not telling me everything, are you?"

What could Drake say?

Arnon slid his chair back and stood up. "I need to go grab some things from the cellar."

The look on Arnon's face as he walked away made Drake's heart break. He should've just kept his stupid mouth shut. With a grunt, he set his leg down and stood up. Leaning on his cane, he walked over to the cellar door but paused. Even from up there, he could hear Arnon weeping beneath the steps. Drake leaned his back against the wall with a sigh. When Arnon was young, Myla always worried that he never cried. Drake never thought he'd be the first to get it out of him.

The Mill and the Map

Geoffrey's tattered shirt flapped against him as the wind stirred dust across the open landscape. About half-a-dozen guards stood to his right, and his heart pounded against his chest. The crowds of gray-shirts shuffled their feet through the gate, while the guards unshackled their chains, one at a time, then they passed beneath a brick underpass between two buildings. Just in front of him walked Burlan, with Bartholomew behind. Dust caught in his mouth, and Geoffrey let out a hack as he spat on the ground.

He was told that just after the guards unlocked their shackles, there would be a brief moment when the gray-shirts crowded the underpass, with the only guards outside on either end. If the door was open, that would be their opportunity. They would walk in, dawn the uniforms, hide out until night, then they'd make their escape. This plan was so absurd that Geoffrey spent more time imagining how they would kill him once he got caught, rather than if it would even work.

A Daecish guard unshackled Burlan. Geoffrey stepped forward and lifted his wrists. With a turn of a key, the shackles clanked on the dirt ground. The sun vanished as Geoffrey stepped beneath the underpass, glancing back at Bartholomew, who followed closely behind. About twenty feet ahead was the door on the right. It was closed. But was it locked? Burlan purposefully kept his pace slow as the crowd of gray-shirts began to tighten. He glanced back to Geoffrey with a short nod. Geoffrey took in a deep breath and shook his tingling hands.

They inched their way to the right of the underpass. Geoffrey's shoulder rubbed against the brick wall. He walked with a slight limp as a broken blister on the bottom of his right foot rubbed raw against the dirt ground. Over the days, it would scab, but he always managed to break it open again. Burlan gripped the doorknob, and it swung open as he slipped through. Geoffrey held his breath and stole in after him. Lastly, Bartholomew hurried inside and closed the door to a crack.

They all stood silence, only listening. The crowds seemed to continue with barely a murmur.

Inside, the shadow of Burlan searched around earnestly below a window, where the barren land beyond brought in the only light. He rummaged around a desk and slipped something beneath his shirt. Then he bent over and glared into what looked like a cellar vent grate near the floor. "We gotta get out here," he whispered to Geoffrey in a harsh tone. "Now!"

Geoffrey's whole body locked up.

"Why?" Bartholomew glanced back at the door.

"There ain't no uniforms! Now go!"

Without another word, Burlan peered through the door crack.

"But—" Geoffrey began, but Burlan had already opened the door and slid out.

Geoffrey knew this was it. They'd get caught.

Bartholomew passed by him, and Geoffrey closed his eyes as he stepped back into the underpass. When he opened them again, crowds of gray-shirts were still there. One old man looked at them peculiarly for a second but looked back down as he continued on. No one else seemed to notice. Geoffrey let out a sigh of relief. He was probably in there for less than ten seconds, but it felt longer than any day he'd spent in that place. Burlan glanced over his shoulder. Even in a Daecish prison camp, he managed to part his black hair to the side, but his teeth were starting to look grime-filled and blackened.

"That may not have worked," Burlan told him. "But there is some good news."

"What's that?" Bartholomew's brows angled down in what Geoffrey assumed to be either fear or frustration. His teeth didn't look as bad as Burlan's, but his scraggly beard made up for it. There was even a hint of gray in his hair that Geoffrey never noticed.

"Well, we now know we can sneak in and out without getting caught. And there's a grate in there that slides up. We can crawl in and hang out 'til night. I don't know how deep it is, but it's big enough for us to lay in." He patted his chest. "And I found something."

Geoffrey waited for him to say what it was.

"We'll talk about it tonight," was all Burlan said.

"I don't reckon I can go through that again," Bartholomew admitted.

"Then you can stay behind. But now that I know there's a chance, I ain't staying any longer than I got to." He shot out a breath through his nose. "I gotta get back to Egbert. If he's even still alive."

They stepped out from the underpass, and the sun shined bright in Geoffrey's eyes. He lifted his hand above his brow and let out a gasp. He hadn't seen green grass since Runevast. There were no trees, just smooth low-lying hills, below which ran a deep river winding to the west into a large reservoir. A wide brick building rose above the waterline on the other side, where the water plummeted into three dark archways with a deep and thunderous roar.

Around the reservoir, many gray-shirts gathered with a few guards wielding what Geoffrey could only assume were the muskets he had overheard some of the Daecish talking about. But even with the firearms, they still had short swords sheathed on their sides. To Geoffrey's left ran an iron track, where a small carriage rolled along, pulling a wagon, full of a dull-gray powder. Steam whistled from the carriage, but there was no horse. An eerie shiver ran down his spine. He understood enough to know that it was steam-powered, but having never seen something like this in motion, he couldn't shake the thought that it looked like it was being pulled by a ghost. It continued running along the track toward another brick building to Geoffrey's right. From that building's center towered a tall circular chimney, with smoke billowing from the top.

Two guards, wearing the short-brimmed hats, stepped forward and moved the men to different areas. One took Bartholomew. "Fifty-nine," he said with a nasally voice. "Go with them." He pointed to a small group of gray-shirts walking toward the carriage. "Help unload the dinkies. You," he pointed to Geoffrey and Burlan, "to the mill with the rest."

Geoffrey kept close to Burlan as they headed to the brick building where the black smoke drifted into the clouds, which was apparently the mill. He scanned the wide landscape beyond the river. "Why don't we just escape from here?"

"It'll never happen," Burlan answered. "I've seen a few men try to escape here during the day. Killed on the spot." He pointed to a tall iron tower behind the mill. "You can't tell from here, but there are towers all around with lookouts."

"What about at night?"

"They shut the gate on this side of the underpass."

If that was the case, then how would they escape at all? "Then where will we go once we get the uniforms on?"

"Just outside of the camp fence, before you get to the underpass, there's a road to the east."

"I think I know what you're talking about," Geoffrey replied, looking back, but the buildings blocked his view.

"I see guards walking that way all the time. It's guarded, but there's no gates or nothing. If we keep our head low, we shouldn't get caught."

As they approached the mill, another guard stepped forward. "Forty-three." The guard gave a nodding gesture.

"Sire," Burlan replied.

"You think you can handle running as clot today?"

"Yes, sire," he replied.

"Good. Don't forget to keep dashing it with sand." The guard looked at Geoffrey with a calm expression. There was even a hint of kindness in his eyes which Geoffrey wasn't used to seeing in the Daecish. For just a second, it brought back a strange feeling of the comforts of home, as if he was simply going to work for the day. "You'll go to the mill," the guard said, "knead the clay. They'll show you where to take it afterward." The guard walked off.

As they continued to the mill, Geoffrey peered at Burlan, dumbfounded. "That guard. He just talked to you like you were a . . ." He didn't even know what to say. "A person."

Burlan chuckled. "It just depends on the guard, but some of them ain't as bad as the others. He ain't never told me his name, but he showed me how to mold the clay into bricks the other day. Perchance he figured I can handle it on my own now?"

"What will I do in the mill?"

Burlan whistled as he shook his head. "That's hard work, that is."

Geoffrey groaned. They'd been given more food and water in recent days. He didn't know if it was because enough gray-shirts died to meet their budget or if it was to give them the strength needed to slave over making bricks.

"You basically take that clay powder over yonder," he pointed to the carriage as it disappeared through a large opening in the side of the mill, "add some water and sand, then you knead it like dough. Once you're finished, you'll load it up in a cart and roll it to me or one of the other clots."

"That don't sound so bad."

Burlan raised an eyebrow at him. "You're starting to sound like you were raised in Astford."

Geoffrey laughed at himself. Living in Everwind, working among the Daecish had softened his Sunderian accent. But now that he was actually in Daecland, strengthening it made him feel more at home. He didn't know what he would do if Burlan and Bartholomew weren't there.

"It's harder than you think," Burlan went on. "That clay gets thick, and we'll be working a good fourteen hours before they take us back to the bunks."

"Fourteen hours?" Geoffrey sank into gloom. Would they get fed at all? Wasting away in the camp didn't sound so bad anymore.

Suddenly, a loud wail broke across the yard. Geoffrey held his hands to his ears and recognized it from his first day there when Claude was killed. When it stopped, Burlan glanced behind him. "Sirens," he said. "At least that's what the Daecish call 'em."

"You think they've got men in that ring again?"

"Don't know, but I hope I don't ever have to go back there."

It was well into the night or early in the morning; Geoffrey wasn't sure by the time he was taken back to the camp. His arms hung like lifeless ropes, and his legs felt like they weighed a hundred pounds. Opening the door to the bunkhouse, a single lantern hung from the ceiling. Everyone was asleep, and every bunk was taken. Burlan and Bartholomew had already filled up the last two in the other bunkhouse, so he knew there was no use looking elsewhere. He found a spot on the floor, curled up, and slept hard.

When he awoke, it was barely dawn. Some man had knocked him in the head with his foot as he stumbled out of the door. Geoffrey sat up, rubbing his hand through the knot below his hair. He was so tired, he felt sick and sore all over. He knew the bunkhouse reeked of a mixture of sour sweat and human waste, but he couldn't smell it anymore. Forcing himself up, he walked out the door. Just around the bunkhouse, he found Burlan and Bartholomew sitting in their usual spot, with their backs against the outer wall. Geoffrey sat next to them. "How much sleep you think we got?" he asked Burlan.

"I probably slept one, maybe two hours." He glanced at Bartholomew. "I don't think he slept none."

"Where did they send you to work?" Geoffrey asked.

The bags under Bartholomew's eyes were so dark they looked black. "Where they diverted the river," he half mumbled. "We had to dig up the clay and lay it out to dry." He slowly blinked his eyes. "Hardest work I ever done."

"It'll keep you alive, though," Burlan said. "Keep your blood going." He glanced around the camp, then turned his back, so he faced the outer wall of the bunkhouse. "Anyway, I got something to show you." Slipping his hand into his shirt, he slowly pulled out a piece of paper. Both Geoffrey and Bartholomew squinted as they peered at it.

"Is that a map?" Geoffrey wondered.

"That's what it looks like," Burlan replied.

"How'd you get that?" Bartholomew asked in a quiet tone. Something looked wrong with him like he was deeply troubled. But Geoffrey figured they all looked like that.

"It was right there on the desk in the room we broke into." Burlan smiled. "I got to looking at it last night in the bunkhouse. There wasn't much light, and I can't read too good, but I did notice this." He pointed to the top of the map, on the right side, where a legend marker, apparently for a city called Fingate, was located. He traced his finger down a road to three other markers, labeled the "Dilution Sites," each marker labeled One, Two, and Three, respectively. To the east of the Dilution Sites, the map was bare, but to the south ran several zigzag lines in a south-westerly direction until they ended at sea. The lines were labeled "The Mountains of Einarr," but the sea was blank. On the coast, however, was a dot labeled "Fiskerstrond Port," from which several shipping lanes ran south-west into the sea, or bent south-eastward, where they returned to the shore on the other side of the mountains. There, near the bottom of the map edge, was what looked like several copper mines, and in big letters, "Sunder."

Geoffrey pointed to the Dilution Sites. "That's where we are, isn't it? I've heard the guards talking about Section Three."

"I think so." Burlan pointed to Fiskerstrond. "And I bet we could find a way to Sunder from there."

For the first time, a glimmer of real hope welled up in Geoffrey. At least from the map, Sunder didn't look that far from the port. "You think we can traverse the coast, around the mountains?"

"Maybe."

A sudden anxiousness came over him. He had no idea how his family was doing. Did Sarah get arrested along with him? Did she survive the childbirth? He would do whatever it took to get back. That much he knew. "So, when do we make our escape?"

The shuffling of men stepping out of the bunkhouse started them, and Burlan shoved the map into his shirt. "I say next time we go out to the reservoir." He looked to Bartholomew. "What do you think?"

Bartholomew furled his brow.

"What's got you down?" Burlan asked.

He was quiet for a moment, then he took in a breath. "While I's working yesterday, some of the guards were mocking us. They said here in a few days they'll be taking half of the gray-shirts outta camp to some other section. They said . . ." He choked on his words. "They said we'd be burned in the furnace." He lowered his face into his hands and began to cry.

Burlan drifted his gaze away. "That just means we gotta escape before then."

"What if they don't send us back out before then?" Bartholomew asked, swallowing deeply.

A few days could mean a week or even less. The thought of having hope arise, only to be taken so quickly, brought a sudden weariness over Geoffrey.

"If that fat knacker Abbot hadn't betrayed us," Burlan said with a scowl, "we wouldn't even be here." He slammed the outer wall of the bunkhouse with the back of his heel. "We'd all be back in Sunder with our families."

Bartholomew wiped his eyes. "I'm sorry," he said. "I'm so sorry."

"You got nothing to be sorry for." Burlan braced his hands against the wall. "You're here with us."

"You don't understand," Bartholomew said, snorting in through his nose and wiping it. "I've been trying to hold it in, but I can't take it." He glanced at Burlan. He shook his head and, with a deep sigh, looked back over at Geoffrey. "Not long after you left Astford, the Daecish came to the inn. Asked if I had housed you, and thinking nothing of it, I said I did. They asked if I knew what you were up to, and I only told 'em you were there for training purposes, just like you said." He wiped his face. "They told me you were working in the Silent Hither and was sent from Everwind. They asked if I knew anything, and I told 'em no. I swore on my life. But they didn't believe me." He sniffed in and wiped his nose.

Burlan's face turned red, but he didn't say anything.

The timeline didn't make sense. Geoffrey knew enough to realize that Bartholomew didn't sell him out. Someone from Everwind must have ratted him out before he even left Astford, but who? "Then what happened?" he asked.

"You know I can't lie. I ain't never been good at it. The moment they asked, I got all flustered like and started stuttering."

"What happened?" Burlan asked in a cold tone.

"I remembered that note you wrote Geoffrey, asking if he would meet you at the Alcove Tavern." He kept his eyes down, still shaking his head. "They kept pressing me, and I gave 'em your name. I'm so sorry."

"You told them?" Burlan's voice echoed across the camp, and a few of the surrounding men shot them a glance.

Bartholomew clenched his eyes shut and nodded, his voice lowering. "Then they drafted me and took my daughter."

A deep sorrow overcame Geoffrey.

Burlan suddenly let out a howl and threw himself over Bartholomew. "You traitor!" he spat.

Geoffrey lunged forward and tried to pull Burlan back. "Stop it!" he shouted. "Let him alone!"

With his arms going limp and his head dropping low, Burlan broke into a sob. Geoffrey fell backward with him still in his arms as Bartholomew skidded back.

"Why?" Burlan cried out as he sprawled over Geoffrey. "Why was I so stupid?" He crawled off Geoffrey and laid in the dirt. "I should've sent that boy back into the hills when I had the chance."

Geoffrey sat up with shaking limbs. Bartholomew still pressed himself against the bunkhouse wall, jaw trembling. "It's not the boy's fault!" Geoffrey exclaimed. "And it's not yours, or Bartholomew's, or anyone else's. It's just what happened."

Burlan moaned as he rolled over to his side, but he seemed to calm down.

"Maybe we're being judged by Theos," Bartholomew said quietly. "Maybe it's the end."

Wiping the snot and dirt from his face, Burlan dragged himself off the ground. "Just 'cause we're out here don't make it the end. The rest of the world's doing fine while we're rotting and dying."

Geoffrey didn't say anything. Maybe Bartholomew was right.

"But Theos kill me if he don't judge you for what you done to us," Burlan told Bartholomew. He stood up and walked to the other side of Geoffrey.

"Watch your tongue," Geoffrey snapped. "Bartholomew did nothing to us. You and me both participated in the Silent Hither on our own accord. Bartholomew here was only trying to make a living for his daughter. If anything, we're to blame for dragging him with us."

Burlan didn't say anything, and neither did Bartholomew.

"Besides," Geoffrey continued. "We may all be judged for the things we've done. None of us have a right to judge the other." Neither of them would have guessed it, but he had plenty of things he regretted. All of his life, people only talked about how good of a man he was. But not all of it was true. Sure, he had kept all the laws. He'd never stolen anything. He'd never cheated on Sarah. But he did all the right things for the wrong reasons. For most of his life, whenever he did do something he regretted, maybe a lie or hateful word spoken in anger, he didn't feel guilty because it was wrong or because it hurt someone. He felt embarrassed because his own pride was hurt. Because it made him look bad.

Burlan spit on the ground. "You may be right about the judgment, but it ain't gonna be here. I refuse to die in this place."

A commotion arose from a small crowd of gray-shirts by the fence. Several guards conversed amongst themselves on the other side before walking through the underpass and out of sight.

"I wonder what's going on over . . ." Geoffrey began, but Burlan had already stood up and walked over to the crowd. Several in the crowd held wide eyes as they murmured to one another; others paced around with scowls on their faces. Two guards marched back over to the fence and pulled out swords, banging them against the iron. Soon, the crowd dispersed, and Burlan hurried back over. "What was that about?" Geoffrey asked.

Burlan sat back down with wide eyes. "Some feller over there by the name of Matty, apparently from Llynhithe, said when he was working by the reservoir last night, he overheard the guards talking about some telegram message. He couldn't say what that was, but it somehow mentioned a shipment of wheellocks and muskets to Sunder." He stared grimly at Geoffrey. "And something about a fleet heading to Everwind."

"Of wisps?"

"Don't know."

Bartholomew sat up straight. "Why would they send a fleet to Everwind?"

Burlan slapped his thigh. "Y'all know as much as I do."

Geoffrey's heart pounded. He'd only seen a fleet of wisps once when Daecland conquered Sunder. Why would they need a whole fleet in Everwind? Picturing his family being slaughtered beneath a torrent of cannons and wheellocks, his desperation to leave suddenly escalated with his racing pulse.

Bondage to the Body of Death

I t's all right, it's all right," Adelyne said as she patted Acton on the back. For the past half-hour, he wouldn't quit crying into her ear. With a flustered face, Sarah rushed into the kitchen, wiping her hands on her apron. There were now seven girls in the house, and getting any of them to help was more difficult than either Adelyne or Sarah had expected.

"When Agatha gets back," Sarah said, taking a sip of honey wine, "I'm afraid we'll have to tell her that it's enough for now. We've got barely enough food for those already here, and they'll have to start putting in some effort if we want to make it through winter." She set down the pewter mug and walked back out of the kitchen.

Adelyne's stomach growled. By enough, she knew Sarah meant two small meals a day.

She gazed out the window. It felt like it was yesterday when she was working for the Dark Horses. Things were so exciting then. But so much has changed. So many people have died. Poor Murdock. She heard his body was finally found beneath a collapsed wall. At least Quinn was still alive.

Letting her eyes wander around the empty kitchen, she couldn't control the anxiousness growing inside of her. Was this her future? To be stuck in a house all day feeding babies and listening to countless sob stories from these girls? If she didn't get out and do something more adventurous soon, she'd go crazy.

More than once, she imagined what it would be like to just go away with Arnon. To get married and have a family. How that was any more adventurous than this, she didn't know, but the thought still made her smile.

Hearing the front door swing open, Adelyne walked out of the kitchen and peered down the hall. Agatha stepped inside with Cydney following her. Adelyne felt sick.

Still in her cream-colored dress—though by now, it had tinged a few shades darker with what looked like blotches of dried spilled ale on the front—Cydney fiddled with her fingernails as if she was embarrassed to show herself in that house. Then she looked at Adelyne, drawing a smile across her face.

Maybe she really wanted to be free from Three Rivers Tavern? But Adelyne couldn't see how. There was a wild side to that girl no one could tame. And she never ceased to get other girls caught up in her trouble. But Adelyne knew she couldn't blame her for everything she had done. She thought about mentioning to Sarah that Cydney staying there was a bad idea, but what if she really needed a place?

Agatha disappeared into the fireplace room as Cydney walked toward her, gently patting Acton on the back. His crying had eased, and he fell into a whimpering sleep. "Never thought I'd ever walk in here," Cydney said as she examined the hall. From behind her yellowed teeth, her breath smelled like an acrid mix of onions and sour milk.

"It's a good place," Adelyne managed to reply.

"How long you've been here?" She twirled her curly black hair.

"I helped Sarah move back in, and we started the house together."

"Oh." Cydney raised her eyebrow. "I figured you'd of come here for help like the others."

"Is that why you're here?"

Cydney shrugged. "Agatha came by the back door and offered food. It's running low over there at Three Rivers. And I'm tired of giving myself over to men every time I want to sup. Besides, Fletcher ain't spoken to me in two days. You know how he is. Acts like he loves you one day, then the next he's courting some other girl."

Adelyne's jaw tightened. She wished she had never met him.

"He talks about you a lot, you know?" Cydney said with an almost jealous tone. "Says he misses you."

With a sudden desire to leave, Adelyne glanced over her shoulder, hoping to find an excuse. But even then, a strange attraction welled up in her. She hated Fletcher, but for some reason, she liked that he missed her. It was as if his words made her feel like she was worth something, and in a twisted way, it sparked that sense of adventure she craved.

"Egbert!" echoed the voice of Sarah from a back room.

Both Adelyne and Cydney turned.

"What have you done!" Sarah exclaimed, storming down the hall and into the kitchen.

Agatha stood in the bedroom doorway with a deeply apologetic look on her face. "Egbert," she barely said.

Taking the opportunity to get away from Cydney, Adelyne hurried toward the back bedroom. With bits of bread and a few corn cobs littering his lap, Egbert sat on a straw bed, laid out on the floor, with a mouth stuffed full of food. Holding an empty milk jug in his right hand, he wept as he occasionally spat out wet crumbs onto the floor. Adelyne dropped her mouth. It looked as if he had eaten enough food to feed the whole house for two days.

"What are we going to do?" Agatha asked, pacing the floor.

Adelyne wasn't sure what to say. "Just make sure he doesn't eat anymore." She handed Acton to her and hurried back down the hall. Ignoring Cydney's shocked expression, she found Sarah sitting at the kitchen table with her face in her hands.

"We don't have enough food." Sarah wept. "I never thought things would get this bad. I thought the girls would help more. I should've been better prepared."

Adelyne knew she had to do something, and she didn't want to spend another minute in that house with Cydney. "Don't worry about food. I'll go to Drake and see what he can spare. If not, I'll find Arnon. We'll figure something out."

"Thank you," she said with a sniff.

Walking out of the kitchen, Cydney stood in front of the door with her shoulder leaned against the wall. "You know," she said, curling her hair, "if y'all are that desperate for food, there's ways you can get it."

Adelyne really felt like hitting her, but she just wanted to leave.

"Fletcher cares for you," she continued.

Adelyne paused with her hand on the door handle.

"You give him what he wants, and he'll make sure you're taken care of. I know he will."

"Please, just go away," Adelyne said as she opened the door, forcing Cydney to step aside.

Her mind was so consumed with thoughts that she was nearly to Drake's tavern before she even realized it. If there was any man who actually cared for her, she believed it was Arnon. But she also knew there was something she desired—a desire for something Arnon couldn't give her. He was too honest. Too innocent. Adelyne paused in her step and braced her hand against the outer wall of a house, wrapping her fingers around a thin dried branch that stuck out from the daub. Her stomach churned, and she was afraid she would throw up. "What's wrong with you!" she shouted to herself. Why did she feel like this? Why couldn't she just change? For just a moment, she imagined the branch was her father. With gritted teeth, she ripped it from the house and snapped it in half with her hands. Her grip was so tight, one end of the branch drew blood from her palm. She cast the shattered ends to the ground. Every part of her abhorred that man.

Taking in a deep breath, her stomach settled for a moment. She would get food from Drake, go back to the house, tell Cydney to leave, and everything would be okay.

She continued south and eventually stepped up to the front door of the tavern. With another deep breath, she turned the knob. Inside, the lanterns were lit, but the hearth was dead, and the tables were empty, except for Drake, who sat across from Bell.

"Adelyne," Bell said as she stood up and walked over to give her a hug. "How's my darling?"

Adelyne faked a smile. She was never as close to Bell as she would have liked, but she always imagined her like a grandmother. "I'm all right," she replied.

"The milk's been a blessing to you all, I trust?"

Starting with that question made Adelyne realize how difficult it would be to ask for more. "It has," she said. "And I know how much of a sacrifice it was for you. But if it's possible . . ." she hesitated, almost already expecting them to say no. "We need more if you can spare it."

At first, Drake gazed ahead, then he eyed Bell with worry in his eyes. "Times are getting tough." He wiped his face. "I ain't hardly had no business. My stores are running low." He shook his head. "Now Merle should be shipping in some meat and milk from his farm, but it won't be here for another week. It won't be much, but I'll spare you some."

They would need food before then. "Can I buy some now?" She needed him to provide her food for more reasons than just for her and the other girls to eat. It was her excuse to stay away from Fletcher. "I've got a few aracs saved away."

"Ain't no one taking aracs anymore, dear," answered Bell.

Adelyne's chin trembled.

With a groan, Drake leaned onto his cane and stood up, hobbling over to the bar. He picked up a pint of milk and a small cheese wheel. "Take this," he said.

She held the items loosely in her hands. It wasn't enough, but she knew it was more than he could give. "This was your meal today, wasn't it?"

Drake waved a hand to dismiss her. "I'm full," he said, sitting back down.

A conflict arose in her mind. She tried to ignore it as she gave Drake a hug. "Thank you," she said.

There was a glint in Drake's eyes as he looked up at her. "Now you go take care of Arnon. You mean the world to him." He smiled.

She couldn't even nod. "Thank you again," she said before walking out the door.

Outside, her pulse began to race, and her whole body tingled. Part of her felt sick. The other part felt overwhelmed with desire. She could just go to Fletcher. She needed food for the girls, and she knew he would give it. It all made sense, and it would just be one time. A sudden sharp pain shot through her stomach as she thought of Arnon. How could she even consider doing something like that? He would be so heartbroken; it would kill him. And she loved him. She had never felt that away about anyone.

She walked north. The cheese wheel fell from her hands, and she feebly picked it back up.

But she knew it would never actually satisfy her. It would just leave a gaping hole in her heart, and she'd probably regret it the rest of her life. It was wrong, but maybe that was why she wanted to do it as if the wrongness itself was what excited her. She had already messed up so many times in her life. What's the difference if she did it again? Her father had already ruined her. And as soon as Arnon found out about her past, he would leave her anyway.

With a sudden sniff, tears filled her eyes. She knew she had already given in.

The Forest of Valor

Søren stood beneath the tall hemlock trees, looking down at his arms. It was hard for him to be sure, but his tunic sleeves seemed to run shorter and fit a bit tighter than when he had first put them on in Astford. By now, all of his scars had long disappeared, even the one on his knee, which he has had for as long as he could remember. With his right hand, he gripped the hilt of the sword. The pummel was rusted a golden red, and the edges of the blade were getting there. For several days, or maybe several weeks, he had been wandering north, down the mountain slopes of a dark forest. Time seemed to dissolve there. In one sense, it felt older than any other place he had ever been, as if the trees and mountains only sat there, growing slowly through the changing seasons. Yet, at the same time, it felt wild and perilous, as if anything could happen at any moment.

Most of his days were spent procuring food. Before he drowned in the Finnvard River, he had never so much as spent a single day in the woods, much less having to survive in them. But he had a new instinct that he never noticed before—an awareness of sounds and smells, so vivid and clear, he could look directly at the needled branches and caves from which they echoed and seethed from. Colors and light were also more vibrant and crisp, and he was able to make out even the faintest of details from the darkest shadows.

In bare feet, Søren walked down the leaf-riddled mountain slope in a zigzag fashion, pushing the limbs away from his face. He paused at the edge of a mossy bank and washed the pine sap from his fingers. He parted his hair, which now reached to below his nose, and took in a mouthful of cold water as the stream rippled and bubbled over the smooth rocks. With the swaying branches, sighing and moaning in the wind, the forest sounded like music to his ears. He breathed in the scent of the spicy cedar and wet earth. Since the day the shadow entered him, he was at peace, and he never felt alone, even in the midst of that desolate place.

Over the remainder of the day, Søren walked west, following the stream. He wasn't sure where he was going, but he felt as if he should just keep walking. High up, on a dead branch, a round-faced white owl tilted its head as it stared at him, with dark eyes and thick long feathery lashes. He paused to look at it, but just as he did, the owl spread wide its golden-white wings and flew off across the river and out of sight.

Birds acted strangely in that forest. He looked behind him, gazing into the canopy. Dozens of ravens were perched on the high branches, flying from one tree to the next as they followed him, or at least it seemed that way. They would stop when he stopped and fly toward him when he walked. Although they always kept their distance. Each day there seemed to be more. He could do nothing about it, but the thought of it piqued his curiosity. Maybe it had something to do with the shadow within him.

At times the mountain laurel grew so thick, Søren had to either hack his way through with the sword or ascend the slopes of the western bank to gain clearer ground. More frustrating was the occasional briar field which he would find himself caught in, scratching his legs and snagging his tunic and arms.

By late afternoon, the ground had leveled, and the river eased as it slowly winded beneath deep undercut banks. A few times, fish jumped upstream against the current. He attempted to catch them before but never had any luck. Most of his diet consisted of bird eggs, grubs, worms, anything he could find. Once, he ate a hard-shelled beetle of bright colors. It tore his stomach up so bad he had to lay down for two days. All he could do was drink water from a nearby spring before he mustered enough strength to raid a log of termites.

In all his time in the forest, he never saw any sign of humans. As always, he thought of Eirún. Though the words of the shadow had led him to believe he would not see her again, or at least not any time soon, he somehow knew it would be okay. He never again wondered whether she loved him or not. He just knew she did. Often, he thought about what she was doing. Was she still at the orphanage, or did she go on to Vagholme? He didn't know, but he hoped she was happy. On occasion, he thought of Burlan's words about Theos, and at times he found himself talking to him. Although he never heard anything back, he liked to imagine he was listening.

Approaching a stretch of the river, which ran straight with a glade on the far bank, and leafless hardwoods overhanging the river on the west bank, Søren slowed his steps and narrowed his eyes. Sitting beneath a large oak sat the outline of a man, but his details were hidden behind the tall grass. Søren held his breath. It didn't take long for him to realize who it was. With his hand on the hilt, Søren approached the tree.

The prisoner looked up at him. His uncanny smile had been replaced with a look of disappointment.

"Good evening," the prisoner said, looking back across the river.

Søren didn't respond. He could see the darkness creeping from the prisoner's heart like a plague.

"I see you've refused to listen to any of my advice."

"I refused because you are a liar."

The prisoner cocked an eyebrow. "You believe that?"

"I know it."

With a laugh, the prisoner scratched his wrist beneath the iron shackle. "And what makes you so sure?"

"The shadow t—told me." Søren's heart remained calm. He was not afraid.

"The shadow told you? Did the shadow also tell you that you are doomed?"

"I have a fate, but it is not the doom you spoke of."

The prisoner bent his bruised legs and rested his thin arms on his knees, which were barely covered by his tattered brown shirt. "You will never do what it requires of you."

"But I will."

"No." The prisoner laughed again as he shook his head. His long, dark hair clumped together in greasy mats. "You're too weak, too small." Søren felt his cold gray eyes pierce his heart. "Too prideful."

Søren pulled his gaze away from the prisoner. Pride. That was for men who had it all, who had strength and courage and boasted about it. "I'm not prideful," he replied.

"No?" The prisoner let out a hacking cough, then he spat on the ground. "You have the worst kind of pride. The kind that doesn't look like it. You want everyone to feel sorry for you, see how small and helpless you are. You expect everyone to do everything for you. Disgusting self-pity."

At those words, Søren's heart quivered. He knew that was true, but he also knew that he was different now. Ever since the shadow entered him, he had a new strength and saw things from a different perspective. "So, what of it?"

"No matter what you do for the shadow, Theos will never forgive you. You've always cared for yourself only and brought grief to too many people in the process. Even now," he let out another cough, "Eirún weeps in her own misery which you have brought on her."

Søren closed his eyes. He didn't know if Theos would ever forgive him, especially for the way he treated Eirún, but something inside of him told him to be at peace. He looked hard at the prisoner again. "You once told me that all who I meet are wrought within my doom. That they will die in ruin."

"I'm glad you remembered," the prisoner replied.

"Then I'll be your death as well." At that, Søren walked past the prisoner.

Further downstream, he found a boulder beside a deep pool at the base of a waterfall. He sat down and rubbed his cold, wet feet. The air quickly dampened his tunic, and he slid off the boulder, searching for dryer ground further from the spray of the falls.

Approaching a small glade, he stopped. Beneath the sunlight was the alphyn, sleeping in a thicket of tall grass. It looked normal once again, but it no longer seemed hideous to him. Rather, he felt a bond with the beast. Besides the shadow, the alphyn had been his only companion since the mines. But more so, the shadow had come over the creature, as it had him, and that was a connection he could share with no one else.

Before long, the shadow slowly manifested itself and hovered above the alphyn like a thick shapeless cloud. The same sound of flowing wind moaned through the air as rays of sunlight seemed to draw into its darkness. It was as black as a bottomless hole, and Søren put his hand against his heart. The force of its presence pressed against him.

"I thought," Søren began, but he wasn't sure what to ask. Did the shadow disappear that day on the mountains, or did it enter him? "I thought you were inside of me," he said at last.

"I am in you," the shadow spoke. The forest suddenly went quiet, and the sun dimmed as if it was hidden behind a cloud. "But I am not bound to you."

Søren peered at his hands. A storm of questions he had been wanting to ask swept over him. "What's happened t—to me? Why do I feel so different?"

"The old you has passed away, and you are now being made new, but you are not yet who you will fully be."

Søren thought back to the river he drowned in. Is that what the shadow meant by passing away? Did he actually die? "Did . . ." he began to ask, but the thought of it terrified him. "Did I die in the river?"

"You were never truly alive, to begin with. Not until I entered you. And now, you will never taste death again."

The answer was more than he anticipated. Never taste death? And what about his eyes. Why did people always talk about them? He would have kept asking questions about it, but he wasn't sure he could handle any more. "Why are you here?" he asked instead.

"I have come to take you to Norfrost. The time has come for Daecland's Blight."

His heart suddenly pounded. What would the shadow have him do in Norfrost? And why did the shadow need him at all? Søren was nothing compared to the power of the shadow's presence. "I'm just a boy. Why do you need me?"

"You are not needed. You are wanted."

Søren suddenly desired to fiddle with his fingers. "Are . . ." he trailed off. "Are you Theos?"

"No," the shadow answered promptly. "I am a shadow. Theos is the substance."

"But Theos wants me to go?"

"Yes."

Søren dropped his hand and looked back up. If that's what Theos wanted, then he would do it. But what if the prisoner was right? What if Theos knew about him and never forgave him? "But I'm afraid," he confessed.

"Do not be. The blood that runs through your veins is not your own." Then, as if the shadow could read his thoughts, it drifted into the alphyn, and it transformed once again into a walking shadow beast with glowing blue eyes. It stepped over to Søren, and the cool, soothing breeze brushed against his face. "Do not be troubled," the shadow spoke through the alphyn. "You have sought forgiveness, and it has been given to you."

Søren felt his heart calm, and his fears subside. The alphyn lowered itself, and Søren saddled over its back. Without another word, it turned and rode north toward Norfrost.

* * *

Gunnar raised his eyebrows, but his lids felt so heavy he was barely able to keep them open. Nevertheless, with Eirik's orders to Ónarr in his left hand, he walked down the ramp, breathing in the stale smell of the port docks of Llynhithe. He had only been there once, and it didn't look any better than it did then. The shops lining the boardwalk, across the way on the water, were of mostly Sunderian architecture—simple thatched roofs and dirt floors, but some held a Daecish flavor, which did more to diminish their appearance than anything else. What few glass windows there were, were either out of pattern or crooked, as if someone threw them up in a hurry. The occasional thick oak door didn't match, and the trim looked like scraps they found lying around, hammered half-heartedly into the wattle and daub. It was a disgrace to Daecland. They must have hired Sunderians to do the work.

Several onlookers marveled at the two massive wisps still humming behind him. Even though an entire fleet of wisps rested in that field, they must have not seen one in operation since the invasion. Up ahead, Halvard and Dagr stood with their hands behind them. Dagr still held that cocky smile, and his pointed nose looked perfect for brown-nosing Ónarr. Gunnar would have felt better if he wasn't there. But Halvard—that was a good man. If he kept it up, he would replace Asger in Norfrost one day. But that thought only reminded him that he had to tell Halvard that he was about to lose his position as Commander-in-Chief in Sunder. He wasn't looking forward to that. And what about Eilívur? Did anyone know if he was even still alive?

"Commander Veurðr," Halvard said as he curled up the corner of his mouth. "You look terrible."

"I've barely slept in a week." And he never got a chance to see his family. It wouldn't have been so bad if he hadn't have been so close to them in Norfrost.

Dagr didn't say anything but held a bored expression. Halvard motioned behind him to a horse carriage. "As soon as we saw the wisp, King Ónarr ordered a meeting." He smiled. "The look of fear on his face made me think he half-believed King Eirik was onboard."

Gunnar thought of some reply, but with Dagr present, he held his tongue. Halvard led the way as they walked to the carriage.

Dirt roads never made for comfortable carriage rides, but it was better than being on a wisp. He still couldn't get the humming out of his head. Heading south, the streets were somewhat empty, but otherwise, the city appeared untouched by the events surrounding Everwind.

"Have you seen any of those creatures in Llynhithe?" he asked.

Dagr didn't answer, but Halvard tilted his head in thought. "I heard there were a few on the west side of town. Some of the citizens were calling them alphyns or something of the sort. But it hasn't been nearly as bad as Everwind was that day."

Remarkable. He would have expected much worse. "Has the economy been affected?"

"It has," Halvard replied. "But given the lack of any Silent Hither here, no riots have broken out." He motioned a hand to Dagr. "Commander Dagr has helped oversee several improvements."

"We tried handing out doles," Dagr said. It was the first time Gunnar heard him speak that day. "But that only increased laziness among the people. So, rather, we created new jobs."

"Really?" Gunnar asked. He was genuinely impressed.

"We've started work on a new palisade wall outside the city." He pointed north. "As well as the construction of several launch pads for the wisps."

"And Sunderians are working on them?"

"They're doing whatever it takes to feed their families."

"That's ironic. Do they not know they'll be used to invade Everwind?"

Halvard laughed. "I guess that explains why you've been sent to Llynhithe?"

Gunnar chuckled. "Surprise."

Dagr stretched an arm in the cramped space. "We've held to the possibility that Asger or even King Eirik would make an appearance. So, we've been preparing."

"Preparing?"

"We have two full legions armed and prepared for orders."

Gunnar tried not to look surprised. Maybe Dagr has changed? He was certainly on top of things.

"Have you brought orders from Norfrost?" Halvard asked.

"I have." Gunnar held them up in his hand. He almost forgot about the firearms loaded in the stowage wisp. "And I think you'll be in for a surprise when your troops get issued their new weapons."

Approaching the town hall, they stepped out of the carriage and were welcomed by several of Ónarr's officials, dressed in gray suits. Other than losing paperwork and opening doors, Gunnar never understood their purpose. Nevertheless, he followed them inside the dark entry hall. The torches, rough wooden floors, and the stale smell of oil immediately made him realize how far from home he was again.

"Right this way," said one of the officials as they turned left into a large room where Ónarr stood, overlooking a map of Everwind on the desk before him.

Even though it had been just over a week, Gunnar swore Ónarr looked thinner. "Commander Veurðr," he spoke aloud.

"Your Majesty," Gunnar replied.

The king held out an open hand, and Gunnar gave him the orders. Though he didn't look his best, his eyes were still sharp and bright blue beneath his light-red hair. He sat down, broke the wax seal, and unfolded the documents. After a considerable length of time, he reached out his hand, shaking Gunnar's. "Congratulations on your promotion, Commander-in-Chief."

Gunnar glanced his eyes to Halvard, who gave him a sarcastic sneer. He felt a pat on his back. "Congratulations," he whispered.

At that moment, a short, plump officer, whom Gunnar had never met, stepped into the room.

"Admiral Bjarke," the king said.

"Your Majesty," he replied, now standing beside Dagr.

"Admiral Bjarke will be assisting with the invasion." The king looked back to Gunnar. "And both wisps have arrived, correct?"

"Yes, Your Majesty."

"Good," he said in a loud tone. "I've been looking forward to the firearms for quite some time." He motioned to Dagr. "Commander, arrange for the unloading of the stowage wisp. We will begin training on the wheellocks and muskets immediately. The orders state that a fleet should be arriving from Norfrost in two weeks. That doesn't give us much time." He eyed Bjarke. "In ten days, I want our own fleet serviced and ready to go. Our troops will need to begin their march within the week."

"Yes, Your Majesty."

"Within the week?" Dagr questioned. "But Your Majesty, there is much we must get in order first. Preparing two legions of troops is going to take longer than—"

"We have no choice. Their march east will take considerably more time than the airborne armada, and I aim to have both fleets and the legions to arrive in Everwind at the same time."

"If I may, Your Majesty," Dagr protested.

"You may."

"Two fleets of wisps and two legions of soldiers. That is a bit excessive for taking back Everwind, is it not?"

"Commander," the king said as he stood up and folded up the papers, "we do not simply aim to retake Everwind, but to take it and Denhurst, and to keep them!" He shot his gaze at Gunnar. "I will leave you, Commander-in-Chief, in charge of the legions. Admiral Bjarke will oversee the Airborne Armada, under your leadership, of course."

"Yes, Your Majesty."

"Commander Dagr," the king continued. "You will remain in Llynhithe to maintain city defenses."

"Yes, Your Majesty."

Gunnar held in his sigh of relief. He did not feel like putting up with Dagr on the long march to Everwind.

"What of Commander Tyr and our prisoners of war?" Halvard asked.

The king waved a dismissing hand. "This Sunderian Army has sent no dispatch for negotiations. I doubt our men are even alive."

"If they are," added Admiral Bjarke, "we'll have an infirmary land just outside of the city."

"Very good. Now, gentlemen . . ." The king walked around his desk as they all turned to keep facing him. "Eirik has ordered a total war. First in Everwind, then Denhurst. Do I make myself clear?"

"Yes, Your Majesty," they all replied.

Gunnar couldn't help but feel uneasy by the idea of total war. The last time Daecland was involved in such warfare, they had sieged a city in Kalestrond until the people starved to the point of cannibalization. By the time they broke through the city walls, there was no one left to fight. "Will it be a siege, Your Majesty?"

"No," the king replied. "Our wisps will suffice in storming the city upon arrival. But we will take no prisoners. We will make no treaties. All involved in the rebellion will be executed, and their buildings burned if necessary. I will leave the tactics on how to accomplish that to you, Commander-in-Chief."

"What of the women and children?" Gunnar asked.

The king gazed across the entrance to the room for a moment as he clasped his hands behind his back. "I will only accept unconditional surrender. If anyone resists or flees, they are to be executed. The women are just as guilty as the men in their rebellions, and those brats will one day grow up to take their parents' place. I mean to end this now. We will crush their hearts once and for all."

Gunnar's bones ached at those words. He understood that the rebellions needed to end, but the women and children? He didn't know if he had it in him to command such a thing.

The Lament of Eadig the Wise

With a growling stomach, Drake stood in the kitchen pantry. He was tired of filling himself with ale, but the remaining cheese wheels and salted meats were going to have to push his business through the winter. He laughed at himself. What business? The few people that came in barely had anything to barter with, although one old gentleman, a widower, offered his wedding ring. Drake gave him the bread and refused the payment, but it still made him feel sore. The fact that Three Rivers was apparently thriving didn't help matters.

Drake walked out of the kitchen as Bell was lighting the hearth. "We expecting customers?" he asked, hobbling around the bar.

"No," she said as she straightened herself. "But I figured we might as well eat something before we wither away."

With pain shooting up his thigh, Drake sat in the chair and pulled up his pant leg. The wound was swollen and purple, with some yellow fluid dripping down to his calf. Byram the butcher, the only doctor in his district, had already come by and applied some herbs to help with the smell. Other than that, his only option was to cut his leg off. Paired with his throbbing head and cold shivers running down his back, he knew this would end up for the worst.

"How you feeling?" Bell asked, grabbing a cooking pot.

Drake lowered his pant leg as bell hung the pot from the spit. "I'm fine, but I'll be doing better when I get some food in me."

She sat down across from him. Her gray hair pulled up into a bun. "I heard people were going out and taking alphyn meat."

"They eat that?" Drake thought he might gag.

"They do what they got to do."

"They smell horrid as it is. Don't know if I could swallow it." He looked around the room and sighed. "It's sickening though, how some people choose to thrive in all of this. I can't reckon why Theos would let people who are living in wickedness fill their stomachs while those who are trying to do right starve."

There was a short silence as Bell gazed at the hearth. "I don't know," she said at last. "They may be filling their stomachs, but their dying on the inside. Those poor girls." She kept looking into the fire. "If men would just quit going, it would stop. They think they're all just having a good 'ol time, but instead, they're draining the life from their souls."

Drake knew that was the truth.

Bell peered around the room. "You ever think we'll dance again?"

"With this leg?"

"Not you. I mean the folks coming in the tavern just to have a good time. Hear the old tunes and jig a little. Like the old days."

"Oh, well, I appreciate your sympathy for me," Drake replied.

She smirked. "You never could dance anyway. At least now, you'll be saved from embarrassing yourself any further."

He tried to think of a smart reply, but Bell went to humming an old tune. The sound brought such a memory to his mind that he couldn't speak. For as long as he could remember, his tavern was filled with laughter and life. Music rang within those walls even when his own father owned it before him and his father before that. Drake looked at his leg. His father died when he fell from a horse, and the injuries went for the worst. They never healed. They only turned green until he caught a fever, fell asleep, and never woke up again. Maybe he'd have a similar fate.

A commotion thundered outside the front door. After a second, the door pushed opened, and Quinn's back poked through. "Careful!" he shouted. "Don't ding it!"

"I'm trying," came Arnon's voice from outside. "But my fingers are going to get caught!"

"What in Theos' name . . ." Drake began to say, but as Quinn shuffled his feet backward, a grin stretched across his face. He could see the dark curved wood and green-silky fabric. "Don't you tell me you hauled that thing all the way from City Hall!" He stood up and hobbled toward them.

"It wasn't that bad," Quinn said, panting for air, just as Arnon had stepped in. They set the couch down with a thud.

Drake's smile was so wide it hurt. "You brought this in for me?"

"You can't expect that leg to heal sitting in those chairs all day," Quinn said as he tried to catch his breath.

Drake couldn't believe it. No one had ever done something this nice for him before. "Look at her," he said. There were even lighter patterns swirling in the green fabric, which he didn't notice in the darkness of City Hall. He sat down and stretched his legs over the arm on the far end. "Ain't this nice."

Arnon stepped back outside, and Quinn looked at Drake, then the rest of the room. "Don't you want to move it somewhere else than right in front of the door?"

"Nah," he replied.

Bell rolled her eyes. "We'll move it whenever he gets up."

Quinn crossed his arms, observing the room. "It don't match this room too much, does it?"

"Who cares?" Drake replied. "I tell you what, though. Maybe we ought'a grab all them couches and line 'em around the room. We could advertise it, and we'd get all sorts of business like never before. People would come from all over the city just to sit in 'em."

Quinn smirked and wiped the sweat from his brow. "If you want them that bad, you can haul them over here yourself."

Stepping back inside, Arnon held a bundle of hares and squirrels from a leather strap.

"Where'd you get them?" Drake asked, sitting up.

Arnon grinned. "I've got a few traps just outside the city. I checked them this morning and figured you could use some food."

"I appreciate you," Drake replied, and he meant it. Those hares looked nice and fat for any winter. "But I know some girls who'll need it more."

"You mean Sarah?" Arnon asked, setting the bundle on a table.

"Aye, helping those poor girls get out of the streets is costing her dearly."

Arnon looked out the door as if in thought. "You go ahead and take this. You need it, too. I'm gonna go hunt a boar."

"A boar? Where you gonna find one of them?"

Arnon crossed his arms. "You forget who my father was."

Drake laughed. "Aye, you got that right. I reckon he knew of all the best hunting spots around the city."

With his expression shifting to a troubled look, Arnon looked away. Drake feared he forever ruined the memory of his father for him. He would never forgive himself.

"Has Galvin or Porter mentioned anything about the dispatch to the Crossroads?" Arnon asked. "It's been close to a week."

"I ain't heard nothing yet, but be patient. It takes time to move that many people across the countryside."

That didn't seem to encourage Arnon any. And if he was honest, the thought of Myla and the girls roaming out there with alphyns put images in his own mind he wished to forget.

* * *

Sarah laid her lips on Acton's forehead. She didn't want to acknowledge it, but he still felt hot. One of the girls was already in bed for two days, sick with the fever, and rumors were beginning to spread

611

that it was coming out of the Southern District. She could only pray the plague wasn't returning.

Agatha stepped into the kitchen, carrying a small bone knife and a thick rag. She gave a sympathetic look. "I know you already said no, but for the baby's sake, I think it's time we bleed him."

Sarah tightened her grip around Acton. "Agatha, you're very kind, but Geoffrey has always been against it. He thinks blood-letting does more harm than good." She hoped she didn't sound too rude. "I would never forgive myself if he died because of it."

"But I fear he'll die if we don't."

"He's in Theos' hands. If it's his will, he'll live. If not, then he'll join his father."

Agatha wrapped the knife in the rag. "You're his mother, and I know you mean best." She glanced out of the kitchen. "I wanted to apologize again about Egbert and the food. I fear I've only brought trouble on you."

"There's no sense in staying sore over it. It wasn't your fault, and he meant no harm. I doubt he'll do it again."

Agatha smiled. "He still hasn't forgiven himself."

"Then you can tell him that I have, and he shouldn't stay put out." She peered into the fireplace room where Langleigh sat on her low bed with a psaltery resting on her lap. Beside the fire, Lilly played with her doll. "How has Langleigh been?"

"She's doing better. She still doesn't talk much, though."

At that, they both fell quiet, hearing the thrumming of the psaltery, and Langleigh's soothing voice softly hum in the tune of an old melody. She strummed the strings against the cherry wood as if she had played it her whole life.

"Where did she find that?" Agatha asked.

"The psaltery?"

"It sounds beautiful."

"Geoffrey purchased that many years ago." Sarah smiled. "But he never learned how to play it, so it just sat in an old chest. When Langleigh mentioned that she liked to play the dulcimer, I told her she could have it."

Agatha didn't reply as Langleigh shifted from humming to words. With Acton asleep in her arms, Sarah followed Agatha into the hall to listen. She recognized it as the Lament of Eadig the Wise:

Hear my plea and weeping
My heart and bones are breaking
Will you forever turn away your face
Like a father careless and disowning
How I long for your grace

O how we bear the prices
Of our own evil vices
How long will you leave us in this place
To endure the sorrows of our devices
How I long for your grace

Pity! I shout and cry
For our young mourn and die
And though we bury them in disgrace
You've made a promise and cannot lie
How I long for your grace

Hope appears under stars
One which heals our deepest scars
Our young and old, we again embrace
All your promises are now made ours
How I long for your grace

Langleigh drifted her words into another gentle hum, and Agatha disappeared down the hall. Sarah closed her eyes as she held Acton close, stroking his hair. Although she hungered for bread, the truths Langleigh sang were enough to feed her soul. The last time she heard that song was when she was a young girl when her mother sang it to her. Even though Eadig had lived only a century ago, his laments captured the heart of Hælend's Ballad the best. That even the darkest sorrows cannot extinguish the joy and hope of grace.

She almost couldn't believe how quickly everything was falling apart. Geoffrey. The lack of food. Now Acton was sick. Everwind was in political and economic ruin, and she could only guess what the other cities and villages looked like. And for the first time in Sunderian history, alphyns openly wreaked havoc in the countryside, with the occasional breach into the city. It was terrifying and deeply saddening. But it was also a sign. A sign that the end was coming, and then everything would be made right again.

To be at peace. To never feel sadness again. Part of her wished it would come tomorrow.

The front door slowly creaked open, and Adelyne stepped inside. Over her shoulder was a brown sack and in her right hand was a pint of milk. She kept her eyes down as she walked toward Sarah. "I brought some milk," she said in a low voice. Her neck looked dark. In the lighting, Sarah couldn't tell if it was a shadow or bruising. "And some bread and cheese." She said nothing more and disappeared into the kitchen.

Sarah could sense that something was wrong. At first, she thought about giving Adelyne her privacy, but she really didn't want to. She was determined to help that girl. She walked down the hall just as Agatha was leaving Egbert's room. "Could you hold him for a moment?"

"Of course," she replied, taking Acton from her.

Sarah walked into the kitchen, hearing once again the voice of Langleigh flowing through the house. On the table by the window, the sack was laid on its side with several loaves of bread and cheese wheels scattered from the opened end. Adelyne stood with her back to Sarah and her hands planted on the table. Her body shook in a quiet sob. Sarah walked over and placed a hand on her back but shuddered at the appearance of her neck. It was red, with brown and purple splotches, almost in the pattern of fingertips. Adelyne suddenly bent down to her knees with her forehead against the end of the table, breaking into a loud cry. The sound of her shrill voice, as she tried to inhale, sent a shiver down Sarah's spine. She looked and sounded like a girl whose soul was cut out from her.

Sarah didn't want to believe it, but she couldn't help but guess at how Adelyne got that food.

May Theos Protect You

Eirún peered out of the window. Directly below, the landscape lay green, but ahead, near the southern horizon, stretched a flat and barren sea of sand and dirt until it ended in the gray western marches of the Mountains of Einarr. Inside the cabin, several sailors looked busy as they walked to and from the cockpit. She knew they would be landing that day in the Dilution Sites, but how Hrunting was planning on stealing this wisp left her in a constant state of cold sweats. She removed herself from the window and headed to the aft. The hatch to the sleeping quarters was closed. She knocked and heard Hrunting rustling around.

He opened the door. "Eirún," he said in a positive tone. He stepped back, allowing her to walk in, then he closed the hatch behind her. Their bags were packed, and the bed was neatly made. He occasionally shook his hands with nervousness.

"Why did you pack the bags? I thought we were leaving in the wisp?"

Hrunting scratched his head. "I'm not sure why I did that. I think I was just trying to occupy my mind."

She understood. Whenever Søren got himself into trouble, or if she was fretting over something, she'd habitually sweep the floors, even if she had already done so that day.

"I figured that when we land at the Dilution Sites," Hrunting said, sitting down, "we'll walk off with the rest. Given the small amount of crew and the fact that that we've been in the air since we left Fingate, I would assume all the sailors would step out at some point."

"What happens if they don't?"

"Based on how they operated when we landed in Fingate, the worst-case scenario would be that there may be one or two men left onboard for watch rotations. But for such a small place as the Dilution Sites, I don't know. But just in case," he reached into his bag and pulled out a wheellock, "we may have to use this."

She stifled a gasp. "Do you think that will be necessary?" She had never seen one fire, but she had heard enough from Geirleif to immediately feel uncomfortable around it. "You're not going to actually kill anyone, are you?"

Hrunting laughed quietly as he gripped the handle. "To be honest, I don't think I could, even if I wanted to."

"Even if you wanted to? Does it not work?"

Hrunting scratched at his stubbled beard. "No, it works. I'm just not sure *how* to work it."

Eirún was surprised. He seemed to have more knowledge than most men she knew combined.

"The funny thing is," Hrunting said with a slight blush, "I helped engineer the barrels." He chuckled. "But for the life of me, I can't exactly remember how the arm and priming pan works. I thought about loading it, but I can't very well test it to see if it works, can I?" He raised a finger. "But don't be nervous. I can still operate a wisp, I assure you."

Eirún forced a smile, but just the thought of pointing that thing at somebody and stealing the wisp felt like a plan for disaster. Did he actually know what he was doing? She let out a long breath. At this point, she had no other choice but to trust him.

"And I trust you will never tell Geirleif that I can't operate his wheellock!"

Eirún laughed.

"I'll never hear the end of it!" The clank of someone walking past the hatch rang out, and they waited for a moment before saying anything else. "The Quartermaster has informed me that we will be landing within the hour," he continued. "Remember, you are Lady Signy Hrunting."

Eirún felt the ring around her finger. It was a little too big, but despite the tension of the moment, there was a part of her that enjoyed wearing it. She would have never thought about marrying Hrunting, but she imagined that if she ever were to be married, a gentleman like him would be nice.

By the time the wisp began to descend, Eirún was in the main cabin again, looking out the window with a hammering heart. Directly below meandered a dark river, where it filled a reservoir, from which the water channeled through a dam as it poured out into a white froth on the other end, making its way north toward Fingate. South of the reservoir, the green land turned a yellowish-brown, where several buildings arose, forming a rough triangle. In between them were many towers, all wrapped in iron fences, with voltaic copper wiring running from building to building. The only movement to be seen was the form of small bodies, no more than dots to her eyes.

"Hydro-voltaic power," Hrunting said, standing beside her. "That's what the dam is for. And it's cost us dearly."

"What do you mean?" she asked.

Hrunting glanced toward the cockpit, then back out the window. "There are some things that are probably better left unsaid, but the work that goes on there is the kind of the stuff our country will look back on in shame a hundred years from now. At least I hope so." He gave her a half-smile. "But now is not the time to worry about such things. We are about to land."

The quartermaster stepped into the cabin. "It's time to get fastened."

Both Hrunting and Eirún sat down on the benches and pulled down the leather straps over their shoulders, buckling the ends into the floor by their feet. A moment later and the wisp vibrated and rattled as Eirún shut her eyes and clenched every muscle in her body.

The smell of smoke billowing up through the floorboards brought on a nauseating headache. The shouting of the sailors only intensified the stress. Although she experienced the same thing when they landed in Fingate, she expected the wisp to explode at any moment.

Soon, the wisp jarred as it landed. The roaring of the engine and propellers eased into a steady hum, and she let out a sigh of relief. Looking down, she realized that Hrunting was holding her hand. He sheepishly drew back. "You looked afraid," he said with a boyish smile. Even with the faint graying in the sides of his hair, he appeared young for his age.

Eirún blushed and unbuckled the leather straps. "Thank you." She went to stand, but Hrunting motioned for her to hold on.

"Wait a moment," he said. "My nerves are shot, and I want to get this over with if we can. Let's see how many depart first."

The quartermaster stepped into the cabin, slicking his hair to the side, matching his perfectly groomed beard. "I trust that wasn't too exhilarating?" he asked.

"It was just fine," Hrunting replied calmly. "Thank you."

"As soon as the wisp is fastened, you'll be able to depart. Captain Holger will escort you to Section One for your proper permits."

"Thank you, again," Hrunting replied. "But if you don't mind, I think we'll stay onboard a moment. We're both feeling a little bit of motion sickness."

"Very well." He pointed out the window to a low brick building. "When you are ready, you can join Captain Holger in the entry facility. Just keep in mind that we will be departing at sunset."

"That is more than fine," Hrunting assured him. "It won't take me more than a few minutes to gather the blueprints."

"Very good, sir." The Quartermaster departed to the cockpit.

Eirún looked at Hrunting. "Now what?" she asked.

"We'll just wait and stay low for a moment. Then I'll take a look around and see who's left." He paused in thought. "We'll just have to go from there."

Eirún shook off her cold fingers and wished she wasn't sweating so much. And the headache didn't help. She began to realize why Geirleif often looked so stressed around him. Hrunting seemed to take everything as it came. And he seemed to like it that way.

Hrunting patted his gray outer coat where the wheellock was stuffed into his pocket. His gaze was fixed ahead in deep thought. Before long, sailors walked past them and through the outer hatch. The captain soon followed, tipping his hat at Eirún.

Outside, the sailors were tying down cables that attached the wisp to the wooden landing pad. Beyond was the entry facility, where the captain was now walking towards several other men. To the right ran a barbed wire fence. She could just make out the dam, as well as several men in gray shirts hauling dirt in wheelbarrows to a tall building, which blocked the rest of her view in that direction. To the left of the entry facility ran an open passage between the building and another fence. There, in a wide yard, sat two wooden buildings with many other men in gray shirts, sitting or idly walking around. A lump rose in her throat. Although there were too far to make out many details, she could still see that they were all horribly thin. Several of them were missing limbs. One man relieved himself by the fence, right in the open, with no pants—only a shirt, barely long enough to reach his thighs.

Hrunting was looking out the window as well. "I can't wait to be in Sunder," he whispered. He stood up, wiping his hands on his coat. "Wait here. I'm going to have a look around in the mess deck below."

Tearing her face from the scene, she kept her gaze on the wooden floors beneath her feet. She couldn't help but wonder what Sunder would be like. She was probably wrong, but she imagined a warm climate with small towns—very different from her own world. The people were nice, and there were lots of children. Maybe spring would arrive earlier there.

Hrunting appeared from the ladder well. "No one's left below." He walked past her toward the cockpit. After a moment, he walked back and slowly closed the hatch door, leading outside.

Eirún suddenly found it difficult to breathe.

"The Quartermaster is the only one left," he said. "Poor fellow. He'll have to go with us." He pulled the wheellock from his pocket, took a deep breath, and walked back to the cockpit.

Eirún stirred in her seat. She wanted to tell him to wait, but she had no reason to. Should she follow him? Stay where she was? She decided to stand up and peer from around the steam engine. Hrunting held the wheellock behind his back as he looked to the Quartermaster, who seemed to be observing a map.

"So," Hrunting said as he cleared his throat and bounced on his feet. "I imagine they've got you on board for the watch?"

"Unfortunately." The Quartermaster looked up. "It always is the Quartermaster's job to keep to the cockpit."

"Just one man, huh?"

"It's sufficient unless we're in foreign or hostile territory."

"Interesting," Hrunting replied. "How long did it take you to learn how to fly this?"

Eirún gripped a copper pipe until her knuckles turned white. What was he doing?

The Quartermaster smiled. "I just finished flight school last year."

"Very interesting," Hrunting said again, looking around the cockpit aimlessly. He nervously shook the wheellock behind his back, and Eirún was afraid he might drop it. "You have any family? Wife? Children?"

"Oh, no," he replied. "I'm only twenty-two. I'll get around to it one day, I'm sure."

"Well, that's good," Hrunting said, letting out a deep breath. "That'll make this a bit easier on me." He suddenly pointed the wheellock at the Quartermaster's head. "I'm terribly sorry about this. But I'll need you to take her back up."

The Quartermaster trembled. "But—"

"It's not an option."

* * *

From the camp gate, Geoffrey peered at the wisp, sitting just a hundred yards in front of him. Sailors were just beginning to walk out as they tied down thick-looking ropes mounted against the hull.

"Wish we could take one of those," Burlan whispered in his ear. "We'd be in Sunder in no time."

That would have been great, but Geoffrey knew it would never happen. Their best option was the western coast, and he didn't feel like making any rash decisions that would ruin that. Following Bartholomew in front of him, they soon stepped beneath the underpass. Imagining the joy he'd have when he saw his family once again, he prayed the door was unlocked. This was his only chance. For all he knew, if they missed this, they may all be burned by the next day.

As the crowds tightened, Bartholomew glanced behind him, then lifted himself on his toes to peer over the heads of those in front. As soon as they approached the door, Bartholomew opened it and slipped in. Geoffrey hurried behind. He flattened his back against the dark wall, chest tight, as Burlan stepped inside and closed the door to a crack. Immediately, Burlan began looking around the room. Through the window, Geoffrey could just make out the back end of the wisp.

"Praise Theos," Burlan said in a whisper. He lifted up a stack of clothes. "Quick, let's put 'em on, then we'll hide in the grate." But as he unfolded the clothes, a frown furrowed his brow. He glanced around the room again and even under the desk, then he looked up at Geoffrey with pursed lips.

"What is it?" Geoffrey asked.

"There're only two uniforms."

Despair knotted up Geoffrey's insides. "Are you sure?"

Burlan looked around again as Bartholomew gripped the hair on his head. "This is our only chance!" His voice came out hoarse and raspy.

"What about in there?" Burlan asked.

Geoffrey stepped over to a narrow cabinet and pulled open a drawer. Just a bunch of papers. "Nothing."

Burlan began pacing around, then he stared at Geoffrey with eyes so helpless he looked like a lost child, stricken with fear. "One of us will have to stay back. We've got no other chance."

Geoffrey's head throbbed, and his jaw felt so tight he thought it would crack. Was Theos playing some kind of game with them? Why did there have to only be two?

"Me and Geoffrey's got kids," Bartholomew told Burlan. "You should stay back."

"Quiet!" Burlan hissed. "Let's think this through." He pulled his hair and paced back and forth. "What if two of us dress up like guards and we carry the other one out as a prisoner?"

Geoffrey shook his head. "That won't work. No one's ever seen a Sunderian leave this camp. The moment they ask questions, they'll know we aren't Daecish."

Bartholomew buried his face in his hands. "I ain't never gonna see my little Langleigh again, am I?"

Geoffrey closed his eyes. He could see Lilly sitting in the kitchen, in her little woolen gown. Sarah, still pregnant, walked toward him, reaching out her arms. As she hugged him, the warmth of her skin pressed against him, and the sweet smell of her hair floated in the air. His eyes watered, and a tear dripped off his nose in the darkness of the room. He opened his eyes. "May Theos protect you both." He stepped toward the door and grabbed the handle.

"Wait," Burlan insisted.

Ignoring him, Geoffrey walked out and shut the door behind him. The crowds were still moving forward, and he joined the mass as his head went foggy; the reality of what he had just done barely registered in his mind. As he stepped out of the underpass, the sun warmed his face despite the cold air. The crowd of gray-shirts began to thin as some were sent to the reservoir, others to the mill.

A loud commotion came from up ahead.

Several of the gray-shirts were looking east, through the fence, behind the brick building to his right. He walked over and peered in the direction of their gaze. Half a dozen Daecish guards were shouting out orders as the wisp roared and the propellers quickened their speed. Steam sprayed from black circular objects beneath the flat bottom of the hull. Other men, who appeared to be in sailor attire, an outfit he hadn't seen since the invasion, ran around with no apparent order.

The gray-shirts all stumbled back as the wisp rose from the ground but faltered against the tension of the ropes. Dust whipped up from the ground in all directions, and Geoffrey turned as it stung his face. Peering below his shielding hand, he watched as more guards ran toward the wisp, their hats blowing off against the wind, but the ropes snapped, splintering parts of the hull in all directions.

The wisp effortlessly raised into the air as the guards still scrambled around in a mess, except for two, who walked along the fence line with their faces down. Geoffrey squinted. It was difficult to make out much through the dust, but the uniforms didn't quite fit right, and their faces appeared dark, likely from their beards.

Soon, they both disappeared down the road, beyond a low hill, and no one so much as looked at them. Geoffrey let out a smile. It seemed they didn't have to wait. Theos had given them the perfect distraction to escape. At that moment, peace came over him. He knew it wouldn't be long now, and for the first time in his life, he looked forward to the hope of what laid beyond death.

Death Runs Deeper Than the Flesh

Wrapped in a wool blanket, Adelyne sat against the back wall of the room with her elbows propped on her knees. The fireplace heated the left side of her face. A dozen makeshift beds scattered the room, with the wooden furniture tucked into the opposite corner against the half-timber walls.

Since yesterday, she had been in her bedroom upstairs, but Sarah made her come down for breakfast. The quarter loaf of bread still sat untouched on the pewter plate in front of her. Her eyes felt raw, and her chest ached. When she had woken up that morning, she first thought it was all a nightmare, but the pain from the bruising around her neck reminded her that Fletcher was real, and she could never take back what she did.

She had slept with other guys for aracs in the past. But this time, it was different. She couldn't just swallow her guilt down. Just the thought of Arnon and how much she loved him made her want to fall asleep and never wake up again.

In front of her, a girl slept on a low bed, shivering beneath her dark gown. Adelyne didn't know her age, but she looked very young—ten, maybe. She tried to recall her name but couldn't remember. The only thing she knew was that the girl came from a brothel in the Eastern District and had a fever since she arrived. That morning, Sarah had said that the girl's fever felt better, and even in the midst of her own torment, it gave Adelyne hope that Acton's fever would break too.

Sarah stepped into the room. Dark bags had formed beneath her red eyes as she sat down in front of Adelyne. "How are you feeling?"

She felt like dying, but she didn't respond.

"Now I know you won't talk, but if you hold it in, it's only going to make it worse."

How did she know it was only going to be worse? Had she done something like this? Probably not. Adelyne was done. She had no more hope. Arnon would find out sooner or later, and he would never so much as look at her. She may as well end her life now.

"If you won't talk to me," Sarah said in a soft tone, laying her hand on Adelyne's elbow, "you need to talk to Arnon. You'll never forgive yourself if you don't." She hesitated for a minute. "And I say this out of love. But he needs to know the truth."

Adelyne hid her face in her arms. It was easy for someone like her to say that.

Sarah picked up the plate and stood up. "I'll bring you something fresh in a little while. You'll need to eat if you can." She walked out of the room.

Hearing the voice of Cydney as Sarah walked away, Adelyne sank into her knees and peered in the entry hall. She wished she'd leave, but apparently, Sarah didn't have the heart to tell her. Maybe if she knew what she was really like, she would. Seducing men was just a hobby to her—a game. She even seduced married men, then afterward, she would spread the rumors, hoping the wife would find out. It was as if she enjoyed watching the hearts of other families rip apart.

Was she as bad as Cydney? She didn't think so, but if Sarah knew about either of their pasts, she'd probably kick them both out.

She peered forward, and Cydney and Egbert stepped into view. Cydney gave that flirtatious smile as she curled her hair. With her other hand, she poked his chest. "What have you got there?"

Egbert looked down and grabbed on the end of a long necklace that hung from his neck. The straps were leather, but at the bottom was something Adelyne had never seen. It looked heavy and expensive. Egbert took a step back. Cydney giggled, then she placed both of her hands on his shoulders. "I just want to look at it."

Egbert shook his head.

Cydney's smile turned to a grin. "I bet I can convince you to take it off."

Cydney was disgusting.

"Egbert," came Agatha's voice stepping from behind him. She gave Cydney a cold look and took Egbert's hand as they walked out of view. Cydney glanced into the fireplace room and examined Adelyne. With a sigh radiating boredom, she walked over and sat beside her.

"I bet that'll get us a good amount of food," she said, nodding back to the entry hall.

Adelyne remained quiet.

"You look sore; what's wrong with you?" She peered at Adelyne's neck. "Fletcher, huh? He can be rough at times. But you should be happy. You're all he wants."

Adelyne's chest quivered again. She couldn't handle crying anymore. "Please go away."

"Some people," Cydney scoffed as she stood back up. "Don't matter what happens, they'll never be happy. I'm gonna get that necklace." She walked off.

For the next hour, Adelyne was left alone. She spent most of her time in a haze, trying not to think. But whenever she did, she thought of ways she could talk to Arnon. How to justify it. Excuse herself. But every time, her stomach ended up in knots. There was nothing she could say to soften what had happened. But why did she tear herself up so much about it? And why did she love him so much? They weren't even married. Sarah was wrong. He didn't need to know the truth.

The front door swung open, and Adelyne held her breath. Part of her wanted it to be Arnon more than anything else, and the other part would have rather died. She let out a deep groan and felt as if her bones were wasting away. Sarah stepped out of the kitchen with wide eyes as she peered at the front door. Adelyne still couldn't see who it was.

"Where did you get that?" Sarah asked.

"I killed it this morning," came the voice of Arnon.

He stepped into Adelyne's sight with a boar slung over his shoulder.

Sarah held her hands to her mouth, then she rushed forward and gave him a hug. "You don't realize what you've just done!" she exclaimed. "You've saved us!"

Adelyne lowered her head. She went through all that for a few loaves of bread and some cheese. Was it really worth it? She bit her lip. Did she actually go to Fletcher just because of the food? She knew that wasn't the case. When she looked up, Arnon was looking back at her with narrowed eyebrows.

"Adelyne?" he asked. "Are you okay?"

He glanced to Sarah, who tried to look normal, but the worry in her own eyes was too obvious.

This was it. He was going to find out what she had done.

* * *

Eilívur sat against the stone wall, lazily gazing through the bars of the cells to his left. Of what little he could make out, there must have been over a hundred men crammed into those tight spaces. Fights had broken out in recent days. One man bit off another man's ear. Others wailed and paced around, picking and scratching at their sores. Feces puddled everywhere. All evidence that the early signs of starvation had already passed. At the foot of the iron bars to his own cell sat a scrap of half-baked dough, molded and soggy. The ground beneath him was wet, leaving his pants constantly damp, while his fever sent cold shivers down his body.

The last time he could remember being this cold was when he was a young child. It was a bad winter, and all he and his family had was a small wood-burning stove to keep them warm. But when his birthday came around, his mother had given him a navy blue peacoat. It was his father's when he was a child, and it looked just like the real kind sailors wore. He was so excited he even slept in it. Of course, it only took him two weeks to snag it on a branch and lose one of the buttons. And being as poor as they were, his mother had told him he'd have to wait until his next birthday to get a new button sewn on. He missed that coat.

At the top of the stone stairway, the dungeon door screeched open against the iron hinges. Galvin Barclay walked down with two other brigadiers. Eilívur never forgot a name, and this man was one of a kind. He held himself as if he was the new king, but he looked like the rest of them—a poor peasant, too dimwitted to see his own folly. The Sunderians never defeated the Daecish; they only aggravated them— stirred the hive a bit. Barclay led a fool's hope, and their days were running short.

Barclay and the others continued down the passageway to the very end, stopping before the cell which held Albern. He'd been so quiet for the past two days, Eilívur thought he was dead.

"Who's that?" Barclay asked, looking into Albern's cell, though his grayed left eye wandered, almost as if he was unconsciously looking toward Eilívur.

Eilívur glanced to where he was pointing. Beside the mass of Albern, who laid under his cloak, was another man sitting in the corner with his legs stretched out before him. He had iron shackles around his wrists and a bloated stomach. His eyes were sharp like silver, but his few teeth were blackened. Eilívur couldn't recall seeing him brought in.

Barclay looked at the brigadiers. "Did you bring him in here?"

They shook their head.

Barclay peered at the man. "You there. Prisoner. Who brought you in?"

The prisoner gave a distressing laugh. "I brought myself in."

"You're as mad as Albern," Barclay replied with raised eyebrows. He motioned his hand to the brigadiers. "Let's take Albern. We'll leave this other feller locked up until we find out how he got there." Stepping into the cell, Barclay put his hands on his hips. "Albern, it's time."

Shifting his legs, Albern's wet cloak slipped from his head as he let out a moan, but nothing more. Clumps of his thinning hair piled on the floor. Did it just fall out, or did he pull it out? If Eilívur had more strength, he would have laughed. Every time he looked at that man, he remembered why Daecland did the right thing in taking Sunder from such madness. If Albern had been given more time, he probably would have started demanding the people to worship him as some god. Sunderians never quite understood what the Daecish had saved them from. But what did it matter? Their kingdom was crumbling anyway.

The two brigadiers pulled the king to his feet and began to drag him out of the cell and down the passageway. Drool dripped from his mouth, and he grunted but made no effort to resist. Barclay relocked the cell and followed them but paused in front of Eilívur as he looked down to the soggy bread on the floor, which was now nothing more than a pile of light brown mush. "Why have you quit eating?"

There was a thread of hope in Eilívur that if they held any value to him as a prisoner, he could convince them to feed his men. Otherwise, he would starve himself, leaving them with no negotiation. "Feed my men first."

"I've barely got enough to feed myself or my people." Barclay pointed to the cell on the far end, where Eilívur couldn't make anything out. "And they are eating. At least, they're drinking the blood of one of their own. I think he died last night."

Eilívur held his composure, but anger seeped into his veins. "You're all monsters."

"If we're monsters," Barclay replied with a snarl, "then what do you call the rape of our women in the mines? Or the children who you left to starve in the slums after you kidnapped their fathers?"

He was aware of the mines, but as to the draft? What was it for? Certainly, there wasn't a war going on; otherwise, he would have heard about it. He did know that as bad as the slums were in Sunder, it would've been worse if Daecland hadn't been there. "You don't understand the first thing about running a kingdom."

"Now that we've taken it back from you, we'll learn!"

Eilívur almost laughed. "Then tell me, what exactly do you plan to do when we take Everwind back?"

Barclay straightened but didn't respond.

"Do you actually believe you've defeated us? In Norfrost, Fingate, even in your Llynhithe, we have legions of armed men. Fleets of wisps. Weapons you've never even imagined in that peasant mind of yours. Do you truly think we're just going to let you have your country back?"

He waited for a response, but Barclay only gazed down the hall.

"But you know that, already," he continued. "You know you never had a chance to actually win back Sunder. You better wake up soon. Your false sense of victory will end in misery before you realize it."

As Barclay walked out of the dungeon, Eilívur knew he had gotten the best of him. And for good reason. Daecish fleets would arrive soon, and these peasants would be crushed.

Eilívur curled the corner of his mouth into a smile. As soon as his rescue came, he'd finally get justice against the rebels. Especially Arnon.

* * *

Adelyne couldn't keep her back from trembling. She had just told Arnon everything. Not of her father, but of Fletcher. She had prayed that it would make her feel better, but the look on Arnon's face made her realize that her worst nightmare was coming true. He had given no response. But what hurt her the most was that she could tell by the cold darkness in his eyes that he no longer felt anything for her.

Adelyne's whole face drained as she tried to wipe her face. "I'm so sorry," she cried. And she meant it.

Arnon's eyes drifted from her as he gazed aimlessly across the empty room. Sarah had taken the girls to the back of the house to apparently show them how to hang and slaughter the boar. Adelyne never felt so alone. She peered at Arnon through her tears, but he was still expressionless, with a tired and heavy posture. For a long time, he stood there, and she didn't know what to say. Then, slowly, he began to walk away.

"Please!" she begged. "Please don't leave me!" But she knew it was no use. She was nothing more than a prostitute. In older days, she would have been thrown into prison if not put down for the betterment of society.

He rounded the corner into the hall. She waited to hear the front door open and shut behind him, but there was only silence. Then she jolted as he hit something against the wall. Then the front door slammed shut.

The Beginning of the End

Galvin grimaced. The straw had already been piled around the wooden block. Cut from the trunk of an ash tree, the top had been carved to fit the neck. Somewhere behind the stable, Clive was dawning his hood. Galvin didn't enjoy forcing him to take up his grandfather's occupation, but that was the tradition. Personally, Galvin thought Clive should be proud to resurrect the bestowing of royal executioner. However, since Clive hadn't seemed too impressed by the role, he'd assured him that given the gravity of the situation, his identity would remain a secret.

A shuffling, dragging sound caught his ear, and he turned around. As the old king of Sunder was dragged across the cobblestone, the crowd stood in silence. Many looked at one another as if in disbelief of what was about to happen. That was interesting, given that an hour ago, they wouldn't quit chanting for Albern's beheading. Perhaps they didn't expect to actually get what they had asked for.

Galvin rubbed his icy hands. Beside him, Porter hollered out a sneeze and wiped his red nose with his arm. Porter leaned toward his ear. "You sure we won't regret this?" he whispered.

Perhaps. Galvin himself wasn't entirely comfortable with it, but the people had spoken. "It's what they want," he replied, pointing to the crowd. "And the brigadiers voted in favor of it. I won't stand in the way."

Galvin glanced to the side. From the stable, Clive slowly made his way to the block. The black hood did a good job in hiding his face. Galvin wondered how he could even see through the tiny eye holes. Albern was led by two men, who positioned him before the crowd.

With hands bound in rope and trembling bent legs, the king practically leaned against one of the men as his glazed eyes wandered behind his greasy hair.

"Good people," he barely mumbled. "I've come hitherto . . ." His balance wavered, and he stumbled backward. He kept mumbling something, but Galvin couldn't understand any of it. The crowd remained silent. Almost breathless.

Giving him no more time to speak, the two guards blindfolded the king and dragged him to the block. Galvin winced. In the old days, an official would announce the king's execution at this point, along with a list of the crimes he had committed. Galvin had prepared something, but he couldn't bring himself to speak.

With the king's neck in place, Clive gripped the ax handle and made eye contact with Galvin. Galvin simply gave the nod. Clive's arms visibly shook. The man had felled trees for over thirty years, and yet he kept repositioning his grip as if he'd never held an ax before. When he, at last, lifted the blade above his head, several in the crowd turned away.

The ax swung forward, but Clive had missed the neck as the blade hacked into Albern's shoulder. The king howled. The crowd moaned, and several cried out in disgust. Galvin hid his face in embarrassment.

"Dispatch him quickly!" Porter hollered.

Clive pulled at the ax while another man held Albern down. The old king twitched but otherwise made no more noise. The ax swung down again. This time, Clive's aim was true, but it took another two blows to completely sever the head. The straw soaked up the blood which ran down the block, and one of the men held up Albern's head by his hair.

The crowd gasped, and Galvin lost his own breath when the king's lips continued to move. He knew this happened at times, but he couldn't help but wonder if the king was somehow speaking a curse over the people for their deed.

"Theos, save the House of Burgess!" shouted the man holding his head, and the crowd echoed his call.

* * *

Arnon marched north along Merchant's street. His mind was filled with anger, but he tried to keep his mind off of her. He was tired of trying to help people. He was tired of everyone he loved letting him down. He shivered and wished he had never given his father's cloak to that Daecish coward. What was he thinking? And how could Adelyne have had sex with a man for food? Did she not trust him? That he would take care of her? She was just using it as an excuse, and the boar he killed would certainly prove that. He hoped every bite would remind her of how thoughtless she really was.

Approaching the castle courtyard, which stretched out to his left, he noticed the shutters were open to a small blacksmith shop to his right. The stone foundation sagged into the cold mud, and on the other side of the small window was a table. On it sat a single loaf of bread.

He wasn't even that hungry, but he wanted it. And he had every right. He had fed all those girls at Sarah's and did everything he could to help this city. If everyone else did what they wanted, why couldn't he?

Hurrying to the window, he glanced around and snatched the loaf of bread. He took a large bite and rushed across Merchant's Street to the castle. Passing the fountain of the wolf to his right, he tried to erase his memory of the day he had walked around the courtyard with Adelyne. His bones felt hot, and his head ached. He had had enough of it all—Galvin, Porter, Adelyne, even his own father. Was nothing left unruined?

Pausing in his step, the bread in his mouth turned bitter. He looked at the remains of the loaf and suddenly felt disgusted with himself. Did he seriously steal this? He threw it onto the ground and spit out the rest.

For a while, he just stood there, lost in a sea of memories. All of them were dark and tainted. He pictured Adelyne and Fletcher together. Maybe he should just go the way of Haiden. Find some cliff and throw himself off. Don't be stupid. But he did want to run away. And that's exactly what he was going to do. With clenched fists, he hurried up the castle steps. If Galvin didn't have any information on his family, he would take a band and leave for the Crossroads himself. And there he would stay.

When he placed his hand on the castle door, grief threatened to overshadow the anger pumping through his veins, but he swallowed his sorrow and, with a deep breath, wiped his nose and pushed the door open.

His feet echoed into the ceiling of the great hall as he made his way to the door on the far right. Mounted on old hinges, the door often stuck against the stone frame, and he had to jerk it to pry it open. Now heading down a dark hallway where the air hung thick with burning pitch from the torches, he glanced into the council chamber, where a few thin windows brought in more light. Galvin sat at the head of the table with a brigadier, whom Arnon didn't know by name. Drake stood at the corner of the table with a red face.

"When did this happen?" Drake scowled.

"At dawn," Galvin answered in a sullen tone. His burgundy tunic was well maintained, but his beard had grown wild, and his face sagged, thin and weary.

Drake's hand trembled against his cane. "And at what point did you all vote to have him beheaded?"

Who did they behead? Arnon could only hope it was some Daecish officer.

"Last night at our meeting," the brigadier replied.

"Why wasn't I asked to join?" He pointed to Arnon. Apparently, they all knew he was standing there in the doorway. "And why didn't you ask him?"

Galvin let out a sigh. "Because the council is for brigadiers only."

"And who gave this tyrannical army the authority to kill the king?" Drake hollered. "Suddenly, you're in charge now?"

Arnon didn't say anything, but mad or not, he couldn't believe they'd killed the king. The House of Burgess had continued unbroken for thirteen-hundred years. This would have far bigger consequences on the minds, and the hearts of the people than Galvin likely realized.

Galvin stood up. "The Free Sunderian Army is the reason this city is protected! Who else is feeding the people or rebuilding their homes?"

"I ain't seen that food, and neither has anyone else I talked to!"

"Drake, my friend." Galvin tried to calm his voice. "Keep to your tavern and leave the welfare of Everwind to those who know what they're doing."

Drake peered at Galvin in the eyes as if he was trying to read his thoughts. "You and your army murdered the king. It's treason, nothing less." He turned and walked out.

"It was the people who wanted him dead!" Galvin called after him.

Walking past Arnon, Drake disappeared into the hall.

Galvin slammed his hand on the table, and his face burned red. "Arnon," he said, looking down, "I'm hungry. I've got riots breaking out at the grain stores in the Southern District. I'm accused of being a tyrant by my enemies and my friends. I'm trying to do what's right." He looked up. "Please help Drake see that."

Arnon stood quiet. He saw things as Drake did, and he feared that corruption was already beginning to show itself, but at that moment, he couldn't think straight enough to even give an answer. Part of him pitied Galvin, and he wanted to say something, but the other part of him obsessed over Adelyne, and he wanted to crawl inside a hole. "I'll talk to him," he replied at last. But he didn't actually mean anything by it.

"Thank you," Galvin replied.

Arnon glanced through the thin window on the wall to the right, barely able to make out the lawn outside.

"And Arnon?"

He turned back to Galvin.

"I want to ask for your forgiveness. I spoke about your character without thinking in the Keld Valley. And you should know that your father was a good man. The best."

Arnon didn't want to hear anything about his father. Drake already told him enough, and Galvin would probably say anything right now because he was afraid of losing the peoples' trust. "Has any word been sent from Crossroads?" he asked instead.

Galvin sat back down. "Unfortunately, no, but it still may take more time."

There were two dozen families, including his own, whose fate was entirely unknown. "Have any of the other men left to check on their families?"

"I'm not giving leave for anyone until we stabilize this city."

Arnon tried to untense his shoulders. "It's been long enough, and I fear the worst. May I have permission to take a band to Crossroads?"

"Everwind is too frail and our army too small to let any more go. But if you wish, I'll give you leave. You can use my own horse."

Knowing there was nothing more to be done, Arnon performed a half-hearted salute. Galvin wasn't looking up and didn't salute back. "Thank you," Arnon said as he walked out the door.

As he stepped outside, he could see Drake sitting at the bottom of the steps just before the courtyard. The buildings across Merchant Street looked livelier than the previous days. Shops appeared to be open, and there was a certain canter in the people's steps as they strolled along the cobblestone walkways. But even with that, there was still a settling grayness in the atmosphere—an underlying hunger and desperation. It was as if the people longed for normalcy, and if they couldn't have it, they would at least pretend it was so.

He walked down the steps and sat beside Drake, whose temper seemed to have cooled as he looked ahead to the crowds. "I don't know how much more I can take," Drake admitted. His breath smelled bitter from ale, and Arnon knew he was drinking more than usual.

Arnon picked up a pebble and pressed it between his finger and thumb. "Me neither," he replied.

"If this world don't end soon," Drake said, "you've got your life ahead of you. But me, I'm running out. I got fever. My leg's infected. My tavern's empty. I'm forsaken by Galvin, perhaps rightly so. No, I don't reckon I'll be around much longer."

Arnon didn't want to hear it anymore. Right now, the last thing he needed was to lose Drake. "Don't say that. You're all I've got."

"Ain't true, boy. You got Adelyne."

"No, I don't."

Drake laid his arm around Arnon's back. "I heard what she'd done."

Raising his eyes, Arnon looked at him.

"I heard it from Bell, who heard it from Sarah." Drake shook his head, smiling with just the corner of his mouth. "But you know how women are. Once a story goes through so many, you don't know what's been added or changed. But the look in your eyes tells me I heard the truth."

"Then you know why I have to leave today. I'm going to get to my family."

Drake squinted an eye as he observed him. "I'm gonna tell you something. I probably should let her tell you herself, but I reckon she won't." He looked ahead and let out a deep sigh. "After her mother died, her father went to drinking too much. And he, uh—" He took in a long breath through his nose. "He raped her, Arnon. For years."

The muscles in Arnon's jaw trembled, and he sank as if a heavy weight pushed his chest to the ground.

"None of us knew at first." Drake wiped his eyes. "Otherwise, we would've stopped it sooner. Praise Theos Darragh got drafted when he did."

All Arnon could picture were the bruises on her neck. Then he remembered the bruise on her cheek when he first met her. He wanted to kill Fletcher. He wanted to kill Darragh. And Adelyne, he didn't know what to think. He was still angry with her, but he pitied her all at the same time. "Drake, what am I going to do?"

"I reckon most would move on to someone else. And I don't blame you for wanting to."

Move on. Arnon wanted to do that more than anything else, but the longer he sat there, the harder it was to imagine himself without her.

"Let me ask you something," Drake said. "And you answer me straight." He waited for a second. "Do you love her?"

Arnon didn't want to, but he nodded. He loved her more than anything else in this world. He would've married her if she'd let him.

"All right, then you best learn now that ain't nobody perfect. Every single one of us got evil in us, though some worse than others. And though we don't deserve forgiveness, we've got to forgive one another. Otherwise, not a single one of us will be able to stand on the Day of Reckoning, you hear?" He rubbed his face as if trying to keep himself awake. "Now, that don't excuse what she done with that feller. It was wrong, and she's gotta turn from it. And if you still want to leave her, you got every right to. You can forgive and move on. But you said yourself that you still love her. And what she needs is a man in her life that'll show her what real love is."

As much as he resisted it, he felt a glimpse of sorrow penetrate his anger. And despite the pain in his chest and the grossness he felt over the whole thing, every part of her was still beautiful to him.

Drake patted Arnon on the back. "At least tell her your mind. It may be your only chance before you leave."

"I'll see you soon, Drake," he said, standing up. "Don't die before I get back from Crossroads."

It was late afternoon by the time Arnon made it to Sarah's place. His whole thoughts were consumed with what to say, and at the same time, a new wave of grief and anger swelled up in him. It was all so much to take it at once.

He pushed open the door. Inside, the house looked busy as several girls chatted in the kitchen. In the hall, just ahead of him, was Sarah and another girl with a pale blue ribbon tied in her black hair.

"What do you mean?" Sarah asked.

The girl held her hand against her stomach. "I think I'm pregnant, and I don't know what to do."

"Cydney." Sarah's face grew worried. She seemed to be at a loss for words. Looking across the hall, she spotted Arnon and placed her hand on the girl's shoulders. "Give me a second," she said and walked toward him. "I hope your here to talk to her." Her eyes watered. "She hasn't left her room since you left. I'm afraid she's going to starve herself before it's all over."

Arnon gazed at the stairway. "I'll talk to her." He walked up the steps. The lanterns on the hallway were out, and the sky looked gray behind the single window on the back wall. Two doors were on the right, with a single door on the left—Adelyne's room. He stood in front of it and placed his hand on the knob. What could he even say to her? He still loved her, somehow even more so. But he felt sick about what she had done and couldn't just be okay with it.

He quietly prayed before he turned the knob, and the door swung open. Curled up beneath the blanket was the shape of Adelyne. Her hair sprawled out over the long bolster pillow. Arnon walked around the bed. Her eyes were blank as they stared forward.

As he sat down beside her on the floor, she glanced at him and her face twisted into grief. She tried to mumble something incoherent, but she seemed to barely muster the strength to move her lips. Arnon immediately leaned forward and wrapped his arms around her. She tried to talk, but a sudden sob kept her from getting a single word out. Before he realized it, tears were pouring down his cheeks, and he ran his fingers through her hair. "I love you," he told her.

"I love you so much," she finally got out.

For what felt like an hour, they laid there together, saying nothing, as he kept her wrapped in his arms. The mildewed scent from the moss stuffing in the pillow filled his nose as he gazed at the wall, with his cheek resting on her hair.

"Why did you come back?" she eventually asked.

At first, Arnon thought about telling her that he knew what her father had done to her, but he didn't think it was the right time for that yet. Then he remembered Drake's words about how no one was perfect. "I'm not as good as you probably think." He paused for a moment as she turned, squinting at him peculiarly. He leaned back and picked at the bedsheets; tiny black bugs crawled through the woven fabric. "I'm selfish. I say things without thinking. I once called my sister a horse."

Adelyne raised an eyebrow.

"That doesn't sound like anything, but she's looked up to me her whole life, and when I said that, she could never see herself as beautiful. I've stolen things, including food, from hungry people. I've told so many lies. I've thought things I would never share because if I did, no one would want to be around me." He shook his head in shame and began to habitually wipe his hands again. "When I killed those men at my homestead . . ." he couldn't get it out. "Something cruel came out of my heart. It wasn't justice; it was hatred. I'm not good. I need forgiveness for more things than I can count. So how could I not forgive you?"

She leaned forward and hugged him. "You're not as bad as I am, though."

"That's not true."

"But it is. You may forgive me, but I don't think Theos ever would." She closed her eyes and sniffed in with a whimper. "He doesn't just know what I've done. He knows everything about me. I'm afraid that when I die, I'll find out how much he hates me."

Arnon took her hand in his. "Listen to me. The only reason anyone will be able to enjoy the life after this one is because of mercy. Every single one of us needs to be forgiven. You, me, our own families."

She didn't respond, and he placed his other hand on her cheek. "He knows all of your thoughts and everything you've done, and he still loves you more than you could ever know. You must trust in that."

"But doesn't he punish evil? Isn't that what Hælend's Ballad is all about?"

Arnon thought for a while. "My father always told me that those who want forgiveness will have it. But those who refuse to admit that they need it won't. It's almost as if Theos gives us what we want."

"But if you keep doing the wrong thing, will he keep forgiving?"

The question bothered him. He loved her, but he also knew he couldn't handle her ever being with another man again. If they were to be together, she would have to commit to him. "When you experience the forgiveness, you want to change." He thought carefully about how to say the next words. "It doesn't mean you'll be perfect, but, for me at least, forgiveness brings a desire to run from the wrong things and to do what's right. When I killed those men, my mother told me she loved me no matter what. And all I wanted to do at that moment was be her innocent son again. To be washed clean."

Adelyne rolled over so that her face was hidden. Arnon couldn't help but wonder what she was thinking. "I love you," she said.

He smiled. "I love you too."

As he laid beside her, letting his mind wander to what their life would like together, he was reminded of his family. The last thing he wanted to do was leave her, but he also knew he couldn't wait any longer. He needed to make sure they were okay. "I have to tell you something." He hesitated for a second. "I have to leave today, but it won't be for long."

Her face suddenly dropped, and she gripped his hand. "Please. Not now."

"I have to. My family has been at Crossroads since before the battle. I don't even know if they're alive. What if they need me?"

"Can't the Army send someone else?"

He leaned over and kissed her on the head. "Unfortunately, they can't. It's a three-day ride; I can make it in two if I'm quick. I'll be back before the week is over."

"But what if you don't come back?"

"I will," he insisted. "And when I do, I'm going to marry you."

A Winter Stroll Through Sunder

Eirún's eyes burned when she finally blinked again. Through the front windows of the cockpit, the green and white landscape seemed to rush upon them.

"What do you mean we can't land in Runevast!" Hrunting hollered. Gripping the ship's wheel, his eyes seemed to almost pop out of his strained face. "And what's happening to the wisp!"

With his hands tied to a pipe, the quartermaster motioned his head to a gauge beside Hrunting. "The engine's rattling because we're running low. We only had enough steam to make it back to Norfrost. I've been trying to tell you that!"

"No!" Hrunting argued with his eyes still locked on the landscape outside. "All you said was that we had enough steam to get back to Norfrost! Based on the map, I took that to mean we could also make it to Runevast since it wasn't much further!"

"If you were flying straight, then yes. But you've been sailing all over the place. If you don't land this soon, the balloon will deflate, and we'll crash!"

Dizziness swamped Eirún as the wisp continued to descend. She stumbled out of the room, bracing her hands against the bulkhead, and forced herself down on the leather bench.

"Buckle yourself in!" she heard Hrunting holler after her.

Snapping the buckle into the floor, she straightened her posture, trying to calm her breathing. She glanced outside the window behind her. Beneath the clear sky, the snow-laden hills rolled into the mountains of Einarr. Through the window across from her spread the gray expanse of some sea. Suddenly, the wisp wavered and tilted to one side. Eirún's head flung back as it knocked against the window.

"Brace yourself!" Hrunting shouted. "We're going to land!"

"W—What about me?" the quartermaster stammered. "We can't land with myself bound like this!"

"I'm sorry!" Hrunting replied. "But I can't take my hands off the wheel!"

Holding the back of her head, Eirún shot her gaze around the cabin. Did she have enough time to untie him? There was a sudden jolt as her body shot up against the leather straps which held her down. Her neck whiplashed as the floorboards in front of her erupted, uplifting the engine onto its side. Steam surged from the piping with a deafening roar, cloaking the interior of the cabin like a scalding white cloud.

When she opened her eyes, she wasn't sure if she had passed out or not. Steam still spewed out from the engine. Smoke filled her nostrils. Rays of sunlight broke through the ceiling. The floor was a disheveled mess of broken boards, piping, and shattered glass. She bent down to unbuckle the belt, but it was already hanging loose, torn from the floor mount. Standing up, she held on to her throbbing head. Her neck felt sore, and she could hardly keep her balance. She stumbled her way across the cabin and peered into the cockpit. Hrunting lay forward, the side of his head running red onto the ship's wheel. The Quartermaster was piled in the corner—the pipe which once held his bound hands was broken as oil dripped onto the floor.

"Hrunting?" she called out.

There was no answer.

She shook his shoulders. "Hrunting!" she called louder.

He moaned and slowly slid open his eyes. "Did we land?" he asked.

Eirún looked out the window. In front of her was a rising hill, backdropped by a blue sky. "Yes."

Hrunting straightened himself up. The wound on his head bled down the side of his face and onto his gray jacket, but it didn't look deep. He looked over to the quartermaster. "Is he all right?" He leaned toward him, but after a moment, he covered his face with his hand. Eirún then realized that part of the broken pipe was sticking out of the quartermaster's stomach.

"We killed that poor boy," he said with barely a whisper. "I didn't think we had to land so quick." He suddenly kicked against the gauges on the dash in front of him. "I would've untied him if I had just had the chance!"

Eirún startled at his shout, but she knew his anger wasn't toward her.

For a long while, Hrunting sat without saying anything.

"Should we bury him?" she asked at last.

"We must."

Outside, the air bit far colder than she would have expected. Although Hrunting had given her his coat, she still shivered as she watched him dig a hole at the base of a hill not far from the wisp. All he had was a wooden plank and a scrap of steel from the hull. With rolled-up white sleeves, he kept wiping the sweat from his brow as he continued to dig up the earth. It didn't look like he was getting very far. A wooden plank probably wasn't the easiest thing to use.

"Would you like some help?" she asked.

Catching his breath, he leaned against the plank. "Just a little more," he replied.

She wasn't so sure.

Soon, he threw the plank down. "All right, let's lay him in there."

Eirún didn't want to say anything, but even she could see that the hole wasn't very deep or very long. Hrunting walked behind her and grabbed the quartermaster by the shoulders. He dragged him over to the hole, but his feet stuck out about an extra foot.

Resting his chin in his hand, Hrunting made a humming sound as if he was working out a problem in his mind. "Maybe if I . . ." He titled his head to the side. "No." Then he walked over and pushed the quartermaster's feet into the hole, bending the legs at their knees.

"Hrunting," Eirún said in as gentle of a voice as possible. "I don't think it's deep enough."

"Nonsense." He took the plank and began covering the body with dirt. When he was finished, a knee and part of an elbow still stuck out. Eirún even thought she could make out the ends of the hair on his head. Hrunting put his chin back on his hand. "Maybe you were right."

Yes, she knew that.

He dropped the plank. "I'd dig more, but we need to get moving before we lose all of our daylight. He looked at the grave for a minute. "Should we say something?"

Eirún didn't know. Whenever they did funerals at the orphanage, an ambassador of the constable would stop by and say a few things. But it was all read from a paper and didn't actually mean anything.

"We come this day," Hrunting began awkwardly, "to honor the death of Mr. . . ." He looked at Eirún. "Did you know his name?"

She shook her head.

Hrunting grunted to himself as he bit his lip. "to honor the death of Mr. um—" he cleared his throat. "To the quartermaster of this fine wisp, which he sailed so bravely over the mountains."

He wasn't sailing; he was tied to a pipe. No one else was even around, and Eirún felt embarrassed.

"He just earned his pilot's license," Hrunting continued, "and now he will keep it with him, forever and ever."

Eirún snorted in laughter.

Hrunting blushed. "Look, I've never done a funeral. Would you care to say the next part?"

"No, no. I think you did a wonderful job."

"I believe you're right," he said, straightening his sleeves and holding his chin high. "Poor man. We didn't even know his name." He turned to Eirún. "Do you still have the map?"

Realizing she was wearing his coat, she pulled it out of his pocket and handed it to him. He unfolded it and followed his finger along the coordinate lines. "I believe we are here in this vicinity." He pointed to just above Everwind, near the north side of the Swelling Sea. Then he pointed west. "If we head in that direction, we should reach a road along the coast. We can head south from there toward Everwind."

After they had gathered their two suitcases, filled with mostly sailor's rations, three canteens of water, and a single change of clothes for each of them, they began the long walk west. Occasionally there was a sinkhole or a deep trench, marring the otherwise smooth hills which rolled like a rippling blanket. Mostly, the air smelled like winter—thin and fresh, but at times, a gust brought about a putrid smell she recognized only from her ride to Norfrost.

Making their way up an incline, she held up the bottom of her dress and quickly grew irritated at her aching toes, which cramped in her white, laced up steeple boots. She wished she had something with a lower heel. But as always, Hrunting was kind enough to hold her hand when she needed it.

Dark, leafless trees, mostly oak and walnut, sporadically grew in tight clusters. With the sun now high, what snow was left on the ground turned into a wet slosh. Her shoes soon went damp, and the briar, which often blended in with the tall grass, snagged her dress until dozens of loose orange and white threads hung about it. At first, she worried Hrunting's sister might not be too happy about her ruined dress, but then she figured they would never go back to Daecland anyway.

After a few hours, with only the occasional short rest, they crested yet another hill, and the Swelling Sea came into view as it sparkled beneath the sunlight. Massaging her sore thighs, she tried to catch her breath. She wished she could take off that troublesome corset beneath her dress. Daecish fashion, at least for women, could not have been more impractical. Why women suffered such an irritation for mere looks was beyond her.

Hrunting pointed in the distance. Not far from the beach ran a dirt road, really nothing more than a trail to her own eyes. "There," he said, glancing back to his map. "We'll follow that, and we should be in Everwind in a day or two."

"A day or two?" She scanned the countryside, her chest seizing at the thought of spending the night out there. They had no shelter and no means to start a fire. "But what about the cold? What if it rains?"

"Then we must move quickly. Maybe there's a village nearby." Hrunting raised his hand above his brow. "Look." He pointed south. On the road, not far from where it disappeared around a low ridge, was the small form of someone walking with a cane. Or maybe it was a staff. "Come on," he said, taking her hand. "Maybe he can help us."

"Wait," she said.

"What is it?"

"You said we would need to change names again."

"I believe you're right." He lifted his hand to his chin. "I doubt anyone would guess we are here, but just in case, how about I'll go with Halvor, and you can go by Eerika? We'll say we traveled from Llynhithe."

She wasn't sure how much she liked the name Eerika, but it was only for public appearance. "Okay," she replied.

They hurried down the hill as her dress flowered behind her and her toes hurt so bad she feared they were bleeding. By the time they made it to the road, whoever it was ahead of them had stopped and turned around. It looked like an old man with a hood over his head.

"Sir!" Hrunting hollered, waving a hand.

They hurried down the road until they stood before him, catching their breath.

The old man studied them peculiarly with a tilted head. "What can I do you for?" he asked.

Eirún wasn't sure if she understood him.

"We're on our way to Everwind," Hrunting said, straightening himself, though he still sounded winded. "Do you know how far we are?"

The old man rubbed the white stubble on the loose skin of his cheek, then pointed over a low hill to the east. "Lots of bandits on the roads these days," he said. "It's safer if you go that-a-way. But I reckon you won't be there 'til evening on the 'morrow."

"Excuse me?" Hrunting asked, squinting his eyes. "My apologies, sir, I'm having trouble understanding you."

"You ain't gonna make it by tonight," he said louder. He stepped forward and examined Hrunting in the face. Then he looked at Eirún. His breath smelled terrible, but the stench from his clothes was just as sour. "How'd you get here?"

Hrunting glanced at Eirún. "We traveled from Llynhithe," he lied.

The old man squinted again. "That ain't how you pronounce it. You tell me the truth now. I can tell right 'way you ain't Sunderian."

Eirún's pulse raced.

Hrunting seemed to battle with himself, then he shrugged at Eirún. "We're from Daecland," he admitted.

"I figured that already, but how'd you get here?" He kept his eyes on Eirún.

"We took a wisp," she said. "Over the mountains."

The old man licked his crooked teeth in thought. "I don't recommend going to Everwind. They don't take too kindly to Daecish folk." He poked his staff at her. "They ain't never seen a girl from that land neither."

"Is there somewhere else we should go?" Hrunting asked.

"Back to Daecland, if I's you."

"But we can't," Eirún said. "Haven't you a place we could stay?"

"Miss, I ain't had a home for a long time." The old man looked at the ground for a minute, rubbing his chin. "And you very well can't make it to Llynhithe or Astford on your own out here. Everwind's just about your only option. I'd be careful, though. Try to stay outta sight."

What did he mean by staying out of sight? Eirún only knew a little about the Sunderian expeditions, but as far she understood, some of her people were at least living there on friendly terms.

The old man dropped his weathered sack to the ground and took off his brown cloak, revealing his white hair and a faded-red shirt, which went down to his knees, with a single belt wrapped around his waist. "I've only got one, but you'll need it." He handed the cloak to Hrunting.

"I can't take this."

The old man waved a hand. "I get too hot in it anyway."

"But why do I need this?" He rubbed the leather in his fingers.

"To hide your hair and skin. You both look just about as Daecish as they come."

Eirún's stomach suddenly turned to bile, and Hrunting didn't look any better.

"If your gonna go on ahead, you might as well camp with me if you'd like. The hills are barely any safer than the road." He began to turn but paused. "The name's Benedict, by the way."

"Benedict," Hrunting replied. "My name is Halvor, and this is . . ." He motioned to Eirún.

She bowed and lifted the bottom of her dress, just as Geirleif had taught her. "Siv," she replied as she faintly smiled at Hrunting. That was a better name than Eerika.

Hrunting glanced at her and huffed out a laugh. Then he looked back at Benedict. "Now, what do you mean the hills are not safe?" he asked, throwing the cloak over his suitcase.

"Alphyns." Benedict waved his staff in the air. "All over this place. You's gotta be careful. Nasty things, they are." Then he tapped the bottom of his staff on the ground. "They mostly stay down there, though."

Below the ground? The creatures that had appeared just outside of Norfrost came to Eirún's mind.

Benedict pointed to the sea. "And wyrms be coming out of there before long, too!" He let out a gristly cackle as he began to walk south.

They both followed him with cautious steps as Hrunting leaned toward her ear. "Either this man is mad," he whispered with a half-smile, "or we've come into the strangest country I've ever heard of."

She knew he was only trying to make light of a situation that likely concerned him as much as her, but she wasn't so sure Benedict was mad.

By nightfall, Benedict had led them off the road to a dry hollow in the hills. On the eastern slope sat a cluster of oaks, bare and leafless, with large roots dangling from the dirt overhang. From within the trees, beneath the scant remains of snow, the damp rotting stench of vegetation kept nagging at her nose. Benedict laid down his sack and sat down, massaging his feet. Eirún promptly took off her own boots as Hrunting sat beside her.

"What is that caused from?" Hrunting asked, pointing behind Benedict.

Eirún looked up to see a wide sinkhole on the northside of a hill, with mounds of loose dirt around its edges.

"Alphyns," Benedict said.

Eirún froze with a boot still in her hands. "Shouldn't we stay somewhere else?"

"Nah." Benedict laid down on his side and propped himself up on his elbow. "They don't tend to come out of the same hole twice. Sometimes they do, but it ain't often."

That did little to make Eirún feel any better.

"Should we at least light a fire?" Hrunting suggested.

Benedict shook his head. "They come out at night. That'll only attract them."

Since she and Hrunting left Norfrost, Eirún looked forward to being in Sunder, but now she would do anything to be back in Daecland, or at least beneath the cover of the wisp. "Do you think we'll be safe?"

"We ought to be," Benedict replied.

"So, tell us about this land," Hrunting asked, probably trying to change the subject to something more pleasant. "What are your people like?"

Benedict laughed. "You've come at the wrong time to be asking 'bout us. This here world is dying."

"What do you mean?"

"The Day of Reckoning I mean."

"The Day of Reckoning?" Hrunting crossed his legs. "Now, what is that exactly?"

"All our old tales speak of it, especially Hælend's Ballad. It's when Sunder's Bane comes."

"Sunder's Bane?"

"From dark and hidden shadow, he'll bring judgment on the world."

"How interesting," Hrunting replied, balling his hand beneath his chin. He seemed far too interested. "So, this bane of yours will destroy the whole world for the evil in it, I presume? Even Daecland?"

"Aye," Benedict replied, "but Sunder's Bane is just a man. The instrument. The judgment comes from Theos."

"A man, you say? Is he special in some way?"

Benedict shook his head. "I don't reckon I know, but tradition says he's just a man. An outcast even. And shouldn't surprise us none. Theos uses even the lowest men to achieve his greatest works."

Hrunting's eyes seemed to dance with questions. "Now you said Theos. Is this your god?"

"Aye, but I don't reckon folk like you believe in that sorta thing, do you now?" Benedict chortled.

The whole idea of some god destroying the world was deeply disturbing to Eirún. "Why would you ever believe in such a god?" She put a hand to her mouth. She didn't mean to ask it out loud.

They both looked at her.

"I mean," she cleared her throat and suddenly felt nervous. She was always taught to leave such controversial subjects to herself, but she felt this to be a real problem. "Wouldn't you rather believe in a loving god rather than something so hateful? It just seems absurd to me to believe in a god who is bent on destroying everything he creates as if it's their fault."

Hrunting only continued to look at her with gentle eyes. She thought he would agree with her or at least say something, but he remained quiet.

"That's difficult," Benedict admitted, "trying to understand all of Theos' ways. But it's us who choose to do evil. You. Me. And his judgment," he lifted a finger, "is an act of his hatred *and* his love.

"What do you mean?" Hrunting asked.

"Judgment is both a display of his hatred of evil as well as his love for justice."

Eirún wasn't convinced. It didn't address the problem. "But don't you ever wonder why he ever allowed evil in the first place? Or at least why he doesn't end evil now?" She threw her hand in the air. "What is he waiting for?" She didn't say it aloud, but she would have been far more satisfied if this so-called god would have never created her, rather than making her endure the life she had.

A frown formed on Benedict's face. "I don't reckon I know why evil's allowed. But I do know that I'm not good, so who am I to be a judge of such things? But I'll say this. I'm glad he ain't ended evil quite yet."

Hrunting raised an eyebrow. "How so?"

Benedict laid down on his back. "'Cause evil comes from here." He pointed to his chest. "So, if he did end it now, none of us would wake up on the 'morrow. I can blame Theos night and day for allowing it, but I'm the one to blame for my own choices. I've done evil 'cause I wanted to. I deserve his judgment. Which is why I'm thankful for his patience. And his mercy."

"Mercy," Hrunting mumbled. But as he ran a finger through the wet grass, he seemed more interested in pondering the meaning of the word in his own mind rather than whatever Benedict's answer might be.

"Mercy," Benedict continued, "I reckon is the only time Theos ain't fair. He don't give us the judgement we deserve."

Eirún didn't know what to think. Her whole life, she had considered herself a good person. Of course, she had done some wrong things. She did steal a large sum of Audin's money, most of which she still carried on her. But who wouldn't have? He deserved it. But then there was the quartermaster. His death was their fault, wasn't it? She glanced at Hrunting, who looked troubled. Maybe he was thinking the same thing.

But his death was an accident. They would have saved him if they could have. And besides, she had always tried to be kind to others. She let out a sigh. That was until Mathios. She knew that most people would probably brush off her feelings as nothing, or they would maybe even say he deserved her neglect because he killed Søren. But the fact that she never forgave him or even spoke to him when he asked to see her wrecked her conscience. It was too late now, and she could never take it back.

The next morning, Eirún awoke with a startle. Lifting her head from the suitcase, she darted her eyes around the hollow. With a quiet sigh, she sat up and rubbed her sore shoulder. All night she had heard distant roars across the black landscape and was hardly able to even close her eyes. She glanced down at the two men, still sleeping. At

Benedict's bidding, all three had slept next to each other for the warmth. She was in the middle, with Benedict's back to her, as well as Hrunting's, out of respect. But she could never get that terrible smell from Benedict out of her nose. Below them stretched out the leather cloak, and several layers of their clothing were used as makeshift blankets. Soon, Hrunting stirred and rubbed his eyes.

Although the cloak kept the ground dry, their clothes were damp with cold dew. Standing up, she carefully stepped over Benedict and walked over to put on her boots, with Hrunting's coat still bundled around her.

"When Benedict wakes up," Hrunting said. "I want you to wear the cloak."

"But you'll freeze."

"I'll take my jacket, but you wear that. You heard the old man. They've never seen a Daecish girl." He leaned forward and lowered his voice. "And based on his character, I don't know what to expect. I'd rather be safe than sorry."

"But what about you? Won't they recognize you as Daecish?"

"It'll be fine. They'll assume I'm a Daecish officer. We do occupy Everwind, in case you've forgotten."

The thought did make her feel better.

As she tied on her boots, Hrunting walked over to Benedict. He bent over to wake him but paused. "Benedict?" he asked.

He didn't move.

"What's wrong?" she asked.

Hrunting placed a hand on the old man's shoulder. "Benedict?" he asked again. He felt the old man's cheek, then turned his face, revealing his cloudy eyes. "He's dead."

The Setting and Rising Sun

By evening, Eirún and Hrunting had made their way south-east, following the map as best as they could. They eventually came back to the road, which soon split into a fork, with the city of Everwind sitting on the southern horizon. Interestingly, some of the buildings, which peaked above the wall, looked vaguely Daecish, but it was too far to know for sure. Thankfully, they never encountered any bandits or those creatures Benedict spoke of. She hated that they had to leave his body in the open, but with no tools, they didn't know what to do. They did wrap him in Hrunting's spare shirt as best as they could, but it didn't feel like they did enough for the old gentlemen. And like Hrunting, she still couldn't get over the fate of that poor quartermaster.

Maybe it was her lack of sleep, or maybe it was the conversation they had with Benedict the previous night, but she felt herself getting low. Bitter even. The fact that she had to hide her blonde hair beneath the leather cloak didn't help either. She was supposed to be free here. But she wouldn't let it get to her. It was just for the time being. Soon, everything would be okay.

"Which way should we take?" Hrunting asked, now wearing his gray jacket once again.

She pointed to the left road, leading to the northern side of the city. "That way is closer." Honestly, she really didn't know if that was true. But the other road ran west toward the sea, and the thought of wyrms, or whatever Benedict called them, slithering out of there made her skin tingle.

"Very well, then," Hrunting replied as they continued on. "Are you nervous?"

Of course, she was. She had not the slightest idea of what to expect. "A little."

"I'm sure it will be all right," he comforted her. "I won't let anything happen to you. But if, for some reason, something should happen, whatever you do, don't do anything that would expose yourself as Daecish."

Eirún stopped in her steps as Hrunting turned. Was this place going to be another prison where she had to constantly hide?

"What's the matter?" he asked.

She trembled with anger. "This whole thing is the matter! I left Daecland to start a new life so that I didn't have to hide anymore. I already have to change my name." Her eyes began to water. "Again! And now I have to hide not only from my own people but from the people here as well. Am I to be cursed wherever I go?"

"Come now," he said, giving her a gentle hug. He took a step back and looked into her eyes. "It's only for now. We must heed the old man's warnings until we know we are safe."

"But what if it isn't safe?"

"Then we will go somewhere else." He held her hand. "But we will never give up. I promise you that."

She wanted his words to encourage her, but the depression threatened to slip back over her like a black veil.

"Listen to me," he said to her in a gentle tone. "I know you suffer. I know you carry a burden over you. A sadness you cannot shake. But do not let it be your master. Whatever happens, keep moving forward. And as long as you'll let me, I'll be here to help you."

She wanted to say that she felt useless. That her life had no meaning. But his words gave her courage, and she yearned to believe them. She made herself believe them. "Okay," she replied. He looked at her hand and smiled. "You don't have to wear that anymore if you don't want to."

She looked at the ring on her finger. She had completely forgotten about it. "It slipped my mind," she said with an involuntary smile.

As they continued on, the sun touched the horizon, and a foul rotting smell lingered in the air. Peering toward the city, she thought she could make out certain details on the high stone wall, though it was still too far to make out anything.

"What on earth is that smell?" Hrunting asked.

Rounding a small hill, the road ran south to the city gate. Scattered along the ground were bones and dried flesh, where vultures fluttered their frayed wings. Several of the bodies were more intact than others, dawned in familiar-looking uniforms, but they were torn and weathered against the thin sheets of snow. Eirún lifted a hand to her mouth as Hrunting grabbed her by the arm.

"Are those Daecish bodies?" she asked.

"It appears that some of them are," he replied in a calm voice, but his eyes looked deep with concern.

They continued forward, and Eirún couldn't keep her eyes off of one body, whose leathery gray face and white clouded eyes peered lifelessly toward her. She suddenly felt Hrunting's hand squeeze her arm. Pulling her eyes from the scene, she looked upon the wall, and her strength left her as if her bones liquified. Hanging from leather straps were nearly a dozen naked bodies, dismembered and twisted in grotesque fashions. Her legs locked up.

"I—I cannot go any further," she stammered.

"What kind of place is this?" he said almost to himself.

Just as she was about to demand that they turn around, a man appeared at the gate, waving his arms for them to come over.

"No!" she told Hrunting in a trembling voice. "Please! Let's leave!"

Hrunting looked at her, then the man.

"We're closing the gate!" the man shouted. "Hurry before the alphyns come out!"

"I don't think we have much of a choice," he told her.

"But, the bodies on the wall. What if they're Daecish?"

"We don't know that for sure." He glanced behind him. "We cannot survive another night out here. It's dark, our clothes are wet. What else can we do?"

With great hesitancy, she let Hrunting lead her to the city gate, but she kept her eyes away from the walls. Tremors ran through her body, and such a fright fell upon her; it was as if she was walking into the gates of death itself.

"Ain't safe after dark," said the man just up ahead. Dressed in old leather armor, he had a long beard, with a spear in his right hand. As they walked by him, the man stared peculiarly at Hrunting. As soon as they stepped onto the cobblestone street, the man waved to several others, who shut the gate behind him. "Now you hold up right there!" he shouted, holding up his spear. Hrunting immediately stepped away from Eirún and lifted his hands as the men surrounded him. The crowd grew, and she backed up against the city wall as Hrunting continued to back away in the other direction.

"Where you come from, pale-face?" one of the men shouted.

Hrunting frantically shook his head. "I'm just passing through," he stammered. "I mean no harm!"

Resisting the fear that threatened to capture her, Eirún reached a hand toward Hrunting, but he shook his head. He intentionally kept his eyes off her, and she knew he meant for her to try and escape while she could.

"You been hiding with the rest of 'em, ain't ye?" a crooked old man demanded.

"Please," Hrunting pleaded while he held up his hands. There was terror in his eyes Eirún had never seen before. As if the confidence he seemed to always possess simply vanished like a vapor. "Please," he said again over the crowds, but their shouts grew too loud for her to hear what he was trying to say.

Scurrying backward along the city wall, she found herself beneath the shadow of a wooden stable. She quietly wept and pulled the cloak over her face as the men kept yelling at him. Hrunting was soon bound in rope. Everything in her wanted to scream, but with a tightening chest, she forced her shaking lungs to hold it in. The crowds only grew, and she lost sight of him as they moved south, lost between several buildings.

The distant shouts soon faded, and everything went quiet. She glanced to several brick and wooden buildings to her right. She looked down the alleyways. As her heavy breathing fogged into the air, she tried to wrap her mind around what just happened. Where were they taking him? What was going to happen to her? For a second, she considered running after him, but she knew it was pointless.

The sun was now set but still managed to cast a pallid light across the sky. Few people were left in what looked like a ruined courtyard. In its center piled a mound of churned earth with a mass sticking out. No legs, just a mound of raw fat and muscles tangled in fur and blood. Two women were standing around it, cutting out chunks of meat and throwing the thick slabs into sack cloths. One of the women looked up and noticed her. Eirún backed further into the stable until her back hit a wooden gate.

The woman walked over. Eirún glanced around for an escape.

"Dear?" the woman asked.

She tightened the cloak around her hair and stared at the ground.

"Dear?" she asked again. "You all right?"

Eirún quickly nodded.

"Do you need any help?"

"No," she mumbled.

The woman put a hand on her hip. "Now, don't you think I'm just gonna let some helpless girl hide out in this stable." She squatted down until her face was level with Eirún's. She was older, with dark eyes and brown hair, held up in a bun. "Where you from, darling?"

"I'm . . ." she didn't know what to say. She thought of a town she saw on the map. "I'm from Astford."

The woman looked at her peculiarly. "We've got a few of you come in as of late. You have a place to stay?"

Eirún shook her head again.

The woman glanced over her shoulder at the courtyard. "You were with that man, weren't you?"

Eirún swallowed.

The woman's face softened. "It's all right, dear. Don't fret." She grabbed Eirún's hand. "I won't let no harm come to you. My name's Naomi. Can you tell me your name?"

Eirún couldn't think straight. She had lost any hope of staying safe in this dreadful place, and she was tired of always hiding and pretending. "Eirún," she said in almost a whisper.

Naomi let out a gentle sigh. "You're from Daecland, aren't you?"

Her eyes blurred, and she let out a whimper. "Please, don't hurt me."

"Oh darling," Naomi said as she held Eirún close. "I already told you I won't harm you." She leaned back. "But you gotta tell me. How in the name of Theos did you get yourself in Sunder? We ain't never seen a Daecish girl before."

Eirún sniffed and wiped her nose. "That gentleman they took. We took a wisp here together. To try to start a new life."

Naomi patted Eirún on the cheek. She observed Eirún's right hand. "Was he your husband?"

Eirún could still feel the ring on her finger. Just as she was about to say no, the thought came to her that if they believed he was, they might bring him back to her. She nodded.

Naomi lifted her hands to her mouth as she closed her eyes. "Theos have mercy."

"What are they going to do to him?" Eirún asked.

For a long time, Naomi didn't give an answer. "If there was anything I could do," she said at last, "I'd do it. But your husband . . . I'm afraid . . ." She hesitated. "I fear you won't see him again."

At her words, an onslaught of sorrow burst from Eirún's lungs, and she slunk to the ground with a wail. How could this have happened? The nightmare of her life kept beating her down until there was nothing left. She didn't want to start a new life. She didn't want Hrunting. She didn't even want Søren. She just wanted it all to end.

Naomi continued to hold her head against her breast as she wept. "It's going to be all right. I've got you."

By the time Eirún's tears dried, the moon was high, and the clouds had parted. With swollen eyes, she placed a hand on her aching chest. Naomi continued to hold her, humming softly as if she was a small child. "It's going to be all right," she said several times.

Eirún found a strange comfort in the woman's embrace—like a motherly love she hadn't felt in a long time. And Hrunting's words kept coming back to her. She must keep moving forward, no matter what happens.

"Do you think you can walk?" Naomi asked.

She didn't feel like going anywhere, but with Hrunting's words in her heart, she refused to let her sorrow master her. "Yes," she replied. "But where are we going?"

"With that pretty blonde hair and fair skin, there's only one place in this city where you'll be safe." She ran a finger in Eirún's hair beneath her cloak. "The House of Good Hope."

* * *

The sun arose blindingly in Gunnar's eyes, reflecting against the armor of the legions before him like glistening diamonds. Marching through the green and white fields, their raised muskets reminded him of the reality he was about to face in Everwind. He wasn't going to fight, just some army. Families would be involved. Unless they surrendered, their fate would be the same. The hardest part was his written orders to execute anyone trying to flee. But whether he thought it was right or not didn't matter. Orders had to be obeyed.

Running his finger through his long mustache, he gazed north toward the mountains of Einarr. Dark clouds gathered in the sky behind them, black and eerie, as if the sun had not the power to penetrate Daecland. Must be a bad storm. He hoped his family was doing well in Norfrost. And hopefully, the storm wouldn't delay the arrival of the wisps. They would be soaring into Llynhithe to join the southern fleet before too long.

Halvard rode up beside him. "If we stay close to the sea," he said, "We'll make quicker time."

"The only issue is the banks," Gunnar replied. "The road isn't wide enough for all of us."

"Couldn't we just break the legions into regiments?"

Gunnar didn't like the idea of stretching out the legions, but neither did he want to try and march that many men through the rugged hills. Those creatures were undoubtedly out, although he had seen none yet, and it would be a significantly slower trek. "Go ahead and order the regiment officers to break off and head south. Once we reach the road, we'll camp for the night and continue on as you suggest."

"Yes, sir," Halvard replied, galloping ahead of him.

* * *

Arnon had hoped he'd be at the Crossroads by that evening, but the changing landscape indicated he had at least another day to go. Since he told Adelyne that he would be back in a week, he knew he barely had any time to spend before he needed to leave again. Even then, he realized he had miscalculated. Not only was it further than he thought, but with two dozen families, it would take at least twice that time to trek back to Everwind. Maybe he could ride ahead of them? That probably wouldn't work. He hoped Adelyne wouldn't worry. But then he let out a smile. She was actually going to be his wife.

As the road gently winded through some cornfields, Arnon caught sight of something shining at the top of a low manmade bank to his right. Probably from when the road was first made. He dismounted and pulled out his father's sword. The last thing he wanted was an alphyn to come out while he was on foot. Narrowing his eyes, he peered at what looked like a torn leather helm with a rusted iron-nose guard and studs. He gazed across the barren cornfield. A few weathered strips of burgundy fabric were tangled in the broken stalks. Walking toward it, he got startled as a small bird flew into the air. Then he froze. Near the fabric was a dark spot on the ground—dried blood. About a yard to the left was a long thick leg bone, cleaned and shattered on the end. This must have been what happened to the dispatch Galvin had sent. Besides those scant remains, nothing else could be seen. He hurried back to the horse and continued east.

By the evening of the third day, Arnon reined to a stop. With the sun setting behind him, a band of deep crimson streaked through the pink clouds as if the sky itself were bleeding. The Crossroads stood isolated and quiet in the distance, like a ghost town. Besides the Green Carrick Inn and a few other small cabins and thatched-roofed cottages, the only things sticking out of the flat landscape were scattered birch trees, their white bases tangled in thorn and briar. Ravens cawed in the evening air. Arnon breathed in through his nose and glanced to either side of the road. The thick smell of alphyns hung heavy, but there were none in sight. Gripping his father's sword in his hand, he gave the horse a kick and continued to trot along the dirt road.

Keeping his eyes on the buildings, he waited for any signs of people, but no smoke rose from the chimneys, and all the windows were dark. He began to fear the worst. Maybe they went further east? But he doubted that was the case. The closest village was about thirty or so leagues away, nestled on the edge of the Amyrran forest.

A roar broke the heavy silence, and Arnon's heart leaped into his throat. His horse reared, throwing him to the ground. It bolted to the town, and Arnon rushed to his feet and shot a glance behind him. About twenty yards back stood a gray alphyn. Although smaller than some of the others, its height still appeared to be over his head. With black beady eyes, it looked straight at him and drew back its pointed ears. Opening its long mouth, sharp yellow teeth appeared dripping with thick saliva. It lowered itself onto its hind legs, digging its front talons into the earth.

Every muscle in Arnon's body clenched tight as a tremor throbbed up his chest. Just as the alphyn leaped forward, he opened his mouth, but nothing came out. He made his legs turn and flee. His feet stomped along the dirt, the earth trembling behind him. A loud roar made him glance over his shoulder. The alphyn sprang forward. Arnon threw himself to the side of the road. The alphyn turned, stumbled over its feet, and fell on its side.

Fighting off the tingling numbness in his limbs, Arnon gripped his sword as he staggered toward the beast. Theos help him; he'd stab it in the belly. But the alphyn struck the blade with its paw as it scurried back to its feet. The hilt was almost wrenched from his hand as the blade swung against him. Arnon tightened his grip and pointed it forward once again. Their eyes locked together, and the alphyn let out a low rumbling growl as it paced around him. Gray fur hung thick and matted below its jaws, and its hot breath reeked like rotting death.

Distant voices echoed from the buildings, but the alphyn blocked his view. It pounced with open jaws. All Arnon could do was stick his sword out—it pierced the alphyn above the mouth. The beast reared back with a howl, and Arnon jumped forward. He struck the alphyn above the right ear, but the blade barely cut into its flesh as it turned its head toward him and snapped its teeth over his forearm, the blade sticking out of the side of its mouth. Arnon took in a deep-throated gasp as the teeth sank through his muscles.

In that same instant, he took his left hand and clawed it into the alphyn's eye. It shook its head as tendons, and bone from Arnon's arm ripped away just below his elbow. Blood drained from his face as he squeezed his hand tighter until eye fluids burst into his palm. The alphyn stumbled backward with a whelp, dropping his arm and sword to the ground. Without a thought, Arnon went for his sword as blood poured down his side and leg. With his missing finger, he was unable to grip it tightly, so he held the crossbar with the hilt tucked in his armpit. He lunged himself forward, but just as he did, his head went dizzy, and his body fell limp.

Peering Through the Gates of Death

The lens felt cool and hard in Egbert's hand as he gazed through the kitchen window. Although the glass waved and bubbled, he could just make out a brown bird as it landed on the stair railing. It let out a single chirp before flying back off. He always wanted a pet bird, but Burlan said he couldn't have one. His stomach growled. He had hardly eaten the past couple of days, but he felt so bad for what he had done, eating so much of their food. But he couldn't help it. He was so hungry.

Sarah walked in from the hall and opened the cupboard as Egbert tucked the lens back beneath his shirt. In her left arm, she carried that little baby, Acton. He had dark hair, just like Egbert's, and he was named after a hero. Egbert wished his name was Acton.

"Good morn'," Sarah said to him.

Was she just trying to sound nice because she wanted to see the lens too? That Cydney girl did. Egbert didn't trust her. That lens was his and his alone. "Good morn'," he replied.

Adelyne walked in, and Sarah handed her Acton. "Would you lay him down upstairs for me?"

Taking Acton in her arms, Adelyne nodded, but she looked troubled.

"You all right?" Sarah asked.

Adelyne took in a shallow breath. Her dark auburn hair curled down just below her shoulders. She and Sarah were as pretty as fair maidens. Especially Adelyne, but he wouldn't even let her touch the lens.

"It's only been four days," Adelyne said, "and I can't help but worry about him."

"Arnon will be fine," Sarah replied. "He's a strong man and will be here before you know it. He said by the end of the week, didn't he?"

"Or sooner." She sighed. "But what if he doesn't come back? What if he changes his mind?"

Sarah walked over to the counter and grabbed a brown sack. "Now, don't fret like that. You'll only torture yourself for no reason. He'll be back; just trust him." She peered into the hallway. "How's that girl doing?"

"You mean Eirún?" Adelyne said in almost a whisper.

Sarah nodded.

"She seems okay. She doesn't talk much, but she helps out around the house a good bit." She glanced over toward Egbert and spoke quieter. "You think it's safe for her kind . . ." she said some other things, but Egbert couldn't make out the words.

"I don't know," Sarah replied, "but she's more afraid than we are. And I mean to help her as best I can." She wiped her forehead. "I still can't figure out how she got in Sunder. The whole thing's strange."

Adelyne didn't reply. Instead, she walked out and up the stairs with Acton in her arms while Sarah went back to organizing something in the cupboard.

A knock sounded on the door. Sarah set the sack back down and stepped out of the kitchen. Egbert peered out the window. He couldn't be sure, but it looked like Agatha with two of those men in burgundy uniforms. What could they want? The front door opened and one of the men started saying something. Egbert soon lost interest in trying to hear and wondered where Sarah may have hidden the dried oats.

Sarah walked back into the kitchen, followed by Agatha and the two men. There was a look of worry in Agatha's eyes, and one of the men's hands was on the hilt of a sword. "Egbert?" the man asked. He was tall with dark eyes and a really big chin. The other man, who was a bit smaller, stood in the back by the doorway.

Egbert gripped the lens beneath his shirt, but his fist shook. "What's this about?"

Agatha stepped forward. "Give me a moment," she told the man. She sat down across from Egbert. "Don't worry, we just need to ask you some questions. Is that okay?"

What were they planning? He didn't do anything wrong.

Agatha looked at the man, then back at Egbert. "When was the last time you was with Cydney?"

That was a good question. He saw her a couple of times inside the house. Once outside. But the order was a little blurry. And the way she talked to him made him feel funny inside. Uncomfortable. "I don't know last I seen her."

"Do you know where she is now?"

Egbert shook his head.

Agatha reached over and gently held his hand. Warm and delicate, as usual.

The man took a step forward. "The girl's been found dead in an alleyway, not far from here. She was beaten and strangled. Several folks in the street said the last person they saw her with was a man who looked like you. Now you speak the truth!"

His eyebrows shot up. Dead? He never killed her. At least he didn't think he did. He remembered her being sick in her stomach or something, but he didn't kill her. Why was he outside with her? He couldn't remember. The man still gripped the hilt of his sword as the smaller man took a step forward. Sarah stepped out of the room.

"Egbert?" Agatha asked. "Did you kill her?" The look on her face sent a sudden shiver down his back. She looked so heartbroken.

Egbert quickly shook his head. "I didn't, I swear! I ain't killed no one! Never!" At those words, a violent well of guilt caused him to choke, and he gasped for air as he held his chest. An image of Henley suddenly rushed upon him. He had killed him. He was nothing but a murderer. But he couldn't keep it a secret anymore. It had to come out. He let out a loud wail. "I's sorry!" he shouted. "I didn't mean it! I's sorry, Henley!"

The man gripped him by the right arm. "Who's Henley!" he demanded.

"I didn't mean to do it," Egbert pleaded. "I didn't mean to kill him. It's just that he wanted my . . ." He looked down at the lens, and sudden anger broke through his tears, and he ripped it off his neck and threw it against the wall. He keeled over onto the table and let out a blubbering cry. "I'm just a murderer," he whimpered to himself.

Agatha stood up and backed against the wall with her hands over her mouth as both men lifted Egbert by the arms. They strained to drag him across the kitchen floor. They yelled at him, probably for him to get on his feet and walk, but Egbert hardly paid attention. He was lost in his own sorrows and disbelief at what he had just admitted.

As he was marched across the city, Egbert's head wobbled back and forth, having lost all his strength. Drool dripped down his cheek and neck. The men never spoke to him, save the tall one, who called him "a half-wit, no better than the Daecish." Egbert's feet throbbed. They didn't even give him time to put on shoes.

When he finally drifted his eyes up, a single stone tower, on the back corner of a large castle, seemed to pierce into the sky. His heart raced as they pulled him toward a wooden door, just to the left of the tower. Were they going to kill him? Was this it?

"Help me," he mumbled. He knew Burlan couldn't hear him, but it made him feel better.

He soon found himself walking down a hallway, damp and cold. It was so dark he couldn't even see his feet as their footsteps echoed around him. He was led down a set of steps and into a dungeon.

On his right ran several cells, where a foul smell of bodily waste and sour flesh emanated from the mass of Daecish men lying around.

Most looked alive, but barely. The last two cells were less crowded. One held only one man, obviously a Daecish officer. The skin around his eyes was so dark, it looked bruised. The last cell held four other men—all of Sunderian appearance.

The tall man unlocked the last cell and shoved Egbert in. He sat in a puddle. The lock turned with the sound of grinding metal, and both guards walked back out.

"I didn't mean it," Egbert mumbled.

Of the four other prisoners in his cell, three sat together. The oldest of the three had a bald head and a band of white hair around his ears. The other two looked about Egbert's own age but were thinner and harder in the face. All three of them stared, almost as if they were afraid, at the fourth prisoner who sat in the back corner alone. Long and dark hair matted over his shoulders, and his wrists were chained together with iron shackles. Of all the men there, he alone looked like he had been there for decades, rotting and withering away. With his face down, he appeared to be asleep.

Egbert turned his gaze as the dungeon door creaked open again. Another man in a burgundy uniform walked down, but with more decorations on his sleeves and shoulders than the others. He had short brown hair, a full scraggly beard, and a gray eye that awkwardly wandered to the left. With his right eye, he looked at Egbert with a stern face. "I'm General Galvin Barclay. What's your clan name?"

"D-Dunhaven," Egbert barely got out. He twiddled his fingers, his hands sat on his belly. He let out a whimper as he pictured Henley. Then he pictured all those hungry girls just because he had a problem eating too much. "Forgive me," he mumbled. Although his heart ached so badly, he thought it might stop beating at any moment, at the same time, his guilt was lifting from his heavy bones. In a bizarre irony, the locks and chains around him meant freedom. Everything had come out into the light. He had no more secrets.

The General raised an eyebrow. "From Astford, then?"

Egbert hardly heard the words.

"From Astford?" the General asked louder.

Egbert nodded.

"My brigadiers tell me you confessed to killing a man, and possibly another. Henley, they said his name was. Was he of your own kin?"

"No, sire." He could barely move his mouth.

"Then how did you know him?"

"He helped take care of me."

"Speak up!"

"He helped take care of me!" Egbert said louder, followed by a loud cry.

"Then why'd you kill him?"

The very question made Egbert want to die. "I didn't mean it. Well . . . well, I did, but . . ." Just the fact that he tried to hide it again brought out a deep moan from his chest. He laid down and wept.

The prisoner sitting in the corner cackled. Then he let out a cough and spit out something slimy and black. He lifted his bound hands and wiped his mouth. The three men beside Egbert scooted further away until their backs were against the iron bars.

"Something you want to share?" the General asked the prisoner.

The prisoner continued to look down. "A feast for birds be given, the flesh of beasts and men. The warmth of the sun be hidden, all souls exposed within." He spoke the words with a certain bounce and a hint of boredom. Egbert wasn't sure why, but the prisoner's words seemed to harden his own heart, and for a second, his sobs stopped, and his sorrow faded. Darkness hung around that man, as though he had done something so terrible it couldn't even be spoken about. And it was infectious.

The General straightened himself. "Why do you speak of Hælend's Ballad in such a tone?"

The prisoner shot a glance at Egbert with sharp silver eyes. And although he said not a word, Egbert felt as if he screamed "murderer!" at him.

But the prisoner remained silent and only looked back at the General. "You're blinded by the fear that creeps in your heart. Be careful. Your time is running out."

"You sound like the rest of them," the General said as he pointed to the older of the three men in the cell. "That's what got that feller in here. He was a blacksmith in the Eastern District. Before the depression, I imagine he did pretty well for himself. Then he stabbed his apprentice for stealing a loaf of bread. 'Course, the apprentice denied it and blamed some other man who stole it out of the window, but this feller said Sunder's Bane's coming anyway, so he didn't care."

The prisoner laughed again. "I'm not talking about the end." His eyes suddenly went wide as he stretched his mouth into a grin, revealing his dark rotting teeth. "I mean the pale-faces. They're marching from Llynhithe as we speak. That's the only bane you need to fear."

The General observed the prisoner for a long while. "Where did you hear of this?" he finally asked.

The prisoner only smiled with a hoarse giggle and dropped his hands, his chains clanking against the stone floor. The General eyed him for a moment before he walked over to the cell with the Daecish officer. The officer sat with one knee up, his armed propped on it. His eyes were open, but his lids were heavy.

"I trust you've been eating now?" the General asked the officer.

The officer nodded, almost indistinctly.

"I've removed the dead ones," the General continued. "And I've rationed food for those left, but I can only feed them so much at a time. We'll bring some more water down shortly."

The officer didn't respond, and the General walked out of the dungeon.

Not wishing to see that dreadful prisoner any longer, Egbert rolled himself over so that his back was to him. He closed his eyes and felt his heart ache once again. The prisoner was saying something—cold and repulsive, but this time, Egbert let his mind drown out all noises. For a long time, perhaps even hours, he thought of Henley. He thought of the girls who might go hungry and anything else he may have done that was wrong. And the longer he laid there, the more came to his mind. With flowing tears, he didn't just beg for mercy; he yearned for all the wrongs he had done to be made right.

* * *

Fleta sat in the chair, gazing at Arnon from across the upstairs bedroom, built of sturdy, rough-cut logs. Sleeping on a straw bed, the stub of his right arm was wrapped tight in wet cloth. Hazel was sound asleep on a pallet beside him. When they first brought him inside, his pale skin had been covered in so much blood, she thought he was already dead. The last time she cried like that was when she left Hazel in the cellar in Denhurst.

But even so, a numbness spread in her. So much death and violence had happened in the past few months, she quit trying to process it all. When brigadier Redfield bound the cord around Arnon's left arm before he cut off the stringy remains of his tendons, it barely even fazed her.

She tried not to imagine how she'd feel if Arnon died. Normally, she would have been afraid that her family wouldn't be able to provide for themselves, but Arnon hadn't really been there for them anyway. They'd managed just fine on their own. She knew it probably wasn't his fault, but she resented his absence, especially for Hazel's sake. She hadn't left his side since he arrived.

Fleta stood up and walked over beside him, and sat on the floor. Above the wrapping, his arm appeared less swollen than the day before, but it was still purple and bruised. His cheeks were thinner than last she saw him, and dark rings formed around his eyes. She wasn't sure if his body was reacting to the injury or if he hadn't eaten enough. With a low moan, Arnon opened a glazed eye. It lazily wavered around the room before it met hers.

"How you feeling?" she asked.

Arnon raised both eyebrows, but his eyes barely remained opened. He looked at his arm. "Other than a headache," he mumbled. "Not too bad."

Fleta laughed. "You're handling this better than I expected."

Arnon wryly smiled. "It may have got my arm, but I got its eye."

"And more than that," she said. "When we found you, you were laying on it with your sword in its neck."

"I killed it?"

"Not quite. The soldiers finished it off, but it probably would have died after a while anyway." She smiled. "Everyone's been talking about it. Some even nicknamed you Wrecan."

"Soldiers?" he asked. "I thought they were killed by alphyns."

"They were attacked on the way, but about eight or so of them survived and are staying here at the Crossroads."

Arnon scrunched his eyebrows in confusion. "Why haven't ya'll come back to Everwind yet?"

"The families are waiting for more soldiers before they go back. It's too dangerous out there."

Arnon closed his eyes. "No more's gonna come. They won't let them leave Everwind."

Fleta knew that would upset the families, probably even the soldiers. Just about everyone there was growing weary of living at the Crossroads. Both the smell of smoke and lantern lights at night attracted alphyns, so cooking was minimal, and by the time the sun set, everyone locked themselves inside and laid down without making a noise. Every night the howls came. Sometimes alphyns walked up to the outer walls sniffing and snarling. The people were surviving, but only at the cost of losing their minds.

"What of that boy you were talking to?" Arnon asked with a brash grin.

Fleta's cheeks warmed.

"What was his name?"

She cleared her throat. Since they met on the journey from Denhurst, she had seen Beckett nearly every day. Myla knew they liked each other, but she didn't know that they kissed in the cellar about two days before Arnon arrived. She was fourteen, and many girls her age had already been married off. But because Beckett was only fifteen, she knew her mother wouldn't allow it. Not until he could at least inherit some land or provide a dowry. But Fleta liked to dream it could happen sooner. "Not sure who you're talking about."

Arnon laughed but cringed as he placed his left hand on his side. "Beckett, I think," he managed to get out.

"Oh, him."

Arnon laughed again and pointed his finger at her. "Your face is red. You're a terrible liar."

She couldn't help but smile.

He placed his hand on her cheek and sighed. "Be careful. You're an attractive girl, and not all guys should be trusted so easily."

Fleta knew that wasn't true. Arnon probably meant she was attractive on the inside, but she loved him for being so sweet to her anyway. Beckett, on the other hand, looked at her in a way no one ever had before. Being around him was the only time she ever felt beautiful. "I will," she replied.

Arnon dropped his hand. "How long have I been asleep?"

"Three days," she replied.

Arnon's eyes went wide, and a sudden panicked look came over him. "Three days!" He groaned as he tried to sit up.

Fleta placed her hands on his shoulder. "You can't get up yet," she insisted. "What's wrong?"

"I have to go back!" His eyes watered as his back fell back against the straw. "I told Adelyne I'd be back. We've been here too long!"

Who was Adelyne?

The wooden door swung open, and Myla walked in. "Is he all right?" she asked. She hurried over and placed her hand on Arnon's head. "Arnon?"

"I'm fine," he replied, but his face was furrowed in pain.

"Praise Theos, you've got no fever." She looked at his arm and then rubbed his head. "My poor baby." Her eyes watered as her lip quivered. "My poor boy," she kept saying.

"Mama!" came Hazel's voice as she sat up, rubbing her eyes with a pout.

Good grief. Everyone was crying. Fleta felt like it was time for her to step out.

"I need to go," Arnon muttered. "We all need to."

"You've got to rest," Myla replied. "When more men come, we'll all go back."

"No more's coming," Fleta whispered in her ear. "That's what he told me."

Her mother did well to keep a straight face as Hazel stumbled toward her, reaching out her arms. "We'll need to let Redfield know. Will you go fetch him?"

Fleta eagerly nodded and walked out the door.

* * *

The next morning, Arnon was moved to a cot downstairs, by the stairway, much to his relief. The front door was propped open, and several soldiers and men walked in and out, carrying sacks and supplies.

It made him feel more a part of what was going on, even if there wasn't anything he could do to help.

Looking at his arm, there was nothing below the stub of his seared elbow, but for some reason, he could still feel the pain as if the rest of it was still there.

Fleta sat across the room at a trestle table, with Beckett sitting beside her. They giggled and whispered to one another, and she attempted to secretly hold his hand beneath the table, but Arnon could clearly see it. Despite his pain, he couldn't help feel happy. Beckett looked a little funny, with his over wide cheeks and big lips, but he seemed to really care for her.

The previous night, Arnon had told his family about Adelyne and how he was going to marry her when he got back. Of course, his mother was ecstatic, but he couldn't help but wonder if Fleta and her would get along. They seemed to be very similar. Independent and strong-willed. That might not be a good thing when they're together.

"I've got something for you," came Hazel's voice as she sat down beside him with an overly large grin and bright eyes.

Clenching his chest tight, Arnon lifted himself up on his arm. He had already eaten a dense breakfast of cornmeal and rye bread and could feel the energy flowing back through him. "And what would that be?"

She pulled out two wooden figurines and carefully set them upright on the cot. It was a yellow owl and what appeared to be a red fox, but its head was missing.

"Where are the rest?"

"Well . . ." Hazel replied, fiddling with her fingers.

Arnon laughed. "Have you already lost them all?"

She didn't reply, and her mouth slowly fell into a frown.

Arnon leaned over and kissed her on the head. "I have an idea. How about you keep the owl, and I'll keep the fox. That way, if we ever have to be away from each other, you can look at your owl and remember that I love you. And I'll do the same."

Hazel picked up the headless fox and set it in Arnon's lap. "Yours doesn't look like he's feeling too good, though."

Arnon laughed again, but Hazel stuffed the owl back in her pocket and stepped out of the room.

Soldiers continued to walk in and out, and Arnon peered at the stub of his arm. He could still feel his lower arm and fingers, despite nothing being there. Brigadier Redfield had been informed of the situation, and the families were preparing to leave that afternoon. Arnon was surprised they reacted so quickly, but Redfield worried that he may need better medical attention if he caught a fever or infection.

Hazel walked back into the room, carrying a bowl as she mixed dirt with what smelled like old ale. "When I get done," she told him, "you take this. It'll make you feel better."

Arnon grunted. "If you think so, Hazel."

In a gray gown, with her hair pulled up, his mother walked down from the upstairs bedroom carrying a wooden box. She sat beside him. "I have something for you."

Arnon quirked an eyebrow as she set the box in his lap. He ran a finger over the decorative lid. He tried to open it, but he really needed a second hand.

"Oh dear, I'm sorry!" Myla said as she opened the box for him.

He peered into the box and noticed two silver woven rings. "Are these?"

"Your father would have wanted you to have them." She picked up the rings. "Before this one was mine, it was his mother's. And now it will be Adelyne's. And your father's ring will go to you."

Arnon did well to hold himself, but the rings meant more to him than his mother could have known. His marriage to Adelyne suddenly felt like a reality, and his father was now a part of that. "I love you," he managed to get out.

She leaned over and kissed him on the cheek. "I love you too."

"It's ready," Hazel said as she stood up from the floor, carrying the bowl of brown muck.

Arnon raised his eyebrows. Wondering how he was going to get himself out of this, he leaned his head back as she shoved the bowl in his face. Fortunately, Redfield stepped in from outside.

"The wagons are all loaded." He looked at Arnon. "Commander Greystrom. Glad to see you sitting up. How do you feel?"

Commander Greystrom? He still couldn't get used to it. "Better, thank you."

"Glad to hear it," he replied. "You lost a good amount of blood. We worried at first, but it seems you're a quick healer. You feel ready to depart?"

"The sooner, the better."

"Good. You'll ride with your family. If all goes well, we should be back in five days." His freckled cheeks stretched into a smile. "If I can help it, you'll be decorated before too long."

Decorated? For what? He didn't think he did anything greater than anyone else.

Doubt and Depravity

In the back garden, Adelyne barely pulled the husks from the dried corn. Her fingers were trembling, and she never felt like eating. Her bones ached as if she was constantly homesick, and she couldn't even remember the last time she smiled. Arnon said he would be back before the week was over, but it had been nine days since he left.

Sarah had tried to encourage her, but she just knew that Arnon was either killed by an alphyn, or he decided to leave her for good and stay at the Crossroads. Of course, he did. He probably came to his senses and realized he would never marry someone like her. Maybe she would go to the Crossroads herself. Even if it meant her death, it was better than slowly withering away. She tugged at another husk, pricking her finger. She should quit being so foolish. He was only two days late, and he could still come back at any time.

It was warmer than it had been the previous days, and most of the snow had melted. Across the table, in the garden, Sarah had taken the opportunity to show Eirún how to cut the brown asparagus stocks and cover them in manure and straw to help preserve them through the rest of winter. Most of the boar had already been eaten, although a few flanks were left. Despite still having a limited food supply and the continuing spread of the fever, the rest of the girls had learned well how to help around the house. But with the recent death of Cydney, most were afraid to go in the streets.

As much as Adelyne disliked Cydney, she couldn't imagine what would have enticed Egbert to kill her in such an awful way. And she was pregnant.

"What's bothering you?" Sarah asked.

Adelyne glanced up from the corn husk. She thought Sarah was talking to her, but she was looking at Eirún, who was spreading the dirt with hands. She didn't respond.

Despite the lines of weariness on her face, Adelyne couldn't believe how beautiful Eirún looked. She wished she was tall and fair-skinned liked that. And her large green eyes perfectly matched the color of the emerald dress Sarah had given her to wear. It was a little short in the sleeves, but she still looked dazzling. Usually, her blonde hair was put up with a hood to cover it, but today she let it fall to her lower back.

Sarah straightened herself, placing her hands on her hips. "That's good for now. Let's have a drink." She walked over to the table and sat across from Adelyne. Eirún wiped her hands on an old apron, hanging over a wooden rail, and sat down as Sarah poured a pitcher of water into pewter tankards. "You're likely the most interesting person to ever step into Sunder, being a Daecish lady, and yet you've barely spoken a word."

"There isn't anything to tell," she replied.

Sarah set a tankard in front of her. "When that kind lady, Naomi, dropped you off, she told me about your husband. I know that what you're going through is unbearable, but many of us here have lost our husbands." She spoke more softly. "And you don't know his fate yet. There's still hope."

A sudden cool breeze moaned from the back alley, rustling the corn husks off the table. Adelyne held her stomach, but her queasiness never went away. It was like being constantly sick from a heart that felt stretched out and thin as if the other half of it was somewhere far away. Maybe Arnon would come back today.

Eirún wrapped her fingers around the tankard but only stared at it. "He wasn't my husband," she admitted.

Sarah tilted her head. "Isn't that what you told Naomi?"

Eirún tapped the mug on the table. "I had hoped that if she thought he was my husband, she might be able to say something to those men and bring him back to me."

Sarah opened her mouth to speak but hesitated before going on. "I've already asked Bell to talk to Drake," she said eventually. "See if maybe he can find your man in the prison there. We'll see what he can do."

"Thank you."

"You loved him, though, didn't you?"

Eirún shrugged. "I don't know. Maybe?"

Sarah glanced up to the wooden overhang and took in a long breath. "We don't know why Theos lets bad things happen to those we love, but he's good, and all we can do is trust him."

Eirún slid the tankard away from her. "I've heard a lot of talk about this god lately. Do you mind if I ask you a question?"

"Sure," Sarah replied.

"Have you ever seen him? Has he ever spoken to you?"

Adelyne's eyes widened, but Sarah only held a look of pity. "I've not seen him, and I've never heard him speak. But I know he's there."

"Forgive my bluntness," Eirún said, "but how do you know he's there? Or that he even cares?"

A lump rose in Adelyne's throat. She would have never asked that question so frankly, but she often felt the same way.

"Because I know him," Sarah answered, "and he gives me joy. I feel it."

"Because you feel it?" Eirún went on. "Anyone can feel anything. That doesn't mean it's true. Do you have any reason to believe in this god other than you want to?"

Her words were directed at Sarah, but they cut into Adelyne's heart. Was she right? Was there any reason to actually believe in Theos? She didn't feel him the way Sarah did. She tried to hold on to what

Arnon told her before he left, but his words began to slip away. Maybe Sarah had a good answer.

No, Adelyne was hanging by a thread. She needed Sarah to have a good answer.

"I understand what you're saying," Sarah replied, "but Geoffrey, my husband, was better at answering those questions than I am. I wish you could have talked with him."

Adelyne couldn't believe it. It was almost as if she tested Theos at that moment. If he was real, why was he letting all of this doubt cloud her heart? He didn't care about her suffering. He wasn't going to work it to the good; he certainly wasn't going to forgive her because he wasn't even there. And neither was Arnon.

"Where is your husband?" Eirún asked.

Sarah's eyes went heavy, and she remained silent for a moment. "The Daecish took him." She quickly shook her head as if she was snapping out of deep thought. "I didn't mean to say it like that. I hope I didn't offend you."

Eirún softened her expression, and her shoulders lowered as if letting down her guard. "I'm sorry."

"You shouldn't be. You didn't take him."

Eirún took a sip of water. "I've heard the other girls talk about the mines they came out of and some of the things they had to live through. And that's not just here. Similar things take place at home." She looked at Sarah. "But not all of Daecland is like what you've experienced."

Sarah patted Eirún's hand. "After meeting you, I now see that." She glanced over her shoulder as if she could see down the alleyway. "And as you've experienced already, we are capable of doing just as much evil."

Eirún appeared lost in some thought and didn't respond.

"What's troubling you?" Sarah asked.

Eirún's expression was blank. "I doubt you would understand."

Sarah cocked an eye. "Try me."

With a quiet chuckle, Eirún situated herself on the bench. "You ever feel like you're in a dark tunnel, and despite how hard you try to get out, you never find the end of it?"

"Like depression?"

"Yes," she replied.

Sarah picked up another husk of corn but mostly fiddled with it. "I've often been there."

A glint appeared in Eirún's eyes. "Really? How do you deal with it?"

"Well, for me, it wasn't so much a tunnel. It always felt like I was dragging a massive stone. Everyone around me seemed to move fine, but I had this weight I couldn't get rid of."

Adelyne never thought of herself as a depressed person, but she felt like that all the time. Except every time she tried to move, a voice always yelled at her that she was inept. Filthy. Unwanted.

"But how did you get out of it?" Eirún reiterated.

"I didn't," Sarah replied. "You don't get out of it. You get through it."

"My husband—" Eirún began, "I mean, Hrunting said something similar to that, and I think it's helping. But sometimes I just get so tired."

"I understand," Sarah replied.

Another breeze sent a shiver down Adelyne's legs. Tired. That's the perfect description.

"Don't you ever get frustrated at your god for making you go through all of this? I mean, wouldn't he want to stop it if he loved you?"

Clasping her hands together, Sarah thought for a moment. "I've wondered that many times. But I must confess, it's in the moments of my depression that I grow closer to him."

"How so?"

"It's difficult to explain, but when my life is going well, I tend to forget about Theos. But in my dark moments, I see him more clearly— kind of like a candle. In the daytime, you can barely see it. But when the night comes, that's when it shines the brightest. So much of the way I feel depends on my circumstances. Happiness, anxiousness, sorrow. But Theos gives me a joy and a peace that transcends whatever problems I may be going through."

Eirún seemed to be working out something in her mind. Adelyne remembered what Arnon said about how music stirred up a longing in the heart. As if we were made for something more than the temporary things in this world. And even though Sarah's words were almost too perfectly tailored for what she was going through, she couldn't feel Theos the way she did. She wanted to, but it was as if her soul was numb.

She got to her feet. "I think I'm going to go inside for a minute."

Girls filled the hall, moving busily from the upstairs to the kitchen. One girl carried two waste buckets while others held bundles of old straw and moss used as mattress stuffing. There were probably chores Adelyne could do herself, but she didn't really feel like doing anything. Maybe she would go sit on the front stairs.

Stepping through the front door, she sat down at the top of the steps. Old Birchton Way was beginning to look less maintained. Dirt and mud ran over the cobblestone from the alleyways, and the Daecish were no longer around to ensure that it got swept. At the corner of the western Road, an old man was boarding up the shattered window to the Tea House while several other younger men were walking in. From inside flowed the sound of music—some stringed instrument and singing, but it was too faint to make out the tune.

She glanced up the road to her left, and her heart sank. Fletcher strode down the sidewalk. He still wore his black coat, but his top hat was gone, revealing his short brown hair. She stood up to walk back inside.

689

"Wait!" he shouted after her. "Can we just talk?" He hurried up the stairs.

Her stomach ached. "Please go away."

He grabbed her hand. "I know you don't want to see me, but just hear me out."

Taking in a quivering breath, she looked at him but ignored his gray eyes.

"I can't . . ." he started to say before he glanced behind him. He faced her again and held her hand in both of his. "I can't stop thinking about you. I can't sleep. I can't eat."

He was a liar, and she knew it. "You hurt me. You hit me." Her eyes welled up. "You don't love me. I'm just an object to you."

"I'm . . ." He let out a sigh as he continued to look at her. "I'm different now. I'll never hit you again, I swear."

"It doesn't matter," she replied. "I'm going to be married soon."

A sudden look of sorrow came over his eyes—a look she had never seen. "To who?" he asked.

"Arnon Greystrom."

"I ain't never heard of him."

She cleared her throat. "He's a commander in the Free Sunderian Army. And he loves me."

Fletcher glanced at the door. "Can I meet him?"

She shook her head.

"You're telling me a lie, aren't you?"

"No. When he gets back, we'll be married."

"How long's he been gone?"

Adelyne shrugged, but she could feel her limbs go weak. "Less than a week," she lied.

"Being a commander, he'll be gone a lot, I reckon." He lifted her chin with his finger. "You're gonna have to get used to that, and I know you can't. He'll be gone months at a time."

She tried to control her shivering lungs, but she'd never thought about that.

"I may lose my temper at times, but I ain't ever gonna leave you, you know that. I never have."

He was right. She had known Fletcher since she was a little girl. He had always liked her and was always there if she needed him. It was her that always left him.

"When I saw you on these steps, you looked upset. It might do you some good to get some air. You wanna go for a walk with me?"

She knew she shouldn't. They would probably go back to Three Rivers. And what if Arnon did come back? He would never forgive her again if he ever actually forgave her in the first place. But she knew he came to his senses and probably decided to stay at the Crossroads for good. And Eirún was probably right about Theos anyway. He wasn't real.

Adelyne could feel that same pull drawing her to the same lie. She felt weak and powerless. "Okay," she told Fletcher.

She walked with him down the steps. It didn't take long for Three Rivers to come into view, and with her hand in his, regret swept over her as her skin tingled with rising panic. Was she really doing this all over again? She prayed that Theos would save her from herself.

* * *

A full day had passed. Sarah stood beside the kitchen table, looking out the window. One of the girls told her that she saw Adelyne walking up the road yesterday with a man. She never came home last night, and Sarah's chest felt so tight she could hardly breathe. She was trying to save the prostitutes, but by bringing them into her home, she feared they had influenced Adelyne for the worst. She should have known better. She clenched her eyes tight and massaged her temples.

She wasn't doing anything right. Her gut told her to not let Egbert stay there, and when she did, he murdered one of the girls. She silently let out a prayer and tried to calm her nerves. She couldn't take it back. Egbert was locked away, and the girls were safe. And Agatha went to go find Adelyne. She told herself she would just have to wait until she got back, but the anxiety was too much. She sat down and rubbed her arms. Langleigh was caring for Acton and Lilly for the afternoon, and she was more than thankful for it. Although Acton had eaten more than he had the previous days, he still had a fever, but that never deterred Langleigh from helping all that she could. That girl had the best heart of them all.

When Sarah opened her eyes, she caught sight of Egbert's necklace piled on the floor in the corner, where he had thrown it before he was carried away. She leaned over and picked it up. It was heavier than it looked. And by the craftsmanship of the glass and brass components, she immediately could tell it was Daecish. How on earth did Egbert get his hands on something like this? Glancing at the window, the shape of someone walked toward the house. She set the necklace on the table and ran to the front door, and pulled it open.

At the bottom of the steps stood Agatha. Damp strands of her red hair clung across her washed-out face.

Sarah's entire body trembled, and her throat tightened. "Where's Adelyne?"

Agatha wiped her tearing eyes. "She's at Three Rivers. But don't go."

Sarah went dizzy and couldn't breathe. She forced her trembling legs down the steps as she leaned against the rail.

"Sarah, don't."

Ignoring her, she ran toward the tavern as her legs burned, but she couldn't get there fast enough. Several people stopped in their step as they gazed at her. What did Agatha mean? Was she hurt? Was she dead? She would never forgive herself for this. Theos have mercy.

By the time she made it to the tavern, she turned the knob as the door swung open. Suddenly her legs locked, terrified of what she might find. Through the thick haze of smoke stood a small crowd of mostly girls in front of the bar as they stared into the hallway, which ran along the back wall to the right. Behind the bar stood several men, including Bale. She barely looked in their direction, but she did notice one in particular, who stood in the corner. His clothing appeared ragged, even for that brothel, and although she doubted her eyes, it looked as if his wrists were bound in iron shackles. He was the only one in the room smiling.

The whole room reeked of sour beer. A baby cried somewhere, and a little girl wrapped her arms around the leg of one of the prostitutes, probably her mother. Every girl stared at Sarah, like sick patients, barely hanging on to life. One girl, who had curly frizzled hair and sagging cheeks, pointed to the hall.

Almost involuntarily, she felt her feet walk forward, but everything in her wanted to stay put. She turned down the dark hallway. Black singes from the lanterns marred the already filthy-looking walls. All the doors were closed except for one on the left. Sarah continued forward but closed her eyes as she faced the open doorway.

When she opened them, it was too dark to see inside. She gently pushed the door against the hinges.

Adelyne lay on a stained wool blanket on the floor with open, still eyes. Her clothes were stripped from her body, her face and neck purple and swollen.

She was dead.

Sarah's stomach violently clinched tight. She raised her hands to her mouth and fell backward against the wall as she let out a loud wail. Tears poured from her eyes. "Why!" she screamed into her hands.

The others only stood there, except for the frizzled hair girl who walked over and sat beside her.

"What happened!" Sarah yelled with heavy sobs.

The girl only held a painful expression. "It was Fletcher."

"Why didn't you do anything!" she shrieked and smacked her hand as hard as she could against the girl's leg.

The girl scooted away. She didn't say anything.

"I'm sorry," Sarah said, gritting her teeth. She let out a deep moan. Her heart felt like it was going to give out. "Did no one try to stop him?"

The girl glanced back to the others. "None of them were here. The men, I mean. And we was too afeared."

Sarah managed to calm her breath for a second. "Tell me exactly what happened."

The girl swallowed. Her face was covered in freckles, and she appeared no older than twelve. "She came in with Fletcher yesterday evening. She looked upset, like she didn't want to be there. She tried to go back out, be he wouldn't let her. We wanted to help, but he's a big man. When they got into the room, he closed the door." She hesitated for a moment. "We heard her crying. Saying that she was sorry for something and begged to leave. But . . ."

"But what?"

The girl bit at her thumbnail and avoided eye contact. "Then it stopped. We didn't know what happened 'til today."

Sarah turned her gaze and looked at Adelyne's body through the open door. She knew there was some dark secret Adelyne wouldn't share. And as much as Sarah had tried, she couldn't help her.

From Waters Deep and Cold

Gunnar gazed east as the legions curved south around the Swelling Sea. They were on schedule and would be in Everwind in two days, but he was getting impatient. The moments leading up to a battle were worse than the battles themselves. Sweat already leaked down his neck and back, and his fingers fidgeted around the horse's reins. For the past week, he remained at the rear while Halvard had taken the front. He was a good leader, and Gunnar was thankful for his friendship.

Hearing the clomp of hooves, Gunnar glanced over his shoulder. A soldier bearing a dispatch flag galloped toward him. He already knew what message he'd receive. The wisps were likely setting out soon from Llynhithe, if not already. Gunnar figured the legions would arrive in Everwind a day behind at the most. Ónarr may not be happy about it, but that was as close as it could have worked out. The dispatch pulled the reins of his horse as he came alongside Gunnar's.

"Commander." The corporal saluted, his bay mount snorting. He handed Gunnar a letter.

Halting, Gunnar opened it up and read through its contents. The wisps never arrived from Daecland, but the fleet in Llynhithe would be setting out anyway. "When did King Ónarr write this?"

"Two days ago," the corporal replied.

Gunnar raised an eyebrow. "You ride quick."

The Corporal didn't respond but only held a stern militaristic expression. He was probably all protocol and no personality. He couldn't stand new recruits like that.

"King Ónarr means to send out just the single fleet from Llynhithe without Norfrost?"

"Yes, sir."

"When will they depart?"

"Today, sir."

Gunnar gazed at the mountains on the northern horizon. The dark clouds beyond the peaks seemed to grow. That storm had been there an awfully long time. Was it that bad that they couldn't send the fleet from Norfrost? A terrible thought came to his mind, and he envisioned a storm ripping apart the roof tiles of his home. "Did a dispatch from Norfrost inform you that the fleet would not be arriving?"

"As far as I was told, we've heard nothing from Norfrost. The fleet just never arrived, sir."

Gunnar let out an unintended chuckle. He had never heard of such a thing. Why hadn't Norfrost been in touch? He handed the letter back to the corporal, trying not to think about it. He needed to focus. "Ride back swiftly. By the time you return, we will be at Everwind. Let King Ónarr know we are on schedule."

"Yes, sir," the corporal replied as he reached for the letter. Suddenly his horse neighed and shied off the side of the road. He almost lost his balance as he gripped the reins.

Gunnar's own horse pranced into a trot. He pulled on the reins, but the black stallion only went faster. "Hold back!" he shouted.

Ahead, the divided lines of the legion began to break up as horses bucked and neighed, riding off the left side of the road, away from the sea.

Peering across the water, Gunnar made out something strange about the glistening silver swells. They moved and shifted against one another as if strange winds came from different directions. He squinted. For brief moments, dark shapes emerged from the waterline, only to sink down again.

"What on earth?" he muttered.

He pulled his horse in short. Distant shouts broke out, and the soldiers pointed at the sea. One fell from his horse, and he ran north. A chorus of loud shrieks, echoing from the sea, lifted up as large slick heads slithered toward the shore. At first, he thought they were fish, or maybe whales, but their long gray bodies, which coiled and winded up the beach with opened mouths, made him question his own eyes. A sudden torrent of fear shuddered his spine as one of the serpents struck forward, swallowing a man whole as its sharp fangs dug into the back of his horse, lifting it into the air.

The legion broke into chaos, and Gunnar's own horse bolted forward. The wind rushed through his hair. Glancing to the beach, more serpents were slithering out. Dozen's even. Several of the soldiers fired their wheellocks and muskets, ripping apart the serpent's pink flesh as they hissed and coiled back. But even with their weapons, he knew they could never take on such monsters.

"Retreat!" he hollered. "Ride north!" He galloped through the legion on the northern flank as he continued shouting. Horses reared and fell beneath the thick bodies of the serpents that continued devouring his men. "Move north!"

By the time he made it through the mess of the rear legion, his heart hammered and he saw Halvard on his horse, staring in Gunnar's direction. Behind Halvard, the front legion lined the road. "Ride!" Gunnar shouted. "Now!"

Halvard turned his horse and galloped south. A good amount of the cavalry rode hard after him, but nearly all the footmen were caught in the chaos behind. Gunnar continued to catch up with Halvard as he tried to block out the screams of his dying men.

* * *

Eirún stood in the hall with her arms crossed, listening to Sarah and Agatha weep together in the kitchen. She had hardly ever spoken to

Adelyne, but she seemed like a sweet girl who was supposed to marry that other man. How terribly sad. Why would she throw herself away like that?

She glanced to the front door. Hopefully, she would hear word about Hrunting soon. Maybe he was okay. Sarah had asked if she loved him, but she didn't know. But part of her wanted to. She was fairly certain that he had feelings for her, though.

Hearing Agatha and Sarah pray together, she thought about Sarah's words to her two days before. It was one thing to have a discussion, but the way they were now pleading before Theos for mercy and understanding, that was something different. It was almost as if she could actually feel the peace and relief they had, even in the midst of their sorrow. She thought about praying herself, but she could never force herself to talk to something she knew wasn't there.

Letting out a sigh, she dropped her arms. She needed to help with something. Maybe she could cook some more food. Despite being in an entirely different country, so much of it reminded her of the orphanage. Maybe that's why she felt she finally had a purpose again. But more so, it was the reminder of Hrunting's words that encouraged her. No matter what happened, no matter how she felt, she would take one step at a time.

Deciding to try and comfort the girls, she walked into the kitchen. Sarah and Agatha sat across from one another at the table. Eirún walked over and sat down, but just as she did, something on the table caught her eye.

Her mind went blank.

Was that? Impossible. "What—" she tried to get out, but her whole mouth trembled.

"Eirún?" Sarah asked.

Eirún reached over and grabbed the lens. She stood up, knocking the chair to the ground. She'd lost her mind. It couldn't be. Almost afraid, she turned the lens over, and there it was—the crack in the glass.

Her hands trembled so much she dropped the lens onto the ground and covered her face. "Where did you get this?" she wailed, stumbling backward and falling to the wooden floor.

Both Agatha and Sarah hurried from the table. Eirún glanced around the room, but she couldn't see through her tears. "Is he here?"

Sarah looked at Agatha, then back to Eirún. "It's all right. Calm down. Now, who do you mean?"

Eirún tried to answer, but she couldn't quit weeping into her hands. Finally, she pointed to the lens. "I gave that to him before he died. That's mine." She gritted her teeth. "How did you get it?"

"You gave it to Egbert?"

"No!" Eirún cried. "I g—gave it to Søren!" She hit her fist against the side of her head.

"Theos have mercy!" Agatha exclaimed.

"We want to help," Sarah insisted, as she tried to calm Eirún down by rubbing her arms, "but we don't know how. Who's Søren?"

"He—" Her chest quaked, and her head throbbed. "He was my son." Her own words broke her, and she fell over and laid on the ground.

Agatha's eyes widened. "I know him."

Eirún's heart felt as if it stopped. She didn't hear that right.

"Was he small?" Agatha asked. "About nine or ten?"

Her weeping faded, but her lungs continued to shake. How? Was he actually still alive?

"Did he have blonde hair?" Agatha asked.

Eirún sat up. "Where is he? Please!"

Agatha hung her mouth open. "I'm—I'm not sure."

"How do you—" Her hands shook in front of her. "Is he here? Is he alive?"

Agatha swallowed and looked at Sarah. "He's alive. But last I saw him was in the mines."

"Where are those?"

They didn't answer.

"Where are the mines?" she demanded.

"Just east of the city," Agatha answered, "but you can't go there. He's left."

She knew she was going to wake up. This was just some bizarre dream. "Where did he leave to?"

"I don't know," Agatha insisted. Her voice began to quake. "He rode north on this animal out of the mines, but—" her voice cut short.

"Did he come here? To the city?" Sarah asked as she wiped Eirún's cheek with her apron.

Agatha held her mouth open as if dumbfounded. "I don't know. I don't think so."

"It's all right," Sarah pleaded. "Let's just think this through for a minute."

Eirún stood up. She couldn't stay there a second longer, and she didn't care about thinking it through. She ran out of the kitchen and through the front door. Sarah and Agatha's voices fell distant as they called out to her. She only knew of one way out of the city, and there she was headed. Her leather shoes pounded against the stone. She cut north through an alley. With heavy coughs, she tried to control her breathing but never stopped or slowed her pace. Søren was alive. She didn't know how, but she didn't care. She would never stop until she found him.

By the time she made it back to the main road, near the northern end of the city, she passed through a large gate, which she remembered walking through with Naomi. Holding her dress, she hurried across the cobblestone. Along the sides of the streets and in front of shops, people stared at her. She had forgotten to pull her hair up, and she didn't have a cloak on her. But she would die before she let anyone stop her. Nearing the outer city gate, she glanced to the city wall on the other side of the ruined courtyard.

From the long row of gallows, several men hung by their necks. When her eyes caught sight of Hrunting's body, her feet faltered, and her breakfast came out as she threw up on the ground. But then she quickly wiped her mouth and nose and kept running until she made it outside of the city.

Daecland's Blight

Riding upon the alphyn as he ascended the rising road, Søren gazed up. He could just see the light of the sun behind the swirling black clouds in the sky. Otherwise, a blanket of darkness laid over the land, almost as if Daecland was caught in an eternal night. Although he couldn't put his finger on why he felt as if even time itself had slowed.

A strange smell hung in the air, like a mix of rotting fruit and mothballs. It almost felt as if the outside world had been abandoned for a thousand years. Still and lifeless as it slowly decayed.

Despite the gloom of the landscape, in the vicinity around him, all was bright as light crept out from the alphyn like a lantern shining alone in the grayness of the land. At the same time, slender rays continued to flow into its black form like streams of wind being drawn from the air. It was strange to see light and darkness swirling together in such an unnatural way. Even his sword glowed white. He would have been terrified, but the light seemed to enter into him.

Peals of thunder echoed across the mountains to Søren's left, and it reminded him of the thundering army behind him. The first day he came out of the forest, he observed an alphyn roaming the landscape. It began to follow him, and at first, he was afraid, but whenever he and his alphyn stopped, it stopped as well. Then, over the course of the next three days, more alphyns began to follow until hundreds rumbled behind him as walls of dust picked up like a brown-gray cloud.

Behind the alphyns, hundreds, if not thousands, of ravens flew high above. Their shrieks were so loud at times, Søren could hear nothing else. He wasn't sure what it all meant, but he knew it would be something terrible.

As the road turned north, he faced a towering mountain. At its peak lay bands of clouds, wrapping themselves around a rising city. Wisps were in the air, more than he had ever seen in his life. They seemed to be slowly heading east as they made their way out of a large building near the mountain peak.

He could feel his blood surge through his limbs as he gripped his sword in his right hand. Although he trusted the shadow, he wasn't sure what he was supposed to do. All he knew was that Norfrost and maybe even all of Daecland would meet its end that day. A sudden thought came to his mind, but he was almost afraid to know the answer.

"Is Eirún going to die today?" he asked aloud.

"No," said the shadow through the alphyn. "I've taken her from this place."

"To where?"

"Sunder."

Sunder? Was she there the same time he was? "Will we be going back to Sunder?"

"We will."

A sudden hope filled his heart. "When?"

"Before the sun sets."

Søren didn't expect that answer. It had taken him many days to just travel across Daecland. How could he possibly get to Sunder before nightfall?

"As the world dies, so does time," was all the shadow said.

As he tried to figure out what the shadow meant, the clouds thinned further up the road, and a large gate came into view. Before it laid many other alphyns, slain and lifeless, with blood running down the paved road and over the edges. The alphyn continued walking forward as Søren glared at their gaping mouths and long talons. A thick foul smell plagued the air. Behind the city gate, soldiers ran in all directions, hollering out to one another. Several men braced iron beams against the gate

Suddenly, the alphyn quivered and seemed to grow and shift its shape as a deep thunder from its body rent the air.

* * *

Geirleif sat by the window at the entrance of the Norfrost Precinct. His hands were locked in cuffs in front of him. Despite his situation, he was thankful for two things—Eirún seemed to have escaped with little problem, and he was able to be home for a while with his family before they left to stay with Eilis' sister on the second level. They would be safe there, and Eilis was charged with no crime. As much as he hoped, he couldn't talk his way out of his situation, so he took full credit for housing Eirún, and he even confessed that he helped her escape on foot to a town in the mountains. He wasn't sure how this would work out for Hrunting, but it was the best he could do.

He peered through another glass window in a door. There, Chancellor Thialfi was talking to the Chief-of-Police. He knew it would do no good. No man was above the law. He only wished he could save the embarrassment of being held in such a public place. He was a lord, for goodness sake, not some petty criminal.

Outside the window beside him, the gloominess in the atmosphere alone was enough to make a man go mad. Pulling out a golden pocket watch, he turned the winding crown. Despite being relatively new, the second hand had already begun to tick too slow, and it was several hours behind. He wound it again, almost to the point where he feared he'd break the spring, but it didn't help. It only seemed to go slower.

"Blast it," he said with a grunt as he slid it back into his pocket.

Thialfi walked back through the door. His expression didn't look hopeful. He sat down in front of Geirleif. "Four years," he said. "That's the best I can do."

"Four years?" Geirleif replied with a gasp. He thought his maximum would have been three. "What was it before then?"

"Eight."

Geirleif laughed. "For housing a girl?"

"For willingly housing a wanted murderer, Geirleif."

"She didn't murder him," he corrected. "She was protecting herself."

"That's only what she told you. How do you know she was telling the truth?"

"If you met her, you would understand."

Thialfi wiped a bead of sweat from his forehead. He looked thinner than usual. "And you haven't heard from Hrunting?"

"Not for over a week."

"You know they suspect you of foul play there."

Did Geirleif hear him, right? "Foul play?"

"You hid a murderer, and your servants testified to you engaging in long conversations with Lord Hrunting. Some of which consisted of conversations about that girl. Then suddenly, he disappears and is nowhere to be found."

"What are they accusing me of?"

Thialfi hesitated. "Possibly murder."

Geirleif rolled his eyes. Even with Hrunting gone, he was going to get him killed. Geirleif thought about just mentioning the wisp to the police, but they would figure it out sooner or later. "I will not say anything, for his sake. But he is fine, I assure you. You will find that out soon enough."

Thialfi peered at him with questioning eyes. Then his expression softened, and he rubbed his face. Looking behind him as if to make sure no one else was in the room, he let out a long sigh. "Geirleif, I cannot begin to process it all. You are one of the best men this country has ever had. And I don't know what to do."

"You can do nothing," Geirleif tried to encourage him. "You're a young man and a good leader. You have a country to help run. My time is over. I'm an old man. You don't need to worry about me."

"You don't know the half of it," Thialfi replied. "The economy is still falling. These creatures are still roaming the countryside. And a few days ago, we received a telegram from Scathwold that Folkbjörn has apparently been all but destroyed."

Geirleif almost swallowed his tongue. "Destroyed?"

"The whole town, as far as we can tell. The reported death toll was nearly the whole population. We've sent several telegrams to the constables, but since yesterday, we've heard nothing back. Not even from Scathwold."

"You must be joking?" Geirleif sank in his seat. "Why haven't I heard about this?"

Thialfi smirked as he motioned to Geirleif's cuffs. "For obvious reasons."

Geirleif only shook his head. He gained four years in prison and lost everything else. "I suppose it's the way it must be. But those poor people. What could have caused such a thing? Was it a storm?"

Thialfi laughed. "You wouldn't believe me if I told you."

"I doubt that."

Thialfi rubbed his head beneath his thinning hair. He was so young; it must have been from the stress. "The telegram reported," he motioned his hand in the air as if he couldn't come up with the words, "sea serpents flooding out of the Finnvard River." He chuckled in his throat. "We had a fleet scheduled to leave for Sunder earlier this week, but since all this happened, we had to cancel the orders. We just now got each wisp re-supplied with emergency relief provisions. They're heading east to Scathwold as we speak."

Geirleif could barely hear the hum of the fleet from outside. "Why were they heading to Sunder, to begin with?"

"King Eirik insists on taking back Everwind."

Geirleif didn't know Everwind needed to be retaken. But the thought of the serpents was a more astonishing thought. Thialfi was right. If it wasn't for these other creatures, he would have never believed him. The painting of the serpent wrapped around the ship in the ceiling of his stairway came to his mind. Is that what they looked like?

"I'm run out, Geirleif. I don't know what to do. It's all madness. Our country will be forever changed."

Geirleif wanted to speak a word of encouragement, but a sudden roll of thunder took their attention. They gazed out the window. Geirleif couldn't believe it, but somehow the sky looked even darker than it had been, as if night had fallen several hours too early. He pulled out his watch again, but despite turning the winding crown, the cheap thing had quit working altogether. He shoved it back in his pocket.

Thialfi frowned, and his lips pinched in as he stood up and walked out the door. With his hands still cuffed, Geirleif followed him outside. He wasn't sure if he was allowed to, but he didn't really care.

Dozens of wisps soared below the swirling clouds as they made their way east. At the end of the block, soldiers surrounded the city gate as crowds began to amass along the sidewalks. Another rumble of thunder boomed so loud Geirleif winced, wishing he could remove the cuffs to cover his ears. The soldiers frantically stumbled backward, pulling out swords and firing off muskets through the gate. Thialfi took a step forward with a look of shock over his eyes.

The gate exploded inward. Soldiers were flung into the air, while others ran north for their lives.

Geirleif's heart melted.

Through the gate walked a horrid creature. Solid black like death. Larger than any animal he had ever seen. Its small blue eyes, set behind jaws large enough to swallow a wisp, pierced his soul. Smoke, or a black mist, emanated from its body, somewhat concealing its shape, but each step from its thick legs shook the ground as if the earth itself trembled in fear. On the creature's back sat a small boy with a sword raised high in his hand, from which shined a burning light, like white fire. Geirleif froze to the marrow of his bones.

With an outstretched arm, the boy pointed his sword forward, and suddenly, dozens of those creatures which the city had been fighting off swarmed through the gates.

"What on—" Geirleif muttered, but the muscles in his jaw lacked the strength to finish his sentence.

Soldiers fired off their muskets, but there were too many. A sudden vibration rumbled through the air, causing the hair on Geirleif's arms to stand. The smoke around the creature transformed into great throngs of black tentacles as they raced up toward the clouds like stretching fingers. Wisps began colliding into one another as flames from their engines broke out across the sky. Burning wood and metal fell to the earth, crashing and exploding into the buildings. It was as if the sky itself rained fire upon the people whose screams echoed through the streets. At that moment, a deafening sound, like a roaring cyclone, burst out, shaking the very foundations of the city. Dust billowed into the air while buildings collapsed onto themselves.

The last thing Geirleif saw was a swarm of blackbirds flying down into the city.

Geirleif shrunk into himself. "Thialfi!" he shouted.

There was no answer, and the city went quiet. Never in his life had he heard such a terrifying silence of nothingness. Wrapped in despair, he couldn't even hear his own breathing. All was black, and his feet were locked in place. His chest shook. What was happening? Was he dead? An unnerving sensation fell upon him as if he was utterly alone and yet before a million eyes all at the same time—like his soul was naked and exposed. Long forgotten memories began to appear so vividly, he thought he could see them in front of him.

In his mind, he now stood in a desert, lifeless men stripped of their clothing piled up before him. Their hollow faces were ash-colored with cracked skin around the eyes, which bled from their tear ducts. Swollen tongues hung out from of their lipless mouths, revealing black teeth and gums. Their bodies were skeletal, with stomachs sunken in beneath their ribcages. Most were dead; some faintly drew in their final breaths. The horrors of dehydration had taken their full toll.

Geirleif's face fell. "I didn't know," he said. But he did. He had written the approval for the live experimentation and deaths of countless men. But it was all for the sake of the betterment of society, wasn't it?

The bodies vanished, and his latest mistress stood before him. She was young and beautiful. He knew she was money-hungry, but he never cared. His wife was there as well, hiding behind her shadow, ignorant of his double-life. But she was always in the shadow, wasn't she? He rarely thought of her. He never pursued her. His mind was always on other things or other women.

His face hardened. "That was years ago! I broke that off."

Other men did it, didn't they? Too much was expected of him. He couldn't be perfect. And the reasonable thing to do was not tell her. Save her from the pain. And for all he knew, she probably cheated on him as well.

Then there was Sylvi, now standing before him. He had sworn to raise and protect her, and he meant to. But she was mute and dumb. She couldn't confess anything to anyone. And more times than he could count, he took advantage of it.

At that moment, Sylvi disappeared within a blanket of light. Geirleif was left in darkness as a well of guilt poured out of him like black vomit, splattering over his feet onto the ground. His whole life had been a masquerade—his title, his public image, his charities. It was all a deception to show himself as a good man in society—to cover up the shame of his dark secrets. And it worked. His own family never knew, and until that moment, he had managed to bury it so deep, it was only a vague memory to himself as if it was all just some nightmare which he had awoken from. Like a mist, he allowed it to pass from his mind.

But there it was. Exposed before him. He hung his head. "I'm sorry," he confessed in a shallow murmur. But he wasn't. He was afraid of what was going to happen to him—petrified of it—but he wasn't really sorry. Somehow, even in that terrible place, if given the opportunity, he would have done it all over again. Just as he always had—going back to his shame and numbing the guilt that always threatened to expose his darkness.

A darkness he loved.

* * *

Geoffrey shivered. By the look of the dim light peeking through the window, it may have been mid-day, maybe not. Save for nightfall, all the days looked the same—a depressing overcast of shadow and gloom. Two days ago, he had caught a fever, and the diarrhea had left him dehydrated and oftentimes delirious. But it came and went, and all he could do was go through the motions of what little time he likely had left. He waited for the rumor about the burning bodies, but it never came. Maybe tomorrow.

Burlan was no longer there to help him, and neither was Bartholomew. But they were free. Just the simple thought of Bartholomew seeing his daughter again filled him with a quiet joy, and he knew he could die in peace.

He pulled himself from the wooden bunk and stood up. His head felt as if a rock were in it, rolling one way as he tried to look the other. With a lump in the back of his throat, which he couldn't seem to swallow, he stumbled to the door. He needed water. Stepping outside, he watched his feet as they slowly made their way across the sandy ground. Glancing up, he saw several gray-shirts sitting beside the trough, their eyes fixed on the sky.

To his relief, Geoffrey stumbled to his knees and bent over the iron lip, and peered into the water. The reflection was supposed to be of him, but the thin face and scraggly beard set beneath the dark sockets of his eyes left him unrecognizable.

He closed his eyes and sunk his face into the stagnant water. After taking in several gulps, he leaned back and wiped his face. That was when he noticed the gray-shirts still looking up—even the guards.

The sky was as gray as usual, but toward the north-eastern horizon, it seemed to be swallowed up by darkness, as if the sky itself had been peeled back to reveal only nothing. A harrowing silence settled around the land as if the earth itself was dying. Such a sight brought Geoffrey to his senses for a moment. Was this it? Was this the end?

A sudden howl rose in the distance. Several gray-shirts turned their gaze toward the mountains. There was another howl and then another from behind them. Although they seemed far away, it felt as if the camp was being surrounded by wolves. Several guards ran through the underpass, shouting out orders. Gray-shirts began tripping over themselves as they stumbled toward the bunkhouses. Even though a shiver rose from Geoffrey's feet to his head, he couldn't shift from his gaze. As terrible as the view was, there was something other-worldly and mesmerizing about the sky. The blackness was so vivid, Geoffrey wasn't merely looking at it, but he could feel it as if it was some great mass pressing against his soul. He thought if he stood there long enough, it would crush him.

A siren broke out across the camp, and Geoffrey startled. Gripping his ears, he realized he was the only gray-shirt left outside. He hurried to the last bunkhouse and slammed the door behind him.

Bury My Heart in the Shallow Grave

A s the wagons rolled onto the cobblestone streets of Everwind, Arnon held the rings in his hand. He could almost feel a weight lift off of him as he looked forward to seeing Adelyne again. He wouldn't wait another day. As soon as he saw her, he would give her the ring.

But first, he needed to house his mother and sisters. As the head of the household, he had already decided that they would all live together in their old family home until the marriage ceremony. With help, he would fix up Adelyne's home, and the two of them could live there. It would be small, but he figured they could have enough room for several children.

He looked at the stump of his right elbow. Even his left hand was missing a finger, leaving him practically useless. His mother, as well as Redfield, told him not to worry about providing for himself or Adelyne, but he still couldn't worry that she might feel him to be inadequate. Husbands were supposed to protect and earn a living for their families. He could do neither. And he still couldn't figure out how he'd managed to get the sword through the alphyn. When he passed out, his body must have fallen on the hilt and pushed it through. Some of the folks at Crossroads called him a hero, but he felt like a fool. The reason he got attacked was that he lingered too long on the road, and it was only by sheer luck, or by some miracle, that he even put a dent in that creature.

The other wagons had long departed as the families went on to find their husbands and fathers as his own wagon made its way down Fellhouse Street. The soldier in the front began to mutter something, and although he couldn't make out the words, Arnon could hear a concerned tone in his mother's voice as she replied. He pulled back the canvas and watched Myla as she stepped out of the wagon and walked across the street.

Arnon puffed out air. The thatched roof to their home had caved in with the topped western wall, leaving a pile of rubble in the alleyway. He tried to recall the last time he had seen the house. Was it really since before the battle? He should have at least checked on it. Fleta and Hazel now walked across the street, and Arnon slid himself out the back of the wagon. The soldier hurried around to help him, but Arnon raised his hand. "I've got it."

"You sure, sire?"

"I'm sure." He took a few steps. It felt weird, but he felt stronger than he would have thought. Still in his burgundy tunic and leather boots, he made his way to his family.

"It's been so many years," Myla said with a hand over her mouth. Her eyes watered as she poked at the broken remains of her old life. Arnon couldn't imagine how she must feel right now. "Your father built that house himself."

"I'm sorry," Arnon replied.

Hazel tugged at Myla's faded mauve dress. "Where we gonna stay?"

Myla wrapped her arm around her.

"I know a place," Arnon said. "It'll be cramped, but it'll have to work for now." He made the offer, but he wasn't sure if Sarah had any room or not. It was that, or they would have to stay at Drake's place, and he'd rather not stay there again. Unless, maybe, he got any more of those fancy couches.

A sudden holler from a soldier on the eastern end of the road rang out. Several other soldiers were running north, followed by two sergeants and a chief. Arnon made his way to the wagon. "Do you know what's going on?" he asked the soldier sitting in the front.

The soldier narrowed his eyes as he stared down the road. His thin neck and small chin gave him a bony look. "Not sure, Commander, but I'll find out and let you know."

Arnon glanced back to his family, who was walking toward him. His mother wasn't crying, but he hadn't seen that look on her face since his father died.

"Before you go," he told the soldier, "take us to the House of Good Hope in the Western District first."

"Yes, sire."

The rest of the ride remained quiet, although some distant shouting echoed from further north as they passed King's Lane. It was probably nothing. Arnon kept his eyes ahead, waiting for Sarah's house to come into view. When it finally did, he gripped the railing on the side to keep himself from jumping out too soon. He only hoped Adelyne didn't worry too much. He said he would be back in a week, and it was nearly two at this point. And hopefully, his wound wouldn't frighten her. Surely, she would still love him the same.

When the wagon stopped, Arnon slid out the back and walked over to his mother. "Let me talk to Sarah first, then we'll bring our stuff in."

"Okay," she replied.

He rushed up the steps, took in a deep breath, and opened the door. Inside was fairly quiet, although some girls chatted in the fireplace room. He peered around the corner where Langleigh and Lilly sat by the fireplace, but no Adelyne or Sarah. He headed to the kitchen. Sarah sat at the table, with her cheek resting on her propped-up hand.

"Sarah?"

She startled and turned toward him.

Arnon felt a blow come against him like a taunting spirit, and he almost lost his balance. The weariness in her eyes and the lines in her face made it look as if she had aged twenty years. A strange, uncanny feeling welled up inside of him. "Is everything . . ." he began to ask, but even from across the kitchen, he could see her shake. His throat tightened. "Where's Adelyne?"

She suddenly sniffed and tried to hide her sob.

Something was wrong. His body went heavy, and he found it hard to stand. "Where's Adelyne?"

* * *

Galvin stood in the hallway, running everything through his mind. With the rise of fevers around the city, people began to declare it another plague. A curse from Theos. The Day of Reckoning. And rather than trying to help the city, many were using all of this as an excuse to commit more crimes. He thought Sunderian beliefs were meant to bring out the best in people. Instead, it brought the worst. The whole thing put a bad taste in his mouth.

To top it all off, that morning, a scout confirmed a Daecish legion marching south. With fifteen-hundred men enlisted, they could handle a legion, but he still couldn't shake his nervousness. Maybe they only wanted to establish terms? It wasn't abnormal to send a legion for that, just in case terms weren't made. But he doubted that was the case. If they wanted to, he knew Daecland would take Everwind right back. He groaned. What had he brought upon his own people? He straightened himself. He had done the right thing. He had fought for their freedom, and he would continue to do so.

He had ensured that the northern walls were well guarded. And he prayed they wouldn't have to retreat. They probably wouldn't, but he also didn't know if other legions were on their way. He needed to be prepared. He was at least thankful that Redfield and Arnon had returned that day. Redfield was a good leader, and he was glad to know that Arnon was safe.

He touched the red aiguillette in his hand—the Mark of Valor. Earlier that afternoon, Redfield told Galvin about Arnon's courage against the alphyn. Missing arm or not, he still couldn't believe he killed the thing. Lombard was twice his size and probably couldn't have done such a feat. Arnon had certainly earned the decoration, and Galvin was glad to give him his own. He'd had it since Landon gave it to him when he first became a Dark Horse. That felt like ages ago.

The door to the dungeon swung open, and Porter walked up, followed by Quinn. A man by the name of Fletcher had been brought in, along with half a dozen prostitutes who were sent to the cells at the old Daecish Quarters.

"How'd it go?" Galvin asked.

Quinn had red eyes but remained quiet.

Porter wiped his forehead. "That man didn't hold anything back. He's sick or something." He pointed to his head.

Galvin crossed his arms. "He confessed to the murder?"

"And more," Porter replied, spitting on the ground. He glanced at Quinn, who wiped his eyes and tried to compose himself. "Fletcher said he killed another girl as well. Went by the name Cydney. Said he got her pregnant and didn't want to pay the bastard bonds."

"What of this other one he killed?"

Porter glanced to Quinn again. "She was a Dark Horse. Drake and Quinn knew her well." He paused to cough in his hand. "And I don't know if he's just making stuff up, but Fletcher said she was gonna marry some other man, and he didn't like it. Said if he couldn't have her, no one would."

"Why would he be making that up?"

Porter laughed and shook his head but held no smile. "He said the other man was Arnon Greystrom."

"Good grief," Galvin rubbed his face. At least it now made sense why Arnon was so sympathetic to the prostitutes. And she was a Dark Horse? Wesley just let anyone who felt like it join, didn't he? And what was Arnon thinking, marrying a girl like that?

"Young men got their head in the clouds," Porter added. "They see a pretty girl and can't think straight."

Quinn narrowed his eyes at Porter from behind him. Galvin knew Porter had his own issues with prostitutes. He never publicly announced it, but he docked his pay twice for it.

"All right," Galvin said with a sigh. "I'm gonna see what I can't get out of Commander Tyr. You all know your positions. One legion shouldn't be too difficult, but we need to be prepared for more."

"Aye," Porter replied. He walked off with Quinn following behind.

Galvin raised a hand for Quinn to pause. "Are you all right?"

"Aye," Quinn replied.

"So, you knew this Adelyne?"

Quinn rubbed his eye. "She was one of the best girls I knew."

Letting out a sigh, Galvin set his hands on his hips. "I worry about Arnon. If you're willing, go inform Drake about Fletcher. Then tell him to go find Arnon and comfort him. He looks to Drake like a father." He handed Quinn his aiguillette. "And give this to him. Arnon's earned it."

Walking down the stone steps, Galvin almost dreaded talking with the Daecish Commander. Their conversations were always short, and even though he had fed him and his men more, they never seemed to be pleased. But they were prisoners; what more could he expect? Passing the cells, more men were sitting up rather than lying down. And they had been given more waste buckets, but it didn't help the smell any.

He approached Commander Tyr's cell, but the pale-face was asleep. Galvin thought about waking him but knew he'd probably get nothing out of him anyway. All he really wanted to know was whether Llynhithe still had functioning wisps. He knew if they did, Everwind would be through. He let out a heavy breath like a man at the end of his years. The people still had hope, but deep down, he knew there was none. There never was. They fought for the freedom of Sunder, but the more he thought about it, the more he realized that his people may have been better off if they never resisted. If the Daecish really wanted to, they could burn the whole country of Sunder to the ground.

There was laughter from the last cell. With Fletcher, there were now six men in there, and every single one of them sat in the opposite corner of that one prisoner. For being a cold-blooded murderer, even Fletcher looked like a coward as he hid behind the other men and peered at that prisoner with wide eyes. What in the world did this ghastly man do to make five grown men act like that?

"You're right to be afraid." The prisoner spoke with a rotten gurgle in his throat.

The fat one, Egbert, pointed his finger. "Don't you listen to him. He's a liar!"

"Afraid of what?" Galvin asked, ignoring the warning.

"Wisps are coming. A whole fleet."

How could he even know that? "That's ridiculous," Galvin replied.

"They'll be here by the morning," the prisoner continued. "What are you going to do?"

"Shut up!" Egbert shouted. "I see right through you." His eyes watered. "You're the father of murderers. Everything you say's a lie!"

The prisoner never even looked at Egbert but continued to peer into Galvin's eyes. He thought he might be crazy, but he wondered if the prisoner could read his mind. "How do you know this?" he managed to ask.

"I already told you the Daecish were coming, and now they're marching south, aren't they?"

Galvin felt hot, almost delirious.

"You weary over tales and prophecies, which have brought nothing but misery on your people. Fathers slay their young and abandon their wives, all in the name of Theos. Merchants cheat, and beggars steal. Prophets lie, and leaders prey on the weak." The prisoner pointed out of the cell at the dungeon stairs. "I'll tell you again, as I've told you before. Your Sunder's Bane isn't in your stories. It's marching toward your city. It's sailing over the Swelling Sea."

The prisoner's words wrapped around Galvin's heart and choked out the frail amount of belief he still held on to. But he'd seen it himself. Hypocrites who knew the ballads and lays of old by heart. Singing about sorrows of their evils of old, all the while claiming they wanted to bring about a better city. But it was all the same. They cared only for their own gain, even when it cost others dearly. It's why every single one of those murderers were in that cell with the prisoner. "What do you suggest we do, then?" he asked sarcastically.

"You have but one choice. You must take your army and flee back to Denhurst. You'll be stronger there with more arms and men."

"That's foolish talk," Galvin replied.

"If you stay, you will all die. But if you flee, you'll live to see another day and save Sunder. Countries are never won so easily as taking one city. If you want to be free of the Daecish, you must prepare for many hard years."

As much as he didn't want to admit it, the prisoner made sense, and a faint glimmer of hope flickered in Galvin's chest. Maybe they didn't have to take on all of Daecland; maybe if they just resisted long enough, Daecland would give up and go back over the mountains. In the past, strictly defensive wars had worked in the Southern Kingdoms. It could work again, but he knew they would have to flee to Denhurst first. Only then would he have enough strength. But they would have to flee quickly. "Then, if we must, we'll take our families and flee."

The prisoner shrugged. "If you can take the old and the young with you, then by all means. They'll probably slow you down, though, then you'll all be as good as dead."

Unfortunately, Galvin knew that was likely true, but the thought sickened him. He wasn't giving up yet. But this prisoner, he knew things. There was uncanny wisdom about him. Maybe he could be useful.

Before he even reached for the key on the stone wall, the prisoner lifted up his bound wrists as if he knew Galvin was going to release him. Almost as if he wanted him to. An eerie shiver ran down Galvin's back, but he ignored it.

He unlocked the cell door as it swung open. Fletcher quickly leaned forward to run out, but Galvin slammed the bottom of his boot against his face, and he fell back against the ground. He pointed to the prisoner. "Stand up." He picked the prisoner up by the chain and walked him out, relocking the door. Fletcher moaned as he gripped his face and rolled on the ground.

Galvin examined the prisoner's shackles. There were no keyholes or connections. It was as if the bonds were forged around his very wrists. "How did you get these on?" he asked.

"They've been there a very long time." The prisoner smiled.

Galvin headed up the stairs and pulled the prisoner behind him.

* * *

Just south of the city wall, between the Southern and Eastern Gates, Arnon stood before the shallow grave. He couldn't see them, but a few yards behind stood Drake, Bell, and Sarah. By his side were his sisters and his mother. The weight of Adelyne's ring in his left hand felt like a heavy stone in his heart as he stared down at the pile of rocks. On his own finger, he wore his father's ring. He couldn't even remember when he put it on.

Sarah tried to explain to him that based on what the other girls had said in the tavern, Adelyne tried to get away, that she didn't want to be there. But how did she end up there in the first place? But it didn't really matter, did it? She was gone.

The last time he spoke to Adelyne, he told her that she needed to be true to him. And at that moment, he knew that if she couldn't be, he would have to leave her. But sitting at her grave, he would have forgiven her a thousand times if he could just have her back.

He bent down and removed a rock from the pile. He looked at her ring and examined the woven silver before he let it slip into the grave and set the rock back over it. For a long while, he just knelt there. No one said anything.

He pictured her standing in the courtyard outside the castle with those little flowers woven into her hair. The first time she kissed him, he felt like he had fallen into a dream. And the look in her eyes when he stumbled through Sarah's door after the battle. That was the first time he could tell that she loved him just as he loved her. He could still smell the jasmine when he buried his face in her hair.

Myla rested her hand on his shoulder. She knelt beside him, and he clenched his teeth behind his closed mouth and his eyes watered. "Mother . . ." his words mumbled from his trembling mouth. "I can't do this anymore. All I want to do is lie down and die."

He didn't look at her, but by the tremble in her hand, he knew she was crying. After a minute, she stood up and took the girls out of the way. Drake wobbled over. With a loud grunt, he sat beside him, setting his cane on the grass. Arnon looked up at him and could see tears in his own eyes.

"This probably won't help none," Drake said, "but I heard they caught the man who did this. He'll pay his due."

Arnon already knew who did it. He just had a hunch. But Drake was right. It didn't help. "I wanted to kill Fletcher myself, but I'm useless."

Drake sniffed in his tears. "Killing him ain't going to fix nothing. I know."

Arnon peered at him. What did he mean by that?

"I tried to save her," Drake said, wiping his eyes. "But I couldn't." He looked over his shoulder, almost nervously, then he peered back at Arnon.

He appeared like an old man now, withered and thin, as if he was dying. Just at the beginning of winter, he and Drake were at the front of it all—leading and fighting, filled with the excitement and hope of a new Everwind. But now, in such a short amount of time, everything had changed. That afternoon, the soldiers spoke of a Daecish legion marching south, but the Free Sunderian Army was in charge now. They'd already manned the walls and battlements, and in their condition, he and Drake couldn't even help. But he didn't really care. Let them come.

"I reckon it's the end," Drake continued, "and I've got to get it out somehow." He took in a deep breath.

"Get it out?"

"I've done cried to Theos for forgiveness, but maybe you ought'a know yourself." He nervously glanced behind him once again. "Her father wasn't ever drafted. I found him drunk one night, probably right after he finished his routine with her. I drug him through that hole in the city wall, and I did him in. I'd had enough of it." He wiped his cheeks. "I thought it would fix the problem. But it didn't. All it did was bring me more guilt."

Arnon's brain stuttered for a moment. Drake murdered a man? It was an unnerving thought, but nothing surprised Arnon anymore. He knew he would have killed her father, too, if he'd had the chance. "I guess no one could have saved her."

"If there's anything I learned through this," Drake said, "it's that there's only one who could have saved Adelyne." He motioned at the sky. "And it ain't you or I."

Arnon let his face fall, and he closed his eyes. Every bone in his body pleaded with Theos that she was with him, that she was healed and forgiven. But he had no idea what went through her mind before she died, and a terrible fear haunted him. What if she didn't want to be with Theos? What if she never wanted to be forgiven?

Drake lifted himself back to his feet. "The Daecish will be here in the morn' and they've already shut the Southern Gate. Which means we got to go around through the eastern gate, and the sun's about to set. We don't want to get caught out here all night." He peered north with his hands on his hips. "And there's something peculiar about the sky on the northern horizon. They say it's just a storm, but I don't like the looks of it."

Arnon didn't move.

Drake grunted. "Now I know you plan on staying down here dying and all, but you got a mother and two sisters to care for. So come on, get yourself up."

He knew Drake was right. But what could he even do? They'd be caring for him his whole life. He stood up and wiped his face with the sleeve of his jerkin.

"And here," Drake said, handing Arnon a red aiguillette. "The highest decoration awarded to the Free Sunderian Army. That was Galvin's."

"Why's he giving it to me?"

"Cause you're the only man to single-handedly kill an alphyn since Wrecan. I guess he thought you deserved it." He patted Arnon on the shoulder and walked back to the others.

Arnon ran his finger along the silky rope. He had already buried his tunic in the ground, along with his father's sword. The last thing he wanted to wear was this decoration. Throwing the aiguillette on the ground, he slowly followed behind his family to the Eastern Gate.

The Invasion

Just as the sun was rising, Gunnar stood beside his horse on a high hill. Everwind sat just a league before him, nestled beneath a haze of smoke and fog. In the short time he'd been gone, the city had already settled into disrepair and ruin. He was too far to see anyone along the battlements, but he assumed they were aware of their presence. Although he had nearly a full cavalry of two-hundred and eighty, he had lost nearly three-hundred men to those serpents. Thankfully, they were mostly swordsmen. He didn't like thinking that way, but it was true. His men could still accomplish their task without them.

The regiment officers counted a total of three-hundred and seventy-six muskets and wheellocks, but they did lose an entire siege engine squad, leaving only two more. As a result of his losses, Gunnar was forced to merge the two legions into one. But paired with the arrival of the wisps, Everwind should still be re-taken easily enough.

He kept his ears alert, waiting for the sound of small humming black dots to appear over the sea. He was surprised he made it before the Airborne Armada, but that was better than being late. All he knew was that the fleet would press against the city from the west, but Admiral Bjarke would arrive ahead of it and land near the legion to strategize with him on how to maneuver both land and air forces for a swift victory. Minimal communication between the wisps never made it an easy task, and Gunnar was thankful he joined the Army instead.

Beside him stood Halvard. He had rarely spoken since the serpents, but by the paleness in his face, he was obviously a wreck on the inside. As much as Gunnar needed him to get his act together, he couldn't throw off the shakes himself. Paired with the creatures coming out of the ground, it was like the world had suddenly gone mad and began spitting out monsters from people's worst nightmares.

"Your regiment officers ready?" he asked.

Halvard nodded.

"Are you ready?"

Straightening himself, Halvard nodded again.

"Are you sure?"

"I'm fine," he replied. "It's just those serpents." He lifted his chin, and he stared up for a moment. "And the sky."

"You feel like something's wrong?"

"Something is wrong." He shook his head, jaw set. "And yet everyone's just going on as if everything's fine."

Gunnar felt the same, but he knew his men couldn't do anything about it. None of them could explain it, but they still had a job to do. "When we get this over with, we best prepare for a heavy storm."

"Yes, sir."

"We'll send in the two siege engines first." Gunnar pointed to the Northern Gate. "We'll cover them with four squadrons equipped with muskets. As soon as we breakthrough, you'll lead the cavalry in. I'll send in the footmen afterward. The wheellocks and muskets should do the most work. We'll leave the swordsmen for cleanup." Halvard nodded again, but Gunnar feared his current mental state would bring about a militaristic disaster. "When you get in, the first thing I want you to do is go to the castle. See if you can't find Commander Tyr. If he isn't in the dungeons, go to the Military Quarters. They may be holding him there. Order your first regiment officer to take him and any other of our men you find through the Western Gate. Once the wisps arrive, they should have an infirmary out there. If they're still alive, I imagine they'll need medical attention."

Halvard nodded and took in a deep breath.

Gunnar tightened his shoulders to try and keep himself from trembling, but all he could picture were women and children being fired upon by his own command.

* * *

Fleta stood in the back bedroom with a sack in her hand. Myla had set the rest of the luggage on the bed, set against the half-timber walls. It was the nicest house she had ever been in, but it was hard to appreciate. Not only did she feel intrusive with all the other girls in the house, but Arnon was depressed, her mother was depressed, and Hazel whined all day. The whole thing was miserable. Beckett said he would try to find her, but he probably thought they would be staying at her old family home.

Even with all of that, what upset her the most was the whole idea of a Daecish legion just north of the city. Shouldn't they flee or hide or something? Yet everyone just went about confused and uncertain. She prayed their army could stand its ground. Maybe she should talk to Arnon. He would have some answers. But she'd also never seen him look so miserable. When he said he wanted to die, she knew by the look on his face that he meant it.

She dropped the sack on the floor beside a straw-filled pallet and stepped into the hallway. After she first peered into the empty kitchen, she walked over to the fireplace room. Several girls sat around the pallets. Four were lying down, looking thin and weak. Another girl sat against the wall, holding a baby in her arms. Despite her tangled hair and the stain of dark soil on her hands, a wide smile stretched across her face as she stroked the baby's hair. If Fleta remembered correctly, that was Sarah.

A taller, red-haired girl walked over to Sarah and sat down, placing her hand on the child's head. She let out a quiet laugh as she covered her mouth. "Langleigh told me that Acton's fever had broken this morning. But I just couldn't believe it."

Sarah looked up at the girl with bright, glistening eyes. "Yesterday, he felt so hot, I was sure he wouldn't make it through the night. But, then . . ." She kissed the baby. "He just got better."

"Praise Theos," the red-haired girl replied, now letting the baby wrap his little hand around her finger. He let out a coo as his big eyes wandered around the room.

Fleta didn't want to look like she was eavesdropping, so she stepped back into the hall. Since she had returned to Everwind, she couldn't shake the hopelessness that seemed to saturate the entire city. But seeing the joy on those women's faces filled her with new optimism. Despite how dim everything had become, it seemed that even a single glimmer of light could chase all the darkness away. With the sudden urge to hug her mother, she walked back to the bedroom.

Myla rummaged through her sack. Hazel slept on the bed beside her.

Fleta wrapped her arms around her mother and rested her cheek on her back. "I love you, Mama."

Myla held on to Fleta's arms. "I love you too." She chuckled. "But I haven't known you to hug me like that in a long time. Where did that come from?"

Fleta dropped her arms and smiled with a slight shrug. "I don't know. I just wanted you to know."

Myla patted Fleta on the cheek but narrowed her eyes and peered to the wall behind her. "You hear that?" she asked.

"Hear what?"

Myla walked past her and out of the bedroom door. Fleta followed behind as she opened the back door leading to a small garden which ran up against the city wall, with a thin alleyway running along it.

"What did you—" Fleta began to ask, but her mother raised a hand.

After a second, a low hum arose from somewhere in the distance. Myla's eyes widened. "That's a wisp," she said.

Although Fleta had never seen or even heard a wisp, Porter and her own father had told her enough terrifying stories to keep her up at night. All she could imagine was some flying mechanical ship coming to kill her. She tried to hold it back, but the fear of death caused her to cling to her mother.

* * *

By late afternoon, Arnon stood beside Drake in the castle courtyard. From the Northern District, popping sounds erupted as smoke rose from behind the walls. Entire bands of soldiers and officers hurried south as Galvin barked off some orders. Panic welled up in Arnon. Clearly, the fighting had begun, but surely, they couldn't have been retreating already. Maybe the Daecish were attacking from the south as well? In his condition, Arnon wasn't even sure why he was standing there. All he wanted to know was what the army planned to do to protect the families.

After Galvin spoke to two brigadiers, he caught sight of Arnon and hurried toward him. "Arnon," he said, breathing hard and sweating profusely. He eyed him up and down. "Where's your uniform?"

Arnon lifted the stub of his right arm. "Don't think I'll be of much use in it, but what orders do you have for the families?"

The popping sounds grew louder, and Galvin kept glancing over his shoulder, but he didn't give an answer.

"What's that noise?" Drake asked.

"Don't know, they're like . . ." Galvin's eyes shifted from side to side, and he held his hands out as if holding something. "They're like hand-sized canons. They're slaughtering our men."

"So they're abandoning the Northern District?" Drake asked as he and Arnon both peered back at the disappearing bands of soldiers running south.

"We held them off as long as we could, but it's too much. And wisps are coming. Possibly a whole fleet."

An icy chill fell over Arnon, and he had a sudden urge to run back to Sarah's. On the one hand, Galvin's words shocked him, and yet he knew this would happen. Of course, they brought wisps. It was as if he and everyone else had been living in a false dream where everything was just going to work out. But at some point, they had to wake up.

Drake's face remained calm, but he stared hard at Galvin. "We need to get the soldiers to evacuate the families. We'll head south."

"And they'll run us over before we get a single league into the country," Galvin replied. "They'll kill every one of us."

"Then what do you suggest?" Arnon asked.

The popping grew louder.

Galvin peered at Arnon. "Go grab Myla and the girls. We'll take who we can, but if we want to live to see another day we can't be slowed down."

"What does that mean?" Drake questioned in a stern tone.

"It means if we try to evacuate everyone, we'll all die. But if we can get the army," he looked back at Arnon, "and a few of our families, then we still have hope."

"But you can't just leave the rest to be slaughtered!" Drake hollered.

"I don't have a choice!" Galvin replied, his words taut. "I'm trying to save as many as I can!"

"Then leave the army to hold back the Daecish while the families retreat!"

"They have wisps, Drake!" Galvin shot his finger west. "They'll kill the army, and the women and children'll starve on their way to Denhurst! The army is our only hope for maintaining strength in

Sunder! If we give up Everwind, the Daecish will remain, and we can regroup in Denhurst. If we keep the pressure on them, they may give up. It's happened before."

Drake took in a frustrating sigh. "They're Daecish; they'll never give up."

"Then why did we ever fight them, to begin with!" Galvin's eyes suddenly welled up. "It was always a hopeless cause, wasn't it?"

Drake didn't respond.

"Maybe the Daecish will let the families alone," Galvin continued in a calmer voice. "It's the army they want." He wiped his hands down his face. "Go get Myla and the girls, but I've got to go. Porter's already loading up the storehouse of grain." Without another word, he walked toward the road.

Drake only stared ahead as though he never noticed Galvin leaving.

Arnon bore down on his teeth. What were they going to do? Was this it? Even if the army made it to Denhurst, they would only prolong their fate. "Somehow, I saw this coming," he said just above a whisper. "But I thought we were the good guys. I thought we'd win."

Drake took in a hard sniff. "Ain't nobody good—not the Daecish, not us."

Arnon knew that was the truth, but the whole thing was still unnerving. "But it's just so unfair. So many people are probably going to die."

"There's a lot in this world that's unfair. A lot of sad stories. But that's why my hope ain't in this world, but in the next one."

"So, what can we do?"

"The way I see it, we got two choices. We can die trying to save ourselves, or we can die doing what's right."

"What's right?"

"I've been part of this cause long enough. I ain't going with that cursed army. They're selling the lives of women and children for the sake of saving their own name. I'll stay and get as many of the folks out as I can. I probably won't get too many, but even one child will be worth it."

Drake was right. If they didn't die now, they'd die in Denhurst. "We better get going then."

Suddenly, a low humming droned from the west. Both he and Drake peered at the sky but couldn't see anything as the castle blocked their view. Numbness threatened to overtake him.

"You go on and run," Drake said. "I'll be too slow. I'll rally up all the men I can 'round here. Maybe there's still some brave enough to help the families. Send those you find to the Eastern Gate. Tell 'em to stay along the southern wall. They'll be safest there. If by some grace we survive this, I'll meet you on the outside."

Arnon realized this might be the last time he would ever see Drake. There was so much he wanted to say, but his mind went blank. "Thank you, Drake. For everything."

Drake patted him on the back. Along with the humming, the popping grew louder and now sounded more like explosions echoing through the streets. "You're a good boy, but every second counts. Get going!"

"I'll see you there!" Arnon shouted as he quickly ran to the road.

* * *

Even through the stone walls, Eilívur could hear the firing of muskets. As excited as he was, he couldn't believe it took the Daecish this long to get there. But they did bring muskets. He got to fire one once in Varghoss, and that was many years ago, but he could still remember the power behind it. He could only imagine the slaughter going on above him. Maybe after this, they could finally bring stability and sanity back to this wasteland.

731

The other Daecish men talked amongst themselves, their voices fast and animated. Now that the prisoner was gone, the fat man and the others sat apart from one another and kept to themselves. Eilívur could only hope that Gunnar or Halvard would be there looking for him and his men. For all he knew, they may have forgotten about him and would never even think to check the dungeons.

The musket shots soon faded. The other men gazed at the ceiling as if waiting for something to happen, but for the better part of an hour, they all sat in silence.

At last, the upstairs door swung open. Eilívur pulled himself to his feet and stumbled to the iron bars. He first noticed black boots walking down the steps, then the familiar blue uniform. He let out a grin. It was Halvard.

"Commander Tyr?" he called out.

Eilívur waved a hand through the bars. "Here," he tried to shout, but barely a rasp escaped his throat.

Halvard marched over with several soldiers behind him, carrying a handheld contraption in his hand. His mouth dropped as he stared at Eilívur.

Eilívur laughed. "I know I've seen better days," he managed to get out in a quiet voice, "but you're not looking at a ghost, commander."

Halvard glanced along the wall and found the set of keys. He unlocked the cell, then handed the keys to one of the soldiers as they unlocked the rest. He shook Eilívur's hand. "Glad you made it."

"What took you so long?"

Halvard smiled. "Paperwork."

Eilívur laughed, but he could see a look in Halvard's eyes that something troubled him.

"Who are they?" Halvard asked, pointing to the cell next to him.

"Sunderians. All wanted for murder as far as I could collect."

"Over here!" Halvard motioned to several of the soldiers who hurried over. "Shoot them," he commanded.

The fat one went wide-eyed as the soldiers unlocked the cell and lined up in front of them. They lifted the contraptions, apparently some sort of firearm. There were several loud bangs as Eilívur jolted, covering his ears. The fat one was hit in the face, and the other men crumpled over as blood poured from their bodies.

"Is that. . ." Eilívur asked, lowering his hands.

Halvard took one of the weapons from the soldier and handed it to Eilívur. "Self-priming wheellocks. Like the muskets."

"Incredible," Eilívur said, examining the gun in his hand.

Halvard took it from him and handed him another one. "That one needs to be reloaded. This one will serve you better." He showed him how to fire it and then motioned up the stairs. "We've breached the Northern District with little resistance."

"They're that effective?"

"More so than we thought. The Sunderians fought for a while, but many fled."

"They retreated?"

"Apparently, a whole battalion was seen heading east."

Of course they did. "Cowards," Eilívur replied. "They just gave us the city, then?"

Halvard shrugged with a thin smile.

"Will we let them go?"

"About three hours ago, Admiral Bjarke arrived with a fleet of wisps."

"A fleet?" Eilívur couldn't believe it.

"He landed just north of the city, while the rest are hovering outside the western wall. He met with Commander Veurðr, and, as far as I know, they're sending half the fleet to take out the fleeing battalion."

Feeling weak, Eilívur leaned against the iron bars. "What about Sunderian soldiers left in the city?"

"King Ónarr's orders were to eliminate all resistance. We're taking no prisoners."

"And the civilians?"

Halvard's expression turned solemn. "Unless there's total surrender, Ónarr assumes they're resisting."

Eilívur flinched. He could kill a man on a battlefield without a second thought—even the murderers in the cell next to him. But the order to kill civilians? "What if they're running from the city?"

Halvard didn't respond at first. "That's Commander Veurðr's call," he said, looking away. "But his orders were to eliminate any possibility of future uprisings. Anyone fleeing will likely be considered a future threat."

A series of sudden explosions echoed from somewhere outside, and all the men hunkered down. "And that would be wisps!" Halvard shouted as he motioned for the men to head up the stairs. "We need to get you and the rest to the western gate! There's an infirmary there, and they'll take you all back to Llynhithe."

"We'll follow your lead," Eilívur shouted, and they headed out of the dungeon.

Sunder's Bane

Eirún walked along the base of a bluff, which arose to her left. On her right, the ground plummeted into a steep ravine of broken boulders and scattered hemlocks. Though she couldn't see any water, she could hear the roar of falls up ahead. It had been two days since she left Everwind in a panic. She was utterly lost, but for the moment, the only thought that consumed her mind was getting a drink of water. Pulling at her tattered dress, she followed the sound of the water.

Soon, a shallow free-stone stream came into view. It ran between mossy banks until it curled over the top edge of bare rock and fell into the ravine below. Falling to her knees, she took in long gulps of cold water.

Afterward, she wiped her mouth and gazed up the stream. The reality of what she had done sank in the first night. She knew that finding Søren in the middle of the wilderness was an impossible task, but the shock of him being alive took the best of her. In the fields, she could have made her way back to the city. But not from here. This forested gorge choked her view of anything more than a hundred yards away.

Her thighs and feet ached. All she could do was head uphill, but every few feet, she had to stop and rub out the cramps. She was hungry and tired. Søren could've been anywhere in that country. Or maybe it was all just a crazy coincidence, and he really was dead. Agatha probably saw someone else, and the lens just happened to look like hers. Why did she run out like that? Another couple of nights, and she'd die in this place.

She forced herself up to her feet and began walking east, following the stream uphill as she stepped over roots and small stones. She was surprised at how dark it was. It seemed dawn was only a few hours ago. Maybe it was because she was in a forest.

The sweat beneath her green dress caused it to stick and rub against her skin, bringing on burning rashes between her legs and beneath her arms. When she pushed her way through a thicket of rhododendron, she found herself standing at the edge of a wide glade of tall briar and brown grass. Several walls and foundations of a weathered stacked-stone structure lay scattered around, but everything else looked wild.

Her heart sank.

Beyond the glade, the ground continued to rise again like an endless set of giant stairs—one incline after the other, with the top still eluding her sight. She wasn't sure how she would make it through the briar, much less out of this cursed place alive.

She imagined the trees growing thicker and darker around her—closing in on her like her own depression whenever it began to cloud her mind. But that's all it was. Just her own mind wanting to slip back into hopelessness and sorrows.

"No," she said aloud to herself.

She knew that she had to keep walking, but her mind tried to hold her captive. She tried to think of something else. She reminded herself of Hrunting's words, but she couldn't hold on to them with the same courage as she had before.

"Stop it," she said. Don't let it take over again. She tried to think of something else—anything to keep herself from falling back.

Søren.

What would happen if she actually found him? At first, all she could imagine was hugging him and saying how sorry she was. Then she pictured sitting in a house somewhere, listening to his stories of how he ended up in Sunder. But the more she thought about it, the more she realized it couldn't be so. She still doubted that he was actually alive, but even if he was, so much had happened in her own life. She was not the same person when she last saw him. He might not be the same either. And what would they do? Could she actually raise him as her own son in Sunder? Impossible. And she couldn't go back to Daecland.

Then she had a thought. One that seemed to come against her own will. She didn't want to think it, but it kept hammering on her as if she came to a realization she didn't want to accept, but she knew it to be true. Maybe being with Søren wasn't what she needed most. Maybe she needed something more. She peered up at the dark gray sky through the swaying branches and thought of Sarah and Agatha praying. If Theos was real, why hadn't he shown himself to her? And why did he put her through so much misery?

The lens in the kitchen kept coming back to her mind. She tried to convince herself that it was a coincidence, but she knew it was hers. The crack was exactly the same. It was missing a small rivet in the same spot. Even the leather strap was thicker on one side since she helped her father cut it from cow skin. How on earth did she stumble upon it in the middle of Everwind? Was it all really an accident?

She wasn't sure why, but in that desolate wilderness, she crawled onto her knees and planted her face on the wet earth. She didn't have any answers. She didn't know her purpose. She had no idea what to say to this Theos.

In a whimper, she moved her lips, but no sound came out. She begged for mercy, but she wasn't even sure for what—for not forgiving Mathios, for being angry with Søren, for holding on to her own self-pity. She cried for mercy on Søren. Whether he was dead or alive, she hoped that he would have the kind of peace Sarah had. And she prayed for Hrunting, that he found the meaning in life he sought for. Then she prayed that maybe this Theos would take her depression away completely. And maybe he would make sense out of the mess of her life.

After a minute, she didn't hear anything. There was no voice from the sky—only the sighing wind and rattling of branches. But somehow, she felt better, even if it was just to get it all out. The depression still sat somewhere in the back of her mind. It hadn't gone away. But maybe it was there for a reason. Maybe it served a purpose she couldn't understand.

She stood up, wiped her nose, and pushed her way through the thorns.

When she made it across the glade, she began to work her way up another long, steep slope. She didn't know how she made it this far. She had no strength left. Yet, she somehow kept moving. Keeping her mind focused on each step, she made it through several more inclines until the forest grew so dark, she could barely see in front of her.

Then, something caught the corner of her sight. A subtle ray of light broke through the sky, revealing the top of the ridge. She had assumed it was night, but there was the sun, giving just enough light to show her the end of the gorge. It wasn't very far. Taking in a deep breath, she pressed on toward the light, leaving the darkness behind her.

* * *

Galvin took the rear as nearly eight-hundred men rode down the Eastern Road in front of him. Hundreds had already been slaughtered, and many refused to leave their families. He never saw Arnon or Drake either, and so he assumed they had stayed behind as well. He could only hope that the Daecish would spare the people. Part of him felt guilty, but what else could he do? Hope or no hope, the only reason he breathed was to see Sunder freed from Daecish hands, and he knew the cost would be more than most could bear.

It was early evening, but a shadow from the northern sky spread like a black blanket. The westering sun shone brilliantly against the weathered green landscape around them, but in the sky, it couldn't seem to penetrate the darkness, as if a line was drawn where the light itself was being swallowed up. It created such an unusual pattern in the sky that men began muttering verses from Hælend's Ballad. But he'd had enough of it. He had disregarded the stories of old for nonsense. Based on all the hypocrisy he had seen, the country would be better without it anyway. Galvin couldn't explain the sky, and he didn't care to.

He glanced beside him to the prisoner, whose chain was tied to the back of a mule, as he stumbled over the dirt and rocks. He still couldn't figure how that man knew the things he did, but he reckoned he would be useful somehow. Looking ahead, he could no longer see Porter or the grain wagons now that the front of the army crested over a wide, low hill. It would be a long journey. Hopefully, the wisps wouldn't come after them.

Just as that thought came to his mind, his shoulders sank. From the west arose a distant humming. He didn't even want to, but he looked behind him. Sure enough, black dots rose up into the sky.

"Brigadiers!" he hollered as he pointed a sword to a ridgeline running from east to west, which marked the southern end of the Keld Valley. "Move to the base of the ridge!"

As he hollered, other brigadiers repeated the order down the road. The wisps were still far off, and he was thankful they at least had enough time to make it to the ridgeline. He kicked at the sides of his horse and galloped north from the road. Behind him, the mule followed, dragging the prisoner along the ground. He knew he was probably putting his army into a trap, but if the wisps landed, he might have time to take the army through the Mouth and into the southern end of the valley. That would at least give him a fighting chance to hide out in the hollers.

To his right, the landscape inclined to the east until it leveled with the top of the ridge. He couldn't see Porter, but he could just make out the wagons lagging behind.

An object arose from the ridgeline in front of him. He squinted, and his breath was sucked out of his chest. A small boy sat upon what looked like a black alphyn as it walked to the edge. The boy held a sword high in his hand.

Sunder's Bane? No. It couldn't be.

Suddenly, his horse faltered and collapsed, and he was flung forward. The wind knocked out of his lungs, and he felt a dull snap in his left arm as it landed beneath him. Letting out a gasp, he rolled over onto his back and tried to shake the initial shock away. All around, horses neighed and bucked, throwing men to the ground.

If it hadn't been for his utter disbelief, fear would have consumed him. He kept running through his mind every rational reason he could think of, but he could not explain what was happening before his eyes.

The boy pointed the blade of the sword down, with the hilt raised high above his head. Then he thrust it into the ground. A tremble echoed beneath Galvin's feet as the ground ripped apart beneath the blade, sending a crack through the ridge as it ran across the field to the right of him.

Theos, let him live through this.

Men screamed and cried out as they tried to escape. Another deep rumble came, and the ground opened wide and swallowed the eastern half of his army. Their screams faded as they fell into some abysmal black hole.

Darting his eyes, he futilely pressed his body against the earth, hoping it would hide him. Running his hand on the ground, he went to pull his sword from his sheath, but he froze as black tentacles flung out of the hole and pierced what men were still alive. Then as quickly as they came, the tentacles vanished like a black mist. The men looked around with terror-stricken eyes, frantically feeling their chests and stomachs. Then, eyeing one another, they began to scream as they lifted their swords and rushed toward each other. Galvin scrambled to his feet and ran to his horse, but it was gone. Finding a boulder, he hid behind it and observed the scene as his own men hacked at one another's heads and arms. Some tackled each other; others gnawed at their brother's flesh until they bled out onto the ground.

From behind the ridge, a high-pitched chorus arose. The boy aimed his blade toward the army as a great black wave of thousands of birds flocked from behind the horizon, screeching and cawing so loud Galvin's ears bled. They swooped down upon the dying soldiers and began to devour their flesh. Galvin stood up with trembling limbs and stumbled southward. Others ran beside him, and fear shot through him as a black tentacle ripped through his body and faded. He didn't know how, but he knew the other soldiers were going to try to kill him. He held his broken left arm against his chest but pulled his sword from his sheath with his right hand and ran toward a corporal, bringing the blade down upon his shoulders as the corporal's feet tripped and collapsed beneath him. Just as Galvin pulled his sword back, he glanced to his right and watched one of his own brigadiers charge toward him with an ax raised high. Galvin's limbs locked in place as the blade fell on his head.

* * *

As Eilívur and his men followed Halvard down the road, he looked at the western sun in horror. They had been moving for an hour, and the sun not only never finished setting, it actually seemed higher than it did before. More than that, darkness spread from the north as it began to wrap around the sun, splitting the sky as if day were on one side and night on the other. Several of his own men had already fled from the regiment and ran into buildings. Somehow that made him feel better because he thought he was losing his mind.

Halvard only gazed ahead as he continued leading them forward. A few skirmishes were going on as muskets and wheellocks were fired, but not many Sunderians were left to fight. Of those left alive, most had probably fled or were hiding in the shadows of their own homes. Only about a dozen wisps hovered over the city, occasionally firing into towers and wall battlements, sending thick dust into the air, making him cough.

Several full regiments cleaned the streets with their firearms as they slowly marched behind him. From the alleyways to his left trailed the voices of women, maybe even children, as they ran east. It would have been better for them if they just surrendered. He would have told them himself, but by now, it was pointless.

After they passed King's Lane, several civilians, mostly younger-looking girls, ran south from Old Birchton Way. They kept close to the wall and darted their eyes in his direction before disappearing behind the buildings. Soon, another small group of girls ran south, followed by a man, who glanced over in Eilívur's direction. Although he appeared to be missing an arm, Eilívur immediately recognized him as Arnon Greystrom. Quickening his pace, Arnon followed the girls across the road until they disappeared from sight.

"Commander Halvard!" Eilívur hollered.

Halvard paused and turned toward him, his eyes dazed.

"I'm going to head south. I'll meet you outside of the Western Gate shortly."

Halvard didn't say anything as he continued to walk forward, glaring into the sky.

Gripping the wheellock in his right hand, Eilívur hurried down a dirt alley toward the southern wall.

* * *

Arnon rushed behind Langleigh and Agatha. Other than three other girls, two small families, who were running from their homes near Birchton, had joined them. His mother, sisters, Sarah, and Lilly, had already left an hour prior. He wished he could have gone with them, but he knew he needed to get as many out as he could. Like everyone else, his family was to take the alleyway routes until they passed the Palace of Ingvar. There they could continue along the southern city wall until they made it to the Eastern Gate. He had planned to follow that same route himself, but the presence of Daecish moving west made him realize it was too late for that. Then he remembered the hole in the city wall that Drake showed them. He wished he had thought about it earlier, but at least he could now get the rest of them out that way.

Agatha kept slowing down as she stared into the sky. "Don't look at it," Arnon insisted. "We don't have time. We've got to get out of the city!" She picked up her pace. To his left, he could make out the corner of the Fire and Water Tavern just before it disappeared behind another building. Wisps hummed high in the air, and the last he saw of Everwind Castle, barely a single spire still stood. He didn't want to say anything, but he didn't think any of them would live long, even if they did get some ways out of the city. Maybe the Daecish would be merciful, but he doubted it.

Despite his own advice, Arnon couldn't help but look up at the sky. The sun sat once again above the city wall. It was as if time was going backward. He had no idea what it meant, but if he ever had any doubt about Hælend's Ballad, it was gone now.

By the time the wall of the Palace of Ingvar came into view, Arnon searched for Drake's hole. "Here!" he shouted.

He ran between the girls and families and, with his left arm, began pulling away the stones. Langleigh stepped over and helped him. By the time they got the stones out of the way, he sent the children through first, followed by their parents. Afterward went Agatha,

Langleigh, and the three other girls. Just as he bent his head down to crawl through, he caught sight of someone to his left.

Standing before him was a Daecish officer, or at least what used to be one. His clothes looked large against his thin frame, and his blonde hair was matted and greasy. He lifted something in his hand. It was shiny and metallic, with a hollow iron rod at the end. His expression was blank, and Arnon recognized him from the dungeon. In an instant, an explosion and a billow of smoke shot out of the contraption. Something hard slammed against Arnon's forehead. He felt his body being thrown back, and his eyesight went blank, except for different colors dancing in his mind. Then nothing.

* * *

Outside of the city wall, Fleta had lost her mother and sister as crowds of families drew together near the Eastern Gate. Searching through the throng, she spotted Sarah standing near Drake. She pushed her way toward them but stopped when Beckett approached her. With a sigh of relief, she ran over and hugged him.

"How long have you been here?" she asked.

"Not long, they say we've got to go quickly, though."

Many from the crowd were already hurrying down the road. She scanned along the people but still couldn't spot her family. Her vision distorted, and she struggled to breathe. "Mama!" she hollered out.

At the sound of her voice, Drake and Sarah glanced around, but they didn't notice her.

"Drake!" she shouted. Maybe he knew where they were.

An eruption of screams broke out from the crowd. Fleta raised herself to her toes and peered across the road. A large regiment of Daecish moved south, and the crowds were being cornered back toward the city gate. Mothers picked up their children as they wept and tried to run. Several explosions broke out with clouds of smoke. Fleta hunkered down and gripped her ears. Some of the people fell over. Before long, she found the crowd pressing against her as they were moved back into the city. She still couldn't see her family, but Beckett was gripping her hand tight.

Soldiers pushed them along the inside of the city wall, and Fleta's heart pounded. Along the road and streets laid the bodies of several men and women, including young children, in pools of blood. It was obvious that she was about to die, and her body began to tremble. To her right, the families were lined side by side with their backs against the wall. She finally spotted Hazel and her mother standing beside Drake and Sarah, with Lilly beside her and Acton in her arms. Her mother looked around frantically. Fleta cried for her, but the screams and shouts of others drowned her voice out. Just as tears began to fill her eyes, Daecish soldiers lined up in front of the frantic crowd, and her head went so light she thought she would pass out. In their hands, the Daecish held long devices of wood and iron. There were smaller ones as well, shining like brass in the soldiers' grips. To her left stood an officer. His own face looked sorrowful as he raised a hand in the air. A soldier pointed a device directly at her. Staring into a long hollow cylinder, she couldn't stop crying. She wanted to shout out or do something to make them stop, but she was helpless. Fear overwhelmed her, and all she could do was hunker back against the wall and close her eyes.

"Fire!"

There was a loud explosion, and the last thing Fleta felt was Beckett's grip loosen in her hand.

* * *

Eilívur stumbled his way north. Bracing one hand against the stone wall, his legs shook, and the wheellock in his other hand slipped from his fingers. He tried to blame it on his health, but shooting Arnon without a trial put a weight on him he couldn't shake. Did he deliver justice? Or was it just revenge?

He coughed and wiped the blood from his mouth. The Western Road was not far ahead. Another cough escaped him, and he had to pause to muster what little strength he had left. Bracing his hands on his knees, he let out a loud hack from his lungs, spitting more blood on the ground. He cleared his throat and pressed forward.

His stomach twisted into knots. Killing his brother's murderer should have made him feel better, but it didn't. It was just the death of another young man. Why didn't he arrest him? Give him a fair trial? Eilívur tried to convince himself otherwise, but his own principles haunted him. He failed to uphold the justice he had wanted for so long. Just like Arnon, he was now a murderer. Was he even sure Arnon killed his brother? Maybe he got the evidence wrong.

No. Wesley himself affirmed Arnon's crime. And by King Ónarr's own orders, countless other men, even women, and children, were being shot that day without trials. Arnon would have been among them.

With a deep breath, he settled it in his mind that he had only done what he was commanded to do that day. Thinking no more of it, he continued stumbling through the mud. The Western Gate was just ahead, but his head began to go light. If the infirmary just had clean water, he would feel better.

Bracing himself against the wall, he suddenly paused in his step and stared at his feet. He wasn't certain, but he thought the ground had just throbbed. There were sounds coming from the other side of the wall— strange sounds, like deep crunching and muffled thudding. A soldier abruptly stumbled through the gate as he ran east and out of sight. Eilívur narrowed his eyes, but he pushed himself forward. The sun was now bright and high in the sky as if it was midday, but the blackness continued to spread around it like water running around a large rock.

The noises grew louder as he approached the gate. Several screams echoed before cutting short. He peered out of the city and gasped.

Slithering along the ground were what looked like hundreds of long gray serpents. Their eyes were black, but their mouths were gorged in red. Barely a man was left in sight, save one screaming from inside one of the wisps, as the serpents coiled themselves around it. They began to move toward the city, like piles of dark worms slipping over one another. They poured through the gate, and Eilívur could only look on as one coiled back and struck out at him, digging its rows of thin sharp teeth around his body.

The Desert and The Fountain

S øren straddled the alphyn's back of swirling black shadow. He gripped the sword in his hand as they made their way down the western edge of the ridge. To his right arose many jagged rocks until the earth plummeted into a deep forested valley. Turning south, around the bottom of the ridge, the alphyn stepped over the butchered bodies of the men who had slaughtered themselves. Few birds were now left as most had already flown west, filled with the flesh of men and horses. He glanced behind him to the fleet of wisps, burning in scattered piles of ash and rubble, just like in Norfrost. In that same direction, although far in the distance, he could just make out the last dying screams of men in some distant city until a haunting silence fell all around him as if the whole world had died.

Approaching the edge of the gaping hole sat the prisoner, still bound in chain. A look of fear glinted in his eyes, but he still smiled as Søren and the alphyn stood before him.

"What are you going to do to me?" he asked.

Søren didn't give an answer as he dismounted, gripping the sword tighter in his hand.

The prisoner laughed. "You can't kill me. You're just a boy."

At that moment, a vision unfolded before Søren. Eirún stood at the brink of the Finnvard River with a chain running between two shackles around her wrists. Through a bleak, gray twilight, she was taken west. A shroud of darkness hung about her, and her posture was heavy. With flowing tears, she seemed to be clawing at the iron shackles, but as Søren peered closer, she only tightened them until the black iron sunk into her flesh. She continually looked back at the river with cold, painful eyes. Søren wanted to call out to her, but from the sky above, a sudden glimmer of sunlight broke through the clouds. It shined upon her, but she never looked at it. Other figures, featureless, like dull shadows, came around her, but she never looked them in the eye, only continued tightening the shackles.

The darkness around her soon began to dissolve beneath the now-broadening sunlight, and at that moment, she fell on her knees and looked up with a great wail.

Søren reached for her, but she vanished, and suddenly he watched Geoffrey being pulled from a carriage just outside of Everwind. As Geoffrey looked desperately back at Søren, he too was clasped in shackles and dragged through lofty black mountains of shadow until he was thrown into a pit of corpses. Made of bone and shriveled flesh, the corpses walked around a desert like living people, but there was no breath in their lungs, and their rotting hearts never moved. Geoffrey only sat beneath the sunlight. Though weary and thin, he appeared peaceful and calm, as if he knew he would not be bound forever.

Now Søren was looking through iron bars. There was no sunlight in that place. Only a soft glow and the echo of dripping water. At the base of a set of steps stood Egbert. With slumped shoulders, he stared at Søren's lens, which laid on the ground. Søren reached between the bars for it, but it was too far. Egbert's eyes turned wild as he stumbled toward it. Like the others, he too was bound in iron. When he picked it up, Søren shouted at him, but he had already taken it and ran.

As Søren tried to ponder these visions, his heart suddenly ached. From Eirún, Geoffrey, and Egbert, he saw their own fates entangled with countless others like a spider's web. Although some he had known, many he had never seen before, but all of them were bound in chains. Søren wept as death came upon many of them. Others were tightening the shackles around their wrists as Eirún had. Still, others gazed up at the rays of sunlight. It was then that Søren noticed that all of their chains ran from their bound wrists and tangled together into one large chain leading toward a bleak figure, locked in a black cell.

The vision vanished, and Søren found his eyes locked on the chain between the prisoner's wrists. Somehow, he could feel the prisoner's spirit. He could see inside his soul. Since before the mountains themselves were born, the prisoner was full of hate. Always he sought to shame and destroy, for the only thing he thought would bring him happiness was to bring everyone else down to the level of his own misery. But he was never in control, was he? He was just a pawn caught up in a greater plan than himself. He sought to kill everything, but he failed to see what lay beyond death. And how ironic. In his own scheme, he found himself upon the brink of his own damnation.

"Liberation," Søren barely got out in a whisper as he stared at the prisoner. He placed the tip of the leaf-shaped blade against the prisoner's throat, whose eyes went wide.

The prisoner leaned back until he laid on the ground. He opened his mouth to speak, but Søren thrust the blade into his flesh. A gurgle escaped from the prisoner's throat, and blood ran down his neck on either side. After Søren pulled the blade out, he got on his knees and pushed the body over the edge of the black pit, sending it into the depths.

The earth groaned as it swallowed the prisoner. Dust broke from unseen cracks and was caught in the wind, which sighed low and mournful. Up above, the darkness began to shift over the entire sky, barely letting the sun give its light. Søren looked back at the alphyn and was surprised to see that it looked normal once again, except it was lying on its side with open eyes. It was dead.

Surprised at the sorrow which overcame him, he stepped toward it, reaching out his hand. But as he did, the lifeless creature reminded him of all that he had seen. All that he had been used to accomplish. The destruction of entire cities. The deaths of countless men, women, even children. Søren lost the strength in his legs and fell to his knees. How was any of this good? Was this really the will of Theos?

As he continued to stare at the alphyn, he didn't understand it, but he pondered the words of the shadow when it had talked to him on the mountain. That death was not an end. That something greater would come through all of this. Maybe the shadow represented a goodness higher than his own. A goodness beyond his own understanding, and yet one from which every good thing on earth was a small reflection of. And it was that greater goodness that used him to bring about all that had passed. A scurry to his right snapped his attention. At the top of the ridge, the form of someone stumbled to the edge.

Søren dropped his jaw and felt like shouting and weeping all at once. Looking across the horizon stood Eirún in a torn emerald green dress, with dirt staining her limbs. As if he had awoken from a long dream, he dropped the sword in his hand.

"Eirún!" he shouted.

She shot her eyes in his direction. "Søren!"

He ran south as fast as he could until the ridgeline lowered enough for him to climb over, then he ran up toward her. She reached out and stumbled forward, wrapping her arms around him.

"I'm so sorry!" she exclaimed. There was such distress in her voice Søren broke into tears.

"No," he replied, hugging her tighter. "I'm sorry for everything."

Neither of them moved for a long while until she loosened her grip and looked at him. Despite the lines around her darkened eyes, she looked just as he remembered her—a perfect mother. He hugged her again but soon felt something brush against him from behind.

He turned to see the shadow again, but only as a thick hovering cloud as the last rays of the sun continued to drift into it. Eirún stepped away from him as her eyes widened. Trembling, she walked toward it with her face down. Søren couldn't be sure, but she seemed to be listening to it, but he couldn't hear it speak. After a while, she turned to Søren. Tears still streamed down her cheeks, but the weary lines in her face began to fade, and her green eyes shined bright with joy.

The sun went out as the last stream of light flowed into the shadow, and the whole earth went black.

"Eirún?" he called.

There was no answer—only a deep silence.

Although he couldn't see anything, he kept his eyes on where the shadow had hovered. Then, in an instant, a burst of light erupted from the shadow like rippling water, dashing colors and warmth in all directions. Søren's own body tingled as light penetrated him, sending out black shadows which writhed and dissolved like serpents caught in a flame. The same thing was happening to Eirún. Soon, everything in him felt renewed and full of life. He couldn't explain it, but it was as if he was an empty vessel and was suddenly filled up with love until it poured out of him. He looked at Eirún, but she was gazing ahead at the most beautiful landscape he had ever seen, expanding in the distance with the stretching light, like a wave rolling in all directions.

* * *

Geoffrey opened his eyes. A white insipid light gleamed through the open windows of the bunkhouse. Blinking, he glanced around. He was the only one inside. Dust and sand covered the floors, and the door banged against the frame against a strong wind. He stood up, still feeling weak and weary. How long had he been asleep?

He stumbled toward the door and pushed it open. Outside, dust swirled in the wind. The fence around the camp was twisted and jumbled in several areas, and not a single soul was in sight. He wasn't sure what caused the fence to look like that, but the other gray-shirts must have escaped through. Above, the entire sky was black, save for the sun, which shone like a dim lantern in a dark room. Everything looked ashen as if all the reds and tans of that barren place had been saturated into dull grays.

The iron gate lay in broken pieces. Trying to swallow, Geoffrey realized how thirsty he was. He stumbled to the trough, but it was dry. He observed the gate for a moment, but his legs held him back. Where were the guards? Was this some sort of experiment? Scanning the outside of the buildings, he finally mustered the courage to walk through to the reservoir. He needed water. Passing the eastern road, he glanced down it. Dust continued to swirl in the air, blocking his view from seeing more than a dozen yards or so.

Now beneath the underpass, a gust blew against him, banging the door to the office back against the wall with screeching hinges. His feet turned heavier with each step, but the thought of plunging his face into the water kept him moving.

By the time he made it back outside, he paused. What seemed to be green only a week ago was now as barren and gray as the landscape behind him. He limped forward as his hands hung heavy at his sides. Stumbling to the reservoir, he fell to his knees and looked on in disbelief. Not a single drop of water. Even the mud below the banks was as dry as dust.

He sat for a long while, not really thinking, just examining the cracked earth before him. He slowly looked west, over his shoulder. One of the towers was toppled over, and the large brick building with three large archways had crumbled in ruin. The iron fence must have fallen over with the tower.

Lifting himself to his feet, he made his way in that direction. He knew he'd never make it to the shore, but if he was going to die, he wanted to die heading home. His head wavered with dizziness as he stomped through the dirt and sand.

Before him, at the end of the toppled tower stretched a vast flat desert. There were no features, only shifting sand blowing across the ground, which seemed to run on until it blended with the darkness of the sky. There was no horizon. He took a few steps but stumbled when everything went black as if his eyes quit working. He couldn't even see his hand when he lifted it to his face. He tried to take a few more steps but was unsure of his footing. Before long, he found himself crawling on his hands and knees until he finally gave up and laid down.

After a while, he thought he could see a glowing dim light from somewhere far away, but maybe his eyes fooled him. But it soon began to grow, and the silhouette shape of the land came into view. A burst of light rolled over the gray mountains to the south and rushed toward Geoffrey like a mighty gale, and he covered his face with his arms.

Keeping his eyes closed, he waited until the wind died down and the sun warmed his body. The dirt suddenly felt soft and lush beneath him. He barely lifted his arm, allowing his eyes to adjust to the thick green grass in front of him. On a single blade crawled a small spider, not even the size of his fingernail. It let out a strand of web and quickly disappeared as it was caught in the breeze.

He sat up and rubbed his eyes. The green of the rolling hills was so deep, they looked blue as they ran up against the mountains in the far distance. He glanced behind him. Where the bleak brick buildings once stood now sat a large flowing fountain as it bubbled up from the earth like a mighty spring. Geoffrey crawled on his hands and knees until the water sprayed over him, cooling his warm skin.

His fingers sloshed through the cold, clear water, with the fountain rising just before him. He fell forward and took in long gulps of the sweetest water he had ever had. The coolness soothed him to the soul, breaking away burdens and weights he didn't even know were there. Such a feeling of freedom flooded within him, and he burst into an unexpected cry. All of his time in the camp, and ultimately his entire life, seemed like a vapor compared to the eternity welling up in his heart. All of his fears and doubts washed away as he looked into the water as a new man.

When his breathing calmed, he sat up with his clothes and hair dripping wet. Looking west, a dark shadow had formed not far from the fountain. He lifted his hand to shield his eyes as it thickened and shifted toward him. The fountain fell quiet, and the spray dwindled to a low bubbling until it ceased altogether into a quiet pool. It was so smooth it looked like a sheet of glass. From the shadow, a wind blew against his clothes and hair.

He couldn't explain why, but such a beauty pressed against him, and all he could do was lower his gaze and fall to his knees. "Forgive me" were the only words he could get out. From the shadow, there was no response, but Geoffrey somehow knew it had heard him. He kept his eyes down, locking his gaze on the green grass beneath the clear water. "Are you?" he began to ask, but his voice was weak. He wanted to ask if it was Theos, but something told him it wasn't. And yet, he could feel that it was pure and good. "Did I die?" he asked instead.

"You have been resurrected."

The voice from the shadow soothed his bones, and he found himself relaxing, almost sleepy. Then, he dared to lift his head, and he gazed at the shadow, taking in the splendor. The shadow was not dark in a dreary way, but one which absorbed all colors and light at once, and yet they never fully disappeared, creating an effect Geoffrey had a difficult time wrapping his mind around. Every cloudy ripple seemed to whisper and sing, filling his ears with a melody so sweet he wanted to shout with joy. He sat there for such a long time that if someone told him afterward that he hadn't moved for many years, he wouldn't have been surprised.

When, at last, he found his words, he asked, "Where am I?"

"You are in Daecland."

"But I thought since I died, I would be . . ." He felt the skin on his face, ensuring he was really there. "In the after-life."

"This is the beginning of life."

Geoffrey glanced at the mountains to his right. They seemed like the same ones he saw from the camp but a little different. Larger. Greener.

"You are in the Daecland which it has longed to be," the shadow said.

A Daecland as it has longed to be? The restoration of the world mentioned in Hælend's Ballad came to his mind, but then he thought about his family. "Are—" he began to ask, but he was afraid of what the answer might be. "My wife and daughter. Are they okay?"

"They are. As well as Acton."

Geoffrey's heart leaped within his chest. "Acton?" He laughed aloud. Sarah hated that name. "Where are they? Can I go see them?"

"They are in Sunder."

He peered at the mountains again. He could never cross those. He would have to go around and pray that there was a path along the shore. He wished he could fly.

"You cannot fly," the shadow answered. "But you can walk, and you can run. You will find the mountains will no longer stop you."

Run over the mountains? Geoffrey didn't know how, but he knew the shadow was right. A new strength pulsated through his veins. Just as he was about to leave, another thought came to his mind. "Is everyone here in this new world?"

"Everyone who was thirsty. For those who longed for life, to them, life has been given."

"But does not everyone want life?"

"No. Being bent only toward themselves, many longed to twist and destroy life according to their own passions. Their hearts desired destruction, and so destruction has been given to them."

"But surely," Geoffrey looked across the green fields, "if they saw this, they'd—"

"This place would only be a misery to them, for it is a place no one can corrupt."

Letting those truths settle in, Geoffrey knew exactly what the shadow meant. There were good things in his life, but to his own shame, especially in his younger days, he had manipulated them in perverse ways to fill a dark appetite he craved. But just as those terrible memories were brought to his mind, they suddenly seemed distant, as if they belonged to someone else. "Then why am I here? I've done wrong things. Is it because I also did good things?"

"No man does good as he ought to. You are here because you looked not to yourself or your own works but to the only one who could save you. It is an act of grace, not merit."

What about some of the people he cared for? He felt as if he shouldn't ask but rather trust. Nevertheless, one more question burned in him. "Is Søren here?"

"He is with his mother in Sunder."

At that, Geoffrey asked no more. He looked at the mountains and took in a long breath. Then, he began to run.

* * *

Arnon opened his eyes with a shout. He glanced around the alleyway and scurried to his feet, feeling his face. The last thing he remembered was a piercing pain through his forehead. But everything felt okay. Sighing out of relief, he dropped his hands and searched for any signs of the Daecish officer. But just as he did, he slowly lifted his hands again.

He dropped his jaw and flexed his fingers. He moved his right arm. It was actually there. Even his little finger was back on his left hand. Looking down to his jerkin, he laughed out loud. It was cleaner than he had ever seen it, but it was certainly his. For a second, the shock of the moment caused his head to spin, and he almost lost his balance as he gripped the stone wall. What happened?

Catching his breath, he remembered the girls and his family. He glanced through the hole in the wall and crawled through it and stumbled out on the other side. Staring across the rolling landscape, his entire body tingled. It was still too early for spring, but there it was, in front of him. The green hills were dotted with patches of orange and yellow flowers, wavering with the grass in the warm breeze. He could scarcely take the colors in. Shades and hues which he had never seen before filled his eyes. Smells, fresh and sweet like honey, seemed to satisfy him as if he was being filled up by the beauty of the landscape itself.

A mother deer pranced to his right, followed by a young fawn. Near the horizon rolled a deep green forest of towering trees, which he knew wasn't there before. From out of it ran a clear stream, weaving its way to the Swelling Sea, which sparkled bright and blue. At the bank of the stream stood a horse, stooped low as it drank from the water. In disbelief, Arnon brought his hand to his forehead. The horse looked just like Ansel, and he couldn't believe his eyes, but an alphyn laid down beside it, eating grass. The thought of it made him laugh again.

Shaking himself, he looked east. Did his family make it out? He picked up his feet and jogged along the southern city wall. Occasionally, he shifted his gaze up, looking out for any wisps. Not only did he not see any, but the sky looked normal once again, with scattered white clouds lingering around the high sun. He took in a deep breath. The wind, the humming of bees, and the chirping of birds all blended together as if the earth sang out in a chorus of exultation.

The wall soon curved to the north, and the Southern Gate came into view. The large oak doors, framed in iron, were swung open. He would have been afraid of the Daecish spotting him, but he still couldn't get over all the colors as wildflowers bloomed all around the grass, right up to the stone walls themselves.

When he approached the doors, people were standing in the streets. To his surprise, they seemed calm—even happy. Several

Daecish men were chatting to his own people. Some looked around with awe-stricken eyes, but others were laughing, and one Daecish man held a noose in his hand and was pointing toward the Northern District before he let the rope fall to the ground. The whole scene boasted of a camaraderie and fellowship that was foreign to everything Arnon had known, and yet as he gazed upon them, all he could think of was how good and natural it looked.

To the right of the crowd stood a Sunderian who almost looked like that strange man, the large one, who had been staying in his room. Egbert was his name, except there was something different about him. Standing straight with his hands on his hips and his gaze fixed on the sun, he looked nothing like the imbecile he had remembered. Even from that distance, Arnon could see, almost feel, the joy radiating from his face. He would have walked over and asked him what had happened, but thoughts of his family stirred him. His gut told him they would be on the Eastern Road, and he didn't want to waste another moment.

Picking up his pace, he ran as he leaped over low rocks, but just as the wall took another curve, he stopped. A few hundred yards in the distance stood the figure of a girl. He could just make out her white dress. An image of Adelyne's grave rushed to his mind, and for a second, his knees buckled. He shook his head in disbelief but forced his legs to run. As he approached the girl, she was looking away, but a glimpse of white flowers braided into her dark hair caused a sudden cry to break from his chest. Through his tears, he watched her turn and face him. The wind blew against her white dress, and she drew the hair from her eyes—the woven silver ring was on her finger.

"Adelyne!" he tried to get out, but his strength escaped him as he fell forward with heavy sobs. She ran over to him, and he could feel her hands over his. He looked up. She sat before him, dressed like a bride on her wedding day. It was her. She was alive. Her glistening blue eyes peered into his, and she was more beautiful than he ever remembered. He embraced her. "I love you," he said as he breathed in the jasmine scent of her hair.

"I love you so much," she replied, holding him tight as she wept.

When he finally opened his eyes, he looked over her shoulder where crowds of people walked along the Eastern Road. Just as he had, they looked as if they were in a daze, observing their surroundings. Through his grin, he let out another cry. He could see Drake, Langleigh, and Sarah with Acton in her arms and Lilly walking beside her. There was even Hazel and Fleta, who held hands with that boy she liked. There were so many others, but what struck his heart the most was that he could see his father, holding his mother's hand, as he pointed to something beyond the city behind him.

"Look," he heard Adelyne say.

"I see them," he replied.

"No." She leaned back, and her watery eyes widened as she smiled. "Look."

When Arnon turned around, his eyes fell upon one who took his breath away. As he gazed upon such beauty, his soul felt as if it was being washed clean, and he somehow knew that neither he, nor Adelyne, nor anyone else could do wrong, nor ever even desire it again.

At that moment, his recollection became so clear, it was like having a perfect mind. He remembered everything, even lost memories from when he was very young. But as it all came back to him, he understood, or maybe he was shown, how every second of his life, the suffering and joy, the evil and good, were all used to bring him into paradise that day.

The Lost Stanzas of Hælend's Ballad

None could say who all were there
But joy went on unending
For all who hungered and thirsted in prayer
Were forgiven their offending

On that day it was said a man
Hurried from a fountain
He found his family in his own land
Beyond the lofty mountains

Listen closely to their cheers
For the Giver of life has won
He's wiped away all their tears
After the rising sun

A mother in an emerald dress
Danced with her new son
On the fields their hearts were blessed
Their sorrow and pain undone

Then out went a fair-haired man
And found that son and mother
He reached out and took her hand
As one they remained forever

Listen closely to their cheers

Ian V. Conrey

For the Giver of life has won
He's wiped away all their tears
After the rising sun

Haiden awoke and sang new songs
Clear as running waters
Dead and defeated were all the wrongs
Rejoiced the sons and daughters

The dark-haired bride dressed in white
Along with all the others
Beheld the One of joy so bright
For he was their true lover

Listen closely to their cheers
For the Giver of life has won
He's wiped away all their tears
After the rising sun

About the Author

Ian Conrey is both a teacher and student of history and theology, who actively fights against human trafficking and is working toward an M.A. in Religion. In his free time, he enjoys reading biographies and ancient mythology, discovering early American folk songs, and exploring the Cohutta Wilderness. He lives with his wife and three children in the North Georgia mountains.

CPSIA information can be obtained
at www.ICGtesting.com
Printed in the USA
LVHW052345141222
735274LV00014B/1372